THE
MEASUREMENTS
OF
DECAY

K. K. EDIN

metempsy publications

Published by Metempsy Publications

ISBN: 978-1-7320622-0-7

Library of Congress Control Number: 2018902810

Original cover painting: Badr Ali / badr-ali.com

Cover design & interior formatting: Mark Thomas / coverness.com

To my mother, my father, and my sister. Without your love and support,
nothing I do would be possible.

And to my little palm tree, in whose shade I would sit for eternity.

CONTENTS

"To an understanding endowed with magnificence and the contemplation of all time and being, do you think it possible that human life seem anything great?"
Plato, *Republic*

PROLOGUE

Eight years earlier, he is renegade. Burning purpose, and cigarettes if he can find them. His skin has paled for fear of open areas. He has taught himself to write, and he writes manifestos in defiance of the sun, which no one will ever read.

The heavens did favor him at a young age. They told him of history gone and still to come, from which he has been misplaced. He does not yet understand their betrayal. Since age seventeen, he has navigated the galaxy's labyrinth and slept under shifting skies.

Four ships and as many planets between him and Sol on a compass that cannot shake out a clear direction. That first journey shows him the majestic fixtures of the universe, which appear to him immovable. The hum of speech is around him, but he does not dare participate. He keeps his pact a secret. His name is Tikan; this much, he remembers.

On Earth, he hopes to blow the dust off his most known origins. There is nothing there except a jigsaw of ancient buildings resembling valleys of slanted tombstones and silver spires without windows not unlike those of home. From above, the planet appears as a grotesque infant atrophying gold.

He moves on, spends years like the fugitive that he is on worlds each dismal in its own way. The junk-steel walls of decrepit stations funneling crowds. Dark, glacial Europa. Venus and her fire crown. The false wind of Mars whistling through the alleys of griming districts. Whispers and shades fleet the underground and fly up to scatter in the dawn.

Still, he is searching, wildly afraid of stopping.

To the Dog Star. To a planet shrouded like a mystic's ecstasy; to waterfalls, to gardens thronging outland tropics and oceans frothing marble foam. He brings others to see this unmarked paradise orbiting the twin fires of Sirius in the pattern of infinity. To him, the soil is a fistful of carnelians and jaspers and agates. The clouds are pregnant with opals, the oceans birth jungles, and the horizon beyond the shore is showering in daylight stars.

But to his recent companions, he is a madman. They see only a scorched surface, a dead world withering its skin to the void.

He presses his face against the departing shuttle window and tracks the expanding curvature of the planet lined with diamonds. They are fading. They fade with the few who have at times journeyed with him.

He is scurrying up walls and through crevices, that he might yet answer the celestial call. It is distant, and taller barriers are springing up.

On Eris, the miners are cold as that once-unhinged string of comets on which they work. There is little there save machines and their oilers. Mauve dawn a year hence, and he is chased out through ice and mist under those cooling spheres trailing silver into black space.

They are fading, too. His face he hides well. He shuffles aboard a departing ship and sweats anger in the darkness.

The cracks through which he once slipped have since sealed shut. Stalked and hounded and beaten, he stalls now aboard a freighter threading the voided corridors between the stars. But the largest defeats are yet to come. And the icicle teeth of malevolence have already sunk into those universal fires he still watches and watches.

❧ I ❧

SOPHIA AND HER LOVER

I spent the day making the sun tiny between my crooked and shadowed hands, contorting them as if they were bound in string. It was the ritual I used to perform at the end of a long and aimless walk. A childish invocation, at best, but a way to keep myself from feeling powerless.

As was my habit, I followed the afternoon to the ocean and ended up lounging on a shore of corroded boulders. The waters golden, the horizon blood. The squawking of mindless seagulls. Alone, leering at passersby, I grinned as Saturn brightened and watched feral waves swallow the fireball, savoring the taste.

By dusk, I was mortal again. My flesh rattling off its frame, my fists clenched into pink hammers against the cold, my teeth chattering, my chapped lips rumbling out maledictions. I frowned the entire way home, where Sophia was waiting.

Upon my return, I let her eat dinner by herself while I made phone calls far past the appropriate hour.

But, see my dismal apartment while I rove in frustration. All of its objects and fixtures arranged to reflect the byzantine blueprint of my mind. Gray carpet, rotten desk, half a bookshelf for a library. There is one window, and it offers a cramped view. Already the glass is fogging. The heater whines. The ceiling is a maze of dust-clogged cracks. The air is so stuffy that breathing becomes a conscious effort. A horrible place to live, would you not agree? I'm sure it isn't too different from your own. Near a university, or a bank, or a homeless shelter. Somewhere in the first world, somewhere fixed on a grid. Or perhaps none of these.

There, at the unlit end of the room, stood Sophia. Her lone figure was diminishing in my view, while she continued to regard me with pity. Unemployed for a few months, I had let my teeth file each other down to fangs and my nails rip each other into jagged talons, and allowed morbid creases to form around my eyelids. No company had yet returned my calls.

"There'll be time," she said.

I ignored her.

No, how could I answer? Red fumes were swimming out of cracks in my soul. Responding to her in my stead would be a malefic creature conjured out of the lamp beside me. A sinister and untamed thing, the form my own, but grotesque, lumbering and reaching out of the circle I was drawing as I paced the room, foot after foot.

"Answer," I grunted into the phone, while beginning to periodically look up and shoot Sophia venomous glances.

I chewed my nails and paced. Plastic in hand, thoughts grinding each other into hard granules painful to the step. "Answer me."

Sophia simply stood there.

As the phone called its insults into my ear, Sophia went to sit on the bed. She could not stand long on her feet.

Meanwhile, the moon bulged silver out of a parting cloud. Frost crept along the windowpane in a veiny fog.

The job recruiters I was calling were, of course, far from their offices at that hour. But that was irrelevant. It was about Sophia and me. How much pity could I extract from her? How many of her sighs could I vacuum up into my heart? Despite the poverty of my wallet and of my soul, I was in the habit of squandering treasures.

You likely already have a low opinion of me. But I advise you, my best critic, to sheathe your sword for now. Otherwise, you might prematurely blunt its blade for when you need it most.

"I can't believe this," I said, watching her bury her face in her hands. "It's just not right. They should've called me back at least to tell me they don't want me. This is becoming absurd. I couldn't have given them a better interview. You know I don't care. They've just wasted my time."

Her face emerged from her hands, and she stretched it at the temples before sliding her hands down together under her chin, as though fixed in prayer or some such meditation. She took a breath and opened her eyes.

"Don't you want to just... take a break? And maybe think about something else so we can relax for a change? It's already getting late, and I don't think you should let this affect you so much. It's been like this every night."

I grimaced, defying her to offer some further practical advice.

The ringing cut to the voicemail greeting again, and with gritted teeth, I slammed the phone on the table. It is not enough, at times, to merely keep hostages. Better yet to make oneself the victim.

Sophia was beginning to look wan as the moon.

"I don't want anything like this on our minds either," I said to her, bottling up my resentment. "And I'm trying, really. It's been more than a month. I'll be thirty soon. Should I just sit around and wait?"

"Don't you think it's time to start looking at other options, then? Forget about it for a while. We'll manage fine without you getting that kind of position."

"No. I set myself a task and I *will* finish it."

"I'm not asking you to give up. Just to take it a little easier and stop letting it get to you like this. I know it's disappointing and I know you were expecting more, but this is what we have. Can't we just let it be and watch a movie tonight?"

Leaning against the desk, I thumbed the wood beside the phone. It was not long before I was digging out splinters with my nail. Sophia seemed infinitely far from me now. With one wolverine dash and swipe, I threw the phone into a cupboard and slammed it shut.

My anger subsided after a few breaths, and I stretched out a clump of my hair again, as I had done repeatedly throughout the evening, and sighed as I sat down next to her.

"This isn't even what I want to be doing," I said. "Or what I saw myself doing. It makes me feel sick. I don't get anything done and all I do is wait and wait, and it's made me feel worthless. Yes, worthless. Did I ever think that would happen to me? Never."

"That's how the world is, I'm afraid."

"Sickening?"

She gave me a questioning look. "Disappointing."

I shook my head. "It doesn't have to be."

"What do you mean?"

A glazed, dreamer's look developed in my eyes. "I could fix it."

She said nothing, waiting for me to finish whatever thoughts were then swinging me from anger to folly. "You know I could."

"Make the world a not so disappointing place? Fix the way of things? It sounds like you'd be setting yourself up for even greater disappointment."

"Fix the way of things," I said to myself, staring absently ahead, as if afraid of having my utterance recognized as anything more than a passing daydream of a thought. "Damn it, why does it sound so naïve? I want to fix humanity and the world and I want the means to do it. And I want to fix you and me, too."

"We were fine until you started picking us apart," she said. "Looking for problems where there weren't any."

I ignored her, and stared off again. "Don't you feel like, as time goes on, we understand each other less and less?"

"What are you talking about?" she said, though she knew very well what I was referring to.

"I'm saying I want to be a good person. I want to understand people."

"It's not that hard."

"It is. It is hard. If it were easy for people to understand each other, there wouldn't be any wars or anything like that."

She shook her head. "Why don't you go and actually do something feasible like feed people, if that's your worry?"

"No. Anyone can do that. That's like sprinkling droplets onto a fire. I want to do the kind of work we always used to talk about. The kind that's like lightning in a bottle not because it landed in there by luck, but because you had to reach through the storms and strike an axe at the clouds and pull down thunder from the wound and—"

"And me?" she interrupted.

"And you."

I could not help it, then, but to kiss her cheek. She was more to me in that moment than she had been all evening. She was the ghost of our university days together. There had been no consequences for mere possibilities, then. We had lived in a present built on tomorrows. Wasted tomorrows.

I had fooled myself into thinking that I was some great sage, that the words of true wise men had been my own all along. There, in the tomes and tomes we read, in the speculations we made, in the arguments we had, I had seen a false reflection of myself.

Yes, those nightly discussions with Sophia, in the sanctuary of low oaks and chestnut benches, among those watchers who had listened in, had tied our minds together. We searched and scrounged for knowledge—of each other and of all the mysteries scattered in our path. Bound in every way, in every minute idea, depth of pleasure, or corner of experience, unhappy to let the other ache alone in mind or flesh. And we destroyed the outside world together. We deconstructed it piece by piece and trampled it in pride, until the only thing left of it was the tenuous wisp of some distant and vaguely remembered dream fit to scatter like ash off the reality we knew. Bright days, arrogant days. Our souls burning like those fiery pits of the sun I so seek to dominate.

That night years later, if I had sent a hand through the threadbare mesh of our bond, I might have found only a living twine or two. Frail and innocent as worms between my fingers.

"I just need the time," I said. "If I had the time, it wouldn't sound like a joke. I'd actually get some of the work done. If I just had the time to think. I…" I trailed off.

She looked completely exhausted. "Are you still going on about your treatise? God, it's one obsession or the other. Just stop it. Forget about it. It'll drive you mad. It's driving me mad."

"What?"

"It's a mess. The whole thing."

"How can you say that? You said the last draft reads like Hegel!"

"Yes, in the pejorative sense."

I remained quiet and seethed.

"It's indulgent, it's convoluted, and it's given you a big head," she continued. "So just stop it. You've rotted the whole idea out. And I don't even know what it is you're after. You always talk about this and that, but what about here and now? I still haven't heard a word about it that makes any sense. Not immediately, anyway."

"A word—if only! How could I speak it? Knowledge—you know— the problem. We're not free. Not free to utter a single innocent word. There's no freedom at all when even a grain of knowledge is out of reach."

"What are you even saying? What does any of that mean?"

"I mean, I can hardly understand you. And what am I saying now? Of course none of it's clear. What do you know about me, really? You have my face, the color of my eyes—sort of—the scraps of thoughts you've heard from me over the years, but otherwise, what?"

"Enough to care about you. I think," she said, losing patience.

It was pathetic. I felt like a mute wrestling with a dictionary. "What do you want me to say, Sophia?" I erupted. "Damn it, I don't even know what I would say. Every time I try to speak, to say anything, it's as though I'm trying to pour—no, vomit—all of myself out, and I only manage a little drop while I clench my ribs. They hurt, my ribs. It's as though I'm expecting each word or phrase or sentence to represent everything I've ever wanted to say to you, to everyone. A single word that contains all of me. Where is it? Where's the time for it? I feel mentally constipated, that's what it is, but simultaneously starved. That's disgusting, isn't it?"

She sighed at me. "What do you want to do about it then? It's not right to suffer that way."

"No, I need time to think, need space for it. If I could just explain it to you."

Blessed creature. I envied the very aura that teemed around her. She had the fullest presence: a completeness of being that extended past my understanding. I could see hints of it here, there—a tranquil lake for a mind—and I wanted it.

"Try," she said.

"I can't. I need time."

"Well, whatever it is. Research? You could start today. You really could, if you didn't obsess so much over what's not in your control, and if you spoke to me a little more lovingly, maybe. Do you think every great artist, or philosopher, or scientist had the luxury of time you want? A lot of them didn't even have the kind of salaries we're making right now," she said, and gave a bleak little laugh.

I stared at the wall ahead and huffed. "We live in a different age," I said. "Even though we have more time, it's the wrong kind of time, Sophia. Everything moves so fast, and there's barely a moment to stop and think, and—"

"'And people don't understand each other at all, and we have wider but more superficial knowledge, and good ideas get lost in the noise.' I know. I know what you're going to say, because you always say the same thing. But don't you think that every person who's ever lived has thought the same thing? That they don't have the kinds of advantages that their predecessors did, or that their children will have? I think they probably all did, because it's normal to know how to complain about the present. And everything you'll ever experience will be in the present, so stop it."

"I suppose," I muttered. Of course I was wasting my breath trying to explain. Could not explain, not even to myself. And if she could not grasp it—she, in whose power it was to contain what was possible of me, of us all—it was certainly lost. I gave her another spiteful look, and though she caught my glance, she had the patience to stomach this last affront.

"So I think you should just let it rest for a while," she said after inhaling. "At least while you look for that job. It'll take longer, and you won't have the kind of time you're hoping to have, but at least you'll get somewhere. And have a few peaceful nights, I hope." She put a hand on my lap while I sat there, motionless, unwilling to even look at her.

"What a stupid thing to say," I said. "It shows how little there is—" I stood up, casting her off like a rag. A dark, long-festering hubris was flowering out of me. I found the courage to at last grip the bars of my life's gibbeted cage, and shake them.

She raised her voice and frowned, wrinkling her forehead. "How little there is of what?"

"You know what I mean," I almost snarled. "When was the last time we could look at each other without trying?"

With a sudden crease in her brow, she observed me gravely, as if contemplating something far more serious than me. "You're not wrong," she finally said.

It would be a lie if I said I felt no sudden moment of regret, but I was quick to quash it.

"So leave," she continued while striding over to the desk. She spilled a few volumes off the shelves and then tossed the last one at me. "If there's nothing left, if you're this great misunderstood sage, if I'm just too stupid to understand your work or your ideas or why you're driving us into the ground, then get out."

My hands were planted listlessly akimbo, as though I were ready to sigh out my lack of enthusiasm. "I didn't call *you* st—"

"Either sit down and forget your treatise and your obsessions and hold me, or get out. I'm sick of it."

My stomach churned at the thought of sitting beside her again. It entailed work, real effort, and to what end? No. I was Prometheus under the receding sun, serving cycles of my punishment in hours, not eons, and the eagle would never pause on Sophia's account.

"Well?"

We stared at each other in silence. She was different now, and tiresome. I loathed her for having once been so exciting. My lips were dry and stuck together like a blister, and I was frowning as though I had something sour in my mouth. The moment lingered, my expression said more than any misstep in speech could have, and her face dipped.

As a few lines of her bundled hair fell across her face, she looked on at me with sorrow, and said not a word as I stuffed my feet into my shoes, left the room, and shamelessly closed the door behind me. It was time—she knew it—that much was clear.

Follow me now, dark-hearted and gray-souled, as I stride on into the mist. If all ends are sown into their beginnings, then there is no other storm but this one. But hear the crash of those electric rains shrink to a sizzle. The howling of the wolves drowning out to a feeble whimpering... Those immense robes of wind are only a distraction. Yes, there is time to listen. There is gold in my failures. Hearken to me. The stars are calling, the suns aching to wake, but we needn't pay mind yet. You must listen, and try to wring out what sympathy is possible.

Away then, to split Sophia from her lover, though I did still love her.

THE FIRST BETRAYAL

Dusk was settling behind the hills of Ionia, dragging the clouds down with it and propping the stars up into place. The wind blew an early frost through the puzzle of thatched roofs and swept dust from the ground between houses before sending a firm chill down the spines of sleepers and waking wanderers alike. It was not yet winter, though the dying fires and thin walls betrayed its coming.

It was only months after her birth. She was not yet called Sielle, though the name has always belonged to her, as if her soul were branded with it. A couple found her whimpering in the bushes, the twilight glimmering through the leaves. The wife snatched her from the ground and brought her home.

In a house not far from the lowest hill, overlooking the sea and the rest of the brown hamlet, the couple held a conversation in whispers. Lamplight broke a dim circle into a corner, where a stack of hay supported the little pink and white bundle. The two figures loomed frantically over the baby.

"It's the spirits' doing, I'm sure of it."

"Stop that. Don't say these things. You can't know."

"There can't be any other way."

"We have been here all day. There was nothing and nobody."

"No. But they play tricks sometimes."

"Who told you this, your father?"

"And if he told me? It's something everyone knows."

"What the spirits do is for them. This... look, this is for us."

Below the quarrelling couple, the baby squirmed. She reached into the air, groping, amused with herself. The woman emerged out of the shadows, kneeling down to touch the child.

"Don't!" yelped the big man beside her. "She could be a spirit."

Above the lamp, his nose protruded out of his owlish face. He grimaced wildly at his wife's gesture towards the child below.

"Oh, by Hera, don't be so scared about everything," she told him.

They spent much of the night battling his superstitions and his skepticism. He asked his wife if Zeus had fathered the child. He invoked the evil eye of his neighbors, and his own neglect at the temple. At last, once his wife had calmed him down, he bent over slightly to take a closer look at the child.

Reluctant at first, he bent lower, but not before throwing his wife a last worried glance. He extended a finger to the baby's tiny fat hands. Just as the child curled her little stubs around the callused thing, the man retracted his hand as though he had stuck it in a beehive.

"Don't make her scared like that, old woman!" his wife said, slapping his shoulder.

There was a pause, as the lamp sputtered and oil dripped onto the floor beneath it. The man pulled the lamp back with alacrity and stamped his feet where the oil had dripped, twisting his head to see if any of it had landed on the child beside him.

"You see? You love her just like I do, big coward. If it's from the gods, then it can't be something bad."

The man's eyes snapped between his wife and the child. "Maybe... Maybe, if we take her to the temple, and if I honor the white rooster, and if we have her blessed. Then maybe."

His wife beamed at him as she raised the child up to wrap her in thicker cloth. "Our daughter! Our wonderful daughter."

At sunrise, light flooded the couple's house and warmed the big man as he wriggled himself awake. He shut his eyes hard and rubbed them while trying to raise himself from the bed.

Sitting up, he tried to understand what was blaring through the room. Memories of the previous night fell on him like a waterfall. Not yet fully awake, he turned to look for his wife, but found only the empty bed. He heard muffled wailing followed by whimpering from the far end of the room.

His wife was in the corner, crouched over an empty stack of hay.

꩜ 3 ꩜

THE EQUULEUS

Tikan sat at his desk in the officer's lounge of the Equuleus with a worn book folded over his knee. The stars shone half-light into the room, casting it navy. Each one made a final glimmer before passing out of sight. Far away, the swirl of a distant galaxy faded.

There through the glass, the void was playing with his perspective. In the span of a moment, his perception of the darkness switched from emptiness to the binding of all that *is*; from sun eater to tapestry riddled in holes leading to a more frightening place yet. His thoughts wandered to dimmed memories and hopes. He was incapable of seeing the whole from where he was. He was like a fool trying to survey a room through a keyhole.

His thoughts shrank, and he returned to his sober loneliness. He passed his hand over the mottled leather of the book on his knee. Many years prior, he had found the tome on Mars, among other heirlooms of the old world. Ever had he turned to it for knowledge of the past, though it felt more and more impenetrable to him as the years wore on.

Suddenly, light slashed through the room as the door behind him opened, and a tall silhouette walked in. The flash caught the corner of Tikan's eye. He spun in his chair without turning his face from the

Tikan's eye. He spun in his chair without turning his face from the window. Then he took the book from his lap and slid it to the edge of the desk.

"And what have you found out in black space today, Mr. Solstafir?" Captain Amozagh asked, as the door slid shut to the floor behind him.

Tearing himself from his thoughts and the window, Tikan stared at the door and postponed his response for a few seconds. "The stars, captain. The old fire. They have many truths I can't yet tell."

"Should I be worried? Only madmen and seers speak to the stars. And you sure aren't the latter."

They looked at each other, and Tikan could not help adopting the captain's infectious smirk. There was a festive sarcasm without which the old jester could not begin a conversation, an obnoxious humor that somehow turned into endearing charm.

"I tend to do more listening than speaking, these days," Tikan said.

"As it should be. All that dark emptiness around the stars is made of speech, if you ask me."

"Ask *him* about emptiness," Tikan said languorously, pointing at the misshapen figure of a third man seated on the other side of the room.

The buzzing, slouching flesh was arranged in the corner like some dumped cargo. Somewhere, in a room light-years from his body, Naim's soul was vacationing. With his back slumped against the seat and his legs outstretched, and his fingers quivering as they dangled close to the ground, his body struggled in unsteady rhythms of contortion. He groaned periodically, with saliva hanging off of his lips. There were droplets of his drool scattered about him, making a clicking sound whenever it hit the floor. And his eyes were open and jailed in their sockets, trembling in microscopic shudders, the dark honey irises dilating and contracting in epileptic non-patterns. They vibrated as though in disagreement with the dusk blue of the room. If Naim's sense of hearing were not muted, he would have heard Tikan kick the floor, and his office chair rumble against it.

"He is far, far away," Amozagh said, chuckling as he strolled in.

The old captain trampled the shadows with his easy gait. He

leaned against the wall to rest his gaze on the stars, where Tikan's had once again landed.

"And us? How far are we from Proxima?"

"A jump or two, maybe more."

They did not speak for a moment, but instead listened to the grunting exhaust of Naim's abandoned flesh.

"Come on, let's play while I still can," Amozagh said, throwing a stained pack of cards onto a nearby table. He shook the cards out of their uniform pile and began languidly shuffling them.

Tikan swiveled in his office chair and paddled with his feet over to the table where Amozagh was sitting. "You're starting to like the game."

"It's a lame old game. Reason you can't find easy replacement cards, I bet, is because they didn't print many. Nobody plays it now; nobody played it then."

Tikan shook his head. "You get to play it with a real person."

"Get to play it with a washed-up cripple."

"A cripple?" Tikan laughed. "You're getting meaner in your old age."

They drew their cards, then, and began to play. Amozagh placed a dented and scratched little portable air filter on the table and switched it on. Then he lit a cigarette and made sure to blow the smoke into the filter's suction.

They drank purified water and matched wits and were in the habit of slamming cards down onto the table upon their palms while they played their game, which was a patchwork of other games whose rules had gone neglected for centuries. As their laughter came to overtake the sounds of Naim, and after the pile of cards in the center of the table grew sizable, the hour elapsed.

"The king of hearts." Amozagh said, grinning, pulling out a king of hearts whose corners were peeling and whose hearts were turning a sickly green. "Do you think it's any fun, ruling a kingdom of hearts?"

Tikan shook his head dismissively.

"Are you going to come to the surface with us?" Amozagh asked.

The starlight rotated across Tikan's face in crescents. He looked up at Amozagh with a degree of irritation, and inhaled. The cards smelled of must. "You know I can't."

"I know you don't want to."

"No."

"Come. This time we won't take the throughground. I promise."

Tikan tossed his cards into the pile. "Ridiculous."

"Yeah, I just don't know why you hate the place so much," Amozagh said. "It's the same as Earth or any other place, just prettier."

Tikan shook his head at him. "Come on, it's a pain enough having to explain myself to others. Shouldn't have to do it with you. Draw six."

"Does he know?" Amozagh asked, pointing at Naim just as he made another mindless sound. He drew his last hand.

"Of course not. He's just happy to obliterate himself in metempsies all day."

Amozagh sighed. "You know, I don't think there's much of a difference between what he's doing and what you do, reading that torn thing all day. Or playing this game. Has it started making sense yet?" he asked, pointing at the book on the desk.

"There is a difference."

"Right," Amozagh said, standing up. "It's much better, that's what."

"Sure it is."

"Anyway. The dinner's starting in the lounge; I should get going. But, I don't know, Tikan," Amozagh said, dropping his comedic tone. "I am starting to feel sorry for you. How many years have you been here now on this… this pilgrimage to nowhere? No metempsies, even. Go back to Sirius, or Earth, and find a family. Leave this old ship to its old captain, before you get too old, and take that fool with you while you're at it," he said, pointing at Naim as he made another groan.

"Won't get much farther than the airlock without a procrustus," Tikan said, incessantly reshuffling the cards, though he had already made four perfect rectangles of them.

"Look, you don't want to metempsy, fine, but the world runs on procrustiis. You've got some noise in your head, that's all. But, go ahead, stay here. It suits me just fine. I told you I enjoy our talks."

Tikan's jaw tightened. "And why would I go?"

"Go and live."

"You've got a strange idea of living."

"Yeah," Amozagh said. "That's why I'm on this ship with you, 'cause I don't know how to live. Right?"

Tikan got up and slammed his fist on the wayward jack of spades, revealing the sleeve of burn scars coming down his forearm to the front of his hand. "You've got no clue. You really don't."

Amozagh let out another sigh. "Metempsies, metempsies, procrustiis and the galaxy in flames. Bad excuses if you ask me. You—"

"And what else?" Tikan almost yelled.

As the tension between them lingered in a brief silence, Amozagh furrowed his brow, and put his hand on Tikan's shoulder.

Recognizing Amozagh again as his one living confidant, Tikan's gaze softened and his shoulders slackened, and he fell back into his chair. "Every time we sit together to play cards, and relax, you try to pull some story from me that you think I've got neatly laid out in my mind. You want to know what happened to me? I've lost years to the question. I've killed and stolen and harbored myself here, in the middle of space, precisely because I have no answers."

He has seen galaxies die, after all. All devoured and forgotten. He has watched the universe fall on its own sword, though he will not invoke the images any longer.

The sound of heavy breathing filled the room, punctuated by the aberrant sounds coming from Naim. Tikan turned to the dark and the stars outside again. He ignored Amozagh's glare.

There was a prolonged pause between them, during which Amozagh took a last drag from his half-wasted cigarette before putting it out. The top of the captain's face was obscured, though his graying beard caught the light of his cigarette, the little curls brightening in orange detail.

They both refrained from speaking and listened to the hum of the ship. Then Naim's seat squeaked after another of his errant movements, and Tikan's rolling chair started to grate the floor.

"I'm sorry," Amozagh said. "I've tried to understand and I can't, but I'm sorry. Maybe if my imagination still worked right I could understand." He knocked his own temple as if his head were a faulty device. "Stay here and have your peace. It suits me just fine."

Just as the ship made another jump through space-time, the window twinkled out a series of crescent lights across Tikan's face.

"So, tell me, captain," Tikan said, regaining his composure and exhaling through his nose. "Any chance dinner will be any good tonight?"

"On this damn ship?"

They broke into laughter. They turned back to the window and watched their common view of that great canvas against which all was absent. And before Naim's body could make another interruption, Tikan pushed his chair against the desk and rolled away from the window.

"I'm going to try and sleep for a few hours, then," he said, rising and sliding his book into a cupboard in the desk while exhaling a final breath.

"Okay, then. Let's hope this fool comes back from his holiday before his shift starts. If you can't sleep, I'll be in the lounge. Otherwise, I'll see you in a few hours. I'll try to keep you a bone or two in case you get hungry."

They walked out of the room together, leaving Naim to his visions and his convulsions. Amozagh slapped a hand on his friend's back. After a final chuckle, they split at the ship's midsection.

Somehow uplifted by his conversation with the captain, Tikan started to make his way to the crew quarters. He passed the long hallway and the kitchen. The smell of grilled meats and sautéed vegetables wafted out into the ship's principal spine before being sucked up by vents in the inlets of the ceiling. His hunger was roused, but he continued on, only glancing at the chefs busy at their stations.

He passed by the passenger dormitories and caught a glimpse of a person in a metempsy whose lips were now pressed lasciviously to a lampshade. Another was sitting down, also metempsying, far more immersed and therefore possessing a more docile body, but regularly calling out absurdities such as, "Meteorites are people too!" or "My first true love was myself," or, "You'd have an easier time finding matches in the sun." A few younger passengers were gathered in a circle, metempsying a sport together, their fists squeezing red as each of them won while the others lost.

Farther down the halls of the crew quarters, he slipped into a vacant room to find his sleeping pod, which resembled a giant test-tube.

4

THE THREE GORGONS

In the waiting area near my departure gate, I sat and stewed and leered bitterly at a child across from me. Stewing, yes, the contents all Sophia.

I grew vexed, the longer I sat there, thinking over how she had implied that I should abandon writing my philosophical treatise. But, as with most of my ill feelings towards her, it was not long before these led back to my own shortcomings. I had been happy to speak about the work on countless occasions, while reserving its execution uniquely for an ideal time in the future when I would be at my highest intellectual capacity and physical form, free of all constraints and able to change the world in one stroke of brilliance. Soon, it would begin.

The call for boarding broke me from my thoughts, and I joined the queue.

"May I have your boarding pass, please?"

I reached for the paper card without looking at the person. The machine inhaled my pass and spat out a green light.

"Thank you, sir. Just down here."

Down I walked through the long walkway and up to the side of the plane. I tried to avoid seeing the nauseating blue of the carpet with its small, whirring little squiggles littered all around. A swoop of cold air rushed me as I stepped into the cabin.

"Thank you, sir. 12D. To my left, down the aisle."

I may have replied something. Probably it was just a half-uttered grunt that sounded like a "thank you" in my head. The miserable shuffle through the plane started.

I was behind jaded businessmen with their luggage trailing too far behind them and a mother struggling with too many plastic bags from the kiosk at the terminal, each of her children clamoring for a different distraction. I wanted only to watch the city become a speck of dust, before the clouds would cover it completely, and those people were making the process painfully slow.

Then came the cheery and smiling student, probably on his first flight, probably for some foreign exchange program that would later disappoint him, carrying a cased cello on his back and trying to swim against the current. Let his innocence burn through the cynics like sun against chalky vampires, and then move. Move. Move. Move.

Finally, 12D. There was a toothpick of a man in the seat next to mine. He was tracing a finger up and down the page of a thick book with a dulled cover. I wished I had been given the window seat, but I was too tired to ask, and instead settled for an opportunity to distend my contemptuousness. With my seat belt buckled and my earplugs in, I was able to keep my eyes open just long enough to watch the Earth sink.

I slept through most of the flight, though I woke into brief, semi-conscious dazes at certain points. The drag of takeoff had taken a substantial toll on me, and the toothpick beside me proved to be pleasantly soundless and studious. In my few waking moments, through the hum of the engines and the gush of compressed air, I could sense the flight attendant buzzing around me, preying on me, waiting for me to show the slightest sign of alertness so as to pester me. *Bother the toothpick. Pick your teeth with him. Bother him while I dream.*

I woke to a sudden landing. The plane bumped and jerked to a halt. The pilot gave his dreadful speech, announced the temperature, and then retreated again to his fortress.

More cramped shuffling, this time accompanied by the smell of travel sweat and the sound of a teenager's distant and tiny music from out of his earphones filling the few gaps left between miserable strangers. A boy who visited musicians for philosophical advice, no doubt. He looked around, hoping to catch someone observing the rapturous intensity to which he was subjecting himself. How was anyone to know, little man, what powered those drums? The cymbal crash of a failed romance? Childish. The snare of ambition? It does capture us all. No, hear that bass drum kick out the trauma of your very birth!

We all stepped out of the plane's orifice onto more blue carpet, and *Bienvenue à l'aéroport Charles-de-Gaulle.*

A poster with a cellphone caged in a stop sign caught my eye upon entering the baggage claim area. I checked my pockets. Nothing. Of course, I had left it in the cupboard along with the string that had tied Sophia to my heel. How good it felt to be free of that toxic heap of junk! The sign had it wrong: the cellphone was the cage, and the observer was inside.

Leaving Sophia felt like leaving all restraints, but it wasn't only her and her stifling aura; phones, wallets, keys—these, too, had been anchors in my pocket, which had ever bound me to places or times or persons. Vile little things, promising to facilitate our union but only driving us apart more deeply.

Yes, how terrible and worrisome when those externals became like organs, unfastened by bones or flesh to their hosts. Victims, all of us, to a life eroded by digital rain, pickaxed apart by bits and digits, with the small death of ring after ring ghosting through the cracks—each one a momentary, thin spike slid into the ego, bruising it, whispering, "You're nothing" into it, compounding fractures in it, year after year, until the result was a paranoid beast unable to disconnect its mind from its pocket as it bulged with a poisoned treasure.

And those who purchased these amusing mores from society fooled themselves. They drew some image of a sophisticated self over the cave paintings of their ancestors, when, in truth, these little tokens only funneled their primitive instincts into controllable channels; where, as a herd, they could agree to the same sour illusions; where, as oppressors, they could curb the innovators, the thinkers, those who could soar but were weighed down by the pathetic talismans of the modern world: the phone, the key, the wallet. The three Gorgons in plastic, metal, and leather: serpents at my feet, no longer.

Returning to myself at the airport—I must mention Sophia again, since my thoughts continued to circle around her. My love for her had been violent, during those first years; and then it simply was. Unchanging, uninteresting, and unmade. Even as I had wandered the freezing streets out of our home, during the night of our argument, I had not found resolve in my decision to leave. Until, at dawn, the sunrise let me drink up what courage I was missing. I would travel, far and out of reach, and I would pursue my hermetic quest.

Out of the terminal I breathed the fresh air.

When I said would travel far, I meant to Paris, and when I said out of reach, I excluded my friend Pierre. I had called him from a payphone at the airport before departing and explained the situation to him.

Before Sophia had taken to consume my life, we had been very good friends, Pierre and I. In our university days, he would entertain my tirades and long speeches filled with half-completed thoughts and ideas about the nature of *something*, and he had done so with calm interest. In a way, Sophia had taken the mantle of muse right off his back, providing me—for a short time—with a taste of the satisfaction of mind I came to crave.

When I called Pierre from the airport, he had filled the crackling call with promises to help me until I got back on my feet, and with jealous proclamations such as, "Well, I never liked that bitch. You're better off, now." Still, our contact over the years had been limited, and I hadn't expected his kindness.

I paced the pavement for some time, hoping Pierre would recognize me despite having not seen me in years. The new cold had me rubbing my hands and puffing out clouds of breath while looking for shreds of sympathy in the faces of people rushing out to the world again.

Then, from around the corner, what looked like a refurbished getaway car, black and lean, circled and swerved, too fast for an airport parking area. The smell of petrol mixed with searing tires as the car stabbed the sidewalk. He was an odd person, Pierre. He honked in off-beat rhythms and lowered the window, sticking half of his long head out and yelling, "Hey, *gros salaud*. Here!"

I walked briskly to the car and slid into the front seat.

"How the hell are you? Ah, never mind. Obviously, you're not great. But, how are you, you know, generally? I mean, how was your flight?"

I blinked at him rapidly. Somehow, his French accent seemed to have almost evaporated. Not that he had had a strong one to begin with, for he had been sent to study abroad at a young age, but it was still somewhat remarkable, considering he had returned to France.

"I'm well. Quite well. Better than I've felt in a long time."

"Oh. Well, that's good. Great. I'm glad you decided to come here, after, well, all *that*, you know. You couldn't have picked a better place. It's good. We haven't spoken properly in a long time," he said, twisting the air-conditioning knob into the red.

"No, we haven't. And I'm sorry about that. You know, with Sophia and all. It's been hard. But that's how it ended up, and here I am. We'll make up for all the lost time, now," I said, trying to grin.

"Yes! And it's going to be great. I'll show you all the great places. We'll catch up, and chat like the old days. I've set up the place for you. Tonight we can just hang out, or get dinner somewhere. There's a great Chinese place near the apartment. However you like."

"I'm looking forward to it."

"So what's been going on with you? You know, other than, well, her."

The green scenery next to the concrete ramps of the highway passed us, blending together into one mammoth bush. I tore my gaze from it to reply.

"Nothing good. It all fell to pieces, really. I was trying to land a job as a manager or consultant somewhere. It didn't work out. I'm more than qualified. I don't know why they never called me back. None of them. I think I'll start on a project I've waiting to start for a while, instead."

I stopped myself before letting the tide of bitterness in me triumph again.

"Ah. Projects. *Those.* You always said you were working on something. What ever happened? Get any done?"

"Well, that's what I want to work on, now. I've put it off for too long. I just never really had the time; it was always just one thing after the other. But now I'll have a fresh space to work in. I have so many thoughts, ideas, piled up in my head. They've been swimming around there for so long. It's more than I need to write about. How about you? How are you doing these days? What are you doing?"

"I'm great, actually. My internships out of college sent me straight here. They like the cosmopolitan background, these companies. Local who speaks four languages and studied outside? Be slightly competent at your job, and you're in."

"That's great. Really great. I'm happy for you. How about on the side? Have you met anyone?"

"I could, if I was interested in that." He eyed me for a second while giving me a roguish grin. "Things are moving automatically for me. I'm enjoying the trip. Steering with my feet and enjoying the cocktails, you know."

I flinched at his bizarre metaphor. The conversation paused, and I squirmed in the seat, trying to disperse the soreness in my muscles. His car smelled like it was brought out of the showroom the previous day—that odor had always been putrid to me.

"Okay, Okay. Well, don't worry. Don't feel uncomfortable, or scared," Pierre said, after glancing at me and taking in my pitiful shape, and no doubt misconstruing the way I had flinched. "I'll help you find a job, a good one, you know, I work at *Technologie-Dupont.* I have good contacts there. I can help get your application in easy, no problem."

No. No. Not that. Anything but that. I was finished with

corporations and jobs. At least until my ideas could be safely exported and stored where they could not be interfered with. You understand, don't you?

"To be honest, I want to take that slowly, the job hunt and all. I said I'm alright, but it was taxing, with Sophia and all, and so I'm still recovering. You understand, right? I think I want to take some time to do some personal work."

"I understand. Yes. But you know, after two weeks or so, when you feel ready, I can help you," Pierre said with a full grin.

I shuddered, without saying more on the subject. He had changed. I could sense it through the off humor and the well-reconstructed character of his youth. Job, job, job. What a terrible way to start. No, this Pierre was not going to allow me to thrive. I would have two weeks to find a new dwelling, before cutting him from my life as well.

THE ORPHAN

FROM THE PRIVATE JOURNAL OF DR. CLYDE BOOTH

Patient: Jane Smith

Age: (Approx. 5 years)

9/17/1956

Received a call this afternoon from Sunrise Children's Home. Stern voice. Distressed. Administrator mentioned a girl of theirs—Jane Smith. Anti-social, removed from the other orphans, refuses to participate. Speculations about whether she is foreign, since she understands English but does not speak it. Asked to see me and evaluate the girl. I'll be meeting with her tomorrow.

9/18/1956

1:36 PM meeting with Randall & Eloise Carpenter.

The orphanage administration is worried that Jane Smith has suffered some trauma. They describe her as "lonesome," "emotionally disturbed," "disaffected," and "un-childlike." Generally not hostile, but defensively anti-social, from what I gather. They mentioned she appeared at the door a few months ago by herself. Likely a runaway, but apparently police have no leads. Meeting with Jane in 20 minutes.

2:03 PM meeting with Jane Smith

The child seems normal at first glance. Slight darkness under the eyes, but certainly not "disturbed" or "un-childlike." My preconceptions led me to think she would use her dark hair as a shield, but instead she seems intent on confronting her conversant intently with her gaze. She refuses to speak when I ask her name. At first one could mistake this for shyness, but her generally confident posture, straightforward gaze, and raised tilt of the head conflicts with that account. Indicates a distrust of adults, and perhaps other children, too, given Carpenters' testimony.

I talked a bit about myself to build trust. No results today, though she did seem to perk up at mention of my weekly hiking this past August. Perched head forward at mention of thunderstorm the other week, and at talk of crepuscular rays or woodpeckers. According to the Carpenters, she is not mute.

9/19/1956

9:06 AM meeting with Jane Smith

Brought soda with me today, thinking Jane would like it, but she just asked for water instead. Seemed to flinch at the soda can. Got her talking, at least. I asked her why she doesn't like soda but she just made an expression like she had something sour in her mouth and shook her head. I wonder if this is just distaste for cola or if it is motivated by something else.

I caught her looking out the window behind me while I was trying to make conversation. She was looking at a bird tending to her nest. We talked about wings and wind and the way leaves fall in the winter but grow back. She has a funny accent, and gaps in her vocabulary. I'm guessing she's a Soviet refugee, or some other kind. Tried to move to other subjects of conversation, but she just clams up. At risk of losing progress, I did not push.

9/20/1956

9:30 AM meeting with Jane Smith

Today she asked me whether looking at a painting of the moon was looking at the moon or just at paint. Smart kid. Got me thinking. Shows intense, joyful wonder at the natural world, but little interest in social matters.

1:01 PM observations of Jane interacting with the other orphans.

Though she mostly keeps to herself, notice her, at times, eyeing groups of other children. Her body language indicates that at first she intends to approach these more socially active groups, but almost immediately retracts. Recoils, more like. When she is noticed by them, they mock her accent or generally deride her. This appears to affect her not at all.

She hovers about the more isolated children. She even tries to approach one of them—another girl seemingly without friends——but her status as a pariah appears already cemented. Contrary to the original testimony of the Carpenters and of my own previous observations, these situations do indeed seem to cause her some emotional distress. That is, she is not disturbed at all by how she is perceived or by the fact of being generally ostracized, but she is indeed affected once her approaches are rebuffed. It is not the other children's reactions which seem to disturb her, exactly, but rather that she has compromised herself in the first place.

Must investigate this matter more carefully. Starting to build basis for a formal report.

9/21/1956

Beginning to suspect that Jane is not emotionally disturbed, but instead is a victim of Kanner's Syndrome. Not the most popular explanation for this sort of behavior—but I think it fits. Kanner uses the word "autism," after all, to refer to the psychological need children have to escape from reality. Jane appears to me unfixed. Not necessarily unwilling to participate because she finds a problem with the other children, the home, or the Carpenters, but because they do not appear as entities to which she can fix herself in the first place. Perhaps she is not autistic, then, because she is not escaping. Rather, she has already escaped, or she is not captive to whatever ails the autistic to begin with. Fascinating.

9/23/1956

Sunday, 6:14 PM emergency meeting with the Carpenters.

A few hours ago, Jane cut the webbing between a boy's thumb and index fingers with a pair of scissors during arts and crafts. The damage was not severe, but the staff is understandably distressed.

6:45 PM meeting with Jane

Trying to understand her motivation. She looks confused by the commotion around her actions. Exchange went something like this:

Me: Why did you do it, Jane?

Jane: I don't know...I wanted to see if it's like cutting paper.

Me: Paper and a person's hand aren't the same thing. Don't you feel pain when you get cut?

Jane: Yes, but that's me.

Me: Others don't get hurt?

Jane: I think so. But they're different.

Me: How are they different? They look like you. They mostly behave like you. Can't they feel like you?

She does not answer much else. Frown indicates that she is aware that others feel pain. Mostly, she seems confused. Will return tomorrow and attempt a deeper understanding.

9/24/1956

9:00 AM experiment with Jane and Thomas.

It struck me last night that Jane may not fully appreciate that others have minds. In order to investigate this I've decided to run an experiment.

I called in another orphan, Thomas. While Jane was still in the room, I asked Thomas to leave the room. I then removed my wristwatch and hid it in one of the filing cabinets. I then asked Jane where she thought Thomas would look for the watch when I let him back in the room. My hypothesis was the following: If Jane said Thomas would know the watch was in the cabinet upon returning, despite her knowing that he did not witness me hide it, then her understanding of other minds could be described as highly problematic.

When I asked her where she thought Thomas would look for the watch, she just shrugged. Initially assumed that the hypothesis was disproved. Then, I asked her why she didn't think he would look in the cabinet——just to be certain. Expected her to say, "Because I saw him leave the room. If he wasn't in the room to see you hide it, then he can't know it's in the cabinet."

Instead, she looked at me with an innocent smirk and asked, "How can someone find something if they can't see it?"

9/26/1956

Received a call from the Carpenters today. Jane has gone missing. The other kids reacted harshly to the scissor incident, would not stop harassing her about it, and apparently made her cry. Hard to believe. Did not think they could affect her like that. Unsure of how to proceed.

6

THE CHOIRS OF PERDITION

Beyond the veil of sleep, sweeping, alarming sounds circled the world. Submerged, almost inaudible at first, but gently the noise was rising. Perhaps in a dream stretching out in the final moments before waking, the world seemed to sway and tilt. It was all taking on weight.

Tikan pressed his fingers against the circumflex window above him. They twitched, bending to make claws, then straightened out in search of slivers of the cold outside. He repeated the motions, and then opened his eyes to fogged glass. Each breath burdened his throat. Heat swam out of the synthetic black leather and smothered him. Outside, he heard screams racing. There was another tilt, and a rumble through the ship. He tried to focus in zigzags, and the glass lit up as he jerked forward.

A series of colorful sleep analytics floated above him on the tube's window. A log reading *four hours*, graphs, pie charts. He swatted it all away and scrambled to exit. The shield of the tube opened with steam and precision. After pushing himself from the pod, he stumbled groggily out of the room.

The hallway was a blur of hot lights. Bright, far too bright. And the walls were sending out sharp reflections. Tikan threw an arm across his face as he made his way out of the crew quarters. His head throbbed to the sound of boots like dull hammers on some nearby floor, although he had yet to see a single person. The commotion seemed to be coming from the lounge, where the passengers had been spending their time. The ship rumbled again.

He drifted out into the long walkway that ran through the ship while coughing out remnants of the compressed air that had been pumped into his lungs. Still in a daze, and staring too long at mundane peculiarities in his surroundings, he made for the lounge.

There was a lull before the tilting started again. Then the ship started to shake, and the floor vibrated. With a sense of impending danger, Tikan fell chest-first against the beam of a nearby doorjamb and pressed both hands to its outer walls. The walls turned slippery, and in his confused state he questioned for an instant whether they were beginning to melt. Then the rocking started. And the ship dipped and spun onto its starboard side. The artificial gravity lapsed, and his feet were sent up into the air. He hovered off the ground for a moment, clinging to the steel of the outer doorjambs. As soon as he landed, shockwaves from the port side tore through the entire structure like detonated mines. His hands were ripped from the doorjamb's beam, and he was flung back across the hallway into a nearby door.

The ship mended back to its original position, and Tikan wiped his hands and raised himself, almost tumbling over, then started again down the walkway. The walls were now burning in earnest. He looked around. There were other passengers arriving, as if from nowhere, rushing.

The rhythm of Tikan's heart and his skittering eyes told of a dark suspicion now festering in his chest: that he, and he alone, was the cause and anchor of this emerging violence.

An orange glow emanated from the corridor, followed by a low, deafening blast. Tikan cupped his ears. Sparks, flames, and smoke poured down a column of screams from the front of the ship. Fire and bodies rolled by, and people began moaning in agony. Tikan kicked himself up a final time and hurried into the security room just in front of him.

Nobody was inside. It was dark, the blue light of the security feed's display streaking the walls and painting his inflated shadow across the room. The anodized gray rifles on a rack to his immediate left caught his attention first. He grabbed one and slung it over his shoulder. With the rifle not yet settled across his back, he raced for the light at the far end of the room.

All of the live feeds from the lounge had been destroyed save for two. In the second, he could make out a torn and bloodied Amozagh leaning against a dented wall.

The surveillance projection jittered with the image of the battered captain. He was almost fully veiled in smoke, surrounded by fresh corpses, severed limbs, and bouquets of electronics erupted from their casings. Shadows swayed through the fumes encircling him. Then fast, through fleeing wisps, a hand plunged through the smoke to Amozagh and drove him against the wall by the throat.

Black-gloved fingers curled around his neck and pressed into his arteries. The old man was then forced back down to the floor. There was a brief pause. Before Tikan could resolve to do much else, Amozagh looked up at his assailant with bloodshot eyes widened, and in his old arrogance he tried to form a grin.

His grimace lasted half a second before he received the hard butt of a rifle in the mouth. Tikan gripped the chair he was leaning against. Blood burst from Amozagh's gums and lips, spilling down his chin and vest. It glistened against his skin. He opened his mouth again and spat a red glob at his attacker through broken and missing teeth. The hand hovered tensely about him, as though disembodied and ruthlessly inanimate.

Tikan cringed and turned, an eye half lingering on the projection, ready to run down the hall. Then a loud zap screeched through the live feed. The captain's head was gone, disintegrated and replaced by a smoldering stump for a neck and a mural of violence on the wall.

Tikan held his breath. He moved toward the room's exit in a slow nausea. He looked up and saw a group of other crewmembers looking in, not all of them security. They cleared the way for him fast. A churning started in his stomach, a deep sickness, and he lunged out of the room past them.

On burning legs, Tikan raced back down the corridor, away from the lounge and the bow of the ship. Past the galley now empty, clanging loose pots and pans, through the quakes still rocking the ship, and to the officer's lounge.

The door slid open. Inside, the same solemn starlight fell against the walls and shook above a figure in the far corner whose head was against the floor, eyes closed.

"Naim," Tikan called, running to the unconscious man. "Naim!" he roared, the word tearing out of his throat and distorting. He pulled Naim by the collar and tried to shake him awake, then slapped his face.

Naim stirred, grunted, and lifted his eyelids. He had spent the past few hours living the full lifetime—from childhood to death—of a lost colony's sole survivor. Scavenging for food, pilfering old supply caches, learning to nurse fabricated memories already sepia with nostalgia, and ultimately failing to make contact with the stars. The metempsy had allowed him to experience the full breadth of those fifty-four years, and that life was now gradually dissolving, along with most of its memories and its identity, into the back of his consciousness.

Naim at last recognized his friend. "Tikan, I—"

"Shut up. The ship's on fire. Get up, we're moving."

"What?" Naim said, rubbing his bleary eyes. "I need to finish my— the satellite repairs—when can I get back?"

Tikan bared his teeth. "Shut up. Something's happening in the lounge, and we need to go."

"I—what? I—no. What do you mean? I just need another hour in there."

"Forget your damn metempsy. Amozagh is dead, and more people are dying."

Naim's face tensed into a frown. "I didn't mean to switch from one metempsy to another. This must be a mistake." He rolled his eyes up as if to begin troubleshooting his own mind.

"This isn't a damn metempsy. It's real. Get up."

Still confused, Naim pushed himself off the floor. Then the two of them ran from the room, back again towards the lounge.

They stood, slick with sweat and soot, with their backs to the wall just beside the corridor into the lounge. Tikan's lungs felt like two slabs of gravel in his chest. He peered just slightly into the passage beside him. The air was thick with smoke, and the sound of rushing feet filled the ship. The compulsion to stage an assault on the lounge bubbled in him as he strangled his rifle.

Tikan and Naim were at the stern end of the lounge, far from the scene he had witnessed in the security room. The feet of the invaders pattered just beyond the threshold into the corridor. The coordination with which they moved unnerved Tikan. Their steps seemed perfectly choreographed.

Flash.

Croaks and howls escaped out of the hallway, followed by trails of smoke that reeked of burnt flesh. Tikan edged his head closer to the doorway, about to take another peek at the carnage unfolding just beyond the threshold, when Naim whispered in his ear. "I don't think it makes sense for us to go in there. Let's think of another way."

Tikan opened his mouth to respond, to confess that in his heart he believed himself to be their objective. But just then, a familiar bulk landed beside them.

"Don't go inside. They're crazy, those people," Alec said with bated breath, cradling a trembling rifle. "How did they get aboard? They— they killed Amozagh."

The others who had taken point nearby all looked as rattled and terrified as Alec. With such bloodshed unheard of during their lifetimes, they were now the first to reenter the long-shut maw of war.

"Amozagh is dead," Alec repeated.

"We know," Tikan said, feeling a mountain form in his stomach.

"They just piled in and threw him on the ground and then burned his face off and—" Alec trailed off.

Trying instead to notice the movement of the invaders, the others did not reply.

"They're not normal, those guns they're using. They aren't normal. They cut through the walls like—I don't know—the word's forbidden. And I was just on my bunk, about to metempsy, or something, when all this started. I—they're just killing people. Passengers, us, everyone," Alec continued in frantic whispers.

"Calm down," Tikan said. "Just stay quiet." He surprised himself with the calm in his voice. "They look trained. And you're right, those guns aren't normal." He looked over at Naim for confirmation.

The three crew members on the opposite side of the room looked at Tikan with impeccable focus. They stood there, nervous and sweating in their uniforms. One was muttering something to herself. Another was digging into the fabric at the end of his vest.

"You four," he continued, pointing at Alec and the others, "hold this chokepoint until we come back."

"Where are you going?" asked Alec.

"To find Mira. We should have all been gassed by now. Something's wrong in the cockpit."

"Gassed?"

"There's an emergency protocol the pilot can activate that puts the whole ship to sleep. We'll find her and seal this gate from there."

"No. No, have you seen their gear?" said one of the men on the adjacent side of the threshold.

"It's not the kind of gas you're thinking of. It's designed to pass through airtight suits and pores. It will work," Tikan replied.

"How do you know?"

Everyone ignored the contrarian and focused instead on the makeshift plan.

"But—I—the cockpit's at the front of the ship. How are you going to get past them?" Alec asked. His misgivings about being left to hold the gate against probable death were plain on his face.

"It'll be just like a metempsy," Naim told Alec. To Tikan's surprise, this advice did, in fact, seem to comfort the man somewhat.

"We need you three here, otherwise the whole ship will go. You have cover and you have some time. We'll hurry and take the engineering tunnels. Just don't move from here," Tikan said.

Just as Tikan and Naim were about to head for the nearest engineering shaft, they had to stop to ground themselves from another detonation. Flames vented out of the corridor on a new wave of terror for the unlikely battalion. They shielded their heads with their hands, voiding themselves of any lingering courage.

Between the new fumes that were thickening and drifting in past Alec and the others, a group of figures could be seen shifting. They stalked their territory while the clouds streamed dense and grim around their shapes. They stood in the center of the clearing smoke unbothered, as though that graveyard fog were some incorporeal beast summoned to presage and decorate the coming of death and its agents clad in decay.

And as enough of the smoke cleared, the figures could be seen grasping people by their throats or bloodstained collars, dragging them up to question like the inquisitors of an order unheard of since the long history now obscure and buried on Earth. They picked up the doomed and, in spite of their shrieks, with hands glistening red, pulled out bones from ribcages, or spooled out strings of guts, or crushed larynxes like filled paper cups jetting their contents, or pressed heads into the ground by pushing those same talons into eye sockets, and then making crimson tracks along cheeks by squeezing them for answers.

The innocents yet untouched writhed as though their spines were strung of loose vertebrae. They contorted expressions at one another, each squirming in clothes half-burnt, their blackened shins exposed under the teeth of newly singed seams. Their skins were plastered in dust like ceremonial powder in preparation for the methodical and merciless ritual waiting to make use of them.

Others, who had been metempsying at the moment of invasion, remained mutely and eerily standing, smiling, or otherwise acting as if nothing were taking place. One woman was dancing by herself, pirouetting, a coryphée in the carnage. A man was chuckling joyously to himself, metempsying a family picnic while the black suited invaders butchered his true family beside him.

The dead or dying they kicked aside like bags of trash blocking passage. They walked not like men but like a coterie of chthonic demons released from out of time and millennial tombs of sand to punish any who might have forgotten their taste for violence not seen since the universe's youngest and most mythic days.

Tikan and the others stood mesmerized at the gate. All their schemes were at once arrested.

With a hand trailing bits of viscera, one dark figure stopped its patrolling and stood prominent among its peers. A loud voice screeched out of the lounge. Though no mouth could be seen behind the helmet, the still figure was certainly the source. The voice was distorted, the sound of myriad cursed souls collapsing into each other, the space in a throat insufficient to contain the bursting volume.

Cold ran down Tikan's back, the hairs on his neck springing up.

This presumable leader stood in front of the others as they continued their business. "Friedrich Farabi," he screeched. "Friedrich Farabi," he repeated, like it was the name of some criminal escaped from perdition's highest sentencing. He emphasized his final utterance by driving a full arm through the chest of the hostage he had in hand, as though the rifle in his possession were some useless ornament.

A pale Alec looked over at Tikan. Tikan nodded uneasily at him before turning with Naim and making for the walkway behind them.

7

LOVE AND HATRED

The days blurred together. Before I knew it, a week had passed. I had hardly moved from Pierre's little guest room. I wore the same clothes for days, and I ate there too. Half prison, half sanctuary. The room had long khaki walls that dropped shadows and a single, thin window, which I took to block out with a dirty towel. The room became dank with the smell of sweat and toast. I killed enough fruit flies by the radiator to fill a child's grave.

Much to Pierre's dismay, I avoided spending too much time with him. We did play cards one night, and it was entertaining, but ultimately a distraction.

It bothered me greatly to see a few pop science books on string theory, astrophysics, and neuroscience strewn about the apartment, their corners far too clean for him to have done more than skimmed them once and convinced himself of his own comprehension. Nonetheless, I used him over two other dinners to discuss ideas for my work, but he seemed to have long abandoned his capacity for my interests.

"Not this again," Pierre laughed, without spite, slapping the dark wood of his dining table with a fork. "That's all speculation. Thoughts that go nowhere. This is the real world, so let's talk about real things."

The words did little to damage my notions of what was important and what was not; instead, I saw my old friend replaced by an accountant now compensating for his own death. At least the jester in him remained.

I seemed able to convince him of my depression with my deplorable sociability, and thus bought myself more of his sympathy and more time to find an alternate place to live. Meanwhile, Sophia was already ceasing to occupy my thoughts.

There was a desk there, in that tiny space of mine, and there I sat, and there I toiled away toward nothing. There, I could agonize over my treatise, hunched over the glow of my laptop. The keyboard developed a film of grease from my fingers in a matter of days. In that one week, I started and restarted the work perhaps six or seven times, never passing more than two pages and hardly writing anything of worth. The ideas were difficult at first, but that was fine. To be expected, really. I recall the army of dead first sentences, rewritten into each other:

It is for the cause of understanding and compassion that I begin this discourse.

Human understanding has largely been a failure.

A person is born completely ignorant and must fight to come out of that blindness.

There is no freedom without complete knowledge.

Each part of the human capacity for comprehension and compassion must be actualized out of the fullest potential of its parts so that the negated whole may be resurrected and may thereby earn the benefit of its own negation.

The vehicles of language and logic must be expanded to include in themselves all of their possible content.

The innate inclination towards psychological technologies that do little to refund their content or to supply an a priori *fulfillment of ideas and of that which generates them requires revision.*

Which concept preceded the other? Which was more logical? How could these things be determined, when the concept was not even complete in my head? And they devolved into more pitiable attempts, too:

There is an objective and it is necessary.
Meaningless.

The universe is
Unfinished

Synergy is an elusive concept, which has its roots in
Unfinished meaninglessness.

I find myself searching for the humility in others.
Unrelated.

I am the king beneath the waves.
Childish.

It is only by avoiding certain types of grapes that humanity can be
Absurd!

Pierre did come in from time to time to check on me. As the days turned into weeks, though, his words of encouragement became blatantly tinged with annoyance. The jester in him disappeared, too. The jolliness of those first few days seemed to have been nothing but an instinctual reenactment of our university days. Now, there was Pierre the Accountant, Pierre the Financier, or whatever his job with numbers was.

On the third Sunday, he started to openly suggest that I take him up on his offer to find work for me. *Work in accounting.* What a miserable suggestion. He said that I could stay for a while longer, as long as I contributed to the rent and the grocery budget. Unimaginable to me, of course, so I pleaded. I told him that my work was coming along and that soon I would be able to publish something and return to form in that way. So, he asked to see what I was working on. What a thorn he was!

I had nothing. Hardly anything. I had no more than a few paragraphs of a draft, without context, which I was far from happy with, and which I told him was a snippet of page seventy-three of my treatise. It read:

ON THE NECESSITY OF PARADOXES FOR THE POSSIBILITY OF TRUTH

When I apprehend a universal, when I think of it, I particularize it in my act of thinking. Though I am thinking of the universal form of tables, and not this table before me, is that universal form not made particular, given a particular form, when clenched in my psychic fist? Is the reverse not also true when I think of the particular table before me? Particular universal: is this not a contradiction in terms?

Now step in the river twice, and it will be found that contraries lie on a plane of infinite expansion. They lie in perfect opposition to each other and they sustain each other through this opposition.

Let us take passion as an example. Suppose an individual is in a state of passion whereby he may be compelled to love, or possibly to hate.

Let us say love. To increase his capacity for love, it is necessary for him to reach its borders and certainly not to idle at a so-called golden mean.

Now, if this individual, in his state of passion, were to experience the most extreme form of love possible, on the precipice of hatred, the scope of passion would extend. He will require, if he wishes to be capable of love again, a stronger state of passion in order to reach the new point of the extremity by traversing what will become a greater gulf between love and hatred. This is a careful balancing act. If he is not careful, he may accidentally traverse love and arrive at hatred (or be slung across to it?).

If we then apply this principle to the universe as a whole, in its opposition of one and many, and of stability and flux, we will find that the borders of the universe are in constant expansion due to its limits being perpetually reached. This is why bodybuilders increase their muscle strength by exhausting it. But, like love, and like the body, and like mankind, the universe has limits in its capacity for expansion, as all things must follow these principles. There is only so much content to be unpacked by means of exhaustion, and therefore, a distinction between potential limits and actual limits must be drawn.

Now, passion is not composed solely of these sets of opposites. In the sphere of passion are various other sets of opposition (for subjects can themselves be points on the plane of other subjects). Further, the midpoint of love and hatred lies in opposition to passion itself: apathy. Not friendship, as might otherwise have been said, had we not pitted Heraclitus against Aristotle. Thus, we have an odd set (Love—Apathy— Hatred), and to accommodate the dualistic nature of the universe, a fourth must occur, and this will, of itself, generate a second midpoint, or a fifth opposite, and so on, ad infinitum.

The process of generating resolutions to this forever-incomplete program is what is infinite, and which gives the principle its paradoxical character. And it is this process alone that sustains the whole. Like the plant cell reflecting the whole cosmos, so too is the system reflected in its tiniest pieces.

Pierre stared at the page, and then eyed me, and then looked back down again. "I like it," he said.

"You think so?"

"Sure. Yes. Very original." He opened his mouth to say something and then thought better of it. "The stuff about plant cells—that was interesting."

"Yeah, yeah—the microcosms, 'the system is in its tiniest pieces.'"

He nodded. "That part. Yeah."

"Do you think it's true? What else did you find interesting?" I asked. I had a momentary, intense fantasy of being interviewed by some important journalist and, when asked about this line, mentioning Pierre's awed reaction.

He scanned through the page, trying to find something else to talk about. After a while he just scratched his head. "I mean, it's interesting, but what's the point?" he said, crushing me instantly. His irritation over the past weeks was packed into his words.

"What do you mean, 'what's the point?'"

"I mean, okay, let's be honest here. I'm being honest because I think you don't just want me to pat you on the back, right? This is like some pseudo-science mixed with outdated philosophy."

"What?"

"You make a lot of broad claims that don't really seem to go or come from anywhere. You can't even name your subject, or whatever it is. It's all muddled and not even in an artistic kind of way. Nobody would ever take this seriously. That's the point, right? It's pretty funny. It sounds like New Age bullshit. Is it for an ironic philosophy blog or something? Not sure many people will get the comedy, though."

His words stung. I could have torn his face off in that moment. Torn it off and gone searching for that of his younger, submissive, attentive self.

"It isn't pseudo-science, it's metaphysics. And there's no such thing as outdated philosophy," I said, the calm in my voice hovering just above the rage I was suppressing inside.

"Wait, you really are serious—what the hell?"

"Yeah, of course I am!"

He shook his head. "What the hell does metaphysics even mean to you then? Trying to explain physics with love and hate—which I'm not sure you even understand properly—and vague, pedestrian references to theories in physics?"

My nails went to war with each other. "No, no. Did you even read it properly? I'm trying to explain the originary rules of things. It isn't about love and hate building the universe, it's about first principles! It's about how love and hate exist in the universe in the same system by which the universe and all of its components can themselves exist and function and—"

Pierre blinked a few times. "I mean, why not just leave it to the physicists? I remember we used to talk about this stuff all the time, but come on. Isn't this the job of a physicist? Or at least a qualified philosopher? Aren't they the ones figuring out how this stuff really works? Besides, *you* don't even have a PhD in this stuff, how are you going to bring anything new to the table? How do you know someone hasn't tried to say the same thing thousands of years ago? I love it, I think it's interesting, but you can't sit around all day doing...*this*."

I ignored his more biting comments and shook my head without looking at him. "The earliest scientists were philosophers; science came from philosophy. It was called natural philosophy. And I mentioned similar thinkers in the —"

"And now it's called science. There's a reason why it *used to be* philosophers. Because the physicists figured out how these kinds of things *actually* work. And whatever, I'm not saying philosophy is outdated, but there's a reason why philosophy and science are separate fields. Anyways, I don't know that much about philosophy or how it works, but this doesn't seem academic, what you wrote. I don't think you should be throwing around names like Aristotle when it doesn't seem like you get it, really. And I mean, '*man*kind'? Come on. Isn't that a bit sexist? Who uses that anymore?"

My neck throbbed as violent blood coursed up to my head. "I don't care about that. And I'm not even doing natural philosophy. Like I said, it's metaphysics."

"Okay, fine, let's say this project you've developed is a real work of modern, reflective, well-informed philosophy. Let's see," he said, scanning through the printed page. "Why is the universe *naturally* dualistic? This seems like a statement you took from nowhere."

"It's something that's observable."

"Observable. Meaning, scientifically, no? As in through systematic experience, or induction, right?"

"Yes, and, well—no. I mean, it's obvious. It can be dedu—"

"Things *can* exist in threes, though. It's not obvious at all, what you're saying. It's simplistic. People don't write books of calculations for nothing."

"Yes, but only within a larger set of twos, and *that* was my point, anyway, that threes come about but need to be resolved as twos."

"Why?"

"Because—well—because that's how it is, and—"

"And here," he said, pointing at another line, "If I follow what you're saying, isn't apathy in opposition to passion? Doesn't that make it a perfect four?"

"Apathy is in opposition to passion, yes, but it's also the midpoint between love and hatred, and there are midpoints between those and so on. The idea is that a third midpoint will always emerge. The regress has to go on forever."

"The regress has to go on forever," he repeated patronizingly. He took a moment to think about it, to find a hole in it. "So why did you just choose love and hate to be the only features of passion, though? What about obsession? What about dedication? What about desire and enthusiasm and a lack of control?"

I shook my head. I looked away from him. "You're being too specific, that's your problem," I said, fumbling to rescue my argument. "It's about categories, and having a system of logic that—"

"So why is this something scientists, or mathematicians, can't figure out? You just made up your own premises about it and ignored every contradiction. It's silly."

"Because they address their own particular things! You think love and hate are chemicals? You think the universe is just a clump of matter?"

"Look, look, I get it. I'm not against philosophy or anything. I enjoy it. I enjoyed it in college, in the requireds, and when we used to talk about it. I know how worthwhile it is to think about the big questions, or whatever. But it looks like you're trying to explain the universe expanding by taking a giant leap from abstract stuff like love and hate and passion, and even...bodybuilding. For God's sake, did you even think about that analogy? Don't you see the problem?"

"The problem is that you haven't read the whole thing. It will be an academically recognized work. Not that it matters. And, yes, all you've read is a page. Of course, the connections will become more clear as you read the rest of the work."

There was a pause as Pierre eyed my laptop.

"Do you really have over seventy-three pages of this stuff?"

The room's atmosphere thickened with his words. Blood was pumping through my body with seismic force.

"It all needs...editing."

"Show me."

"It isn't finished."

There was silence. He sprang, racing for the laptop, and I dove into his chest with my shoulder, and then launched an open palm to smother his face, pushing him away as though I were a bird protecting her nest. He ripped my hand from his face. Red drops slithered from his nose. My adrenaline left me. His face turned somber in the dim light. With a contorted frown, I fell into shame. He saw through me in that moment. Pierre the Inspector, ravager of my lies.

"I'm working on it. I've deleted a lot of stuff, and I'm editing other stuff, and—"

"Get out of my house."

And so I breathed the fresh air again.

8

THE SURGERY

In a room at the farthest end of the crew quarters on the Equuleus, someone was grunting at even intervals. The place was mostly deserted as people ran and screamed outside. The grunting came from an older man of about fifty or sixty who sat with his back to a wall, facing a sleeping pod and carving a hole into his own head.

He was wearing a full bronze environment suit, save for the helmet, which rolled back and forth on the floor in front of him. What little hair he had left was matted with blood, and his scalpel gleamed crimson every time he brought it close to the wound. He was slow and methodical. He held in his lap a tiny plastic box, which got speckled with red droplets every time he flicked his scalpel. An empty syringe rocked on the floor beside his left thigh in a little puddle of its own clear liquid.

He dug and dug, and winced every so often, though he was not particularly affected by the blade cutting into his skull. With only the sense of pressure to guide him, he would pinch up the skin of his scalp, allowing the scalpel to visit his brain. Every few minutes, the ship would shake, making the task difficult. The not-so-distant turmoil swelled in the periphery, laying siege to his focus. As a result, he drew his angles of incision very carefully, lest a random shockwave or distraction send the knife diving straight through his cerebral cortex.

"What are you doing?" a voice came from the door.

The man almost jumped and dropped the scalpel into his lap. Standing at the threshold of the room was a passenger. His head almost reached the ceiling and he had a cut along the left side of his pointy nose. His hair was dripping. The newcomer wiped his forehead while observing the perfectly calm and bleeding man beneath him.

"I have an itch," said the older man, after recovering from his surprise.

"An itch?"

"An itch."

"You're...you're bleeding."

"I'm aware of that."

"Well...would you like some help? I think there are medkits lying around here somewhere. Did you hit your head in the explosions, or what?"

The two stared at each other without words for a short while, the older man's head looking like some outland chimera's hideous egg heated by brimstone and doused in ceremonial paint shortly before its hatching. Then the younger man knelt down beside the bloodied stranger to examine his wound. The older man followed his movements with squinting eyes, almost ready to dismiss him, when he noticed a sudden wave of black hair across the doorway.

"What's your name?" asked the old man, looking at his conversant again.

"James."

"Well, actually, yes, James, you might be able to help me—but wait, who's that?" he asked, pointing at the door with his scalpel.

Standing with her back to the wall just outside of the room was a young girl of no more than three or four, bouncing off of the steel with her hands behind her back as children do, completely bored and unaware of the crisis at hand.

"That's my daughter," said James, turning his head and heading for the doorway.

Grasping the doorpost with one hand, James leaned into the hallway. "Don't come in here, okay?" he told the child. "The man here is hurt, so go hide in that room and close your eyes. I'll come and get you in a few minutes," he said, pointing at the room adjacent to the one where the old man had resumed his bizarre surgery.

The girl did as instructed.

The old man was now peeling back the flap of skin on his head and slicing its corners to create more space. Blood slid between the creases.

"Hey, wait, what are you doing? You're going to make it worse! Let me find you that medkit."

"No, no. There's no need for that. Now stand here, yes, there, and look at this," said the older man, pointing at the well of blood in his head. "Now, I'm going to just do this here, quickly," he said, and broke off a small but significant piece of skull with his blade.

"Suns and moons, what are you doing, man?"

"Relax. Now, this stuff is only good for few more minutes," he said, pointing at the syringe on the floor. "After that I'm going to fall asleep, maybe die, but either way I need you to be quick. I'm going to stretch the skin open, and I'm going to need you to look for a small memory tape looking thing. When you see it, just pull. Now, you're going to see some needly looking things; they're going to stick to it, they're going to look like they're trying to hold on to it. Forget about them and rip it out. Then, you're going to stick this thing on them," he said, opening his case and pulling out a film that looked just like the description of his unwanted cranial object. "Understood?"

"I—Yeah—Are you sure about this? Are you a doctor or something? I mean, this sounds like brain surgery. Are you sure this is the best time to do this?" James asked, barely looking at the thing in the older man's hands, unsure of the situation he had fallen into.

"Yes, I'm a doctor. Now, are you ready?"

James nodded and readied himself.

Just as he was about to search the blood-drenched mess with his fingers, the old man released his torn flap of skin and said, "Oh, and one more thing. If I do pass out while you're ripping that thing out, I'm going to need you to spray the whole of my head, the inside of this helmet, and the whole room with this when you're done. Then put the helmet on my head. You can just leave me here after that." He casually pulled a small gun with a vial of liquid propped into it out of his pocket and handed it to James before resuming his gory task.

After placing the gun on the floor, James scanned the wound. Chaos. Gunfire thundered on the fringe of every moment. Each roaring, muffled sound flinging his eyes to the door.

"Well, it isn't going to pull itself out. Stick your fingers in."

James followed the instructions with skeptical diligence. He approached the old man while still eying the exit. With constant glances at the old man to confirm that he was performing correctly, he slowly inserted trembling thumb, index, and middle fingers into the wound. Wet, fleshy bumps and grooves, under the fragile dome, between bone and brain. It felt like a warm, pulsating sponge. When there was not too much blood obscuring the organ, he noticed networks of capillaries spread around bulbous lumps. The weight of all this man's memories, thoughts and ultimately being at his finger tips.

Outside, the screams and stampedes were loudening and threatening to overcome James as a great tide. He pressed deeper. The wound oozed and spat. His focus depleted as he struggled to keep track of every form of chaos presenting itself to him. He was exerting too much pressure, trying to get under the skull. He was certain that he was killing the man.

"Don't tie the raspberries unless they've been bad," said the old man, his eyes like stones, red and fixed on the wall in front of him.

Now that the old man had gone delirious, James felt abandoned. The walls narrowed. And the air was finishing. James would kill this man, and then be trampled by the crowd outside, if not outright blasted apart. Of this he was growing more certain, though he could not recoil from the bloody procedure to which he had committed himself.

Then, with a mixture of relief and terror, he pinched the end of what felt like a plastic clothing tag, inorganic and thin, jutting out slightly from between two bloody creases of brain. He gripped the thin little film. The patient's eyes returned, rolling up at the pretend doctor like those of a possessed man.

"Suns, is that your procrustus?"

"Don't worry about what it is, just rip it out!"

James pulled as instructed, and as he had been warned, the little film resisted. The brain bled a tantrum to keep it. He pulled until there came a loud break, and another chip of skull cracked off, and finally the tag could be peeled off. And release. Out it came, dislodged with a hard pull, and *horror*. An army of thin and furious black tentacles leaped out of the wound, still stuck to the little strip, holding it down and pulling. James stepped back, though he did not let go. He made some mulish sound. Then, like an angered cove of leeches, more tentacles sprang out through the skull and set their hooks into the film. There were hundreds of thorns along their bodies, embedded deeply in various parts of the brain as well as the film.

The old man ground his teeth together as blood spat out of the hole in his head. James pulled with all his might, legs anchoring the heave, when suddenly—

"Are you finished yet? It's getting really loud outside."

"Little girl, whatever you do, *don't* come in!" James yelled at the top of his voice, still pulling the tag with his dripping red hands. Sweat was streaming down his face. His thoughts raced in different directions as he tried to keep them bottled and focus on the worsening task.

The girl's feet pattered towards the room like drops of the storm outside. She peered in and, with widening eyes, took in the horrific surgery, the gore on James' hands and the old man's face, the streaks of blood against the wall, the fire screeching across the entrance to the crew quarters.

"*Don't* come in here," James roared, still fighting those lashing wires.

She did not listen. She stood there with her mouth open and her eyes skittering.

James shook his head. "Get out!"

Still she did not listen. All the while, James continued pulling, pulling, regardless of the brain, yanking. And the latched wires snapped off, one after the other, whipping back like vines. He dropped the film to the floor as it came free and scurried for the item in the old man's hand. It looked identical to the little film he had just removed. The black wires were spinning, writhing around, some slinking back into the brain while others raged in place. Horrified, he pressed the new film onto the jutting bed of tendrils and watched as they attached to it and fastened it down into place across a lump of brain, just where the old film had been.

The girl was hyperventilating. Her brow was creasing with knowledge unfit for a child. At last she spun around, ran back towards her hiding place, and disappeared.

"Finished?" came a voice from the ground.

"How *in the world* are you still awake? Alive, even! And what were those things? The ship's coming apart, for sun's sake. Is that…what we all have in there? Does that mean I have those too?"

"Afraid so. Oh, don't look so bothered, they're just like little…helpers."

James stared at his blood-soaked hands.

The old man tried to wipe away the crimson river running down his temple and cheeks, before giving up and reaching for the medical gun on the floor beside him. He pointed it up at the wound first, pulling the trigger to let out a cool spray. The sea-foam mist clouded around his head and started to cake a similarly colored crust where his brain had been exposed. After emptying half of the vial, he retrieved his helmet and sprayed it all along the inside. Content with the sterilization, he placed the helmet over his head and snapped it to the rest of the suit. Then, he whisked the gun around the room with the trigger held down, letting clouds of the mist fall about.

All the while, the impromptu surgeon could not remove his eyes from his own outstretched and browning hands.

"Well, thanks for your assistance, but I'm going to have to ask you to leave now, yes," said the old man, muffled by his helmet.

James' eyes widened, and he gave him an incredulous look.

"It's quite alright. I'm going to take a nap now."

"I—What—" But he no longer had the patience. The gunfire outside was making its way closer, and James turned, remembering the girl. "Okay. Alright—I—are you sure you'll be okay?" he replied, unsure of what he had just been subjected to, or of what else to say to the fantastic person before him. He wiped his hands on his pants, then made for the door.

"Sorry," James heard, just as he was about to take a step out. A ray of heat tore through his lower back and out of his upper abdomen. He had time enough to twist his head back and see his assassin-patient's eyes roll behind the tinted glass of the helmet and collapse to the floor with him.

9

THE ENGINEERING TUNNELS

F ire bloomed along the Equuleus' innards. Sparks burst from wall panels in loud discharges, and the stink of burned plastic clung to the air. Shouts and screams raced back and forth along the long walkway, travelling up melting walls and down the collapsing ceiling, crashing and rising together as a hellish choir while flames ate up the oxygen.

Tikan and Naim navigated the chaos as best they could. They ran clutching their rifles, under wires hanging from the ceiling and spraying electric gore. They slipped through gaps in the crowds and darted along the walls and sidestepped tumbling runners. Some passengers moved out of their way at the sight of their uniforms and their armaments, but most were too consumed by fear to notice. Far off, an unfortunate few were being trampled, skin and bone breaking under the stampede. The two pressed on. They gulped air and their lungs burned. Their visions throbbed with each pump of their hearts.

The crowd thickened as they neared the end of the walkway and the ship's midsection. Many passengers had recognized where the danger was coming from, and they had clotted every inner corridor leading to the dormitories.

With sweat streaming off his skin, Tikan stopped in front of a red wheel fixed on the wall. It was accented by a touch of the haunting blue light spilling out of the security room.

Naim forgot about Tikan for a moment and observed the flurry of passengers. In the eye of that maelstrom, he noticed a stationary pair. There was an old man in a helmeted, shiny outfit, squeezing another old man's temples. Naim squinted at them. After a moment, the shiny old man got up and dragged the other man, now unconscious, into the dormitories. Just before passing out of sight, he shot Naim a glance, as if he knew Naim were looking at him.

"Help me spin this thing around. We can enter the tunnels from here," Tikan huffed at Naim, gripping the bottom of the wheel and pushing it at an angle with all his weight. The steel slipped in his moist grip.

Naim ignored him. His head was still whirring around, eyeing the crowds. "How did this start?"

"I don't know. I was sleeping. You were supposed to be on duty, you should know."

"They didn't look normal. Not like, you know, criminals, or anything I've heard about. Do you think there's something valuable on the ship or something? Do you think they'd let the rest of us go if they found it? It has something to do with that guy, Farabal, err, Fereby, or whatever that guy said."

Tikan was too focused on unlocking the shaft to answer. "Help me," he commanded, still pushing the wheel hard. He clenched his teeth at Naim, until he joined the labor. They pushed the slippery wheel until it came loose.

When the shaft opened, Tikan stopped, took a breath, and looked at Naim. "Those people don't give damn about letting anyone go," he told him. "Now, let's go."

"So we're going to Mira?"

Tikan gave him an exasperated sigh. "Yes. We're going to crawl under the floor and pass under whatever's happening in there. I'm going to assume that, whoever they are, they have biosensors. So, we're going to have to be careful. Very careful. And quiet. Can you do this with me? I trust you."

"Wait, if we can just gas people from the cockpit, why hasn't Mira done it yet? Maybe there's no point in going there."

Tikan took a few hard breaths and looked away. He tried to calculate the odds of his plan succeeding and tell himself they were not slim. Screams were building up beside them. A passerby fell and twisted his ankle, then limped on to the dormitories. All was falling away, whirlpooling out of coherence and into the void outside.

"Mira," he said. "She might have been somewhere else—eating, showering. She might be dead. I don't know. I don't know. But, this is the only solution I can think of. We're dead either way if I'm wrong, and I'd rather die in those tunnels than groveling at their feet. Are you coming?"

There was a pause. Naim lifted his head after gazing pensively at the floor. He flung his head one way, then the other. "Just a second," he said, unflinching as he turned and ran into the security room.

Tikan hurried behind Naim and found him digging through documents opposite the live feed. "What are you doing?" he almost yelled from the threshold. "We have to go. Now."

"The ship's manifest. Have to destroy any proof in case we survive," Naim said as he continued pilfering the filing lockers with the determination of a man he had embodied a few metempsies ago.

He pulled out an analogue file and a memory reader from a cupboard and relayed them to the desk projecting the live feed. The blue light made the beads of sweat on his forehead shine like melting sapphires. He took two steps back and waved for Tikan to stand away. Then, he pointed his rifle at the bundle of documents and set the entire wall aflame, just as the projection made its final flicker. Fire hurried up the wall, curling and falling backwards. He swooped the gun back over his shoulder.

Tikan motioned for him to hurry, grinning as his friend sped out of the room. Without a word, Naim rushed the open shaft and scurried down the ladder. With a last look over his shoulder before taking on Orpheus' curse, Tikan jumped in after Naim and sealed the light out behind them.

The air was thick down in the engineering tunnels, and no less full of smoke than the main corridors. They wiped their foreheads and exhaled smoldering breaths. They trudged in a crouch all the way down a slim walkway of manifold pipes, tubes, and circuit boards, their steps chinking beneath the crew quarters and for some distance beyond. Their mouths were dry and tasted of salt and ash, and their lungs felt swollen with heat after only a few breaths. Soon enough, there was no telling how much distance they had crossed. Claustrophobia lurked behind each nearer wall of darkness, waiting to snatch away the mind of the first man to lose his nerve.

Walking ahead of Tikan, Naim kept his head low and balanced himself by running his hands against the uneven walls of machinery.

"You okay?" Tikan asked.

"I'm alright. It's just...a little hard to walk down here with a rifle and everything."

"It probably doesn't help that you're kind of tall for a place like this."

Naim's quiet laugh rolled down the tunnel, and he shot Tikan a weak grin through the shadows. The passage was, in fact, miniscule. It was designed primarily for automatons, which were sent down to fix leaks or other minor problems in the lesser guts of the ship. Nonetheless, it was large enough for the occasional human visit, however lacking in accommodations. The floor was little more than a thin, grated sheet of metal under which more of the ship's intestines wove together. Besides whatever dire thoughts may have wandered into their minds during that solemn trek, they were accompanied only by the clacking of their boots.

"Do you think they have friends, or family?" Tikan asked in a low voice.

"What do you mean?"

It was difficult to speak, but he pushed himself. "I mean those people, all ruthless. If they're people. Do you think you can have family and friends when you're something like that?"

"Maybe they're just like that here."

"How does that work?"

"When they go home they're like you and me, then when they're here, they kill people like they're ants."

"I don't think they're the same as you and me. Isn't the worse monster the one who can go home to friends and family afterwards? If you can find it in yourself to care about any other person than yourself, it's because you're willing to accept that you're not the only one alive. That you can agree to there being a history as vast or vaster than yours in another."

"So you're saying you have to love everyone?"

"No. No, I'm not saying that. I'm saying it's strange to me that someone could just ruin a person, so completely and so easily, you know? Reduce them to some sack of meat. It's like those people, the ones who metempsy to gory accidents for the thrill, or to harden themselves, or who knows why, and don't feel some sort trembling in their core. What about the memories?"

"What about memories?"

"There's so much in a mind—you could never know how much. The character, the people that knew them, every feeling or thought they've ever had, all the things they've seen. All of that complex stuff— it's familiar, isn't it?"

"I think so."

"Then how could you so easily smash it?"

"I don't know. You ever kill someone?"

"Yes." He paused. "It's not the same, though. I'm not talking about the act; I'm talking about the person who does it and what it does to them. And why."

"What's the difference, in the end?"

"The difference is that—"

Footsteps rumbled above them, followed by shouting. Muffled howling. They focused their eyes upwards and tried to listen, and the conversation was brought to an anxious end. They could not discern what was happening. Breathing hard, Tikan lightly pushed Naim and tapped him on the shoulder to signal him onward.

"We're probably right under Alec," Tikan whispered.

"How will we know if we're near the suits?"

"I'm not sure. I hope we'll be able to hear them from down here. From what I saw, those boots of theirs looked heavy. Probably magnetized to protect them from hull breaches."

They scurried on, bracing the walls as though to keep the place from caving in, fighting off the nausea feeding off of their hunger; and just ahead, they noticed the darkness lighten. The tunnel was growing a fat lining of dusty light. Naim stopped and looked back at Tikan. Both of them stood still and surveyed the way ahead.

There was a breach in the ceiling of the engineering tunnel just ahead, which nearly exposed them to the lounge above. Their hearts dropped. Bent pipes spat steam into the gap. Ashes trickled down the white curtain of light and fluttered about like necrotic butterflies in the rays. Beyond this collapsed section, where debris had piled up, the covered, shaded tunnel continued.

Naim caught a glimpse of one of the black suits just beyond the lit veil of steam, and with speeding heart and fast hands, he turned around, his face aghast, and pushed Tikan backwards into the shadows, lest the raiders see them. There was a lull in which they held their breaths, not certain yet whether they had been seen.

They stopped and waited and tried to measure their breathing. Amid the wreckage of exploded electronics, opened pipes, and cracked metal were the remains of several dead people from the massacre above. Three corpses had fallen into the net of wires and pipes below, some wholly dumped into the tunnel, others in limbo between Hell and Hades. The falling ashes finished their angelic glide atop these broken forms. In addition to the full corpses were fragments of singed or blackened flesh strewn about, along with a full head caked in blood and grime with an eye still open, which looked straight at them. A set of steps grew louder on the grille above them, and their focus shifted away from the dead until it passed.

"Get ready, we're going to run through in a few seconds," Tikan said beneath his breath, barely audible even to himself.

Naim gave him the most sincere look of shock of the entire ordeal. Sweat was dripping from his eyebrows, glossing his brown skin, and his eyes grew rounder. He looked at his friend and, without speaking, mouthed an exaggerated "What?" at him.

Tikan grabbed Naim's head and put his mouth to his ear to breathe aggressive instructions into it. "As I said earlier, they probably have biosensors that'll go off when we get close. We can turn this to our advantage. We're going to run, dive across the gap and the debris, back into the tunnel on the other side. Then keep running. They'll look back once their sensors go off and they'll see a bunch of corpses and sparks. At best, they'll assume one of the corpses was still alive. Maybe the sparks will throw them off. Worst case, we keep going and rush the cockpit. We can seal it if we get in fast enough."

"You're crazy. One them is probably a medic. They'll know right away that those burned up guys are dead. Look at that!" he said, pointing at the watchful head.

As Naim mouthed those last words, another troop of footsteps clacked above them. A new blast of heat raged through the lounge, and a fresh corpse was dumped into the pile.

"Now."

Naim did not question him, but only frowned a moment and then powered down the bit of still-covered walkway, his hands sliding down the tube and his head low, and then ducked to anticipate the first strike of light on his skin. As he dove, with his elbows bracing for impact, he caught a quick glimpse of the lounge above him before passing through the debris clogging the tunnel. Wires. Corpses and pipes. The gap. His lanky form made it through the space under a broken support beam like a thread through a needle's eye.

Tikan followed just behind Naim. A metal step echoed from above just as he reached the exposed section of the tunnel. His heart palpitated. His legs swelled, and he dove.

The light flashed over him for a half-second like a white scan across his body. He passed across the debris, through the hot, cloudy steam, and crashed down, sweating, into the new dark. Not as graceful as his friend, his right foot caught the beam just as the rest of his body cleared it, and, without a second to think, he pulled it with abandon. With his foot free of the girder, he bolted up. The mangled structure shook with the shaft's release, but there was no time to look back.

They sped down the remaining gauntlet. Naim turned to look at Tikan and beamed, face wide in euphoria. Their steps began clacking over the thin grate. Then the sound of screeching metal bellowed from behind them as the cluster of debris and part of the tunnel collapsed at their backs, leaving them in pitch darkness.

Suddenly, a scorching discharge blasted through the right wall of varicolored tubes in a diagonal line, lighting the tunnel in a momentary orange surge and taking Naim in the leg like a harpoon, sending him tripping through the tight space. He lost speed and paddled the floor with his hands. The smell of charred flesh trailed behind him. The air turned hot in his throat.

Tikan pounced on Naim as soon as he started to falter into the side of the walkway. He crushed Naim's mouth with a bestial grip. Down, with the strength bulging in his forearm, down like an unmuzzled beast, he pushed Naim farther into the wall before lowering his head to his ear again. "Its fine. Relax. And don't close your eyes. The crash startled them, that's all. They don't know. It's my fault. I'm sorry."

Each word fell from Tikan's mouth as he panted. He could feel Naim's breath trying to escape his hand. The footsteps above moved away and became more distant as the heat settled around them. They remained for some time coupled against each other, backs to the side of the tunnel, the sound of suppressed breaths and Naim's squirms of agony the only noise now in the tunnel.

Tikan released some of the pressure in his grip without wholly removing his hand from his friend's mouth. He looked at Naim's ravaged thigh as it bubbled in the dark. It was difficult to tell the extent of the damage, but it was likely that whatever flesh had been struck had been badly mutilated.

"We're going to get you to the cockpit. There's probably a medkit there," he whispered. "If I remove my hand, are you going to scream?"

Naim shook his head, his tears running between Tikan's fingers.

Tikan removed his hand and tried to get Naim up by lifting him under the arm.

Captive to silence, Naim's pain condensed and freely roiled within him, causing him to tremble and wince. Why was he here? What was this pain cratering through his leg? He tried to force himself into a metempsy and thereby abandon his body, but Tikan continuously shook him out of it.

Both men collapsed again into the side of the tunnel. Far away, the sound of repeated gunfire was starting again. They looked backwards, but saw nothing beyond the impenetrable blackness clogging the place.

"We have to move. That's Alec and those others shooting at them. There isn't much time," said Tikan.

The injured Naim tried to lift himself with his good leg, but fell again. In his delirium, he groped and tore irrationally at the edge of his vest, searching for a tourniquet for his smoldering leg.

"Don't. There's no need. The wound's cauterized. There isn't anything we can do for it now except get to the cockpit," said Tikan.

"O–Okay."

Tikan lifted his friend again, this time letting the full burden pile in his legs. He took a number of deep breaths and then stomped onward to the cockpit.

10

L'HÔTEL DU PUITS

After being ejected from Pierre's apartment, I took to roaming the streets of Paris for some morose tourism. Forget the Tower and the Arc. Forget glossy Elysian Fields where Socrates pushes Achilles from the scaffolding of the cosmos so that he may disappear for good. To alleys! To dumpsters! Few of those in the Périphérique, but nevertheless. I sought carpets of tossed fruit peels, of candy wrappers and cans all prepared to resist erasure forever and thereby blight the world. The poetry discarded out the windows of sages in high towers above. The desanctified wreckage of Odysseus between residential straits, all splinters and shattered cisterns and masterless ghosts awaiting their captain's return for eternity under the world's watery coat. How else to hunt down inner nectar but to begin with the abandoned rind? Out of trash, the true legacy; out of waste, the origin. From these, at the bottom of rubbish bins, I tried to eke out some inspiration.

He was a fool, Pierre, that was certain. Someone in dire need of compassion. Perhaps someone like Sophia could right him, hah! No, Sophia could not, never would. As for me, I still had funds, enough to last me a while. But it was liberating to be completely cut off. No more human anchors around my work, no more judgments over my shoulder.

I took the metro and got off two or three stops away from Pierre's apartment. Then, having gathered sufficient thoughts from those smelly areas of the city, I set about accomplishing serious work. I sat in parks and between buildings, and through cold and wind my fingers clacked away on the keyboard. Mostly, it was to delete failed ideas, and this eventually drained the battery.

Night fell fast, and the streets emptied. A ruthless car or two would tear down the road every so often, but mostly I was alone. Meditating, wandering, shivering, searching. I turned bitter fast, truth be told. I considered, for a while, sleeping in the gutter, but abandoned that notion quickly. The lamplight was just too strong and unavoidable. How could I sleep with that artificial glow in my face? No. And the pavement was hard—too hard for the philosophical excavations I was to undertake.

But I stalled there nonetheless, in the gutter, in rebellion against the city. Curled between two dumpsters, hoping for the numbness in my toes to pass. Until I decided to seclude myself appropriately. That is to say, between warm walls and not far from room service.

I got up and scanned the street. Near me was a dilapidated building. A hotel that looked as though it had been built some time after the Second World War, as though nobody would have noticed its pseudo-classicism in that period of recovery. I sprinted over to it, splashing through shallow puddles and their skins of ice.

I stepped into the dim and dank lobby of L'hôtel du Puits without many expectations. It was awful, regardless. The walls were narrow, the carpet stank, and the floor creaked with each step. A dingy old place, with no amenities save for the breakfast. And I had little appetite for food.

The owner and resident manageress was a fat woman who dragged three bulldogs around as though she were perpetually investigating crimes or conspiracies against her. All three could have been her children, given the resemblance. She sat by the only lamp, behind the front desk, reading a magazine with perched eyebrows and wielding a fuming cigarette.

"Bonjour," I mumbled, leaning over the creaky wood.

"Bonne nuit," she corrected without looking up.

"I'd like a room, indefinitely."

She leered at me, a half-shadowed mass from where she sat, and gave me a look of disgust. I ignored it as best I could.

"I'm on important business," I pressed.

"Business?"

"I've only just landed in Paris and I'm conducting some work. I'll need absolute privacy."

Still, her expression did not change. I sighed, and produced my credit card. Its gleam caught her eye, and she gave me the key to one of the six rooms in the miserable place.

I strode to my room between mottled beige walls whose paper was peeling off. Wet patches on the ceiling dripped rancid water from leaking pipes. There was a certain uncleanliness to the place. It likely had not been renovated since the sixties or seventies, probably when the grandmother of the bulldogs owned the place. Very little décor, though there were some paintings misaligned along the corridor. Most of these were poor, even for a place such as this. They hovered between post-modern tripe and technical failure. I would not have been surprised if they were indeed the works of that vicious woman, hung up in some mythomanic pride, some unbridled desire to impress whomever, deranged in their soul, would agree to stay in such a place.

But the words started to pour from me in that hotel room. An uninterrupted river of thought from my mind to the laptop. The bedroom walls were thin, betraying me to the winter with glee, and the place smelled like clogged dust or wet pillows, but it mattered little. The work was well under way. Ten pages, then fifteen.

Pierre will see. Sophia will know. All of them will beg for forgiveness.

My bitterness climbed with the word count.

In the mornings, I would snatch my breakfast from the door, lest the man outside, likely the husband of the witch, be allowed to interfere. There would be no entangling banter with any nonpersons.

Twenty pages, twenty-five, thirty...and then *stoppage.* It was sudden and unexpected. Everything had been going perfectly, and then the river was dammed. Two weeks in that place and I had been thwarted at thirty pages—thirty well-revised and twice-rewritten pages. I took lengthy breaks, even to cough out cigarette smoke near the window, but could not overcome the impasse. The next days were spent rereading what there was of the draft and editing it until it no longer made any sense.

My daily meal had been difficult enough to commit to, but now I fasted as though to purify my meditations. I paced the room, afflicted by mania, and chomped at my nails. The window, the window would inspire me. Window: a portal to the outside world. There was a wall around it, a brown wall, dim lights, a filthy bathroom in its reflection, dirt caked between the tiles. Through it cars were visible, and people. A man in a phosphorescent work jacket, though it was day. People. People, out there, animate. Clothes.

Nothing.

I squirmed and rolled on the bed, buried my eyes under my palms, and ceased to think. Only the impasse was real, everything else a distraction.

I slept.

The morning after, the knock came, at precisely eight-forty-two, and I gagged before opening the door.

"Hello, sir. Breakfast for you."

A human being: well of inspiration under coats of flesh.

"Hello. Thank you. What was your name again?"

"George, monsieur."

"Right. George. Come in, please."

The man was rattled by my request, as though the past two weeks had been a calculated program of habituation designed to throw him off in that one moment.

"Where would you like it, sir?" he asked through his thick accent, pushing the tray of stale bread and sealed preserves through the door.

"Oh. Anywhere. On the bed, thanks."

"Bonne journée," he said, turning to leave.

"No, wait. I want to ask you something. How long have you been working here?"

"Five years, monsieur."

"Ah, so you're not related to...her?" I asked, pointing downwards.

He grinned boyishly. "No..."

We exchanged a hearty laugh, his genuine, mine manic. I picked up a small pot of jam and juggled it in one hand.

"She is very terrible, but also she is kind when you know her," he said, choosing the words with some difficulty.

I stared at him, perhaps too long, still juggling. "What do you do when you're stuck, George?"

"Stuck, monsieur?"

"Yes, stuck, as in, you don't know where to go. Or, you have too much bottled up and you don't know where or how to empty it."

"I look for where I want to go," he said, his expression jumbling as he sought to understand whether my query was indeed as strange as it seemed or whether it was by some failure of his English that he was confused.

"And how do you do that?"

"I think about it, sir."

I failed to catch the pot of jam, and it fell to the floor before rolling under the bed.

"*Merci*, George," I said with uninhibited pretention. "For your troubles."

He grasped the last of my change and then walked out, confused.

A few seconds later I heard his voice, dampened through the walls, say, "Il est fou, ce mec," and it saddened me.

I snatched my food from George on the mornings that followed without saying much. It was clear now that he, and by extension all others, were useless to me.

I quested inward.

When I ate, I ate as little as I could, and tried to close my eyes when I did it. I could not help but begin seeing food as a sort of deception. It was as if every slice of toast or forkful of egg was a part of the external world whose essence I could digest as well as its matter, though this essence never showed itself between my teeth or in my gut, and I was reluctant to begin looking for it.

Time passed, and my frustration only multiplied. Half the work should have been finished by that point. I should have been in the midst of e-mailing universities, contacting publishers, or writing the crowning summary. Instead, I sat beside the laptop, unproductive for hours, and only sipped my coffee when it was already twilight.

There was little I could do but writhe in bed. I twisted and stretched like an alley cat on the lumpy mattress, itchy feathers piercing me through the sheets, surrounded by used earplugs, for what seemed like a week or two. There were breadcrumbs of varying age gathering in the sheets.

Unable to sleep due to my body feeling like an old mine field, I rose and paced at odd hours of the night, and raked at the dark under the bed for the pot of jam, and washed my face or gargled mouthwash, but was faced each time with failure. Soon my funds would dry up, and then I would be finished.

Then, one particularly maddening afternoon, as I lay on the bed with my eyes locked on the ceiling, I was confronted with a graver problem. Deep in introspection, I came across film reels all tattered and disused in the shadowy backstage of my mind, disconcatenated memories I'd long ago edited out of my life as if dissatisfied with some director's work. I passed by the scaffolding of my old selves, now devoured by mites, on the verge of collapse. There were not only vermin in the infested woodwork of my consciousness; the wood itself was rotted, neglected for years.

I had little time to examine these psychological troubles of mine, as I came under attack. Intrusive thoughts, there to defend whatever darkness I had come across. They interrupted my thinking, chucked me out of those deeper regions of my mind, out through the stage curtains like some vagabond.

There I was, groaning in my bed; and inly cast as a gladiator in nothing but a loincloth, facing unfathomable horrors, creatures procured by an emperor too friendly with the underworld. My will against fiery impulse. They were volatile, barbed, kamikaze notions that burst into the spotlight, forcing me to attend to them.

The attacks came as vicious compulsions, statements such as: *"To hell with metaphysics,"* or, *"I slit the throat of literature,"* or, *"David Hume is my slave."* Other times, they were clear and sadistic images, such as the cathartic destruction of my laptop and of the desk, or the burning down of the hotel; or the spontaneous assault on George in the morning, smashing the tray into his mouth until all of his teeth were shattered and blood frothed from the wreckage; or even the murder of the bulldogs while they slept. The most aggressive and unrelenting of these images clasped my mind like an iron maiden. In it, a giant tenebrous beast, certainly not human, chased Sophia through a labyrinth until she ended up half bent over a windowsill. The creature rammed her without restraint as she reached out in desperation for lunar safety.

I tried and tried to rip these thoughts from my mind, but it felt as though I were lying on train tracks and being repeatedly slammed by speeding carriages every time I tried to rise. And the thoughts repeated, post-nausea, again, and again, and again. As though I had lost control of whatever part of me was responsible for imagination, given up to some demon jester to play with.

For days I made worthless attempts at auto-exorcism. Sometimes running my head under a cold tap helped, but by the time I began shivering, it had begun again.

The days rolled on, and my condition did not improve. Behind one of the routine breakfast knocks one morning stood not George, but

Madame Hugo, the mother of the dogs. She shoved her weight through the threshold and pushed me aside. Her nostrils contorted after an exaggerated sniff. Her dogs sat leashed at the edge of the room, which began smelling of unwashed canines.

"Monsieur, I must ask you how much longer you plan to stay, and how you expect to pay for your considerable bill," said the fat woman in a laughable and forced British accent.

"Ah, Madame, welcome, welcome," I said, eying the dogs.

Know that there are few things I despise more than animal lovers, besides domesticated animals themselves. Pestilential creatures with no place on man's Earth. The rank of their saliva, the inarticulate growling or squawking, the dumb frenzy for base desires attended to by a servile master. It's enough to make even the coldest intellect forget reason and do unspeakable things.

And let me tell you, yes, that I would be lying if I said I hadn't fantasized about taking care of those beasts; that I hadn't, in the dead of night, tip-toed my way through the corridors, down the creaky stairs, across the lobby to their three smelly bodies, and with maximum effort not to inhale a breath of canine air, a butter-knife in hand one night and a steak-knife in hand a subsequent night, stood there stabbing myself lightly in the leg, resisting the urge to make ribbons of their necks, ultimately dissuaded purely by the thought of their filthy blood touching my skin.

"Please, not to worry at all," I said to Madame Hugo. "I will be paying you by card soon, quite soon. I am finishing my work here in Paris, and then I will be returning to London," I continued, readily exploiting her apparent fetish for the English.

"Ah, but your accent did not tell me you were from England. *Bien, bien.* You did your education outside? Yes, like me. You know that I studied in England? Many years ago. I lived in St. John's Wood."

I rubbed an ache in my leg. "Ah, wonderful. That's fantastic. I have many friends there. Alas, my family's estate is in Kensington, closer to Hyde Park."

"Oh, my. That is very nice. And so…" She forgot what she wanted to say, and I saw the opportunity to strike.

I sprang, all eight of my legs at the fore, and plunged my fangs into her buttery neck. "Oh, but you are so very charming, Madame Hugo," I said, giving her a lascivious grin and raise of the eyebrows, suddenly thankful that I had showered for the first time in days. "And these lovely little ones, are they your children?" I asked while maintaining eye-contact with her and petting her three ugly dogs.

Bitch, bitch, bitch. Mother of dogs! Was running through my head all the while, and I fought the compulsion to run to the bathroom and wash my hands. *Calm down. Ca-BI-lm d-Bitch-own.*

"Yes, oh you are so good with them. This is Victor, and Abel, and Eugène," she said, pointing out the three beasts.

"And they have a beautiful," *Sto-Bitch—p,* "mother." *of-stop- dogs.*

And, like a wretch, uninvited, I went and I kissed the manageress on the cheek, while somewhat wiping my hands of her dog's filth on her dress, and not without the complimentary vision of tearing her head from her shoulders as I did so.

She blushed, and she turned and walked from the room.

"I will come to you to ensure that the bill is well and settled before I depart, Madame. You have my word," I said after her.

R-Fu-e-c-l-k-i-metap-e-hysics-f.

"Oh, *bien sûr,*" the old bag said, almost skipping down the hallway. She was so fickle. A hypnotized mongoloid at the word "Kensington."

BABA YAGA

There is a letter tucked away in a drawer somewhere in Moscow. It is buried under a battered old rock and frozen dust, in a building long abandoned. Only the spiders and the rust have visited these ruins. There is a memory in this letter, a memory rotting away with the desk that holds it. This letter reads as follows:

To whom it may concern,

I am not entirely sure that I deserve to be writing all of this down. In many ways, I am a poor woman, and usually it is people who are prosperous in one way or another who write things down. I am poor because I have a wasteland inside me, and truly, a well-cultivated garden is the only sort of wealth I can see as being worthwhile. I've been poor my entire life. Some days I've felt as though that barren soil of mine could grow something, anything, but the seeds have always died before they could sprout. This is what is the truth, anyway. What I remember is different.

I grew up in a small home, in a village near the Tosna River. The smell of fish fills my memories of that place, along with images of burly fathers and weathered mothers. When I remember those days, there always seems to have been a drunk somewhere in the scene, too.

That was a long time ago, another life, even. I have a few memories of my family in those days, too. The love of the Orthodoxy, and of our Little Father —those things I remember my mother speaking about often. She would even cry about them. She often cried when father was around, too, but she never said why.

I have never seen my mother again since those days, but I've come to know my father again. He's quite different now to how I remembered him, but then, I was only a child, and he was a lot younger.

We speak regularly these days, though he doesn't have much at all to say. Or maybe he's embarrassed for some reason. I've stopped asking, honestly. I'm just glad he's back in my life. It reassures me that those memories are real, and that I didn't just invent them or something. He's the only tie to those memories of my youth I've got. And did I mention my mother used to sing? That's how I remember her most, sitting in her chair and singing while I sat at her feet and listened to her. I loved her.

Still, I am a poor woman. And my father knows I'm a poor woman. He knows this, and that's why he won't listen to me when I say crazy things. I know they're crazy, but it can't stop me from saying things about them, because for me they are real, my sister and my daughter. He says he only had one child, but I remember it differently. He says I'm a poor, poor girl, and that my mind is dying like his bones.

He also said my soil was dead from the beginning, and that my husband (God rest his soul) had only a dead sea for me. Sometimes I think I'm the only link he has to our past, too. Maybe that's why he's so careful with me. He says I can't remarry, even though I'm not gray, yet.

But I want to write about my sister and my daughter. If it's too crazy for him to hear, then maybe he can read it, and if he can't read it, at least you will read it, and you will laugh with me, even if you don't know my name and even if you will never know me.

They were both beautiful. The only girls in the family with black hair, and the same eyes, cold and blue like our winters.

When my mother was still with us, in the days of the drunks and the fish, we would sometimes walk to the river and she would speak to me about her favorite things. The Orthodoxy and our Little Father, usually, but sometimes she would tell me about father, and about Uncle Josef, and sometimes about secret things she did not tell father, or her sisters, or her friends.

One day, by the river, she told me I had a sister, "only one year older than you," she said. "You will care for each other and become like twins," she said.

But she also said father was not to know, because he had too much drink in his heart to care for one more in the family. She said that my sister was a gift from Our Little Father, and that the other villagers would not understand, so my sister lived with our Auntie Mariya. Poor girl, she was forbidden to leave the house. Maybe this is why her skin was so white, like my daughter.

One year we were allowed together. Me six, and her seven. She did not speak our language in the first months, but when we played, I told her the words, and we danced and ran and peeked out of the window to see the adults. We laughed a lot, and giggled, mostly at our Auntie Mariya and her big nose.

In the nighttime I begged my father to let me sleep in the house of my auntie, and for the first few nights he said yes, maybe happy to get rid of me. But father did not like mysteries. He asked me why I liked sleeping there so much, and if I thought she and Uncle Anton had a nicer house than he did. When I said I only wanted to see my auntie, he became angry, and he shouted, and he told me to stay with my mother. My poor mother, she could not say anything to him because she was afraid of him finding out about our happiness.

I did not understand, and I asked my mother when we were alone. It was the first night my father did not let me sleep at the house of my auntie, after he was sleeping like a bear. I asked her why father did not let his daughters stay together, and she said, "Don't ask your father these questions. He works a lot and he likes you better, so never mention your sister to him. He can't love her like he loves you."

My heart was broken, and the whole night I lay with my eyes on the window, planning my big escape to the house down the road. I never went, *because father snored too loud and scared me every time I walked near the door.*

When I finally saw my sister again, we went to play in the woods near the river. Father forgot about me if I forgot to ask him to go to my auntie, and I always forgot to ask him after that night when he had become mad.

My mother did not let us near the river alone, but she said we could take our sticks and run in the woods before the dark. So we went, and we became red from how much we laughed.

Mother came with our auntie when the sun started to go away, and they laughed with us, too. We smelled like grass and earth the whole day. Out of my entire life, except when I saw my little girl for the first time, this was the happiest day I can remember.

When we came back, there was time to sit in my auntie's house and whisper stories. My sister didn't speak much. Not only that time, but whenever there were adults, even after she learned how to speak our language. Sometimes I think she forgot she was there with us. When we didn't play in the woods and the snow, she didn't even smile a lot. But we loved each other very much. I know because one day she came to me with tears and with a small rock she had found in the woods the day we had run together. It was a few months later, so I didn't understand very well why she had decided to give me the rock. She said it was so I could remember our special day. My poor little sister.

I said it was one year that we spent together, and I think this is right. I am not sure. It's difficult to tell time when you are small, before your parents and your work teach you how to measure it. I think it was one year. One happy year.

When we went into the woods every now and again, we continued a long story that we invented each time. We were two Princesses, Vassilisa and Vasiliya. Both of us against Baba Yaga!

The first time we played in this story, Auntie Mariya came looking for us and we screamed "Baba Yaga! Baba Yaga!" at her. She knew the old story well and was not happy with us, so she asked, "And which one of you two is the Princess Vassilisa? There can't be two."

So we stayed, and we looked at each other, and my sister said, "She is the Princess Vassilisa, and me, I'm the Princess Vassiliya."

"Who is this new Princess?" my Auntie Mariya asked.

"The one that arrives to help Princess Vassilisa against Baba Yaga when she is alone."

My Auntie laughed, and she played with us that first day, pretending to be Baba Yaga and scaring us before bringing us into her arms.

Near the end of that year, our story became longer and longer, and drifted away from the stories they told us when we were smaller.

My sister, the Princess Vasiliya, she became like the Baba Yaga against Baba Yaga and her evil friends. Strong, and always arriving with strange news and powers against our imaginary fairy monsters. The Princess Vassilisa was always the one Baba Yaga came after, but Baba Yaga was scared of the Princess Vasiliya. She ran after Baba Yaga with her magic stick, and behind her, I, the Princess Vassilisa, ran screaming for help from the nasty Baba Yaga. Only the special Princess Vasiliya could defeat her!

One day, we ran and ran, chasing the invisible hag. And when the dark started to run after us, too, we kept running. We forgot the way home when the trees stopped glowing, and my Auntie was shouting my name through the woods. We looked and looked, and then we came to the river. I shouted and told my auntie we were there, but she did not come, she only kept screaming my name.

The trees were not very far from the river, and what happened was very quick. I cried as soon as it happened, when I heard the splash through the ice. My poor sister. My poor Princess Vasiliya.

They sent Uncle Anton to look for her, and he dove and swam in the ice, and he caught a very bad cold, but they never found her frozen little body. My mother said Our Little Father took her back because she was an angel, but I know my mother cried every night. And she died, too, one night, alone in the house. I only have the rock left from my sister. I keep it in my cupboard and I bring it next to me every day when I pray for her.

After mother died, father became like a monster. Angry with drink all day and always smashing things. I could not speak to him about anything, not my dead sister, and not even my dead mother. So I spent all of my time in my auntie's house, and Uncle Anton was there more often, too.

He was kind, my uncle, but not a very happy man. Always tired and making strange remarks about things. Well, I lived with them after father left to fight in the revolution. But when the soldiers came to our village, my Auntie Mariya and Uncle Anton and I left for Moscow, a long way away, to try to work and find a nice husband for me, and not starve, as we had started to in those last years.

The first five years were hard. My Uncle Anton put me in school, but the schools always closed down. We lived in a small room, the three of us. It was bigger than their house near the river, and it was warmer. Uncle Anton worked in one factory, and then another. He helped me learn to read and count at night, although I don't think he knew how to read very well himself.

My Auntie Mariya was always there, but she was less happy since we had moved, and since my sister had died. When she spoke to us, it was usually about the violence in the country, or of how the Little Father was a liar. It made me think of where my sister was.

It was hard, but the years passed, and then the revolution finished, and then it was hard again. But I was older, sixteen at that time, and my Uncle Anton had moved from the factory to work in an office, collecting and organizing papers for someone more important. Maybe he wasn't that bad at reading.

Some days I went to his office, and I waited for him to finish his work. It was a small place, but it was very warm. Everyone there was nice except for Uncle Anton's supervisor. He always kept my dear uncle late to make him do extra work. He didn't let me sit with my uncle while he worked, so I always waited nearby, in other rooms, but usually in the lobby.

There was a nice man who worked there. Andrei, he was called. He worked with my uncle, but his job was higher ranking. They said he would be the next supervisor if the old man died soon. He was very young, too. Only twenty-five at the time. We talked a lot, about small things, like the seasons, and our childhoods, and I remember that I blushed whenever he came to speak to me. He must have noticed, because one day, maybe only six months after we had met and started speaking, he went to my uncle to ask for my hand.

My Auntie Mariya didn't think much of him when I came to her, excited and joyful. First, she asked me his name, and I said, "Andrei," and then she asked me for his family's name, and I said, "Belyakov." But none of this impressed her.

Then, Uncle Anton came to her and told her that he was a good man, with a good reputation with the party, and "a good job if that old geezer ever croaks." So my auntie agreed. She said it was a good choice for my future, and that I could have wonderful children and live a good life, and that she wanted the best for me.

And so, less than a year from when he proposed, Andrei and I were married. We lived in his apartment, which was very large, and had very nice furniture. Fine wood and some mirrors. He said his father had handed him all of his affairs after he had died, and Andrei was also lucky to able to do many favors for the party, for which they rewarded him often.

One year passed, and then two, but no child ever came. It made us both sad, though we were happy together, at least in the beginning. Andrei became more and more frustrated as the time went—he was quite desperate to become a father—and as his job stopped advancing, and especially the day the doctor came and told us a child would never come.

He started arriving home from his work later and later each day after that, saying the party was giving him extra work, and becoming angry with me if I asked too many questions.

I never knew much about the party, except that Andrei said good things about them, and that my Auntie Mariya did not leave the house because of them. Uncle Anton said he liked them, but I saw his eyes worry, as if looking for someone listening to him every time he said it. Well, my poor uncle must have said something without looking, because one day they came to his apartment and they took him away. We never saw him or heard from him again. I cried with my auntie, and we spent the week worrying at the door, waiting for him to come back and tell us it was all a big misunderstanding.

I asked Andrei about it. I asked him if he could talk to his friends in the *party, to save my poor uncle, because my uncle was a good man. But no! He smashed a vase on the table and said that if I kept asking him I would kill him with worry and questions. I cried, and he hugged me. He was not a bad man, only an unlucky one.*

My uncle never came home, and so my auntie wrote to my father, asking him to come work in the city and take care of us. My father did not write back, and my auntie spent her days crying and eating very little. She kept hoping that one day Uncle Anton would come through the door, but instead, what came was the news that he was going to be killed, along with other traitors to the party.

I asked Andrei what this meant, and why my dear uncle would be accused of something like that, and all he said was that my uncle had probably used documents belonging to his supervisor to help the Trotskyites. I could not believe it. My auntie kept saying it was only because his old, nasty supervisor didn't like him.

I asked Andrei if she could come and live with us, but he refused. He said that he could not be seen with the wife of an enemy to the party, and that I should be careful to even be with her myself. I cried, and he hit me. We had stopped hoping for a child before, but it was difficult to even look at each other after that day.

My Auntie Mariya died in the winter. Her dear Anton never came home, so she stopped eating. Less and less every day, until she looked like Baba Yaga. I miss her very much, and I wish my beloved Andrei had tried to help her, or at least let her live with us so that we could have taken care of her.

I miss him too, these days. We became closer, after my auntie passed, and he never did strike me again. The old geezer at his office finally expired, and Andrei became the new supervisor. If only my dear uncle could have seen that day.

Some more months passed, and life moved on. My father even wrote to us. The letter was addressed to my auntie, but it said that he had decided to come to the city and look after us. He said he had finished with his drinking, and warring, and that he wanted to see his little girl and her husband. I was excited, but a little sad. The last time I had seen him, he had been shouting at my mother's ghost.

Before he arrived, though, I fell very ill. It started one afternoon, but became an illness that stretched into a month or more. I don't remember much of it. I was very, very sick. Saying many crazy things, like I do today. Andrei was kind enough to take care of me. The last days, the ones just before I started to become better, those I don't remember at all. Always sweating and sleeping. The first thing I saw when I woke up from that horrible disease was the white face of my small darling daughter.

I didn't understand at first, but Andrei said that I had been pregnant, and that my sickness was nothing more than the difficulties of the final months. He said he had called a doctor, who had delivered our baby girl for us. I told him that I hadn't felt pregnant at all, and that I didn't remember seeing any doctor, but all he said was that it was because of the fever. And there, in front of us, was this beautiful little child. And I knew she was mine, because she looked just like my sister, with the same snow-white skin and black hair. It was like waking up from a long nightmare when I understood that she was real.

We played together, and I took care of her, and fed her, and I wish that she were still here. Andrei loved her, too. He called her his little snowflake.

But Andrei's work became tougher, and he started spending even less time with us. Some weeks passed, and while I was holding our baby, a knock came at the door.

It was Nikolai, Andrei's coworker, and he was worried. He said that I needed to go with him right away, because Andrei was in trouble. So I dressed, and I wrapped up our baby, and I followed him to the office.

Andrei was sitting with two men, going through some papers. He looked terrified. I didn't understand, until Nikolai whispered to me that they were from the party. The party. The party. Always the horrible party!

Andrei saw me through the glass, and then he stood up. He went quietly to the door and said something to the two men inside. Without any more words, the two oafs beat him, then took my husband by the arms and carried him out through the office. When they passed me, I was too shocked to say anything, so I watched. And Andrei looked at us, his little girl and I, and he could not keep his eyes away from her.

One of the oafs said, "Is this your wife?"

But he replied, "This contemptible woman is like a dog to the party. I spit on her."

And I understood. Dear Andrei was a good man, but an unlucky one.

And so we were alone, my daughter and I. I missed Andrei in those days that followed, but they were not the saddest days, because at least I had her, my little snowflake.

At night I started reading the story of the Princess Vassilisa to her, only I told her the version that my sister and I would act in the woods. I told her that one day she would be like the Princess Vasiliya, stronger and more beautiful than the Princess Vassilisa. I told her that Baba Yaga would cry from hearing her name, and that I would always be there to help her. I wish I never said the last part. I am a bad mother for lying to my poor little girl.

My father arrived one morning, knocking at the door and calling my name. I was so excited for him to meet his granddaughter that I could not help myself from crying. I ran to the door and I hugged him. He did not cry, but he was happier than I have ever seen him before or after. And he said, "There is my beautiful daughter! And where is her dear Andrei?" And the room became darker.

I had to tell him the whole story, about Andrei, and about Uncle Anton and even poor Auntie Mariya, and he said he could not believe it. He looked so broken when I told him my auntie and uncle were both dead. I felt sorry for him.

He said he would go straight away and sort the problem out with the authorities. But I wanted him to meet his granddaughter first, so I begged him to wait and to see her. It was no use; he was too angry. He said she would wait for him, and he ran out of the door again.

I waited some hours for him to come back, and in that time the strangest feeling started to hug me. Slowly, at first, but then louder and louder in my heart. I felt like I had fallen into a nest of hungry insects.

I could not find my daughter anywhere. I searched in my room, and in the living room and the kitchen, and even in the bath. She was nowhere. She was NOWHERE. How can I explain? This page is like a prison for me now. I want to write a scream into it, so that you can hear the only thing left in me. I wept and wept, and threw up, even.

If I became crazy it was in those moments, not before, like my father says. I thought that maybe he might have taken her with him for some reason, maybe to plead for my husband's innocence. But he never even saw her. How distressed I was, how horrible I felt.

And when my father returned, and his first words through the door were, "Your husband admitted to being a traitor, and he said you are a vile woman who licks the boots of the party," all he heard in return was a howl from my torn throat.

My sister and my baby were real. I know that if Andrei were still alive he would tell my father the truth, that she was born in the house he lives in. And I know if my Auntie Mariya were still alive she would tell him the truth about my sister, as well.

Father thinks his bones are dying, but his heart was buried with mother.

And me, I am nothing now. All I have is you and this letter. The days eat me away, and father will die soon, too, I know it. They say there is war starting in Finland now, and I think he will go, even though he is old. Then I will be alone, and I will die, too.

I love you, because I know you believe me. Because I know I don't have to show you their bodies for you to know that I loved them.

Sincerely,

12

THE UNIVERSAL FIRES

More than an hour had passed in the engineering tunnel. Having abandoned their rifles in the darkness far behind them, Tikan and Naim were away from all sounds of violence now, though they could no longer discern their location along the ship's arterial passages. In that darkness, they could not tell whether their eyes were open or not, although they stung enough to keep them squinting. Their faces were soaked and still streaming, with their breaths curling back black against them.

Guided still by those stars no doubt furious outside, Tikan plodded forward, supporting Naim's slippery form as he limped on. As they advanced through the baking cylinder, Naim grew drowsier, his eyelids heavy as oceans and promising relief. His head dipped continuously, and his eyes rolled. Beneath him, his spoiled thigh seemed to fizzle and seethe as though it were some manifesting incarnation of the pitch darkness they were infiltrating. He heard Tikan whispering something as they slugged on.

"What...What are you saying?" Naim whimpered, trying to twist his head to look at his muttering friend. The other did not reply. Naim's thoughts were like bruises still forming. His memories flickering in and out. As discomfort overtook him, he let his head dip.

Tikan felt his thighs bursting with each step. At times, his head grazed the ceiling, glancing now and then off an exposed section of wiring or protruding girders. He kicked a hammer someone had forgotten on the floor, and his toes recoiled. Behind him was the faintest sound of screaming and gunfire starting again, soaked up and muffled by the shadows around him, inferior now to the throb in his head.

Naim was beginning to writhe and groan feverishly. Somewhere above him, Tikan continued whispering.

Eventually, Tikan caught hold of a jutting pipe in the wall, and he leaned on it as though it were a support rail. Though it managed to hold their weight, the pipe also periodically creaked, and eventually began to crack and hiss out waves of steam. With a scalding wave overcoming his face, Tikan gritted his teeth and marched on.

Some time later, Tikan's wrist knocked against a stile, and he stopped and caught Naim from falling. He reached out and found another stile, perpendicular to the first, and the rungs between them.

"This is it," he said, shaking Naim.

The other man roused himself, prying open his eyes, fighting his crushing fatigue to look at the vague shape.

"The ladder. We're at the bow, just under the cockpit," Tikan said.

"I—Go inside—Come back after."

"No."

Tikan lowered Naim to the floor opposite the ladder, and then climbed up. He spun the small wheel in the dark. After the metal disk creaked open, he poked his head out into the light, which blinded him immediately.

His eyes burned as they adjusted to the new brightness and the acrid smoke that streamed around his face and siphoned into the hole. It reeked of incinerated plastic and fuses and bodies. Yellow fog obscured the place. He focused. His bearings swirled out of unison for a moment before they returned to him, and he recognized where he was situated.

The exit through which he peered was at the very end of the lounge, in the corridor at its bow end. Far to the right, past the full and vile smoke, he could see the black suited invaders firing at Alec and the others. It came as a great relief and surprise to Tikan to find that the others had held out so long. Perhaps the black suits had ignored them while they finished up their business, or perhaps Naim had been correct, that certain metempsies inadvertently served as suitable training exercises.

Tikan dropped back down the shaft before he could see anything else, and he lowered himself to Naim's level. He lifted Naim under the armpits and dragged him to the ladder.

"You're going to go up first," he told him. "Once you're out, just cross the open space so they can't see you. The cockpit's close. I'll be right behind you."

"No—leave—after," Naim groaned.

"You're not staying here, and I can't lift you from up there. Wake up. We're almost through."

With arms outstretched, Tikan pushed his friend up the ladder. He was careful not to touch the wound, which was now revealed in full as light poured in through the exit. The crater of the wound was surrounded by black crust that stained down to the bone, with the surrounding fabric baked into it. He ignored it and lifted Naim out of the portal. Naim tumbled out of the hole the moment his torso cleared it, and his wounded leg scraped the silver rim on the way out, though he did not cry out.

Tikan scrambled up the ladder after him. Before exiting, he surveyed the area. There, on the floor, Naim was about a meter from him. Naim was crawling, dragging himself on his good side, halfway out of the lounge. None of the black suits were nearby or watching.

Tikan scuttled out of the hole and strode in a panic through the smoke to Naim, his lungs straining. He gathered up Naim's limp body and, stumbling, dragged it to cover.

They sat against a wall, panting, with their backs to the lounge. The cockpit was ahead of them, down a last corridor. Though it was not as dark as the underworld they had just wormed through, most remaining lights were fogged behind thick smoke. Naim looked at Tikan, his eyes whirring, open and searching to stay alert. Their throats burned.

"The cockpit, it's there. This is it," Tikan said, pointing ahead of them, down another narrow corridor.

"I—yes," panted Naim.

They got up again and hurried through the corridor, trying to control the impact of their steps. A line of ceiling lights popped down from above. Hunching like a pair of runaways whose backs were mangled after years of confinement, they hobbled down the gauntlet, with fear flashing in the dark periphery behind their skulls, with the wet nuzzling of paranoia's hound about their ears.

When they reached the end of the corridor, they came upon a circular metal gate sealed all around like a vault.

"Here."

Still holding onto his battered friend, Tikan scanned the giant disk before him and then smashed it with the base of a closed first. There was no response from inside. He tried again. Nothing. Blood pumped through him. He was moments from panicking, and he spun his head right, left. There was a screen beside him, which remained unlit and threw his ragged face back at him. He prodded it, still holding Naim, and typed until it bleeped and opened a voice channel into the cockpit.

"Mira, It's Tikan. We're injured. Please, if you're inside, please open. Fast. There's no one else but us," he said, watching the volume of his voice lest it rise too high, still scanning the space behind him as he spoke.

There was no answer. The blood was ready to burst from his ears. Naim was drifting off again, lashing his head up every other second, his breaths dwindling to quiet huffs.

"Whoever is inside, please. This is Tikan Solstafir, please, we—"

The gate steamed at its edges. It slipped out of its seal and slid into a socket to the right. With an almost blank expression across her face, Mira stood before them.

There was a gash running down her bald head to her brow. She opened her mouth to speak, but Tikan stepped forward and dumped his companion into her arms before she could say anything. He turned to the counterpart screen inside, typed, and watched the gate shut again. It closed out the brightness and left them in minor shadow again.

"What's happening?" the bald woman asked, leaning backward and struggling with the load she had been handed.

Tikan did not answer. He was busy scanning, searching, looking for the emergency controls, pressing screens and twisting analogue knobs. The cockpit was cramped. There were no seats, only a cold empty stage surrounded by cabinets and screens, and a piloting station at the very bow end of the room, which looked like an enormous marine arthropod resting its girthy tentacles into the steel around it.

"The gassing protocols. Where are they?" he demanded, turning to face her.

"What? Why? What's going on?"

"You...You don't know what's happening?" Naim said, as Mira lowered him into a corner. There, his body was made stark by the angle of the light against it, and his eyes sank. He laughed deliriously when she was slow to answer.

"I...No," she said, as though trying to remember.

"Mira, wake up," Tikan said. "Were you sleeping? Piloting? Did you not feel the crash?"

Mira gave him a concentrated but vacuous gaze. "I...yes. I fell. I..." She touched the gash on her head. She was only just waking up, red-eyed and confused, and could remember little. She searched her memories. There had been a loud crash and a gravity lapse, and she had been sent headfirst into a wall. She could remember nothing afterward.

"The protocols. There are people on board. Invaders. We're all going to die if you don't activate them right now."

Mira did not answer. Instead, she turned and strode to a nearby wall, an eye still on Tikan, and lit up her security feed projection.

"The ship's networks are down and there are barely any cameras online. What's happening?"

Tikan walked to her briskly and pointed at one of the last surveillance feeds, where the black suits could be seen. The feed showed the corridor where the others had bottlenecked the passage to the rest of the ship. Three security personnel were dead already; only Alec and another remained.

"Look. The ones in black suits. Everyone else is hiding in the dorms. There isn't time. Look at what they've done in the lounge. They've killed the captain," he said, swallowing a moon as he stared at her.

"Oh, suns...Everyone's dead," she said, looking at the grim remains of the lounge.

"Not everyone yet. Gas them. Knock everyone out. Do it fast."

"Knock everyone out?" she said, eyeing him intently. "Is that what you think the gas does?"

Tikan stared at her in silence. The nausea was starting again in his stomach.

Then came a demented guffaw from maddening Naim in the corner of the room. "Why in the pits of the sun would transport freighters be equipped with lethal gas?" he said, hurling the slurred words out of his depleted, feverish body.

"Did you really think a little sleeping gas could stop people like *that*?" Mira said, pointing at the feed. "If they aren't gened against it, they're probably on enough stimulants to wake up a brown dwarf. You think after Mars they weren't going to mandate every transporter to have kill gas?"

"What's the point of killing everyone on the ship? To save people?" Naim laughed his mad laugh again. "People like this don't exist, they just don't. When was the last war? The Mars attacks? One hundred years? Do you think war is even real? It's not," he spewed, only moments from losing consciousness. "War's not real, never was, and neither are these people, or attacks on Mars. I've fought a thousand battles, killed generals and galaxies, I know. You think we would have come off Earth if we were like that? We can't. They say it hasn't happened since, and it isn't. No. No reason to save."

As Mira observed him, she noted his feverish state and spoke to him less firmly. "It's designed to save history, not people. But wait." She turned to Tikan and crossed her eyebrows. "He's right. What is this? Were these people on board from the start?"

Tikan's gaze was glued to the surveillance feed. Alec and the other remaining security officer stood in dark wet outfits firing at those black solids in the smoke, who returned fire more precisely and in barrages, and who walked as though the entire exchange was little more than a necessary waste of time. Another officer lay on the floor beside them with a shriveled crisp for an arm, trying to claw his way to the dormitories.

"No. They boarded us," Tikan said. "I felt it. I don't know how. I don't know what they want. Someone called Farabi. Look, we're out of options. Is there anything else we can do?"

Mira looked at him, wide-eyed, half-grinning incredulously. "Wait, *they boarded us?* They boarded the Equuleus? No. We're between systems and between jump gates. Even if you said they boarded us in orbit, I wouldn't believe you. Forget the logistics, try finding a ship first. We're interstellar. Not in Sol, not in Proxima. We're in *dark space*. This doesn't happen. This can't happen," the pilot said. She frowned, and a trickle of blood oozed from the wound on her forehead. "You're right, either way," she continued after half a pause. "This is insanity. We just have to gas them."

Tikan continued to watch Alec and the other man struggle. The man who had been crawling away now lay still, and Alec was firing blindly from behind cover. Tikan squinted hard as though he were in some pain.

"No," he said.

The surveillance feed showed the man beside Alec poke out of cover for a moment, only to have a fiery hole widen in the center of his chest. He looked down his sternum in sheer awe before total agony overtook his expression and he collapsed to the floor. As his final companion crumpled beside him, Alec cried out, red-faced and soaked.

"What do you mean, *no?*" Mira said. She strutted defiantly to a wall of consoles in front of the piloting station.

Tikan intercepted her and grabbed her arm.

"Stand aside. They have to die," she said.

"I will not let you."

The image flickered. Though Alec was still firing without aiming, his opponents no longer returned fire. He sat on his knees, rocking himself, and clenched his whole face and shot his rifle, which was half dangling out of his grip. The doomy band marched through the corridor.

"Why are you doing this? Didn't you come here to stop this?" Mira said.

"Switch the surveillance to the dorms."

Mira looked at the projection and squinted at it. A second image appeared, showing a complex of rooms packed with frantic faces and crying children.

"Are you going to condemn all of these people, too?" Tikan said. "You can't."

"Condemn? Me? I'm not condemning anyone. What are you saying? They were all dead the minute those monsters climbed into the ship. What are you talking about?"

Another laugh came from the madman in the corner. "She's right. Do it," Naim said, before writhing again in his waking discomfort.

"No, she isn't. They're still alive."

"Have you lost your mind?" Mira said. "There is *nothing* we can do for those people."

"You can't know that. You can nev—"

"*Stop this.* I want answers. I want to know who these people are and why they're here, and how they boarded us. I want—I want to kill them."

She tried to consume Tikan in the frosty viridian of her eyes.

Though his cheeks seemed to sag in despair, he stood, unmoved as Citium's most stalwart son.

"That's not justice," he said.

On screen, Alec stopped firing, and he slumped against his cover. He took a last few measured breaths in resignation as feet shuffled out beside him. Four or five invaders streamed into view.

"Justice? What's justice? What the he—ah," she flinched as she tried to speak some forbidden word. "What do you know about justice?" she snarled, immediately recovering.

"I know—"

"You think it makes a difference who kills them? You think—oh, moons. Let me go, Tikan. Now's not the time to lose sight."

He tightened his grip on her wrist.

"Tikan, there," Naim said, pointing at Alec with a quivering finger.

He remained stoic and repeated, "No."

"They're going to come after us afterwards, you know that right?" Mira said, her voice trembling.

"Then we'll die. And the world will be no better, but no worse, either, and—"

"Oh, just stop," she shouted. "Stop it, just stop. Give them mercy and give them vengeance and stop it. Nobody cares what we do. We'll crash into the nearest star after this, and then it'll all be gone, and the least we could have done is this. Now let me go."

"Mira, do you know what I think?" Tikan said, bringing her gaze to his. "I think this ship, this body, and the galaxy can burn. Let the planets fall, let the suns collide, but not by my hand."

She looked at him in disgust.

The remaining invaders emptied out of the corridor and formed a circle around Alec. He cowered when they took him by the collar, like Amozagh. They rammed him below the eye with the butt of a rifle as he tried to throw a fist. His collapsed eye socket filled with blood.

There were no questions for Alec. For him, there was a punishment doled out only for those most egregiously misaligned with power at its most incarnate. They dented his head against the wall and blood sprayed across the metal. They dropped their guns in a clatter to the floor and dragged the bloody pulp half way to the ceiling, streaking the wall in crimson. He was no longer fully conscious, but still they plugged fists into his abdomen and then struck him to the floor. And they stomped, stomped, stomped on his head until it resembled a crushed grapefruit, violence cooling out its oozing center. Then they turned around uniformly and streamed into the rest of the ship.

Tikan winced at the carnage on the screen but would not turn away.

"You're mad, Tikan, you bastard. Like them. Like them, but at least they know what they are."

"Mira, look at me. Just look. I'd boil out of this room, and—"

"Then *do* something, or let me do it."

He considered her a moment. "Can't let you," he said. He paused and held up her wrist. "Listen, I promise—I promise. After, if we survive this, we'll find them. You'll have your vengeance. But not now."

She shook her head and started to beat her free hand into his chest.

They watched as the black suits streamed single file into the dormitories and dispersed through the crowd. The passengers, all huddled together, began screaming and cowering into corners. In the chaos, they fell atop each other and fought to distance themselves from the guns now firing.

The word *Farabi* soared, distorted, as the crowd thinned. Scarlet fumes needled about the doomed as though those wisps were their blood-bound spirits not yet ready to leave their bodies.

The black suits made their patrol through the growing mass of bodies. After the initial slaying, they roamed around gunless, massacring barehanded and scanning heads with slim devices. They walked like risen ghouls clad black for eternity, and they slaughtered the children first, discarding them without concern.

Mira turned away, her wrist still in Tikan's grip. She wiped her cheeks before looking up at him with clenched teeth and trembling jaw and a look of near-hatred. Then she pounded his chest with her free hand again and wept.

Watching his choice unfold on screen, Tikan battled his own tears, with the soot around his eyes now tracked with a clean line or two. In the corner, Naim's eyes closed, and he slumped against the wall.

Tikan released Mira's wrist. "You can try it now, the gas. There's no one left there that deserves to live," he said.

She had no words for him, only a look of deep spite. Then she turned to face the console.

"Look," Tikan said, pointing at the surveillance projection.

Two of the black-suited men were crouched down, holding the head of an old man. A third arrived, broke open the old man's skull, and tore at something in the bloody mush.

"Are they...?" Mira said.

"That must be Farabi."

"Well, the gas is spreading down now. Looks like we'll both come out of this satisfied."

He focused at once on the live feed. The invaders, now finished with their business, had walked back into the lounge. Tikan and Mira watched, horrified. The screen flickered with data indicating how much gas was filling the atmosphere.

Twenty percent.

Then the black suits stopped midway through the lounge, just in front of the boarding gate.

"What—what are they doing?" Mira asked quietly.

They had recovered their rifles and pointed them in unison at the wall beside the gate. All together, these slim rifles spat out white-hot beams that made an orange circle of melting steel.

Thirty percent.

"I...I think they're trying—*oh God*," Tikan said, for once incautious of his language. "They're trying to blow a hole into the hull! Seal the lounge off from the rest of the ship. Hurry."

"R-Right."

Almost tripping, Mira ran to a console on the other side of the room and drummed another screen with her fingers while her eyes jittered at it.

Forty percent.

Meanwhile, the metal ring those ritualists were drawing slagged at the edges.

"Seal the gate. Now. We can't pay the hole. You have to seal the lounge off from the stern. Fast," Tikan shouted.

She did not answer, but began sweating profusely.

The liquid metal dripped off until, in a soundless instant, the disk was ripped out to nowhere and there remained only a black hole which greedily inhaled all debris, human or otherwise, and smoke, and guns, and flames.

The gas percentage plummeted from fifty percent to zero.

The black suits swayed like trees in a hurricane, though they stayed firmly rooted.

The ship's stomach was being pumped. Light flickered away. And yet, step after heavy step, the black suits trod towards that entrance to the void they had carved out. They approached the mouth of the abyss, and the foremost member of their group stood and tapped his chest with precise little prods.

There came a flash from out of the hole, into the lounge. At once, through whirling debris and apocalyptic lights, the dark visitors ejected cables from their chests out into the breach. They were pulled out of sight, zipping and bent like strung bows, out into black space on taut cables. And then silence.

"What just happened?" Mira said.

"The lounge, or we're dead with the life support."

She scrambled, sweat dripping from her nose. "There. There, it's done. It's sealed."

Mira collapsed onto her knees and buried her face in her hands, while Tikan watched out of the blast windows running along the front and ceiling of the cockpit. An aquiline sliver of a ship burst through space like a rogue star, enshrouded again, gone into infinite dark.

13

THE WITCH

See the void unobstructed. Negative flesh and soul.

Then: Mercia in the Middle Ages. A village whose huts look like they are sinking in mud. The villagers gnarled and dirty and mean. A single donkey braying in a rundown stable. The clouds are graying again for a second downpour. In one month, bannermen shall ride through to collect the men and the boys.

The crowd forms round an unlit pyre. They have gathered here before, many winters previous, with different girls tied to the stake. Now they are thespians, practiced in the glut of hysteria.

Sielle tried to explain herself, but her language was not theirs, and was therefore demonic. Within an hour of her appearance, she was excommunicated and sentenced. The trial took place knee deep in the mud, with her body tossed around by men and women wrinkled by calluses, with shrieks and pitchforks in the round.

The blacksmith, who dragged her out of his home claiming she had appeared from hell's gullet to tempt him, is now ruining his voice denouncing her over the crowd.

She smirks. Over these past fourteen years, she has learned to control the powers for which she has been accused.

Sorcery, they jeer.

The priest is uncertain. His eyebrows are creased in doubt. His years at the monastery, last sanctum of Europe's knowledge these dark centuries, have tempered his mind enough to be cautious. He waves the torch about nonetheless. The clouds bulge darkly from behind the pyre.

"Burn her!" they call.

The priest recites his prayer, then whispers another under his breath, and tosses the torch into the pyre while looking away.

Her smirk widens and, without struggling against her bindings, she begins laughing. Her eyes redden with the flames. Cackling, staring the blacksmith down, her gaze mirroring the blaze of his forge.

The crowd jeers at the mad girl.

Just as the downpour drops from the clouds as one thick curtain, she vanishes. The flames curl inward, rushing to fill the space she has vacated. The pyre hisses in the rain. The villagers reel in euphoria. Even their most resolute and vocal members are in shock, as if simultaneously aware of their previous imprudence and their now absolute justification in the echo of her laughter.

Out of the flames, she aims for the moon. There, she spends a few days watching ships depart for the new horizons of Mars and Venus. Earth's old satellite bored through and turned into a conduit to the new world.

Days later, she is standing outside a television store. The year is nineteen-sixty nine and Armstrong makes his small step. To her, the crowds are amusing, their enthusiasm difficult to comprehend in light of the broad history she has witnessed, and shall continue to witness.

She had intended to leap off the moon and plunge into the marvels of the universe, but she could not yet will herself to it. It was not always a simple matter for her to break away from the world, or to correctly direct her flights. Throughout her childhood, fear or near-death alone could spark her power, fling her through space and time.

The older she has grown, the more accurate and precise she has become.

She travels on, stitching consequence into the past and antecedence into the future.

She works for a baker in Victorian London. The dour basement, the other workers prepubescent with misshapen backs. Her affinity with humankind is already withering off her soul, but such sights can still break her heart.

For two weeks, she travels with a Syrian caravan, growing unusually close to her hosts. Dates and poetry at dusk. The desert's creases frozen in the moonlight. A young man whose outline straightens in her presence. She does not understand his words, but his pulse under her thumb quickens as she steals a glance.

A cloud of dust on their heels in the daytime indicates a Frankish ambush. The camelback archers circle around the advancing iron column. The cross cuts into the caravan, spills its gold and spices and blood. In defense of her first love's corpse, she drives a lance into a crusader's back.

With tears on her cheeks, she escapes again. The cycle is becoming dull, persons and attachments as firm as wisps. Even the temperate few she meets appear to her more like machines than souls. From her freezing station, she wanders on. Soon she will leap for the stars.

❧ 14 ❧

IMMANENCE AND
TRANSCENDENCE

Progress on my treatise was still not forthcoming in the following days. In fact, it was wholly paralyzed, as my condition deteriorated. I had parasites for thoughts. Every morning when George came in with his tray, I had to suppress the image of his untimely end. The same went for Madame Hugo, as she would trot down the hall quite conveniently at every crack of the door that I made in those split seconds of the morning when I retrieved my meal.

I had that buffoon of a manageress in my pocket, and so, with my stay extended indefinitely, I formally decided to put my treatise on hold and address this very serious deterioration of my conscious mind. I sought to address not only my intrusive thoughts, but also those deeper concerns previously mentioned, which I took as the foundational problems.

As a child, it often seemed to me as though the world was not in fact populated by true objects and people, but by props and sets. The thought had sprung out at me while I was standing in line at a grocery store, waiting behind my parents and listening to the digital anthems of the cash registers finishing transactions. I was stretching the arms of a flexible toy action-hero when the realization struck me from the abstract on high. I kept my sight fixed on the toy, but ceased paying attention to it.

From there, I spiraled into what can only be described as a sea of overwhelming thoughts, composed not of rational reflections, but, as might be evident from the limited vocabulary and rational powers of a child, of wordless intuitions and sentiments foggily stringing together a narrative.

I looked up at my parents, and it suddenly became apparent to me that I could never experience existence as they did, nor as the cashier, nor as the impatient stranger in line behind us. And that even if I could have existed as them, I would, necessarily, have had to abandon my current existence to do so. I recognized that, insofar as I existed, I was fundamentally alone. And if I could not *be* anyone else, if I could not inhabit others, I could not know or understand anyone else, and no other mind was therefore *real* as far as I could tell.

It therefore seemed to me as though I was the only person truly alive, and that everything else—people, objects, the sky—all of these were constructions designed solely for me. Though, I was unsure of whether the physical world was created for me all in one instant, or if it was being produced as I traveled it; if, by some stroke of luck, I might turn a fast corner and witness the construction in progress.

I became haunted by the desire to peek behind the curtain of reality, so to speak; to witness the scaffolding of the farcical world I inhabited. Further, I began wondering about who had created everything for me, and, more importantly, why they had done so.

And so I imagined the architects. The watchers, as I came to conceive of them. Humanoids, but with the colossal heads of flies, with myriad bulging eyes and mechanical curiosity, operating on incommunicable knowledge that they immanently passed amongst each other by the act of collective research alone. For every street I walked or action scene I orchestrated with my toys, I would look over my shoulder, here—there!—thinking of those hideous, bulbous spectators and their panoramic vision, ever observing me from the rafters of reality. They were not concerned with my moral decisions or my thoughts. They simply wanted to observe me. They were ideal scientists.

As I grew older, however, I forgot about these fantastical fly-headed watchers. At the age of ten, I crushed my first pair of glasses in my hand. Within a week of having been prescribed them, I had become irreconcilably bothered by their interference between the world and me. Watching two fat shards of lens buried in my palm within an oozing perimeter of blood, I was confronted with the world more intimately, though I yet felt a great distance between myself, my pain, and the rubies in my hand.

What remained was a notion of the material world, as I pictorially conceived of it at that time, as nothing more than a thin and flimsy wall behind which was absolute darkness. A wall which I could peel off with ease, if my hand were not a part of it. People, clouds, grass: all of these were animated matryoshka dolls, shells within shells, metaphysically packed to the core in only layers of their outer casings, and therefore leaving no room for any real content.

In fact, it was not so much that I felt the external world to be hollow, but rather that I felt *I* was a hollowed out part of it. That I was negative space somehow occupying matter, cleaved into the world as the only real substance, somehow able to participate in a realm not my own. I ate from the material world, I chewed with it, I breathed from it, I walked through it and in virtue of it, I scratched my head with it, I grew hair out of it; but I, the conscious *me*, was not *in it*.

I learned to appreciate interiors. I learned to appreciate a page for the way it confronted me as a limit, as a lettered stop sign indicating that I should gather the words and retreat inward, away from the world. Likewise, I learned to appreciate only artificial lights, whose illuminating properties are paltry compared to the infesting reach of the sun, but unlike the autonomous sun, dependent on the flick of a switch, and ultimately, my finger.

Now, in Paris, with this old infection of a thought spreading again, I could not help but feel bitter and unfulfilled. I felt robbed of a metaphysical depth perception; I felt that the world had become emotionally and cognitively dull to behold. As though I could taste, but not taste things. More than anything, I gnashed my teeth at the memory of a boy I had once been, who had sat for hours on salty piers, aching for all the luster promised him by the waves.

What's that, now, you want to hear more about my childhood? You think yourself a psychologist, some causal detective prepared to locate the particular flaws or misfortunes which drove me to my lunacy? To reduce my follies to the thousand stories and accidents we could tell and yet arrive at the same outcome? Please.

So, I sat in my secluded hole, with cold fingertips, and with the evil in my head reddening, and more fiendish thoughts baying just at the gate. I hunched over the desk and pulled out a piece of paper, preparing to purge myself in ink.

My pen circled the empty page for a while, as I waited, expecting the answers to pour from me. I eyed the laptop several times while I stalled, but—no, that was a place solely for clean, pristine reflections, not the hideous and visceral place I was going to.

The pen did eventually reach the page, and it did write, but it funneled only counter-catharsis out of me. Messy scribbles and smudged ink, hands to strangle away my time. I paced the room between failed attempts, clutching my hair, focusing on the order of my steps, pulling apart the stained curtains by the window to peek bitterly at empty cars, soaking in the solemnity of the full moon enthroned in clouds that only made me more furious and maddened me like some impotent, hairless, defanged lycanthrope stuck mid-transformation.

I visited the desk again every so often to churn out pointless reflections such as these:

Spaces between..........these..........paragraphs

(or are they separated expressions? How can I rejoin them as one?)

are..........the..........purest..........frustration..........They are like necessary c

r a c k s in my thinking..........I wish were notnecessary.

– stop it. Stop wasting time by observing irrelevancies when I should be focusing on the -focus- of this. --Focus--. Attend to it. Hold it.

But this is it. Is this <u>distraction</u> not part of the problem?

Its one question after the other, stacked in a regress. No answers

I don't want the answer next to me. It feels like being smothered when there's an answer, mentallysmothered.

But it's not. It's not like a thought or something similar to a thought. It's very visual in essence.

Sometimes I think its too visual to be a thought.

But there are no images like this. It's not an image, not a picture, and not a thought, either, really. Is it even conceptual?

It's closer to the negation of an image.

What I mean by a thought is difficult. I am thinking even when I'm just seeing, smelling. I know I can think about pictures in my head. I know I can have sentiments. These are not pictures, and I have sentiment only about them.

Is it a negated thought?

That's not what I mean. I mean...

Colorless color. Is this closer?

Surely a contradiction in terms can't be it.

Again (or is it the first time, again?) I'm smashing concepts together and...Useless.

Fuck you.

I'm sorry. I wish I hadn't said that. I deserve better.

There is no solution here. I am an irrational beast and I have wilder creatures running in my head and we all need to be broken in. Try, then.

Use the sieve.

I am entirely incomplete: u
Sophia has betrayed me: q
Pierre is human trash: r
I am sick in the mind: p

$$\textit{This is empty: s}$$
$$\underline{\hspace{2cm}}: t$$
$$((q{\cdot}r{\cdot}s{\cdot}u) \rightarrow p) \leftarrow\rightarrow t$$
$$x \leftarrow\rightarrow y$$
$$x = y$$
$$x = x$$
$$x$$
$$\therefore$$
$$\cdot$$

No, no that's not the way! Stop that. That's nothing. That's —
Stop contradicting me.
I am contradicting me, not me.

I'm sorry you had to see that. It went on for quite some time. Perhaps you can begin to understand why Sophia grew tired of my writings and me.

Still, even after those hours of frustration, I tried other ways to cure myself, with which I will not tire you. It was all of little use. The quest continuously turned on itself, and ultimately, I dug deep circles around what was probably not what I was searching for. Soon, even my capacity for mediocrity would empty, and I would abandon looking into the fractures of my mind. So I collapsed, and slept for a short time over the desk. I skipped the hours in abyssal stillness, felt them pass like seconds.

It was still dark when I woke, late in the predawn, and the room seemed less like a cage. Quieter, even. The cars outside were still parked, and the clouds still congested the sky, but a slight calm had settled around me.

The creatures in my head seemed to slumber, and I wondered if perhaps I had somehow exhausted them. No. They were still there. I could sense them. Awake, breathing like hounds, waiting for me to begin my serious work again before striking.

I cried, then. Whimpered, more like. It was a pitiful scene. Anger pricked me as I wept—little prods—just enough to hold me from becoming completely pathetic. Light started to rise behind the clouds as they separated, and I fought the impulse to shut the curtains again. Instead, I sat, and I wrote a half-felt poem about dawn.

~~Of~~ Dawn

> Helios is ~~standing proud,~~ bound
> In cracked white robes
> And he ~~orders~~ begs ~~S~~ the ~~M~~ moon: ~~"die"~~ "rest."
>
> --
>
> Gone is the cloak of night, feasted on
> And the sunbirds gloat of their swallowed dark
> Heralds of the vast sun, colossus of light,
> Rejoicing ~~without shame~~ in the advent.
> The ~~tyrant~~ watcher drags his burning weight over the horizon
> And his gaze (--) cleaves ~~my~~ the darkness;
> He watches skins smolder atop molten cliffs
> The blistering which details ~~un~~certain colors
> As barks burn to cake the animal mirrors
> In a layer of permanent ash ——————;
> Waters are stirred ~~monstrously~~ by his wake;
> And there is ~~more~~ silence ~~than can be known.~~
>
> --
>
> But it's me who's sipped the remnant shadows
> Bloated ~~and diseased and sick and a wretch and I can't sing these demons away because they live in my voice and in these words and they're~~ of darkness I've made my own;
> It might be best if I
> Drink the sun as well—

I tore it up as soon as I wrote it, as though it were some blasphemy.

Now the morning was a pleasant gray, and cars were beginning to rumble down the street, and people were milling about to work or early morning errands, some alone, others in pairs or groups. I stood pressing half of my face to the window and fogging it with my breaths of disdain, watching them all with contempt like a rueful prisoner.

Then I thought of Sophia, the kindliest soul, and suffered an autumn's worth of gloom and cold and regret. Where was she, now? A part of me began to hate her for having not yet rescued me. Had she really taken me so seriously as to think I would just depart forever without a word? That I had truly lost my love for her? I felt at once the desire to punish her for believing me. To vindicate my actions, and not reveal myself to have been a fraud by crawling back to her.

And with that, I set out to prove myself true to my own capricious pretenses.

15

THE INCORRUPTIBLES

Tikan and Mira sat in silence with their backs only a wall away from desolation. The shock was only now pulsing through them.

Part of the galaxy was projected against the cockpit's ceiling: a wavering tapestry of purple smoke and stars, fading at the edges, as though this ceiling were an observatory whose whole dome was its telescope. They scanned the sparse throng of stars in search of a point that had made an odd blink of hope every ten minutes or so. It did repeat its lighthouse flash, eventually, though the cockpit remained dim.

Meanwhile, Naim dozed beneath the universe. With his head aimed at the floor and his legs spread, he was completely oblivious to that eternal weight above him.

"It's probably a dying star, you know," Mira said, moody as her opposite.

Her glare cut through Tikan's brooding. He sat, looking small, in his own private misery. Though he would have seen himself as cross-bearer, Mira had painted him a coward and a fool. She rose, striking him with razors for eyes, and then faced away from him. To avoid her, he looked up, and sought refuge in the stars. Then, with a squint, Mira made the galactic tapestry above flicker and turn into a slate gray ceiling.

"I'm going to sleep for a few hours. Try to, if you can," she said snidely.

The cold shelf Tikan leaned against dug into his back. "Where are you going?"

"Down."

Still in his sulky mood, he observed her as she drifted past slumbering Naim. She stopped before the room's only vacant corner, adjacent to Tikan and opposite the enormous piloting station. A section of floor tiles zipped open to reveal a flight of stairs.

"What's down there?" he asked, trying to shake the discomfort between them.

She ignored him. Her footsteps resounded as she descended. From his vantage, Tikan could see a counter and the edge of a sofa in the room below.

"An apartment?"

The floor whizzed solid again and removed her from sight.

Hunching in dejection, Tikan buried his head in his hands. He gritted his teeth, looking like a man capriciously unaccustomed to shame.

"Naim?" he called. But the man's eyes were still shut, and his chest was slowly rising and falling. Tikan sighed, and resisted the urge to persist.

Then he searched his pockets and pulled out something unexpected. The king of hearts card Amozagh had waved around during their last conversation. It was damp with sweat and now almost peeled to the middle. He sank against the cold wall and closed his eyes.

"I couldn't sleep. I couldn't sleep, Tikan."

The words thinned the churning molasses of Tikan's mind as he woke. "Hmm?"

Mira was standing over him, breathing hard. "How could you sleep? Do you realize what's happened? How could you sleep? Do you realize we're going to starve or freeze when the ship's power runs out?"

Tikan shook his head at her, though the panic bubbled in his chest, too. "We won't die."

"We're going to die, and you took away our chance at revenge! Revenge!"

"We're not."

"Oh, yes we are. Better face it now. I'd metempsy if only it wouldn't take my mind off revenge."

"I want revenge, too," he said, without much intonation.

"Liar. Coward."

"My whole life I've wanted revenge," he shouted, looking up at her suddenly. "I'll swim back to Earth if I have to."

"Idiot. We're going to die. Right here. A month, a year, twenty years from now. Suns, I hope it happens soon."

"We're not going to die."

"Think about it," she said, letting the panic overwhelm her, tears suddenly streaming down her face. "We're in a tiny metal room, surrounded by so much empty space you'd go mad trying to imagine it. Mad. The engine's off and we're drifting, we're going to drift forever now, till a few pebbles hit the ship and the life support and the power goes and we choke and freeze, looking at each other face to face. I don't want to look at you, Tikan. Your face is death, and I don't want to die. What you did makes me sick. Sick. I should just kill myself. Oh, suns. If my procrustus'd let me I'd kill myself right now. And—"

"Shut up," he said. Her words had infected him, and he, too, was now panicking. He got up and grasped at the walls, then smashed them with his fists.

"That's the way, savage! Break down those walls so we can get it over with quick."

He turned in place a number of times, running out of breath and growing dizzy.

"The walls are so narrow," she continued. "I've lived here for months, but now they're narrow."

"Mira, stop it. You're going to kill us."

"We're already dead, Tikan. Already dead. And you could've taken those people down with us, you bastard."

He leaned against the wall and slid down, putting a hand through his hair and hyperventilating at the ground. Mira, too, started hyperventilating. Her maudlin streak ended abruptly. She grasped her head with one hand and turned away from him, utterly disappointed and afraid.

They said nothing to each other for a long while. Exhausted by their wracked nerves, both of them fell asleep again on the floor of the cockpit.

They woke up hours later, still agitated but no longer in the grips of hysteria.

With a trembling hand, Mira pinched the bridge of her nose and exhaled. "How long do you think until his leg's better?" she asked, fighting back tears and pointing at Naim. "He's been asleep for nearly twelve hours."

Tikan stared up at her. "How long have we been sleeping?"

"I don't know. Six hours."

To shake the buzzing from his legs, Tikan rose and made a short march around the cockpit, taking long, deep breaths. The galaxy was still paved over in metal. The only light in the cockpit, dim as it was, detailed Naim's face. It looked petrified, like the byproduct of some volcano's fury centuries earlier. Tikan went over to him and crouched to inspect the leg.

"How did you sleep?" he asked Mira as he prodded Naim.

She just nodded at him. She paced the room in silence, leering at him as he handled Naim's bandage. Though she avoided bantering with Tikan, she could not wholly make a nemesis out of him, for they were now bound by survival.

"Yourself?" she found herself asking.

"Alright, thanks."

The bandage was damp in Tikan's hands. It was tattered and dirty. He raised Naim's leg over his knee and started to unroll the gauze. He had some difficulty unbinding the wound without touching it or tearing off its scabbing. When the last thread came off with sticky resistance, both he and Mira flinched. The thigh was a misshapen bulge of pale sea-foam cream peppered with emulsified flakes of blackened flesh.

"How is it?" Mira asked.

"Not a medic or anything, but it already looks better than it was. A lot of the muscle's regenerated, and it looks less infected. But I think he still needs some hours. I'm going to clean this layer off and reapply the mist. Then we just have to let him rest."

Mira handed him the platelet gun as he dug at the end of a roll of fresh gauze. They gave each other sympathetic looks. With the new gauze prepared, Tikan began cleaning his sleeping friend's wound.

"We can't just stay here, you know. I don't care if there's enough food forever," she said, watching him work with a scalpel.

Tikan cleared off layers of dead flesh in coagulated mist, remaining careful not to aggravate the raw surface of the wound.

"I know," Tikan said. "Have you thought of a plan?" He wrapped Naim's leg in fresh gauze and glanced at Mira.

"No, but that's not the point," she said.

"What do you mean?" Tikan asked, lowering Naim's limb and rising to face her, wiping his hands off on the front of his pants.

"Well, the lounge wasn't exactly closed off as soon as the decompression hit. We sealed it in time to stop any real damage, but the sudden temperature drop and flying objects set off the emergency motion sensors and suspended engine function."

"You can't reactivate it?"

"Not from here. It has to be done manually."

Tikan's muscles stiffened around what could have been mere hollow bones. "It can be done, though, right?" he asked, setting his shoulders back.

Mira's avian features wrinkled. "Well, let's say we get it up and running again. Where do we go?"

The obvious answer hung over him, and he remained silent.

"That ship—the last co-ordinates they displayed were in the direction of Solic wormholes, not Proxima," Mira continued.

"Well, with the kind of stunts they were pulling, I don't think we should be in the same system as them, not with this ship," he found himself saying.

"I thought you said we'd go after them." The gash on her bald head had scabbed, and now it creased into a red mark of anger as she frowned.

"Yes, but let's think it through. They don't even know we're alive. They probably think this broken heap of metal is drifting off between fire and gravity wells. If we show up with it back in Sol, they'll probably come finish the job. Or—I don't know. Who knows what they were even after? I think we should head for Sirius, away from all this. I know a few people in Sirius, I think. On Proxima they'll ask too many questions, and we'll probably get held up somewhere while they investigate what's happened. At least we'll be safe for a while in Sirius."

Mira grabbed her head and sighed. She was about to agree with Tikan, but then suddenly changed her mind. She frowned and tried to squint away a headache. "No, that doesn't make sense," she said. "There aren't any stable wormholes to Sirius in this sector. And in case you forgot, the ship's barely together. As I see it, Proxima is our only real option. It's a lot closer, and with that hole in the hull, we can only do orbital docks."

"Why?"

"We'd break apart reentering any normal planetary atmosphere. So, either way, I think we're stuck with Proxima. I don't even know how long this thing will last with the kind of damage it's taken. We might not even get to Proxima, let alone Sol or Sirius." Her temper cooled and deflated.

"That's true," Tikan said quietly.

"So, for now. The engineering bay—How do you plan on crossing that vacuum?" she asked. "I'll stay here and operate the doors."

"Do you have an environment suit somewhere here, or down there?" he replied, one hand scratching his head, the other pointing at her apartment.

"Yes."

"Okay, we're sealed off," Mira said, her voice repeating smooth and crisp through Tikan's helmet. "You're going have to be very careful, because those magnetics in your suit aren't very strong; not at all like the ones the black suits had. And the entire ship from here until the end of the lounge is vacuum. Call for me to shut the cockpit entrance fast once you're out. Otherwise, the oxygen won't refill inside, and we'll die and you'll just get sucked out."

He stood alone in the cockpit, catching faint glimmers of half-light off his shoulders, and he faced the gate. "Are you sure you're both safe down there? Is the seal airtight?"

"No, I'm not sure. And you have the only environment suit, so don't get sucked out. I'll climb back into the cockpit and help you from there if everything goes well."

The exit was that same circular steel disk on which Tikan had first collapsed, carrying his maimed friend. Now, this obsidian gateway before him loomed higher and surely kept clogged up the condensed wailing of each and every corpse preserved against the all-darkness of star-snuffed space. There were quarter circles on the face of the gate, converging on each other in a complex locking mechanism. Each one a round plane of suffering, dark on one side and glinting heaven's fire on the other. The silver piston doorposts could have been black pillars or charred trees, deceptively flameless and offering not a glimpse of the victims kept like the treasures of some ruined outworld vault. In the dim light, a faint, faded inscription could be seen above the lintel, likely a disused and ignored safety warning. Now there was no Virgil to guide him through, and no Limbo ahead. Ahead, there was only an abandoned inferno, its fires and denizens long extinguished to make room for some darker presence yet.

Tikan resolved. He pressed his hands together, and his gloves magnetized. Then he did the same for his boots against the floor, and traction swelled under them.

"I'm ready," he said.

"Opening it now," Mira said.

Sweat streamed from his enclosed face at her words. Then Antaeus moved to show him the Ninth Circle. The new airlock hissed open.

There howled the howl of a gargantuan banshee, and the room's contents were pulled out. Papers, a torn strip of dirty gauze, and the sundries of their reprieve all flew out. The void, under the guise of balance, was infesting this last pocket of oxygen.

Tikan stood exposed before the abyss inhaling before him. Half of him was heaved forward while his feet stayed planted on trembling magnets. It was as though the talons of some monster had lunged out and dug into his waist to pick him out. With only furious dark ahead, he ambled hesitantly forward until his steps turned into an unwilling stampede, and his eyes bounced around in their sockets even as his wrists bashed the lintel.

He remained suspended in the gateway a moment before the disk even finished sliding open, skating over a lake of ice and juddering like a flag. He shuffled sideways, though his arms conformed errantly and his feet danced loosely to the spastic pulse gluing them to the ground.

The disk slid into its socket, and steam flickered from its edges.

"What are you doing? It's getting cold. Be fast," buzzed throughout his helmet.

With his chest stuck to the gate's curved jamb, Tikan slid around to the inner cheek of the maw. As his hands started losing traction, he pressed and smashed at the wall with a fist chaotic as a meteor on a string. Then he remembered Mira.

"Now," he cried out and shut his eyes.

The gate slid shut. He went limp, and with his other hand still stuck to the wall, his legs floated outward. Heat bulged from his face, and Virgil was barred from making a late arrival.

Tikan dragged in jagged, titanic breaths. When he exhaled, the air raced against his visor, faster than the pump in his head, and cooled the sweat on his face in large swoops.

"Good. We're all still alive. Now make sure you don't accidentally float out of the hole," Mira said, clear through the equipment but vaporous through his senses mired in adrenaline.

"I-I can't see anything. It's all dark," he said.

"Turn on your light."

There was a slight indent on the upper right side of his helmet, and when he pressed it, a beam burst out from atop his head. Its cone was narrow, and it looked as though it struggled to keep from collapsing under the weight of the darkness.

"Are you both okay, then?" he asked while regaining his composure. He rotated his head around to make frantic illuminations, which revealed gray halos of steel.

"It's cold. Really cold. But yes, we're okay."

Tikan kicked the floor, propelling himself upward, and he floated to the left, away from the gaping wound in the hull that lingered somewhere opposite.

"Will it get warmer?" he asked. "I don't want you both to freeze before we get anywhere."

He landed a magnetized arm and leg on the left wall, then stood on it, making it the new floor, and began trotting to the other end of the lounge.

"It'll warm up a lot faster once we get the primary functions running again," Mira said. "It's not so bad, and our friend is covered up."

As Tikan advanced, he scanned the floor. Those organic objects that remained hung in near stasis, burnt objects turned pale and icy.

"All right. That's good to hear."

The hole in the ship kept him out of breath. There above was the immensity of the universe, beyond imagining and therefore terrible. He was like a mariner wandering a vessel sunk to the ocean floor. And dread came not from space, but from the breach itself: a far less comprehendible monster, proximate as the violent and unforeseeable death that has ever breathed down men's necks. He crept beneath the void like a servant in the presence of a sleeping master.

"I never knew you had nice quarters like that," he said as he tried to focus his gaze on the runway of light he aimed for himself. "No wonder we hardly see you."

"I guess," Mira said. "They've made it pretty comfortable for us. It's mostly to isolate us from everyone else on board, but it's hard to complain. I get a proper bed with all the stabilizers, a sofa, updated metempsies—though I usually just stick to a few good old ones—and enough space that it's more than just, well, just crew quarters."

Tikan's eyes skittered at the edges of their sockets, as if to reach the darkness wrapping his skull and his body, which were not afforded a place in the light.

"What about food?"

"I have a food printer. I don't get to have the natural stuff they make upstairs, but you can't really tell the difference, if you ask me."

"That's nice. Cozy," he said.

"It is."

"Lonely?"

"You don't become a long-haul pilot if you're not happy to spend a few months by yourself."

"So you never come out?"

"Not really. I have everything I need here."

"I understand that."

"Well, you don't understand it. You're not me," she said calmly.

"I know," Tikan said. He crossed his eyebrows, trying to navigate both the conversation and the ship. "I didn't mean it that way. I mean I can imagine why you would like it. But, tell me why."

"Why what?"

"Tell me why you became a starship pilot. Even though most people don't like speaking to each other, they also start to panic when they're thrown out alone."

She raised her voice. "What's the use in being with others? Everyone's always by themselves anyway. You know that. That's why you always sneak those old books aboard—don't think nobody's noticed."

Tikan could hear her breathing in his skull. "And the stars have compelling words for you?" he asked after a pause.

"They don't speak their brilliance. They're like—" She paused a moment. "There were birds on Earth. Before they deleted the records, I used to know what they were called. Damn it. Wait." There was another pause, and it seemed to drain out the hostility between them. "I can't remember. I should've stored the memory. Well, those birds, they caught everyone's eye. They showed all their colors in a fan, and you saw it and knew that that was all they had to say. Those are like the stars."

She was not permitted the word, though its referent meant the world to her.

Tikan did not respond. A great sadness overwhelmed him, for he knew of peacocks and of loneliness, but could mention neither of these to Mira. Least of all now, as her ire at him persisted in each of her breaths. Whether she even remembered an image of peacocks, or merely held on to a vague idea of their fans as her mind struggled to erode it, he could not tell.

As he walked, still treading on ash-streaked metal, the thought crept up on him that the hole was now directly above him, alive, bearing down like the Sword of Damocles, inverted to pierce no man's head but rather the sky above him. Suddenly, the light on his head seemed a match dropped in the ocean.

Tikan breathed to steady his heart, and listened to his own breath against the visor. He made faster steps, but not so fast that he would slip and float upward.

"I'm at the second gate," he exhaled, standing before a second wall of intricate disks.

"This is probably going to be a little easier," Mira said through his helmet. "You're going to be fighting to get in upstream, now. So stick to the entrance and you should make it. Just call it when you're inside."

"Okay."

Tikan pressed himself against the wall to the left of the gate, locking his four magnetic limbs to the surface. Then he scuttled sideways like a crab scaling a rock until he was exactly adjacent to the disk. "Wait," he said. "I know the gas we deployed got vented in here, but is it still live in there?"

"No. Doubtful. Whatever was in there got vented out fast when they melted the hull. I shut it off after that."

"Okay. Open it," he said.

Without her confirmation, the disk spiraled open. It was louder this time. A violent gush poured out, small objects launching from its stream into the null.

"You didn't mention the debris!" he called, almost inaudible to himself.

"I forgot about it. Just be careful. Quickly. Remember the life support won't last long in vacuum."

With nerves afire, he inserted an arm into the airstream and scuttled around. This time he was better prepared and had more control. As he inched closer to the other side, a rushing body smacked the gateway and bent in two before flying through, the impact sending out chunks of its inner organs in icy cubes as though out of a shotgun. Larger debris sped along with an irregular stream of cadavers.

He managed to grasp the gateway's jamb and pull himself in through the windstorm.

"Close it," Tikan gulped as he swung around the narrow passage and pinned himself to the wall.

The gateway tightened shut. A menagerie of corpses struck the floor with him. Some even landed across his lap, knotting him into a maze of limbs.

"What am I looking for?" Tikan asked as he walked, his boots decoupled from the ground and subject to gravity again.

"Head down to engineering. I'll guide you from there," Mira said.

The back end of the ship was a gallery of tangled corpses and electronics that had burst from the walls like unraveled intestines. Despite this arcade of horror, Tikan walked faster through the ghost ship.

"How's the life support?" he asked.

"It's fine. No damage."

"And our friend?"

"Let me go and check on him, actually. I ran up to manage the doors," Mira said, before leaving him in silence.

The corpse piles increased in size as he made his way. In each room were mounds of bodies arranged differently. Tikan stalled in the doorways, peering in and casting a feeble cone of light. He passed by the galley, and the crew quarters, and the security room. It was now all still and dark and disordered, like a large theater left un-swept after a large production. Past these rooms was the long walk to the engineering bay.

"He's all right," Mira suddenly crackled in his helmet. "He woke up, actually, for a few seconds, and asked about what was happening. I told him to go back to sleep."

Tikan stopped at her voice while staring at a disembodied face missing a chunk of jaw. "That's good. We can wake him up properly when I get back," he said, and then tore himself from the grisly sight.

"Why don't you take off your helmet, by the way? We can metempspeak," Mira said.

"I feel safer with it on."

"The life support is working fine, though. You have oxygen in the air."

"I know, but it's cold. And I don't want to take any chances."

"Fair enough," she said.

He was now stepping over large mounds of corpses, paying special attention to his footing so as to not step on the remains of any children, the bodies of whom he could not bear to look at.

"What's wrong?" Mira asked.

"Nothing, why?"

"Your breathing. I can hear it through the channel."

"Nothing. It's nothing."

"Are you passing the dorms?"

Tikan peered into the dark hall whose floor was lumpy with bodies.

"Yes."

They fell silent, and paused. He could hear her restrained breathing through the channel.

"They were digging around people's brains earlier, looking for something. Do you want to see if you can find anything?" she asked sharply.

He hesitated. "Yeah, I could. Are we fine, though? I mean, with the engine room."

"Yeah, you have some time."

"All right, then," he said, and began trudging over the corpse mounds.

Under his narrow light the hall appeared as some plundered catacomb: bodies entwined together, faces frozen out of decay like Incorruptibles. The slaughtered children he avoided completely, circling around them.

"It was an old man, right?" he asked.

"Yeah, I think so. They weren't very gentle with him. His head probably looks like a mess. Look for an un-cauterized head wound; I saw them digging into his skull barehanded."

Disquieted, Tikan scanned skull after skull before reburying them. He lifted persons out of graves of limbs, by torso or by waist, or dragged them out by their stiffened arms or legs before moving on to the next pile.

On this somber excursion he could not help but discover little bodies. One with a hand jutting out of a pile, browned and missing a thumb or more. Another was curled in a fetal position, as though in an attempt to reverse life's cascade of traumas and escape the telos of suffering in which he had been preserved.

Tikan walked this carnage, relieved when a gap between bodies allowed him to plant a foot on steel rather than on human flesh. Outside of his exoskeleton there was a growing stench: flash-frozen corpses now slowly thawing, the rank of a fetid burial ground intended for cremation but abandoned instead.

Sweat pumped from his pores with every heave and pull, and the light from his helmet shook against the walls. There, by the far end, was an outcast corpse. Its head resembled a blooming red flower with petals of pale, wrinkled skin. A slop of brain bulged out of the skull, bulbous as an enormous pollen node torn apart by an overzealous hornet. Threading this cerebral blossom like filaments were the black wires of the man's procrustus.

"I found it," he said, bending to examine the abominable wound.

"What does it look like?"

Tikan drew the head closer to him and angled the wound towards him. "It looks like—Oh, God. It looks like they ripped out his procrustus."

"His procrustus?"

"Yeah, it—"

Tikan stopped and tried to twist his head, but his suit was not mobile enough. A hand had reached out from the shadows to grasp him. He flinched in horror; sprang up and spun around.

There before him was a shining figure, bronze as Talos.

Tikan recoiled in shock and tripped over human debris, his foot caught in a tangle of dead arms. He stared up, out of breath.

The visitor stomped towards him in a heavy environment suit, looking like an awakened deity fresh from a thousand-year slumber and roving his own tomb out of nostalgia. The visor was obscured but starkly lit from below as Tikan jittered about.

"Who are you?"

The figure advanced on him, stepping over the mystery corpse on the floor.

"What's happening? Is everything okay?" Mira asked through the helmet.

Tikan ignored her. "Who are you?"

"Calm down," said the intruder. "I'm not one of them."

16

THE HUNTRESS

Sielle walked between skeletal birches shining silver in the winter sun. The cliffs towering above her were covered in snowy moss and teethed with rows of icicles. Since morning, she had drifted to the chirping of sunbirds quite far from their natural place. Off by a frozen brook, whose bed was littered in varicolored stones. Her hair was dotted with snow. She was bundled in a thick cloak and wore a man's worn kyrtill overtunic braided at the collar in bright wool. Her leg wraps were caked in frost up to her knees.

It was now noon, and she began making for home against a light gale. With the shadows of crooked branches swaying around her, she looked as though she were a woodland augur deep in communion.

Often had Sielle lived in hard stone, or steel, or concrete. The nightlights checkered down skylines, the tents pitched near freezing camels. More attractive to her were the waters down the malachite banks of spring, or autumn's cracked leaves, or sand dunes pale as salt in the moonlight, or the summer buried under snow. For three years now, this Nordic valley had soothed the violence of her existence.

By the late afternoon, she was returning from her hike. With the winds gusting down the valley and rustling shrubs of lingonberry beside her, she came upon black smoke spiraling above the brow of the knoll ahead of her. Her pulse quickened and she stomped up the slope, watching the black pillar gain density as it continued to wreath up.

When she crested the hill she saw, stark and true, flames undulating from the roof of her house in the distance. It was spewing out fumes against the backdrop of a halo sun. She bolted down the hill, her tracks snaking up to the fire.

After stopping abruptly before the house, she squinted up and breathed hard until the icicles in her lungs melted. The structure's logs crumbled out of order and sputtered out flames. She set about edging in through a collapsed corner, traversing a thick wall of smoke as though it were a portal to some high demon's sanctum.

Inside, the hearth was roaring wild fire. The ceiling's dirt was spilled over the floor and baking. Already the wind was sweeping ash out of many new exits, and the cold cerulean sky was exposed through gaps in the ceiling. She crawled under a fallen beam and hurdled over fire as smoke rolled through the house.

"Far!" she called. "Far!" but to no answer.

She buried her mouth in the crook of her arm and started to cough. After rounding a corner, she found three serried figures burnt like effigies by the far wall. They were blackened all the way down, and their features were demolished. A misshapen lump on one of them looked like it had once been a nose. She rushed to them, dodging a pit of fire. Her brothers gone, and thinning still. They were long past smoldering, and already what had been their skin was flaking off and breaking apart in the wind.

After briefly inspecting these bodies, she turned from them and ran from room to room until she came to her own. Red logs stuffed the doorway and spat hot ash at her. The room's ceiling collapsed before she could take a step inside. Her eyes stung from the smoke, forcing tears down her cheeks.

Still reeling, Sielle heard wheezing from behind her. She ran into the opposite room, which was free of flames. A barrel-chested and aged man was bent against one of the house's few stone supports, his chest rising and falling unevenly, his mouth half roasted off.

"Far!" Sielle called, running to the man and seizing him under the arms. He was too heavy for her to lift. Instead, she crouched and dragged him out into the snow. The man's wheeze turned into a cough as Sielle pressed his chest. Her arms were trembling.

Suddenly, his eyes whirled open, blood-red and unfocused.

"Hva har skjedd?" Sielle asked.

"Sielle, jeg—" But he could only cough, and he coughed blood and then vomited over himself.

She took a step from him, removing her hand from his shoulder and wincing at the snow spoiled by his dying.

"Sielle ... menn kom ... fra sør ... dro videre. Reis nordover." His body quaked, and he coughed again. "Sielle, brødrene dine ... brødrene ... ta vare på dem ... de tok alt ... vi har tapt alt. Bare du. Nordover til ..." His eyes stirred and swiveled until they froze in place.

Sielle did not shut the man's eyes. She stood up and turned from the house, just as logs crashed down through the roof. At the edge of the wreckage were two seax daggers smoking their new coat of ash.

For three years, she had lived with these people, come to think that perhaps their warmth could be permanent. Two winters ago, when their mother had died of pneumonia, Sielle had felt the permanence of loss eviscerate her for the first time. For every blue morning, when she taught her two of her brothers how to fish and hunt with the frost on their cheeks, she now felt a tightening in her chest.

For an hour she screeched into the valley, listening to the echo of her sorrow gain a vengeful quality. Then she picked up the daggers. The man who had for a time been her father remained, head frozen skyward, and she started south.

Hours passed as Sielle stalked down the valley. At sunset, she surveyed the land from a rise. The horizon was a vermillion slash across the world's waist, vaporous blood arcing out of it. With the sinking of the sun, she cupped a hunk of snow in her hand and watched it crumble through her fingers.

She hurried down through the birches, spruces, and pines, while gusts whipped her dark cloak. The wolves strode on nearby hills and howled a celebration for the moon. Perhaps they knew of its dust still at her heels, or its light lacing her skin fluorescent, or its reflection striking a kindred bloodlust in her eyes.

Come midnight, a turquoise aurora hung over the land. Not as a fragile drape gliding down against the stars, but as a slow whip to bleed the firmament of its mysteries. As though out of those celestial wounds she would divine the whereabouts of the men she hunted. Because she had at times rearranged the constellations to suit the patterns of her mind and not of myth, to her the stars were playthings, the moon her kite. She strode down the snow with the frost climbing up her legs, while tracking the aurora.

Half-covered footprints surfaced every few hours. There she found twigs and branches snapped by less graceful feet, and crushed draba camouflaged in the snow. Half a day's trail, if they were not foolish enough to make camp.

In the predawn, the aurora dissipated, and with it the cyan evaporated from the snow. She persisted through the thickening woods. The frost had crawled up her body as if she were turning into some demon of ice, who would slink down into the snow under the roots of the pines and the birches and wait, patiently, unwearied, until the whole land could erupt chthonic for her and strike.

Her pace remained high until faintest dawn, when she began landing against the barks of the trees to rest and watch.

While the sun was erupting from the world's edge, she came upon four thinly ploughed tracks of snow like shallow trenches, winding ahead. It was not long then until she heard them barking through the trees and saw them trudging slovenly.

"Gå raskerer, Bjørn, din tulling," one man said to the other. "Tror du vi har mat nok til to dager til? Fjols! Hvis vi ikke rekker frem til byen før det blir mørkt, skal jeg koke deg og spise de fete armene dine."

Sielle shuffled through the trees, descending catlike behind them.

"Hold kjeft. Vi har ikke byttet på å bære på flere timer. Bare hold munn, slutt å skråle som en narr. Vi rekker frem til byen før kveldingen."

On that sharpening slope, still hiding in leaves burdened with snow, Sielle watched them and listened as they began to argue. They were both complaining to each other, about winter and about who would carry more of the load before nightfall.

The second man bore a large pack. Inside were the few items they had pilfered from her home.

"Jeg kan godt gå fortere hvis du bærer din del av denne 'fantastiske skatten', din drittsekk."

"Hvem kaller du drittsekk, tosk?"

The treeline was ending. Soon they would exit onto open white plains.

"Deg, Rolf, og de tåpelige innfallene dine," said Bjorn.

They had confused her family for nobles living in the country, and plotted to make their fortune. Now, with mere trinkets and cheap heirlooms not worth two strands of silver burdening their shoulders, they traded blame while their toes numbed.

Bjorn stopped at the very edge of the thinning wood, turned and looked at Rolf. Not four trees away from them, Sielle tightened her grip around the hilt of her seax daggers and exhaled a cloud of mist.

"Du kan bare våge å kalle meg tulling en gang til," said Bjorn.

"Du er en forbasket tulling, og du er tjukkere i hue enn noen stein jeg noensinne har satt foten på," replied Rolf.

"Din drittsekk! Jeg skal—"

Both of them dropped their packs and began to wrestle, arms woven into each other, struggling above the chest to throw each other to the ground.

Sielle relaxed, and she drew her seaxes. She leapt off the knoll and flew downwards like a death-starved raven. She plunged both blades into Rolf's back. With tears running down her cheeks, she pulled them out of his back and slammed them back in, growling.

Bjorn lunged at her, and the three of them hurtled down the icy slope. The sound of mild sucking and gurgling started. Rolf coughed out a patch of blood as they rolled down to flatter land. His head half twisted right, then contorted left, seeking answers he would never receive.

In their tumble, the knives came loose from Rolf's back, and a brighter red stream started to color the snow. Rolf dug and crawled out of their heap, coughing crimson, mouthing maledictions he could not speak. After a meter or two he ceased to move, and his face dropped into the snow.

Meanwhile, Bjorn swiftly escaped the tangle and pounced on Sielle with his blade drawn. He drove it reversed through her left shoulder as though he were planting a stake. Then he sat atop her and pinned her at the neck with his forearm.

"Hvem er du?" he breathed at her in a mixture of anger, confusion, and odd gratitude.

She smirked and then laughed, though not without wincing at the cold sting in the soft of her shoulder.

Bjorn relaxed and began to look at her lustily. "Hvor kommer du fra, vakre møy?"

She only grinned at him hideously.

Bjorn laughed. "Jeg skal la deg bli igjen og råtne i snøen som de—"

Suddenly, his face reddened, and his cheeks swelled with air almost comically. He exhaled in great discomfort. His mouth quivered at the corners, and his forehead creased. When he looked down, he gave a look of surprise at the blood dripping from his sternum down to Sielle's chest.

She had stuck both of her daggers to the hilt up under his ribcage, wedging them between the organs resting within. A gelid wind swept up Bjorn's hair as he bared his teeth and made his mortal grimace and finally coughed blood at her face.

Then she lifted him up with her teeth clenched, gory faced and beaming malefically like some folkloric nightmare come to life. His eyes were bursting from their sockets, transfixed. He could not understand, even in those last moments, how the she-devil, the blade still resting in her shoulder, had turned the situation on him. And as he slumped backwards off her lift, the sword lodged in her shoulder fell to the snow.

She vanished.

∼

With her will aimed at soothing the wounds in her spirit and in her shoulder, Sielle streamed across the galaxy and across epochs.

Gripping her perforated shoulder, she arrived in a metropolis, the sun flaring red at her. The constellations now were reordered in the form of harpooned whales, satellites, and chemical compounds.

In her ancient rags, Sielle strolled this new place, unwilling yet to make sense of it. Here, they used a language she had known more often than not, although the accent was not recognizable. A few bewildered passersby indicated the nearest medical facility when she asked.

The floor of the clinic was white with polish, almost bordering on beige. The room was decorated with evergreens and bromeliads. Sielle sat in a cushiony chair for a time, wincing, gripping her leaking shoulder, and there she locked gazes out the window with a red sun throbbing in the black of space. The pulsing, crimson majesty of it began to mesmerize her. She put a hand in the way of its scarlet rays and watched them slide across her skin.

Just as she started breaking from her star trance, she was called in for surgery by a pudgy woman in a purple blouse and frizzy hair. In automatic metamorphosis, Sielle's seat rearranged its pieces to a more compact form as she rose from it. She pulled away from the thing and followed the woman into the hallway.

While following the woman down the hallway, she could not help but marvel at the ceiling. Though she could clearly discern its limit at first glance, upon a moment's concentration it seemed to go on forever into a vague, beige infinite. The arches serried along the corridor folded into the infinity of the ceiling before they could meet.

There were also plants of varying color—one with a seafoam stalk that gave cyan leaves, and one mauve with magenta shoots and flowers—lined up against the walls, looking as though they had been extracted from the gardens of a planet solar systems away from Earth.

All this marveling she did in quiet, lest they find extra reason to suspect her, especially as she had entered the place in bloodied and alien rags.

There did not seem to be any rooms along the walls. The hospital attendant trotted on and looked back, smiling, at Sielle. She smiled back. Then she gazed up at the arches ribbing the place again. The architecture was not entirely unfamiliar to her. She ransacked her memory for it, but could find it nowhere, and she smiled again despite the twinge in her shoulder. Just as the purple-bloused hospital attendant stopped, a section of the wall swooped up beside her.

"Thank you," said the lanky technician inside.

In a windowless room, he sat beside a machine hanging off the ceiling like a fat mechanical spider, which was situated above a hospital cot without rails.

"Sielle, is it?" he said, squinting at the woman as she left. "Have a seat."

"Here, doctor?" she asked, motioning towards the bed.

"Yes there," he said, frowning at what she had said for some reason. "Oh, that is… quite the outfit. What is that exactly?"

"It was a project. For school. Historical."

"I see," he said, crossing his eyebrows. "Not sure what that is. Anyway, not that it's my business, really. Just lie down and we'll fix it. It's a messy wound."

"It was an accident—I fell holding a knife in the other hand."

The man frowned again. "Where in the world did you find a knife?"

"In the kitchen."

The technician shook his head. "Hmph. Look, I don't want to know. Please lie down straight."

"Yes," she replied.

Grateful to not fall under much suspicion, Sielle lay down under the machine.

The technician only looked at the machine and squinted the way he had at the hospital attendant. Another, smaller arthropodic looking device, oval shaped and shelled, emerged from the machine's bottom and scuttled over the wound. Its mouth opened, and it filled the wound with a thick blue gel. Sielle shuddered at the cold, but there was no pain. Once the wound was plugged blue, she rose.

"Do not touch it for at least an hour," the technician said, as he wrapped her shoulder in gauze.

She nodded, and they did not say goodbye.

Sielle left the room with a child's grin on her face. She paced out of the clinic, too happy with herself to give more than a passing glance at the corridor's infinite ceiling. When she exited into a boulevard, she was confronted with the full breadth of the metropolis, under the glass dome shielding it from the sun.

❧ 17 ❧

OLD WORLD CRUELTY

M adame Hugo had become insufferable. She had started with the peeking in at breakfast, and then moved on to skipping romps of faux-concern down the hallway at mid-day, speaking with trumpets in her throat and stumbling by my door with the grace of an elephant. In case it was not already clear, let me pronounce it: I loathed her. The violence I conjured up for her in that dark sanctum of mine was infinite, and the subject of her various fatalities and tortures came to almost—almost, but not quite—rival those intrusions which such thoughts of Sophia continued to make.

What began as Madame Hugo's ridiculous infatuation with me gradually turned into a full assault on my privacy, escalating into ill-footed attempts at seducing me for my charms and what she no doubt still believed was my noble British lineage. Is there a more absurd predicament you could imagine me in? These bothersome attempts— no, campaigns—to capture my already fraught attention culminated in shameless knocking at my door in the mid-afternoon, on a day when I felt somewhat vulnerably more at peace.

"Monsieur, if I may," came from the door.

"At once, Madame Hugo, at once."

Curse her, curse her, curse her. I swung the door open, overly attentive and half dressed, my shirt hanging out of my pants and my hair in tangles.

"How may I help you, Madame?"

"Monsieur, I was only wondering about your stay," she said while stomping into my room, all ochre as her desires.

It was difficult to even look at her. The blackness of her gums, the yellow of her teeth, the old nail polish, the shape of her hands like two meaty clubs, the calluses on her knuckles. She was like a miniature Scylla bursting through the doorway with her dogs wreathing her feet, and her shape metamorphosed hideously in the half-light.

"I am very enchanted that you are here," she said, "*vraiment*, and I must ask you how much longer you will be here. The last time we spoke, you said it would be a little while longer, and now it has been more than a month and a half that you have been here."

Her eyes slithered at me, and we became locked once again in our flirtatious game to see who would display the greater old-world politesse. She took a step forward, almost tripping over her dog's leash, and caught herself by planting a fat hand on the bed. Meanwhile, I tried to dodge her and struck my heel against the corner of the dresser. The pain flashed in my foot, and I gritted my teeth.

"Yes, of course," I said. "Well, you see, my work has taken new shapes, new forms; expanded, in fact. I overlooked many aspects of modern Parisian culture insofar as they factor into my research, you see, particularly with regards to the socio-economic implications of—"

"Ah, ah, *mais vous êtes si intelligent.* Please, you are welcome to dine with us tonight. We would love to have you. Please, dine with me. You are living here for so long, we would love to know you better," the monstrosity said.

Her eyes glittered. She smiled in such a vile way, too, that I had to show the restraint of twenty ascetics not to destroy her right there and then.

"Madame, you honor me, but truly, I have much work to do, and I cannot afford to waste time."

"A waste? Monsieur, s'il vous plaît, ne m'insultez pas."

"Look," I said. "If you think anything about that kiss—it was only a kindness, a polite 'hello' and 'goodbye,' you see?"

She scowled. "Hello, goodbye? Ne soyez pas malpoli, monsieur."

She approached: slow, languorous, brimming and oozing with fetid desire, yet with the outward sensuality of a hippopotamus. Eying me as she approached, she liberally exhaled her rancid, tar-caked breath.

I pushed her away. I could not stomach it.

"Monsieur?"

It was too late, beyond the chance to correct the situation. Despite all the colors I'd added to the chameleon thus far, even this reptile could not help but to now shed his rainbowed skin.

"No, Madame, I am sorry but I think you misunderstood my actions, I was not trying to suggest that, well...that I was interested in you in any sexual way."

She blew up at my words, instantly, her face sore in disbelief like a putrid fruit. Now, as I took her fantasies and her dignity in one fell swoop, the intrusive thoughts burst again into my mind's theater like hooligans. They took up residence in the box seats, and in all their mischief called out commands to the stage and rejoiced.

"L'arrogance," she said. "You—You think I was frappé by your stupid kiss? You think I am such a little woman that I am like a schoolgirl, who melts because of a stupid rich boy? Jamais. You are a disgusting man, Monsieur. You do not shower, and you do not change your clothes. What kind of recherches can you be doing in this room all day? And, you do not even eat more than breakfast—what kind of man from Kensington cannot afford proper meals? Vous avez l'air d'un fou, franchement."

It was finished, the end of our genteel antics. I huffed to myself out of restraint.

"Madame, let me, now that we are being frank with each other, be perfectly clear with you," I said. "I think you are a loathsome old bag, a blimp of bile and pus, both in appearance and in character. You are twice, perhaps nearly thrice my age, and yet still you have insisted on pathetic, juvenile attempts at courting me. Have you no shame? I kissed you, accursed as I am, only so that you would leave my room and feast from the trough of your delusions elsewhere."

"Mais quel mythoman! Quel fou! Je n'ai jamais avoué une chose pareil. Vous êtes—"

"And while I am on the subject of your shortcomings, let me address other concerns that you may wish to take into consideration, but that I know you will certainly ignore due to your inimitable self-love. Your paintings make me sick in my stomach; they remind me of a schoolchild's work, which only garners praise out of pity. But we forgive children and their arrogance. You, on the other hand, could not hope to be redeemed by the most illustrious, the most talented, the most attentive teacher who has studied under the spirit of every great painter since time immemorial.

"Your hotel is dusty and dilapidated, and your presence makes it unbearable. So I want nothing from you, certainly not your body, especially not your dinner or even this conversation with you. Your three dogs, ugly as they are, are more pleasing to look at than you. Now, get away from me. I'll be leaving tomorrow morning at eight o'clock sharp and taking my stay elsewhere."

She stood, flabbergasted, her face scowling red.

As for me, I was enlivened. Each of my breaths after the long speech was euphoric. I had taken all of the old-world charm I had summoned to beguile her in those weeks and transformed it into old-world cruelty, a type of cruelty that is at once satisfying and elevating, as opposed to crude, graceless, regular cruelty.

Of course, you suspect me of omitting half of her speech, to protect my identity and my pride, and selectively make her out to look like a blundering, emotionally compromised fool. You think I am some kind of deranged psychopath, or a misogynist of the worst kind. Your thoughts wander back to my poor treatment and sick fantasies of Sophia, and you take me to be a fiend, rather than a victim of my own frustrations. How can I win with someone like you, who refuses to understand me despite my best efforts?

"George!" she shouted, throwing her voice up at the ceiling.

We locked eyes as George's footsteps bumbled up the stairs; hers fiery pits, mine phlegmatic and blasé. I reveled in each wrathful huff she made.

"Oui, Madame," said George as he stormed in, panting.

"Ce *bâtard*, cet *enfoiré*, cet homme de *merde*, il nous quitte demain matin. À la première lumière de l'aube. Je n'veux plus voir sa figure. Fais en sorte qu'il nous paye," she yelled, and then turned her still sanguineous face and stomped out.

"What did you say to her?" George asked.

"The truth."

He looked at me with a shrug and raised eyebrows, as though to say, "Well, no wonder."

My lies would unravel soon, but first I let the hours darken the night. The end was still at my fingertips. George, the poor bastard, had been sent to wait outside my door to ensure that I would not leave without settling my account. Would I invite him in with friendly banter, and then fulfill a tray-less rendition of my previous macabre prophesy for him? Or would I throw myself from the window? The window, the window seemed a better option. I was not a killer, though some part of me was trying to convince me. I could not listen to it yet.

Strolling, pacing—not entirely stressed—in fact, invigorated. I peeked out at the street while leaning against the glass. It was not too far down, and there was a small mountain of trash that could cushion my fall, perhaps. Perhaps, yes, perhaps. My breath fogged the glass. Pacing, pacing.

I approached the door and stuck an ear to it. George was awake, reading to himself. I was about to knock, my knuckles cocked and ready—but no. I returned to the window, and—the laptop—I could not forget my work. Laptop in hand, I lifted the window.

The sky was streaked by gray wisps. The stars could not be seen. I looked down. It was only one story down; I could make it. I could. I slid one leg over, then the other. The opposite window was shut, and its curtains were drawn, and the sculpted busts of petrified justice or courage jutting out on its flanks and guarding it had their eyes closed.

Snow drifted into the room, and I started shivering. The laptop bag was slung around my shoulder, and I clutched it tightly to my chest. I shut my eyes and took a long breath. With the moon careening me over, I slipped off.

The wind gushed up my trousers as I shot straight down, and it rushed up louder past my ears, as though to yell a quick "watch out," as I sped down. It lasted a moment, and then my feet struck the hard black bags beneath. It was as if, in that instant, my body were no longer an ensouled or possessed animal, or even an animal, but a mere object in flux and collision, like all inanimate things. A sudden and harsh reminder of nature's uncompromising laws.

I felt crippled. My ankles felt shattered and my knees buzzed in pain. *It was only one story*, I kept saying in my head as I writhed in the garbage. The reek of coffee and rotten bananas and other foods blending together in decay. The arm of a broken coat hanger in my side. The shards of glass bottles prickling my shins.

The snow fluttered down and built a consoling blanket over me, the pain turned to twinges, and then serenity overtook me, as I lay there on the concrete and the whitened rubbish.

❦ 18 ❦

TALOS LIVES

The man towered above Tikan and stuck a shiny arm out at him. Tikan reclined farther into the pit of corpses, almost blanketing himself in them for defense.

"Onasus Loptar. My name is Onasus Loptar. Don't panic."

"Explain yourself," Tikan said.

"Tikan. *What* is happening? Answer me," Mira pressed.

"I knew this man," the bronze man said, pointing at the corpse of the old man with the destroyed head. "Friedrich Farabi. I was traveling with him. Now, we'll have plenty of time to speak after we… well, after we sort out this trouble with your ship and clear these corpses from it."

"What?"

"The engine room, the corpses," Onasus said. "It's all got to be sorted if we're to make it out of here, yes?"

"Mira. There's a man here, in an enviro-suit. He's saying for us to sort out the ship," Tikan said in frenetic gasps.

"Well, who in the fiery moons is he?" she asked.

"He says his name is Onasus Loptar."

"Oh, for sun's sake," Onasus said. "You don't have to keep talking about me as though I'm some menacing specter. Now, stand up and let's get all of this sorted out."

Tikan pushed himself from the floor and faced Onasus, directing the light into his visor and thereby revealing the face of an older man with dry red streaks caking his every wrinkle, like the warpaint of an Indian chieftain. They stared at each other, visor to visor.

"Well," Onasus said. "Let's make for the engine room. I'll fix it so that we have light and heat and power, and so that we can jump to Proxima—that is where you plan on heading, isn't it? Yes. Anything else would be preposterous—and then we can all go and have warm chocolate in the cockpit."

"Wait—who—we don't even know who you are—"

"Yeah. Find out who he is. Can't trust anything," Mira said.

"Oh, enough of that perfunctory rabble, both of you," Onasus said, coming close to Tikan's enclosed face, as though to speak to Mira as well. "We'll speak at length in short enough time. For now let us survive, fine?"

Neither spoke as Tikan sized him up. "Fine," he said. "But after this is settled, you're going to tell us about this Farabi person and why those black suits did this."

"Well and good. Now, shall we?"

Tikan followed Onasus Loptar as he half-waltzed, thick and bronze, out of the dormitories and through to the central walkway, between thinner corpse piles and towards the engine room.

"I wish you could just turn off that stupid light above your head," said Onasus, as the two neared their destination.

"I'm sorry?"

"The light on your head. You would think that they would let you poor bastards have technology from this century. You know, night-vision, infrared, sonar, phase-contrast imaging, atomic reconstruction, the standard equipment, you know. Instead you have that ridiculous beam dangling around. Pathetic. It isn't a wonder that you were decimated so quickly."

The passage to the engineering bay was clear. Both men passed through unhindered and descended the spiral staircase down to the engine room.

"It's hard to think about how many people..." Tikan mused morosely as they walked into the engine room. "We're the only ones left."

"Yes, well," Onasus said. "You two seem to have decent enough heads on your shoulders if you escaped that mess. Yes, with you two aboard, I'm certain we'll devise a solution to all this. But enough of that—look there, our 'engine.' Our magnificent gate-pryer, our co-ordinate de-randomizer, our telescope and rudder both, if we're going to be archaic," he added, approaching the titanium contraption taking up most of the chamber.

"Why does it shut off in case of sudden decompression?" Tikan asked.

"To make sure we don't get cooked inside. If the heat dumps get knocked around and the cooling systems fail while all of that is still running hot, well, we all fry with it. Space doesn't simply soak up the ship's heat, you know."

They made their way around on railed walkways surrounding the engine, which had a slick outer cylinder for a shell, replete with machinery only hinted at and tucked away inside. The whole machine was aimed out of a true window, looking like an enormous cannon for the new age. There were almost no consoles.

Onasus approached the closest guardrail and squeezed it. The cylinder lit up bright silver and began spinning and blaring out a loud, monotonous buzzing and whirring. The whole room glowed iridescent platinum.

"How did you do that?" Tikan asked.

"Do what?"

Tikan pointed at the engine. "Activate it with your procrustus. Not even the captain can—could—do that."

"Oh. Well, I suppose you should know. I have clearance that civilian procrustiis don't."

"What do you mean?"

"What do you mean, 'what do you mean?' You know how procrustokinesis works, yes? You activate the sensors with your thoughts, yes?"

"Is it technical, or what?"

"Ah, of course the public is unaware. There are levels of clearance, even for thoughts."

"Yes, I know that," Tikan said defiantly.

"Do you now? Interesting," Onasus replied slyly.

"So what is it, technical clearance? You an engineer?"

"Of course not."

Onasus turned to walk on, and then spun back around to face him. "I did not expect a—well, a lowly grunt like yourself to know about the clearance hierarchy. Let me enlighten you further. There are a few people in the galaxy with unilateral access, often to hidden sensors. But you don't need to know about procrustus clearance, do you?" he said in a tone that implied a grin despite his helmet.

Tikan stood, unsettled. Before he could reply, Onasus walked away, unfazed and comfortable.

Tikan chased after him to the other end of the engine room. "How did you survive the invasion? You were wearing your suit and that's why you didn't die in the decompression, fine, but how is it that you're the only survivor out here?"

"Aren't you also a survivor?"

"You know what I mean."

The engine hummed and spun a greenish-silver sunflower of light above them.

"Those kinds of questions need to be discussed at a table, with tea, or coffee, or water, even," Onasus said. "Not here in this doomy pit. No. Now, tell your friend that everything is running smoothly and, once we're in that dreadful hallway, tell her that she can now seal this gate and that she should do the same for all rooms with critical systems in them. Life support, especially."

Without another word, Onasus strode to the staircase again, almost prancing, floating, unimpeded by any questions or concerns, and he waited upstairs for Tikan, who dawdled along behind him.

They stood before the gate to the lounge, Tikan behind Onasus.

"Mira, the engine is up," Tikan said. "You should be able to seal off the life support and the other systems now."

"All right," she replied, worry in her voice.

"Tell her to hurry," Onasus called.

"You're in a rush?"

"A rush to get away from these awful rotters, yes." He kicked aside a head poking out of a nearby room.

"Have some respect."

"Respect? For what?"

"The dead."

"And whose fault is it that they're dead?" Mira buzzed in his helmet.

As though he had heard Mira, Onasus did not immediately reply. Tikan clenched his teeth. Like a troubled monk, he closed his eyes and measured his breathing.

After watching this with some degree of satisfaction, Onasus spoke. "Now, you can bang your head against the wall about the dead, or we can move on and do what we can, okay?"

"Let's go."

"Wait a moment. Let her secure the life support, that we might flush out the carcasses."

"What?"

"We'll run across the lounge through both airlocks," Onasus said, as though it were a simple matter.

"And just send them out to the void like trash?"

"The void?" he asked incredulously. "Absolutely. Did you think to bury them in steel graves?"

Tikan huffed in his helmet. "It's not about graves, it's about...meaning."

Onasus shook his head in disbelief. "Meaning? Are you some kind of mystic? Some sort of olden moralist? An overly enthusiastic student of ancient philosophy and religion? I had no idea these subjects were still investigated. Look around you, boy," he said, pointing at a pile of corpses nearby. "Another breath's the only meaning you should be worried about right now."

"Just—Just shut it," Tikan said, pushing past him. "I don't know you and there's—"

"Will you two shut up and come back here so we can find out who this guy is and what our plan is?" Mira interrupted.

Onasus moved close to Tikan's visor, and tried to speak his words into the microphone so Mira could hear him. "Sanctimonious, isn't he?" Onasus said lazily, and then spun to face the gate again.

Tikan seethed for some moments, his eyebrows crossed. He waited behind Onasus and gritted his teeth again. "Are you sure you're going to be able to do this?" he asked.

"Do what?" replied Onasus.

"Get us through two waves of decompression without being ripped out into space."

"Of course. Do you think this suit is as flimsy as the paper you're wearing? In fact, just hold on to me."

Tikan remained immobile. He appraised Onasus' heavy gloves and boots.

"Just hold on to me," Onasus instructed. "Otherwise, we'll be here for a while trying to rescue you."

"Are you sure?"

"Yes, I'm sure. Now stop asking so many questions, hold on, and tell your friend to open the gate and keep it open. We want to flush out all of that evidence before it causes us problems."

Tikan folded his arms around Onasus' waist and held. He took a few deep breaths, and then spoke. "Mira, please open the lounge gate for us, and keep it open. Make sure all systems are sealed up before, though."

"Keep it open? Why?"

"Our friend says its best to send out all the corpses."

"I suppose so," she said. "Ready?"

"Yes."

As the disk slid aside, air streamed out. They remained firmly rooted to the floor. Tikan felt the slip and slide of bodies rush past him. A few brushed him on their way out, but he held on. Luck alone, or some unspoken calculation of Onasus', kept the corpses from crashing into him and his unlikely anchor.

As the ship's innards emptied out, and the white noise charged about their skulls, Onasus set out. They stomped through the gate into wild darkness, the winds lashing them. To their left, they felt the pull of that hole to the galaxy, which was now active like some wakened monster feasting awfully. Out they fled, in the storm of Thanatos' beating wings, opposite the whirlpool stamped into the ship's hull.

The pair traversed the lounge before long.

"Mira! Get downstairs," Tikan yelled, though he could not hear himself, or any response if it came.

Onasus ploughed onwards, each leg thundering down to the floor, grounding them. He seemed not to take any account of the cyclone around them. He shuffled his shoulders and surged on. After clearing the arena of racing bodies, they arrived at the narrow corridor before the cockpit. There, the winds were focused into a shrill.

They closed in on the entrance to the cockpit, and it spun open with blurry light as though in response to Onasus' mere presence.

Now both airlocks on opposite sides of the lounge were open, each gushing out its vortex. Onasus slowed somewhat as they neared the light. Then he lost his footing for a moment and almost lost Tikan, but righted himself and caught the other by the wrist. They stomped on, with their muscles weakening and bottling acid in their exoskeletons, Tikan hugging Onasus again. The light glowed ahead. They pushed on, their titanium legs hanging off the bone.

Once they passed the threshold, the fangs of the gate circled inward, and the disk slid shut, and they collapsed on the floor of the illumed cockpit.

❦ 19 ❦
PROXIMA

F ar below the glass dome wrapping the metropolis planet like a
bubble, Sielle walked the streets aimlessly. At certain angles, the
sunlight broke into glimmers on the dome like crimson stars.

Some time after wandering out of the clinic, she had found herself
among sparse crowds drifting through an open boulevard, which was
divided in two by greenery. There were rows of angel-white buildings
on each side of it. The smell of pines wafted as she glided along the
pavement, alabaster and pristine like the rest of the city.

She spent some time gawking at the architecture, and tracing new
myths into the constellations with her finger. There in the city, each
building, road and monument wound together in platinum and glass.
And as the red sun broke all over the glass, the whole city gained a
scarlet tinge.

Though at first she was drawn to the pines dividing the boulevard,
eventually she could not help but recoil from them. The pretend scent
of spring and the perfection of each leaf left her feeling nauseous.
Sielle crossed the boulevard, almost skipping, to the streets again.

Some passersby creased their foreheads at her, but her eyes just
glazed over them. Only slightly more animate than the other objects
in the metropolis, most people she encountered had dead, empty

expressions. A few broke the monotony of their faces with a random grin, but Sielle could only guess at what had provoked it. Aside from their footsteps, they made few sounds.

She avoided the more direct stares of those pedestrians who looked more awake. If their heads were not tilted towards the ground, they regarded her and her frayed rags from centuries past with expressions of discomfort. Their own clothes were simple tunics in pale colors. Lithe garments which almost bordered on regal in certain quiet flourishes.

"Where can I find clothes like this?" she found herself asking an onlooker. The woman, who was clad in a salmon dress, was frightened into a faster pace.

Out of the other end of what could hardly be called an alleyway due to its pristine sheen, Sielle arrived within view of a building made of glass, save for its specular floor. She approached it and found a crowd bulging at the front entrance.

"Yeah, the new ones are supposed to have better physics. More realistic," she heard someone saying as she drew closer to the crowd.

"Why would I want more reality, though? If I wanted pure reality I'd just live life. That would be so boring. No point in metempsies if all you want is everything to be fully realistic," another replied.

"No, but I mean, realistic—like it all feels real, you know? Like I can believe it more."

"I guess. It doesn't have to look exactly like real life for me to be able to lose myself in it completely."

As Sielle joined the crowd, the building made a shift toward the opaque, and then it shined with gold and crimson and silver, brighter and brighter with each step, taking on colors not uniform with the rest of the city. She stepped backward at the sudden contrast, and watched the structure regain its original, translucent form.

"Love the outfit," came a voice just behind her. "Is that for *Yggdrasil's Sap* or *Terra Obscura?*"

It was a boy some years younger than she. He bit his nails as Sielle looked at him.

"I'm sorry?" she asked.

"Your costume. I think it's very good. I was wondering what metempsy it's supposed to be from."

"Oh. The first one you said, *Yggdrasil*."

"*Yggdrasil's Sap*? Wow. I can't wait for it. They say it's like having a new procrustus it's so real. Just like being on old Earth."

"Yes. It sounds exciting," she said, her laconism lowering the boy's face.

"I wasn't expecting so many people here."

"You know everyone's excited because these metempsies are supposed to be different, right? Some people who got inside were even saying that they forgot who they were completely the whole time they were in them. Isn't that amazing?"

"It is," she replied, hardly paying attention to him. "Do you know anyone else here?"

The boy frowned. "No. Why, what's wrong?" he said with a light quiver in his voice.

"Why is no one else dressed up?"

"I don't know. Nobody really does that anymore."

"But you complimented me on it."

"I just thought it was nice, you know? Bringing metempsies to the real world, instead of the other way around."

"I see. Well, thanks."

The boy nodded. He looked at up at her with gems for eyes, and she saw the opportunity to mine these and pick him for information.

"How are these metempsies different again, by the way?" Sielle asked. "I knew they were working on updates, but I didn't really pay attention to the details."

"I don't know too many details yet either, but people inside are getting to see for themselves before it releases next week. The ones who've come out say they don't remember too much of what happened in the metempsy, though they remember the whole metempsy. Isn't that weird?"

"It's really weird. Tell me more."

"You ever want to just, be another person? Like in metempsies, except you really forget who you actually are the whole time? Like those people that are really good at metempsies, but without any effort."

"Sure."

"I heard it's just like that, now. I mean, you're still yourself, but in a way you're someone else, too."

"I see," she said. "But what's the point, if you don't remember it afterwards?"

"Haven't you had a really strong metempsy before?"

"Of course."

"Then you kind of know what it's like. You do remember it afterwards, but it's hard to remember what someone else did. I have a friend who's really good at metempsying, and he says it's always like that for him. In the metempsy, he doesn't remember himself at all— it's like being born again, and then going back to your old life when you're done with the new one."

Sielle was beginning to understand. Unlike some mere virtual simulation, these *metempsies* were drugs of the identity, smugglers of memories and hijackers of being.

"Okay. And how do you do it?"

"What do you mean?"

"I mean, how do you become someone else, the way you're saying. I want to try it."

"I don't understand. You just *do*."

They gave each other looks of suspicion and confusion.

"You said you had to be good at it," Sielle said.

"Yeah, but that's not what I mean. I mean—" the boy stopped and began to express discomfort, pained by the harsh limits of his linguistic capacity.

"You mean there's no skill in it," Sielle said.

"Yes."

"You mean, you're either totally immersed, or you're not, and it's not something you can easily fix by trying."

"Yes! You're really good at this."

"Yes, I'm great. So tell me, what's it like for you?"

"Metempsies?"

"Yes. Do you remember who you are? Are you happy when you do it?"

"Happy?" he repeated, and then looked ponderous for a few moments. "Yes. But. But—It's not really like that, you know? It doesn't matter if you're happy or not, because you're just someone else for a while. And it usually works for me, but sometimes I remember myself and it's not nice. That's why I can't wait for the new ones."

The boy stared at her in silence. His expression was a mixture of deep thought and perplexity. It was as though he were considering the nature of the phenomenon in question for the first time, and experiencing an avalanche of new ideas as a result.

"Interesting," Sielle said.

"You're excited, too, right?" His eyebrows lifted and his lips parted only slightly, and his eyes took on their sparkle again.

"Of course. And, actually," she continued, motioning her hand to dismiss the matter, "I think I should go and change into something else. I didn't think I'd be the only one dressing up for this, or that there would be so many people here. Do you know where I can find some simple clothes nearby?"

"You mean, to buy them?"

"I would buy them, but I have no money."

"What's money?" His youth afforded him little in the way of skepticism. Rather than ask further questions and risk embarrassing himself, he resolved to guess her meaning. "Why don't you just go home and change if you can't have clothes dispensed?"

"It's a bother. And I want clothes like that," she said, pointing at a woman in an azure tunic.

"Oh. I think you look great, though."

"Do I?" she asked, leaning towards him.

"Your costume, I mean." He looked at the floor. He had seen her face in a dream or in a metempsy, though he only vaguely remembered it. "Your costume is really amazing. You are too. Not, 'too,' I mean you are amazing. I—"

"I know, I know," she said languidly, placing a hand on his shoulder. "So where can I get those clothes?" she asked, brightening his face to a latitudinal pink and demolishing all of his fumbling attempts at expressing his confused enthusiasm and desire. "Can you show me?"

"Yeah, yes," he said. "Down near Road Thirty-Four, all the shops are there. But come back before they let us in and—"

"Thanks," she said, turning away from him before the 's' left her mouth, hurrying down the street.

All throughout her walk to the shops, an alien feeling tugged at Sielle from inside. Everything around her was pretty and spotless. The city seemed like a giant circuit board, the kind one of her fathers had shown her in the garage, days after man had reached the moon. And despite the token trees, despite the glittering sky, the city felt as artificial as people regularly did. Props designed for a camera, for a temporary and unreal perspective.

She walked on, and buried her thoughts until she arrived at the shops. Though they appeared as austere as the rest of the city, they lit up in her presence, and she drifted into the quietest looking one.

"That's a funny outfit, miss. Were you just at the metempsy expo?" said the elderly shopkeeper, smiling as she walked in.

"I was, yes," Sielle replied, wandering into the tiny aisles of the store.

He showed her around the store, describing various pre-printed designs and fabrics of differing price. What price meant in the absence of money she could not tell, but she guessed that this society must operate on some kind of credit system. She glided her hand through the racks of clothes, fiddling with the fabrics.

"You said these were less expensive," she said, turning to face the shopkeeper again, and grasping an outfit. "How can I pay?"

"How can you pay?" He gave her a peculiar look. "My dear, you just walk out of the store. Have you never made a purchase before? Or is it that you haven't yet been registered under your guardians?"

"Yes, I have, but I'm not from here, you see."

"Okay, so you're from Sol, or another system. And? Sol is not *that* backwards; I visit it every few years. It's all galactic, you know. The sensors will gauge your future worth, and you'll be procrusted for your purchase regardless of where you're from."

"Yes, of course. So it works even away from Earth?"

"...Yes," the man said, crossing his eyebrows at her and leaning in to gently grasp her shoulder. "Are you all right?"

Sielle kept her eyes downcast, and then she shook her head in a practiced act of distress. "Yes, I'm all right, I think. It's just those new metempsies. They're so real. I felt like I completely forgot who I was."

"Oh, dear," the shopkeeper said, bringing her to a nearby chair. "My wife always dislikes it when I spend too much time metempsying. She partakes so little, I think it affects her more strongly. Perhaps you're of a similar cloth. Here, let me bring you some water, and then we can discuss your outfit, all right?"

"Thank you."

The man disappeared through a backdoor. Sielle began tapping her feet on the ground and glanced out at the exit, planning her next moves. She could have the shopkeeper make her a tunic like that other woman's, and then she would exit, and then perhaps she would exit again if trouble started.

"Here you are, miss," the shopkeeper said as he emerged from his hidden grotto holding a tall glass of water.

"Thank you."

"How old are you?" he asked as he approached.

"Twenty," she replied, before taking a sip.

"I see. Yes, well, not that young, but you were dabbling in those powerful new metempsies, and you likely have a lower threshold. Sometimes I wish I was more like you, that I could just forget myself in them. I've long since adjusted," he said, trailing off.

"Yes, you're right. I'll have to just be careful from now on."

"And so," he continued, after she had drained her glass, "Will you still be wanting to take out a new outfit today?"

"Yes, and I've decided I want to design my own."

"Excellent, excellent. Yes, we have fine configurations at your disposal, but first, if you would just stand, yes like that, and spread your arms out, yes, thank you," he said, pulling out a sensor thin as a wand and shaped like a snakehead. He aimed it at her and pressed it twice, and it beeped.

"Okay, now, if you would kindly come to this monitor, we can make the design."

"And my measurements?"

"Ah, well, we just took them," he said, smiling. "Yes, sometimes I am a little fast, and customers don't notice it." He chuckled to himself, and Sielle forced a smile.

He brought her to a screen close to where he had disappeared, and a collection of shapes and colors appeared on it as she approached.

"By the way, have we met before? You look so familiar to me."

Sielle shook her head.

"Oh, well. As you can see from this menu, we have a wide variety for you to choose from. And if you wish to have the items procrusted so that you can print them elsewhere instead, please let me know."

She stood at the console for some time, deciding.

"This," she said, pointing at her configuration on the screen.

"Are you sure you don't want to peruse our wares further before making a decision?"

She eyed the clerk suspiciously, noting that his vocabulary was strangely more sophisticated than anyone's she had yet met here. In fact, his whole persona seemed somehow out of time, as if he had been grafted into the city from a previous age. "Yes, I'm sure. Shall I return in a few days to collect it?"

"What for?"

"Well, how long will it take?"

The shopkeeper laughed, shaking his head. She noticed him wipe his brow, which had a peculiar, faint pinkish color to it.

"Miss, I suggest you return home and take a long rest. That metempsy experience must have rattled you somewhat. Here, let's print it."

A whirring sound started from behind her as the man squinted at the screen. He then drummed his thumb impatiently on the glass desk. From a large device resembling a small hollowed-out rocket at the other end of the room, her outfit was already assembling. The machine spun the thread fast, whizzing, burring, and within seconds it was finished, the garments suspended from the top of the needle that had wrought them.

"May I change here?"

"Of course. Please, the changing room is over here."

Forgetting herself completely, Sielle strode over to the contraption and snatched her prize, then disappeared into a room of mirrors.

There she removed her rags from ages past and changed into her new attire. The light in the room was harsh, and reflected to infinity on the specular walls. She half-tripped as she sank her limbs into the powder blue trousers and tunic.

"What a wonderful choice," the shopkeeper said as she exited the changing room. "Now, do as I say and get some rest. No good walking around with a strained procrustus."

Sielle did not listen to him, but took a moment to feel the new clothes, still warm from the machine against her skin. She smiled as she made for the door. Then, her heart started racing, as it did whenever she thieved in unknown places. She prodded where the wound in her shoulder had been, hoping to find some crust or scab to pick at, but it was all gone. Only clear skin remained.

"Thanks, and goodbye," the shopkeeper said.

Sielle ignored him. Adrenaline was cascading through her. As she walked to the exit, her nostrils flared out columns of air. She stepped out, flinched at the harsh night-lights, and took another breath.

The sky above stretched wide and shimmered with blood rivulets of light. No sensors or alarms or shouting. She exhaled. Whatever system bound the galaxy, it attended only to those already in its clutches, and could not detect, or even fathom, an outlier such as herself. She grinned. Still reeling from the episode, she beamed down the open pavement, no longer drawing suspicious stares, and began striding towards nowhere in particular.

Some hours passed as Sielle lost herself in the streets, but night never turned to day. Ever suspended above, the sun poured its blood over the planet. There were no vehicles in sight, only sparse crowds and distracted people. No neon or excessive writing plastered around street corners, and only within close proximity did buildings reveal their purpose in a stark metamorphosis, like that glassy building where the metempsies had been showcased, or the row of stores from which she had just stolen her new clothes. Were it not for the actual people that walked around, there would scarcely have been a trace of humans actually living in such a well-kept, automated place. In fact, so little motion occupied the streets that it was hard to understand how anything functioned at all. Though buildings and objects transformed and livened at close proximity, this, too, seemed empty artifice.

In the sky, against the dome, Sielle saw boney-looking objects lined up at an angle. Some penetrated the glass membrane of it and came to a halt, and others lifted off and passed out of the dome. They did not look altogether dissimilar to certain shuttles she had boarded in years past.

"What's there?" she asked a pedestrian, pointing up at the moving ships.

"The docks," the woman replied.

"And what's the fastest way there?"

"Take the throughground," the woman said, pointing at a nearby set of stairs leading below ground.

Without a second glance at the woman, Sielle darted off down the steps, running her hand along the wall to feel the cold steel of it, whipping back her hair. She descended, and even in this supposedly public place of transportation, there was nobody.

From the base of the stairs, she hurried through a dimmer gauntlet still lined with sun-like spheres glowing along the walls, and then she stopped at the end and stood on a platform facing a number of dark tunnels. The platform was too small for what otherwise seemed to be a train stop. It was perpendicular to a set of horizontal and vertical passageways that came to form a cylindrical cross ahead. She waited.

Then she jumped at a sudden, startling noise. A panel shot out of the ground before her without warning, shouting, "PLEASE STATE YOUR DESTINATION," at her.

"Docks," she replied hastily, sending the obnoxious but well-mannered thing back down into the ground.

Within moments, a rush of wind soared through the lower tunnel ahead of a speeding object. A streamlined, silver vessel, which somehow resembled the tube-trains of old, rushed out from beneath the platform at blinding speed. It stopped with a sudden jerk, propped up like a rocket before takeoff, ready to melt off its excesses.

Then a solid section of its body opened, inviting her into a small, solitary compartment, above and below which she could see the other passengers of this metallic caterpillar. Some of these people looked bored in their seats, others drowsy.

She stepped inside and sat down. A set of safety belts shot out from all sides and tied her up like a mad person. The train took off. It flew through the manifold network of tunnels at all angles, coursing the bloodless, silvery veins of the city. Sielle breathed hard, and her grip tightened around one of the straps across her belly. She peered out and watched the walls shift at speed, free of the sun's ruby glare. Though her booth was cramped, and the window almost pressed to her face, she remained spellbound.

After a few minutes in the train, Sielle heard the same voice from the platform shout from behind her seat, "EJECTING SEGMENTATION FOR ARRIVAL AT DOCKS," still stone-neutral, but warping as the argent snake coursed.

And thus, without any further notice, she was ejected from the whole, cast out of the moving set of linked booths, hers propelled down its own pathway at feathery speed. No harsh twists or turns. The single pod fluttered through the remainder of the trip before landing gracefully on a platform identical to that of her departure. The safety belts unstrapped her and receded into their slots, and Sielle marched out and up the stairs.

When she emerged from the transport station, she found herself high above the city, just under the glass barrier in the sky, where ships of various sizes and design streamed in and out from a number of double airlocks in the dome. From here, the city looked like a tiny model of itself.

The docks were composed of thick glass platforms, connected together like overlapping, two-dimensional bubbles. So high above the city, people walked atop rouged doubles of themselves, spectrally gliding across the platforms. Unlike the near-ceremonial cleanliness and symmetry of the city she had seen thus far, the docks were busy, crowded, and loud. People bustled about and chattered, performing their rituals of farewell or of welcome. This seemed a final, errant cultural leftover from the distant past.

No one paid attention to her as she wandered about, watching the dispersal of containers of various provenance on unmanned vehicles, the slow drift of inbound ships, and the way ships exiting to space stretched into needles and finally as twinkling steel dots in space.

"Where are we, exactly?" Sielle asked a man, tapping him on the shoulder and drawing him halfheartedly away from his group.

"The docks," he replied.

"But where are the docks?" she pressed.

"Proxima, where else?"

The words settled in her mind as the stranger turned away from her. She searched her memories for the distant yet familiar name.

Not far from her, on Dock Nine's platform, people were gathering, grouping together in mutual concern, mumbling to each other, their heads cocked upward. Sielle attended to the bubbling commotion as she returned from her fruitless thoughts. She walked up to the crowd and looked up with them.

The teeth of the airlock above spun open and admitted a long transport vessel. It limped in as if on crutches, gliding through the glass to reveal a ruined hull with a gaping hole in its side.

20

THE VAGRANT

Paris was unforgiving in the months following my great escape. And the words started to fall away from me, quietly, unceremoniously; I lost the will to say or write anything. I wandered the streets without clear aim, shuffling from alleyway to alleyway, scrounging for food in cold dumpsters, suffering the weight of pity. My hair became disheveled, my clothes ragged. Sleep was forbidden. Yes, and the city was against me: all lampposts and sidewalks and stone gargoyles animate and viciously conspiring to keep me from warmth, shelter, and other jewels.

Meanwhile, I convulsed in the frost, dark after dark. I roamed, and like some lost jackal, tried to feed where there was no food. I was the wraith of the city, the one who haunted himself. Trash became treasure and shelter. Dumpsters became friends, and train stations lovers.

I consorted with others like me, eventually. It was accidental at first. Perhaps a week after the fall from the window, I found a man sleeping in the metro at night whose beard sank to his chest and whose torn and layered rags spoke of years in the knowledge of homelessness. Some sleeping augur, no doubt, asleep for centuries.

I approached him with a broken expression, against the shadows leaping out from the tunnels, and I prodded him. He would not wake. Again, I shook him, harder. When his eyes opened, he just coughed to himself. I didn't understand. He drew a slow smile, like a crack spreading through a tablet bearing arcane wisdom. Then he started laughing, sitting up like an overly amused child, filling the empty tunnels with toothless cackling. Still, I didn't understand. He stopped, and then stared at me, as though to consider whether I was serious or not in my sorry demeanor, and then he demeaned me again.

It was my face, my *will you please help me, I am newly dispossessed, and you seem to have been here a long time* mien, which sent him into that maniacal frenzy. We crossed the boundaries of language without speaking, for he replied to me, with that crazed guffaw, *buckle up, because no one is here to help you, and you're ridiculous for even thinking I will.*

I did meet more communitarian street dwellers in the metro stations, those temples of the exiled. To think that, years before, these underworlds of the Périphérique had been pristine. Now they were ratty and filthy as freedom's newest bastion, or better yet, the tumor of man's failures infiltrating the world at last.

I met Claude, Karim, and Jean-Louis together at the Port d'Italy station. They were rather accommodating, almost friendly, though they still wore the de facto survivalist fortress about them. Nevertheless, I could see how these three pleasant men would eventually turn into that concentrated manifestation of cynicism who had destroyed me with his laughter. Our interactions were not free of pessimism or sneering jabs. Through them, I saw how I could become such a thing, broken down by the world, reduced to a comedian whose favorite audience is himself, who laughs because, underneath his torment, he has found the glorious absurd.

Jean-Louis had been a store clerk, Karim a woodworker, and Claude a builder. This last man yet retained employment as a purveyor of fine addictions. All they knew about me was that I had decided to stay in Paris for the architecture, that I was some sort of deranged monk, a wide-eyed tourist-ascetic, one who denies himself all but his own peculiar brand of sorrow.

Of course, they could not actually believe me, but it was the formality of my false identity that counted. No, I could not let them know about my laptop, trove of my work, container of my life's last light. I never showed it to them.

They were nice enough, either way. They showed me the pockets of free warmth between the public places of the city, and though I did not live with them by any means, we did form a disconnected alliance of commiseration. We would meet every so often, sometimes for days at a time. We played cards by the fire and exchanged stories; I remember one evening holding up a triumphant king of hearts after a successful game of Liar. My tales were always fabricated, of course. The language was a problem, but, in many ways, it was entertaining to attempt breaches of that barrier together.

We made tortured puppets of our hands and shook our heads to understand each other. It was a refreshing change from the usually uncomfortable introductions one regularly makes in one's own language. Karim and Claude, in particular, made efforts to teach me. Accidental shadow puppets born of those gestures streaked the walls in the late-night metro gatherings as those two turned the place into a classroom.

As I got to know him, Karim came to visit less and less, and began to constantly look over his shoulder as if followed by government intelligence. I dismissed it as some psychic scar he'd earned over his years of hard living. Sometimes, he would meet alone with better-dressed persons; when I advanced on these meetings he would turn aggressive and drive me off as if I were vermin. I learned to ignore it.

When they travelled off to the suburbs or to other areas outside the Périphérique that I dared not yet venture to, I would practice my French alone, or confront pedestrians with creative new reasons for why they had to assist me. "Catch me, the world as it is in me, that you might see the value in a packet of cigarettes!" I rasped at one man who was busy on his phone.

Months passed, and I began to feel hopeless. Regardless, I was determined to continue my work. I would sit, during my lonesome nights at the train stations—not the usual metro, with its prying eyes, but the ground-level sanctuaries which traded me cold for privacy, where a wall socket was often nearby, and thus, where I could write, a bearded wreck of a man with a pristine piece of technology. The contrast appealed to me in quite a significant way. It told me that I was more than just a lowered beast in rags, that I was not yet finished, only set back.

I continued from where I had left off at the hotel, and I found that I hated all that I had previously written.

Delete.

And I started again. The first words were automatic:

It is important to fully embrace moments when the habituality of existence reposes.

I felt proud of those words, content. I knew that they were uncontrived and honest. That I had, at last, expressed my exact sentiments as I sat cross-legged against the station's checkered walls; suddenly feeling human, and not in some sort of cloying, sentimentalistic sense, but in quite a physical and perceptual sense.

I felt the fragility of my organs within me, and I felt the blood rush into my eyeballs, and that was the first time I understood how to conquer the gray haunting in those layers of the world like prison walls. But it required concentration. It needed to be a deliberate effort, a special attentiveness.

And so I continued:

There is a difference between the physical conditions for the possibility of consciousness and the subjective a priori *experience of pure consciousness. The former we leave to men of science to discuss.*

Consider, then, that while one may introspect to clear out the haze of the self, which is at times more opaque than any sensed particulars, one may also apply oneself to a different sort of self-investigation. In fact, the word "investigation" is not suitable for this purpose, as it implies a rational principle. What is being suggested is a mindful focus on the senses and their end in our general awareness. It is to refrain from linguistic thoughts, or rational theorizing, and with great effort, to inhabit the self completely. To close the plastic bag of our experiment over our theorizing heads, to fill up the boot of the foot, the hat of the scalp, the glove of the hand, the jacket of the torso, and so on, with the body-shaped spirit. Were a dog so disposed, it could perhaps achieve this, though the value would be lost on it.

It is a process of pure intuition, and nothing else. Yet it requires immense focus. It is to recognize our intuitable sphere of being. I remain vague on what this sphere delimits, for the simple reason that any successful meditation of this sort would be hardly communicable. It would take into account all of collective history and all of one's private, subjective history. It would destroy the purity of the experiment.

We are not, here, speaking of a mystic experience, either. It is simply that the spaces between any letters, or, worse yet, words, attempting to apprehend the matter, would only succeed in slicing up parts of what is otherwise only valuable as a self-contained whole. And any cut, therefore, would be critical. And to speak would be to section off the consequent experience from antecedent causes that have no basis in language to begin with.

The point is to make aware the flesh, as flesh or as ensouled body, for it has real existential nectar. We deposit all that we can into the flesh, and, without abandoning that stream of experience, we eject our rational selves, so to speak, and wholly apprehend this continuous stream. It is not an aesthete's gambit. It is to touch glass and search the sensation absolutely, not for pleasure, or for reason; and then, coupled with the touch and all its particular essence in the act of consciousness aimed at it, to embrace the bundled sight of it: its smell, if it has one, or its lack thereof; the pictures or sentiments drawn up and expanded over time (or time itself as colored by myriad collections of this sort) in the pure realm of the self and all its cascading extensions.

Indeed, this sort of meditation is for a regaining of the self, for consciousness as more than a tired cog. Further, it must be noted that in order to clarify the nature of the relation between objects appearing in consc—

I closed the laptop after those imperfect but satisfying few words, and I ran them over in my mind, until they were etched in my mind and soothed me towards sleep. It was going to be all right. Everything was going to be perfectly fine; I would write my treatise on the back of that gentle epiphany, and it would raise me in mind and body from the gutters.

I started to drift, alone, there, in the dark. Peace and quiet, at last. I slept with the laptop resting on my chest.

And in the morning,

it

was

all

gone.

I could barely keep together a coherent field of vision. There, in that early morning rage, before the mind is equipped to lay precise blame. Where? Where was my prize? I walked in a mad circle scanning the floor near where I'd slept and when I found nothing on those tiles again and again my orbit widened and on that ireful ecliptic I found nothing but polish harsh to the eyes and I got close on all fours and dusted the floor and broke nails between its tiles as though to force open a hidden cache between them and I sniffed the floor and prowled the floor with my nose to it looking like some freakish anteater warped and sent back grotesquely malformed from a nightmarish plane where space itself is tormented and whose bones are roiling anger and I searched the floor beneath bench seats and atop bench seats and around these seats and made aberrant grunts and half-caged howls while jittering and I jumped down to the tracks before the trains arrived and no there no nowhere in the same mad circle the floor the same polish and no I looked and pleaded no and almost prayed no and but no.

No!

My mind was a sulfur cloud. And the world all clouds. Hah! The flimsy film of existence. The thinnest peel that made me want to rip out my own arms. Hah! But, no, this was no time for laughter. That feathery white nest laid the previous night in my head was full afire.

I shouted, in broken French and in English, and stumbled, as the early-morning commuters appeared at the station. They observed me like pedestrian scientists, each noting the aberration before them and assigning half-guessed causes to my state. Fools, all, an Antarctica for each heart!

But who was the thief, in fact? Claude, *that filthy drug dealer*. The suspicion rioted around in my skull. Who else would have taken it? But he couldn't have known where I was. No, not him. And we had a code, honor among the broken. *Then who?* An unknown. A thief! A rotten, abject monster of society with a northern waste in his chest more frigid than all others, but a creature as victim as I.

He was gone, probably selling my treasure, if it was not already sold. Paris had done this to me, that sick, golden parasite on the world's breast. Wretched city. Broodmother of the irredeemable. It was mine. That work was mine, and the laptop was *mine*. My beautiful treatise; the beautiful harmony, gone, captive. I would take it back. I'd take revenge on the city. Claude would help me. He was brave, Claude. He sold counter-poison, yes: a real hero—heroin the heroine, medicine to the machine.

～

"Claude! Ou est Claude?" I yelled through the solemn halls of Port d'Italy.

"Ici," he said, from behind a pillar.

"Ton flingue. Donne le moi."

"Pourquoi?"

"Parce-que c'est fini. Tu m'entends? Je m'casse."

"Arrête de faire le guignole."

"No!" I said. "That's it."

He revealed a crooked tooth or two at the foreigner's plight, and handed the gun over.

I found myself, then, under a moonless and star-robbed night, standing in front of a quaint Parisian grocery store, fiddling with my thoughts and with Claude's handgun. There was more than blood hammering through me, that was certain. I stood there for a good ten or twenty minutes, letting the neon of the store wash over me as I scraped together an escape plan.

I was right next to the Maison Blanche metro station; with the right timing and a quick dash down the stairs, I could easily make the one-fifteen stop and be on my way. My mind scurried through a half-remembered map. *I could get off at Tolbiac, or Port d'Italy, yes, or—*No time to think.

I stumbled into the shop like a drunken clown. Not surprisingly, I began having violent spasms, which I could not discern as being of body or spirit. Well, in my anxiousness, I did not take the time to pace around and pretend to browse the aisles of packaged candies or newspapers before unleashing my weapon. No, from the threshold I swung my arm up in a clumsy arc aimed at the clerk. His face sank and he immediately raised his arms.

I was trembling. What was I doing? How had I arrived at this juncture, out of all possible worlds? Flashes of Sophia's face appeared in my mind, and somehow legitimized the artificial fury I was trying to summon. *I wouldn't be here if she were with me. She wouldn't have let me. Curse her!*

I was stuttering when I told him to, crudely translated, "Open the fucking register and give me what's inside!"

He began fumbling in his nervousness. Nervous—the fool. No one alive had more electrified nerves than I. I eyeballed him up and down. I scraped at the skin under my beard. Oh, he was careful, the clerk, nodding meekly and such. Meanwhile, my thoughts attacked: *Am I being convincing enough? Does he take me for a joke? Port d'Italy—anyone else watching?—the police?*

"Ouvre cette putain d'caisse!" I repeated, loud and hoarse.

Just as I finished yelling, there, fast, the clerk dove for cover under the cash register, and then erupted like the delayed sight of lightning with a rifle. I panicked, and held my breath, shut my eyes. There was nothing else to do. I squeezed fire out of the gun.

Then a cacophony of other gunshots rapidly succeeded my own, as though the result of some labyrinthine Mexican standoff, though there were only two of us. I waited there, trembling, with eyes shut and teeth clenched, sweating tremendously.

Certain of the end, I held my breath for a small eternity, but nothing happened. There was only ringing in my ears, and then a faint gurgling sound coming from somewhere in the room. I felt sheltered behind my eyelids. As though closing myself off from the visual world allowed me to sidestep the whole enterprise and enter some irreal sanctuary, remove myself from the equation and every decision that had led up to it. I stood there, trying not only to bracket existence, but to wholly seal it off. But, as I could not darken the rest of my senses, I grew panicked again.

I dropped the gun and looked out. I patted my body down absurdly in search of bullet wounds. The store was so brightly lit it made me sick, sicker. And when I moved on to survey what I'd wrought, I half expected to be prancing, skipping. No, in fact, I was shaking even more now, as it became apparent that there was nothing in the room except for that thick gurgling.

I staggered to the counter. There was a single bullet hole in the wood, which had clearly come from where I had been standing. I had missed. Of course I had. Had I thought myself some desperado gunslinger at first shot? Hah! Hah, *what a ridiculous notion this whole robbery has been, what a pleasant diversion*, hah!

But before I could become too comfortable, it occurred to me to see where the gurgling was coming from. I peered over the desk. Though I had missed, the clerk was lying slumped against the now red-streaked soda machine behind him, sucking gravely for air.

I inhaled deeply, the air all sugary artifice and bodily iron. He wheezed breath after breath despite the two holes in his chest leaking crimson. He was straining his delirious eyes at me. They spun in their sockets, as he tried to either curse me or ask for help with a few pathetic hand motions. He sputtered blood at me, and flicked his wrist a last few times. But suddenly I didn't care. I wasn't feeling horrible anymore. As though tempered by his blood, I had stopped shaking, and had finally achieved that elusive confidence I had been seeking. It wasn't hard for me, then, to slip my hand into his pocket—our eyes still locked—and take the key to his cash register. The clerk's eyes rolled; I turned to take my prize, and *horror*.

A deathly tall and hideous thing loomed above me. I charged, bolting up and full of fear. *Port d'Italy.* Colossal arms dragged down through the air and cracked my head as I sprang.

21

TEA, CHOCOLATE, AND CONSPIRACIES

"This really is wonderful chocolate," said Onasus, still in his bronze shell, now hunched over a mug. "I daresay it tastes even better than the original stuff. Amazing how far we've come as a species. Isn't it? That we can sit here while half the ship is coming apart, in the middle of dark space, enjoying a fresh hot chocolate—or tea, in your case. Without our story behind us, this little scene of ours would look entirely absurd."

In Mira's quarters beneath the cockpit, the group was huddled together, all wearied, on two small couches bordering a coffee table. Despite their sullen mood, Onasus Loptar kept up his sprightly banter. Tikan sat across from him at the other head of the low glass table, waiting for his opposite to finish his trivial ruminations. The tea in front of him remained unsipped.

"And you," Onasus started again, this time turning to the awakened Naim, who lay on the couch beside him. "Are you sure you don't want anything to drink? You don't look very well at all. Maybe some coffee to wake you up?"

Naim stared at what looked like the outline of a continent of dried blood on the top of Onasus' head. "No. I'm all right. Thank you. I'll have water. After."

"Suit yourself. Watch that leg, though. You need to keep hydrated if you want those neutral platelets they keep spraying on it to work right," Onasus said.

"Yes, thank you." Naim closed his eyes again and winced, looking away from Onasus.

Their new haven was a small one. Furniture and oxygenated air. The soft sheets of Mira's bed and the lifelike plant in the corner beside it too neat, the kitchen and its appliances too convenient. Outside, the world was burned, the ashes not yet settled.

"Have this," Tikan said, pushing his drink over to Naim. "I'm not thirsty."

Naim curled his fingers around the handle, and he swallowed a few sips of the tea.

"Well, that's somewhat rude," Onasus said, flinching with an exaggerated look of offence. "Last time I offer you a drink."

Naim gave him a weak smile before taking another sip.

"You know, I think it's time you tell us about yourself," Mira said, cutting through Onasus' carefree aura.

Onasus sighed loudly. "Have I not yet earned enough trust for a brief reprieve?"

"You may as well have been doing yourself a favor. You're also marooned here with us."

"Am I?"

They paused.

Onasus squinted hard at Mira, and then at Naim, making the same expression as when he had activated the ship's engine. Mira continued to eye him suspiciously, certain that, were it not for his bronze suit, she could easily accuse him of being complicit in the slaughter. She and Tikan crossed glances and shared a wary expression.

Mira opened her mouth as if to say something, and then, with some consternation on her face, closed it quickly.

Onasus cleared his throat before taking a final gulp of his chocolate. He set the mug down on the glass. "My friends, and that is what you are to me, necessarily, for you have been both gracious and accommodating to me in this bleak test of survival, inviting me down to this cozy, homely, toasty shelter as we drift across the dark: I speak the truth when I say that I mean you no harm. You will forgive my secrecy, my evasiveness, when you hear what I have to tell you."

"You do know what happened then?" Mira said.

"Yes, I know of the plot. I know of Friedrich Farabi, brilliant scientist and brave soul. Let me tell you, however, that regardless of what you will do with the information I am about to provide, you are all already implicated in this saga. No, not as of this moment, of course, but unless you plan on staying aboard a ghost ship for the remainder of your lives, you are all now fugitives and criminals of the highest order. Throughout every sector of conquered space, yes. Yes, even you, Tikan Solstafir; you most of all, for when it becomes clear to them that you do not have a procrustus—no, do not interrupt, please—they will have double the reason to seek your capture."

Silence swallowed the room. Tikan set his eyes on Onasus and he gripped the armrests of his seat, struggling to comprehend the viper's knowledge of his inmost secret. He could feel the sudden focus shifting, the inquisitorial eyes bearing down on him. Probing, questioning. Beside him, he heard Mira huffing lightly.

"You what?" she asked, her thumb and index nails tearing at each other.

With the shame now bubbling in his gut, Tikan stayed quiet. Mira ripped her gaze away from him and tried again to process the revelation. She bared her teeth at him, gritting them as if she were in great pain. She breathed heavily through her nose, flaring her nostrils, and she forced her own mouth open and made a sound, but then went quiet. She glanced over at Naim, whose eyes were shut in contemplation and whose chest was rising faster than usual. They said nothing to each other and instead they waited for Onasus to proceed.

"Having established this," Onasus continued, careful not to shatter the tension he had so carefully constructed, and shifting his gaze between each of his interlocutors, "let me now explain the circumstances. As you know by now, I am Onasus Loptar. What I am now is without title. Not long ago, however, I was a researcher under the great Friedrich Farabi, a man whom you had undoubtedly never heard of before the events that have transpired over the last few hours. This is to be expected. He was, until quite recently, chief engineer of the procrustus, in charge of the constant maintenance, revision, supervision, and most importantly, enhancement and development that it re—"

"You mean for Earth?" Mira asked.

"Earth? You think Earth is responsible for the procrustus?"

"Well, Sol is, the Ministry of Information and Mind of the Celestial Assembly of Sol is, right?" Tikan added, enthusiastic about his private research on the matter.

They looked at him as though he were some alien or diseased man quarantined and not yet released.

"My friends," Onasus said, grinning incredulously. "I do not wish to offend you when I say that you are all painfully ignorant on the matter. This is not your fault, of course, for that is by design. The Ministry of Information and Mind is a sham: an empty, pointless, pathetic apparatus that serves only as a distraction, and as a place where hope may be lost along with other applications and forms. It is necessary for a bureaucracy to exist as a place to filter out the zeal of the masses. Yes, for otherwise, where else would people focus their natural ambitions for change and improvement? Ah, but it was understood long ago that change and ambition should not be allowed in the arena of governance, rather they are to be entertained on the side, so that the architects may work in peace.

"No, Tikan, it is not at the Ministry of Information and Mind that the procrustus is developed; and, no, Mira, it is not done at Earth's behest. Earth is nothing more than a vestigial fount of jingoistic humanism, regardless of how much supposed clout it has in galactic politics. The Celestial Assembly, along with all of its institutions and participants, are just as useless as the Ministry, only more perfunctorily relevant, and larger in scale."

They looked at him, dumbfounded. Both Naim and Mira had adopted a curiously strained look: arrhythmic breathing, frowning, gritted teeth. It was as if they both had something incredibly difficult to digest in their stomachs. Tikan, meanwhile, paid them no mind as he leaned in and listened, forgetting Onasus' affront for a moment.

"No, you are all wrong," Onasus continued. "For it is in the shadows that the procrustus is developed. Always far, far away, and more advanced than what is trickled down the pretend institutions. It is engineered by a group, ever shifting, ever moving; corporations and politicians and independent powers together, none of whom actually know what they are doing, all of whom are perfectly and truly innocent."

"Innocent?"

"I mean it, yes: they are innocent. Very few actually know why the procrustus exists, and none knows what the exact driving forces behind it are. I can tell you first hand that the great Farabi and his team did not fully understand what they were dealing with, either. We assumed we were working for the Ministry, or some other government, or some legitimate authority."

Tikan shook his head. "Then how could you have been hired if you didn't know what you were doing?"

"All of us were picked out as cherries from this job or that," Onasus said. "Most of us theoretical physicists, if you know what that is. Transferred to a secretive post, few details and high salary—enough future worth to last a lifetime. The work itself was always in bits and pieces. It was like building an engine without knowing about the spaceship it would be used for. The system itself demands the procrustus and directs its evolution. We are all pieces in it, you see, unable to do anything but to assume roles in satisfying its own emergent desires."

"A system?" Naim asked. "Like a computer?"

"No, of course not. Computers are involved, certainly, just as the politicians and the others are, but innocently. No, by *system*, I mean the whole. Everything. The total interaction of all human beings, together; the combined activity and thought of every element: that is the system."

"What are you talking about?" Tikan said. "Not everyone's always wanted it. I knew people who refused. I was with them. People who—"

"Your very acts of rebellion, you and your sorry band, have fed the demand in their own way."

Tikan remained silent, lest Onasus reveal more of his past to the others.

"You provided the system with an object to negate, and thereby advance itself. It is because each human being's life, from prehistory till now, has been an expression of demand for the procrustus," Onasus continued. "You and I are just as responsible for the procrustus as the Celestial Assembly is. That's right, yes. Minor cogs in the great Cog. Bits of reason within Reason. Every desire has a material consequence; every complaint voiced, every selfishness enacted, carries over the centuries like a rotting echo. Every hedonist and monk and mystic who ever sought annihilation or unity; every empiricist and rationalist toiling to abstract himself into a perspectiveless arbiter of general laws.

"Of course, demand is only half of the equation, complex as it may be, and it is not a merely economic or spiritual demand, but a process which encompasses all wellsprings and lodestones in between. And there are certainly organizations that are more directly involved in the procrustus' creation, though the exact structure of supply and design and manufacturing has become so complexly obscure and automated that one could go mad trying to point out its processes. It is, as one of my forbears once predicted, 'the ever-accelerating progress of technology and changes in the mode of human life, which gives the appearance of approaching some essential singularity in the history of the race, beyond which human affairs, as we know them, could not continue.'

"Now, you will ask how even the procrustus' very designers can work on such a project without real knowledge of it. Well, the exact consequences of its unleashing on humanity are so insidious, stretching out over centuries of conditioning, of massaging the public psyche into submission, that they cannot correctly fathom them. To these designers, the procrustus is just some common fact of life. They are like car manufacturers in the nineteen-forties, unaware of the damage petrol shall do to the Earth, or how it would change the organization of social life. They do not have the trans-historical insight to see it for what it truly is."

Over the course of Onasus' speech, the uncomfortable expression on Mira's face had turned to agony. She was now holding her head in her hands, shaking it, and exhaling hard. Naim, too, had been stirring in discomfort, though he was now silent and calm.

"I…I didn't understand those words you used," Mira said. "'Car,' and 'monk,' and 'lodestone,' and…"

"It's quite normal," Onasus said. "These are concepts you have not been afforded; the words not included in the current vocabulary package."

"What's going on?" Tikan asked Mira, ignoring Onasus for the moment. "Are you okay?"

She glanced up at him with bloodshot eyes, still holding her head, and through much effort spoke. "It's just a headache. A very bad one."

"Shall I take a look at it?" Onasus asked.

"No." She shook her head, and though she was still in visible discomfort, she managed to address Onasus. Despite her worsening condition, she did not cease to eye him with great suspicion. "Listen, I don't understand. You're talking about the procrustus as though it's some horrible thing. Who cares? I want to know about the black suits."

"Well, yes, that was the thrust of my next point, the fact that—"

"But it is horrible, Mira," Tikan almost whispered, his eyes downcast. He raised his voice. "The procrustus is a chain on every mind. You can't convince people. You can't show blind people what colors are like. But I know it. I've lived it."

Mira leered at him. "What are you talking about?" she asked spitefully. "Apparently *you* don't even have a procrustus. So how do you know anything about it?"

"That's how I know, damn it, Mira—because I don't have one. Listen. Stop looking at me like I'm a monster and listen to me. Have you been to the unnamed world orbiting Sirius A and B?"

"The one with the burnt surface? Yeah, I've seen it."

"That's just it," he said, growing almost fanatic. "There's nothing burned. The paradise of Sirius, the garden world they talk about as myth alone, it's all there. Locked out of each mind or eye, I don't know. I've seen it. They say it doesn't exist anymore, but I've seen it, smelled it. I've brought people there, walked through the tourmaline jungles and shown them amethyst oceans hardening on the shore, pointed at the blood comets arcing the sky like red claw marks, and held up pearls of crystalized thunder rained down from the clouds before their eyes, but they won't even believe."

"Beliefs are generally composite," Onasus said, as though to intentionally deflate Tikan. "And composites usually have a broken piece or two in them. How could you think to have a creature that operates on simples alone understand you?"

"I don't understand," Naim blurted. "What's the difference? I see Sirius all the time. The trees and the water, everything. How is it different?"

"You see it in damn metempsies," Tikan said. "That's not truth. That's not knowledge. Nothing in your life exists. And soon you'll all just be made to *know* the wrong thing. And—damn it!" Glaring at cold, uncaring space just a wall beyond him, with bared and gritted teeth, with pupils like livid whirlpools, with chest like a bursting cannon and fists clenched into maces, he stopped himself from saying more. He crossed gazes with Onasus, who was observing him with an anthropologist's belittling enthusiasm.

"But—" Mira started, and then fell silent.

She and Tikan stared at each other, both hearts agitated. Onasus took a sip of his cold chocolate, watching them from the edge of his mug.

A pillow fell from Naim's grasp. He observed their quiet moment from the side while twirling a loose strand of the gauze around his leg. He shook his head to the side as if shaking off a fly or some other nuisance, and then spoke out. "How do you even know what this guy is saying is true? His head looks cracked open. He could just be some metempsying, insane person. And Tikan, like Mira said, you don't even have a procrustus, how do you know what in the world you're talking about? Do we all just look like robots to you, or something? Idiots that can't think for themselves?"

"Why should an idiot be a slave?" Tikan said.

"It just makes life easier," Naim replied. "Can we just finish? My leg hurts. I want to—"

"To metempsy?"

They stared each other down.

"And so what?"

Tikan looked at him in disgust. "You've been dying to jump back in from the moment you woke up. Am I right?"

He did not reply.

"You're addicted," Tikan said.

"Are you addicted to breathing?" Naim returned.

"That's exactly the problem," Tikan continued, smirking to himself and looking up. "It's funny. I almost have to stop myself from laughing. I look at you and I want to weep, but I feel like laughing. Do you understand that? How ridiculous you are? If you think—"

Onasus struck his mug down on the table, commanding their attention. "Perhaps from a different set of principles, you and I can agree on this Tikan," he said. "This is the concern, yes, and why we think it so need not matter. We have our paradigmatic case of tragedy before us, indeed. But more than this, in a way that you may have envisioned only in some nightmarish thought experiment, the end looms far worse."

"Worse?"

Onasus gave them all a grave look. "Yes, worse. And this brings me to the explanation of what caused the assault on your ship. You see, when Friedrich—Dr. Farabi—and I worked on upgrading the procrustus, we did not work on the whole thing. It was not some preplanned, well-envisioned project. We were handed parts, segments. It was all in pieces, the end goal ever obscured, likely even to the murky taskmasters from above. The equations were always taken away before they could be linked to the greater whole. How to keep a scientific unity under such conditions? And yet, through his brilliance, through an insatiable curiosity that will no longer be possible if what is intended comes to pass, our dear Dr. Farabi discovered the unspeakable plot that had been unfolding under his very guidance."

And Onasus stopped, and drank again from his bottomless mug, and then paused absently.

"Well?" Naim said, looking almost insulted by the orator's long pause.

"Forgive me, but you seemed disinterested in what I was saying," Onasus returned, giving the couch-ridden man a hard look. Then he cut him off before he could reply. "It is, truth be told, that I am no longer certain I should be divulging the details of the machinations at hand, even to natural allies such as yourselves."

"What? Why?" Mira barked, suddenly jerked from her dark, pensive mood.

"Because he thinks we might try to sell his information to free ourselves," Tikan said.

Naim folded his arms and writhed in his seat. He switched his gaze from Onasus to Tikan. "Well, that's just dumb. Whoever those people were—and by the way, I still don't understand how they knew to look for your Dr. Farabi if this whole scheme is so disorganized—they won't let anyone with that kind of knowledge live."

"That's true," said Onasus. "And you would do well to remember it. As for your other question—and my, we are full of tangential questions today—let me say that you make a mistake in interpreting my account of the system's emergent plot as 'disorganized.' Decentralized, yes; not disorganized. Those black suits knew exactly what they were looking for, but certainly not why. I would bet that they were not even fully human, probably very cyberized, yes. And, whoever gave their orders likely did not know the full reason why, either. In fact, their orders most probably came in bits and pieces, too, put together by the unlikeliest of forces, you see, small enough to keep the whole obscured."

"No," Mira said, shaking her head. "It just can't be that random and lucky. They boarded us in dark space; I won't forget it. That's not something you just do on a whim based on dodgy orders from who-knows-where."

"My dear, you assume so many things," Onasus said in patronizing way. "You assume that I am suggesting luck or chance had anything to do with this: not so. You assume that I suggest the assailants did not know where their orders came from, or that there was arbitrary faith in some reasonless operation: also not so. This is no absurd gambit. The plot to murder Friedrich Farabi and extract the sensitive data on his procrustus was quite a deliberate one. Enemy of the galactic order, they painted him, probably; or treasonous scientist; or rogue, celestial terrorist, hoarder of destructive secrets. And for such a grand enemy, of course the most surgical, cutting edge methods will be employed. Boarding in dark space? Please. If you only knew half of what can be accomplished today. But those plotters are pawns, often mostly to themselves. The internal deceptions among them are all part of the puzzle as it comes together.

"When I said the individual parties are innocent, I meant only insofar as they are knowledgeable about the true ends of their actions, not with regards to what they *believe* they are doing. No, no, absolutely not. War criminals and thieves abound! Their intentions are just as rotten, but quite far removed from the greater things at work."

"So, why do you have dry blood on your face?" Naim asked almost immediately. He leered at Onasus.

Onasus twitched, but in an instant he turned his look of surprise into a half-grin. Tikan observed how he made his careful expressions.

"Tangential. Almost random—but it's all right," Onasus said, smiling. "I will answer your questions, though I do hope you come to trust me, for it is only together that we will—"

"Tell us what Farabi found, then," Mira demanded.

"One question at a time, please," he said, squinting at her again. "In fact, both are related, yes. And I will tell you the deeper story, but know that this incriminates you all even further. No longer unfortunate accessories or abettors; if you are caught, you will all be tortured and treated like me, for you will become like me: a traitor."

The gravity of the words weighed down on them. Tikan sighed, and looked around the table in an effort to gauge the others' thoughts. "Just tell us. We've come this far."

"Fine. You have been warned, yes? So be it. You see, as we worked, we quickly realized that we were developing forthcoming upgrades to the procrustus and its systems. You understand that technology trickles down at a molasses-like speed, yes? Right. Well, this was years ago, and even now we have room to breathe and scheme, for the end is far from fruition. But, that is no reason to celebrate much, for there is little but us four standing in the way, at present. But, I digress.

"We developed the technology thinking that we were working to improve the functionality of jump gates. The technology is all derived from quantum mathematics, yes, for both the procrustus and jump gates, you see; and, in fact, both are partly based on the same theoretical concepts. Although we would only become aware of this late in the game. But yes, we toiled away, looking to eliminate gravitational collapse, trying to reduce and suppress levels of quantum decoherence, racing to turn the Quantum Zeno Effect on itself so as to effectively create perpetual, self-sustaining jump gates, free of the random, spontaneous whims of the firmament.

"'Imagine it!' we declared; 'consider the implications!' we said to each other. We wanted to permanently freeze the decay in each spatial tear, and Farabi said this would accelerate travel and progress by light-years. Imagine it, yes: end-to-end tunnels live forever the instant they're pried open. All engineered to be activated by long-range burst waves, radio-like pulsations through the universe. And with the Quantum Zeno Effect in a self-fulfilling feedback loop, well, that's it, that's all. Well, not *all*, of course, but that was generally our enterprise. That was the plan, in any case.

"As our initial tests started to show promise, we were set to attempt a first live implementation on a nearby wormhole, near where they have that asteroid mining operation set up in the Belt. We targeted a set of gates close enough to each other that the mutative pulse we sent out could reach both ends of the portal within the same fraction of a second. And it worked. It's still in operation, in fact: that single, useless, permanent tunnel through space-time. A waste, really. I do sometimes think it is unfortunate that we discovered the true purpose of our endeavors before affecting a more useful route through the galaxy."

Mira gawked at him in astonishment. "Wait, what do you mean? You created a permanent set of jump gates?"

"That's right, yes."

"How? I don't understand."

Onasus paused a moment before speaking. "Do you suppose the passage of time moves all objects, or that it is the movement of objects that controls the passage of time?"

Mira's eyes rolled to the upper right. "The second, I think."

"That is correct. Time is the succession of events in the world. Now, how do you suppose these objects change and move at all?"

"Because of something else," she said.

"Correct."

"Something bigger."

"Or smaller," Tikan jumped in.

"Smaller—yes," said Onasus, anxious not to spoil the story before his would-be students went through the steps themselves. "Fundamental. Subatomic. A complex web of fundamental, unpredictably dynamic singularities whose slightest movement rearranges the whole universe built atop it."

They all paused to digest the information.

"But... what moves *them*?" Mira asked.

"Exactly! What indeed? The answer must be nothing," Onasus said. "They move themselves. Unmoved movers. It was our task to locate these gems beneath the universe, and cast our own light through their prisms."

The others stared at Onasus, each with his or her own wild set of abstract shapes and nebulae of thought flashing through the mind.

"In any case, yes," Onasus said, resuming his story. "Immediately after our trial in the Belt proved successful, the team was somewhat jumbled, the lesser members cast away, transferred or fired. A group of four remained: Farabi, myself, and two others, and we were given new work. In no small part due to the unparalleled genius of our mentor, our reassignment was to a different area of procrustic research. The department of nano-neurological auto-surgical development. An offshoot project of our scientific inquest into neuronal automation. But, this is all probably gibberish to you; let me continue.

"We did not spend much time on this new project, for it became strikingly obvious to Farabi, then, when he was afforded another thread of the procrustic tapestry, what we were dealing with. Farabi was undoubtedly the only individual to ever acquire such vast knowledge of the procrustus. Unlike your average imbecile tinkerer or death-fascinated scavenger, who toils without mortar or rope, without signpost or sun, looking for a way into the impervious fortress that is the procrustus, Farabi almost made it to the throne room. I think it was a flaw in the system that such a man was allowed so close. It isn't perfect, of course, the system."

"And so, the 'system' targeted you? Scheduled you for purging after your discovery?" Tikan asked, his eyes wide and his lips parted, staring with intense focus.

"No," Onasus said. "The reason for our persecution resides in a second, more incriminating discovery, and our subsequent actions. Once the implications became clear, once Farabi brought us in on the matter, revealed to us the grand design, he also redirected most of our resources to secretly creating a blueprint of the procrustus. This part was easy, for we had the majority of the requisite knowledge by this point, and the tumblers all fell into place. And then, once the nature of the device, both its physical, auto-ameliorating capacities and its capacity to virtually replicate mental substance, became known to us, well, we were then also able to discern the trajectory of its future upgrades."

"How did you figure out those details?" Tikan asked.

"The procrustus upgrades itself, you see. It knows its own trajectory and how to propel itself. Sometimes it just needs an extra nudge, a push. To accomplish this, external resources—researchers, events, history, works of art, us humans—are manipulated and mined.

If one can observe its architecture, and note its patterns of change...
Well, then it becomes possible to make a causal prediction."

"And so what did you find?"

"Yes, and now for that abstruse devil hiding, deep, deep down in
the details," Onasus said, nodding as though he were a teacher
responding to a precocious student's question in class.

Naim, for the moment, seemed to have fallen asleep again. Mira
was looking at the floor with her head in her hands, struggling with
her migraine again.

"Tikan, your fears at present are somewhat negligible given your
current knowledge about the device and its effects. If the procrustus
were indeed but an impartial tool, its features determined purely by
free demand, then certainly: let the human race drown in its own
stupidity. But, there is more to it than that. Not everyone is innocent,
as you have no doubt been suspecting. At first Farabi and I believed in
our own myth, that the procrustus was simply the result of an
emergent intelligence, produced by cosmic patterns beyond
observation. But..."

"What?" Tikan said. "Who are the 'they' you keep talking about?
Some group? A shadow council? Speak!"

"I don't know. They—it—someone—exists, who pulls the threads.
Perhaps inhuman, or not, or—a single source to which every
transmission we received could be ultimately traced, to no location, to
void space, and..." He trailed off.

The others felt their skins chill.

"It doesn't matter for now," Onasus continued, staring off to the
side as if recalling some unspeakable tragedy. He looked back into
Tikan's eyes. "Let me finish, and tell you what we discovered. The
procrustus' final aim, which, as I said, is still temporally distant,
though causally near, is for total unification: for the synthesis of every
mind. Decentralized centralization, you see. Each person, each node
of thought, whether in full embrace or dragged kicking and
screaming, will be thrown into a great crucible, and there all will
dissolve into each other. All minds to be forced into one, all people to
be duplicates of each other, the originals destroyed. All for one mind,

ensouled in countless bodies. And this will not be a subtle, self-inflicted disaster. It will be a deliberate act on behalf of the headless, bodiless puppeteers—and thus it cannot be allowed."

They all sat in deep contemplation and said not a word. The smell of tea and dried chocolate lingered in the air. In silence they rummaged their feelings for answers. Mira looked up, and through her agony she furtively shook her head at Tikan, who looked away lest Onasus note their misgivings.

Tikan's gaze was locked in place, and his nostrils flared to the rhythm of convictive thought. He wished that Amozagh had heard the tale, if only to hear the dead captain make a contrived remark against his now iron proof.

But the path to take was yet unclear. He felt the urge to soar out and grasp in hand every glory promised him from youth, to embark on a perilous quest and strike the deathblow to the procrustus and its world. The call renewed, irresistible.

And what of Mira, and Naim? Their consent mattered only in principle, for in practice, they would follow him to darkest space and back, irrespective of what surface anger they held towards him.

But he was hesitant. And he grew angry with himself for lapsing into such naiveté. All through the speech he had noted Onasus' obscurantist manner, the excess of opaque and convoluted language, the shadows of contradiction lurking beneath the surface.

There were no windows in Mira's apartment, or even projections of the outside. With his hands clasped together, leaning over his knees, Tikan looked out at the others. Mira stared at him, a few tears of pain in her eyes. He tried to wring out her thoughts from her expression, but it was no use. He turned to watch the empty quadrant of the room.

"I don't—" Mira suddenly said and, before she could finish her sentence, croaked in agony.

"This isn't normal," Tikan said, standing up and walking over to her. "What's wrong?"

She ignored him, shut her eyes hard enough to make crows feet appear around them, gulped, and then, through much consternation, attempted to speak again. "I don't believe you," she said.

Naim opened his eyes. All heads turned towards Mira..

"You don't believe me?" Onasus asked. "You think I'm making this all up? Inventing? No. Never. All that I have said is based on facts. Yes, I know it seems somewhat preposterous, and anyone other than dear Tikan over there will find it hard to swallow. It is also the first time you are hearing half of these words, no doubt, for I have temporarily suspended the linguistic sanctions from your procrustiis. These new words you are hearing, understanding; these fresh concepts forming —they are likely the cause of your headache. Poor creatures! Compromised by language and also deprived of its riches. Hear us!"

Naim shook his head almost angrily. "Let me—"

"And I should point out, for it was perhaps not made clear," Onasus interrupted, taking on an academic tone again, "that there is still time before the end. Yes, it is a steep hill to which all will be shepherded. First, the passions are diverted and dampened. You see this, yes? Most are made so dissatisfied with their existence that they are more content to waste away in false realities, or in doctored memories. Yes, I am talking about metempsies. You know this well enough, dear Naim.

"And more. More subtle, before the crushing blow. Notions such as taste and worth are slowly eradicated, the objective and subjective realms collapsed into one false whole, all distinctions blurred together. Names are conflated until they denote only one hideous, mutant conglomerate referent. Think on the stars, on Proxima. We call the star and its system and its capital planet by the same name. Language falls apart and gives way to simplistic propositions of want. I could go on, but you see my point, yes? It's a process of narrowing down the psyche, boiling it down and making it common. In the end, it will all be for a single being, a single, passionless host that was once manifold bodies or minds. For where is pain when all is one?"

"Each person a mere limb of the artificial 'man,'" Tikan added.

"What?" Mira said.

"Imagine a sort of meta-consciousness that treats inferior consciousnesses as resources within it, like psychic limbs," Onasus interrupted again, just as Tikan was about to continue. "The arm serves the brain, and the brain would then serve the over-brain. All would become just slavish parts of a bodiless consciousness presiding over many waking sub-consciousnesses."

"Even if the individual survives, he or she would just be a copy of a copy of an original that never existed," Tikan managed to add, somewhat vexed.

"Astute observations, Tikan. Astute. We may make a scientist out of you yet—"

"This is all…very hard to believe," Mira said.

Naim scratched his head.

"Yes, first you must understand it coherently," Onasus said.

"I *don't* understand. But that's not why I don't believe you," Naim said, alarmed. "I don't believe you because when you were out there, walking through that graveyard, you didn't care. You were just walking around like it was a park. How does that add up with what you're saying, about you caring about humanity so much?"

Mira and Tikan looked at each other gravely. Though they kept their ultimate suspicions to themselves, Naim's tactlessness threatened to compromise them all.

"Naim," Tikan said. "Let's not get into that again."

"No, I want to hear it," Naim said. Then, he, too, began sweating and blinking in pain.

Onasus cleared the sweat from his brow with his big metallic arm. Afterward, he pushed his mug away from himself, and he cleared his throat with an exaggerated gruff. "Now, that is unfair. You all hardly know me, and yet you are making vast claims about my moral worth. As for the indifference that you are accusing me of, I think this is just a perception of me that has come about as a result of Mr. Solstafir's philosophical views clashing with mine. You are all quite enamored with him, aren't you? Captivated, I should say."

"No!" Mira said, "He's killed—"

"It does not matter," Onasus said, waving his hand. "It is good to have a leader, even if he does not lead. Now, about this accusation of yours. If measures could have been taken to prevent the loss of life, by the infinite stars, I would have taken them. But I do not respect corpses, for they are not even the victims of tragedy; they are material residue. And remember, Mr. Solstafir, that you could not have escaped desolation were it not for me. So I decapitate your philosophy, just as you encumber mine, and that is how it is. But, if it offends you, I will not step on the soon-homes-for-worms, though I will not mourn either. Now, I suppose you will allow me my difference of opinion on this matter, for it is not due to insidiousness that I hold it. Fine?"

Tikan and Onasus locked eyes, and Naim squinted before turning away to watch the ceiling.

After a brief pause, during which they all sat in reflection, Mira looked up at the group and scanned each of their faces. "So why have you told us all of this?" she asked. "I'm guessing it's not just a fireside tale while we're lost in the woods."

"I appreciate your archaic metaphor, Mira, I do," Onasus said. "And I'm sure Tikan does as well. It's nice to find people who aren't completely blind to history. Well, yes, anyway, I'll explain why it is opportune that we have met in such inopportune circumstances. There is a way to prevent all of this, you see. But it cannot be done alone. There are places, places where the clock ticks, where shadows collude to bring about the end. There, the machinations unfold. There, we may reverse the process."

"And you," Tikan said, lighting up. "Have you treaded there? Have you walked the dark places of the galaxy?"

The room stirred.

Mira crossed her eyebrows and her forehead creased in suspicion. "Wait, Tikan—" She began coughing and could not finish her sentence. She made a nearly inaudible growl, got up, and paced around the room in search of a book. There was only one—an old maintenance manual that had never seen use—and she brought it back to her seat, opened it, and focused intently on a page indicating how to repair the galaxy map. The others did not notice her.

"I have. I have been one such shadow," Onasus said.

"And you can take us there? Show us the way?"

"Wait," Mira repeated, angrily staring at a page. "Let me speak. I can't weld together what's being said, if you don't give me any blowtorches or spanners. I want to know more before we go flying into broken wormholes or moons know what else," she continued. "I want to know where these places are, which shadows. I want to know—"

"You want me to tell you why Farabi is dead, and why I am here in his place," Onasus said, looking somewhat irritated. "Why we were here, and not there. I will tell you. There are two principal stations from which the procrustus is developed and deployed. In the Arcturus system and in the Vega system. There are others, too, but they are auxiliary. It is from Arcturus and Vega that the poison pours, you see, and there the antidote must be administered. Farabi and I were intending to acquire a ship from Proxima and make for Arcturus. From Mars, our two other companions were to reach Vega."

"Wait, wait," Mira said. "Arcturus? Vega? Half the planets in already conquered systems aren't even finished being terraformed yet. Proxima II is still under construction, and they're still building pseudoplanets around Sol. They've said that Vega, and not to mention Arcturus, are both too far, too risky to start development, or exploration, even. That we don't even have the resources. That going there with current travel tech is like warping to the other end of the galaxy without a way back, or to Andromeda even. And—"

"They lied. There are research posts in every arm of the Milky Way, and Andromeda is only a few decades away from exploration. The people at those fringe outposts do not expect to return. And it is entirely within our means to produce the requisite technology. Momentarily suspending our concerns for the future of our race, consider the work our team accomplished on jump gates. Had it been applied to its intended function, the possibilities for interstellar colonization would have risen exponentially. Think of it: a secure, permanent route from system to system, galaxy to galaxy. Distance would come to mean nothing on a large scale. Transport vessels such as this one would no longer meander the cosmos indefinitely, waiting for a stroke of luck.

"But that is beside the point. Your doubts are misplaced. Arcturus and Vega stations are indeed real. Think of it: you yourself had trouble believing that a dark-space boarding was possible, yet it was so. As I said earlier, my story is based on facts."

"I—Fine. They're real," she said. "So you want us to go there? To finish what you started, destroy the procrustus? Is that what this is all about? And how could you even destroy the procrustus? Each person has one in their head."

"Well, Friedrich Farabi is dead; dear Tikan handled his obliterated skull in person. And I cannot assume that the others have survived. You three seem hardy enough to complete the task, if lacking in enthusiasm. As for how to destroy the device, this is a good question. We would not touch the hardware in each skull, but the servers on which they are all dependent."

"But how are you alive, then?" Naim asked. "How come they didn't get you? You still haven't answered."

"Simple," Onasus said. "Tragic, really, that Farabi did not have the time to save himself. It is a little-known secret that procrustiis can, in fact, be removed. Temporarily, only. The connectors destroy the brain to a pulpy mush if enough time elapses without the device returned. We crafted replacement chips for ourselves, thanks to Farabi's blueprint, in case of imminent capture. A way to destroy our identities and the sensitive data on our minds.

"Well, *I* was able to make the switch in time—quite bloody business, you know—and I locked myself in a secluded chamber, and thus evaded capture. Does this answer your long-standing concern surrounding my reddened face, dear Naim? I appreciate the worry, truly, but, well, it's unfounded."

Pushing back his seat, Tikan stood up. Everyone's attention fell on him as he paced around in a small circle, hand cupping his chin and rubbing his growing beard.

"What are you thinking?" Mira asked.

"I'm thinking there's only one path from here."

Onasus lit up. "Good. Yes. That's the only real—"

"We're with you for now," Tikan said, glancing at Mira and Naim to confirm their agreement. Mira gave him an uncertain look, but nodded.

There was a vague chain of circularity in Onasus' story that bothered Tikan, though he did not pursue it. In truth, there was little about what he had said that Tikan entirely believed. But despite every such warning in Onasus' serpentine manner, Tikan would not be so easily precluded from that old destiny ever festering in his heart, in which he would ascend as humanity's prodigal champion to cast off its chains. It would do no good to make known his suspicions, in any case.

"But I want to know about your taskmasters, about those bodiless puppeteers, or whatever you called them," Tikan said.

"In good time. In good time, you will see, yes. You will see. Let's escape this smaller fate, for now, yes?"

With Onasus' help, Tikan carried Naim up to the cockpit by lifting him under the arms. Tikan's body still ached, even hours after returning from the lounge. They lowered Naim into a corner and gazed up at the galactic map Mira had once again invoked.

Mira stood ahead of them, in front of the behemoth piloting station that took up the majority of the room's lateral space. There was a human-sized slot down its center. Its metallic top was like the back of a whale ready to plunge back into the deep. This contraption flowed out into the projection of star-riddled space above and beyond it. At this time, the ceiling had been set to show the whole breadth of the galaxy, to lay out all of its clusters of dust and bloated nebulae.

She prepared herself, stretching her body and inspecting the electronics.

"We're lucky," Onasus said, pointing up at the galaxy. "Look. Yes, there. A wormhole is open. Has been for some hours. It's not far at all, straight to the Proxima system. Best head there. Approximately four hours left before it closes. More than enough time, but best not to dally, considering the poor state of our ship."

The bright purple markers indicating the jump gate Onasus had mentioned flared, and Mira advanced. "When we arrive, are we going to have issues?" she asked, stopping a moment to look back at them. "Proxima has the tightest security of all worlds. They're going to want to scan us, for sure. And if we don't get tagged there by your 'system,' I think Mr. Natural over there is going to raise some alarms."

"That's true," Tikan said. "I always stay onboard whenever we dock at Proxima. Most other places are fine with the malfunction excuse and a written manifest, but not Proxima."

After rubbing his eyes and then blinking and squinting, Onasus walked up to Mira, and stared up at the glittering ceiling. He traced a path through the galaxy map with his index finger, as if he were signing his name into the stars. "It's a good point, yes. Worry not; I have a solution, well, half a solution. The simple truth is, there will be no hiding from the authorities. They will swarm the docks, I am sure. We will lie about what has transpired aboard this ship. We'll say there was a hull breach. Some asteroid fragments too small to notice shelled us, or whatever. What is interesting about Proxima is that it's so closed, controlled, habituated—so sure that everything must fit inside the box—that anything which does manage to slip the cracks ends up semi-invisible. We will exploit this."

"And all the fusion burns all over the place?" Naim said.

"A fire. A terrible fire broke out, running through the ship, yes, and that's how the explosion started, blasting the hull open. Yes, and if we are fortunate enough, the authorities will be late in their realizations and their pursuit, and by then we will be long gone. For, yes, luckily, our final destination is not Proxima, and we will not stay there long."

"And me?" asked Tikan.

Onasus glared at him, small-eyed and tired. His face was difficult to read, as though he were at once in deep strategic thought and lazily annoyed. "And you…"

A few quiet moments passed.

"I destroyed the ship's manifest, if that helps," Naim added.

"Both digital and analogue?"

"Yes."

"Interesting. Well, that makes things easier. Good. Yes. Mira, do be good and get us through that gate. We are in somewhat of a hurry."

"And Tikan?"

"Don't worry about Tikan."

Half shrugging, she turned, and rubbed her hands together. She reveled in the shiver as she walked up to the piloting station. It whirred open in response to her presence, and she disappeared behind the closing slit.

THE MERCY OF THIEVES

I half-woke to excruciating pain bulging out of my head. The place where I had been struck, square atop the fragile cranium, was now a hot well of suffering, and I was sweating profusely despite the stinging cold. I was tied to a wooden chair. My wrists burned between the binds and felt as though they were about to snap.

Through messy squints, I saw what appeared to be an empty warehouse, gray saturating the place. The smell of gasoline fed my terrible headache. The waves of agony arrived in a sluggish rhythm, in which I tried to center myself. It was no use. The extreme discomfort of my monstrously incongruous posture disrupted that Sisyphean tempo in my skull, placing me—immobile, helpless—between two varieties of anguish.

Were the police so cruel? Was a relative of the clerk carrying out his vengeance? No. No, it was none of these. I hoped that it was some mysterious Good Samaritan who had somehow rescued me, but the tautness of the ropes around my wrists and my memory of the shopkeeper's unexplained demise had me quickly dismiss the thought. I would have to wait to learn what had transpired, and I yearned for the safety of sleep until such time. But I was denied this for the moment. My head jerked backward with each propitious dip toward kind oblivion, as though I were on heroin.

So, through great pain, I whirled my eyes up and tried to understand where I was. There was a warehouse, yes, and it was gray, yes, and unfortunately, my sight was sucked into a feverish sort of swamp where the rest of my senses also swirled. But it was nighttime; this I could tell. The same night as that of the failed robbery? Perhaps. Not much more could be discerned from the incomplete and disconnected images running in my mind, which failed to keep a coherent narrative and instead stalled and skipped at random. Only shadowy figures featured in each fleeting frame, moving with deliberate protraction, muttering baleful things. I must have groaned, for those shadows started moving fast towards me not long after I had awakened to my haze. A quick swipe from the heavier blur, and, wish fulfilled: I descended into reverie.

Like any memorable dream, I started mid-activity, present without a causal past and yet in full pursuit of some burning, preset ambition. In this case, I was swimming. Not in water, but in a void gracious enough to uphold me in planar suspension. No downward forces; certainly no gravity; no up-thrust, either. Only variable places of being that happened to coincide.

I searched for invisible threads that might have been holding me, dragging me along, but none existed. All was gray and vast. I had been dropped into Anaximander's principle. It visually resembled a purgatory under construction. Outside, my real head was aching. The murky walls of the dream's shell throbbed and kept the pain at bay.

As the dream progressed, I found myself on a small island. It rested over nothingness, bearing sand and a single palm tree, washed of all but the slightest hint of green. Like some computer-generated texture with no innards, this island did not have an underside. Though I greatly dreaded what I would find underneath this top layer, I lowered my head over the rim of the island nonetheless.

And there, below, shooting out and wrapping me up, were the cephalopodan pillars of the abyss. Non-Euclidean forms atop non-Euclidean forms atop non-forms, all rising outward at me, all beyond reason. Tractricoids without curvatures, asymmetrical tesseracts, million-celled polychora pulsating out of uniformity. Elliptical hyperboloids constructed of malformed dodecahedral honeycombs, restless against the backdrop of a tessellating pseudospheric plane in hyperbolic excess. Madness, all madness. And these descriptions are worthless. Abandon the anchor of mathematics, too.

I felt acutely, now more than ever, as I hovered over the sea of mad cogs blotting the emptiness up, my fragility, as though the yoke of my being were at storm in a cracking shell. I sank. I reached out for the ledge of the island but slipped. And there was no water, though I was drowning. I reached up. I tore and clawed and stretched through oblivion for the palm tree too readily forsaken. I needed more time. I needed the death of space.

The gray shattered. All boundaries collapsed inward and buried me in a rain of shattered glass. I felt another fist smash into my head, probably real-world seconds after the first, and I woke, infinity still burning in the back of my mind, hotter than the blood on my forehead.

Either the cranial knock or the dream must have repaired my vision, for things were less blurry when I woke again. But my focus did not bring gifts. Standing above me was that heavy shadow, now clear. A brute, large and grave. The same beast that had crushed me at the grocery store. Thick, callused hands, fingers like squashed sausage ends, body a wide Frankenstein of fat and muscle, head a pit bull's.

"*Ton nom,*" he said, remorseless garlic pouring down his breath.

"S'il-vous-plaît, I can't. I—" I whimpered, too tired to exercise my months of French education in the bowels of Paris.

The ogre gave me a squint, and then half turned to face the far end of the warehouse all shadowed.

"Bogdan," he called, farther out than my recovering senses could reach.

Cold steps clacked towards me from afar, and the thug was pushed to the side by his umbral companion.

"English," he said to the thin new figure before me.

"English. So, explain. Who are you and why are you stealing from poor old grocers? You killed that man in there, you know. Not good. Immoral."

"No, I—I missed. Someone else—him," I said, ramming my head at the large man beside me like a neutered unicorn.

"Now, shut the fuck up. Don't blame poor Esteban for this; he had to clean up your mess. It was supposed to be silent and clean. A missing grocer, easy. Esteban had to mop up after you. The bones are still dissolving in the van. Say thank you to him."

"I—"

The thin man's hand jumped, and the cold barrel of a gun was slapped across my mouth, tearing the insides of my cheeks.

"Thank you, thank you," I cried, while spitting out blood.

"That's disgusting. Ungrateful shit," he said.

"I'm not, I—"

"I said shut the fuck up." The words echoed. My vision came clearer, and I saw his thin features light up. "Answer only my questions," he said. "Who are you and why did you try to kill Luc the Grocer? Why did you come there, messing up Esteban's work?"

"Money. Revenge. Everything, everything," I replied, shaking my head.

"Revenge?" Bogdan asked, his temper cooling to frosty intrigue. "Why revenge?"

"Why did you want to kill him?" I insisted.

He slapped me with the gun again. "I'm asking the questions. What we do with our clients is our business. What you do with them is also our business."

Clients. Drugs? No, too erratic. Gambling? More to do with vultures and sharks. Protection racket. Yes. Protection racket. Now, fast, on your feet. How to win their ash-black hearts?

"Too much opportunity in this city. Too few people willing to take it," I threw from my bleeding lips, trying to gather up some guile.

Tall Bogdan glanced at his accomplice for a short while and then faced me again. For a moment, his face was caught in a lone shaft of light. He was gaunt, and scarred enough to look shriveled. His nose looked as if it were making a swan dive for his chin. "So you're telling me you are nothing more than a hungry, stupid criminal?"

I winced at his remark but suppressed my ego. I had to focus. Else, I would be washed down a drain as a sickly mush the color of vomit, like that dead grocer.

"Hungry, yes. Looking for work. Skilled. Speak languages. Educated. Can—"

"Oh, would you shut up. We're not interviewing you, darling. We're still not finished deciding if we want to chisel your face down with bullets so your mother won't recognize you," he said, with surprising elegance for a ratty criminal. "So, yes, explain. Only what we're asking. Your name. Who are you? Why that place, at that time?"

And so I spilled for him my name, and I spun a criminally romanticized version of my sojourn in the gutters. "I was drawn here because of the history," I mumbled and then spewed out the rest of the messy, contrived tale as it degenerated into drivel. "The cities themselves are the new tyrants," I said incoherently, among other asinine remarks.

They started giving me strange looks as the half-lies slurred out of my mouth. But, as the time passed, I regained my mental faculties. Somehow they had remained curious enough not to kill me, and now I thought myself eloquent enough to speak death away.

All consistent criminals are anarchists at heart, sidelined kings of the jungle in which all cities are built. Though the areas around my eyes were swelling like two fleshy goggles, and my vision was turning to blur again, I made a special effort to observe these bitter, exiled monarchs and divine from their pouting and their huffing and the winter in their eyes the source of their unanswered royal pleas.

"I mean, what were you, both of you, before this? Waiters? Bus drivers?" I asked.

"Doctor, actually," Bogdan said, finding it in himself to indulge me once without breaking the flesh of my cheeks into my teeth again. "Ophthalmologist, to be precise."

"Chauffeur," Esteban mumbled.

"A doctor, even!" I exclaimed from my splintery prison. "The backbones of society! And here you are, because you know what it really takes. Because you know that the government is just another protection racket taking your money and promising that neither they, nor anyone else will take your house in return. Fuck that. You're here, about to put a bullet through my head, because you know that that poor bastard of a grocer was like anything else you put your work into: yours. Your property. Sectioned off from the rest, to do with as you please. Why do you think I was there?"

"And you work alone?" Bogdan said, suddenly taking me more seriously, the smell of gasoline flaring his nostrils as he looked at me.

"Yes. Alone."

"You must be stupid, then. Only an extreme idiot would go around robbing Paris alone. A hundred years ago I would have called you brave. But you're an idiot."

Though he remained aggressive, it was on the verge of bruising camaraderie.

"Make me smarter, then," I said, my face like hard stone under puffy red bags. "Let me join you. As I was saying, I have skills, useful —" I continued after a brief pause.

Esteban laughed, and Bogdan drew a sidelong grin. He had a little scar running from the left corner of his mouth, which made it look almost unnoticeably disproportionate.

"No one can do that for you," Bogdan said. "You'll have to help yourself. You're a bad shot." He paused, and scrutinized me further. "We'll see," he said, shooting Esteban another sideways glance. "You'll sleep here. No, don't look at me like that, not on the chair. We're not barbarians. There's a mattress lying around somewhere. You'll sleep in handcuffs, and tomorrow we'll speak about what you can do to make yourself useful, maybe even prove your story a little bit more."

"And then maybe that interview?" I asked, the humor almost absurd as I spoke with a cannibal's crimson teeth.

"Maybe," Bogdan said, resuming a steel demeanor and turning from me.

⚜ 23 ⚜

EUCLID AND LETHE

W ithin the piloting station, Mira slunk to fill in the padded mold with each of her limbs. Layers of machinery hummed above her. She positioned herself pitching forward, as if making a swan dive for the very bow of the ship, though her head was pivoted upward and held at the neck as though in some atavistic ritual celebration. She calmed herself as the mold clasped her body, and then she breathed. Once inside this niche, her splitting headache dissipated. She smelled, for a moment, the tea on her breath, and then the burr of the machine started.

From the darkness above, needles swarmed down uniformly and drove into her head where the hair should have been, slipping into her brain to make new neural pathways in a bloodless surgery, tightening in knots until complete.

Then her vision ran at light speed to break apart the darkness that cased her and the ship and she rushed through the full range of the electromagnetic spectrum disembodied as tunnels of stars and oceans of bright dust bent and rearranged until she found full before her, shining and unfathomably wide in scope, the sight of every welkin fire unchallenged by the abyss. In her boundless vision she perceived the whole galaxy teeming. Metempsychosis from flesh into the fabric that binds the stars and from which she imbibed the platinum melting off of each sun.

And somewhere in the celestial frenzy, Mira remained, pursuing a tear in the weave. Somewhere far away from her new mind, all astral ecstasy, hidden away in some insignificant place, the ship buzzed and roared to her will. Somewhere, near that same desolate place, she felt herself coming apart. Somewhere, the ship may not have held. The hull might have broken apart; and what a sweet death it would have been, to be cremated and scattered on the fire map of the cosmos.

But the portal drew close, and the ship labored on. Through that tear, forms bent into non-forms, Euclid drowned in Lethe, and Mira felt herself reduced back into her flesh.

~

While Mira piloted the remains of the Equuleus through the heavens, Naim sank into another metempsy.

On this occasion, he was a bard and assassin named Visage. He was on a dire quest to slay a tyrant in his keep. He was travelling with a number of armed companions. One was a mercenary, another the wizened hero of a politically divided empire, and another a farm boy caught up in events beyond his reckoning. They marched together through the forest bordering the keep.

As crepuscular rays began shining through the leaves, Visage began to sing. He sang of Moerven, their hooded leader; of the branch-shaped scar across his left eye and the eye milky white; of his longbow, whose carved runes shone in what was left of the sun, and his arrows gleaming like solid mercury. He sang of their sylvan trek, of the autumn and the gossamer. Of the meadows glutted with the blood of a nation. His companions wept, for his words were unlike words they had heard before.

By nightfall they had infiltrated the small fortress. One man had fallen to his death off the parapets. Three others had perished in a furious battle to prevent a contingent of guards from sounding the alarm. Swords clattered to the ground. Blood streaked the fire-lit stones of the corridors. And Moerven himself succumbed to a mortal blow during this battle. He had lunged to intercept a sword thrust intended for Visage's back.

In this particular metempsy, the character of Moerven was always scripted to die in a number of possible ways contingent upon his presence in the keep and myriad other conditions. Though Naim had witnessed Moerven die dozens of times before, Naim's mind and identity were not Visage's. Visage was brokenhearted. He wept over his leader's body and whispered an elegy that made the farm boy weep. He scavenged Moerven's bow and his arrows and sent the farm boy home.

Visage snuck past the remaining guards. In the blue moonlight, he used a grapple and hook to climb the highest tower of the keep.

He crept in through the window, and there found a crimson and gold room littered with jeweled trinkets and gold goblets and a mirror framed by sapphires. An old man was asleep on a four-poster bed, which was surrounded by a veil.

"Justice," Visage called out, sitting on the windowsill and aiming one of Moerven's arrows at the old man.

The old man awoke peacefully. He shuffled up and sat on the side of the bed. Visage could see the outline of a long beard and flowing hair. The old man was little more than a silhouette behind the veil.

"Will ye speak the truth, or shall justice alone inherit thy final testament?" Visage called out.

The old man began to laugh to himself. Visage's skin chilled. Though Naim had encountered this same old man as many times before as he had witnessed Moerven die, some deep, subliminal part of him could feel that something was different about this encounter.

Feeling something terribly wrong about the old man, Visage loosed the arrow at him. "For justice, and the truth," he yelled, still locked in the metempsy's narrative.

The old man's silhouette turned towards him, and from his rasping throat emitted a laugh far more sinister than the previous, as if it were transcending the very fiction of the metempsy and addressing Naim instead of Visage.

The arrow rent the veil, but dissolved past it, leaving no closing wound. The old man, still sitting on the side of the bed, reached out for something on the bedside table. Visage loosed arrow after arrow, but it made no difference. Dread began to flood him.

The old man got up from the bed, still cackling with the knowledge of some terrible evil, and thrust his hand through the veil. He held up a small mirror to Visage.

Visage dropped his bow and his arrows and he drowned the room in a scream, his horror so complete as to paralyze him. Naim's consciousness convulsed. The old man's face began to distort in sharp, digital spasms. As if afflicted by an ontological virus, the whole room began to shimmer and warp like the old man's face, while Visage trembled still before the mirror's reflection.

On the ship, Naim's body was convulsing, too. This was not altogether unusual, as powerful metempsies usually had this effect on the body.

Onasus placed a hand on Naim's shoulder.

Tikan went to him, too, and slapped the back of his head a few times. "Wake up."

❧ 24 ❧

SOL VICTUS

N aim emerged from his metempsy to find Tikan's figure before him.

"Have we arrived?" asked Naim. He was sweating profusely. He looked to the side and frowned, trying to recall the end of his metempsy, but soon abandoned the thought and looked back at Tikan.

"We're about to pass through the jump gate," Tikan said. "Look."

They all looked up at the galactic map above them. Within seconds, the geography flickered into a new arrangement.

"Is that all?" Naim asked, unimpressed.

"What do you mean, 'is that all?'" Onasus returned. He was leaning back on his elbows against a thin shelf, and his head was tilted upward at the transformed map. "Do you know what we've just done?"

"Yeah, of course. I just always thought it would be...Slower, you know. More dramatic, or special, the first time I *saw* it for real. It just looked like we skipped over. In metempsies, when I swim through wormholes, it's like swallowing the world. Didn't take half a second here. More real in a metempsy."

"Not for her, though," Tikan said, pointing at the rumbling mass Mira had entered. "We have the map, but she sees the real thing."

Onasus sighed loudly as he pushed himself from the shelf and walked up to the center of the room. "Quiet, both of you. It's there, our destination: Proxima I. And look: Sol Victus, that red, drowsy beast. Marvelous. Did Akhenaten ever see this second sun in his nightmares? Do you see it?" he asked, pointing at the glass sphere of Proxima, which was approaching in the frontal projection.

Off the shoulder of Proxima's dome, there came a crimson gleam. From inside the glass, a white center shone out at them.

"A monument to scientific triumph," Onasus said. "Yes, many small details they had to work out. To redistribute the surface light as it radiates down on the dome. It solved the problem of tidal locking, you see, so everything wouldn't freeze over at the unheated end, yes. Green plants, too! Would have been black without the intensifiers. And people really do want their green scenery, you know. A marvel, a real marvel. The last one, perhaps. Sol Victus, ah, Sol Victus. O, how his brother dreamed..."

"Though he sleeps more deeply now," Tikan murmured cynically.

They neared the glass-wrapped core, and the kiss of the conquered sun reached over the curvature. This ruby wave washed over them, momentarily blinding them.

When the view came clear again, the ship's nose was almost touching the planet's outer shield. Out of the glass, an airlock spun open, and the ship hovered into the maw agape.

❈ 25 ❈

THE DOCKS

At the docks, the crowd ahead of Sielle was swelling. Down it came, the ruined ship, gliding in through the rim of the airlock and provoking looks of disgust in the spectators below with its dented gray and scratched silver hide and its black burn streaks, looking like the casket of a galactic giant.

With the glass sparkling under their feet, the spectators began clustering together on the platform beneath the ship, watching it with perfect confusion. Already, some were sweating and stirring, with their eyes fidgety in their sockets. Others were smiling and calling out their perceptions. Someone even reported the sky to be shattering. Across each platform in the interconnected structure, people gossiped, speculated, and gave false testimonies and rabidly sensationalized explanations.

"This world is metempsy, too!" one yelled.

"I don't believe. I don't believe. I don't believe," another, who looked more frazzled than the others, recited like it was some mantra.

Some only looked up with their mouths open, as though they had been cast straight into an impossible fantasy. A woman with red hair and a lilac outfit had her eyes shut hard, trying desperately to induce a metempsy and escape the trauma of surprise. The more temperate of these pedestrians watched the ship in silence. They skeptically wavered and stepped away from the nucleus of the crowd, as if unwilling to partake in some new blasphemy.

Sielle, meanwhile, swayed at the edge of the crowd and continued to watch the society wake from its sedation. Through the clamor, she slinked through a gap in the crowd.

And then, from the corner of her eye, she saw figures in hard, gray uniforms pouring in from a hidden casern to meet the crowd.

"The sentinels!" someone called as they arrived.

Sielle stood on her tiptoes to watch them over the crowd. Though she had enough wit to discern Proxima's homogenous police force for what it was, she could only guess at what lay under their visors, or at the functions of their suits.

In fact, the grayness of the sentinels was not some poetic statement about their voided hearts, if they had hearts, but rather a practical consideration: whereas they looked like men or women in armor to the naked eye, they could take on any terrifying appearance to one whose brain was procrusted; and the color gray served as the best canvas for this totalitarian art.

The sentinels stopped at the edge of the crowd. They formed a ring barricade before the vessel as it completed its docking and evened itself out against the side of the platform. The noise of the crowd surged up again, and then ceased instantly, becoming muted huffs and sighs of disappointment.

The civilians all stood bewildered and perplexed, turning and rotating in place, scanning above, below, and around as if the ship had disappeared. Suddenly, the docks were enveloped in utter silence, and each individual stood up erect in place, eyes emptily aimed at the sky. Sielle copied them until it was over.

Afterward, the sentinels began herding the pedestrians away from the scene. Some people resumed speaking as they exited the platforms.

"Not for us, it looks like," one woman said to another as they walked from the crowd and passed Sielle.

"Shame. Would have been nice to see what was inside," another said.

Though they looked consternated, the people made no protest. Emptying the platforms to near vacancy within minutes, they dispersed faster than they had come. Sielle looked at the fleeing crowd and back a number of times, trying to understand what had happened. There was now a different congregation formed around the ship, one made up of those gray, dark-visored sentinels. They hankered about its side like jackals around a fresh corpse.

Sielle yanked one of the last men leaving by his shoulder. "Excuse me, but what just happened?" she asked.

"What?"

"With the ship. Why is everyone not interested all of a sudden?"

"What do you mean?"

"I mean, everyone was excited to see what happened to it, and now they're just leaving before finding out. It's still there. They're about to find out what's inside. Don't you want to know?"

"But it's not still there," the man replied.

"It is."

"No. It was, and now it's gone. They announced it."

"Gone?"

"Yes."

"Does that happen often?"

"Of course it does. It wasn't for us. Is this the first time you've had a—"

Out of nowhere, then, one of the sentinels arrived and, with a crushing grip, he swung her conversant around by his shoulder. Before the man could call out, the sentinel lunged at him again and grasped him by the mouth, squeezing his cheeks together.

Sielle stood without moving, jolted to attention.

"This area has been marked for clearance due to an unauthorized perception. It is illegal for anyone to remain and attempt perception. Furthermore, the utterance and recognition of unauthorized perceptions is strictly forbidden under Clause XXI of the..."

The sentinel hauled away the man without so much as a glance at her. Stranger, still: there were now other sentinels swarming past her, completely oblivious to her presence.

Sielle took a careful few steps backward. From a new and more distant vantage, she saw a group of those hoary authorities as they stood abreast of the steaming vessel. Standing in an idle row, each was the exact same height as the other. Others continued to patrol past her without noticing her at all, one almost bumping into her, even. She snorted a laugh and with a wide grin watched them mill about like drones, protecting the invisible and also ignorant of the invisible.

She walked closer, then, to those sentinels standing in a row not far from her, to conduct a brief experiment. She stepped in front of them, craned her head close to the darkest visor, and made exaggerated motions only centimeters from it.

Nothing.

A small, vicious laugh escaped her as she drew back again. She fought the compulsion to cover her mouth, and instead let her cackle ring out. No one so much as flinched. These editors of perception were little more than prisoners, unaware of which side of the bars they were on, or of the outer cages and cages they operated in, only a layer away from the most central jail.

With a mocking wave of the hand goodbye, Sielle turned in time to hear the piston-burst of a ramp shoot up in a glittering hurry from the edge of the platform and run into the side of the docked ship. The sentinels charged up in single file, drew their rifles in a swing, and pointed them at the ship's egress.

Sielle stood in plain view and watched. The sound of releasing pressure rang out to her, and the fuming round gate of the ship split apart to reveal darkness and the glint of bronze behind it.

An unnaturally long moment followed. Her senses slowed and absorbed the orange light bursting from the ship as if it were dawn's sun, and it sent her into a sudden crippling stupor. Creeping, slithering, something ineffable was gyring within Sielle. The shifting of a long and unbroken season, the flutter of autumn's final leaves accelerated to decay, the whisper of time tunneling down her ear; a tide of desperation rising up from the wells between her shoulder blades to swallow, to snuff out her spirit, all as that metallic corpse of a ship steamed open at the side to reveal a coppery gold spark. As though a ghoul's frozen hand had risen from her stomach to clasp her heart.

The feeling worsened, and she staggered backward across the gulf between herself and the ship. She hid behind a silver column, against which her heart could crash and her lungs could heave, though still she peeked at the ship. She breathed and made fists that reddened her hands, but still her dread, which was colored the same as a distant strand of memory, entered the marrow of her bones.

The pile of sentinels at the ship's exit throbbed. Meanwhile, the bronze light at the egress shimmered and burned through the mob. The sentinels made their robotic recital, the same one Sielle had heard as her unfortunate conversant had been reprimanded.

Then the golden Apollo emerged: a man in a brilliant environment suit, thick as armor and reflecting the full brunt of the sun as it flared red.

Her heart's labor threatened to crack the pillar. The sentinels recounted laws and pointed their weapons, but they might as well have been heralding that warden of the sun as he made his upright, confident stride down the ramp. From behind her buffer, Sielle squinted and looked past his gold aura.

There, behind the bronze man, three others disembarked. They were battered and dirty. One man was limping and leaning on a bald woman; the third man was black-bearded and gaunt. They marched down surrounded by guns. Then the armored man made a wave of the hand, and like puppets the other three overtook him. As the brightness of his suit dimmed and the others came closer into sight, her heart relented.

There was no wind to cool Sielle's face as she began to calm down. The sentinels surrounded their captives in a tight circle and marched them away from the ship.

When a slight gap opened in this lasso of guards, the bronze man thrust a shimmering arm into the back of the bearded man, shoving him out of the group without word or recoil from the sentinels.

Though he was discreet, it was not a careful maneuver. It even seemed as though he had pushed the man with some degree of contempt. Nonetheless, the bearded man stumbled out and walked away from the group.

Still in the malfunctioning eye of the authorities, he took a moment to gather his bearings and redress himself. He looked back at his companions and then headed in a stride for the city below.

Now free of her inner din, and cooled of her tumult, Sielle returned to her solemn mood and found herself overwhelmed with curiosity. Who was this golden-carapaced man, spidering into her memories? Where had this ship come from? How had it been removed from the public perception? And, most pressingly, why had she and the black-bearded man remained invisible to the sentinels?

For a few moments, Sielle adopted again her Nordic persona. As the huntress whose boots were caked in the blood-stained snow of a mountain now eons away, she tracked and followed this equally invisible fugitive fleeing across floating glass platforms, his feet trailing sky diamonds, down into the throughground.

Always an expert step behind, she pursued him to the throughground loop dock, where she heard him say, "Road Sixty-Three." When the throughground tube arrived, she waited for him to board and then hurried into another compartment, ever careful to stay out of his field of view. Seconds later, they were both whisked away down the windy tunnels of Proxima, away to Road Sixty-Three.

26

THE CHASE

The man she was following appeared to be lost. Out of the station, he had stomped away in a determined beeline, and then walked street after street, through various passageways and alleys, marching with a knowing gait and yet turning innumerable times to rethink his steps and retrace his path. He was more like a child attempting to prove himself a capable explorer than anyone with a clear destination. Most aggravating of all, he appeared resolved not to ask any passerby for directions, perhaps out of that same small arrogance.

She followed him until it was clear beyond a doubt that he was lost and unwilling to be found. Somehow this irritated her immensely. She had been in the city less than a day and had encountered no problems navigating it. They were beside Road Fifty-Two. The street signs were clear, even to an outsider. The man nonetheless refused to quit his loop between Fifty-Two and Fifty-Nine. Enough. Sielle strode over to him across the street, her shoes clacking.

"Sixty-Three is over in that direction, two rights and straight ahead," she said to him, pointing to the right, her face in his and her nostrils flaring.

"Excuse me?"

"Sixty-Three, where you're going. It's there."

His eyes widened, and he suddenly had the look of a man who had just had a spear run through him. He sprinted off down the street. Half amused and half frustrated with his paranoid manner, Sielle turned her palms over in confusion and then ran after him.

With the sun's evening rays swapping through gaps between the buildings, she chased him through the incarnadine night, across narrow streets and through shadowed alleys. Had Sielle not spent the last few years hunting hares in the snow, she may have missed him slaloming the streaks of sunlight on the ground and shifting like a misshapen cat into backstreets.

In the midst of a snaking alley complex, the man turned a fast corner. Sielle bolted after him, but then stopped short midway through it. There was no sign of him. Only a long shadow corridor with a bright exit lay ahead.

She sauntered towards the end of the alley, breathing hard, looking left and right. There were no other exits, but still she could not find him. For a moment she considered the possibility that she had, at last, encountered another being like herself.

Sielle stopped at the end of the alley, on the fringe of blinding light. When her eyesight adjusted, she could see that the alley led to a secluded cul-de-sac formed of glimmering towers and starkly dying shadows. Believing she had lost him, Sielle relaxed and began panting over her knees.

Had her eyes cheated her? The man had certainly entered the alley. Short of some hidden sideways passage or ladder, he could not have escaped.

Suddenly, she heard a flurry of steps behind her. Before she could react, the man reappeared like a piece of the wall made animate, and pulled her into the alley, restraining her against his chest and cupping her mouth with his hand.

"Who are you and why are you after me?" he snarled into her ear.

Sielle slammed her elbow into his gut and slithered out of his grasp. After spinning around to face him with a feral look on her own face, she considered shedding the world right then, but a glint of fright in his eye made her reconsider.

"I'm not after you. I don't care about you," she said, straightening her tunic out. She advanced on him, and gave him a long look. "Why are you running away? I know they can't see you. I watched you escape. They couldn't see me either."

He frowned. "Who are you?"

"I just want to know why they can't see us. I don't care about you or where you're going."

The man coughed out a few breaths and relaxed somewhat.

"You mean the sentinels? At the docks?"

"Yes. I was standing in front of them and making stupid faces," she said. "I thought it was funny. I was even laughing about it out loud and nobody even noticed me at all. They ignored you, too, when you got off your ship with those others they took away. What was all that about?"

He paused and exhaled loudly. "Were there other people there before, watching the ship dock?" he asked.

"Yes, yes, they were all excited and waiting, and then they just ran away, saying your ship had disappeared. One person who was still standing around talking to me even got carried off. Why?"

"And you could still see it? The ship?"

"Yes, of course. Perfectly fine."

"And you don't know why that is?"

She held her tongue. His skepticism became obvious on his face and in his posture, in the way he was almost circling around her with his slack arms akimbo.

"No. I've been dizzy lately. I—"

"Tell me, where are you from?"

She frowned and raised her shoulders. "What does that matter?"

"It matters, because you might be the only person in the galaxy who doesn't know the answer to your own question."

Her face went red. She looked left and right, like a fugitive about to be discovered. For a moment, the anxiety she had felt at the docks bubbled in her stomach. She could always exit, remove herself. But the planet still teemed with mysteries, and she could not now excise herself from such wonder as this shining ball of artifice hanging in the void. And there was a peculiar sympathy in the man's face, something that kept her tethered to that world for moments longer than she otherwise would have been.

"You don't have a procrustus, do you?" he asked calmly. There was even an odd glimmer in his eyes, hope of some kind. Sielle took another step back, her back now pressed to the wall.

"It's okay. I don't have one either," he said, letting out a comforted sigh.

They searched each other's eyes.

She squirmed against the wall. Beside her, the threshold of the alleyway seemed to extend outwards into the cul-de-sac. The call of survival snarled at her. She closed her eyes and—

"And that's how they do it," he continued. "Through the procrustus. Parts of your brain can be inhibited or altered by it from a distance. My friend—one of the people who was on the ship with me —he blinded the sentinels, and they blinded the civilians; but you and I, we can't be affected by it."

"The bronze one? He made us invisible?"

"The what? Oh, the suit. Yes, him. He has his ways."

"I see," she said, placing a hand on the wall adjacent to the alleyway.

"What's your name?" the man pressed.

"Don't worry about my name."

"Names are important."

"Not if you already know what they mean."

He shook his head, grinning. And for half a moment, she betrayed a smile.

"Tell me, what do you see, there?" he asked, pointing up at the sky opposite the sun.

"What? Why?"

But he did not look back at her. "Just tell me."

She followed his finger up to where it was motioning. A shining point in space. A glowing swirl of marble dust wreathing in on itself.

"A whirlpool," Sielle said.

"Andromeda," said the man, his face now beaming. "And there?" he continued, pointing at another location in the heavens.

There was a bruise on the skin of space, overlaying a group of stars.

"That's a nebula," Sielle said. "I've seen them before."

"So, you're not nobody, then," the man said. "You have the marvels of the galaxy at your feet, unedited, unadulterated. How many can say the same?"

Where others would have seen just a reddish haze of a night, Sielle had found on Proxima the last frontier of humankind, the last jewel in Earth's old stellar crown.

"My name is Sielle," she said, relaxing her shoulders.

"It's good to meet you, Sielle," he said. "I mean that. I really mean it. And so, what are you looking for, running around on Proxima?"

"All of this," she said almost absently. "The stars. This cold luster. What's happened here? And you. What were you doing on that ship? Why don't you have one of those crustaceans?"

Still beaming, the man laughed lightly to himself.

"What's so funny?" she said, grimacing at him.

"Nothing. Nothing at all."

She remained silent and eyed him.

"You know, it's a dangerous set of questions you're asking," he continued, letting the joy seep away from his countenance. "They run deeper than you think, especially in this city."

"I told you, I'm not from here. I'm just passing through."

"None of us are from here, really," he almost mumbled. "We're all just passing through."

"Whatever that means," Sielle said, rolling her eyes. She saw him, then, as aloof and lost, as she had first seen him, abandoned in the city. "I mean it, though," she continued. "I won't tell anyone. And you're not going to put me in danger or anything like that, if that's what you're thinking. Like I told you, I'm leaving this place soon."

"Really, though," he said. "You're making it sound like you don't know how anything in the galaxy works. I'm not stupid. If you've made it this far without a procrustus—what are you, twenty?—I'm sure you already have an idea or two."

"I'm from Earth," she said firmly.

"That's not saying much."

"You're not saying much, either."

He stopped a moment and crossed his eyebrows.

"I don't think you really understand what you're asking," the man said as he shook his head. "If you're alone on Proxima, I think you're more in need of a friend than a hurried story."

"What makes you think I'm here alone?" Sielle asked, raising her voice and stepping forward.

He gave her a look of incredulity. "There's a universal price to pay for keeping secrets, we both know that."

"Of course I know about keeping secrets."

"Then we're alike."

"I doubt there is *anyone* like me."

They paused.

"So…"

"So, listen," he said, even calmer. "Let's stick together for a while."

"No."

He looked dismayed. "Where will you go, then?"

"I don't know. Why do you care?"

He did not respond. He now seemed to her no threat at all; simply an innocuous romantic too knotted up in ideals.

Very subtly, he had even started behaving like certain other men. The distant, intense look in the eyes that spoke of retreat to some fantasy; the way his limbs all seemed to react and point to her movements as if they were metal and she were a magnet; the constriction in his throat as if to control and redress the tone of any word that might pass through; the overly correct rhythm of his chest rising and falling, as if his lungs were mechanized. He was, even then, abstracting away from her, stealing moments of her particularity as pieces for some ideal assembling in his mind.

The moonlike luminosity of the city under them enrobed her as she ceased retreating and walked away from the alley. In response, the man extended his hand out to her.

"I have to go," the man continued. "The others will be waiting for me on the other hemisphere, and I have to pick something up before I go to them. The address you overheard—Road Sixty-Three. Come with me. I can't idle here longer."

Leering, Sielle took a moment to consider his offer. "If I come with you, I want you to explain all of it to me. The ship, the crustaceans —everything."

"Once we're on the move, I will. Your questions are difficult, and they need time."

His hand was still extended, the sweat dried from his face. Sielle she sighed through her nose.

"And what's *your* name?" she asked.

"Tikan."

"Come on, then, Tikan. You're obviously not going to find the place you're looking for by yourself," she said, walking past him and bumping into his clumsy gesture without acknowledging it.

27

THE CHESS OF EXISTENCE

The morning after my ordeal at the warehouse, I awoke to a dulled thumping in my head, child of the lava fount that had sprung there the previous night. The iron scent of blood was under my nose and almost ashy in my mouth; and a great, fuzzy ache was in my right arm.

Forgetting the rusty handcuffs around my wrist, I tried to rise, but was immediately restrained, and fell against the coil-pierced mattress. Sunlight burned through the warehouse windows. Shutting my eyes again, I tried to dive in for more sleep.

But with a sudden kick in the gut, my eyes jolted open to the sparkling chaos of the glass window above me.

"Wake up. Time to talk," said Esteban.

I squinted. The sun outside looked subdued by fat wintry clouds. Esteban groped my numb arm, unshackled it, and then pulled me up. With my headache still crowning me, the giant dragged me out of my corner and through steel doors at the end of the warehouse.

"Ah, you," Bogdan said, appearing at the end of the new room. He was sitting in a circle of foldable blue chairs and consorting with associates, all of whom were new faces to me. "Come, I want to speak with you," he continued, breaking out of the circle and moving towards me as the others continued their meeting. "There's a thing you can do to make your—application for joining us, let's call it— easier. That's what you want, yes? To join us? Yesterday, you were not just making a stupid bargain for your life? I'm correct in interpreting the events this way?" he said intensely, his face close to mine for added menace.

The night of the robbery seemed epochs away. Like some foggy and embarrassing memory, some drunken escapade attended to by a now sober mind. Though the thought of my stolen laptop still prickled me, it was being overshadowed by a new set of ambitions.

"Yes, that's what I want. I can do a lot for you. I want to be a part of this," said I, the philosopher-ignoramus, the redeemer-deceiver, the savior-murderer.

The plan slowly unfolded in my head. No, I was not lying when I said that I wished to join them. To thieve and extort and whatever else Bogdan and his merry band did. It was the fastest way to recover.

Note, that it was not for greed. I was never merely in search of great riches, for any man who takes these as ends in themselves is a fool. What I required was the freedom to return to my contemplating. And I did not need much to support myself: a place to stay, writing tools, and food. These could be furnished by Bogdan. It was nothing but a stroke of luck to have met him.

Yes, for there I was, outside of society, destitute, torn between transformations, between beast and god. What other paths could I have taken? No, it was worth corrupting myself slightly, if corruption it truly was, for any filth on my soul would be washed out and countered tenfold—all corruptions sanctified in the purity of the ideal at hand. In the end, if I could recoup through the travail of honest crooks—honest in their ambitions, that is, unlike Pierre the financier, reverse Robin Hood and self-delusionist extraordinaire—I would be doing myself, and thereby the world, an invaluable service.

But all this justification I add in retrospect. There was no moral dilemma. Just a theoretical argument I entertained for the sake of keeping my intentions sharp.

No, I was not morally concerned in the slightest. How could I be, when knowledge and freedom, the ground on which morality rests, were as yet unresolved? Consider it this way: I had to perform so-called immoral acts in order to solve knowledge and freedom, for only with knowledge of what was immoral and freedom to choose otherwise could I be sure of what never to do. And, just as some fellow skeptics have previously bracketed their doubts for some provisional ethics, so did I thus masquerade as a utilitarian for the sake of convenience.

In any case, morality—whether the eternal prism catching all the lights of heaven, or the helpful fiction we chased through the muddy labyrinth of lawmaking—was such a confining trifle.

It is true that the vast majority of our dirty horde must be shepherded so as to keep things practical and moving; but those, like me, whose intellects and rational powers soar so much higher as to make us the shepherds—well, for us the glass of conformity was shattered long ago, never to be repaired. The scope of law could never keep me in its universe. They would have had to devise an entire legal system for me alone. And still it would not have been sufficient.

No, I had no need to justify myself. At this stage, I had not yet resolved my renewed existential queries, either—and that was a far more pressing issue. I should mention, at this point, that a number of varying possibilities had started to enter my mind.

First, I considered what it meant for others to be unreal as people, or created solely for the purpose of my perception. It meant that, in some sense, there was a fundamental difference between the nature of my existence and of theirs. It also meant, insofar as they were objects in my lonesome sandbox, that my existence was superior to theirs.

But, of course, I had no proof for any of these enticing thoughts. Cursed proof! Cursed proof. Proof: flimsy, false, ethereal fugitive, hiding at the end of a regress that runs out the world itself. No need for proof.

Still, and this leads me into the second consideration, if my existence was special or solitary in some sense, then I would have to consider theirs in relation to it. So perhaps each person was a facet of myself, a creature filling up the greater monster. Esteban, my violence; Claude, my resourcefulness; Pierre, my greed; Madame Hugo, my sexual repugnance. Not that they all represented me, but that they were objects possibly in me, or objects projected out of me to be hated and alienated; or to be approached, like Sophia. And I— the *me* in all this—I would be the central, abstracted command; that which experiences itself, which perceives itself, which thinks itself. Thought thinking itself, yes. In that case, I would be immortal: a god.

Yet, arriving at the second point, if I was indeed a god, I had to force myself to admit that I had no memory of creating myself—that in some sense, I was a defective god. Or, as may seem the more likely case, that still there was a higher power beyond me. And this consideration stung me, sent me squirming within my own mental toilings.

"Ok. Good," Bogdan said. "Then you'll do some work for us to show you mean what you say. There are some people, some rats. You'll go with Esteban and get rid of them. If everything goes well, you'll start with us—small, but a start."

I turned to give Esteban a blank stare. I was harshly sobered by the implication of murder. He fishhooked me under the arm, and led me out of the warehouse and the gaze of its dull, stained windows.

~

"Where are we going?" I asked Esteban, breaking an hour-long silence in the old Sedan. I pushed myself against the tight strapping of the seatbelt. The smell of dust rode the waves from the heater and worked to stuff my nose.

"Clichy-sous-Bois," he said without turning his head.

I slinked down the seat to form a limp posture, relishing the constriction of the belt. The trip wound on in further silence. We drove from the warehouse district and neared the suburbs that lay beyond. The car hummed.

"Who are we going after?" I asked, to no more than an unrelated huff.

Soon the belts would shrink back into their slots and I would be loosed on the individual. The fuel for truth, for brilliance, was perhaps the blood of a wretch—perhaps, and so be it. Sustenance would come—and freedom?

In the car, under those strict belts, I felt the weight of freedom.

Esteban slowed the car as we entered the housing project and expertly wove us through. Each building dripped the slag of clouds off its side, which turned to jagged stains before reaching the ground. We wheeled through the empty streets and found brighter clouds rearing behind the buildings and promising the sun.

"Out," Esteban said, parking across the street from an apartment building and twisting the key from its hole with a jangle.

I stepped from the car into the cold and shivered. Rows of slim windows lined the building ahead, with vestigial satellites hanging from their lips. The whole place looked as if a disease had laid waste to a once-vibrant community, leaving the homes to rot with the corpses. Tombs for rent. Live-in ruins for denizens of this age.

"Was it always like this, here?" I asked Esteban as we walked.

"No," he replied.

"What happened?"

"First riots. People wanting more. They riot, but it is worse if they win. Then nothing, and people forget."

"Why riots?"

"I don't think anyone remembers."

A pallid blue streak ran up the side of the building like some beam of prayer calling the sun to flush out the sky. The color faded to wan and finally turned achromatic before reaching the roof.

Maybe Esteban will do it. Maybe all I have to do is watch.

We crossed the gravel and entered the building.

Inside, the halls were brown with grime and lit only by what daylight was allowed through. A few addicts rested in corners or against the walls beside apartment doors.

Esteban marched down the hall, with me in tow. A hammer started loud work in my chest. In the grocery store, I had missed my haphazard shot, and the whole escapade had been chaos. Far from the night of the robbery, now, this was murder determined from a rational distance.

I tried to distract myself as we walked by examining coats of graffiti on the walls, as though they were hieroglyphs or some other ancient language; and as though the persons littering the floor were the ruined progeny of those scribes. Many of those corridor dwellers were sleeping in dark, wet clothes; others crouched and stared off or whirred their eyes in place. Behind every other door I could hear the sounds of children quarreling or watching loud television. All throughout, it smelled of cigarettes and urine.

"He's behind this door," Esteban said.

The door imposed itself on me. Its flaked jambs, its rusted knob. The frayed welcome mat, written in both French and Arabic. We were far from the exit, up many stairs and deep down the maze of halls. We stood before the threshold of ghastly transformation.

"What do we do?" I asked, my thoughts trailing behind my voice. On the verge of trembling, trying to masticate away the dryness in my mouth, I waited for a freak incident to remove me from the coming trial.

"You take this," he said, pushing a handgun into my breast, one uniformly black and larger than the relic I had taken from Claude. "I break the door. We go inside, and you shoot him. Okay?"

"Okay," came from my mouth. "But—what if he runs?"

Esteban gave me a bored look that lasted long enough for me not to pursue the question. Then he turned to the apartment. I braced myself and waited for him to knock.

I expected the victim to present himself unwittingly at the door for a quick bullet to the gut. But, without warning, Esteban drove his bovine leg through the door, smashing it apart in a flurry of splinters. And then it was my cue. Nothing was as I had envisioned it. This was the freedom I had, freedom from any grasp on the future. Beastly

Esteban frowned at me from beside the entrance. He took me by the shoulder and pressed his gun into my left kidney.

As soon as I stepped off the welcome-mat, the scent of cigarette ash and tagine wafted over me. Dark moldy carpet, stained kitchen floor, and half a toy lying by the entrance. I aimed the gun at the ceiling. I heard feet shuffling ahead. How could I hope, now, for a serendipitous escape in this cramped place? Just as I made my way into the tiny living room where a family had no doubt once crowded the couch, I looked back at the entrance and saw Esteban standing morbidly on the threshold, his gun pointed at me.

There was a closed door on each side of the living room. There was muffled panting coming from the center of the room.

I stood there, behind the cheap couch, all red twirls on white, and torn up as though it were the object of some fencer's practice sessions. It was situated in front of a bulky television more than three decades obsolete. It was no use trying to moisten my lips.

"J'arrête," rose out from the other side of the couch. The voice was painfully familiar. "Aujourdhui. J'arrête," Karim repeated.

I peered over the couch and began to feel sick. He was sitting there in a ball with his back to the front skirt of the couch, unwilling to look at the intruder he seemed to have been expecting. His face was in his hands, either in prayer or despair. The windows were open, suffusing the place in light. He still did not see me.

It was unfortunate. Certainly, it was Claude who had brought this innocent soul in on his drug trade. Claude, distributor of fine poisons: *he* had long ago given up his rights to life. It would have been a simple matter to dispatch that bastard: drug dealer, gun peddler, desolator of lives, scum of the earth. Friend. And here was another friend, another, albeit newer, drug dealer.

The knots in my head had me turn to Esteban, prepared to say, "He said he would stop," but I wrenched myself back at the last second. *Are they not all part of me, anyway?* Corrupt parts of me to squash, yes. Arguments in my subconscious. Pieces in the chess of my existence, of all existence. Mere pieces, hah! It was necessary for me to proceed.

I drew the gun and pointed it at Karim's head. I was sweating so much it almost slipped out of my grip. Cold nights in the metro flashed in my head. Scenes of laughter. Shadows cast by makeshift fires. Broken French rattling along with broken English. A creak came from the door to our left, where two obscured figures watched from a slit into the other room.

Karim was startled and spun around to me. He fell backward in confusion. His arm came outstretched, his palm facing the gun. I took a step forward. His mouth opened, "*C'est moi, arr—*"

It was necessary for me.

Through the head, twice. His blood and brains jetted onto the dirty carpet, the television, and the wall behind him like the tossed meal of a spoiled infant. As he fell backwards, his freshly dripping skull landed against the floor to bubble a pool.

And fast, loud, a young woman flung the door open and ran out, wailing, with tears streaming down her face. A man followed her out and rushed me. One, two, three, four, five, and my ears were ringing, and the man was dead on the floor with a red well for an eye.

Rattled by the kick of the gun, I paused, and watched. The girl stopped, and in her doubled grief, she screeched an utter rejection of life, frantically switching her gaze between the corpses, confused as to which to collapse over. A sister or daughter to my former friend, perhaps? Probably. I executed her as well. A hole through the throat, before she could compose herself.

I breathed rabidly and careened my head around to survey the scene. How far the aspiring scholar had fallen; how far he would have to climb to recover himself.

"Okay," Esteban said, wearing the same bored look.

He walked up to the corpses, drifting into the fuming carnage with ease, and then faced me. I stood, shaking, dripping, the gun still aimed at where the girl's throat had been.

"Go wait in the car," he said.

I turned, and walked to the doorway, passing the dead toy on the floor that alerted me to the likely presence of a child hiding somewhere in the apartment.

But I didn't care. He was just a part of me, in any case.

28

ARCHITECTS OF THE NIGHT

Proxima's steel shone as Tikan and Sielle walked through the streets. The night sky had brightened, and the sun loomed ahead on the horizon, its face reflected across the avenue before them.

While Tikan's speech began to border on monologue, the sun flashed them repeatedly. His hands were aflame, painting pictures and stressing enunciations into the air in front of him. Even the way his sleeves hung off his wrists told of some history of crushed ideals and heroisms.

With her gaze firmly aimed at the pavement throughout, Sielle was engrossed in his tale. It had not taken much pressure from her to make him speak. Despite some initial misgivings, he had been unable to help himself.

During the course of their walk, he had detailed the invasion of the black suits, the death of his friend and captain, and the ensuing troubles. In a few hurried mumbles that Sielle likely did not properly register, he also glanced over an explanation for why a certain fatal gas was not deployed at the crisis moment, and he then dove into recounting how he had marched through rooms of vacuum to meet the perturbing scientist named Onasus Loptar.

"What was it all for, though?" Sielle asked, as the tale wound closer to the dire lecture Onasus had given them shortly before their arrival on Proxima.

"A procrustus," he replied.

Sielle raised her head and squinted in concentration, before looking at Tikan. "What's in a procrustus, exactly?"

"What?"

"I vaguely understand it, but not really."

Tikan paused. "It's okay, Sielle," he said in a carefree manner, like a teacher willing to forgive a lying student. "You don't have to pretend. I'm in the same situation as you. I've been in the same situation as you almost as long as I can remember."

She glared at him. "I'm not acting. Why should I be acting?"

He stopped to look at her. "You don't think I'm stupid, do you?" he said. "Come on. Like I told you, I don't have a procrustus either."

"I grew up on Earth, not here."

"Proxima, Earth—it's the same everywhere."

She did not answer. She refused to look at him.

"It's okay, really," he repeated calmly.

"How could I know about all of that? We hid from it."

"You wouldn't have been hiding if you didn't know what the problem was."

"You sound proud, for someone who hates it so much."

He shook his head. "Maybe. Doesn't mean I wouldn't have it otherwise."

"Why?"

Unwilling to dignify the question, he gave her another incredulous look. "Tell me, where did you really grow up? I've scoured the whole galaxy for a free haven."

Sielle did not respond, but instead continued to gaze obstinately at the pavement.

They strode on down the sidewalk. As they ascended an incline in the road, they were met with a rusty skyline composed only of skyscrapers looming in the near distance. Row upon row of them, aligned like townhouses, but soaring and silvery and reaching so high as to almost kiss the glass dome.

Then, just as Tikan made a sound to begin speaking despite her rebuffs, she interrupted. "I did grow up on Earth." Her eyes flickered, and she restrained herself from biting her nails midway as they travelled to her mouth.

"And?"

"And, that's all."

"That's not fair, Sielle."

"Like most things."

Tikan's expression was almost blank, though he creased his brow. "I don't want your secrets if they're secrets," he said. "God, isn't it hard enough? It's you I want to know about." He paused. He did not believe her, though neither did he doubt her sincerity. It was not an easy thing, after all, to invite trust in the eye of the red sun. But in truth, it was her very reservations that progressively worked to dissolve his own caution. "I suppose you've never heard of the Hephaestus Act, either?"

"I've heard of being polite, and not asking too many questions to someone you've only just met."

"Okay, let's talk about the weather then. It's bright out, don't you think?"

She smirked. "Yes, it's bright and horrible. Someone forgot to turn off the sun at night."

"I bet one of those buildings is the switch," Tikan said, pointing at one of the skyscrapers.

"And how many people do you think it would take to turn it off?"

"You mean to push the building over?"

"Yes."

"I don't think you could count. It would probably be better to have one giant hand."

"It's crazy how tall they are," Sielle said. "And there's so many of them."

"That's because architects are crazy people."

"Why do you say that?"

"I don't know. How many times can you try and hit the sky until you realize there's no end to it? On Earth, you can't even see the stars anymore, the sky's so crowded. That's why they built that glass bubble, I bet, to keep the architects from losing their minds."

Sielle laughed. "You sound like the crazy one."

"Maybe I am."

They walked on.

"I'll explain it, the procrustus, if you're being serious," he told her after a while.

She afforded him a glance, and nodded appreciatively. "Everyone talks about it and it sounds like an electronic computer chip in the head."

"Well, you're not far off. It does work a little bit like a computer, though not really, and I don't think it's electronic. It probably started off like that. I don't know. Nobody really knows what it is; it's more what it does that's important. I guess the best way to put it would be that it's like an organic automaton. Not an animal, but not a machine, either."

"Frightening."

"Very."

"And what does it do? I mean, what's the point?"

"Facilitate life. Enhance life. Or, so they say," he said. He took in a deep breath and then spoke a recitation long revised in his mind, which few had ever cared to listen to. "On the surface—meaning, as far as most people know—it provides auxiliary functions to the mind. Interstellar neuronal reception, some limited mind-to-mind telepathy, distinct visual data storage, perceptual enhancements, memory storage, instant access to banked data or publicly accessible information, procrustokinesis, metempsies, et cetera. I can't tell you about the experience, of course. But the way I always understood it was that it's like having a separate mind glued to your own mind, one that's supposedly a slave to your thoughts but that's also more mechanical and reliable. Memories stored in a procrustus are never forgotten, for example."

His voice rose, and he began to sound as though he were speaking from a podium. "But which memories?" he continued. "How can you remember something if it never happened? It implants every word they'll ever know in one discharge when they're children—but what language? What is language, then, but just one block, turned on or off? Do those words refer to anything, mean anything, or are they just sounds for machines? Where are the words, if they can't be forgotten or learned? They're forbidden. All the procrustus ever did was let people abandon the world to live mostly in their heads. Well, not really their heads. That's the problem, isn't it?"

"It all sounds like a nightmare," she said sincerely, turning to him at last.

With a look of surprise, Tikan could not help himself, then, from adopting a slight smile. She was crossing her eyebrows in deep worry, and in that expression and those uninflected words, she shone out the arcane act of pure understanding, born of words or expressions but ultimately transcending these—the sort of communion that was dead with history, and therefore ever barred from him. "The longest nightmare," he replied.

"And does the night ever end on this planet?"

"On occasion. For certain...events. I've only seen it once."

"Like what?"

"Like more nightmares," he said, trailing off again.

There was a pause, in which Sielle resisted the urge to ask more of him on that subject.

"Okay, so there was some important information on one of the passengers' procrustuses" she said, interrupting Tikan's brief daydream.

"Procrustiis," he corrected her.

She nodded hurriedly, slightly irritated. "But, what was it? Some guilty thoughts he had? And why are you running around here, now?" She looked at him intensely, as though she were about to unravel some grand conspiracy.

Taking a long breath and staring off, Tikan did not answer immediately. He stopped walking and watched the avenue sparkle as though the horizon had garnet teeth. "You're better off not asking me. Especially you."

"What's that supposed to mean?"

"It means—you can never die."

"You're not making sense," Sielle said.

"That's all right," he said, walking on towards the skyscrapers.

Sielle was flung into reflection, squinting at Tikan in suspicion. They had only known each other a day, and already he was making cryptic, grandiose statements about her.

As they continued their walk, Tikan observed her from the corner of his eye. It had begun not long after he had learned that she had no procrustus. Tikan, who hardly knew Sielle or her history, and whose sleeves were ever streaked with his heart's blood, had started taking her as a blank canvas on which to project his own idea of her.

And this idea was, insidiously, an abstraction he made out of her. To him, she was becoming the living symbol of his cause. Despite her flesh and her mind and words—rather, due to these—he began seeing her as a mere ideal of humanity, a fleshless world-soul containing in her the essences of each living person. A spirited, thinking person in a world dispirited and mindless. The torch-bearer and the posterity. The reason, the final cause. In her he saw some image of survival in the ideal unity of freedom. And in some sense, as the moment lingered, it was as if he were aiming his gaze through her, beyond her, and not quite at her.

"Why are you looking at me like that?" Sielle asked, instantly resurrecting the adversarial mood of their conversation.

Tikan himself was not conscious of this idealizing operation, and in truth, her real and ideal selves—her status as subject or object— routinely battled and exchanged places in his mind. She was, after all, too strikingly individual to be so effortlessly generalized. "We'll talk," he said. "About the ship, about the procrustus—all of it. But not now."

"Fine," she said, dismissing him. "And, about that address, it shouldn't be too far from here."

He caught himself and made a low, gruff sound. "Yes, should be one of these buildings. Onasus described the area as a hexagon of silver skyscrapers."

"And Onasus, he's your friend in the golden suit? The scientist?"

"Yes, that's him. Although, I wouldn't call him a friend."

"Why not?" she asked, a slight, almost unnoticeable quiver in her voice.

"He's...difficult to read."

"I—" She stopped herself.

"You what?" Tikan asked, as he noticed her sink back into a sullen mood.

"I think we've arrived."

They walked up to the entrance of the apartment building framed by pale gold arches. The rest of the entrance was chiseled silver in the fashion of dreams belonging to certain industrial visionaries and architects who once reached for the sun by means of its own beams and whose bones had been dust for centuries. Bold geometry and slick rectilinear craft that prized symmetry above all. Rows of this same grand entry repeated identically until the road's end.

They climbed the stairs into the lobby. Inside it was dark as ink. Columns jutted from the walls and shot up out of sight to tenebrous heights above, where gargoyles could have been serving as wardens.

As they walked to the elevator, it dawned on both of them that even the unceasing night outside was brighter than this inner cortex of shadows. They peered into the obscurity above them, trying to discern what looked like the stacked rows of an ossuary. Soon they came to feel that this place, devoid of windows or even artificial lighting, seemed rather like a shrine where the true darkness of Proxima, and therefore man, had been preserved after being imported like excavated marble or pyramid stone from the foulest regions of ancient space and time, which have never borne a stellar nursery or crypt, and to which no iris-shaped nebula has ever looked.

There were no others around. Sielle paced in small circuits as they waited for the elevator to arrive, gazing up at the unending ceiling, while Tikan watched her.

The filigree gate opened, and they stepped into the gold carriage. It was so brightly lit inside that they were almost blinded. The extreme contrast to the murky lobby seemed some odd psychological trick played by the architect. The elevator's walls were narrow and intricately gilded at the edges, and it had large mirrors facing each other so that the reflections could transcend each other to infinity.

The doors clanged shut, and Tikan ordered the fiftieth floor.

"What does Onasus want you to get?" Sielle asked, standing aloof in the elevator as the sound of passing floors zoomed beneath them.

"Parts for some device he wants to build. He said something about it skirting procrustus modules and seeing the universe as it is."

"And you trust him?"

"No."

"Then why are you taking orders from him?"

Tikan smiled at her but shook his head. "Ask me again on the shuttle," he said. "Let's get this package first."

"Fine."

The elevator stopped at the fiftieth floor and opened to another corridor of subdued color which fast replaced the opulence of the elevator. The pair walked out and strolled on through the hallway. They stopped before a segment of wall marked with a dull number *fifty-six* at its head. There was an analogue doorbell on the wall of apartment fifty-six, which no other apartment had. Tikan shrugged at Sielle before pressing it.

"Who is it?" came a muffled voice.

"The seer," Tikan replied.

"And what does he see?"

"Only what he's made to."

There was pause, during which Sielle circled around impatiently. She bounced off the walls with her hands behind her back. The sound of her heels against the floor resounded down the hall. And before long, the door swished upward, and a hand rushed out.

On seeing this particular motion, Sielle was stunned by an intense feeling of déjà-vu. The person appeared for only an instant, and did not show their face. They pushed a heavy chrome briefcase into Tikan's chest before vanishing fast behind the door as it fell shut again.

"That's it?" Sielle asked.

"Looks like that's it."

"So, where are we going now?"

"The shuttles. To Onasus' safehouse on the other hemisphere. They should be on their way there by now, too. He said it would only take them a few hours to be released. It's not too far to the shuttles. We can probably walk there."

"Fine, then. I hope there's a good view of the city from up high," Sielle said, as they walked back towards the elevator.

～

Two hours later, they were standing single file in line for shuttle departures with other persons, each of whom bore a frosty, vacant look. They were being funneled down a tight corridor that ran somewhere above the ground level. It was altogether not too different from the throughground system, although much more controlled.

The men and women of Proxima, looking like drained and gray replicas of ancient sculptures, slugged between the specular walls of the corridor, towards the whizzing of small transport ships docking and departing ahead. Children did not wander in boredom, but rather moved in tow on the short sleeves of their parents. Everyone besides Tikan and Sielle had their heads mostly facing the ground, and their legs seemed synchronized as they advanced. At the end of this robotic march, their cradles arrived like the carriages of Earth's old theme park attractions. The ships swooped down, against half a panorama of the city beyond. The elbow of a distant constellation looked as if it were burying itself into the horizon.

There was little speech, save for the brief and dispassionate chatter of a few. Tikan and Sielle, meanwhile, snuck nefarious words to each other, and gave each other sideways and adventurous glances, and stood and stepped furtively like footpads or like an eloping couple. Every one of their movements left behind it a kind of charge in the air, an afterimage of their rippling, marble souls.

"This is torture," Sielle muttered.

"I agree."

"Doesn't anyone else feel it?"

"Their minds are deep in metempsy. If you ask any of them, they'll say it's to pass the time in dull moments, but really, that's how they spend most of their lives. Have you seen the children aching about without it? The adults are just as addicted. Oh, and a metempsy is a—"

"I know what that is," Sielle interrupted. "I asked others."

"I see."

"But," Sielle said, "why don't they just have machines feed them so they can do it all the time? Metempsy, I mean. It sounds like that's all anyone wants to do here."

"I'm not entirely sure, to be honest. Maybe the mind needs some kind of anchor. It's probably easier, when every metempsy's different, to keep a fixed identity by having a 'real' ground somewhere."

"Interesting. And sad," Sielle said.

"Yeah, I think so."

"They could at least listen to music, or something."

He turned quickly to her. "Music? Have you heard music before?"

She grew apprehensive and replied slowly. "Yes. My mother found an ancient device that could play it, when she was young. We used to listen to it together."

"I've only heard music twice," he told her. "An old friend once pilfered one of those same devices from a derelict freighter drifting out of Sol's orbit. It sounded like blood bursting from a heart. Fountains of blood gushing through a supernova. Or like dying, really dying. I cried when I heard it, both times. I couldn't help myself. It was like hearing for the first time."

"I understand. I sing to myself sometimes, but it's not the same."

"No, it's not. But them," Tikan said, waving his finger about at all those metempsying in the crowd, "they only ever listen to music."

"What do you mean?"

"I mean, there's always music playing in their heads. Theming everything they see or touch, or do, or metempsy. Always running in the background. It's the one thing I'm jealous of."

Sielle looked at the crowd and noticed that their heads were all bobbing subtly out of unison, or their heels were tapping the floor, or their open palms were drumming their outer thighs. It was no passionate reaction to galloping drums or furious cellos, but a cold, bodily response to the mathematical rhythms burned into their psyches.

"Don't be," she said. "Too much music ruins music. And anyway, there's a difference between music out in the world and music only you can hear. If only you can hear it, it's like being underwater. It's all you can hear and it drowns out every other sound. Every thing loses its individual sound, and it dulls the whole world that way."

Tikan nodded at her contemplatively.

While she was half daydreaming, a man bumped into Sielle, pushing her slightly out of synch with the advancing line. She turned to the man and gave him a vicious look, but Tikan gripped her shoulder before she could respond.

"Don't cause a scene," he said. "We're going to have a problem enough as it is getting a shuttle."

"A problem?"

"Yes," Tikan said, as he and Sielle finally came close to the platform at the end of the line. He sighed. "Since neither of us has a procrustus, we're going to have to steal someone's spot. Otherwise the shuttle won't recognize us."

She frowned. "That sounds difficult."

"Not if we do it right. There aren't any sentinels here, and—"

But, just then, a newly docked shuttle cracked open, and out poured a band of gray sentinels. Tikan felt a great frost emanate from his heart. The sentinels disembarked and marched with their same menacing gait, but they did so entirely unaware and unexcited.

"Damn," Tikan said. He straightened his slackened posture, and his eyes darted about.

"The problems are coming to us both ways," she said.

"No. Not a problem. Just wait."

They stepped forward. The end of the line was drawing close, the whimper of cycling ships loudening. Gray sentinels abounded, patrolling the mouth of the passage, scanning the boarders for mental papers.

Tikan began sweating.

"They can't see us. It's fine," Sielle whispered urgently.

"These people could, though," he said, pointing at the pedestrians. "The sentinels can see through their eyes if they need to. And I'm sure they all probably have my name seared into their heads by now."

"What, then?" she asked, all agitated. "Let's go. Let's go back. Your friends can wait."

"No. We're going to move, fast, and take a ship. By the time they figure it out, we'll be gone, out of here. Not now—just wait. Not the ones boarding now. These three ahead of us. As soon as their shuttle door opens."

Another shuttle departed, leaving only two more parties left to board before Tikan and Sielle. The line advanced like one great mechanical centipede.

"You're not making sense," Sielle said.

"Listen," he insisted. "What do you think's going to happen when the line gets held up because a ship can't take us? The sentinels are right there. Can't afford to have people wake up. While they're still deep in their metempsies and their bodies try to board, we'll have a chance to cut ahead and get on undetected."

She looked at him in confusion. "But they'll find out anyway once we take off. What's the point, now?"

The sentinels had taken up positions at the very edge of the platform.

"They probably won't realize what's happened," he said, without much confidence.

"You're not listening. We don't have to go. We—" But she stopped herself, and her face went blank. "Oh, fine. But now, then."

"What?"

"Now, this one," she said, taking Tikan by the arm and dragging him into a sudden run. Without further warning, she stomped ahead and jostled two people in front of her. She slithered the both of them through the party of three still waiting in front, unconcerned with

Tikan's gasps of unpreparedness. They bumped a few of the sleeping drones in line, though none woke.

Meanwhile, the sentinels were stationed ahead like a dual firing squad.

Without much grace, Tikan copied Sielle's slanting and shifting movements and jangled the chrome briefcase along as they slipped through the remaining crowd and the guards. None of the sentinels so much as moved.

The shuttle arrived and opened its gullwing door. The dawdling pedestrians intending to board were rousing from hallucination, about to embark.

Just as one of them stepped forward to board, Sielle elbowed him in the ribs, almost knocking them all down to the city below. They made no reaction save for small grunts, as their minds lumbered back to their bodies. Tikan and Sielle dove into the compartment and slid over its leather seats just before the door shut.

29

SIRIUS

In the almost lightless cabin, Tikan and Sielle adjusted themselves in their seats and panted. Tikan squirmed in place to find a comfortable position, and Sielle nestled into the corner opposite him.

"What was the rush for?" Tikan asked.

"The two trying to board looked clumsy," she said, controlling her breathing. "Looked easy to knock out of the way."

"Okay. Fine. Fair enough," he said. "We're probably safe."

"Won't they just keep looking for you?"

"I don't know. There are probably patrols around. But there's no strategy to any of it, just brute force. We don't exist enough to show up in their system."

"If you say so."

There were no windows aboard the shuttle, and it was shadowy as some clandestine meeting place.

"So much for the view," Sielle said. "I know you said that people aren't awake very often when they wait for things, but it seems silly for this place to be so dark."

"It makes for an easy metempsy when there's little to sense. But it's okay. The flight isn't very long. Just a few hours. You could always try to use your imagination instead."

The comment made Sielle smirk, and then laugh softly. He had not intended it as a joke, but her laugh was infectious to him, and they both chuckled in the dark. Still, Tikan continued to writhe in his seat, restless by long habituation.

"Does every world look like this?" she asked him. "This is the only planet I've visited other than Earth."

"Yes and no. Do you remember Andromeda and the nebula I showed you in the sky?"

"Yes."

"There are whole worlds like that—alive and vibrant, like living jewels. I've been to one of them, orbiting the twin suns of Sirius. I don't know if humanity discovered these worlds or engineered them, but a long time ago, long before I was born, it was decided that we should not experience these things."

"Because it takes away from the power of metempsies if you can actually find beauty in the world," Sielle said. "That's what I'm looking for," she continued, yawning and coiling across the seat. "Beauty in the world."

"Yeah, I think that's right. The whole planet looks like an inhospitable, scorched earth if you have a procrustus."

Tikan waited for Sielle to respond, but she remained silent. It seemed to him, after a short while, that she had fallen asleep curled up in her corner. He did not speak for fear of waking her. He sat in the dark and rubbed his thumb against the corner of the briefcase.

As she slept, he pondered. In his imagination, he built up a vision of the oncoming events. A melancholy journey to the edge of known space, the pride of true flesh and spirit held high, off into what he could only conceive of as vast halls of whirling, ominous towers, the cells of each mind lodged in spiraling pylons of electric ichor. Hall after hall of dark objects tessellating the colors of storm. And behind each peeled layer of shadow, the presence, the illusive force, the council, the hidden masters. There, he would arrive and liberate the mind from its manacles. All without praise, his name driven into glorious obscurity.

"You're leaving, aren't you?" Sielle asked, still curled sideways, breaking the silence and Tikan's spiraling daydream.

There was a lengthy pause.

"Soon, yes," he said. "I can't stand this place."

"I understand," she said softly. "I don't like it much either. I mean it. Not just as a joke. There are no clouds here, and there's no wind or snow or grass. Just a few fake trees and buildings that look like they came out of a factory. And the sun looks tired. It looks broken. But that isn't why you're leaving, is it?"

There was a lull as they faced each other. It was as if they were intoxicated by the shadows around them, which prematurely gave her face the scars of life's meridian.

"Even if I didn't have to leave, I'd leave," he said. "Like you said, we're walking on a planetary grave, we're on the crust of a wound that festers faster than it heals. And, well—nothing."

"What?"

Perhaps the time had come to speak of ill things. Perhaps she was the correct audience. He parted his lips, prepared to whisper the void to her. But he could not. No, he could not find it in himself to lay the weight of time on her. "Nothing. Don't worry about it."

She glared at him. "You said you would tell me everything once we were safe and travelling."

"I did, but this isn't about that."

"Then what?"

"It's something personal."

"It sounds to me like it's all very personal to you. But I still want to hear it," she said.

"I'll tell you we're going somewhere far from here, and from Earth."

"To do what, destroy the procrustus?" she sneered.

He did not answer, surprised that she had jumped so quickly to the truth.

"That's selfish," Sielle said.

"Selfish?"

"Yes. Everyone looks happy the way things are. It's all ugly to me, but what do I care, if that's how everyone wants it?"

"I wouldn't call what they have happiness," he said. "And even if it was, it would still be disgusting."

She paused a moment and ran a hand through her hair. "Then isn't it better for you to just get away from this world?"

"Get away from it? To where? The last place I have is my own head!"

"To that garden world, or somewhere like it."

"What, run away? Look at this cold life I've led! There's a reason for it. And if there isn't, I'll make one. Don't you feel the same? Don't you think it's possible for life to be good and meaningful?"

Sielle exhaled. "Everyone I've known has used those words differently. 'Good' and 'meaningful.' It sounds like nobody actually knows what they mean."

He puffed up his chest defiantly. "Then let words fail, but let them fail between us," he said, pointing at her and then at himself. "When language breaks and I'm alone, it's a thousand glass shards for me to step on. But is there anything better than the ache of two people who can't express their selfsame feeling?"

She did not answer at first. Tikan's heart hammered in his chest as unspoken beliefs continued to pour from him, thoughts he would not have shared even with Amozagh. And there, opposite him, humanity was listening.

"What you're saying is confusing," Sielle replied.

"Why?"

"I feel as if you're saying it's good to suffer in some ways, although you're sick of suffering yourself."

"What I'm saying," he said, righting his posture, "is that people are un-free to be good, to suffer, to be happy, to mean anything."

She almost laughed. "So you're just doing this for freedom, and meaning?"

"Sort of. What, you think freedom isn't real, is that it? That's what Onasus thinks."

"Oh, no," she said. "I know that I am *absolutely free*. That's what I find funny, that you're trying to free *freedom*. You're looking for something you, especially you, out of everyone in this world, already have."

He huffed at her incredulously. "What world have you been living in?" he asked. "You saw it most today. People don't even have the right to their own perceptions. And me? My cell is sky, land, and horizon."

"Aren't you freely speaking now?"

Tikan sighed. "What I mean," he said, "is that it can't be just an illusion."

"No, it can't."

"And it can't just be a little bit of freedom, not just the freedom to choose between metempsies."

"You're wrong," she said, shaking her head. "You can never cut off a piece of freedom. Nothing changes that. Every slice of time is a new and free world that carries over the past only so you don't go mad. I'm definitely free. And you? Some of you isn't your choice, I can see it, but it's built the you that made and will make choices. And the procrustus slaves? They're all free, too, it looks like. They could have followed your way, or you could have followed theirs. They're probably just happy the way things are, and they probably just don't care about 'meaning,' or whatever else."

"No," he said. "What are you saying? Of course they haven't had any choice, not after the Hephaestus Act. And it's much more complicated than that. Even before the Hephaestus Act, for a hundred years you could barely find anyone who hadn't already volunteered to be procrusted. We were conditioned into it, made to like it, made unable to see the world any other way."

"Then why aren't you like them? You're not that old."

"Because I wasn't free to—"

"You know, I've heard my parents, throughout most of time, begging and crying about freedom. It's pathetic. Asking for freedom is admitting that you don't have any. And if you complain about not having it, then you're shouting, 'I will never be free,' to the world. Even if you're tied up and thrown into a dark room, you're still free."

He paused for a short while to consider what she had said,

reclining somewhat and staring at her face, which looked as though it were lit by a flashlight below. "No, I don't understand. What you're saying doesn't make sense, not about any freedom worth caring about. Freedom is more than a choice between drowning and immolation. More than some cogs turning behind my mind."

"That's a very silly way to think about it," Sielle said. Enveloped in shadows, she inspired a chill down his spine. As if she were, in that moment, the avatar of some cosmic Pythia. "Using words like 'more free' and 'less free.' The measurements of something are not that something. And you can't even measure how free someone is because everyone is always equally free, at all times, in all situations. There will always be different and infinite and better or worse options to choose from. The choice between water or soda, between this memory to recall or that, between extinguishing a star or not. Each requires the same freedom, not more or less. And if I thought the way you did, I'd say all those choices make me unfree, since I am forced to choose."

"So I'm free just for existing?" he asked.

"Yes, in a way. All castles are made out of the playground's sand. The only real castles are the monarchs who built them. You are free for existing with me."

He stayed silent and stared again beyond her dimmed face, which was becoming slightly damp with sweat. "Fine, but then it's meaningless to talk about freedom. Meaningless to talk about meaning, or purp—"

She got up suddenly then, startling him. Out of the darkness she leapt across the short distance between them as though shapeshifting into a panther or some other extinct creature, and on her knees she mounted him and pressed her forearm into his neck. Her hair lightly whipped his face. "You're free," she almost barked into his ear.

As he was confronted with the scent of her hair and the pressure of her fingers on his shoulder, he said nothing, but breathed up at her.

She pressed his neck harder, until he began coughing, and she put her forehead to his. "Isn't this freedom? I could kill you right now. I could choke the life out of you and steal your choices and make your meaning mine," she said. They remained in that position for a few tense moments like two embers being smothered. Then Sielle spoke again. "Until you can look at yourself with the eyes of God, stop talking about being or becoming un-free. I forbid you." Then she released him and slunk back to where she had been sitting.

He coughed and kept his eyes on her, just as she watched him. He had some trouble gathering his bearings. Their mere contact, violent or otherwise, had at once destroyed all of his heavy thoughts. He felt enlivened, and at the same time fragile. As though a long-hidden dimension of his flesh-bound condition had at last been uncovered.

And the words she had spoken had struck him. No one had ever spoken to him like this, not even lost friends with whom he had tried to discuss the vague references to such ideas he had found at one time in his reckless youth.

They sat opposite each other in silence and tried to control their breathing.

Tikan leaned back into the darkness, and waited. Still keeping his gaze fixed on Sielle's gaze, he lulled into solitary reflection. The shuttle's hum seemed to louden. The orange lights of the electronics twinkled around them like concentrated, final sunsets. The muted intensity between them seemed, even then, insoluble. The briefcase fell on its side. Across from him, Sielle shifted to the other corner and stretched her legs again across the seat.

"I want to see the garden world," she told him. "That's where I want to go."

"I can't."

She laughed. "There you go again, acting un-free. What's stopping you?"

"The procrustus—the galaxy. I want to see where Onasus goes. I want to see his masters and kill them. I want vengeance and I want—"

"To do what?"

He remained silent, holding his head in his hand and shaking his leg. Though he had, for nearly a day now, been building her up as the mere representation of an ideal, a mere vessel holding in her all of humanity, during their last conversation this pure abstraction of his had been deflated, and he began seeing her for who she was in herself.

"Forget about whatever that spider told you," she said. "I know he's a spider. Don't ask me how, but I know it. Don't let his gold suit fool you."

"I know he's a liar. He's probably even responsible for what happened on the ship. But he thinks I believe him."

"And so what, you want to follow him to his nest? Tell me, Tikan, what does this world have to offer you, and what do you have to offer it?"

He sighed in exasperation. "I fought for years without ever getting a chance like this. I owe it to myself. I owe it to—"

"No. No, no. Stop that. You owe yourself just the future, and nothing else." She spoke firmly, and waited a moment to let the statement sink in. "Now tell me, where were you supposed to go to?"

Tikan hesitated, her ideal and real selves alternating before him. "To Arcturus."

She shrugged.

"It's supposed to be an unconquered system," he continued. "Onasus said the procrustus is controlled from a station orbiting it, and from another orbiting Vega. He and I are supposed to go to Arcturus, and Mira and Naim to Vega."

Sielle grimaced, her face direly re-sculpted in shadow. She sighed. "Let me see if I understand this right. He wants to split you and your friends up, send them off to an abandoned system and take you with him alone on a ship? Of course he knows you're the only reason your friends are alive. They won't make it a day on their own; they'll probably get invaded midflight the same way your ship did. And he'll probably put a knife in your back when you're not looking. Come on, Tikan. Did you really think it was possible, this crazy plan? Arcturus this, procrustus that. He just sounds like he wants to use you for something, nothing to do with the procrustus or freedom or anything. And it sounds like you just want to throw yourself in the fire so you can say you tried to do *something*."

Tikan said nothing.

"He told you exactly what you wanted to hear," Sielle continued. "And—"

"And..."

"What?"

"And he knew I didn't have a procrustus, though I never told him."

Tikan put his hand through his hair and shut his eyes, gritting his teeth.

"Do you need any more proof?"

"You're right. I know you're right. And I don't want to stay on this planet any more than you do," he said. "But if there's even the slightest chance..."

She caught a glimpse of his consternation and knew in that moment that she had convinced him. "Come with me to Sirius. Forget this madness," she said.

"What about everyone else?" he said, trying to convince himself. "Why shouldn't they see the garden world, or Andromeda, or the nebulae?"

"You want to spoil the world on Sirius by letting everyone else have access to it too? You think every person is worth the other?" Sielle said. She shook her head. "Let's go, you and me, and leave them to their metempsies."

Tikan thought of the stars burning furiously beyond the shuttle. Even if he could find resolve enough to persist on his flimsy quest, he could not now abandon Sielle. Whether as the ideal of humankind he had so hurriedly affixed to her, or as the enchanting human being now embodied before him, he was compelled to stay with her.

He briefly considered bringing her with him, introducing her to Onasus and the others, and therefore compromising her as well. He discarded the notion at once—besides, she would never agree. For a few moments, he even tried to reconcile his principles with abandoning the quest, but then he saw her face shift out of the darkness and knew that the truth was simpler: he would sooner destroy the galaxy than lose sight of her.

"Fine," he said after the tense pause. "But if we do this, we're doing it my way."

"Whatever that means."

"It means no rushing into shuttles and risking getting caught. I can't do much against the sentinels if they find us."

"Okay," Sielle said. "I trust you." She repeated the words over in her mind, and wondered whether she meant them.

Tikan, meanwhile, still had a concerned look on his face.

"Stop worrying," Sielle told him. "I know this probably meant a lot to you. Sirius will mean more to you."

Tikan sighed again, but this time partly out of relief. "We're going to have to go underground for a while, until I can find a way to get us off this planet."

He tried to glimpse her expression again as it shifted in the dimness.

"We can always try to steal one of Onasus' ships," Sielle said.

"No. No stealing."

"He's evil, though."

"I don't even know if that's true. He just can't be trusted."

"Trust me, he's evil. I'm certain of it."

"Still, no. Besides, neither of us can pilot."

She sighed. "Then how are we going to get off Proxima?"

"We'll have to find an amenable enough captain willing to smuggle us off. We'll have to find something to bargain with, too."

"We could start by selling whatever is in there," Sielle said, pointing at the chrome briefcase at Tikan's feet.

THE CANNIBAL'S TEETH

The months hurried on after my trial of initiation in the suburbs. Time ran at night-speed, pushing me down a course at full mast between mountainous tides and with thunder against the gloam. Remorseless, remorselessness for it all. But in truth, the memory of that messy business did haunt me for some time, even as similar situations arose not long after.

The blood, the fragments of skull, the wailing—why would Karim and his friends bring such misfortune upon themselves? Regretful. It was regretful that humans were so prone to violence against each other, with such a lack of empathy and understanding, such a lack of *pitié*. Pitiful. Man was pitiful. Something had to be done, surely. My work, my treatise: *the only way*. That was my purpose, after all, the reason for my many massacring detours. Pure understanding, and the end of conflict between all people.

Yet, I was intellectually stranded, without tools or even a bed. My lodging was on the cold ground of the warehouse. Well, at least I had a mattress, and it was better than the streets and the metros, but still insufficient, especially as I did not have a laptop with which to work, or the necessary privacy. I dared not even work by pen in view of the others, and there was always at least one other person around, even though nobody else lived there.

Every day I'd wake up and loiter around the warehouse—which seemed to have once been used to store trucks or other large vehicles —and wait for Bogdan or Esteban to give their orders. I hardly ever left the place. Dreadful, unthinkable. I spent those months in the company of Bogdan and his associates so that I could earn some money, recoup from my catastrophes, and resume work on the cure for the human sickness. Months of following his destructive orders, out and about, with Esteban at the wheel and others unstrapped and wild in the seats beside me, tempting fate and fast traffic.

Night capers through stores of all kinds, escapade after escapade, clenched fists of tobacco cash and swollen pearls, squeezed through our fingers and jangled away from cash registers dented silver and broken display cases. Hostages forsaken and left trembling with their arms bent overhead. Escaping, ramming out shoulder-first through backdoors and into wet alleyways, followed by the nightly rush of rank garbage air that cooled sweat from the face. The petrol pop of a roused exhaust, loud through the dark; loud through empty streets shining with the day's rain. Splashing across puddles glistening under cones of lamplight. Into black getaway cars, jolly with adrenaline; and laughing, laughing as we would peel down the roads with treasure dumped into the backseat. Intoxicating, really, all of it. And there were other tasks, farther from the bombast of robbery and closer to the quietude of blood.

We were a coterie of thieves and killers. But I was not entirely like them. My goals were vaster and more important than they could conceive.

And, unfortunately, beyond Bogdan and Esteban, this group was composed chiefly of grave morons. Excellent at their jobs, no doubt, but incompetents and nuisances in every other respect. Stéphane, Yuri, Samir: the beastly fools. Halfwits who thought themselves comedians, and who usually made me the subject of their comedy.

The daily insults and derisions they slung at me hardly stuck, as there was not a creative bone between the three of them, but it was tiresome nonetheless. Jabbing, jabbing, like gorillas trying to assert themselves in a pack. Half of it was probably due to the fact that Bogdan never officially swore me in. These pesky idiots made it particularly difficult for me to be productive in any way while I was yet unable to afford a home from my illicit earnings.

However, the problem I was looking to solve was coming clearer to me by the day. I observed it between my tormentors. I felt it every time I inhaled the rank of death. It was a matter of somehow eliminating the possibility for misunderstandings. Of making clear the maps of each heart, and the hearts within those. To clasp the hearts themselves. To make an other's sense of worth and self-preservation as intrinsically known as one's own.

Now, you might hold me by the back of the collar as I bolt off toward this end, and tell me I want the unachievable. You might say that to learn peace by means of broken tools is mankind's redemption. Spare me. I am more interested in a solution than in poetry.

In fact, I have suffered enough abuse from you poets. You, who operate on sentiments as opaque as mundane stone, who raise brittle steps over the abyss between words, who weave up glittering tapestries to veil the unspeakable: I would not merely banish you from my republic, but have you all beheaded, that I could at last see the ichor that should have filled your works spray from your necks.

But, listen to this platonic hypocrite! You think I don't understand the emptiness of my own words to you? I am trying to show you.

Having shed your complaints and your poetries, I return now to the problem: the perpetual misunderstanding of the other. As I have alluded to already, the roots of my epiphany were fed with blood. So many nights I spent meditating on my actions and those of my colleagues, half-haunted and half-fascinated, looking to evince from them some answers. Why was such brutality possible between humans? What determined the bouts of violence we, like acolytes of Mars, routinely performed? To begin my war on war itself, I needed to understand its nature—what better way than to investigate first hand?

But it isn't a problem endemic to the warlike alone. Even the most pacific fail at grasping each other's immensity. If I told you, "I would like some water," you would not understand this except by a sliver. You could not comprehend what it would mean to be me, in that moment, given all that I have been and am, and to want water; nor could you comprehend all of what the oceanic notion of water is to me. You would merely sail across this unfathomably deep sentiment. And a simple, seemingly innocuous misunderstanding such as this is sufficient to damn us all.

We need not yet even speak of murder and rape and rapine ever present in civilized and barbarous streets alike. Even when peace is not in full decay, and is draped over cities as a soothing white blanket, it arrives infested with the larvae of war, if even on such a maggoty scale as a homeless man's midnight robbery, or an argument between husband and wife over what to eat for dinner. And so after our little scuffs we return to our apologies, our justice, our tolerance, our settled accounts, our state of *not*-war.

But tell me, has this partial accord been the guardian of peace? The jailer of war? Does this mere gleaning of another's inner bastion by means of public words—themselves opaque—ward off hunger and disease and violence and the ache of words left unsaid? So, get away from me, now, you whole and teeming consciousness, for I do not yet have the tools to deal with you. You've only wetted your fingertips in an ocean and called yourself Poseidon.

As you might imagine, the task of solving this problem required secluded meditation, reflection, and introspection. And, of course, these pure ambitions were not possible in the company of the base and corrupt men with whom I worked. Especially not in that hive of theirs which was my unfortunate dwelling.

But I took it in good jest, as the money flowed. Much money, in fact. I wasn't afforded too large a cut just yet, but enough to keep me satisfied. It made everyone happy. And that was what was important, no? Yes. Soon. Perhaps, optimistically, after securing shelter, I would be free from those mental shackles. Money, money. Eventually, enough to come out of the hole of homelessness. Closer, nearer to the goal each month as we thieved through the spring, and summer arrived in a shower of wonderful, dirty, creased bills.

In August, almost half a year since my criminal beginnings, Bogdan began speaking about a particularly lucrative job. In half-whispers, at first. He would mention it in passing while rounding a corner. Mutter to himself in his cold way mid-conversation. He tantalized us with vague assurances of vast sums for all, enough to relax the group's efforts for some time. I watered at the mouth when he formally announced it. I awaited the day giddy as a child. I would ask about it out of turn at almost every meeting.

Although I'd made some money by this point, it was still insufficient to afford a comfortable home for any extended period of time. What I needed was a large enough treasury to last me a good while, long enough that I could abandon the external world for a time and work to complete my ultimate purpose without trouble knocking, knocking, and banging to break down the door of my cerebral sanctum.

The day came later in the month, closer to September. Bogdan had finally given a date and told us to rest in preparation for the big job. Rested, resting; restless, morelike. Making it to morning proved difficult. As I tried to sleep, my mind was plagued by groundless, eager thoughts that shuffled from branch to branch like spirited monkeys, multiplying and metamorphosing upon persecution; haphazard deliberations weighing down the real curse, as I rummaged around in the periphery of darkness, on the precipice of catching that fleeing, vaguely utopic vision of mine.

The moon cycled through the night, and then the sun bolted up just as I was becoming exhausted. After that messy sleep, I writhed and twisted in the morning light. My eyelids turned to bothersome pink shields. Then came the echo of work boots against the rubbery floor. The others were arriving, gathering near me as I struggled to keep a few more minutes of darkness.

Esteban gave me one of his signature, listless kicks. Sharp and slow in the gut, the pointy end almost driving up under my ribcage. I woke up winded. After a few moments of worming in place, I forced myself up.

My eyes opened to a focusing blur, and there I found Yuri hovering over me with crossed arms, observing me from a short distance. He and the others were laughing at me, as usual. Muggy light filled the room. I tried to squint my way to clarity, but the glare from the humungous windows made it exceptionally difficult. I rose from my rock mattress with a sweaty hand on the wall.

Their laughter subsided into silent disdain, and they began chatting with each other. The doors of the inner warehouse flew open, and Esteban called us into the meeting with a stern, "Shut up. Bogdan is waiting inside."

We all sat in the circle of foldable blue chairs, giddy and tense. Bogdan stood facing us beside a blackboard, turning the chalk between his fingers into a caterpillar. It felt like a classroom, an afterschool detention for the most meddlesome of students, directed by the most fraudulent teacher.

Yuri was tapping his feet against the floor, drumming out inconsistent rhythms to which he tried to nod along.

"Stop it," Esteban said, glaring over at him.

"What we have here," said Bogdan, drawing everyone's attention to him and ignoring the small fuss, "Is a rare opportunity. You all know Banque des Citoyens. I bank there myself. I think, Samir, you do also. Good bank, reliable. Anyway, it's a small bank, and it's become very ripe this season. I got a very nice tip about it. Want to hear it? Let me explain, because you're all looking at me like idiots. Wake up, idiots. And pay attention."

Bogdan turned to the blackboard and tapped more chalk lines into it to define our schedule and groups. The rest of us sat with legs outstretched. He then spent the next thirty minutes methodically going through our plan, handing me a military-grade M4 he'd procured, and warned us not to be stupid. I was thoroughly impressed, and also a little afraid. When I'd first encountered Bogdan and his men, they had seemed intermediary thieves at best—drug peddlers, low-level assassins for hire, jewelry store brigands. And now we were about to rob a bank.

After the meeting, we all stood up and shuffled out of the circle of blue chairs, through the doors, and out of the warehouse. It was a bright, hot day, and the sun was rising out from behind the clouds.

It was a solemn ride to the bank, at first. Yuri sat in the front of the van with Esteban. I was in the back with the others, hunched over my knees and running my fingers between grooves in the floor. All eyes were downcast. Everyone was likely envisioning the job. I positioned myself so that I could peer out of Yuri's window at an angle, in order to watch the road and the trees merge into one fast blur.

Yuri suddenly turned in his seat to look at me. "You know, they say jellyfish are immortal," he said with a straight face.

"What?"

"Some jellyfish, *Turritopsis dohrnii*, they're called. They're immortal. I mean, you can kill them, but they won't die naturally."

"Why are you telling me this?"

"They revert to the polyp stage, their stage of infancy, a previous stage in the life cycle," he continued, speaking without intonation, indicating a poorly practiced recital, like something a child memorizes for show-and-tell. "They are able to loop around in their biological stages and never die. The process is characterized by an initial deterioration of the bell and tentacles, and then—"

"Yuri," I almost shouted. "Why are you telling me this? What's your problem? I have a headache. We have a lot to do today."

"Because you think you're smart," he replied snidely. "You think we're impressed by your tricks? Look how easy it is," he said, waving around his smartphone with the article on the display.

Anger swelled in me, doubled by the early morning. "Just shut up. You're nothing. A nothing, got that? Jealous little idiot."

We locked eyes, and he smiled. He started to laugh, and without thinking, I followed. Note: this was not a joint, reconciliatory laughter, or the dismissal of a competitive joke, but a mutual acknowledgment of hatred. Could I have only reached into Yuri's mind, and sat, if for a moment, on the throne of his being, I would have no doubt forgiven him, and indeed, come to love him as he no doubt loved himself. For the moment, I despised him.

"What you need to do is get a PhD," Stéphane said to me from across the van.

Calmed by our mad laughter, I turned to him, thinking I'd at least humor him. "That isn't necessary. Academia is—"

"Pump. Hump. And dump," he continued, not waiting a second to slap his knees and break into crazed laughter with the other buffoon in the corner.

Of course. Complete imbeciles. This was the nature of my unfortunate camaraderie with these people. But they were not so bothersome when on the job, for we were all psychopaths then.

About twenty minutes passed before one of the Neanderthals started chuckling to himself. It seemed a solitary thing at first, perhaps a joke half-remembered during a moment of drifting thought. Then they began darting their eyes between each other and me. Even on the eve of this hazardous task, they could not help themselves.

"By the way, are you upset there's no seat belt?" Samir asked me, still trying to contain his laughter as the others started grinning.

My precautions were a running joke between the clowns. Unlike them, I always wore my seatbelt, even in the heat of felonious escape. It was absurd to them that I should care for my safety, and even funnier to them were my justifications. They passed the time joking about it throughout many long car rides.

"When you're all in the hospital and can't walk, disfigured and shitting in a bag, we'll see who'll laugh," I said, stewing, still staring outside of the van.

"Why do you always have to say these things to us?" Yuri said, twisting in his seat to face me again, unbuckled. "We're just joking around with you, and then you talk about us getting paralyzed. Relax. Life's not that hard, you know?"

"Shut it."

"You need to find a woman is what you need to do. Always upset and angry. Relax."

"I have a woman already," I said, hoping for him to leave me alone, half-thinking of Sophia.

"She must be the one that makes you this way, then. Is she one of those dressed-up girls? You know, the kind that always has that look on their face, the one that says, 'I haven't been fucked by the right kind of millionaire yet.'"

I erupted. I jumped at him from where I sat, but the others caught me, and I clawed at the air in front of him while they restrained me.

"Shut your mouth. You don't know anything about her. You don't know anything. Nothing. You'll never care for anything, ignorant shit."

"Stop," Esteban commanded, though he had been chuckling himself.

I admit, it was a bizarre reaction. While Sophia had been occupying a hateful place in my mind over the long year, I could not contain my defense of her. The suffering she gave me was for me, her gift to me, not for that filthy bastard to use against me. He laughed it off as the other two forced me back into my place, where I remained and brooded in silence for a while.

It was the persecution of the clowns, the inquisition of the jesters. I needed desperately to escape the warehouse and find a secluded place to live. After this job. At least those pathetic jokes at my expense entertained miserable Esteban, who, after hearty, jaded laughter of his own, was kind enough to remind them of my various acts of cold destruction. "Don't forget, he's the one who walked into the bathroom alone and melted that guy in Antony. None of you wanted to do it," he said.

"It's because he's fucking crazy," Yuri said.

No one responded.

The rest of the trip passed mostly in silence, and even fell toward talk of preparation for the job as we neared the bank.

The plan was simple. We were not after anything in the bank, but rather an armored truck set to make a delivery at two in the afternoon. Stéphane and Samir would hide in the alleyway behind the building, where the delivery truck would arrive to unload. They would slay the two guards in the truck and the guards posted in the alley.

Afterwards, they would steal the truck, drive it off to a secluded location, break it open, empty the goods into our own van, dump the emptied truck, and then drive home. Meanwhile, Yuri would enter the bank, pose as a client, and wait. If everything went well, he would exit and meet us later on.

Otherwise, if Stéphane and Samir were to goof something up or if the bodies were discovered too soon, he was to dispatch any guards or troublemakers inside and hold the place from prematurely alerting the police.

As for Esteban and I, we would wait in the van. There would presumably be no trouble, and it would be the easiest money I would ever make; but just in case, I would have my special M4 pointed in view of the bank doors and the street out of the alley, ready to annihilate any would-be heroes.

There were some jokes made about my uselessness, and about how I was essentially stealing a cut from the other three, but good Esteban ignored them, and soon enough, the bank came into view.

It was a shiny little building, with pretty cropped trees all around and an understated logo reflecting glints of the sun into the van. The stooges exited the vehicle to begin their stakeouts, while Esteban and I were left alone for some time.

We sat for a while in silence.

"Do you think there's a world out there?" I asked him without thinking, not expecting him to reply.

He just eyed me.

I tried again. "Do you think we have free will?"

"Yes."

"You've thought about it before?"

"I think about it. I don't think about thinking about it."

"So don't you feel responsible, then? Do you ever feel guilty for what we do, if we're free?"

"No. A man doesn't feel bad. He does what he wants. I'm like this. The world is like this. Nothing to feel bad for."

I gave him a puzzled look. "I thought you just said we did have free will."

"Yes."

"But you also said the world made you this way and—"

"Yes. I said. So?"

I decided not to go on. "So did you have friends growing up?" I asked him after a short pause.

"Many friends. At school, at work. Still I have friends. You think someone who kills can't have friends?"

I nodded at him, somewhat surprised. "You feel like you know them?"

"Of course."

"Really know them, I mean. Or are they just like robots you see a lot?"

"You're really crazy, man. I tell you, you're crazy."

I snorted. "I'm not. I just want to know how you feel about people. You like them, you feel like they do what you say, like they get you?"

He just shook his head, laughing. "Cállate, puta."

I opened my mouth to protest, but he interrupted me.

"I don't want to talk crazy with you," he said. "It's a disease in your head. I don't want you to infect me. Okay?"

I shrugged, and we returned to our silence. After a while, his cellphone beeped, and he straightened his posture.

"It's starting," he said, and started the engine.

He positioned the van so that its back doors would be in plain view of the bank entrance. There, I opened the doors of the van, letting in a fresh ray of light, and crouched and prepared my M4. I pushed the scope into my eye, tucked the butt into my shoulder, and *patience*. The bank had no windows, so there was no telling how well the operation was going. I waited.

"Yuri is inside," Esteban said behind me.

Pigeons were doting around on the pavement, fluttering up towards a perfectly blue sky for a few languid moments before settling their plump bellies back onto the concrete. Their shiny jade and amethyst necks distracted me, and I followed them with the scope. Something in me burned to turn them all into puffs of red mist, but I restrained myself. *To hell with metaphysics* leaped into my skull as my index finger trembled on the clammy trigger.

"Guards are dead. They are in the truck."

I restrained myself. A few moments later, the black armored truck charged out from behind the building. Samir was at the wheel; I could see him through the scope, moments away from a warrantless sabotage on behalf of my unreasonable finger. No. Restraint. I turned the gun away from them as they drove towards us in our moving prize. The treatise, I needed it for the treatise, no time for experiments to test the external world. And pity, pity for the fragile man. I aimed the M4 at the bank then, in case of a problem with Yuri, that I might save him.

"He is taking a long time," I found myself saying.

"Yes," Esteban replied with the only intonations of worry I ever heard in his voice, slight as they were.

The sun was burning around the edge of the scope, its flames focused and penetrating my eye. Fast, fast, exit, fool, Neanderthal, come out of your nimrodic fumbling so that Nimrod might retreat. Sweat was streaming from my brow, making the scope slip and my face sting.

The bank doors opened; commotion followed. Either they'd found the bodies, or Samir and Stéphane had forgotten to use silencers, or they were too loud, or some other mistake had been committed. Tall, inept Yuri was hurtling down the steps, down to the pavement, gun in hand, shooting haphazardly at the door. Idiot, fool, imbecile. Esteban's breathing amplified. The doors lurched open again. Four, five—no: six security guards all clotted the exit and spilled out in pursuit of our friend.

Esteban accelerated a little bit, ready to abandon Yuri, but I shouted at him from behind, "No! They'll kill him. Wait."

Before Esteban could reprimand me, I fired. Hands, eyes, shoulder enflamed. The coarse roar of repeated gunshots crashed down the street, as blood started jumping out of bodies.

Three guards were dead, fallen fast to the floor, then four. The others retreated to cover behind the lovely trees. Yuri was still running, about halfway across the street from us. I sent a hail of bullets to tear through one guard in a flurry of shattering bark, wood splinters chasing garnets to the clouds. There was something immensely satisfying about damaging a body like that. I relished the scene, then I searched for the last one.

Time relaxed its hold, and the sun's flames receded somewhat as I noticed that Yuri was in my line of sight, almost perfectly aligned with the final guard. And what did he have on him except a frantic look? Empty hands and an emptier head. The cargo was secure, ready to be delivered; and there was Yuri: buffoon, botcher of the grand robbery.

What happened next was an accident, in an Aristotelian manner of speaking. His flesh was in the way of my last target; his useless, adrenaline-soaked flesh. I fired into the ground near the van multiple times, and yelled at Esteban, "Get down! They're firing at us." The oaf did as commanded, and lowered his head, and the rest was a pleasure.

The sky was a fiery azure, the clouds like thick, curling steam. I loosed one careful, caring bullet into Yuri's chest. It took a sweet eternity to reach him, flying with infernal grace across the road. He stopped short as the lead penetrated him.

I could not help the glee spread across my face as the scarlet sprayed from his chest. I continued my degustation. A second bullet in the gut, and another in the chest, and he started to melt on the road. He died just as the inevitable puzzled look on his face materialized. And he was insulting me even then, just as Karim had insulted me, just as all others who have ever known me, or seen me, even, and then had the gall to die have insulted me—to die and thereby kill an idea of me.

I finished the last peon behind him.

"Oh, no—oh, God—he's dead," I said, believable fear in my voice, turning from the wet scope. "He's dead—they're all dead. Go, just go. Now!"

Esteban didn't waste time when he saw the corpses and the street glimmering red. The doors closed, the wheels rolled, and my smile flourished in the shadows.

31

THE BILGE

Sielle's vision went red and she snapped open her eyes. Light was suddenly blazing into the compartment. Opposite her, Tikan was writhing out of a discomforted sleep.

As the gullwing door beside them hung open, the sound of rhythmic marching crept in from outside and worked to inflate her feeling of exposure. She snatched the chrome briefcase, took Tikan by the arm, and hurried him out.

They exited to a docking platform almost identical to the one from which they had embarked. Steel gray walls and a snail of dreamers. For a moment, it seemed as though they had never left. And feeding this overwhelming déjà-vu was another band of gray-suited sentinels standing on guard in an identical looking corridor.

Although staggering and disoriented, the two slipped past the authorities, this time without incident. Sielle handed Tikan the chrome briefcase. They ran against the stream out of the shuttle station, careful not to wake any of the metempsying amblers. There were no words between them. They were still drowsy. Their minds were clouds of memories and latent, unborn responses to the discussion they had shared hours earlier.

Sielle's mind wandered between Sirius and Arcturus. Emerald

skies littered with sapphires of the sun. Seas shimmering below a crown of varicolored moons, the galaxy for a horizon. Procrustiis, interstellar ship invasions, dead silver worlds, and sinister plots unfolding in worlds unknown.

Above these mysteries, there hung the threat of Onasus, which she could not understand or shake. She avoided his bronze image, unwelcome in her mind's eye. There, somewhere in her still-waking mind, were thoughts trying to address him. Thoughts of doors venting flames along a corridor. They were little more than foggy images, half-formed or forgotten sentiments.

When they reached the outside, it became apparent to her that nothing about Proxima's other hemisphere was different. The roads had the same flat and strictly gridded layouts, the buildings followed the same pattern in grouped uniform height and had the same platinum glister, and the night still shone a weak red.

They walked on in silence for a while, until they reached a bridge. Tikan went to lean over the railing, looking out at the deserted, sparkling plaza before him and the red horizon ahead.

"Are you okay?" he asked, turning his head toward Sielle.

"Yes. A little tired."

"It was hard to sleep properly in there."

She nodded. "Where are we going?"

"Where captains sometimes go on shore leave. They call it the 'Bilge.'"

For the next few hours, Tikan and Sielle travelled by foot and by throughground to reach the Bilge, Proxima's seediest, most subterranean zone. The journey there was convoluted and required a number of stops. It was the only route on Proxima that Tikan remembered from his youth.

This shadowy lair of the malcontent, the outcast, the defective, was not some criminal haven, but rather a sanctuary for the broken. For those who, in their hearts, did not enjoy an existence spent in virtual boots, but who could not bear to see their own feet, either. Who, by some neurological glitch, or by some grossly improbable psychological reaction, had lost their anchor to the original world, and whose minds were now lost, derelict vessels at sea.

Instead of the pristine, shining staircases or crystal walkways Tikan and Sielle had thus far encountered, their way into the Bilge was a grimy and narrow descent. Fumes reached out of the heart of the place. Its few remaining entrances were covered by debris, or hidden under layered networks of maintenance shafts. It was fully veiled in shadows, save for the blue lights intended to guide maintenance automatons. The blue light mingled with the steam, turning the place into some revenant's haunt. They could smell nothing except the dank of the old water systems.

"Why would ship captains come here?" Sielle asked, as they reached the end of the stairs and came upon a catwalk.

"Starship captains are the least controlled, least slavish people in the galaxy. Among people who have procrustiis, at least. Something about living between authority systems, and being in charge of a whole ship oftentimes for months on end, I think."

Sielle coughed. "So why do they come here?"

"To metempsy, to talk, to barter. To smoke. You can't smoke or find cigarettes anywhere else on Proxima."

"None of them stay on the surface?"

"Most do. But not the kind we're looking for."

"You've been here before, haven't you?"

Tikan did not respond.

They met the end of the catwalk and climbed down another few flights of stairs. Then they followed corridor after corridor, each of which had "Proxima Centauri Station" labeled across its middle.

Before Proxima the planetary city, there had been Proxima Centauri Station, where humanity had planted its first flag outside of the Sol system.

Though none now remembered it, this incongruent piece of Proxima was its first stone. Here there was no silver, or glass, or wide avenues, or garnet-rimmed skies, or perceptually activated signs. There were vents pouring steam and pipes along the ceiling. No pedestrians wearing ironed tunics and blank, distracted expressions, but vagabonds: minds too destroyed to partake in society and yet compliant enough to be left alone.

The other kind of people one might have found wandering into the Bilge were those so profoundly addicted to metempsies that they came to suffocate their bodies in the steam and the dark while they partook. Much of the place looked like the remains of a laboratory, stripped of all its equipment and staff.

"Don't the sentinels ever come here?" Sielle asked. She slid her hand across one of the walls, and then rubbed the condensation together between her fingers.

"Yes, sometimes they do, but infrequently. There isn't much down here except a few broken souls and captains who like to gamble."

The hallways widened and narrowed at intervals, and bore plenty of rooms and vacant spaces. There were furnished alcoves crammed with metempsic degenerates who could no longer distinguish reality from the virtual. They shambled and crept in the steam, sometimes spinning in place like demonic dervishes, the steam twirling like skirts about them; and they madly harangued or spoke words of affection to each other, though they spoke only to phantoms. Some silently writhed like worms; others, in unison, called out the catchphrases of this year's eminent metempsy avatars.

Tikan and Sielle passed through one small lounge in particular, where six or seven people continuously repeated, "I'm Ashley Johnson, and I'm Sol's ninth planet," slightly out of synch with each other. It seemed at first that they were all shouting at Sielle and Tikan as they passed through, like drunks by a seaport might once have; but Tikan hurried on, unconcerned.

There was no Ashley Johnson. He or she was merely the current avatar that every person adopted when engaged in a sports metempsy. Joint metempsies had participants face each other in a shared virtual arena, and each participant believed him or herself to be the great Ashley Johnson. The others appeared as generic weaklings, and Ashley Johnson always prevailed.

There were less confrontational or degenerate inhabitants of the

Bilge, too. Some passed by peacefully, their faces distraught more from living sorrow than madness.

And just as some lived out their madness or sorrow in the Bilge, so too did plenty die there. Along every other corridor, there were sealed rooms full of skeletons and new corpses dragged from the gutters, stinking and grimy with condensation like the subterranean legacy of some treasure-less old pirate too possessive of his crew.

Sielle tracked the hollowed sockets of a skull resting in a throne of dark bones through the porthole to one such tumulus. Tikan avoided them after a single glance. For all their horror, these mass graves, where ruined minds were at last extinguished of their various agonies, where bodies were together relieved of their infinite hungers and their weight, they looked to be a place of communion and peace.

Tikan weaved through dark zone after dark zone as if guided by another sense. For Sielle, the place came to resemble more an underground city than a mere buried space station. There were, at times, ceilings so high as to match the apartment tower where they had retrieved the briefcase; and though derelict, there were also monuments carved of gold, onyx, silver, and gemstone, sitting desolate in the darkness they had been erected to defy. The monuments often resembled no definite figures, but figurative celebrations of the cosmos, now corrupt in the shadow. Invented constellations; hands upholding star systems, now looking more like a symbol of entropy.

Tikan and Sielle even descended into one zone where hanging moss spilled like waterfall off a cliff, leading to a gallery of flowers and cedars on the lower floor. The verdure was often in glass enclosures or behind glass windows, but lately these had failed to contain it. Walls had collapsed, steam infested the place, and oftentimes, mere soil remained spilled over the ground.

After nearly two hours navigating the Bilge, Tikan slowed down behind a rather conspicuous entryway. It had a badly hung yellow neon light framing its door—the only non-blue light in this sunken maze. It reminded Sielle of the entrance to some bounty hunter's bar in the days when lawlessness had still been a possibility. They passed through the doorway and entered into an antechamber.

Two people were sitting on the ground, metempsying for short bursts before waking up, their faces collapsing into expressions of self-hatred, before softening as they returned to another life.

"This is where most of the captains visit," Tikan said, panting through the steam. "Let me speak, okay?" He took a step forward.

"Wait," Sielle said.

Tikan turned around to her. She picked up his wrist and held it up, along with the briefcase he was holding. "What about this? Don't you want to see what's inside so we can sell it first?"

"Well, we can take a look at what's inside, but we can't sell it. You and I can't gain future worth. Besides, no captain is going to deal in future worth. Its too easy to get caught that way."

Sielle gave him a puzzled look. "Fine, but maybe they'll just trade for it. Come, let's go somewhere else," she said, eyeing one of the wrecked human beings on the floor.

They walked out of the antechamber and found an empty room not far away. It resembled a classroom of sorts, with many tables arranged in a grid throughout. They set the briefcase down on a table, angled it into the strongest source of blue light, and clicked it open. A number of mechanical and electronic parts almost overflowed out of it.

"Any idea what this stuff is for?" Sielle asked.

"None."

Sielle grimaced. "And you don't think it's worth anything?"

"It might be. Hard to say. Onasus said they were just parts he needed to build something."

"Fine," she said. "Might as well hold on to it for now. You never know."

Tikan closed the briefcase, and they walked back through the neon yellow entrance and into the antechamber.

They walked past the people on the floor again, and this time entered into the next room.

It was a large hall, which had clearly once been a restaurant, with chairs and round tables unclean for decades, the same blue-lit darkness and thick fumes, ruined tapestries hanging off the walls, and a number of figures whose outlines alone were visible. The smell of tobacco immediately wafted to them. There was a food printer and a tap at the far end, where people filled their cups and mumbled to themselves. To the left of the room was a radiant purple globe on a stand, around which a few people had gathered and seemed to sluggishly dance.

"What's that?" Sielle whispered to Tikan, pointing at the purple globe.

"Just a light. People use it to half-metempsy."

"Half-metempsy?"

"Yeah. They metempsy stimulated by things in the real world."

"Like hallucinations?"

"What's that?"

"It's where people see things in the world that aren't really there," Sielle said.

"Yes, that's it. Except there's usually a story or something going on in a half-metempsy. It's illegal to do it on the street, anyway."

"Interesting."

As they sauntered into the room, Sielle noticed Tikan's expression of disgust as he watched the people metempsying around the purple globe, and those on the floor with their eyes strictly open. She noticed in him the same disaffection with humankind that she had ever felt. Though he could never comprehend the distance she felt between herself and humanity, perhaps he was not so far from her.

They watched a number of red dots brighten at the right end of the room. Wisps of thinner smoke streamed from those red dots to mingle with the steam pouring out of the vents. Tikan and Sielle walked towards one of these tables. A number of people with better clothes and cleaner hair than the lost ones on the floor were sitting with their palms on the table, cigarettes or pipes dangling from their mouths while they metempsied with eyes open.

Tikan sat down at a table with two captains. The captains did not seem to register his arrival. They sat there like two petrified children of the apocalypse.

"Evening," Tikan said.

"Evening," both captains eerily responded together.

"I said *evening.*" And Tikan slammed his palms on the table. The two captains broke from their metempsy.

One took a long drag of his cigarette, the absent look on his face persisting, and then looked at Tikan while exhaling. "That isn't considered polite," he said.

"Neither is ignoring a greeting," Tikan said. "Now give me a smoke. Just arrived from Europa and I still need warming up."

The captain crossed his eyebrows and sized Tikan up. He noted his clothes and his confidence and took him for a fellow captain. He pulled out a hand-rolled cigarette and passed it to Tikan. "Who's your friend?" he asked Tikan while lighting his cigarette for him.

Tikan took a drag and let the smoke sit in his lungs for a while, adopting for a moment the demeanor of his younger, more heedless self. "My pilot," he said while exhaling. "Where are you flying in from?"

"Mars."

"And you?" Tikan asked the other.

"The Belt."

"You here for a while?"

"Just a few days. How about you? You staying up top, or here?"

"Here for now."

"Good," the captain said. "We need a third and a fourth."

Tikan looked at him, dismayed that they were already inviting him to some joint metempsy or other. "For?"

"To blow smoke in each other's faces for three, four days, what else?" the captain said, laughing weakly.

Tikan and Sielle gave each other a glance, and then Tikan forced himself into a chuckle. The bad humor reminded him of Amozagh, and slid a splinter of sadness into his heart.

"What's your name?" Tikan asked the first captain.

"Emilio."

"Emilio—I'm Floyd, and this is Sarah."

Emilio nodded.

"When are you undocking next, and to where?"

"A week or two. Going first to the Belt and then to Sirius A."

Tikan paused to enjoy his cigarette. "Those cigarettes. You got them from Earth?"

Emilio nodded.

"You carry them from Earth often?"

Emilio nodded again, this time more cautiously.

"I need you to carry something else on your next trip," Tikan said. "I'm leaving my ship behind, you see."

"You have some cargo you need me to look after?"

"I need you to take us to Sirius."

He grinned at Tikan. "I think the manifest is full, but if—"

"No manifest. No questions. Just take us to Sirius. A or B, it doesn't matter."

Emilio looked at the other captain, who shortly got up without saying anything and walked off into the shadows.

Emilio looked back at Tikan, and eyed Sielle for a second. "I'm not interested."

"Not yet. But I can tell you're not someone to ignore a good offer."

"How's that?"

Tikan tightened his grip on the briefcase. "Listen. You seen the prices tech dealers in the Belt list for—"

Sielle got up suddenly and marched around to Emilio. She ripped the cigarette from his mouth and hovered the end of it around his neck. "You're a smoker and a smuggler," she said. "Only captains smoke these days, is that right?"

Tikan got up, scraping the chair behind him. He slammed his palm on the table and gave Sielle a burning look.

Sielle glanced up at Tikan and then looked back down at Emilio. Emilio began drumming the table with his fingers, and leaning his neck away from the heat of the cigarette. Sielle followed his neck with it.

"That's right. Only captains smoke," he said.

"You know why?"

"Because we're used to spending a long time in our bodies. It's not the same if you metempsy a cig—"

"That's not why," she snapped. "It's because you're a captain and a smuggler. Because *you can find* cigarettes to smoke." She put out Emilio's cigarette on the table in front of him.

Tikan caught on to what she was doing and sat back down. He and Sielle glanced at each other with approval. She raised her eyebrows at him.

"How's the cigarette trade been doing lately?" Tikan asked, taking another drag of his own cigarette.

Emilio didn't answer. He turned his head, looking for the other captain.

"Not great, I imagine," Tikan said. "Used to find only pre-rolled ancients whenever I came down here—not this roll of... half-burnt residue." He gave the cigarette a sour look. "Did yours taste just as bad?"

"I won't smuggle people."

"You won't be smuggling cigarettes for much longer, either, if you don't take us, it looks like."

"What do you mean?"

"I mean I can tell you where to find old factories. Buried warehouses."

Emilio remained silent. He eyed them both.

"All across the Americas. The two of us together have spent over twenty years on Earth; we know where to find them. I've even heard of a rundown warehouse on the old side of Mars, somewhere around Zone 4."

Emilio paused a long while, staring at Tikan and then glancing at Sielle. "How do I know you're telling the truth?"

"The fact that I'm even down here should tell you I know my way around the galaxy."

Tikan handed Emilio the cigarette. With a trembling hand, Emilio took a drag. He looked back up at Sielle, who was still standing over him, and then stared long and hard at Tikan again.

"Look, give me a few days," Emilio said. "I need to see if it's possible, and make arrangements. And I'm not promising anything."

Tikan nodded at him, and he and Sielle got up from the table.

"I told you to let me talk," Tikan whispered to Sielle once they were out of earshot of Emilio.

"Yes, and I listened, until I realized you were a terrible negotiator."

"Terrible?"

"You shaped up toward the end."

Tikan shook his head. The two of them walked back out into the corridors of the Bilge, teasing each other and beginning to fantasize about Sirius, until it became an ideal so pure and fragile as to be made of glass.

𝕾 32 𝕾

MONKS AND NAMES

In the days that followed, Tikan and Sielle took up residence in a vacant room about thirty minutes from the lounge where they had met Emilio. The Bilge had a number of ancient residences, many of which had vacant rooms due to the propensity of metempsic degenerates to sleep wherever their bodies collapsed. Their room had two single beds and a bathroom that somehow still had running water. There were even a few sundries belonging to the previous residents strewn about. Down the hall, there was a communal food printer.

Tikan insisted that they venture out as little as possible, in case a patrol passed through the Bilge. Sielle, meanwhile, insisted that they were likelier to be caught if they did not remain on the move.

For the most part, they spent the days speaking in their room. They planned their trip to Sirius: the shuttle they would take midflight to the garden world, the supplies they would bring with them, the winters—if there were winters on that planet—they would shoulder together. They began sharing their visions for how their lives would play out together over the coming few years. He asked her if she preferred him bearded or shaved, and when she said she preferred him shaved, he said he would not shave in order to preserve her desire.

When he said it, she smirked and replied, "If it will keep you from your death wishes and your vengeance, you can keep a beard as long as you like. But you'll have to do it on the other side of the house."

"There's a house?"

"Of course. Where else would we live?"

He paused, looking boyish and naïve. "I don't know. I thought we'd live out of the shuttle or—"

"Don't be ridiculous." She shook her head at him, smirking. "If you keep talking like that, you're going to have to start convincing me to go to Sirius with you."

At other times, they explored their environs in the residence complex. They sometimes visited their neighbors on their floor. This was part of Tikan's strategy, for he determined that they would be safer hiding directly among the refuse of society.

One of their neighbors was a man who, battling with himself never to metempsy again, had locked himself up in the darkest, steamiest room on the floor. He sat like a monk, the sweat and condensed water streaming off his agonized face. He was Tikan, if in another life Tikan had been procrusted. Sielle took to calling him *the monk*.

There was a family there, too: a man and a woman expecting a child. Like most couples, they had first seen each other in a metempsy; that is, the interprocrustic network had mathematically determined their optimal compatibility and arranged for them to meet and fall in love by way of subliminal or explicit suggestions. Mostly, they showed up as love interests in each other's metempsies a year before actually meeting, and were therefore conditioned into love at first sight.

This particular couple, however, had decided within six months that they hated each other, and that whatever system had brought them together was therefore evil. Though they themselves could not adopt a monastic life free of metempsies like their neighbor, they wanted better for their child. They had thus resolved to have their child in the Bilge, in order to prevent it from being procrusted.

A number of people had had this same idea over the years, and since such ideas were lethal to a fetus, it usually resulted in a stillbirth.

One afternoon, Tikan and Sielle visited another floor. They walked into an open room with three occupants and sat among them, simply to observe them and satisfy Sielle's curiosity. The trio sat in a circle facing each other and conversed half through their procrustic telepathy, half in speech.

"Yeah, it was the best tasting one, you're right," one said, startling Sielle and Tikan, who had not heard a word from any of them yet.

Ten seconds went by.

"I don't enjoy raspberries without the squish between my teeth, though."

"You can't taste the squishy?"

"Where do you find raspberries here?" Sielle asked.

They did not reply. She looked at Tikan, and he shook his head.

Fifteen seconds went by.

"Yeah, I always forget it doesn't make me full. But it tastes."

On the fourth day, they visited the lounge again and found Emilio. He assured them that everything was being organized, and that they would have safe passage to Sirius by the end of the next week. They thanked him and returned to the residential area.

On their way back to the room, they passed by the hateful couple's room, which was unlocked. Tikan walked on, saying he wanted to wash his face. Sielle, meanwhile, wandered in.

Inside, it was curiously well lit and there was little steam. The husband and wife were there, both cutting vegetables extracted from the old model food printer outside.

"Can I help?" Sielle asked.

"Well, of course you can," the woman said.

"There's a knife right here for you, and I wouldn't be afraid to use it," the man said.

Sielle crossed her eyebrows and approached the man. "Can I have it?"

"That's what you get, that's just what you get for murdering those people!" he said in a furious tone but at curiously low volume.

Sielle took a step back.

The woman pushed a minced onion into a bowl. "Just because I said you could eat all of those fritters, that doesn't mean you should. Now stop that. You'll spoil your appetite."

"They'll never find your body. They'll never find it. Never."

Sielle's skin chilled.

"I'm going to teleport to Earth now and find some real apples for desert. I think I'll make a tart. Would you like some?"

Sielle took a number of steps backing out of the room.

"I threw a whole planet into its sun for you. I did that for you. Do you know how that makes me feel? How many more gallons of blood do I have to boil for you?"

She scurried out and went back to her room.

Tikan later explained to her that these people, having attempted to force apart body and mind, were now deficient in their abilities to metempsy. As a result, their bodies would often express events occurring in their metempsies, their speech doubled in the real world, while their bodies performed unrelated tasks.

On the sixth day, after convincing Tikan to explore the more remote areas of the Bilge, Sielle found an old filing cabinet rife with ancient documents. Tikan was busy examining a monument in the hall just outside, trying to identify which constellation it depicted while Sielle pilfered the filing cabinet.

It was a relic from the Bilge's beginnings as a mere outpost orbiting Proxima Centauri—now Sol Victus. It contained a number of graphs and spreadsheets and other technical information. She also found a dusty old manual entitled *Of the Different Kinds of Metempsies. INTENDED FOR TECHNICAL PERSONNEL ONLY.* She flipped through the introduction, angled the page into the blue light, and skimmed the sections entitled:

1. Passive Metempsies
2. Active Metempsies
- a. Stochastic Narrative Variant
- b. Procedurally Determined Narrative Variant
3. Memorial Metempsies
4. [PROTOTYPE]Intra-experiential Metempsies
5. [PROTOTYPE] Joint Metempsies.

Aside from a few interesting remarks linking the celebrity worship culture of the twentieth and twenty-first centuries to the way metempsies exploited human psychology, along with details about how memories could be replaced by metempsic adulterations, the manual told her little she could not already extrapolate from her existing knowledge.

Sielle yawned and closed the manual. She considered for a moment showing it to Tikan, but then simply tossed it back into the filing cabinet.

On their return to the room, Sielle waited for Tikan to fall asleep before visiting the monk. He remained in his same fixed position, cross-legged and unmoving before the bed, the veins popping across his temple.

"Having a hard time?" Sielle asked him.

The monk did not reply.

She strolled around him, picking up baubles from the shelf and putting them down. "I understand," Sielle said. "It must be hard. I respect it. But do you really plan on just living here forever?"

The monk did not reply.

Sielle crouched down beside him. "You know, you can talk to me. I'd listen and I'd talk. And anyway, wouldn't it help distract you from wanting to metempsy if you spoke to a real person?"

The monk eyed her cautiously.

"I saw that," she told him. "Looking is half the battle. Come on, what's your name?"

"I don't have a name," the monk said, his voice strained. "Names are evil."

"Let's call you Maurice, then. Hi Maurice, I'm Sarah," Sielle said. "How long have you been down here?"

The monk gritted his teeth at her. "Don't name me! Names are vast, empty—nothing! Don't fill me into one—it's prison!"

"Okay, Maurice, there's no need to get angry. You're not in a metempsy."

The monk broke down and leaned over the floor on all fours, vomiting.

Sielle flinched. "That's disgusting, Maurice. Come on."

He looked up at her, still on all fours. "Why would you name me? And how do you know why I'm here? Oh, by the stars—no!" The monk began sobbing. "I've failed. Oh, I've failed! Get away, demon metempsy, get away!"

"You're not in a metempsy, Maurice, and I'm not casting some spell on you by naming you. Just lighten up and try making some friends—I'd rather metempsy than mope in this cell all my life."

Maurice did not answer.

"Maurice?"

He was now curled up on the floor, engaged in his first metempsy in years, the bliss of relief spanning his whole face.

～

They spent the entire seventh day alone in the room, talking and laughing and trying hopelessly to draw parallels to each other's lives. They lay in the blue darkness, with little steam in the room. In his paranoia, Tikan had removed the mattresses from their frames, spread them along the floor, and pushed the frames to block the door.

Sielle had made a whimper of dissent when he had started, but then decided not to oppose it. Now they were both on their sides, each propped up against an old mattress on one arm.

"So where on Earth did you grow up, exactly?" Tikan asked Sielle.

"Here and there."

"Come on. Isn't it time you told me? We're going to spend so much time together. You might as well tell me now."

"Save it for Sirius. Don't you want to have nice long talks by that shore you keep describing?"

He sighed.

"I'm just thinking of the future, that's all," she said.

"At least give me something to look forward to." He sat up and took her hand in his. "You never know when they might just burst in here and bring this little daydream to an end." Her hand was cold and wooden in his, and he felt it give a wriggle of hesitation.

Sielle looked at Tikan and felt a peculiar need to restrain herself, as though there was something about him that compelled her to keep speaking in spite of her better judgment. As though that broken and lonely man who sat beside her were, in truth, a last nomad perfectly doomed on the desert of all existence, and that it might be permissible to whisper some truth to him, for there were none before or after him to whom he could ever repeat it.

"Yes, I'll tell you a little about home," she said. "It's built of thickest blood and silence and all those words you said no one will ever say."

He tossed his free hand into the air and shook his head, grinning.

It was not without courage that she had spoken even that oblique metaphor, but she would not say much more, and instead took pleasure in his lighthearted frustration.

"When I was very young," Tikan said, ignoring her as she smirked, "I used to be proud of this place. Of Proxima. This monument to all science and progress. The idea of it. I used to tell my parents that I wanted humanity to spread throughout the galaxy. I thought I would become an explorer of sorts. I dreamed of eccentric planets, alien architecture, and galaxies bound together by a complete and caring human race. It's funny how this ruin was the first place we built after leaving Sol."

"We all have our childhood fantasies," Sielle said. "When I was young, I used to play with my sister in the woods, and—"

"You lived near the woods?" he asked, astonished.

"Yes, now don't interrupt." She slapped his hand. "We used to play in the woods, and I used to think of myself as a powerful witch who hunted other witches. We used to scream and sing through the trees. My mother was kind, and my auntie was, too. The other girls weren't allowed to do any of that."

"And what happened?"

"I caught a cold, one day, and couldn't play anymore."

"I'm sorry."

"It's alright. I did always try to find that forest again, though."

"It wasn't close to your home?"

"Oh, no, very close," Sielle said. "But finding it was like looking for a marble in a sea of them."

They paused.

"Do you think they're looking for us, now?" he asked her.

"Who? The sentinels?"

"Yes."

She leaned towards him and peered into his eyes, her own reflecting the blue lights like drops of foxfire. "You're used to running from them?"

"Not for a long time now. I did when I was younger."

"Tell me about that time," she said, rolling on her side and pulling him down to lie down beside her on the mattress. They lay there in the dark, listening to their hearts thump into their ears, watching the black steel ceiling as if it were a star-filled sky.

"I thought of myself as one cosmic knife ready to cut the galaxy apart," he said.

"Oh?" she said, facetiously impressed.

"I'm serious."

"I'm sure you were."

He ignored her. "You see, I thought that if I believed strongly enough, my belief would spread to others. Like a virtuous plague or something. I thought I could convince people to be other than what the world had already decided for them. But language isn't enough. For years I raced from world to world with my chin glued to my shoulder, hiding from the authorities and the indoctrinated, sometimes going days without food or speaking to anyone or hearing a word, thinking there were others like me who I could rally to some untouched planet or abandoned station, people who I could count on like those stories I'd heard for years, whispers here and there of groups who'd fought, or who'd escaped—five or a hundred years before me—their names cut out of the language itself so that even the possibility of remembering them was wiped out.

"There's power in a name alone, it leads straight to the thing—they know that." He paused, and sighed a phantom. "It wasn't any way to live, but I wanted to live. Really live. At first there were others. A few people here and there I counted as friends. Some who still knew the names of those who'd fought and lived before us. Then there weren't any."

"And there won't be," Sielle said. "There never will. Nunca. Not in this world. But that doesn't matter."

He turned to her and watched her pale face attend to his, her eyes still flaring with what blue light remained in the room. "No, it doesn't."

In that light, he appeared to her as a wraith looking for his soul, the hollows of his cheeks running aquamarine as if he'd wept it out over a century, and she felt now obliged to share hers with him.

"What does 'nunca' mean?" he asked.

"It's Spanish. It means 'never.'"

"Spanish?"

"Yes. You know, the language." She stopped herself, and her pulse quickened.

Tikan's mouth opened in astonishment when he correctly understood what she was implying. "I never knew there were other languages. I didn't know they had names. How do you know about this?"

"A history book I found on Earth."

"So what's our language called?"

"English. It was the most dominant toward the end of the ancient world."

He turned away from her and smiled at the ceiling. As if each possible language were a log now freshly piled onto the fire of his idealism.

"Books," he continued. "Amozagh used to say they were just proto-metempsies. Things you'd use to escape the real world. He might have been half right, but they also told you about the real world."

"So do metempsies, in a way."

"It's not the same."

She did not reply.

"So, you think they're after us, now?" he asked her.

"Yes, all of them." She smiled, but he did not see it.

"All of them?"

"Onasus and the sentinels and all of them. They're very worried. But they won't find us," she said with her usual nonchalance. She said it while flicking her hand to the side. It was a careless gesture that she occasionally performed, and which, for Tikan, had come to signify the death of a far-off galaxy or another event of such callous magnitude.

Tikan scratched his head. "I haven't thought about Onasus at all. I wonder what they're thinking. Mira, and Naim. I hope they're okay."

"I'm sure they're fine," Sielle said. "But we're having a better time, for sure."

"At least they're not stuck here, out of breath in the dark."

"Oh? I happen to like it here in the dark."

"I suppose next you'll tell me you prefer the steam in your eyes," Tikan said.

"Yes, I just might," she said dismissively. "Now stop saying rubbish." She rolled over and closed her eyes.

Tikan remained awake for a long while, staring at a series of ornaments the room's previous occupants had left behind on a shelf, trying to make out their true shapes in the darkness.

After a while, he heard Sielle whimpering in her sleep. He leaned over to look at her and saw that she was weeping herself awake.

"What is it?" he asked her.

She did not look at him. "Nothing. It was a dream."

"I'm here," he told her.

"No, you're not. You can't be."

"I'm here."

She said nothing. Eventually her sobbing ceased, and she returned to silence. A few minutes went by, and he watched the ceiling again.

"Hold me," she told him, nearly asleep.

He turned on his side to hold her. The rich lushness of her hair brushing his face. Her pale skin burning like an aurora against him.

They slept curled together like two refugees trapped in the boiler room of a faltering ship, who had long ago forgotten any true sense of the future, and whose mutual past was one constellation of sorrow and accident and even blood.

33

THE PYTHIA

The six-way cut became a five way cut, making Yuri's death quite valuable. More so than his life, in any case. His death bought me an extra year or so of solitude, and therefore of work, and therefore his death would help pay for the world's healing. A good, honorable death, no doubt. It was an unfortunate thing, they said; but it was the way these things went. Not much more was said about it. Death, that is.

I was congratulated for my performance, and Bogdan made a semblance of an apology for having been incorrect about the number of guards stationed at the bank. Though, he quickly justified himself by suggesting that we should have expected such resistance, considering the importance of the materiel. It was hard for them to care much about the tragic loss of Yuri when they were all invited to feast on his plump corpse, so to speak.

As for me, I settled somewhat when summer ended. Once the money was all laundered and appropriated, I found a little apartment for rent and ceased to live at the warehouse, at last. The means for this were well within my expanded cut of the verminous pie. Coupling my nighttime criminality with the comforts of a private home made the entire enterprise feel altogether quite legitimate.

It was no palace, no. More a bare box of flakey wood. But it was mine, and it kept the cold away. And not too many cockroaches surfaced between the planks in the floor, and for this I was grateful. Swarms of those nasty things had troubled my nights in the metro and the warehouse.

I was settled, then, when October began to rear its head. Dreary October, gateway to the new frost, dismantler of August's remnant heat. Ah, and October: anniversary of my departure from miserable Sophia. A new computer, too, yes! At last. I fumbled with the cardboard packaging in excitement, at the head of October, that magical month! Even my intrusive thoughts—which had returned, but which I had come to welcome as friends, as visions of possible worlds, some neutral, others warnings—seemed loath to sabotage me then, elated as I was.

But, as I fished the laptop from its womb amid its electric umbilical cords, my delight evaporated and was replaced by an immediate hunger to plunge into the work. I was regenerated, ready to resume the true task. My treatise. The comprehensive treatise for all time, resurrected by a rusty defibrillator, the grimy fingertips of a criminal life.

And what better way to begin again but with the subject of ethics? Not a surprise, perhaps. For, as I gazed into the pools of reflection so wrought of my newfound life, what I found were reddened waters—corrupt or blessed, depending on one's point of view—as though an animal had been suspended atop the basin and had its throat sacrificially slit.

Ethics, yes. Since my trial in the suburbs, the death of Yuri, and the general life I had been leading, the subject had started to germinate in my mind. Not for myself, per se. That entire circus of events served only to further highlight the existence of such detestable acts as those I had witnessed or performed, and that they were quite contrary to what I wanted for others. I was more cautious this time, less dismissive of the idea of morality. It was, after all, necessary for me to establish a moral system for all people. It was not on the knowledge of metaphysical truths alone that wars and all conflict would be ended. And was that not the point of it all? Yes.

And so I set myself up one good afternoon, seated beside a stream of clear light from the windows that colored the wood pale and ran up the wall to breathe into the library of stolen books I had been constructing. Congruously seated, arms at the fore, laptop unfolded.

I made a start. At first I thought it was going well, but that didn't last. After an hour, I found myself drifting away again. Not a bitter straying, as with the previous times. Rather, I just felt tired and resigned. Like a dog defeated by a strict chain around his neck. I won't bore you with a sample of what was written (there will be time to agonize you later). It was a contrived fusion of various moral systems —two or three pages of garbage justification for my behavior, which I told myself would be suitable as a universal system of morals for humanity.

I closed the laptop and knocked it away. The entire enterprise at once appeared to me as a contradiction of my initial quest. What was I hoping to achieve by merely laying down futile rules, as so many others had done? I might have gained some traction that way, maybe gained a following, and perhaps even come to be remembered for my work, but what then? I was not interested in mere glory. And even more repulsive to me was the idea of generating scholarly debate.

It dawned on me, then, how laughable I had been from the start. What kind of impact did I think a haughty treatise would have on the world? Perhaps I thought the ideas would somehow trickle down from the scholars, or something—but no, no, what a delusion.

Even the proven titans of moral philosophy were mostly unknown outside intellectual circles, and few of them were readily convincing. I needed something else. Something far from all well-walked roads and from the desire to be remembered.

The change in consciousness had to be striking, immediate, consuming. Not built of verbose arguments requiring consent or reflection. Rather, an unstoppable, irresistible force, as non-negotiable as a law of nature. The state of mind I required had to be just as an *a priori* condition of mankind's very existence. People had to follow as surely as they breathed or thought, and not by virtue of moral language and its heavy accoutrements. There would have to be only the impossibility of evil.

Thus, I rejected my treatise before ever even producing it. I would re-forge it, somehow.

Eventually.

I collapsed on the bed, pressed my hands to my face, and with my fingers drew harsh lines across my scalp. Squandered opportunity, time turning to ash in my mouth.

If the sudden abortion of my treatise were not enough, then, a friendly old plague made a return. I turned once again to face my longstanding concerns about the existence of others. I was still somewhat convinced that they were most probably animated expressions of my ego, along with the rest of the external world. And, as the concern presented itself in the sour context of my defeat, I took to investigating it quite ruthlessly.

If all people were mechanical parts of my solipsistic universe, then what was the purpose of laying out a moral system for them? Why go out of my way to convince them of anything, if they were me? What was praise, or blame, or anything of meaning, except some trick I was playing on myself?

Look there, a dog on its four legs, chasing a ball I have no interest in. Why? See a man across the street, drinking the lemonade I despise. The sour contraction of the tongue to the roof of the mouth, the acrid layer on the teeth. Disgusting! Without insight into his inner workings, how could I justify him? Why did the wind, of its first principles, blow this way and not that?

I grew frustrated. Time and space were my enemies, of course. I could not gain any adequate understanding of things external to me when everything was given to me in mere profiles dependent on my perspective, or as time's arrow hauled me on before I could gather my bearings.

Then, out of more diseased introspection, the most threatening, synthetic question arose: why was I not in direct control of everyone and everything, if all was me? Why was I even bound to the ground as gravity's slave?

When I watched myself move my arm, it was as any other object of the world, except that I was psychically in control of it. Why not, then, have trees for limbs? Why could I not will bridges to collapse, or oceans to evaporate, the same way I flexed my pinky? Get away from me, thou stewing, malignant doubts! No—come close, let me tear you apart and find truth.

In what might have been my first moment of true self-respect in a long while, I pursued the matter despite my weakening beliefs.

I tried to imagine how the universe and all its elements could possibly be contained in me. My initial suspicion was that the external world was some vital structure of my being that I could never actively grasp in thought. I have already mentioned how I saw each person as a reflection of my own inner self, but now what of the natural world? What were mountains in me, what were rivers through me?

It seemed, on that view, that I was just some knowing avatar of myself, wandering the world in the realest, most cursed introspection. Thunder of my violence, magma of my impatience. But why not have the universe for a body? Why, if I were the only thing in existence, could I not *be* as one great singularity, as one and only monad? Or inhabit the world as a formless ghost? Why this terrine flesh, this hellish shell?

I began to feel the risk of involving consciousness in all of this. I wanted, above all, to keep my individual self, yet still to acquire as a part of my consciousness that of all others. And where was this consciousness? If I had clawed through my own skull, torn my brain to shreds, I would not have found it. That locked-out sphere of unknown substance and horizons, not existing in space and time but somehow containing all of their artifacts.

"Show yourself!" I cried out, hoarse, stretching my forehead apart.

Having not made any progress, I returned to the same answer I had come to shortly after having left Sophia. That all external objects were dormant parts of me—whatever I was—on autopilot, and that it was part of the game of existence to waken them. To synchronize them all to my thinking self. I was not free until I could do this. I was not—*oh, that's enough.*

I won't subject you to these madman's ramblings any longer. This was just one great absurdity born of self-love. Of course this proposed pantheistic self of mine was just a fabrication, something I invented to salve the horror of my limitations. And, of course, I knew as much. If it were even possible to apprehend the subjectivities of others, it would have, of necessity, cost me my own subjectivity.

This was my disease: that I could not, from the beginning, find others in me. Not in that punctured idea of a self now oozing its contents. Not in this earthly shell. Yes, I admit it. Hear me thunder it out of a wounded throat: I admit it!

And even if it were all true, that my consciousness were a solitary machine unpacking itself, still I was contemptuous of the whole arrangement.

You see, if I was more than others, although they were also me, then it follows paradoxically that they would be as much as I was, too, if not also more. This I could not allow. My existence would not be tautologized out of itself. The throat of the universe was for my grip alone. And so I gnashed my teeth at this hellish situation.

Now deeply troubled and bankrupt of answers, I decided to cease thinking. This was a particularly depressing moment. Later, later. The path was long and the answers far off. There was time, even more time found in Yuri's blood.

I rose from my bed, unclasped my face from my hands, and looked up, only to be wracked with shock. I threw myself backward and slammed into the wall. I yelled. There, at the other end of the room, was a most peculiar sight indeed.

The noises in my head were at once quieted. Standing with her back to the door of my studio apartment, was a woman in visible distress.

She was breathing frantically and had grounded her hands to the wall. Her eyes were widening and straining, doom-stricken, and betraying disgust and fascination both. I had certainly never seen her before.

The door was untouched, unbroken, unmoved. No shattered lock or splintered wood. How had she come in? More importantly, who was she?

As shivers crept down my spine, I swung my legs over the bed. She stayed where she was and continued to eye me. Had I been so inly preoccupied that I had not heard the door opening? But enough of preposterousness. I was not so distant from my senses. What, then? She was curling her shoulders up and pressing herself against the door. Only the sound of her breaths occupied the space between us.

I observed her for a while. Her clothes seemed of some silken textures, but they were torn up and bloodied. Her hair was matted with streaks of crimson, some of it stuck above her brow, and lacerations crowned her and marked her whole body.

"Are you all right?" I asked, though my words did nothing but make her breathe faster.

I walked over to her. Still gasping and intensifying her stare, she just pinned herself harder against the door. She tracked me as I moved, as though I were some spellbinding horror. I had questions, urgency, muddled with uncalled desire.

She was not young. With light creases in her face and strands of silver in her hair, she seemed on the cusp of exiting middle-age. And there was something in the way she looked at me that reminded me of Sophia. Though, she was somewhat old for my tastes. But, no. No. I had to quell that inexplicable carnal urge rising in me. Yet, I could not easily rid my mind of Sophia's face superimposing itself, unwanted, over this huffing refugee. And so, I observed her as she observed me, without words, until it was clear that she would not calm down.

"Explain yourself, and I will help you," I said, meeker than I was expecting.

No answer, at first. I opened my mouth to try in French, but she spoke between hyperventilated breaths. "You. You can't see it? Who I am?"

"What? Have you hit your head? Perhaps you'd like some water, or—"

"No, I don't want water. Listen," she said, pushing herself from the door to stand in the pale light. "You have to listen to me."

"Listen to you? Who the hell are you? I'll call the police if you don't explain yourself, I'll—"

She laughed maniacally over my words without changing her expression. Now I was growing disturbed, searching her face for clues and finding only madness.

"Stop it," I said. "Stop that laughing, and I'll listen to you. Speak, and be quick about it. You interrupted me in the middle of some very important work. I'll help you, but—"

"This work. It is for the 'perfect understanding between all people, for perpetual peace, correct?"

The question alarmed me. I eyed her with lethal scrutiny. There was a numinous aura about her, something not quite in tune with the space she occupied. I immediately stopped caring for her injuries and attended to the myriad questions now erupting from me.

"What do you know of my work? Speak."

"Listen to me," she continued. "I'm the answer you've been looking for. Part of you." A neurotic grin formed across her face. She was beginning to buckle under her madness. The glass cannon mania of a martyr intoxicated by the notion of death.

My heart started, and the space of the room doubled. It was difficult to fully appreciate what she—what I, apparently—was saying. Likely she was a hallucination, a child of my cracked sanity. But, there was no proof, not even a desire for proof.

"The answer? What do you mean?" I was ravenous. "I've been slaving over it all for so long. Too long for you to know. What are you going to tell? What do you have that I'm missing? A new thought to offer? I've run through them all. A way to express what's inside me? I've tried them all. I know there's something else. That *thing* I can't access, that sideways door in my consciousness, that's what you're speaking of, isn't it? I've tried to crack myself. Please. Please, if you are with me, unlock us, undam us!"

The woman could not contain herself. She almost bent over laughing, clutching her sides as her shirt started to drip dark, wet scarlet. There was a wound in her side still bleeding. She swayed by herself in front of the blazing window. Her shadow lunged out against the wall in a pagan dance of sickly doom.

"Forget about your work," she said. "Forget about trying to write anything down. It's—"

"Yes! The sideways doors! I've always—"

"No. You don't know anything about sideways doors. You'll never know. *Never.* You speak garbage when you talk about it. Shut up. Listen to me. Listen." There was exhaustion in her voice, and she tried to speak between mad half-laughs and gulps of air. "Till the void in you utterly overflows; till you've exhausted yourself in each and all, and there remains nothing of the man, set out! Till the universe is one mirroring ocean."

Though words were in motion, they were only half of the water that filled the teacup of understanding between us. We communed on such a mystical plane that henceforth only metaphoric utterances could possibly be conveyed.

"How?" I asked, advancing on her.

"Set out! Where the jail walls were cleanly erected, there take a sword to space and time."

My heart would not stop thumping. "Where? Where is this place?"

She was almost gone, her eyes rolling. "Tomb of the great synthesizer."

Fire was crackling from me. Reforged! Restored! And so soon after I had cast aside my previous ambitions. All of my recent accomplishments and milestones seemed to me at once futile and even contemptible. I had a burning urge to destroy the new laptop and set the apartment—no, the whole building—ablaze. Her words were vague, the promise obscure, but still it called to me, fiercer than any black voice in my head. And they were there, the voices. They were gorging themselves on my new zeal.

The woman cackled to herself and collapsed on the floor, fully delirious. Whatever she was, she had stirred me to action.

As suspected, it was not through words that I would redeem man, not through dialectical reason that I would gain the necessary control to do so. There were tools I needed. I spun, not willing to waste a moment, and shut the computer. It was an elegiac moment, a transition away from the life of a futile philosopher to that of a revolutionary, somewhere, somehow.

And the white sun was still drifting through the room when I turned to face her, though I found only her wearied laughter still echoing like some witch's cursed farewell.

34

CIGARETTES IN THE VOID

After the first week had passed, Tikan and Sielle would remove the barricade from their room and head for the lounge once a day. Every time they wound out of the residence hallway, they would pass the monk, who had resumed his metempsic abstinence, and the hateful couple. It was only on their fourth attempt that they found Emilio, sitting in his regular place in the lounge, smoking his cigarette.

They sat down at the table, and he offered Tikan a cigarette. Sielle sat down next to them, clutching the chrome briefcase.

"Everything is prepared," Emilio told them. He took a few prolonged drags of his cigarette. "You will meet us at the docks exactly three hours from now. You will wait for me to take over from my colleague in validating the boarding passengers. Then you will board like anyone else. You will not go to the dormitories, but directly to crew quarters. There will be an empty room at the far left where the two of you will stay."

"Excellent," Tikan said. "Is there anything else?"

"Yes. I need two things from you. First, I need you to provide me with one of the promised locations before we take off. I can search the Earth from the cockpit and make sure of what you are saying. Second,

I need you to promise that you will not leave your room in the crew quarters for the duration of the flight."

Just as Tikan was about to swear his oath to the captain, the door to the lounge flew open. The person entering emitted a growl and a low screech through the steam, which was altogether not an unusual collection of sounds considering the number of broken minds littered about the place, except that Tikan immediately recognized the voice.

"Mira," he said, standing up and turning around. He flicked his cigarette off into the void.

"Excuse me?" said the captain.

Tikan ignored him and strode over to Mira. She was clutching her head, now slippery with water and sweat, and she was moaning inaudible words to herself. She collapsed onto the floor not far from their table. After briefly reassuring the captain, Sielle traipsed over to them.

"Mira," Tikan said, shaking her shoulders.

"I don't want to go, Tikan," she moaned. "I don't want to—I don't want to, no. I want to speak, let me speak. I went there. I went there where it was."

"You don't have to go," he spoke into her ear, shiftily checking his surroundings.

Sielle walked up to Mira and crouched down beside her. "Is she going to be okay?"

"I think so," Tikan said. "Mira, can you stand?"

With her eyes still firmly shut, Mira tried to get up, but failed. Instead, she grunted and crawled on one arm over the wet floor, her other hand still squeezing her head. "I—I need to speak to you."

"Where's Naim?" Tikan asked.

"With Onasus. I can't speak. I need to speak to you. Where been days? Streets. You were gone and we."

"Wait a second," he said, and then turned around and strode back towards Emilio. "Do you have room for two more?" he asked the captain.

"Er-Yes, I don't see why not, but—ok. Fine."

"Okay, good."

"I'll need you to come at the exact time, please," Emilio said. He took a few hurried puffs of his cigarette. "And you'll all stay in the same room. If you're late by just a few minutes, I'll have no choice but to leave without you and—" The captain suddenly stood up rigid as an antenna pole, the legs of his chair scraping the floor behind him. He had a dead stare on his face, the kind one had when metempsying. In rapid succession, all the other people in the room, whether dancing or drinking or metempsying on the floor, also suddenly jumped to their feet and stood like a regiment of trained soldiers.

Tikan's eyes grew wide, and with the adrenaline surging through him like the water of a broken dam, he bolted over to Sielle, who was still squatting beside Mira, and yanked her up by the wrist. He then stood with the same posture as the captain, the sweat pumping out of him.

Sielle watched Tikan and copied him. Just as she was about to open her mouth and ask him what was happening, he gave her the slightest shake of the head, and she fell silent.

With the sound of water at their heels, the sentinels streamed into the hall. They threaded through the crowd, looking at each body now erect and paralyzed, as if they were librarians inspecting an archive. The steam was condensing around their armor.

Mira, unlike every other procrusted person in the room, had some trouble conforming to the procrustic imperative to stand and metempsy so that her eyes could turn into cameras. She was on all fours, her body trying desperately to stand, while she resisted and shrieked. With every attempt to rise, she kicked the space behind her and slipped back onto the floor. While one arm pushed against the floor, another slammed a fist into it.

Tikan watched her dark outline shimmering blue each time she flung her arms into a pillar of steam. The corners of his eyes were twitching.

A sentinel approached the three of them, the steam drifting off his armor like a cloak. He passed in front of Tikan and Sielle and for now observed them only through the eyes of Emilio, thereby validating their correct postures without yet preying on their minds. A chill passed down both of their spines.

The sentinel turned to Mira with his gun drawn after she made another shriek. He bent over and picked her up by her shirt, holding her close to his visor while she continued to writhe like a woman possessed, and began inspecting her mind.

"Go," Tikan told Sielle, and then in one wild bolt he dove into the sentinel, spearing him against the purple globe now surrounded by paralyzed dancers. He pinned the sentinel against it and snatched his rifle.

Hesitating a moment, and gritting his teeth, Tikan blasted the sentinel in the face. The globe screeched and let out electric currents that made the dead sentinel's body convulse against it and the room spasmodically flash purple. The remains of the sentinel's face a horror of wires and flesh. The room and the firefight suddenly took on the quality of a fever dream.

At once, the other sentinels began to converge on them. Tikan scrambled over to Mira, pulled her over his shoulder, and then, with the rifle almost dangling off his finger, he began firing into the solids shifting through the steam. Though they outflanked him, they fired back with care, aiming only at his legs.

Before long, the purple globe was surrounded by corpses like some occult relic activated, the acolytes around it harvested by their very object of worship. One round singed Tikan's thigh, but still he shifted through the steam and picked the sentinels off as best he could, until most were motionless heaps smoking in the dark.

Disoriented, he turned in place a few times and fired another barrage, feeling a cold doom fill him as he remembered Sielle. He scanned for her but could not see her. Suddenly, he heard a clatter of steps behind him, and as he spun to fire he hesitated for a second.

A sentinel stood before him, gun already drawn, a void-like distance between them. Standing at the mercy of this last hollow paladin, Tikan inhaled a mortal breath and, from the corner of his eye caught a shimmer in the steam.

Tikan turned his head in time to watch Sielle shove a paralyzed and metempsying bystander between the sentinel and him. The bystander, stumbling into their gulf, took a series of shots in the back before collapsing. Before Tikan could react, Sielle vaulted out of the dark and in one fluid motion repeatedly fired point blank into the last sentinel's chest and then tossed the rifle out past a veil of lit steam.

"Quickly," Tikan said. He ran to over to Emilio and found him splayed over the table with half a blackened face. He cursed, picked up Onasus' chrome briefcase where Sielle had dropped it, and sprinted for the exit to the lounge, motioning for Sielle to follow him.

They ran into a nearby corridor and secluded themselves in the classroom where they had opened the briefcase over a week before. They squatted there, catching their breaths, listening for the splashing footsteps of their marauders.

Their escape to Sirius seemed now a childlike fantasy, which had always been destined to break apart. They could not bear to look each other in the eye, for each felt ashamed before the other after having invested their hopes in such a vulnerable future.

"What did you do?" Tikan growled at Sielle.

She gave him a confused look. "What do you mean?"

"I mean in the hall, there. That guy you threw, like it was nothing. Why?"

She shook her head. "To save you, what else?"

"And what about him?" Tikan said, motioning vaguely towards the lounge.

"He was metempsying and—and they don't matter! I matter," she said, flustered. "And you matter."

"You're wrong. That's where you're wrong."

"We don't have time for this now."

Tikan shook his head. He put Mira down against a wall and inspected her. She had lost consciousness and was now breathing arrhythmically. "Listen. Mira only just passed out, so she won't go dim to them for a while. While they can still track her, we should split up. We'll meet up at Onasus' place."

"At Onasus' place?" Sielle repeated incredulously. "Split up? You've got to be joking. Let's find another ship and—"

"I won't leave Naim behind," Tikan insisted. "And something's obviously wrong with Mira. I can't. Not now. And we have nowhere else to go."

Though he could not see it due to the condensed steam on her face, tears were now welling up in Sielle's eyes. He gave her a cold hug and a long stare, as if it were the last he might give her in the flesh, and he gave her Onasus' address.

"I'll meet you there," he said. "We'll make it to Sirius. Just don't be reckless."

Then he got up, with Mira on his shoulder and the briefcase in hand, and he stormed out.

∾

With Mira still on his shoulder, Tikan persisted to the lowest, abandoned depths of Proxima. As the sentinels dogged Mira's flickering consciousness, he sprinted past gallery after gallery of Proxima's ancient lore, now dead and dateless like all of history.

He passed a series of sculptures in the amorphous forms of men or women, whose exact features ever depended on the observer's gaze and whose carnelian eyes twinkled past him, as if the sun's beams were being channeled through them. The overgrowths cascading off the ceilings or the onyx-wrought terrace plateaus took on live shapes in his mind, the vines still jade as their first shoots but now crooked, torn, gnarled, crowding the passageways like curtains and the floors like a carpet of ropes. The deeper he went, the more the steam subsided.

By the time the air thinned, hours had passed, and he could hear no more footsteps behind him. When he could run no more, he stopped in a massive chamber almost completely overrun by wild flora.

In this jungle clearing, center of Proxima's buried heart, there lay the ruins of a galaxy wrought in gold. Each solar system extended out of Earth's lowly horizon was there, crumbled with its spheres in the chokehold of brambles.

He lay Mira down, and in the shadows he waited. He had spent hours running, and would spend hours now sneaking back out. Once he had recouped, and the sentinels could be heard arriving at the start of his labyrinth, he made off with Mira back towards the surface.

While Tikan navigated the labyrinths of ancient Proxima, Sielle retraced her path to the Bilge's exit, slinking past the sentinels now streaming into the Bilge by the dozens.

After nearly bumping into a sentinel on her way out, the idea of leaving the world of Proxima altogether began to fester in her mind. She snuck out of the underground with few issues, and spent nearly a full day wandering around the metropolis despondently. Though the hope of reaching Sirius seemed now a dismal prospect, she resolved to meet Tikan at Onasus' apartment nonetheless. She suppressed the memory of Onasus' shining carapace at the docks and the terror it had inspired in her.

She walked towards the blood and black horizon. The glass sky seemed to her, then, a celestial aquarium in which pink or aquamarine nebulae and far galaxies were kept, in the same way that exotic creatures of the deep might have been. She looked for a dust-born nautilus, or a squid curled up and blanketed in its own kaleidoscopic gold and turquoise ink, or a jellyfish made of the cosmos, or the argonauts and Argonauts doubled in brine and the high mythic plane once invoked far from this steely world.

Instead, there preyed only a vampiric sky. There, on the head of Proxima, under that blood haze oozing from the glass lip of the skyline, she felt her curiosity come to disappointment. The silver planet, in all its rigid ugliness, made out of humanity's purest powers of abstraction, had nothing left to offer her save its own collapse.

Tikan emerged out of the Bilge nearly a full day after he and Sielle had split up. He spent hours on foot carrying Mira, and hours more after she had woken up helping her walk. They leaned on each other and spoke little until they crested a rise in the pavement and found a throng of skyscrapers ahead.

"They're running out," Mira said. She had whispered such vague or nonsensical phrases along the course of their journey. "Spilling. Peacocks alone. Tikan. Do you still believe?"

He did not reply.

"Truth and justice, Tikan. The peacocks are fanning."

They descended closer to the mass of skyscrapers and then lost sight of the rooftops as they wound through narrower passages. The journey was not without arduousness. There were no others to be seen, neither in shadow-passages nor in the wide, brilliant streets. The air was thick, too. In that same city where the perceptions of its denizens were edited, the senses were blasted to stupor. Tikan continuously swapped the briefcase between his hands.

"We're close to Onasus' place," Tikan said.

"I didn't want to do it," she replied.

"Didn't want to do what?"

"To go with him. Or to run away. I wanted to live."

"I did too."

Mira coughed and closed her eyes for a prolonged while even as she limped on.

"I thought I could kill myself in the Bilge and live. My words. They don't catch anything anymore. Just empty sounds I know what I'm saying but I can't hear it, I hear sounds. Don't go. Don't say. I know what I'm saying but I don't know if you can hear me because I can't hear myself. I hear one sound and one word's a sound and I see the thing in my mind and I see it there and there but I can't put them together, can't make the sound for the thing. Can you understand me? I only hear your sounds and my sounds, but not words but I know I'm speaking. Help me. Help me, it's prison," She started to sob. "Help."

Tikan held her closer and tried to console her, but it was no use. He did not fully comprehend her predicament.

"Will Onasus help?" he asked her.

She did not answer.

"Mira, I need to know. Were you running away from him? How did you know where to find me?"

She shook her head and gripped Tikan's shoulder. "Truth and justice, Tikan. Still believe? The peacocks are fanning."

~

When Tikan and Mira arrived at the foot of the apartment tower, Sielle had already been waiting for hours. She was waiting in a nearby alley, watching the entrance from the shadows. She stood up as soon as she noticed them, and though she initially strode to the edge of the alley, she stopped herself and continued watching.

Tikan loitered around for a long while, the anxiety on his face, scratching his head and waiting, searching for her. He was grimy and battered. Mira almost collapsed on her feet, and she was motioning for them to go inside.

Sielle considered following him inside, but then she remembered Onasus. She remembered his old face and fire and blood. The dream was dead. They would never make it to Sirius together. And the mere notion of being in Onasus' presence again nauseated her. It would soon be of no matter. He was going to dematerialize very shortly, along with the rest of the platinum carcass that was Proxima.

She watched Tikan spend a few more minutes looking around for her before eventually heading inside. It was a shame. He was a kind man, after all. She had somehow become invested in his struggle, and in the idea that the two of them were indeed two of a dying kind.

But, it was all irrelevant. The weight of time was her treasure, and hers alone. He was not like her, not in the slightest, and he was going to fall away shortly as well, and she would be farther than he could fathom. She watched him walk into the building, and she surprised herself by whispering "goodbye" after him, before the red sun made its final streak against her pearly skin, and she left the world.

35

A MOTE IN THE EYE

A week since the mystical visitation. I spent the time alone, in quiet contemplation, attempting to decipher the message left by my private priestess. To unlock the powers she had confirmed were indeed resting in my soul.

In the dark, mostly, away from light and its material illuminations. Asleep through the days, sunless through most of it, paperless, bedless, pushing away the moon. I tried to purge myself of the sort of linguistic reason to which I had become accustomed, and of passion. To destroy the broken tools with which I was conditioned to think. A clean slate was needed, away from the corruption of thoughts that had matured to near-permanent residents in the structure of my mind. Thought itself: a plague, a lie.

What, then? It was cruel. I had no control; I could feel it. I took a kitchen knife and twirled it around against my forehead until I bled a third eye. I shed my clothes and then tried to peel off my skin with my fingers, starting from the wrist. Was I to introspect, polish myself into immanent resplendence? Or was I to externalize myself, empty myself into everything so as to achieve an ill-conceived transcendence? A tangential thought, closer to my previous ambitions.

The path. The tomb. Those were my new objectives, and yet I had only a frustrating blank as a starting point. I picked up my disused journal and, by pen, tried a final time to expel my thoughts in an orderly way. This time it was without pretension, without the judging audience in mind. But, before I show you this godforsaken work, consider the theme of my madness.

It was a hidden sort of knowledge that I needed, that much was obvious. Something hitherto impossible for the human mind to access. Something ever shifting behind the veil of appearances.

The trouble with appearances is that they are well-meaning deceivers. They want to show you the true thing-in-itself, but they only ever reveal themselves. The thing-in-itself is independent of its sensed appearance. That isn't to say that the appearance in no way corresponds to the thing-in-itself, just that it is a tinted sliver of it. To see something subjectively—say, a tree—is to see it temporally; it is an object floating in the river that is you. It is to witness a profile of it, at an angle in space. To take a stride to the left and alter the angle from which you are observing it is to see the same object, though still incompletely.

Time and space are not simply sensory handicaps, either. To perceive this tree is to perceive it in the context of your own history, as you pass by the park on your way to work. As you spend your one-hundred and ninety-eight thousandth hour and twelfth minute on the world's clock. As the subtle and now subdued texture composed of every jolt of anger or intrusive phone call or thought of charity or whatever other state of consciousness you've been in near other trees underlies—no, infects—your present experience. As you impose on it the rustle and the sway of the thousands of other trees you've seen and the sunlight or moonlight or streetlight or lack thereof between the leaves or the winter branches. As you circle it while retaining a memory of its outer dimensions and expect its next contours and try to glue them together with your imagination, with the resin of the ideal barks you've gathered and conflated over the years. The tree appears to you as an orphan, though you yourself are a part of its lineage.

Appearances can do no more than this. They cannot bring into your understanding the entire history of the universe, past and future, from the simultaneity of each respiring or rolling object's inner perspective.

Only by transcending mere appearances, could true knowledge of the tree be afforded, for apodictic certainty is the only real kind of knowledge. Knowledge all riddled in doubts, or bracketed off, is as good to me as half a bank note. Meanwhile, the veridical tree, with all its profiles and histories, lingers behind the veil. The veridical tree, and the veridical forest, and the veridical rivers, and the veridical seas, and the veridical mind, each hiding itself nakedly in the sun.

Thus, it seemed to me initially as though my new quest was to burn the shroud of noumenal knowledge, of the truth as it hides behind these impenetrable shadows.

Now, before I go on to use the crutch of reason a final time, I must address something. You have no doubt already cupped your chin innumerable times and pointed out, quite patronizingly, that I have what you might call a "God complex." Let me clarify, because you are only in part correct. There is a difference between the philosophic god, conceived of by Aristotle, and the Abrahamic God. I have only ever wrestled with the former.

You may call me egotistical, point at my selfishness—and that may be fair—but be honest as you do so and identify the exact species of my conceit. I have never been interested in being worshipped, or being credited with creation, or any of that. My only transgression, if you want to call it that, has been a dire dissatisfaction with the knowledge I have been afforded after being so ruthlessly thrown into the world.

Although the two notions of God presented above have no doubt at times been confused, there are differences. The philosophic god is merely idealized reason. It is only the arbiter of metaphysical first principles. It has no will in itself, is not a sentient being, is rather the god of science, if pathetic science could apprehend first principles. It is no God, in truth, and none could ever bow to it. The Abrahamic God, on the other hand, is the Creator, wholly unbound, and for the most part, beyond human rationalizing outside the confines of revelation. Do not misunderstand my complex by thinking I would contend with the latter. I am not so arrogant.

Now, quiet! Witness the unfortunate final testament of my rational mind:

I think, I am, but the rest is uncertain. Let me begin with the obvious. I am not God. This is woefully certain, considering I have no memories of creating myself or the universe, and considering I lack any form of verifiable omnipotence or omniscience. The possession of memory, in any case, seems irrelevant to an omnipotent, omnipresent and omniscient being. What I am, reduced in my perspective, is a prisoner, a slave, unable to know anything but his own consciousness as it is chained to time's unceasing arrow. And yet in recognizing this limitation, I feel at once free to reduce myself further.

If I exist, then I have proof that there exists at least one true entity in the universe. Now, having concluded that I am not God the Creator, or the philosophic god, I have only to wonder what use I could be as the only absolute being or subject in existence. I am not so egotistical. I'm not. And I am not a sufficient reason for this.

Either I am the victim of a sealed-off mind, mysterious in its existence and only perceiving its own contents; or, I am in some way related to other entities which exist separately from me. Entities that can become related to me somehow, and in that relation pull me from a static darkness. On this view, the world gives itself to my consciousness, and my consciousness gives itself to the world, and the two are not identical.

It does seem foolish of me to suppose that ideas, other entities, or appearances exist for me only as amnesiac projections of my inner self. As though every time I eat, I were cannibalizing a part of myself. As though my mind were a procedural generation of all conceivable things. As though every time I speak to another, I were resolving an inner knot.

The question, now, regards how the changes in my conscious and perceptual states occur. Consider me as I gaze on a potted plant. There is the perception of the potted plant, and presumably there is the potted plant itself, independent of my perceiving it. Certainly the plant itself remains even when I do not perceive it. Otherwise, it could be said that I destroy it along with the perception of it every time I shut my eyes. What is to help the poor potted plant if there is no longer anyone to perceive it? Must it die? Will God intervene to guarantee it?

But, now getting to the heart of the question: given that something external relates to me (it may not be right to call this external thing an 'object,' or to say it is relational, but let's not drown before putting our swimsuits on) and thus produces my perception of the plant: is it the plant, individually, as a thing, with which I am in a perceptual relationship? Is it an individual, plant-perception-producing thing? Or is it that there is only one external stimulus generating everything in my perceptual state, rendering it rather like the crowded cell of a film reel?

After all, it is not possible to merely look at a plant and only a plant. The plant is in a room, on a wood floor, against a dirty wall, in a cracked pot, with a certain gradient of light across its leaves, with the birds chirping outside, with the smell and moistness of freshly watered soil, and with the baggage of murder and anxiety and curiosity I bring to it.

Given this co-dependence of all perceptions and conscious states within one unitary perceptual state, it seems to me that all I have certainty of besides the perception is the relation itself, or the external stimulation itself, rather than what individually or generally results in my perceptions. What would one general perceptual relationship look like, you ask, as opposed to a set of relations with the plant and the pot and birds? Consider being fed all of your perceptions through a single tube running down your neck, or some device planted in the center of your brain. The relation is with the device only, though it produces many conscious perceptions of sound and texture and color and so on.

Now, if I were related to one and only one externality, a number of other questions emerge. Is the perception already contained in me, awaiting activation? Are the world and I a mere simulation, an engine being run? It seems strange to say so. Though consciousness is opaque to itself in many respects, still there is a degree of distinctness to it. There is a zero-point of interaction with the world, which makes one sensitive to the throne of being. And so while the reality of my thinking being *is illumined and the true source(s) of my perceptions remain obscure, I can nonetheless grasp the truth of an external world as a whole in itself.*

This is promising. It gives me the resolve to say that, though I cannot have full epistemic knowledge of the objects of my perception, I can know, in a general sense, that they are not entirely subjective, internally generated, or illusory. In fact, the senses do not even need to exist for this latter conclusion to be realized. Whether the external world I perceive in fact corresponds with the external world as it is, or whether the external world amounts to the hidden workshop in heaven, there exists some form of an external world.

For even if I were nothing other than a running simulation, still an external force would have had to have sparked the monadic I into being. Something would have had to have built or set in motion the determined theme park that was me. *And if all is in fact contained in my mind and streamed as a reel of panoramic film, then still the ideas, the 'perceptions,' and their mysterious originary first principles, are real as such.*

But we need not go there. What is important is that I recognize the error of supposing that I can be a mere, relationless monad. If thrown out into the cold of existence alone, at the very most I would have been a collection of malformed and wordless understandings, an intellect with only its own idiot self to attend. A consciousness that transcends itself, but to emptiness and back. Far from the prime mover that thinks itself, rather a miscreation of a mind that can only fixate on its own self, bankrupt of potential, lacking any power, and ultimately nothing but a stillborn consciousness.

Thus, I find my own mind, as a solid watchtower scanning the world from above with its spotlight, to be a particular and sharp certainty, whereas the external world could be said to be a general and vague certainty. The epistemic or metaphysical truth of its objects appear to me as blurry shapes to a blind man: certainly there and constituted in the world, but difficult to discern in themselves.

Regardless, the external world can still be established as existent, if only pushed back one layer of reality, and this is an achievement, at least. It is true as a whole, even if all of its contents are illusions. In other words, I find the sandbox to be true, but still doubt the individual grains of sand within it. It is at least refreshing and sobering to know that the universe will not die with me, but also I can't help but feel infuriated.

Now, having acquired some sort of scaffolding, I turn to investigate knowledge from a higher ground. It is possible, given my previous conclusions, to provisionally accept the rules of causality and the appearance of objects, at the very least, for the sake of convenience. It is reasonable for me to believe people are people, and not empty machines.

But I find this reassurance to be insufficient. To be able to describe elements in my subjective sphere or to have confidence in reality are fine for practicality and survival and perhaps even for humbler thinkers, but not for my grand task. It seems to me as though I am still trapped in a moving cubicle, forced to see multi-dimensional objects in a compatibilized, single-dimensional format. The truth presented in mismatched fragments, not even in complete profiles.

Under what conditions, then, could I come to know the full dimensions of a thing-in-itself? My principle certainty is acquired by my thinking and being. I've fixated a lot on logical certainty, but I mean to include the understanding *provided by* intuition *as well. In fact, I think this* immediate *kind of understanding is more important. In any case, if the only pure, certain knowledge I can find is of my own consciousness, solely by virtue of* being *it, then the only way for me to truly and fully* know *something else in all adequacy, as far as I can tell, would be to* be *that thing.*

It is sudden, but I realize upon this last reflection that I have made a substantial error. To be in and for oneself, to know the full dimensions of one's being, and to know that one exists, are three matters quite distinct from each other. Being and thinking afford me knowledge of the first and the latter, only. Oh, and here the frustration and the feeling of only now realizing I have been lost in a maze for days creeps on me again. What a farce! I don't even know myself to the fullest extent, in all immanent and extra-temporal adequacy, the way I insist on knowing that wilting plant in the corner of my somber apartment.

Keep it together—don't let the scaffolding collapse! Oh, I'll keep trying.

How can I know every dimension of a plant if I can't even know my own dimensions? I can confirm my existence, fine, but a confirmed existence does not thereby enumerate or clarify its nature or its contents. Just as I can only attend to one given profile of the plant at once, so too is my whole consciousness impossible to apprehend in one psychic fist. Each of its constitutive elements, each conscious feeler aiming out at the world, ever sacrifices the others, and sinks back down the murky pool forever hidden from my intentional gaze, or they rearrange as the foundation to a different conscious state. To attempt to observe this basic inner structure at the same time as it is in action, is to void the task from the beginning.

And so, even if I could achieve a sort of metempsychotic embodiment of the plant, and come to know it in full existential embodiment whilst somehow retaining my own mind, still, a lot would be left obscure to me, just as much of myself is obscure to me despite my being. This is a temporal concern, too. I cannot inhabit myself at every moment in time, nor do I know my own future, or have a clear map of the past or my past, or of the plant, and I therefore lack complete knowledge of either it or myself in all respects. What a cruel joke. What a waste of time. What a—

Quickly, then. The truth I thought I had been nearing was being wrapped in obscurity in that same predictable way. I fled and scrambled for an escape, as though chased by the dark side of the moon's cold creep. Chased by that sickle shadow as it speeds down, violent and pitiless and hungry.

And, *darkness*.

I spent the next few days reading over it, agonizing over the contradictions and the difficulties and the definitions and the terminology and throwing the whole journal into dark corners before scrambling like a dog to fetch it again.

I twirled my kitchen knife around on the same spot on my forehead, even after it had scabbed over. I then took to stabbing my pillows and my mattress in a flurry of feathers and carving up furniture as if to repurpose the wood and planting the knife into the desk like some pirate owed a debt and even stabbing a full bath of water—which I sorely needed—like a lunatic mariner and slashing the bathroom mirror until I had cuts all over my forearms and fingers. And, reaching the bloody tag end of these cuts, I tried again to rip off my skin, weeping and growling as I did so, grinding my teeth to blood as if to chew the space between them.

You yourself have no doubt already grimaced at the nest of chaos hanging just above us. Have I tried your patience already? Good. Now you have a fragment of the agony I experienced. But don't think it ended there:

Aground again, and no closer to uncovering the cryptic message of the disappearing Daphne. Is it worth another try? Will it take me a lifetime I don't have? What I find, as I continue to pace the impregnable walls of the noumenal realm in all its grand indifference, are my own basic limitations.

But, perhaps I am altogether wrong. Perhaps I am just rejuvenating the same old mistake, magnifying, multiplying my frustration. More than anything, I realize that I don't even know what I'm searching for. Would that the priestess could return to offer a final hint. It's clear I'm still looking incorrectly.

It's not that I don't know myself, but rather that I can't grasp all of what I am. Indeed, the more I consider it, the more I recognize the problem of history and of self-knowledge. Perhaps the thing-in-itself (I won't disrespect the term 'noumenon' any longer by using it in this context) is not a mysterious entity, forever residing behind the object of appearance, in principle inaccessible to the mind.

What if it were, instead, the unity of mind and object, which, once united, obscures the full history that led to its very consummation? What if it is the process that at once makes possible and precludes us from immediate knowledge? The multiple perspectives, spaces, times, and minds which makes an object coherently knowable, but which are, at the same time, impossible to apprehend themselves?

Furthermore, the totality of my thoughts seems well defined before I attend to it or endeavor to pick out some thread of it in letters, at which point it explodes and envelops me in a gangling mass. Let me go! Let me out of this cage! The spaces, the varying shapes, the hole in the 'o' which glares at me like some permanent incompleteness or cyclops' eye, which I would do anything to penetrate and fill up, whose perimeter I would give anything to dissolve, if only it were the real thing and not some damn instantiation. I want to drown in ink.

The difficulty is in the act of trying to pull it out into the light, to speak of the infinite in parts. It makes me feel like a child again, when I was yet freshly raped by language, and gleaned certain understandings of myself only by intuiting the meanings of my sentiments; when concepts were still puzzled together, and I could not express much depth of thought beyond superficial utterances, which, in any case, were usually completely mangled when considered by another.

These are thoughts I cannot find it in my linguistic powers to express. I recall Wittgenstein. He once said of the same problem, I believe: Things that cannot be put into words. They make themselves manifest. They are what is mystical. *Oh, they've manifested, yes, they've mystified, they've tortured and tormented, and it makes me wonder; I wonder, Wittgenstein, whether I should attempt to reach farther than my earthen rind.* Whereof one cannot speak, thereof one must be silent, *he's already responded. And yes, how true, but that's not a commandment! Don't command me, Wittgenstein! It's a vicious condition. It doesn't need to apply to me. I won't let it. Through effort, I can overcome these shackles unduly placed on us all. I can. I will. Drown me in ink, or drain it from this page—that's the only way.*

And this ineffable sense of the greater wealth of knowledge within me is deceptive. I promise you it is. It parades itself around in confidence as a short, summarized thing, ready to be delivered at a moment's notice. Yet, the more I try to pick at such thoughts, pull down the entire tapestry from a loose thread, the more it becomes apparent that what I am attempting to do is section off an arbitrary location in the infinite, and the tapestry unravels chaotically around me.

What I want is to communicate the whole in one fell swoop. What I want is for each of my words—for one word—to be accompanied by the infinity of history, by the history of my body, and of my mind, and of my knowledge, and of the world, and of you, and of their relations.

It seems that what I have tasked myself with, then, is to lasso this monadic cloud and force it down from the ether. Wrestling with such an indistinct and simultaneously complete entity is arduous. The initial or one-off attempts end up feeling like trying to push a rectangular rod through a circular slot; or trying to siphon the whole universe down a tight drain, morelike. The more I try to speak or write, the more the general, unuttered abstraction explodes in complexity and loses its holistic purity and meaning.

They're perfect thoughts, indescribable except in greatly corrupted forms. Inner shadows—that's what they are, and I've just been trying to look at the sun through them. I want to capture those perfect ideas from outside of Plato's cave and drag them in. To eliminate the shadows and the shackles. To destroy the cave, even.

Is it worth cultivating the already incomplete link between that world of nebulous thought and the powers of expression? And even if it were possible, what then? I was told not to write anything down. Could that instruction be extended to mean that I should abandon linguistic refinement, too? The quest is too uncertain. The way of the priestess, of the tomb, of the synth—

The phone rang, then. I rose, swathed in my epistemological stupor, suddenly conscious of the harsh physics that bound my mortal vessel, of the dying tissue beneath my dying skin. I fumbled and fingered for the light switch on the wall. The phone, my portal to the criminal world, was on the bed. I jumped for it, and fell upon Bogdan's urgent voice.

~

It was still dark when Bogdan called me in to the warehouse. Nothing could have been further from my mind than those petty thieves, yet they were dangerous, and perhaps I owed Bogdan some indulgence, at the least. I arrived shortly after the predawn, when the clouds were dull and their underbellies were brightening, and the trees were emerging from their silhouetted prisons.

That foul and rotten hive loomed ahead, looking like some abandoned carnival attraction while the wind gusted coldly about it. I walked towards it in the lucidity that follows the light after a sleepless night, the same near-drunkenness that somehow sharpens the world to excess.

The entrance was empty: no filthy clowns or grumpy Esteban. My footsteps echoed through the place. I saw that the doors to the usual conference room were open. I poked my head in and carefully scanned for Bogdan. His voice reached me before his figure, sharp and delayed in my head.

"Welcome. Come in, come," he said, sitting on a pyramid of crates.

"Hi. You called for me. Is everything okay?"

"Fine, just fine. I wanted to chat with you. See how things are going. Haven't seen you around here in a while. Nice to have your own place, right? I understand."

The sentences came to me fragmented and slow. Everything seemed clear and distinct as a whole, but the parts arrived mangled, and served to create deep, circuitous strains along the surface of my brain.

"Yeah. It is, I—"

"Do you know what I used to do before all this? I told you, a few times. Let's see if you remember."

"A doctor, I think, or—"

"Ophthalmologist. I liked it. I really enjoyed it, and the pay was good. Do you know why I moved on?"

"No."

There was ever a threat in Bogdan's tone, but this particular time, I felt myself in danger. I stepped backward, closer to the large window behind me. Fresh light was beaming in through it, further crowding my senses and warming the room. Bogdan hopped down from his throne of illicit crates and followed me.

"Let me tell you. It's a good story. It'll entertain you. So, I always hated working with people, you know, asking the patients about their health and how they felt." He sauntered around me and then stopped in my face after making a full circle. "You learn, working in hospitals, that everyone is a goddamn hypochondriac. I also hated the research side of it, you know, the statistical shit they make you do when you're working under a lazy big-shot.

"But the surgeries, my God! What a rush to dig into the human eye." His eyes reached out the window, excited at the memory. "I was addicted to it. Organizing the other surgeons, ordering the nurses around, calculating points of incision. You know me by now: I love precision. I love being the clockmaker. Fuck, I miss it just talking about it. I was a licensed surgeon for over five years, and every damn time, I had to stop myself from just forgetting about the job and letting myself explore and destroy the delicacy of the whole thing. Break the glass just to see it break sort of thing.

"One day—it was a normal day, nothing upsetting or anything—I was in surgery performing phacoemulsification on some idiot. Cataract surgery. The nurse was saying something in my ear about emulsification, and I noticed that the idiot's eye was already hollow, and that I should stop and finish the procedure. Well, I didn't stop. Actually, I picked up my scalpel and I started digging into that mushy little hole just to feel the damage. Let me tell you, there is *nothing* like the weight of the knife when it cuts through a person like that—the pressure and release is just exquisite."

He followed his violent enunciations with visceral hand movements. His clenched fist repeatedly slammed into empty air under crazed eyes. "So much blood and little chunky pieces of white. Shattering that guy's sight forever with my red knife. It was excellent. Really satisfying. I couldn't—why are you looking at me like that? Of course, you know what that's like. You're like me. You have the same hungry mouth. You don't want cash. Look at me. Stop walking backward and look at me. You don't want money, you want to be the clockmaker who breaks his own clocks. I know you. That's why—no, shut up—that's why you're here. Stop pretending."

I was too tired to be afraid. The room felt like a strange theatre, where I was both audience and actor. I reclined right against the window and felt a deep sadness for Bogdan and his miserable life. He was in need of help, like everyone else. He lacked pity and understanding of even himself.

"Anyway, I just thought I should share that with you," he continued, the rage subsiding from his face. "But, I needed you to do something, too. I need you to go into the city and…"

I stopped paying attention, as other words were running through my head, bright, consuming, louder than the echoes of the warehouse.

Tomb of the great synthesizer. Till the void in you utterly overflows; till you've exhausted yourself in each and all, and there remains nothing of the man, set out! Till the universe is one mirroring ocean. The voices returned, fuller, too; this time harmonious, demons in saintly garb.

My legs took me away from the warehouse after the murmur from Bogdan's mouth ceased, but I did not follow his instructions; no, I made straight for a burning destination. The oracle was singing in my ears, her voice soaring over the music of revelation.

36

THE DUTIES OF THE SEER

On the highest floor of Tower Thirteen, in apartment six, Tikan was looking out at the city through a broad window. He watched the streets almost buried between buildings, and the avenues shiny against the night and bereft of people, scanning for any sign of Sielle.

He and Mira had arrived an hour previous, and he was beginning to worry that something terrible had happened to Sielle. Had the sentinels caught her, or worse? Or had she simply lost her way? It was unlikely. He tried to put it out of his mind for now and hoped she would just arrive. He turned around to watch the others.

Mira and Naim lay on lilac sofas arranged in a square, half-dozing or lulling in place with their arms resting over high cushions. It was a spacious living room, whose walls were cream papered and whose furniture was vibrant as the ancient cultural shift it was modeled after. Only the sounds of Naim's breathing could be heard, along with the mechanical clicking of whatever Onasus was working on over a dark wood table at the other end of the room.

Since their arrival at the apartment, Mira's condition had improved dramatically. Though she still suffered mild headaches, she was now forming coherent sentences. She and Tikan did not speak about the Bilge in the company of the others. In fact, she barely spoke at all while recovering.

Onasus, meanwhile, had started building his device as soon as Tikan had handed him the briefcase. It entirely preoccupied him, and he, too, said little besides initially ordering Naim about like a lab assistant. Strangely, Onasus had not once addressed Tikan's almost-two-week delay. He had simply greeted Tikan and told him to place Mira on the couch, as if everything had gone according to plan. Tikan continuously watched him from the corner of his eye.

"Mira," Tikan said. "Do you want to come down with me for a minute?"

She looked up at him, rubbing her temples. "Why?"

He was uncertain of whether she remembered Sielle, or whether she had even recognized her presence to begin with.

"There's someone downstairs I want to bring up."

"No. Sorry, but I'm still not feeling well."

Tikan sighed. "The peacocks are fanning," he told her without thinking.

Mira crossed her eyebrows at him. "What?"

"Nothing. Never mind. Naim, how about you? Will you come down with me?"

No response came, save for a deep groan. Naim had started a metempsy, exhibiting slight spasms as he lay starfished on the couch with legs outstretched over the suede.

"I don't believe this," Tikan said as he marched over to the couch to shake the man. "Wake up!"

"What did you say to me, Tikan?" Mira insisted, getting up from the couch.

"I said the peacocks are fanning. Just repeating something you told me earlier. It's nothing."

"No. No I didn't. Shut up, Tikan. I didn't."

"Okay, fine," he said, confused but dismissing it. "Naim, let's go."

Naim did not wake.

"Can you just leave him alone for a second?" Mira said.

"What?"

But Onasus interrupted. "Tikan, tell me about this person downstairs. Who is it? You haven't told him anything compromising, I trust? You haven't compromised us on your little sojourn, have you? And you will discuss the matter with me before bringing him up, yes?" he said, wholly removed from the small argument.

Tikan ignored him and kept his gaze on Mira, who rose to argue with him.

"You treat Naim like he's a complete idiot," she said. "Like he's some child you're trying to raise. He's your friend, not your dog."

"Yes, he's my friend. I care about him."

"Just stop it," she said, frowning and casting aside an invisible curtain. "Stop trying to tell everyone what to do. You're not anyone's keeper. You're just a man. Put your feet on the ground for once."

He flipped his hands over so that his palms faced the ceiling. "What ground? What are you talking about?"

"I'm saying get out of your head, Tikan," Mira sneered.

He took on a countenance of disbelief. "My head? My head!" he said, gripping his head as if he were about to rip it off his own shoulders. "If I could step out of my own skull just a foot farther. What's going on, Mira? I just carried you across half of Proxima. Do you remember?"

"No," she said, holding her forehead. "That's a lie. It's not true. We got off the ship and we came straight here, all of us."

"Mira," Tikan said. He turned to talk to Onasus. "What's going on?" He slapped Naim's head a few times, and angrily asked him, too, "What's going on here?"

"Stop talking, killer," Mira said coldly, staring at the floor. "Yes, now I remember. You let all those people die on the ship. My ship. Killer!"

He swallowed hard, then turned to the window again and paused before turning back. "Killer?" he said. "Killer? Haven't you ever killed anyone? I refused to be a killer, that's what I did."

"No. I've never killed anyone," she said.

"Not even in metempsies?"

"It's not the same."

"Yes it is."

"Nobody died."

"But you still killed them. Why did you do it?"

She breathed hard. "You're a killer."

"Oh, would you both just stop being so melodramatic," Onasus said, sighing over the click-clack of the object beneath him, which was shielded by the raised top of the chrome briefcase in front of him. "Mira, are you still truly mad at dear Tikan for his actions on the ship?"

She leered at them both and then shook her head. Then she nodded. "I—I am. Yes, I am. Yes—and—I was saying—how im-m-mo-moral and un-un-un," she stuttered. "Unjust everything is, when he let those people murder everyone and go. He's a coward and a hypocrite."

"My dear," Onasus said in an elderly way, swiveling towards them in his chair. "He is a fool, perhaps. A man who has glued together the pieces of his shattered spirit with the resin of a misguided philosophy? Certainly. But, he is no coward. It takes a lot of courage to serve the ideal or the invisible, true or not."

"Onasus," Tikan interjected, annoyance in his voice.

"No, let me finish," Onasus said. "If we're going to have this little therapy session, best do it now before it gets in the way of our plans, yes? Listen, Mira, Tikan follows what is, in fact, an old and dead tradition. For this alone you must respect him. He thinks that there are absolute truths: universal ideas that float above us all, which we all have an uncompromising duty to serve. Duty: yes, that is his prime directive. He is a God-fearing man, an idealist and a romantic. You have to respect this for its aesthetic worth, at the least, yes? There are few like him left, if any. Now, Mira, I agree with you, in principle, that this is an absurd way to think. In the end, though, letting your invaders go perhaps bought us some more time, and so it was maybe a good thing, you see? They would have sent more people after us, sooner, if they had known we were alive. The consequences are favorable, so let him have his metaphysical cake, yes?"

"You think I sacrificed those people on the ship to save myself?"

Tikan asked, taking a few steps towards Onasus and staring him down.

"Now, that's not what I said. We've already been through this. I said, considering the consequences, it was not the worst decision that could have been made. What we must keep in our sights is our goal, which will more than compensate the lost." The clack of tools resounded from the table, and Onasus huffed before continuing. "Of course, you and I can have our philosophical differences, Tikan, but at the end of the day we must carry on and be practical—a word you should consider more often."

"Practical," Tikan mused, and then paused. "I don't remember that meaning 'lawless.' There are laws in this universe, and in us, and you'd destroy them, thinking the way you do."

Onasus dropped his tools. It seemed a theatrical move. "Oh, my dear boy, stop it, all right? Perhaps Mira is correct, that you should relax your zealousness. You see, you're a servant of consequence as much as I am. What do you think you're doing when you perform your 'moral duties?' You think there was ever a difference between a mercenary and a priest? The only difference is that my consequences play out in the world shared by all, and yours in faraway heaven. Everyone is a consequentialist. The result of your moralism, if we suppose it is even true and that the universe and the affairs of souls within it are indeed gridded and coded like the contents of some spreadsheet, is that you are further aligned with the universal good. That is a consequence. Without consequence, you are static, your worth is static, your soul is static. You cast your stones first and then, and only then, can you ask who is without sin. Do you see? You let those people die as a means to achieve your private, ideal result. Their death was the means to your universal good. You watered the roots of the celestial tree with innocent blood. Blood gardener, tending the tree of which we are all branches."

Tikan jerked as if to respond, but instead held himself back and dismissed the whole argument. He would not let himself be pulled into Onasus' web. He sighed at Onasus, and then spoke with simple confidence. "What you're saying is wrong."

"Oh?"

"It looks like people are just tools to you, ladders you cast down after you've used them. So of course you'll see it that way. It doesn't matter what I say."

The hands of the scientist reposed, and he squinted over at Tikan pensively.

"You know, Tikan, I suppose you might be right," Onasus said, grinning. "I'll give it some thought, how about that?"

Tikan shook his head in exasperation.

Onasus removed his eyes from the others and quickly returned to his work under a cloud of calculations.

"Tikan," Onasus said, head pointed down behind the briefcase. "You were going to tell me about this person you've met. Who is he, and why did you suggest that we bring him into our company?"

"She, actually," Tikan said in a calmer voice. "A young woman I met who doesn't have a procrustus. Bizarre, I know. I met her by coincidence on my way here. I told her we were leaving soon, and that she couldn't come with us," he added hastily. "But I need to get her off-world. If there's another ship we can spare, or maybe drop her off on the way, or—"

Onasus went pale. "And did you meet this young lady during your vacation in the Bilge?"

Tikan quickly shifted his gaze to Mira, and then at Naim, who was still in his metempsy.

"What, did you think I was unaware? Where else is a vagrant like you supposed to hide on Proxima?" Onasus said, putting his tools down and getting up from the table. "Why do you think Mira came running after you? You would have been caught by the sentinels if it weren't for me."

"How did you—"

"I told you, Tikan. You are already implicated in this saga, and there is no way out of it."

"Did you tell her where we're going?" Mira interjected, to Onasus' watchful, silent approval.

"No, of course not. I just told her we were leaving Proxima, and that our trip was likely one-way."

"Good. That's very good, Tikan," Onasus said, regaining some color after his momentary petrification. "I'm glad you didn't divulge the details of our ambitions. That would have been quite bad, yes. And you think that she was very willing to go with us?"

"No. I didn't ask her. I was just going to help her get off-world."

"Meaning that she wasn't a citizen of Proxima?" Onasus asked, before quickly answering his own question. "Well, I mean, how could she be? Too much procrustic regulation here. You know that better than anyone. Ah, but that is good news, yes. Tikan, I..." His speech ended as he trailed off and stared blankly ahead.

A demonic greed or lust started crawling across Onasus' face. First from the corners of his mouth, a faint but giddy smile. Then his eyes widened and glinted with the sheen of cursed jewels and reached farther off, transfixed like those who have dipped their heads down to the deepest abyss and there seen themselves perfectly reflected.

"Tikan," Onasus continued, not breaking from his trance. He walked up to Tikan and placed a hand on his shoulder. "It is absolutely imperative that you bring this girl up here at once."

"I'm sorry?" Mira said.

"Quiet, Mira," he snapped at her, and then looked back at Tikan. "You need to bring her to us, Tikan. She'll be coming with us. We need as many people as we can bring on this most desperate mission, and another without a procrustus will be very useful to us indeed, yes."

Onasus remained inert and unflinching as Mira stormed towards him. For the first time since before their meeting on the Equuleus, she seemed herself. She flinched a few times on her way to them, like someone with a facial tick.

"Listen, that's not right," she told Onasus, ramming a finger into his chest. "Whoever she is, she's not involved. Don't get more people involved. It's not fair. It's—"

"Mira," Onasus said, twisting his head to face her and adopting a hard look. "I said for you to shut your mouth, yes?"

She stood, aghast, and flinched as if about to receive a blow. Then she grabbed her own forehead again and shot Tikan a look for support.

"Onasus," Tikan said. "Calm down. There's no need for you to talk to us like that. I'll go talk to her and see—"

"Shut your damn mouth," Onasus growled. "You've spoken enough today. What I am planning is bigger than you; it is bigger than us all, clear? Go down and bring her. Now."

Tikan frowned coldly. Immediately, Onasus recognized the danger he had called upon himself and took on a suppliant countenance. For in Tikan's gaze was the snapped patience of a man recently tantalized and subsequently crossed by fate. The cold ashes of his soul enflamed only to have been smothered again.

He lunged at Onasus and wrapped both hands around his neck, pressing both of his thumbs into it, nearly crushing the esophagus. He drove the scientist against the wall and pinned him there.

"You keep your voice down." Onasus squirmed in his grasp, his neck in red coils to his chin. He tried to say something, but Tikan squeezed his neck harder. Onasus' fingers were like worms wriggling on Tikan's hands. He coughed and wheezed and tried to breathe, but Tikan only pressed harder. "I said keep your voice down," Tikan growled. "We're not your toys. Whatever you've been doing to Mira, I know."

Onasus patted Tikan's wrists. Exhaling a large, angry breath, Tikan then pushed himself off of Onasus. He turned for the door.

"Tikan, wait," Onasus said in an almost pleading voice, fixing his collar and clearing his throat. "I'm sorry. You must forgive my attitude, of course. I have been under a lot of strain for the past few years, and now that we are so close, so very close, it is difficult for me to contain myself. I am working on a device that will help us immensely. I am working toward your good, yes? And Mira, too, forgive me. You're right that I am responsible for her condition, but it isn't what you think. I've been helping her to—"

"I don't care. You're going to stop whatever you're doing to her. Now."

Mira was now sitting on the couch again, her eyes shut, massaging her temples.

"Without my help, she would not understand half of what we are saying," Onasus insisted. "The price is a few migraines, but it is worth her staying in the loop, wouldn't you agree?"

"I wouldn't."

Tikan turned again for the door. On his way, he passed the couch and roared, "Naim! Wake up! Wake up, Naim. You better be awake when I come back."

"Tikan, will you bring the girl up?" Onasus asked meekly, the sudden shift in his tone psychotic.

"You're going to help me send her to Earth, so yes."

In his latest metempsy, Naim was revisiting the events of the last month. The destruction of the Equuleus. The crawl through the engineering shafts. The meeting in Mira's apartment and the journey across Proxima. Every day since arriving in Onasus' apartment, he had engaged in this same memorial metempsy, reliving the chain of events.

It always started in the officer's lounge, where Onasus had rushed in to wake him from his metempsy and save him from the flames. Onasus then led him to the corridor before the lounge, where Onasus took command of the ship's defenses. Everyone on the ship already knew Onasus to be a natural leader, but it was in this moment that they truly looked to him for guidance. The subsequent trek through the engineering tunnel was never pleasant, but it gave Naim a chance to appreciate once more the way Onasus had carried him to safety after he had taken gunfire to the leg. He would be dead without Onasus. And in the cockpit, Onasus had made the hard but prudent decision to let the black suits go. Even Mira had not argued with him.

Naim was semi conscious through the metempsy's next day or so, but through this daze he nonetheless managed to witness Onasus healing his leg, smiling in a fatherly way as he did so. Cleaning the wound, spraying it with the platelet gun, wrapping it in gauze. Then, after single-handedly repairing the ship, Onasus spent a long while informing Mira and Naim about all that he had learned regarding the ship's invasion, and requested their help.

The deeper, dormant part of Naim's consciousness nagged Naim-the-subject-of-the-metempsy about the incongruence between Onasus' deep knowledge of the galaxy and the ship's invasion, and his place as longstanding resident and captain of the Equuleus. But eventually, the latter Naim triumphed and gradually replaced the other.

∼

In the elevator, Tikan stood between three mirrors, which detailed each of his dimensions for anyone who might have been examining him. Thoughts warred in his head as he stood watching a panel of lights alternate as the floors passed by.

Squeezing his fists and breathing hard through his nose and curling his toes in his shoes, he tried to tell himself that leaving for Sirius with Sielle was still possible, though he knew it was not. His stomach turned at the thought of Onasus' desperate interest in her, at the way he himself had compromised her without thinking. He slammed the side of the elevator with his fist.

Perhaps they could still manage it. Perhaps they could trick Onasus, steal a ship from him, and—he stopped himself. There was nothing left but Arcturus. Punishment for his selfishness these last two weeks. And the longer he spent away from Sielle, the more ideal she turned again in his mind again. As if her flesh were dissolving somewhere, and the steam of it formed a cloud in her image.

The elevator doors opened, and he crossed the lobby.

The pavement shone, blinding him for a moment as he stepped outside and heard the door to the apartment building land shut behind him. He rubbed his eyes and waited for them to refocus. The blur sharpened and, standing atop the stairs as though they were the raised platform of an alabaster pantheon, he expected to see Sielle wandering somewhere at the bottom or across the street.

She was nowhere to be found. Rows of identical towers lined the other side of the street, and their leaning shadows dulled the pavement. Left or right, he found no sign of her.

She had agreed to meet him here. The scene must have rerun tens of times in his mind as he questioned her absence. It was more than a day since that moment, now. She had been bold and, at times, impulsive. He had shouted at her for saving him. It was not beyond reason that in her bitterness she had taken off to wander Proxima.

He walked for a while around the tower in the hopes of seeing her figure shift out of an alley or from behind a tree. He searched and searched, with the red fire thronging space above him, and he turned the other way to find the gaseous sun almost falling apart while it ballooned to fill the entire horizon at the end of the road. Rows of the apartment towers stretched on into it, the corners of their rooftops glimmering like rubies. There was no Sielle to be found.

Still half convinced that she had not duped him and run, he resolved to check the adjacent apartment towers. He hoped that she had simply entered the wrong building, and that he would find her strolling around a dark lobby waiting for his arrival. She was not in the first. Another tower, and another, and even the unlikely fourth and fifth. He spent over an hour searching, and eventually quit.

He felt at once relieved and crestfallen; for though she would be out of Onasus' reach, he yet had no indication of what had happened to her.

He started back towards Onasus' apartment.

When Tikan returned to the apartment, he found the adversarial mood to have lifted. Mira was standing at the far end of the room near the windows, and Naim was still metempsying on the lilac sofa, his arm slumped over its back.

"She isn't here anymore," Tikan said as the door fell shut behind him.

"What do you mean?" said an impatient Onasus, emerging from behind the table.

"I mean, I couldn't find her. Anyway, it's for the best. I think Mira's right. We shouldn't—"

"Well, did you damn well look for her?"

"Yes, of course I looked for her," Tikan said. "Now lower your voice. I won't say it again."

Onasus scowled. "Oh shut up. Just shut it. You speak far too much." He paused, and pursed his lips. "Damn it, go back out there and find the girl! We need her."

Tikan strode to Onasus, and with one hammer of a fist charged to contain in it the sum of his rage and disappointment, struck him near the eye. Onasus fell to the floor like a heavy mannequin, and Tikan picked him up by the collar, staring directly into his eyes.

"Tikan. Tikan, please," Onasus said. "Please, this is unnecessary. I'm just stressed. Don't make yourself beastly. There's no need for this."

Tikan's bared teeth trembled into each other. He raised his fist again as if to pummel Onasus, but ultimately let him go, exhaling. Onasus stood up and straightened his shirt. A trickle of blood oozed out of the corner of his brow.

"I'm sorry, Tikan. I am," Onasus said. "There's no need for violence. Now about the girl," he said as if nothing had just taken place, dabbing the corner of his brow with a tissue.

Feet shuffled from the corner of the room. Mira stepped forward with a flustered look on her face. She stood just beside rays of light that were penetrating the window.

"Why is she so important?" Mira asked, exhaling as if she'd just finished a run. "We had a solid plan before you found out about her, didn't we? Just let it go."

Gritting his teeth, Onasus squinted at Mira, as if she had just gravely disobeyed him. "I—Yes, in fact, Mira, you are right," he said, visible restraint caging a monstrous impatience. "Tikan, you will forgive me."

Tikan nodded without looking at him. Dejected and sighing, Tikan lumbered towards the couch. He winced again at Naim but did nothing else.

"Tikan," Mira said, rubbing her head and staring off. "Thank you for what you did in the Bilge. I would have died. It was you, wasn't it?"

"Right," he said, giving her an odd look.

He approached the couch and leaned as though about to collapse atop a pile of cushions.

"Ah, no, Tikan," Onasus said, walking up to him and holding him lightly by the arm. "You are right, yes. Both you and Mira, and Naim too, no doubt, for he is also wise. We must continue toward our objective, and we must do so with haste. And so, there is no time for rest, now. You understand, of course?"

Tikan stilled himself in Onasus' grasp. There was a twinkle in the old scientist's eye.

"What do you want from me now?" Tikan asked.

"We must fit you, yes, fit you with the device I have prepared. You must be able to fly, to pilot. And since you do not have a procrustus, or the appropriate training, for that matter, this has been a problem that I have had to circumvent. It is time now, yes?"

"Why do I need to pilot? Can't you do it?" he asked, to no answer.

"Onasus," Mira asked from the corner of the room, a distraught look on her face again. "Onasus, please. Remove the walls. Remember what was said."

"Yes, yes," Onasus snapped back, clearing another drop of blood from his brow.

The room darkened. Tikan shifted his gaze between them and frowned. It was clear that a clandestine, furtive meeting had taken place in his absence, likely something to do with Sielle.

"What's this device?" Tikan asked, giving Onasus a skeptical look.

"It is an extension for you to wear. You will use it to pilot. It will be intuitive and simple."

"Fine. Show me," he said, not yet convinced.

"Good. Excellent."

The two of them walked over to the table, and with each step Tikan grew more apprehensive. He gave Mira a fast look as he moved, and noted that she was distinctly concerned. He frowned again. "Have you stopped messing with Mira's procrustus?"

Onasus didn't answer.

In his uneasiness, Tikan fell into a sort of stupor, his strides turned sluggish, and before he knew it he was already at Onasus' worktable. He stiffened his arms somewhat as though to guard himself.

"Onasus. I'm talking to you."

"Yes, yes. Mira is fine. Don't worry about her."

"I don't see that."

"Not to worry. You will see it all."

The briefcase clicked open, but its contents remained hidden from view as Onasus leaned over it. Tikan stood facing the scientist's back, waiting for him to turn and explain the mysterious device.

"It is a visual extension, you see," Onasus said, still facing away from Tikan and covering the sight of the thing with his body. "So that you can perceive the true nature of space, of the strings between the stars. Like Mira, yes."

Tikan pitched back and forth in place for a moment. The air thickened. He turned to find his friends, who seemed now out of reach. Naim was absent, drowning in another reality; and Mira looked as though held in spectral chains by the corner. He saw her jerking forward, bobbing her head at him and trying to open her mouth as if her jaws were welded together.

With a heavy tongue and dry mouth, he tried to utter something, but Onasus cut him off.

"You mustn't fight it, Tikan. It is your duty."

"Tikan, wait!" Mira suddenly managed to say, stepping forward.

Onasus spun fast and struck, his old face like the devil's. Time slowed for Tikan. For in that breathless moment, color fled from each object, and existence itself seemed to drain from them, leaving behind only the pale, dreamlike scaffolding of reality.

In the deranged scientist's hand was a bulbous steel mask with impressions of a face on its inside and machinery burring on its surface, bulging out to form a lumpy pyramid. Two drills spun on the underside of the mask and fanned Tikan's face in the most noxious air, whirring like miniature turbines.

He tried to speak, to yell, to throw a fist, but Onasus threw himself forward and forced himself on Tikan. Tikan's legs crumbled, his stomach churned. And Onasus drove him to the floor, pinning him by sitting on his chest and barring his arms with his knees.

"It is your duty."

As he struggled on the ground, Tikan caught a last glimpse of Mira's covered mouth and Naim's dangling, dozing limbs.

Then Onasus pressed the mask down on Tikan's face. The drills piled into his eyes. The mask juddered and sputtered blood and covered his face whole like an eclipse of the fleshiest world.

He jerked and writhed and the blades shredded through the two new cavities in his skull. Blood rushed from those smothered fountains against the mask to leak out and pool under his head and wet his ears.

Now the seas, only eternities ago glinting shards of old thunder and hoarding primordial stones or new florae, and all horizons beyond reckoning, collapsed together and buried him in the surest darkness, all siphoned down the drains prying asunder his face.

The turbines roared and spat out the pulp of his orbs. The drills deepened. They reached out for the now-severed cranial nerves. To defile the highest temple. But he had cared about the flesh! How he had cared. They had misunderstood. They had thought his mind the only palace, and had taken this as license to desecrate the courtyard. Now he was Odin forced to sacrifice too much.

It was not possible for him to hear anything but the whine of those rotors, yet 'duty' kept ringing out in the periphery. In that agony which left no room for understanding, he summoned up what strength he had left. His arms and legs lurched out of Onasus' hold. He wrestled with the old demon and also clawed at the mask.

"Oh, suns and moons! What are you doing to him?" Mira yelled, free of Onasus' chains now that he was preoccupied, just as Tikan managed to throw Onasus off.

He bolted up and raced around the room in no clear direction, holding the deathly thing on his face and groping at its sides to try and rip it off. He flung around wildly, stupidly, mute and mad, almost falling over the couch, sprinkling his blood over the lilac sofa and Naim, and then tripping over himself into the beige walls, streaking them red as he made violent contact.

"Stop him!" Onasus said. "He's going to dislocate the damn thing!"

Tikan ran and stomped and writhed and threw himself into each dark space around him, battling blindly to free himself as the thing bored deeper down his emptied sockets.

Mira leaped to Naim and slapped him awake.

"What?" Naim groaned, as his world fell to sudden tatters.

"Help. Please," Mira said.

"Tikan!" he yelped, lurching up.

"No, you fool!" Onasus growled. "Do not interfere, but help. The damage is done. Now stop arguing, and help me hold him. Oh, never mind," he said, and then squinted hard at the two of them.

"Oh suns..." Mira lamented. She flung herself to the floor, and against her fiery will, dragged herself over to Tikan. "Let me go. Let go of my body!"

"What is this?" Naim asked, his voice trembling, shuffling over to Onasus and Tikan. "What have you done?"

"Shut up and help me!" Onasus roared as he tried to wrestle with Tikan, who was hurling himself about like a gagged berserker.

The two ran to grasp Tikan along with the scientist. They clasped his biceps and wrists, full of shame and regret, so as to salvage what was left of him. Onasus then peeled Tikan's fingers from the mask, and they all thrust him back onto the floor, where each pinned a separate limb. Down to the ground like a shot beast still fidgeting, down to the cold floor.

Meanwhile, the machine continued its morbid excavation.

"It is your duty, Tikan!" Onasus shouted. "Remember what duty means to you."

As they held him, his chest leaped up from the ground. He could feel their hands upon him and dubbed these thieves of all the world's luster as betrayers long comfortable in the skin of friendship all tatters and shreds.

"Hold him fast," Onasus barked as he released the left leg and ran back to his crafting table.

"What are you doing now? Oh stop it, stop," Mira said, tears welling up inside her. "Let him go. Let us go."

"The left arm. Hold it tight," Onasus said as he returned, bearing a long, wide knife like the commander of some guerilla squadron.

"Stop it! Stop it!" she screamed, while Naim petrified.

"Don't let him go, or it will be a complete disaster," the surgeon cautioned.

Now they, too, in all their shame, were at the mercy of crazed Onasus. He advanced.

"Your duty, Tikan. The universal good. Duty," he whispered like a macabre lullaby in the broken man's ear.

Then Onasus swung his sword with both hands as though it were a champion's claymore. A single clean slice across the elbow, without mess, wholly separating the flesh and bone. The blood spilled at once from this grisly new wound.

"Tikan, I forgive you. I forgive you," Mira wept.

"Why did you do this? Why?" asked Naim, hands pressing his friend's torso.

"It is his duty, yes? This is his penance. Mira, you agree, yes?"

"Shut up," she cried. "Shut up."

Tikan was no longer resisting them. Only the muffled whizzing of the machine could be heard under Mira's lamenting and Naim's hard breaths. The stump was gushing scarlet, wetting the floor and the two who lay beside it. They let go of their limp and ruined leader's body, and instead leaned over it in disgrace. And then his body started convulsing, his remaining limbs thrashing in shock.

"He's going to bleed out. Finish it," Naim said, bitter distress in his voice.

"Yes, yes," Onasus said.

And as his lifeblood seeped from him, and his consciousness

darkened, Tikan could not but project in his mind's dimming eye a final, feeble, flimsy, misty image of Sielle.

Then there was nothing but the continued degustation of the machine. It was picking at his brain, usurping the optical nerves. In his convulsions, he relented and abandoned himself to die.

Almost falling over himself as he rushed between table and surgery, sweating, Onasus landed beside the exposed and oozing wound. He raised up the stump and kicked away the dead arm.

"Hold the arm up!" he commanded Naim, who rose up, his clothes, like Mira's, brown and wet with blood.

Quickly, then, Onasus wrapped a clear, gleaming membrane around the end of the stump. Then he stood aside and watched it, proud as a master craftsman, as Naim the mortal upheld the scarlet scepter towards heaven.

The fine translucent coating started filling with blood and marrow before turning to a hard substance, which then crusted over into a glimmering, silvery red.

"That's all. That's all, Tikan. That's your duty," Onasus said, his nerves frayed, sighing in relief.

Beneath him was a wreck. Tikan lay in his own gore. In trauma wrung from his very veins. And the machine yet planted on his face continued its buzzing through his emptied sockets, and blood still leaked from the mask to widen the cardinal pool.

"Some hours. Leave him, yes?"

"What—have—you—done?" Mira said with a strained voice as she grieved over him, half of her face smeared red as some savage huntress'.

"Cured him," Onasus replied, before walking away to his bedroom and closing the door behind him.

37

THE MIRROR PEOPLE

Sielle left Proxima in the sourest mood. The towers collapsed and folded under the sky, the dome, and the absent stars. She exited the central causal web, sideways of the colored world, to navigate the backstage of existence. Although, this time she had some trouble charting her course. It was not unlike her unplanned experiences as a child.

Though she momentarily lost all outward perception, her inner sense of time and darkness remained intact; and over many of these jaunts, as a certain weight repeatedly pressed her mind to strange regions, she came to eke out vague subtleties and a fuzzy whole of memory collected of fragments in that realm.

Sometimes her trajectory, such as it could be described, was wide and circuitous; other times it was a quick and simple crossing. It was always close to instantaneous. A will to be elsewhere. An intention aimed across the void—an illusory void, she was sure.

Now she bolted carelessly from Proxima, interminably angry through a second's worth of eternal darkness, to an uncertain destination. Despite this reckless departure, she was yet partly tethered to Tikan, and for this reason centuries elapsed between them, though she arrived causally not far.

It was not Earth she leapt for, or some similar sphere prickled with metal, but an end farther than she had ever previously intended.

Her body reanimated, and she regained the weight of her flesh and bone in sedentary form. The ground lunged up beneath her. A bright flare bludgeoned her on arrival, and she shut her eyes again immediately. She leaned back and made supports of her hands. Colors pulsed beneath her eyelids until she pried them open and squinted until the blur sharpened to unmask the new world. A sheen bounced over the horizon and gave the land a vermillion rim.

The ground felt like a sheet of ice on her palms, though it gave off myriad amber glimmers, like Earth's sea at its most lustrous. She shaded her eyes from this intense brightness with her forearm over her brow.

There, ahead, were two suns burning in the sky, all ablaze but exerting little heat. Two suns, one pink and smoldering north, the other white and dangling in the northwest quadrant. The sky was an ocean blue with wispy clouds drifting across it. She rubbed her eyes. The land was translucent, as though it were made of glass or crystal, and it rolled on for miles into a false infinity like that of her own future.

Beneath its surface, there were massive columns of wiry threads resembling capillaries. They looked like bound ropes, branched together in thicker bunches to form complex networks all through the glassland. They were cerise, sapphire, amaranth, or bone white, but all paled, and no liquid could be seen running through them. It was as if she were standing on the chest of some colossus whose skin was lucent.

She dropped to her knees and brushed the glassy floor with her hands. With some effort, she managed to break its surface tension and drive her fingers through. Her hand was wrist-deep in a sort of jelly.

After she scooped out a handful of the substance, it separated into dense granules, losing its fluid texture and turning murky. The longer she held this batch of hoary pebbles, the louder a ringing developed in her ears. She dropped the granules, and they assimilated back into the ground as liquid. The ringing stopped.

More curious, now, she strode over to a tangle of red capillaries not very subterranean and lowered herself above where they were buried. She drove her hand through the ground, which split again without much resistance, and she grasped the red cords.

Her whole body immediately stiffened, and she shook in place, electrocuted and winded so that she could not cry out. In those brief moments of convulsion, it felt to her as though all of her memories were being dredged out of her mind together in one incoherent heap.

Through great effort she unfroze her hand, let go of the wiry bunch, and fell backward. The wound in the ground closed up with light ripples. She breathed faster, though there was no lasting pain. Ahead, the suns had both switched positions and were heading east on a new ecliptic.

After a brief rest, she got up and walked on towards the suns. She passed spires of capillaries erupted out of the ground and reaching up in bloom. Double or triple helixes, like flowers whose basic genetic code had been tampered with and then abandoned.

And there were other odd structures in her path now and again. Spheres in a pile out of the ground like solid bubbles that sweated something glistening, each containing a soft, organic-looking core. Sculptured shapes like the amorphous essence of tragic heroes distilled bodiless to matter, solitary and stark, and casting no shadow. These edifices melted into each other and rearranged per her distance from them; and they buzzed in a lifelike way so as to make her blood tingle the nearer she came to them, such that she altered her course. Globules hung from ridges, holding in stasis what could have been organs. A mound of interlinked, glass ouroboroses frothed amber paste to the ground in an overflowing perimeter.

Otherwise, all was scintillating flatlands for miles. No humans or animals or ordinary vegetation on this brilliant wasteland.

She walked on. Over the hours, a misty haze amassed around her. It thickened as the glassland started to rise. It obscured her vision, though her breathing was not impaired. The light of those defective suns above broke apart into shards through a glass hill not far ahead. She walked towards it along a track of capillaries that inclined with the land and which, at the hill's apex, tangled into a node beneath the ground.

From atop this ridge, the panorama below looked blanketed in a sea of fog. She leaned over and watched new smoke plume indigo from places where the ground itself bubbled up like blown glass before popping, then thin out and rise far above her as a miasma obfuscating the sky.

Then, out of the blanket of fog, she caught sight of something shifting languidly. It was a figure, striding through the mist, who had her selfsame likeness and clothing. Sielle slid hastily down the hilly ridge on her soles and palms in pursuit of this doppelganger, and the mist cleared the nearer she came to the base until it and the miasma above faded to blue skies again.

She stood, solitary and confused against the flat glassland, while the replica was nowhere to be seen.

After having searched halfheartedly for what seemed now only a mirage, Sielle continued to wander on. Brisk gales carrying a peculiar scent started to blow across her face. It was not strong, and not unlike the smell of pines in winter. It carried also the softness of lavender, and a fullness of body reserved for burning things. She spun in place a number of times and sniffed, but could not identify its source.

She traipsed on like a wonder-struck child along an arbitrary pattern, harboring no thoughts, simply taking in the jeweled vista, until she fatigued and searched for a place to rest. The land had mostly evened out by now. Above, light clouds were gathering beneath the suns.

On that lucent plain, she came upon a ridge which looked like a great frozen tide. She secluded herself under its alcove, and when she looked at her new roof, she saw that the sunbeams were passing through only half smudged. A cluster of glass sacs holding silver and wriggling contents hung from the ridge's lip not far away from her.

She lay down and extended her limbs, and then rested her head on her bicep, ignoring the prods of jagged ground in her side. Her head was angled such that she could watch the sky and its suns, which looked trapped in ice through the ridge's lens. The breeze whistled lightly past her ears and soothed her.

Then, in the stupor that precedes sleep, she saw vague, gigantic shapes moving far off in the sky. Whipping motions, which sundered clouds. But they were too far away to make out correctly, and she was too tired to give them much attention. Instead, she turned her faltering gaze to the glassland sprawling away from her and peered down the glass.

Those same capillaries looked as though they were floating beneath her. Past these, the body of crystal seemed deep as an ocean, and it refracted back the pink and white light from the suns. She kept staring, hoping to find a bottom, until she could do little other than squint, and then she succumbed and slept under the bright, cold suns.

～

The wind still blew over Sielle when she started to wake. It no longer carried any scent. Her face was buried in the crook of her elbow to block out the light. She turned, expecting night, and instead found the twin suns still dangling above.

She shivered, as it was now colder despite the perpetual sunshine on this planet. She rubbed her eyes and raised herself to a sitting position.

Then, the instant her hands reached the ground, she felt a sharpness in her back. With her mind alert and her limbs abuzz, she tried to turn her head, but the object dug deeper and cut her. She gasped, then, and shut her eyes.

"Why are you so far?" came a woman's gruff voice behind her. She was speaking English, though the accent was unlike even that of Proxima.

There was a pause, and the object was pressed deeper into her back.

"Far from what?" Sielle rasped.

"From the group."

"I don't know. Let me stand. I travelled here—I don't know what group. I—"

"Stop," the woman said. "Stand. You need to drink. Your blood is turning."

"Excuse me?" Sielle said, trying to turn her head, but receiving only another prod.

"Stand and drink. You'll come with us, and speak to Elu and Ilu."

The weapon was withdrawn and Sielle stood. A tall woman loomed over her, holding a long metal shaft tipped with opaque white crystal. Beside her was an unarmed man. Both had their faces covered in beige cloth that revealed only their eyes, like the head wrappings of sohei warrior monks, and which descended down below their waists as torn ponchos.

They had wound their joints and abdomens in whiter cloth, which trailed like mummy bandages. And beneath this garb, their chests, shoulders, and joints were padded with thin plates of synthetic-looking armor. Both of them carried mountaineering packs overflowing with supplies and clothes. The woman had a round mirror grafted onto her clothing, just under her left shoulder. Sielle saw herself in its tiny reflection, and saw that her face was flushed, her eyes dark with fatigue.

"Your blood is turning," the woman repeated. "Search the cut."

Sielle groped for the wound in her back. The blood felt warm, close to hot, even. She looked at her hand and found a violet stain on her finger.

"What is this?" Sielle asked.

"You need to drink," the woman said, offering her a plastic vessel glugging liquid.

The wind blew again. With a suspicious glare, Sielle snatched the thing and sniffed it. After a long, skeptical look at both of them, she drank from the gourd. Her tongue and throat seemed to frost with the taste of mint and other alpine herbs. Though she only sipped it at first, she could not help herself from gulping more. Some of it dripped down her chin as she drank.

"That's enough. Too much isn't good," the man said, tearing the half-emptied thing from her.

"Well, I was very thirsty," she said, wiping her mouth.

The woman stepped in front of her companion and cut him off before he could reply. "You said you were not from here," she told Sielle, eying her suspiciously.

"I—"

"They'll want to hear it. Come," she said

"I'll come," Sielle said. "I'm very hungry. But why did my blood turn purple?"

"That you do not know why is bizarre. It's not for us to discuss. Better for Elu and Ilu to explain everything, and for you to explain everything to them," the woman replied.

"What do they want from me? I don't want anything to do with anyone. I was just enjoying the wind."

The woman gave her a grave look in response. "Stop it."

With a step forward, Sielle huffed at the woman. Then the three of them walked against the enormous suns, which were now perfectly opposed to each other as though in preparation for war.

They walked for hours without breaks or much speech on the inclining glass plains, passing capillary trees and roving over hills. Three cloaked migrants indistinct amid the glimmers seen from on high.

From a hilltop, they saw mountainous glass formations scintillating in stark isolation on the wasteland, some resembling the skulls or ribcages one might have found on a desert long ago on Earth; except now of dead gargantuans and not of critters, and out of them crept growths which were not discernably alive, spreading out of cavities and crawling upon the surface like ivy as though preparing to pull each whole carcass down to the planet's veiny core.

"How far now?" Sielle asked.

"Not far," the woman replied. Unlike Sielle and the man, their leader was wiping the sweat pearling on her forehead and running a hand through her hair every so often.

"Neanh, drink. Don't take risks," the man said.

Neanh looked at him in grudging agreement and pulled out the gourd she had given Sielle. She took a small sip from it before continuing on.

They stopped just after cresting a hill and unbarred their brows from their forearms to face the harshening gleam of the suns streaking down the ground in a rippling stream of light.

Ahead of them on those rolling plains, the ground was shattered into giant shards not unlike a collapsed arctic, all broken and piled into each other and threaded by traumatized capillaries, as though a meteor had crashed down into it, or as though some great cosmic whip had lashed it with abandon.

"It's beautiful here," Sielle said.

Her captors did not respond, but only glared at her from the corners of their eyes. They started again down the hill.

"Do you have any food?" Sielle asked.

"Stop it," said Neanh, stopping only a moment to emphasize her severity.

"Here," the other said, pulling something out of his pack. It was not food, but rather a small silver box with a screen. It looked like a food printer, the same kind she had seen on Proxima, but older and clunkier, some relic of a past age.

"Haern, we don't have time for this. She'll eat when Ilu asks her to."

"Let's get her to Ilu, first, no?" Haern replied, a smirk visible through a gap in his headpiece.

He programmed the little machine and then placed it on the ground. With a hum uncharacteristic of the technology on Proxima, the bulky wand vibrated and sank slightly into the ground. It then opened its front panel and expelled a solid white bar.

"You'll have to be quiet, now," he said, handing Sielle what appeared to be food. There was a square-shaped dent in the ground where the machine had repurposed the glass for nutrients.

"Thank you," Sielle said, taking the bar without looking at him.

"Remember your place, Haern," Neanh said, leering at him from a distance.

Haern nodded.

While they spoke in their lower voices, Sielle ignored them and instead attended to her meal.

"Are there animals or plants, here?" she asked as she ate the tasteless mush. "It's all lovely, but it feels strange, almost empty, without them. Those gangly things look kind of like plants."

Neither of them replied, but continued to walk without looking at Sielle.

"Are my questions bothering you? I just mean to say that I like it here," she continued, still to no reply. She followed them on down the hill.

After navigating the perimeter of the great pile of shards, as if those shards constituted some monument residing along the track of a pilgrimage route, they came upon a sharp incline in the land. They hiked up to the very edge, where the wind picked up and streamed down a last stony ramp off the cliff and swept their faces as they gazed upon the desiccated rivulets meandering deeper into badlands of glass.

Neanh motioned for them to stop. Her companion joined her at the ridge, and without speaking, he climbed over the ledge and disappeared.

"Here, the others are not far," Neanh said, waving Sielle over.

"Okay, but I don't want to break my neck. It looks like a long way down."

"Quiet, and hurry."

With a sigh, Sielle joined the other woman, and looking over the ridge, recognized the sharpness of the slope leading to darker glass below. There were pebbles slowly tumbling down this slanted ground.

"It's easy to slip and fall. Be careful," Neanh instructed.

"Yes, I can see," Sielle said.

Then, just as Neanh slung her alpenstock through its holster on her back and crouched to begin her climb down, the wind rose again, and with it the odd scent Sielle had smelled earlier. It was stronger this time, its burned element more pronounced.

"Quickly," Neanh said as she crawled backward, scurrying her legs over the ridge.

"All right," Sielle said, following suit. "But hold on to me or something. I'm going to slip if I—"

"Now."

"Yes, I'm coming."

"I mean *now*. They're coming," Neanh urged in whispers.

Sielle spun in place to look for whomever Neanh was referring to. There was not time to see anything. Neanh suddenly yanked Sielle's left ankle from below her and sent her hurtling over the ledge.

The two tumbled down. Sielle fell on her hands and crumbled. She rolled down on beds of pebbles and occasionally had her skin sliced by jagged glass. The world turned into a cylinder where the blue sky cycled between two uneven suns. Beside her, Neanh had assumed a position on all fours and was skidding down like a stoic, her limbs protected by her elbow-guards and greaves.

A bump in the ground took Sielle's wind and clacked her knees together. She tried to right herself, but she sprang up with an uncertain step and an awkward lunge and fell forward again. The landing impact opened her palms.

And yet she would not leave this world, for its capillaried depths and violent, cold skies were yet calling to the child who had at one time gazed too long at a river of ice. She rolled off the slope and landed at its base, bloodied and unmoving.

Sielle tasted iron on her tongue. Her body ached, and she could not bring herself to rise. The wind was lower, but still blowing. The scent was gone.

Callous Neanh finished her own descent without injury or

complaint, stood up promptly, and walked over to Sielle. She gripped her under the arm, and shook her, urging her to rise.

"Come. We have a while yet to travel. You'll recover later. Get up and drink more, now. You're sweating again."

Sielle was breathing with difficulty and had taken on a look of sincere despair. "Of course I'm sweating," she croaked from the ground, trying not to collapse on her forearms. "You—You've broken my bones."

"It doesn't matter. Drink and your bones shall obey. Drink and get up."

Neanh yanked Sielle a second time, but she was limp.

"Haern, come here. She's being difficult. Help me pick her up."

Haern doubled back towards the base of the slope and squatted to haul Sielle up from the ground. All the while, Sielle's body throbbed with pain. Her Proximaen outfit was now battered and torn. She could not bear to look at the rips and tears in it, for they reminded her of her severance from Tikan.

"Let her drink so we don't have to carry her," Haern said.

Sielle could barely keep awake. "Give it," she mumbled, and was swiftly handed the gourd. She drank from it, and her pains were gradually muted to a mild throbbing. With a few stumbles forward, she regained her form, licked her bloody lips, and took a few steady breaths.

"All right, now come," Neanh said, taking the drained gourd back and marching on.

They walked in the shadows of great crags, whose translucent peaks high above caught the sunlight like fiery beacons, and which turned cloudy halfway down and milky white at the their bases.

They made no camp, pausing only to eat from Haern's little food printer.

Creeping up along the ravines and serpentine paths between the crags were iridescent outgrowths of scarlet that broke out of the ground, not unlike the capillaries but thicker, denser, and rather like coral or crystalized shrubs.

Neanh crushed these under her boots and collected the fragments into an empty vessel, where they would slowly dissolve without sunlight and turn into the liquid they had fed Sielle.

As they continued to descend the land, taller bluffs began obscuring the sky. Through one gap between these milky slabs of glass, Sielle saw again, for a moment, indistinct colossal shapes swinging about wildly between the clouds in the far distance and stirring them out of their bulbous forms into wisps. The others looked oblivious to this, and called her down sternly from her vantage.

Sielle half turned to face them without unfixing her gaze. She opened her mouth with some effort through the seal of dry blood that bound her lips, as though to ask them about what she was witnessing, but instead remained silent and joined them.

They hiked on down obscure and narrow passages. The feet of the mountains beside them looked haunted, all ghostly white as though signposting a way into the underworld. The walls of it displayed thick crimson veins upon their surfaces, like roots harnessing the cosmic energies of the planet itself, or a myth written in a language known only to divine or malefic creatures now extinct.

As the group descended, those looming escarpments, all wreathed in thundery mist, came to look from below like citadels made of ethereal stone, atop whose peaks lorded revenant suzerains. The ground began resembling pulverized basalt in the shadows, and as mists began circling above them and wholly blotting out the sky save some gray light, they entered into a desolate cleaving between the glass mountains, which widened out of a col. In this gap the glass surrounding them was fully opaque, and they stepped on soggy ground.

They waded waist-deep through a creamy morass in which strands of capillaries came decoupled and swung about under the surface like algae. Neanh swept away strange objects bobbing along in their wake with her spear.

When they emerged from this swamp, its viscous water dripped off their garments and turned to hard granules before reaching the ground. Their skins took on a faint teal color, which did not fade for some hours. They made camp on the swamp's banks and slept for an hour or two.

When they started off again, Sielle could hardly stand. They gave her to drink, then continued walking.

It was not long then, after some time navigating those arduous tracks devoid of souls in the nether planes to which they had descended, that they came upon a mountain wall faintly emanating cobalt. The vertical crack in its surface ran down crooked and uneven.

Neanh nodded at Haern as she grabbed Sielle by the back of her bruised arm and pushed her forward.

They slid through the narrow crack, leaning in at an awkward angle and bracing against the walls for support. It darkened considerably as they squeezed through. They shuffled down the passage in a sideways single file with Sielle at the front. As the passage widened, she was able to see into the cave. Inside there were arches and grooves, and the place was dimly lit.

Just as she exited the passage, she came upon two men, who moved aside without a word as Neanh and Haern also emerged from the mouth of the passage. Neanh pushed Sielle onwards, almost knocking her over.

They led her through a network of dim passages. Some had halos of weak sunlight cast against their walls out of small gaps in the ceiling. The anesthetic effects of the liquid were wearing off, and Sielle began stumbling. Her feet crossed each other, and she tripped over herself into Haern.

He flinched as though to catch her, but Neanh shoved him forward to prevent it. The gravel caught Sielle instead. She could not bear to roll over and face the walk ahead. She would have slept face-first in the glass had they not then lifted her up and marched her on. Still, she would not forsake the planet.

It was dim throughout the tunnels, but there was light gradually curling around oncoming corners. It was gentle on Sielle's mind, and it started to lull her out of consciousness. She dangled off of Haern's shoulder, barely conscious. They turned a final corner, and the full brightness momentarily blinded her.

In the cavern's heart, men and women sat on a saffron carpet not dissimilar to a divan, as though part of a majlis, leaning on cushions or sitting cross-legged in a circle. They were quiet and reverent, some lulling in place as though in mystic trance. An old man presided at the head of the gathering. In the center, a pile of gems shone a pale light.

"Haern, put her down, by Zotharra. She's in pain," said the old man. He wore a vermillion gown adorned in mirrors that shone like stars.

"She's fine," said Neanh. "I've given her to drink."

"Don't be barbarous. Let her sit," the glowing man repeated, standing up and letting light pour from his figure.

Haern lowered Sielle to the ground, and she slept as soon as her back reached the support of the walls.

～

"Wake, girl," came a voice.

Sielle squirmed atop hard pillows. She opened her eyes to find a tall and boney woman with long, silvery hair cuffing her delicate hands about her waist. She had a belt of little mirrors, like the old man's and Neanh's. She also had a necklace of smaller mirrors, and a tiara with a single mirror in the center. Sielle almost flinched when she noticed that the woman had a series of mirrors sewn into her skin, which increased in size all the way up her forearms, making her look like she were part of an ethereal, divine species evolved from the reptile.

The cavern was still dim, though a number of standing basket torches were scattered around, brightening the place. Though, it was not fire that burned in the metal baskets, but little gems emitting weak, cyan light.

"Good," the woman said, just as Sielle rose to a sitting position from the pile of red cushions forming a makeshift mattress beneath her. "What is your name?"

"Sielle," she replied without much thought, while dreamily observing her surroundings. "And you?"

The woman gave her a matriarchal smile. "I am Ilu. Come, stand. We have a lot to speak about," Ilu replied, offering her a hand.

Sielle took her hand. Various metal bands, also woven into the skin between the mirrors like threads, ringed Ilu's forearm down to her wrists. These bracelets were paled of their colours and had intricate, geometric figures carved upon them.

Sielle thrust herself forward in an attempt to rise, but she was unable to. Ilu's smile widened, and she gently helped Sielle to her feet.

"Walk with me," Ilu said, before starting out of the hall.

Others milled about while the two women walked. It soon became apparent that the cave was being stripped of its furniture. People collected cushions and circled around carrying rolled up carpets on their shoulders like totems. The place started to look more like a makeshift encampment as it was being deconstructed than the hidden shrine it had first appeared to be.

Meanwhile, there was something calming about Ilu's presence. It was in her swift and calculated motions, all of them graceful. In the way her sleeves hung off of her wrists and in her cold eyes and in her hands, which seemed capable of dark rites when provoked, although otherwise they looked fragile.

"Are you moving somewhere?" Sielle asked.

"Soon, but not before we have spoken."

Though somewhat vexed, Sielle followed Ilu out of the cluster of people and through a maze of passages. They glowed in the gemlight. Ilu's robes were almost gliding along the floor as they trailed behind her.

The two of them ascended a spiraling ramp until they reached a higher floor, and then walked through jagged arches into a new hall.

There were bronze ornaments leaning against the walls and fat pillars of navy crystal, and in the center was a majlis with many cushions. The old man sat like a sage in mediation before a pile of gems anemically blooming light from their cores onto the ceiling and the walls. This arrangement seemed to Sielle now too ritualistic to be mere art.

Ilu strode onwards and sat at the man's side. Sielle stopped at the other end of the majlis, but continued to stand.

"I assume you're Elu," she said, unfazed by the overtones of ceremonial protocol.

"Correct. I am Elu, but that you do not know this, and other obvious things, is to be the subject of our conversation. Can you explain your ignorance?"

"Ignorance of?"

"Of your whereabouts and of your company."

"How do you want me to explain it? I've never met you before. Any of you. I'm not from here."

"Where are you from, then?" Ilu asked, without breaking her knowing gaze.

A short silence followed, in which Sielle redoubled her focus.

"I travel," she said. "No one place in particular."

Elu and Ilu watched her without speaking. Their faces were unreadable. Recalling her encounters on Proxima, Sielle then grew frustrated. The further down the runway of time she traveled, the more difficult it was to remain anonymous. Simply being a human, a traveler, was less and less possible. She had to know peculiar and extraneous details about society in order to remain undisturbed.

"Do you know where we are at present?" Elu asked.

"A cave."

"There's no need for a sharp tongue," he said. "We just want to understand. You told Neanh that you aren't from here. You were also very close to turning, and you had no idea what it meant when they showed you the color of your blood. Had we not tested you while you slept, we might have thought that you were a…well."

"What this all says to us," said Ilu in her gentle way, "Is that you've come from far. Quite far. And you must have arrived quite recently."

Sielle bit her lip. She had spoken too soon, and they had trapped her. And yet, she sensed no threat in either of their voices. The situation was perhaps salvageable.

"Yes, I'm not from this planet," she said.

"That you would even call it a planet is reassurance enough that you are, in truth, very lost," Elu said. "But this calls an even greater question. And I urge you to be honest with us."

The old man's eyes grew stiff, and he fixed them on Sielle, the bags of wisdom underneath them hardening his authority. "Were you sent here?"

"What? No. By who? Who would even send me? I don't know anyone. People are—" She stopped before continuing. "Where are we, anyways?"

"How did you travel here?" Elu pressed, harsher in tone.

"I landed here at random. My ship—from Proxima," she said without thought, grasping at a pastiche of possible explanations.

Elu grew silent, and Ilu's eyes widened. They turned their heads to each other and gave each other severe looks.

"Repeat what you have just said," Ilu said.

"My ship brought me here from Proxima. I was expecting to return to Earth, I—"

"Stop it," Elu said. "Have you told anyone else this? Neanh or Haern?"

"No. They wouldn't let me speak, I—"

"That's good. It would be unfortunate to worry people. Although, I should say that I am now worried."

"Why should anyone be worried? I'm not here to harm anyone, or even to spend time here. If you want me gone, I'll go. I'd be happy to."

"We will explain some matters to you," Ilu said. "But you must let us speak alone for a few moments."

"Fine," Sielle said, somewhat annoyed. With their approving nods, she half-stormed out of the luminescent chamber and loitered just outside.

Once there, she made circles in place, trying to plan her next moves, stewing. On each and every alluring or mystery-tinged world, people had ever only impeded her, blocked her, or tried to break her.

She grimaced, as if to declare that she would bolt off if they menaced her.

She adopted a blank expression, and her thoughts started to wander back to Proxima. Stark images of the red sun and the broken ship, of the chase through the bright night, of the Bilge and of Tikan, of the sheepish pedestrians. Some time passed as she let the loose picture narrative circle and play in her mind, and Elu called her back into the chamber.

"We've decided," he said from afar, as Sielle strolled back into the chamber, "That it is best if you stay with us for a time."

"Do I have a choice?" Sielle asked, annoyed.

"I'm afraid not, but that is not by our design," Ilu said.

"What does that mean?"

"You are a long way from home, Sielle. Earth and its artificial neighbors are far from what you will find here. Our ground is more akin to flesh, and while it might seem apt to call the clouds breath and the water blood, those analogies would not do. Had Neanh and Haern not found you, you would have died, your body turned to something else entirely. Plainly stated, it is not possible for you to survive this world without us. You will have to come with us to Zotharra, our home. You will be welcome there, as you are here."

"And what is this world exactly? Where are we?" Sielle asked, bored with their manner of speech but bursting with curiosity underneath.

"We are among the spheres of Andromeda."

38

THE TOMB IN KÖNIGSBERG

Travelling again, struggling against sleep, nursing the cryptic gift from my precious private priestess, caressing and kissing it in my tormented mind—soon to be healed—rubbing its surface like a jewel with my mental thumb. A hint, a further nudge in the right direction; but it was *I* who had unlocked its meanings. Obvious, as there were commands in it, secret commands for me alone, from me alone. I was far and flying from the miseries of my mortal missions, heading for vindication and vengeance on the doubters and the disenchanters. They would see, and then tremble.

To Kaliningrad, then. To the tomb of the "great synthesizer." Or was it Athens or Rome or Baghdad that I should have sought? No, the bleeding oracle had been clear: it was to the titan of the present that I was to venture, not to relegated stars or suffocated roots. And there was only one said to have pulled all the loose threads of human thought together so dexterously.

No planes or cars or crude vehicles. In spirit, primarily, in mind, defrosted of preconceptions and their cumbrous affections. But there was physical movement, too, for I had to pace and step and pry and dig.

First, through the crossbreed city. Cool winds and fluttering brown leaves, cracking pavements and cloudy petrol. The modern cultivation of European land: the concrete over cobbled roads, the bastard architecture of medieval masonry and office glass, the single-file trees in crippled romance, the industrial rivers under overcast sky; the imprisoned parks, enclaved in the shadows of steel monoliths, found in travel guides and under bicycle wheels; the thin hulls of cars freezing under the light of earliest dawn; the city moving by stalling, growing through collapse. And let us not mention the Russian austerity supplanting German heirlooms.

Running, roving: I was febrile, madly waltzing on a hunt for that most luminous of Königsberg's bequests. The priestess' promise demanded haste. I coursed through the gray streets and up shaved knolls, darkening with the clouds, enshrouded in midwinter steam, misting past houses on marshy slopes. Searching, exploring, dissolving the space behind me like a living avatar of entropy, as a horde of faint stars started piercing the twilight. They brought with them a pregnant moon to launch low tides against the ports, the ships to rock and shake on their steel tethers. Waters silent as I roved on high, pulling out the cloak of night.

Above the city, haunting it like hoarfrost, engulfing it under my terrible wings. I fought off the cold and feasting fog and dove across a solemn old spine of a bridge. The specters in the sky cast me as a paler wraith upon my descent. I bled my dusk into the streets as I crossed them, through to the island at the city's heart, and my prize. There, winding down, I came upon the gothic steeple of the cathedral I so dearly sought.

A winter howl enrobed me as I stalked the holy grounds. I waited, impatient, pacing, trying to murder time with my thoughts. And the snow started to hurry down and blanket the place as I suffered, filling the trees fixed in prayer and dampening the squawks of knowing crows. Waiting, pondering. Escaping! Escaping my narrow booth on that night. Surely, each second a torturous taste of it.

I made myself the hound on the whitening grass, then the spider avoiding the light of sacred windows. Sneaking as I bided my time, my back pressed against the walls of history as I slunk under the parapets, listening and watching for an opportune moment. Night sped down, sliding off the spire and deepening before long, and then the gold pouring out between the cathedral's maroon bricks ceased.

Lightless, hungered, I crawled on the outskirts of the edifice imposing its holiness on me, skirting it like a fiend at the end of his lifelong desanctification, now fearing the judgment which hangs above every pilgrim in those halls.

And so I quested on in the periphery, in the dirt and in the shadows and in the vampiric ache of sin, marring the splendor around me with my mere presence. Stepping lightly, twisting around corners to reach the other end of the grounds, the months of thieving softening my footfalls.

Priests were leaving, worshippers exiting, their feet tapping away on the stone. Faster, then, I lunged from shadow to shadow until I came upon the pink pillars of the mausoleum, square in the dead of night.

The gates were easy to hurdle over. Foot in the gaps between the grille, launching, another step, ascending, then legs astride. I rolled off of my perch and landed in the enclosure, where I found myself faced with dimmed square patterns of orange, red, and turquoise on the ceiling that seemed for a moment to turn inward. I scrambled to the tomb beside me, and lulled for a moment beneath the grave's inscription.

IMMANUEL KANT

1724-1804

The time to defile had come. I walked up the low steps through a sideways gust, prepared to destroy my way through to eternal wisdom.

I stopped before beginning, and recalled a previous epitaph, one that had been emblazoned on a former tombstone not far from where I stood: *Two things fill the mind with ever new and increasing admiration and awe, the more often and perseveringly my thinking engages itself with them: the starry heavens above me and the moral law within me.*

An invitation, no doubt, and a celebration of my ambitions. For what better way to encapsulate my purpose? It was evident. How true the whisper of the oracle was, still wriggling merrily in my ear! Dreadful tool in hand, it was time.

The starry heavens. Crack. *The moral law.* Smash. It all rang through my head as I broke away corner after corner of the tomb, breaching it, causing it to crumble beneath me. Desecrating, desecrating, until my hands were raw and my spirit aflame.

And where the sarcophagus would regularly have been: nothing, an empty grave.

Fool!

But, no. The floor of the tomb, too. I crushed the stone, down to collapse. And beneath me was the light of the oracle's promise, packaged in unyielding darkness. A tight passageway, a staircase that spiraled down into obscurity and invited me in as the lightbringer.

I climbed down the tight helix with my hands against the walls. Darkness deepened with every twist. It was through touch and hearing alone that I managed to navigate that claustrophobic passage without tripping and hurtling down to a broken neck.

My fingers swept the stone of its dust, and my steps rang up as I made my descent. My breathing turned to a wheeze as I drew in the dank, dead air. Careful steps, heavy as I traveled lower into the hidden underground.

Hours passed, but I did not tire. The longer I ringed the coil, the more my appetite was whetted for what truth lay beneath it. Stepping, still. And after I ceased to track the time, after I had forgotten the steps, a faint, orange light started curling up the winding staircase. It grew as I descended, glowing brighter and licking out towards me with each step until I seemed on the verge of a great roaring fire hiding behind the column.

A great room lit by torchlight; a quiet, wide sanctum throbbing with indistinct possibility, inviting me in to examine and make clear what was otherwise a dizzying whole. I hopped off the ledge and observed.

The room was not exceptionally large, and it was somewhat unadorned. In fact, the left wall was missing, revealing piled earth threaded by thin, curly roots. Torches lined the walls and flickered the color of rust. In the center, a white ceremonial sarcophagus lay opened, empty, with its lid leaning over the side. The place resembled an abandoned and forgotten archaeological site, all the treasures and decorations stolen long ago.

I was curious, monstrously so, unable to fix my leaping attention, but sedated by the solemnity of the tomb. I walked forward, mystified, with my jaw hanging.

And there, at the far end of the chamber, a body was resting against a battered wall. I examined the wall from a distance. I saw that deep, rippling circles were carved on the stone surface, haloing the body. They moved outward, unfinished, seemingly beyond the confines of the wall. A trapped section of the infinite, surely, as the strange mural gave the illusion of depth, too, where a flat corridor of rings ran on without end.

I walked over to the slumped body by this wall of concentric loops. It was hard to discern who it was from a distance, and yet the answer was obvious upon a moment's reflection and a closer look.

Of course, it was *he*, the tomb's rightful occupant. There before me was the body of Immanuel Kant, the great synthesizer, whose home I was invading. I should not have been surprised. Although, I was thrown off by his deathless look and clothed foray out of his sarcophagus. His head was downcast, and his hands were resting on the ground, palms facing the ceiling. He was not decayed in the slightest, and it felt to me as though, if I had tried, I could have roused him from nothing but a mere slumber.

Not wanting to disturb the dead or the dreaming, I left him for a moment to massage the circular scars in the wall behind him. Nothing at all. They appeared common, lacking, even. And yet, this was the dubious work of my senses. Of course there was more! Of course there lay globes of shrouded truth behind the wall, which even reason, that conflicted beast, could not address. And what had the priestess said? To abandon that wretched thing. Or was I to refine and elevate it, to find a new path for its maltreated wheels?

In any case, there I was, prodding at mundane carvings, hoping for some other mystical intervention to shine through the cracks. The body beneath me may as well have laughed at me. Laughing, as ever. On marshes or mountains had he ever waited to mock me at journey's end. Undecayed, undying. If only I could have been so fortuitous. In him, then, perhaps: his special head, unchewed by time's teeth— perhaps that was what I needed to excavate.

I lowered myself, and raised his groundward head to level with mine. And—*great horror*! The eyes were missing, scooped out by some precise machine that left perfect pits, without scars or gruesome disfiguration. Only darkness poured out of the empty sockets. And the skin was still full, the lips redder than many alive. What fate was this?

I gazed into the two tunnels, looking, ignoring the dead sage's predicament and focusing on my own quest, hunting for some semblance of reward in the opened depths. Darkness, only. A dent in his powers of sense experience, surely. What was he to do with only reason left? If reason he could. The great synthesizer, benumbed of mind and left an immortally ruined body. The truest tragedy I could come upon. Yet, he was sleeping, surely, eternally, unable to know that sort of suffering.

It was time for rest, time to return him to his right place, in that great sarcophagus; and then perhaps I, too, would return to some sort of rest, or I would hunt down the lying soothsayer who had laughed in a bloody pool on the floor of my Parisian apartment.

I took dear Kant under my arm and raised him up. And as he rose with me, his eyeless head fell backward and faced the jittering light against the ceiling, and a rumble began. The sage was standing upright, scanning the heavens with his shadow eyes.

Where his body had been reposing, the carvings started to dislodge and vibrate. The circles began turning, gyring in on themselves, rearranging. I dared not let go of the philosopher's lifeless form, lest the ritual end. The poor priestess, she had been right, and true. I made apologies to her cherished, delirious figure in my mind. New patterns arranged themselves on the wall before revisiting their concentric origin. A slot appeared at the midpoint of the concentric circles and slid outward, a new darkness widening into a tight corridor.

I held on to the body in my arms, clutching it and keeping it fixed in place. Until, swiftly, as though time had discovered its error and raced to amend it, the flesh started to come apart. Two and a half centuries collapsed in my arms, and the body putrefied and melted, and the bones turned to dust in my arms and flew away with a gust from the black hole in the wall. For me he had waited these centuries, all for me.

I stepped forward, and crouched into the passage.

Down, down, traveling, and this journey was longer, and time was vaguer. Hands astride, I braced the tiny walls of the cylindrical tunnel, bumping each jutting brick. With the exhilaration of an escaping prisoner, I raced in a squat, stomping ahead and expecting the end to flower out in light like a moment of rebirth.

But soon enough, the unending length of the passage revealed itself. The hours dissolved into each other. It was not long before I began to feel as if I were not even moving in any space at all, as if I had entered some terminal void. I tried to run, to pace myself, to forget the journey, but the darkness would not end, and after some time, I started to feel a crushing exhaustion ram me from all sides.

But I pressed on, still, until neither days nor hours had any more currency as measurements of decay, until my bones could no longer hold me; until I, too, seemed on the verge of a wormless death. Was this my fate, then? Was I to be another undead corpse waiting for another hapless thinker to take the grueling baton?

No, the glory was for me. Mine alone. It was *I* who had propped up Kant's eyeless head, I who had walked in through those lightless corridors of his and...and I was losing focus...and I started to stumble...and I slept there, quietly, after a feeble struggle to remain awake.

~

My mind reassembled as I began to wake. The ground beneath me was damp and cold. Not the stone of the tunnel, but mud and wet grass. A burning patch of ice across my back. The scent of wintry pines rousing me.

I opened my eyes to moonlight and was struck at once with the confusion of waking in an unfamiliar place. Leaves and grass, saplings and timeless elders. Crooked branches meandering out in a vast mesh.

I raised myself into a sitting position and looked around. There was a thin ring of trees about me. I was in the center of a clearing. I stood and shivered and searched for understanding. No trace of another, no underground passage nearby. I wiped the dirt from my hands on the front of my pants and looked up.

Huge slabs of rock enclosed this nightmare meadow as if it were contained in a great stone skull. Most of the sky was covered, though the moon did brightly pale the trees. Straight ahead of me, the moon shone out of a natal scar running down from the roof of the rock formation.

I strode on through this narrow and stony birthing passage, and not unlike a newborn did I hold my breath and shield my eyes, blinded by the taunting of the moon above me.

I exited. It was yet unknowable where I was. My senses were waking from the suffocation of sleep and the moon. Waking to wolves ritually baying as though to summon the brume of the forest. Here, the sky was fully exposed. And the moon was belligerent, bearing down, bulging out of its net in the firmament to press me, and beside it the stars were weeping cold fire.

The woods I encountered ahead were denser. With arms cradling each other and legs trembling, I walked through the buzzing of crickets and the cries of sleepless birds, all hiding in the adamantine night. Trees, swaying their full and silver-touched heads in the wind.

The foliage mazing out above filtered the moonlight so that it came down in thin beams to masquerade as some nighttime divinity or magic imbuing the woods.

Wandering deeper into the thicket, I followed a half-lit path on mounds of twigs and moist earth and trudged between trunks thick and gnarled by their anger over the previous winter.

In that forest were oaks and pines and birches and cedars and other unnamed trees, looking as though they had once been haunted, but had since been abandoned by ghosts too melancholy for the task. Some bushes and hanging leaves were caked in rime, and sprigs rustled droplets as I walked through them.

Beneath me, roots bulged water from the ground. Though the animals were all howling or hooting or otherwise signaling their desolate existence, I saw not one. And as I stumbled on in my sadness, I broke off a slab of wood from a trunk and kicked it out, to no response whatever. The stars beyond were not easily defined. The sun was nowhere to be seen.

I walked for some time yet atop beds of dead leaves and twigs cracking underfoot. Searching—for what, I knew not. All the while, I could not shake out a profound sorrow festering in my chest. I took moments to rest against slippery barks, as if the wood were really the skin of some ligneous sage ready to cradle me.

In my selfishness, then, I could have carved myself open and, out the hose of each artery, painting myself red upon earth, wood and leaf, sent my catastrophic essence to be recycled forever through the roots. And as I lumbered under the high branches, all languorous and gloomy, I peeled again at the skin of the oaks and launched myself from them, hands sticky with resin.

"Curse you," I rasped out. "Curse you, O million-faced moon!"

Some time passed, and eventually I came upon the sound of waves suckling at a shore. At first I imagined a nearby stream. I raced out to see for myself, listening to the light splashes loudening, and saw the treeline thin out to carpets of grass ripped out to bare earth, and deracinated plots where trees had once been.

As I exited the thicket, I found not a river, but a vast and ominous thing.

A black lake extended away to distant banks whose trees were wildfires of shadow. The water was pulsing, swirling, beckoning darkly. The surface alive. It seemed almost a sentient thing. I advanced, and gazed at the waves curling like ravens lunging up from the surface. A long portrait of the moon lay in brilliant pieces on the face of the waters.

As though possessed, then, in the purest compulsion, I marched towards the lake. The crickets and the owls blared out of the forest behind me. Mud and grass hung off my heels as I trudged, mindless, drone-like.

I halted a moment, as though on the precipice of the world, about to hurl myself off; not to reconsider my act, but rather to suspend it, that it might take on weight.

Cold water flooded my right shoe as I took the first step in, and ripples pulsed away from my shin. Then I sank both feet in the lake, and watched as clouds ringed the moon and began strangling it. The frozen rain arrived as if it were tears from the moon being dragged from its court. Its image in the waters warped as the waves rose and creased.

I strode on while raindrops shelled my neck. The clouds engulfed the moon whole, and with it the remaining light. The water clapped up to my chest. I shivered and convulsed. And finally, I plunged down with a great splash and sank, wholly limp, through the lake, unwilling to swim.

An anchor in my chest made me sink at the onset. The pressure gained around my head, and after the initial rush of congested bubbles and the rain still pelting the surface, there was not a sound save the slow drift of water by my ears.

I rotated in place so that my back faced the bottom. Only the inverted ripples of the waves could be seen in a shrinking halo as I drifted. And then there was only darkness. I opened my mouth, prepared to inhale the water, but nothing happened. There was no sound, not even the bubbling of submerged breath. The lake caressed me into a stupor, and I did not resist.

With my back bent toward the abyss, I glided down, my arms and legs dangling upward like strands of thick algae. Waters frigid, but my body would not freeze. I refused to close my eyes. I wanted to let in as much of the darkness as I could, that I might siphon it all out and witness the remains. In that umbral bath, I suspended all thoughts and rendered myself blank as the void surrounding me.

Here, all principles of harmony and truth dissolved. Here, like Achilles in the underworld, all small ambitions, arrogances, purposes, and souls outreaching their heroic roofs, died. Here, on the sightless side of dusk, was the far end of a meaningless arc.

I drifted down this bottomless lake for what may have been an hour or may have been long epochs of cosmic recycles. Cities could have collapsed, their stones turned to rubble and ruin; planets could have spun to extinction and wandered out of orbit to crust over in ice; galaxies could have collided into each other, disassembled and scattered like beads of a broken necklace, and not a fraction of the time I spent in that quiet prison would have passed.

And then, long after I had forgotten how to discern shapes and colors, the semblance of a fog began gathering in the black distance. Thin, at first. But it grew closer, and my senses lit up. The mist thickened, and before long I found it surrounding me in a glowing cyan band. Intrigued, I waited, still, and watched this diaphanous circle tighten and condense around me. What new horror was digging in the grave of hope?

At last, the ghostly visitors arrived.

"To sink so far, and learn so little."

A choir of dead voices, ghastly and sonorous and racing around me.

I tried to speak, to yell, but no sounds would come.

Down they descended, the wintry eidolon council. Their faces were shining and terrible. Pure faces, the high features of kings, myths, and legends, abstracted from the body to finer forms, to smoke and cerulean skin. In their incorporeal glory they were crowned in gemmed circlets or headdresses or mitres and clad in the ideal raiments of cultures long lost: flowing and embroidered gowns covered with fur-lined and gilded mantles, or thobes, or togas, or plate armours with sashes hanging off the pauldrons and over the breastplates reserved only for those given up to eternity, or helms embossed with diamonds and jades and sapphires; crafted on no plane to which Gilgamesh or Alexander or Dionysius ever belonged.

They floated together, pallid eyes all aligned and reaching for me. As they fell upon me, I felt myself break apart, the shards barely holding in my fragile, moistened flesh; the great blots of filth on my soul illumed.

"Does this silence match the cacophony in your head?"

Though it was little more than a whisper, it came as a deafening roar in my head.

Again, I tried to utter an apology against their awful words, but I was voiceless.

All of them pressed me with their sapphire auras. Whichever way I spun, one of their faces was there imposed.

They spoke again, their mouths moving little but expelling distilled wrath. "Only now have you been justly anointed in the waters of your ignorance. Do you see it? Did you not feel it pour from you? This is what you have wrought, this endless darkness. And you would have let it flood the cosmos. So sink. Sink to the thankless bottom, and never rise."

Betrayers! Vultures! These were the spirits of blind justice and wisdom, disembodied and beautiful, fleshless and bloodless. I tried again to speak, red-faced against the blue suns, veins popping, the sound bursting from my mortal rind. But my hatred dissolved, and I grew pathetic the instant I spoke.

"Plato, please," I said, absurdly, scanning for the idea as I continued to fall. "I did not do any of it knowingly."

Nothing, no sympathy, only that same smothering aura. Those

horrid unblemished faces, pushing me farther down, still, driving me further into the darkness. I trembled when they spoke again.

"You, who are so attuned to the sorrow that screams from the stars, the suffering that strings them and all the birds and the beasts together, you are beyond excuse. Did you truly think to scatter skies with your reach so short? To reach out with those hands quenched and irredeemably coated in blood? And you have drowned us all with you. There is no justice in you. Death, darkness: that is your domain."

The tyrants, the misleaders, the traitors! Lured me into this dark prison with heart rent open: not a wonder the blood poured! Brought me in with the promises of gold and instead locked me in an empty vault. No. I refused. Even as the pressure gained around the opaque core of my ego to crack and press my inner being, sinking, I would break out. I would be no prisoner of theirs.

"I am Alexander reborn," I roared, roused again to defiance, my voice distorted through the water. "And I have shed the hand of Aristotle. So kneel, kneel that you might be spared the ignorance that plagues the ages. My conquests are a threading of gold through souls, not the restless lust for worlds. And I will drive my needle through you, too. You, who fled to the heavens I sought to bring down to the world. You all, entombed together, who have failed me so utterly and completely. Devils, donning my robes."

No response came, but they continued to watch me, unflinching.

"I will escape this tomb. I will murder you all, flimsy specters. Run. Hide from me now. You are not safe in this silence," I wailed, broken-voiced.

And with that last breath, their veils were torn. Through the majestic smoke of each face, I saw their true forms. Corpses, all of them. Horrible and decomposed, bloated bodies. Bones protruding from flesh marked by ages of slow decay. Jaws dangling from their hinges. And before I could utter another word, their rotten hands extended and grasped me. They pulled me down, down. Crowding me, hugging me, all of them, their skulls to mine, watching me, still, the ethereal spirits grafted onto putrid cadavers.

"Sink now," the wraiths said, as they torpedoed me to the bottom.

No. I would not have them control me. I was my own guide, henceforth. I freed my right arm from their grasp and thrust it through the mist-face of the nearest ghoul, grasping the rotting head behind it.

"You will hand me this kingdom," I managed to say before my arm started to burn.

This was my domain. These ghosts were mine to command. They made no expressions, but their chiseled, gemlike avatars began to fade, leaving only the rot behind, and in that moment their intentions all metamorphosed to my will.

I released the skull and unbound myself from the ring of phantoms. Though they still spun me down, I knew now that it was to no abyss. And just then, after eons and eons, the water filled my mouth and flooded my lungs. They started a low dirge as they drowned me. They made a confession in my ear. And so at last I understood them.

Before we reached the end, these beautiful, decayed souls and I, the violence between us erupted. Like behemoths stomping over the map of history, we wrestled and clawed, and blow after blow I inherited them just as they inherited me. For all their might and for all the adornments of their fists and of their tongues, they could not overcome me, for they were me, and I was them.

And so I let the waters fill me, suffocate me; and I collided with my opponents just as they collided with each other, until their spirits infested me, and their bodies, divested and leeched of vital force, floated out of sight. When the last spirit succumbed, and the last wound in my hide sealed, I was released. The rotting eternals, the ideal corpses. Gone.

Now, alone, hard-hearted and ardent, lungs inundated and full, I lulled in the euphoria of drowning. I floundered for a moment, and in my arrogance thought to forgive them now that I had triumphed to win their fate. But then, as I spun myself again towards the end, a well of light wavered faintly in the distance.

I propelled myself toward the bottom by kicking, kicking the emptiness behind me. The glimmer widened. I flapped and guzzled and thrust, and suddenly the glow exploded, breaking a golden embrace for me through the dark.

There was the sandy bottom. Still frenzying as white bubbles cluttered my vision, I parted wave after wave, as though to part the whole lake in two, and lunged with all my being for that oasis cleaving the shadow.

I was suffocating, moments from losing my consciousness, and briefly lost my grip on the immortals I had sublated. I saw them again, panicked, steaming away from me. A train of their wispy, formless selves. Pieces of the long whole, chasing each other up and down like a gallery of warped, evaporating phantoms. These I gathered up again into one frantic body, one colossus withdrawing out of time.

And at last, when I reached the bottom, I plunged my hand, bloated with their history, into the sand. With each finger, I barnacled myself to the roots buried under the world, and felt the warmth of certainty surge through me, binding the sapphire colossus I'd made of myself and I.

Finally, I let go, and slipped through the warp and woof of space and time.

Eternities were pressed into a half-moment, and the cocoon shattered. *Dawn rises in the Spirit; it discovers focal points; and finally, it attains full consciousness.*

In fire enthroned. Burning, shooting skywards like a rogue comet, streaming through the waters in a column of light and steam. Body ablaze, incandescent, lifting the lake up to the ether.

Flying, rising. I burst out of the watery tomb, high above in a shroud of fleeing vapor, and crashed into the sky like inverted lightning. My kingdom, my dominion. Dread poured from the firmament, and all the creatures wept.

Myriad iterations of the moon ran around the galaxy's band like pearls. It was mine. I snatched it from its cowardly place, all of it, each one, and I cast it down to be purified in the water.

And the meadows were bright, and the clearings shining, and up I flew to gather my panicked brethren and enslave them.

In Paris again, then, or elsewhere, as the metaphors fall away, though their verity clings. In truth, it would be years before I could subjugate the stars and complete the full passage of transformation. And that passage was so far from any human comprehension, so desperately, desperately distant from what can be understood by any other. It was reason, yes, and experience, yes: passion and the irrational and the supra-rational; reasonable passion and passionate reason; empirical deductions and armchair inductions, and conviction, most of all; and a host of other, ineffable processes. Some would call it mystical, but then, that is what all men call the sort of reality to which they do not have access.

Thus, it was necessary to explain to you the mystical by means of mystification. How else to describe that transcendence which you, pitiful creature, could never conceive? How else but to beguile you with romance and allegory? I could have lied, and said that Sielle, the pernicious priestess, had granted me the gift with a magical touch. But I am very concerned with the truth, and that explanation would have deceived, and it would have robbed me of the majority credit. She had pointed me vaguely towards the ladder, yes, but it was *I* who climbed it.

And so, fragile creature, come with me to the window. Yes, there. And look.

Do you see? There is a boy there, playing with a ball. He is also a banker, cheating on his wife. And he is also in a grave, worms in his belly.

39

THE HAND OF HEPHAESTUS

R eturning to Earth. No, not Earth; it was too long lost to be regained. Somewhere else. A place of suffering. Home, then. A fragment. A dream. The memory of a nightmare lived in null space. High above the mists of time. Imprisoned there.

～

The hand of the father was warm, towing his son down the street. Under the glass sky they trekked, towards the glittering, red promise that the sun made the son. And the mother smiled and promised the future as well. Too soon, perhaps, for they were not yet there.

The boy found it difficult to suppress his excitement. He pushed away hunger and fatigue to look for a certain building along the towers and spires.

"What's a Hephaestus?" Tikan asked his father, his gaze aimed firmly out at the horizon and the stars arranged far beyond the planet's glass dome. They looked like pinprick ghosts fading in the azure firmament.

"I'm not sure, to be honest. It's a good question, though. Wait, let me think about it." The father released his son's hand, and he concentrated on the ground. "On Earth, he was the Greek god of craftsmen and blacksmiths," he said after a moment, and resumed his comforting grasp.

"Did he make things for people, too, or just for the gods?"

"Couldn't tell you. There isn't much more information on it, I'm afraid."

And so it was that Hephaestus, smith of the ancients, would design for Tikan a most befitting weapon. A celestial armament with which he would conquer a vague and ill-defined evil: a plotting force distant enough that it was hard to conceive of its purpose yet malevolent enough to instill courage in an idealistic boy's heart. For he was ten, and ten was a glorious age. It was the age of innocent arrogance, of safe heroism, of boundless fantasy and of childhood's last stand. The stars were his to save. In his own, naïve narrative, at least.

They walked for a time through the streets of Proxima, their shadows afraid of the sun, whose full light was today permitted through the dome. All the while, thoughts of limitless adventure picked at Tikan. His soul was leaping in its cage.

At last, they came upon a street flooded with people. The buildings suffused the boy in magenta and cyan and other muted neon as he neared each one. He became nauseous with excitement.

"How long?" he asked, gulping, giving in to his impatience.

"Here," the mother said.

A long line of people stood along the side of the largest building in view. Here was the place of transformation, workplace of the smith god. A sign on the building read: *It is illegal to willfully forgo apotheosis under Section IV of the Hephaestus Act.*

They crossed the street and joined the line composed chiefly of children and their families, though many unaccompanied adults also stood in wait. The line advanced quite fast, but no speed would have been acceptable to Tikan.

"Studies show that early metempsic conditioning leads to enhanced critical thinking and spatial reasoning skills," said a voice, with the text running across screens that were one with the walls of the building. "Further," the bodiless voice continued, as the line moved forward, "Behavioral studies have shown that early apotheosis encourages increased neuronal resource-control, increasing brain developmental potential by up to one-hundred and four percent."

He picked at his fingers in impatience. They were almost at the end of the line.

"Relax," said Tikan's father. "There's no need to be worried."

"I'm not worried! I'm ten."

"We know, and you're strong, and you've got a bright future ahead of you," said his mother. "But your father and I had the operation a long time ago, and we know what it's like. It's going to be a bit frightening at first, but it's all going to pass, all right?"

"Well, that was a long time ago," the father told his wife. "They wouldn't have made it mandatory for children if it was still like that."

"I understand," she said. "I just want Tikan to know, in case he gets worried that—"

"I told you, I'm ten!"

The mother only smiled and promised the future again.

Soon enough, they were at the front of the line. They were ushered inside by a green band perceptible to the parents alone, which began streaming along the building's side with the name *Solstafir* running through it.

They walked in and found an empty waiting room, white as all clinics. The polish of the floor gleamed harsh light from the ceiling. The boy was finding it exceptionally difficult to bottle his excitement. Ahead of them lay rows of closed doors, but no people could be seen.

"Tikan Solstafir?" came a voice beside them. It was a man wearing a white coat, and a nametag that read: *Dr. Julian*.

"Yes, that's me. It's my turn now, right?"

The doctor's steps resounded down the hall as he walked towards them with a smile that was difficult to interpret.

"That's right. It's your turn. He's ready, is he?" Dr. Julian asked the parents.

"Of course I'm ready!" Tikan yelped, almost jumping in place.

"He'll be alright, won't he, doctor?" the mother asked.

"Of course. We've perfected the procedure. He won't notice a thing. Well, except for the dullness subside, but that's the intended effect, isn't it?" he said, expanding his smile to where the tips of his pristine teeth could be seen.

"Come on then," the boy urged.

"I don't know many children your age so eager for apotheosis. You're a clever one, aren't you? Ah, definitely, I can see it in your eyes."

"That's because they don't know what they can do with it," Tikan responded.

"Oh, and what is it that you're planning?" said the doctor.

Tikan looked up at him and grinned, and then noticed that his father's stare was also on him, and he said nothing.

"Well, come on, then. Let's begin. We're just going to go down the hall, and it'll be over in minutes."

The lights were starting to dizzy the boy, though his excitement did little to alleviate the fog stirring in his head. He was almost skipping as the doctor led them down the passage. The doctor turned his head every now and again to grin at the parents, who trailed along behind them.

A door opened along the corrdior, just as they had turned a corner, and another boy walked out with both of his hands grasped by his parents at his sides. His expression was vacant. It was likely that he was too enthralled by his new consciousness to communicate.

Tikan grimaced with envy. He would make more of it than that boy. How could he not? It was a lowly mortal smith who had armed that one, and Tikan had Hephaestus waiting. His mind became enflamed by fantasies of all the worlds he would visit and all the adventures he would have.

"After you," the doctor said, holding the door of the operating room open for Tikan and waiting for the parents to catch up.

Inside, a pale green curtain divided the room in two, and two other doctors along with a technician in white coats waited by a wall console spilling thin wires from its belly.

"Doctors More and Minsky will be helping to raise you up, Tikan," Dr. Julian said as he closed the door behind him. "Now," he said, pulling a straightjacket from a nearby wardrobe, "Please wear this so we can begin."

"Okay," Tikan said, taking the jacket.

"Why, doctor?" his mother asked, uneasiness in her voice as she stood with her husband at the back of the room.

"Nothing to worry about, nothing at all. It's just for safety precautions. The brain is a powerful thing, you know, and sometimes, errant movements—painless ones—can interfere with the procedure. That's all."

"It's all right, dear," the father said, noticing the anxiety in Tikan's face at the mere prospect of having the ritual interrupted.

"Well, if it's for safety," she replied, still unsure.

Tikan slid his arms into the straightjacket. The restriction he felt as the doctor tightened the vest was, to the boy, a necessary trade for the powers he was about to receive. Then, without warning, the doctor pricked his neck with something. He did not see what it was, but he suddenly felt languorous. He marched towards the operating table, which more resembled a massage chair, and sank chest-first into it, letting his neck be upheld by a holster.

"Excellent," Dr. Julian said. "And how are you feeling, Tikan?" he asked, as he strapped the boy into his seat with additional belts.

"Good," the boy replied, trying in vain to turn his head and look at his mother.

"Now, relax. Let's begin," said Dr. Julian, stilling the boy's wriggling head with a firm grasp. "It won't take very long." Then, he motioned for the other doctors to come forward.

"Wha—" the mother said as they hovered around the boy and shut the curtains.

"Now, madam," said Dr. More. "It's necessary for you to stay back. Don't worry, please: we know exactly what we're doing."

The woman stayed silent, and let her son disappear behind flimsy curtains.

The seat was adjusted forward so that Tikan was rotated almost ninety degrees. Additional restraints emerged from the neck holster to prevent him from moving his head. He heard the shaver buzz next to his ear. Locks of his dark hair fell to the ground. They swabbed his scalp with alcohol. "Begin the procedure," he heard one of them say, and then the pressure of incision popped through his head.

"Clip the skin back."

The sound of abrasive drilling filled the room. Still focused on the disorderly mess of hair beneath him, the boy winced. There was pain, somewhere, a small dot lurking beneath its lid.

"I'll need you to drain the fluid now."

The pressure in his brain inflated and inflated, until it seemed to him as though it were a balloon ready to pop. Meanwhile, all clarity of mind was escaping him.

"Feed them in. Be precise about it. Don't let them get too excited."

The pain started turning to agony as he felt a writhing in his skull. He began shaking his legs, rotating his eyes to a hard left. The hand of Hephaestus was too heavy, too aggressive. It kept him pinned to the neck holster.

"Make the adjustments. Cleaner. And measure it. That's the way. Make it clean. Bypass the occipital bridges and fix the temporal lobe. Careful, now."

He intended to move, to run away, and in his imagination he saw and felt his arms come free and his legs scurry, but in reality, they remained motionless. And he tried to make a sound, to scream out for them to stop, but only a whimpering rasp came out.

"Quiet, boy. You can ask us questions after we finish."

They continued their invasion. They piled unspeakable things into his head, which wriggled and refused to nestle into place. The boy felt his lungs strain in the cabinet of his chest as the torment continued.

"Connect the parietal lobe, now. "

The terror was instant, the images latent. A spark lit the room, and the alien smell of burned flesh flooded the place. His body convulsed wildly against shaking restraints.

"Oh, suns! Moons! What? He's going into—? Oh! How? Pull it all out, now! Now!"

The burning spread. It swarmed into his vision, disintegrating the fixed image of the floor decorated in hair. A distant yell from a familiar voice followed him, but died away as the promise broke, and he scrambled to acclimate to the reforging of nature's iron laws as the room fell away and the building sank beneath him and the glass sphere of a planet became a pebble in a whirling vortex of bright dust growing finer, surging inward to a bottomless whirlpool as his mind, disconnected from brain, streamed away from the worlds the world continued to promise, like a lone camera ejected from the premises of a vacant simulation, drifting from the picture of existence. And he fell for time immeasurable into a separate realm, a place without location in which all the objects of being were removed, to the sandbox itself.

His ravaged, anomalous body was taken away to wait for years in a sunless room, superficially repaired as reparation by those petty technicians who had masqueraded as healers. The world forgot about him, cast him out as an invalid. The hair eventually grew back, and the scars vanished from the skin, but the boy was lost.

40

BLOOD AND THUNDER

He began to despair as his body called him back and his mind clarified. There was only darkness waiting for him. Indistinct sounds scuttled around him like a host of insects.

The absence of his left arm crept into his awareness. He tried to clamber away from the ruthless truth. Now, buried alive in the coffin of his body, he began panicking. But above all was a voice, a voice that had slithered 'duty' into his ear as he and the notion of his God had been mangled. A voice that had thrown molten gold over his ideals. A voice that slinked in again and whispered, "Rise, Tiresias."

The sweat was cold on his face. The sockets in his skull were stuffed with now-calm machinery. A few imagined phantoms evaporated before him, and the bruise of immortal regret swelled in him: the glass that could never again be repaired, no matter the innumerable alternate courses forever revised, or the reversals it could have performed in contradiction and insult to nature's laws of entropy. The claustrophobia of his new existence set upon him.

"Betrayers, all," he cried. "Killers! Thieves!"

The cushions beneath him were damp and compressed. He felt

bedsores all along his body. The couch lengthened, and the room's dimensions fluctuated in his mental reconstructions, now built of shadow.

"Now, Tikan, you must rest," said an awful and familiar voice beside him. "Otherwise, you'll open the wounds. We don't want that, do we? No. We want—"

Tikan stiffened as though he were about to convulse in place. A spike of rage was boring through his heart. He tried to lurch up, but succeeded only in coughing out something incomprehensible.

"We want," Onasus continued, disgust in his voice, "to leave this place as soon as possible. You've had an entire week to recover, and it isn't certain how much longer this place will be safe for. You do want to keep your friends safe, don't you? Yes, of course you do. Quiet, then, and listen to me."

Tikan gritted his teeth, and the corner of his mouth quivered. Aberrant perceptions began appearing in his mind's eye: Onasus as a tentacled or satanic shade whose proportions ever ballooned and shrank as he hovered somewhere above in the permanent shadows, spewing his noxious words.

"Where are they?" Tikan groaned.

"Who's that? Your friends?"

"Not friends," he said, the bitterness dripping from his hoarse voice.

"Oh, please. Of course they're your friends. And I'm your friend. I don't understand why you're upset. Not sure why you had to make it so difficult. This is what you wanted, isn't it? To have your throat slit on the altar of sacrifice? Well, I held the dagger, it's true—and look, there, the altar is aglow! And your blood hasn't run out yet. So stop whining."

"Not...like this. Never..."

"Do you want to know the truth?" Onasus said. He approached Tikan's ear and dropped his pseudo-lighthearted tone. "The truth is that they would have betrayed you." He paused. "It's a cruel thing, I know. The last of the Equuleus. Your companions, tested by fire and blood alongside you, and ultimately brittle as clay unsuited to the kiln."

"You're lying."

"Come, now. From the moment we left the ship, they conspired. Did you think they would look on you with trust when they learned you had no procrustus? That your mind was impenetrable to them? That you came from a world altogether foreign and therefore dangerous? They blamed you for the Equuleus. And did you think they would ever find reason to share in your vengeance on the galaxy? If not for me, they would have sold you and me both for freedom and comfort. I've made them your friends, pumped their hearts by my own hand, painstakingly rewired their brains. *I* am the one who's been looking out for you, fool."

Tikan shook his head wildly despite the pain. The movement caused a line of blood to run down his temple. He began hyperventilating.

Onasus fiercely gripped Tikan's head to stop it from moving. "Why else do you think I thwarted Mira when she ran into the Bilge with a trail of sentinels at her call, ready to hand you and your new paramour over? To prevent you from escaping to Sirius? Come, Tikan, my boy. Don't look surprised. I have more eyes and ears than this set on my face. You didn't really think running away to Sirius was a possibility, either, did you?"

"You're a liar. From the beginning you were a liar. You—"

"That's enough out of you," Onasus snarled. "You'll do as I say. You don't have a choice, I'm afraid, as we're both bound for Arcturus together, and you can no longer see. Well, you, me, and the girl, that is. You'll need our help. I implore you not to make it difficult on us."

Tikan petrified the moment Onasus mentioned Sielle. "The girl? Where? She's here?"

"No, she isn't," said Onasus. "I've been searching for her. I will find her. Proxima is quite good for that purpose: ordered, homogenous, controlled."

"You—You—"

Onasus' voice envenomed. "I *what*? You think I won't find her, is that it? Have you hidden her? Told her to run away?"

"No."

"No, of course you haven't," he said in a patronizing way. "Naïve boy. And she is cunning, isn't she? Yes, I can see it in your expression, what's left of it." He almost chuckled.

Tikan remained immobile. He did not say anything for a short while.

Onasus lowered his voice. "If you know where she went, I—"

"The others," Tikan said, more subdued, masking his anger and fear.

"Shall I call them? Then perhaps you can thank them for aiding me in ameliorating you, yes? That's what I'll do. I'd ask you to wait, but that would be redundant." He chortled to himself.

The fiend's footsteps tapped away on the floor, and Tikan remained silent. There was a throb where his eyes should have been, and a sharp pressure along the core of his stump. What horror had they wreaked upon him? What monstrosity had his once-friends carved out of his former self? He would have wept had he been able to; but as the steam in him found no valve, it instead roiled under his skin.

"Tikan," came a familiar voice. "You're looking well," Mira said. Her voice was frail, and sedated. She approached the couch.

"I—I'm looking well?" Tikan asked. "What has he done? What lies did he tell you?"

"Last time we saw you, we were worried you'd sleep forever," Naim said, just as deadened. "It's good to know you're making a full recovery. There is justice in this world after all."

"You were very sick," Mira went on. "Very, very sick."

"Who are you?" Tikan asked, incredulous. His voice loudened into a rasp. "Where are your voices? Speak if you have them! Speak and don't lie, liars. Tell the truth about what he's done and about yourselves and what he'll do and—"

"Quiet," came the scientist's voice from afar. "If you're not going to be positive and speak of progress, then keep quiet. As Mira said, you were very sick. Sick with life. Sick with meaning ever out of reach. Don't you see? Forget about truth, and learn instead to stop lying to yourself. You sick, sick man. Now quiet, and make use of your new health."

The couch sank with Mira's weight. He listened to her breathing beside him. She took his hand and caressed it nervously. "I didn't know," she then whispered close to his ear, almost deliriously. The hotness of her breath lingered on his ear as she withdrew her head.

"Naim," Tikan muttered.

"I'm here, Tikan," answered Naim resolutely. "Are you feeling all right? Do you need me to bring you some water?"

"You're dead to me. Both of you."

"Don't say that," Mira whispered again, this time desperately, and on the verge of tears.

"Mira!" Onasus growled.

She redressed herself robotically at once and stepped away from the couch. She walked out of the living room without another word.

"Come back," Tikan yelled. "What power has he got over you both?"

"Prithee, forgive her, Tikan," Naim said in a voice not quite his own. "She hath been moody as November of late. 'Twas thy blood upon her skin, those sleepy days ago, that hath excited her so." He approached Tikan, who could not find it in himself to respond, and straightened him by the shoulders as though he were a nurse. He drew close and spoke again. "Hither hast thou slept, and hither shall thou sleep another night, and nigh on morning, ere thy next waking, will Mira come in full to her right senses."

Onasus walked over to them and brushed Naim aside. He slid his hand under the back of Tikan's head and grasped his skull as though it were a fruit. "Do you hear that? Do you see how even this once useless, mechanic flesh can be improved, carved into the right tool? Let not language play games on you, boy. You are not so different as this puppet."

Tikan breathed heavy and measured breaths.

"Don't waste words you might be thinking, but listen," Onasus went on. "From the start, it's only ever been you and I speaking, after all. Did you think those walking husks could have opinions without my permission? Do you think the words 'wormhole' or 'justice' mean little more than 'gate' or 'good' to them?" he asked in a manner borrowed from a being no longer flesh or blood or bone but roiling and pervasive spirit. "And we have work to do, Tikan," Onasus told him. He rested his other pestilential hand on Tikan's good shoulder. "It is greater than you, or he, or this man who calls himself Onasus before you. You don't have to like us, or yourself, or what we've done to you—and it was all of us, indeed—but you will have to work with us. You—"

"Get away from me," Tikan growled.

There was a pause.

"As you wish," Onasus finally said, squeezing the back of Tikan's head and sending two fresh blossoms of pain through his sockets before releasing it.

Tikan felt a fresh trickle of blood ooze out of his sockets and down his cheeks. The cage of his broken body only worked, then, to frustrate him to near madness. Using all of his strength, he raised up his stump in a violent arc and crashed it clumsily into Onasus' grip. A column of agony erupted through his mangled limb, and he wailed.

"Leave me! Leave me to die, since you've robbed me of everything, betrayers!"

"That's enough. You're starting to look and sound like a beast," said Onasus. "Another abject word out of you, and I'll have to sedate you. You are still committed to our quest, yes? To pilot us to Arcturus? "

"Pilot?" Tikan asked, trying without success to sit up. "You've taken my sight and my arm. In what world do you want me to pilot? Will you take my mind now, too? Kill me now, if that's your aim."

"You see? This is what I mean. You're given to being very melodramatic about all of this. I've taken nothing from you; I've merely…facilitated things. We'll finish our objectives on Arcturus, and then you can do all the dying you want. Is that fine?"

Tikan did not respond, and instead turned inward to somber meditation.

"It's settled then," said Onasus, taking advantage of the silence. "You should be all healed by after tomorrow. You'll have a new arm, soon, too...in a manner of speaking. That's wonderful, isn't it? Absolutely. In the mean time, I'll continue searching for the girl, and you can sort out your feelings. I do advise you to make peace with your companions before we depart. They won't be around for long, you know. Vega beckons."

Once more, the dark intentions Onasus proclaimed towards Sielle made Tikan seal himself like a frigid clam. The last of humanity's unwanted dream, reduced now to a faint wisp unknowingly fleeing her devourer. She had, in fact, sensed his madness at the first, and this gave Tikan some reassurance.

"I'm off, then," Onasus said. "Do you have any suggestions as to where she might have gone?"

Tikan did not answer. He was wrestling with that question himself.

"No? Fine. I'll see you in two days, then. Rest well. You'll be needing it. And don't forget: as one eye is seeled, another opens!"

The door closed as Onasus left the apartment.

Not too far from the couch, Naim could be heard inhaling as if he had just been released from a chokehold. "Tikan—I. Have you been around here lately? I haven't noticed you...here before. How did you make it off the ship?"

"Go."

Naim did not argue, but instead walked away in a slight hurry, as though to relieve himself.

Tikan exhaled in sorrow. And soon enough, he collapsed back into sleep.

∾

"Tikan. Wake up."

The voice of Naim was comforting by habit to Tikan. Though, on proper recognition, it was anger that he woke to. The rank of his own sweat filled his nose, and his muscles were sore.

"What? What do you want?" he said to the shade of his friend.

"Onasus is gone," said Mira beside him, her voice hoarse.

"Yes, he won't be back for another day or so," said Naim, almost whispering.

"And what do you want from me? To take more limbs?" Tikan said. He was able to move more freely now, and he paddled his legs somewhat.

"Don't say that, Tikan, please," said Mira. "We care about you. And—"

"Only hours ago you called me a sick man."

"That wasn't me!" she said. "It was me…but it wasn't."

"And it wasn't you who brought all those sentinels to the Bilge with her, either, right? Isn't that why you went there looking for me?"

Mira gripped her forehead with both her hands and stretched it apart. There were red marks all across her head, which Tikan could not see, where she had repeatedly tried to reach for her own memories and thoughts.

"He's got something in our heads," Naim added. "He controls the ocean, Neptune does."

Tikan huffed incredulously. "It was always there," he said. "You never listened."

Mira's voice loudened. "Now we understand," she said. "What you said, what you wanted to do. To keep us from speaking words we don't have, it's—"

"That's not it at all," Tikan said. "It's exactly the opposite. It's about truth, and justice."

They did not respond.

"Truth and justice, I said!" he yelled after they remained mute, to no reaction. "Can't you hear me? Truth and justice! Truth and justice!"

"No," Naim said. "Are you trying to say something?"

Tikan's voice shrank in despair. "Are your minds all his, now? Did he make you do this to me, or are you just drones? Are you lurking in their skulls, Onasus? Come out!"

"Do what?" Naim asked earnestly. "Are you okay?"

"Oh, Tikan, it's horrible!" Mira said, bursting into tears. "What he's done to you, most of all. But us, too. I have two different memories of what happened on the ship, and I want to believe one is true. But I can't. I know I betrayed you, but I don't know if I did. When I think, it's between the walls he's built. And the words, I don't know them. And then I remember them, and I forget again—things I always knew but that can't be."

"It's true," Naim said, as if in a moment of sudden clarity. "I—I do feel it's hard to speak when Neptune is around, although I've never expressed myself better. It really does do justice to what I think."

"Neptune?" Tikan asked.

"Yes."

Mira was still sobbing. "He's been calling him that for days. I don't know why. I've told him it's just an old gas planet almost mined to a pebble, but he won't listen. I—We've got to leave this place, fly to Vega and Arcturus," she said. "Every day in this place I feel my mind coming apart. Look at what he's done to him, and you, and to me, soon, I feel it."

There was a pause.

"Arcturus and Vega?" Tikan remarked in disbelief.

"Yes. To get these worms and whirlpools out of our heads. Without *him.*"

"Don't you get it yet, Mira? Proxima belongs to him. There's no getting off Proxima, nowhere to go on Proxima without him. It's not possible."

"It is! I can pilot my own ship," Mira insisted. "I'll go to Vega alone. I'll handle that by myself. You and Naim go to Arcturus. He said you can pilot now. He said it. We can do it. Can't we?"

Her hurried, manic whispers spoke of an agitated and malformed plan conceived under a dominion of fear while Tikan had spent the days dreaming of his amputated childhood.

"What ships?" he asked. "And how do you want me to pilot without eyes, Mira? Do you really believe he did this so I could fly a ship?"

Mira became agitated. "Yes, I know, you're blind, and growing a spike out of your arm, but he said you could—he said."

"That is just the truth," Naim said. "That is indeed what was said, in correspondence with reality. In coherence with all other statements."

Tikan suppressed his anger. "What spike?"

"He did something to—well, to what was left," she said, shuffling in place. "Oh, I wish he'd just died in the cold of the ship so we'd never met him. But what else can we do? Where else can we go? He must have done it for a reason, don't you think?"

Tikan did not answer. He touched his left arm, and instead of a bandaged stump, what he found, with a creep of horror, was half a forearm made of a hard substance jutting from where the wound had been. It was as if glass were growing from it.

"I'm sorry, Tikan," Mira continued. "I'm so, so sorry for what I did or said, and I know you didn't let those black suits go on the ship—I know it's his poison in my head. I know you have a procrustus. Please, Tikan. While I still remember what he did to you, before he kills the memory. The blood and the—I need to remember it. I need us to go to Arcturus and Vega. For memories, and words, and everything, we have to."

"You know, Tikan," Naim said, somewhat interrupting Mira. "Now that you mention it, there does seem to be something off about you. Have you been eating right?"

Tikan kicked a pillow from the couch. "No, why would you remember?" he told Naim.

"Remember what, Tikan? I don't think I was there."

"Tikan, he didn't know," Mira said. "He was—"

"Metempsying," Tikan snarled. "He was there. And now look at the wreck of him."

"Me?" Naim asked.

"Who else but you?"

Naim circled in place a while, like a detective in the process of making a deduction. "I—" Just then, he brushed up against the couch with his bad leg. "I'm not sure what Onasus—" He gasped and electrically straightened his posture. "—What Neptune has done, but I do feel sick beside him. A nice kind of sickness. A seasickness! But whatever it was, I do apologize."

"Shut up. Just shut up," Tikan said with sudden spite. He bashed the back of the couch with his closed fist. They were jolted aback. "I don't forgive you, either of you. You were yourselves enough when he leapt on me. You, Naim, deep in a metempsy, like the rest of your sorry life; and, Mira, gasping in the corner—the last image I have of this broken world. Cowards. You've survived only because it's been my hand that's dragged you along; my hand, now cut from me. You might be husks now, but I won't forget it. And you want the truth, Mira? You want to hear it from my mouth? I *did* let those black suits go. I *don't* have a procrustus."

"I knew it couldn't be true," she said. "Who in their right mind would let murderers escape? Come, let's—"

"Damn you!" he called out. "Damn you, Onasus, and damn you, Mira!"

The others were speechless. Tikan, meanwhile, threw himself off the couch. Mira shrieked. With his good arm he clawed and crawled, thinking it was in the direction of the door, tears red as magma rolling off his cheeks.

"What are you doing?" she asked.

He did not respond. He was not yet strong enough to move properly, and his mouth and nose were in the carpet, his face leaving streaks of blood on the floor as he struggled. "Let me out of here," he cried, when he could no longer move. "Throw me out, to the streets— throw me from the window if you have to! Kill me if you have to."

"Stop that," Mira said. "You're just going to make it worse."

She and Naim carried him back onto the couch. They sat down near him, and for a long while, no one said anything. Tikan calmed down considerably in that time.

"I—I heard what you said. What you actually said," Mira said at last. "I remember it. About the ship, the procrustus. And it doesn't matter. I don't care anymore—I want to believe you were right."

"Why did you say something else, then?"

"Because, I told you—I keep remembering two things, sometimes three things, sometimes more. Every time you say something, even now, I remember it two ways. I try to fight it. I try to choose the real one, or to make it go away. And half the time my words and thoughts come apart. And it's hard. It's really hard. Can't we stop it?" She started weeping again.

No one said anything. They listened to Mira weep.

"I would do it, your plan," Tikan said, exhaling as though his mouth were a steaming vent. "If it made any sense. But there's no way we'll get off Proxima without him, or without him finding us. And there's nowhere left for us to go. And besides..." he trailed off.

"Then where should we go? What should we do?"

"I don't know."

The others did not respond. Meanwhile Tikan carefully massaged his modified limb, trying to accept it. "Why did he do this?" he asked about his lost arm.

Mira sighed. "I don't know. He said something about a map."

Tikan continuously rubbed the edges of the pillar erupting out of the stump.

"I wish," Mira said, composing herself. "I wish we'd known. And seen how far this all went. On the ship, Onasus barely spoke. And what little he said was just a babble about conspiracies. Why did we trust him so easily?"

Tikan tried to sit up again, but did not succeed. He coughed. He gripped the side of a cushion and spoke in a resolute but calmed voice. "Mira, he spoke for hours. You kept giving me looks—I thought we both knew he was lying."

She wept again and did not respond.

Tikan stretched his back and ran a hand through his hair, careful to avoid the device still planted on his face. "It doesn't matter," he said. "It was all lies, probably. But you remember Arcturus and Vega clearly enough. He obviously wants you to remember that."

Then, after nodding along to what Tikan said, Naim pinched the bridge of his nose and closed his eyes a moment. "I know I don't remember," he said. "But inside I feel that sickness, deep in my stomach. I don't know why. I am sorry, Tikan. For whatever happened, I am sorry."

Tikan did not respond. He considered Naim, who had not half the strength of Mira, and felt sadness for this ruined man, whose mind was fully ensnared by Onasus. He lingered, expressionless, on the couch, and then parted his lips a number of times but ultimately said nothing.

"Oh, moons, Tikan," Mira said, despairing again. "We need you, now. So you can't see, and it's horrible, I know, but maybe there are worse ends, and this isn't an end. I was at one of the shops earlier in the week—I went to find some neutral platelets for the gun, I think— and I was trying to talk to the man there. I needed to speak to someone after what happened. About anything. I've never felt like that before. He wasn't even there. His body was there, listening to me, but he just looked at me with glazed eyes. There were no memories forming, pointless as they would have been. There was a woman there, too, buying things. She was gone, too."

She wiped her face, and then breathed. "And I understood it," she continued. "I've never been one to metempsy much, you know that. But the whole thing about needing another's words, warm words, long and real words. It's true, and you told us that before, I think. Years ago, or was it yesterday? Won't you stand upright now?"

Tikan was stirred by her. It was an uncomfortable moment. For all the anger he was impelled to harbor, Tikan did forgive Mira, in some remote alcove of his heart whose exterior dimensions are all illumed. Then, like a man resolved to martyrdom, he drove a finger through the wound of his identity and exiled himself once more from all personal happiness or friendship, rebirthed himself as an instrument of vengeance and the utmost duty—that molested ideal—to then be discarded.

"You know, Mira, Naim," he said in a moment of clarity. "We will go to Arcturus and Vega. And we'll go with Onasus."

"What do you mean?" Naim asked, more timid.

"I'm just a tool now," Tikan said. The top of his face was still obscured by the device, and this made him look oddly without expression, though the corners of his mouth were trembling. "That's how he sees it, right? Let him. I'll go to Arcturus with him. I'm going to find his master, his masters—I know they exist. I'm going to hold them by the throat, drag them from their steel shadows and hurl them into the galaxy's hot heart. You two go to Vega—far from his reach. And if he does find Sielle—the girl—you take her with you." He spoke as though two embers had filled the voids of his eyes, as if by will alone his spirit could transcend his thrice-crippled body to exact all punishments due.

"And Onasus?" Mira said. "If he crosses you again, twists us around again? And if there are no masters?"

"I'll put out his eyes. I might do it anyway. You hear that, Onasus?" he called, in the direction of Naim. "I know you can hear me. I'll put out your eyes, too. And then, once we're in the same dark pit together, only then will my vengeance begin."

"Isn't it a bit late for revenge, now?" Naim said ponderously. "Hath not enough detours and mistakes been committed to start a worthwhile fury? Hast thou not lost the wrong limb to strike the sun? And hast thy ship of cannibals and harpooners not already sunk? Beware the blind man who claims true aim! Beware the hatred of a thing unnamed! Thine heart tumbles down a red brambly gorge, yet youth and vigor long ago escaped thee, and it yet bleeds a streak of hope—follow it not to where blood and thunder shall be mere paint and spark! Or, worse yet, a loveless dark."

Neither Tikan nor Mira understood these words. They ignored Naim, dismissing his monologue as a symptom of his new lunacy.

Mira fiddled with her nails. "Tikan, he—"

"It's the only way," he insisted. "We'll never get off Proxima without him. It's the only thing left to do."

She relaxed somewhat and sniffled. "Only—Only promise me that it'll stop."

"What?"

"The world of echoes that used to be my mind, like a thousand screams from no mouth at all."

🦋 41 🦋

THE MIGRATION

It had been some hours since the tribe had left the cave, meandering the land en route for the City of Zotharra, with the breeze catching their faces and fluttering their cloaks. The suns shone their heatless rays from a clear sky, fracturing through opalescent hills. The city was still a few weeks away.

Sielle lingered behind the others, often climbing atop ridges to watch the line of pilgrims needle into the horizon. Meanwhile, she played with a gem she had snatched from one of the baskets that had lit the cavern. The jewel was gray and empty, now. All of the light within it had fled the moment she had stepped outside. It did not even catch the sunlight. Though, it was pleasant to the touch, given its peculiar shape and texture. She tossed it up and caught it as she trailed along.

Elu and Ilu directed the great snake of nomads. The old man was carried in a ceremonial seat, and Ilu glided beside him, with what could have been a wedding veil atop her head. The rest walked behind in small groups, all of them wearing hoods with their gray and worn rags as though they were monks departing from a monastery.

They were far from Sielle, now. She was closer to the tail, still dawdling down the last decline in the land. The shadows caressing the hills evaporated as she descended. Beside her, Neanh kicked pebbles and crushed many flowering red spirals underfoot. Sielle thought she even heard her mutter disgruntled things under her breath.

A smirk crept across Sielle's face. "So, where is the city exactly? Is it far? Is the whole way going to be like this?" she goaded Neanh.

Neanh had been assigned to guide Sielle and help her become accustomed to the planet. She did little of this. It was quite obvious that what she had been tasked with, in truth, was to keep track of Sielle and ensure that she did not reveal her Proximaen origins to anyone.

Hours into the journey, however, the drudgery seemed to have defeated any sense of duty Neanh may have held. There were no real explanations from her, no elucidations on the erratic clouds or the red formations she so casually destroyed. She merely strolled on and gave others spiteful glares from time to time.

Sielle barraged her with child-like questions over the hours. She eventually had her way, and Neanh stopped even acknowledging her. At most, she would look at Sielle out of the corner of her eye and walk on.

"You know, I'm not holding a grudge against you," Sielle said. "Even though I probably should. So it's rude of you to keep ignoring me."

"The city is far," Neanh stated.

"And?"

"It's far," she repeated, still refusing to even look at Sielle. In the last few minutes, Neanh had taken to looking behind them instead, presumably to check the back of the line for stragglers.

As the snake of travellers made a last bend out of the valley, Sielle stalled and let Neanh walk far ahead of her. There seemed, then, to be an implicit understanding between them. Neanh looked back once or twice, but made no effort to pursue Sielle. Ahead, the suns brightened.

Neanh had explained one matter to her shortly before they had departed, under strict orders from Ilu and Elu. She had spoken of the necessity of finding shade and of keeping the body flooded with that minty liquid Sielle had been force-fed on the way to the cave.

The suns emitted a sort of light which, while bereft of much heat, was quick to mutate cells in the body. The turning of the blood's color from red to purple and to an eventual cobalt was the first symptom of the disorder. These mutations inevitably led to horrors that Neanh did not define beyond vague descriptions of a painful transformation and the eventual death that followed. However, this was avoidable by limiting one's sunlight exposure and by drinking what was known as Zotharra's Blood. Sielle had even despondently been handed a gourd of the drink before they had all set out.

After wandering slantwise out of a last narrow bend in the hills, Sielle was confronted with flatlands encircled by hazy mountains whose various crests looked crusted over with ice in the distance.

She dragged herself down the slope. Scintillations accrued as she descended, until the mountains were swallowed up in brilliance and could no longer be seen. She fixed her gaze on a boulder that wove across the land as though it were the only visible segment of a colossal caterpillar's body, and which then made a subterranean plunge beyond sight.

A familiar voice came after her. "Dear mistress from the stars, I've heard you were lost, up there. Is that right?"

Sielle turned and recognized Haern traipsing beside her. He pushed back his hood, combed his hair once with his hand, and transferred his pack across to his opposite shoulder. Sielle grimaced at him and looked away.

"Yes," she said, looking skyward. "Up there."

"That's fascinating. I've given it a lot of thought, you know. What it would be like to see…all of this…from so high. What does she look like from above?"

"What does who?"

"I mean…the planet. What does she look like?"

"Like a great shining ball," Sielle said, without much effort.

The man looked perplexed, as though he had expected a different answer. He regained his composure, and then made to ask another question, but Sielle cut him off.

"How long have you been out here?" she asked.

"A few months or so. I'm not very good at keeping track of time, to be honest."

"You've only been on this planet a few months?"

"Oh, no. I thought you were asking about this part of the world. We've been here for hundreds of years. Our ancestors arrived here after the night exodus. Honestly, I never knew there were others in the galaxy. I thought we were the only ones. Are there other planets nearby, too? Where were you settled?"

She gave him a suspicious glance from the corner of her eye. "I don't know," she said. "Nowhere. I grew up on a drifting ship; everyone there died when I was very young. Disease, I think," she continued, reciting the lie Ilu had instructed her to give. "I spent years alone."

A look of fear flashed across his face. Anyone less perceptive than Sielle would have missed it. "Oh, I see. That makes more sense. They always told us there aren't any worlds imaginably close," he said, and then paused a moment to contemplate. "I'm sorry you had to endure that. I'd love to ask you more about it, if you don't mind. And about what dark skies look like beyond the suns, or the stars, if any you saw. Oh, and I'm sorry, but I never learned your name. It's funny, I think Ilu's forgotten that I was there when we found you."

Sielle gave him a sympathetic look. "Haern, you seem kind, unlike that one," she said, pointing at Neanh's now-tiny figure in the distance. "She's been extremely unhelpful. Though, you did drop me in the caves. I remember it. Why did you do that to me? I was already in a lot of pain."

They both stared where she pointed, and Sielle noted that those at the head of the line were fast disappearing into the brilliance, with Ilu and Elu no longer visible.

"I'm sorry about that. Very sorry. I mean it. I was exhausted, and Neanh pushed me just as you tripped. You know, you're right about her. She can be cruel, from what I've seen."

"Sielle," she said after a few moments, without looking at him.

"What's that?"

"My name."

"Oh. It's unusual as names go. What does it mean?"

She ignored him. "Haern," she said. "What's this 'night exodus' you mentioned?"

"The night exodus! The lights of the Milky Way turned off. Rotted-out jungles, oceans evaporated, whole star systems collapsed. You didn't hear the legends on your ship?"

"No. I don't listen to legends. Did you get them from a book?"

"Why would we? It's the truth. Books don't have truth. Everyone knows that."

"What does, then?"

"You and me talking—there's truth. There's more than words. No one told you the legends on your ship?"

"I was a child."

He gave her an odd look.

"So you don't have any books?" she asked. "None at all? How do you even know what they are, then?"

"No. No books, no letters or literates. Our ancestors left them all behind, in the Milky Way, and we remember them just so we don't start writing again. Like you would remember a devil."

"You still use words, though. You still speak, and obviously keep history. What's the difference?"

"I'm a person speaking to you, now. In your present and mine. A book cannot speak to you. A book has no mind. You could read a page from a book or listen to me say the same thing, and me saying it would carry truth, but the book would not."

Sielle shook her head. The thought of Tikan flashed in her mind, but she suppressed it. She opened her mouth to argue with Haern, but decided it would be best not to risk compromising herself in any way by upsetting him. "Okay. Well, are you going to tell me the legends, then?" she said after a few moments. "I'm curious."

"I can't."

"Because legends are dangerous?"

"Because silence is the other side of the truth. You don't need books to keep the past alive. But that doesn't mean it's always good to remember. Things can change. Words change their meanings. What I say now, from my mouth to your ear, cannot change."

"But people interpret legends and words."

"Yes, they do. Exactly."

Sielle grimaced in confusion. "Then how do you know what you're remembering is the right thing, without a record of what people thought or said? Doesn't the truth mean that what you say and what *is* or *was* are the same?"

He shook his head. "I'll tell you what I think. I think you're forgetting that we are a community, and not one person. History, to you, is a set of facts. For us, it is a set of meanings. Do you understand? And I think you should be careful talking this way—people might think you carry that disease with you from your ship."

"Excuse me?"

"I just wouldn't go around telling people about what happened on your ship. There are many kinds of diseases after all. Diseases of the body, of the mind, of the spirit, of speech. Diseases of the world, of cities. Just because you're not coughing, it doesn't mean you're pure. You understand?"

She tried to discern whether he was threatening her, or rather cautioning her. "And what do you think? You think I'm not 'pure?'"

He gave her a long stare. "I think you are."

"Good."

"So tell me, do you—"

"Wait. What's going on there?" she interrupted, pointing at the tribe, which now seemed to have disappeared save for a few people, only barely visible through the horizon's glints.

"That's our first patch."

"Patch?"

"Yes. I should explain. We travel the surface faster over black gulfs of sand. We wouldn't make it fast enough to shade without it. I assume Naenh at least told you what happens if the suns fall on you too long?"

"Sort of," she said, distracted. "What happens when you sink in the black sand?"

"Sink?" he laughed. "We don't sink through it. We run across it."

Sielle turned her gaze on him.

"Come, I'll show you," he said, walking past her.

They marched ahead. As though from some hidden inner sun, whose mild flickering generated more heat than the two indolent eyes above, Sielle started to sweat again. They both wiped the sweat from their foreheads. She withdrew her gourd, took a deep drink of Zotharra's Blood, and felt the heat dissipate from her.

"Hot?" Haern asked.

"Somewhat, yes," Sielle replied, partly annoyed by his observation.

"Make sure to keep drinking every so often. Wouldn't want you to turn."

"Turn to what?"

"So they didn't tell you."

"They told me it's painful and horrible, and that you die."

"Well, that more or less sums it up. Except, you don't *quite* die. We don't think, at least."

"No?"

"No."

"And, well?"

"Well, you should ask Ilu for the details. But, you know about Zotharra's children, don't you?"

"No, I don't," she said in a hurry.

Haern did not answer immediately. Sielle noted his inner deliberation, before he finally spoke. "They are others from Zotharra, older creatures than us. We've done our best to keep them out, but it's a problem, sometimes."

"And Zotharra," Sielle said, "How do you keep it? How come it isn't destroyed by these creatures?" She envisioned the city walls of Zotharra, lined with an armored garrison wielding translucent halberds and shields of glass like sharp gems in the sunlight.

Haern did not answer. His eyes flickered, and, ignoring Sielle, he breathed in through his nose. He sniffed the air.

"What is it?" she asked.

He looked left, and right, and then took her hand. "Come."

Sielle sniffed, also, while he was leading her. The air once again carried that mixture of slag and perfume, though only faintly.

Haern led her in a hurry back to the tribe. As they descended their slope, the shimmer across the glass plains receded, and a vast field of black rubble came into view ahead. A few other stragglers ahead of Haern and Sielle were only just approaching it, too. They took off towards it in a run, and were gone in a flash.

Sielle flinched in disbelief. "What?"

"It's fine," Haern said, placing a hand on her shoulder. "Don't worry about it. Just run in straight. Aim for the middle of those two mountains. You see them, don't you? The ones with the bright peaks."

"Yes, I do, but is it safe?" she asked, dipping a foot in what otherwise could have been raven waters.

"It's perfectly safe."

Without asking Haern anything else, she turned from him and walked onto the black sand. At first she almost lost her balance. It felt as though she were levitating while taking only brief, slow steps. Her steps made concentric rings in the ground, which came to look like thick tar, or a massive lake of ash.

Though they had named it black sand, this surface resembled no desert or volcanic beach she had walked on Earth. She reached down to grasp a handful of it and found that it was solid to the touch.

"Go on," she heard Haern call from behind.

One of the suns shot her a blinding glare, and she barred her face from it with her arm. She advanced, and felt beneath her soles a strange buoyancy and a force unaccounted for, which dragged her into a jog. The black substance pooled around her feet, but remained solid.

With each step, she accelerated faster than she expected. She could not have noticed the momentum compounding or the skies shifting or the surface of this black gulf of solid matter rolling beneath her as one great carpet until the winds began blustering and gushing around her ears, and the black streamed below her as a unified mass.

She kicked the hardening membrane floor, and with each stride it propelled her ahead tenfold, and fast, faster, its surface became lucid, as though purified by her steps to form a polychromatic prism housing colours not released since the planet's birth. The suns blurred to a chain atop the planet's rim, rolling above the mountain's two crowns in the distance.

After mere seconds of running, she had already crossed half the surface. She was panting and heaving. She tried to wipe away the sweat now dripping into her eyes and stinging. Still she only took on speed, and did not dare interrupt the cycling of her legs, now possessed. Something rushed past her, then, heading in the opposite direction as she was still powering across miles of radiant mirror.

At first she thought it must have been a member of the tribe doubling back, but then she saw the figure's hair flash like a tendrilled whip, long and black as her own. There was no time or space now to inspect the mirage's return, and she continued on.

As the acid accrued in her legs, the colors around her blended to form an aquamarine highway tinged pink, the mountains a white cluster juggling the suns, the ground an ocean of variegated and specular waves. There ahead, the bank at the edge of the gulf approached like a foamy tide, men and women like ants upon it, and still she had not slowed. Her pulse quickened as to almost leap out the world. Meanwhile, her head continued a steady rhythm as though she were in the midst of a euphoric trance.

The people of Zotharra stood in a wedge formation on the bank. They watched Sielle as she barreled towards them. Without recourse, she vaulted up like an eagle baring its chest to the skies. The mountains rose with her and the suns split them apart. The ground receded to black and then sharply gave to the planet's regular skin.

As her body dipped, she invoked the maw of exile and called its jaws apart. But, before passing through those usual teeth, she opened her eyes and found hands extended to the heavens. She let the net of palms cushion her fall and remained with the people of Zotharra yet.

With her heart pumping and her legs buzzing and her face drenched in legitimate sweat, Sielle wheeled her head back. The sky was still pale and pulsing like her temples; it made another strange, aberrant shift in texture, as she had witnessed earlier. Haern was there, grinning upside down from above; Ilu, too, smiled as they lowered her to the ground.

"I told you it was safe," her most recent acquaintance whispered into her ear. The thought of Tikan entered her mind uninvited again as she stared up at Haern and blinked.

Circling her were proud and elated faces. None of them had previously introduced themselves, nor welcomed her, and Ilu had even abandoned her to cruel Neanh. Yet they gathered around her and beamed euphorically in seeming adoration, as though she had just partaken in a time-honored custom or concluded some rite of initiation.

She lightly shook her head to gather her bearings. And though her senses were overworked, she nonetheless heard a strange chanting somewhere beyond the well of people she had been lowered into. It dwindled to a distant hum before ceasing entirely moments later.

"Be among us, Sielle," came Ilu's priestly voice. She smiled at Sielle in her knowing way.

They made camp not far from the gulf. The commotion about Sielle rose in the days that followed. The people of Zotharra milled about, chatting near her without much discretion, as though she were an outland attraction barred from its own solitude in a cage of eyes.

Sielle was resting on a low boulder, watching the now inexplicably dimming sky. She drank of Zotharra's Blood and leered at the people who lingered too long about her.

"You've got to forgive them," said Haern, approaching her as though from nowhere. His hand was dripping as though he had just plunged it into the ground. "You've come from the stars. You're mysterious and exciting to them."

Just then, the nomads began dismantling their camp. They started again for the city.

Sielle rose from the boulder and walked with Haern.

"It's as if they're trying to study and measure me," Sielle said.

"By Zotharra, no," Haern replied. "'One cannot know another by measurement. That is directly from the wisdom of our forebears.'"

Sielle rolled her eyes. "How much longer will this journey last?"

"We've got a while left to go. Another few weeks or so."

"I thought you said you were bad at keeping track of time."

"You're right. I've made a special effort for you. But perhaps I should ask Neanh how much longer we have yet to travel," he said, grinning, and only barely holding himself from laughing.

"Stop that," Sielle said, though she was grinning and mimicking his tone.

They both snickered like mischievous children while pointing at Neanh in the distance.

For days they travelled. They crossed barren glass until the gulf of black sand dissolved in the horizon behind them. They travelled now along the sides of the mountains enclaving the flatlands. Those monoliths of dense glass provided some shade, and the light breaking through them gave a semblance of twilight.

As they advanced, there rose the same darkening miasma Sielle had seen on her first lonesome trek. The skyline, visible far off in the distance, was nonetheless bright and thronged with unusual clouds.

They spent a span of hours beneath a broad ridge, where they dumped piles of glowing gems into pits to make cyan fires. Then they slept, looking like thieves who had made off with the jewels of paradise.

All night, a contingent of watchmen patrolled the slanted perimeter of the camp with what looked like thuribles of gemmed watchfire. Sielle's own gem remained mute. She watched the gemfire swing through the dark, and she watched Ilu staring, transfixed, into a pit of gemfire like an oracle searching for a prophecy.

When they woke, the suns had rearranged behind the miasma, as though to gain a better view of them.

After packing up their gems, they crossed a ridged plain thick with spindly coral growths and glass dust crusted over the rocks like the white of damaged plastic. The shadows of the crags before them came down thin and raked like the long claw of an incubus. The wind came howling against them.

Before long they were skirting the highlands again. Holes melted into quicksilver slag on the mountain faces as they approached. The whole passage fumed like steam, though it was cool to the touch. As Sielle slid her fingers through some of this watery silver, her perception of shapes altered mildly, before returning to normal.

They passed through these brief metamorphosing tunnels dripping like accelerated stalactites, and when they reemerged, the skies had darkened again. Though, the suns still shone like flashlights through a thick fog.

Over the course of this journey, Sielle learned of the fascination the people of Zotharra had with mirrors. Many in the tribe decorated themselves in specular jewelry or adornments. Some, like Neanh, wore geometrically peculiar mirrors as designations of rank. Neanh even had a small mirror—an item whose creation required precise and masterful craftsmanship—lodged in her left earlobe like a slightly enlarged earing. Sielle discovered, too, that the mirror at the center of Ilu's tiara was in fact stitched into her forehead.

The people of Zotharra spent little time looking into these mirrors, but rather used them as a matter of symbolism, or as if it were important for parts of the world to be reflected, irrespective of an observer.

They made the children wear mirrors on the palms of their hands, especially when playing together or when speaking to elders. Some in the tribe had mirrors permanently sewn into their skin in various places. Mirrors sewn over the heart or the forehead or the palms were the most common, but some had them under their shoulder blades, and others on their shoulders. They even ate out of plates that doubled the images of their food.

Every so often on the journey, they would point large mirrors at the gazes of the suns, and then carefully rotate each one until they were able to merge the beams across the ground. At first Sielle thought this might have had some sort of navigational purpose, but in truth it had only spiritual significance.

Over the course of the journey, Sielle and Haern increasingly bantered and could be heard laughing at regular intervals. Sielle routinely asked him about the planet and Zotharra and the pilgrims she walked among. Haern revealed little.

The others watched enviously as he entertained the cosmic guest, and they came to leer at them and whisper jealously.

It was not long before, one day, Ilu herself took notice of them. Beside her, Elu turned in his portable seat to give the chatting pair disapproving looks from afar. He had seemed entirely disinterested in Sielle after their first meeting. He had otherwise worn a vacant expression and continuously mumbled to himself as they journeyed to Zotharra. Already the old man was pawing at a spirit world in the hereafter.

Eventually, a frantic little messenger called Haern over to Ilu and Elu. Haern stopped abruptly in his speech and walked over to them without saying another word to Sielle.

He stood with Neanh before Ilu and Elu, and they were both reprimanded. The others watched as Ilu berated him for what otherwise seemed like plain, if slightly relaxed, friendliness.

When it was finished, Haern walked back alone in dejection along the outside of the queue. His face was sullen and downcast. When he braved a quick glance at Sielle in passing, he found that she was gazing out over the mountains, no longer paying him any interest. Others gave him looks of disdain, and, preoccupied with his public shaming, he almost tripped on an obvious rock and then passed out of Sielle's sight.

Sielle had turned her attention to the mist curling below the mountain peaks. The fog coiled around spires of opaque glass on the mountain peaks. Every so often, the whole body of fog dipped, forming an inverted crown of ghosts. As they walked on, this band of wisps grew to blot out the suns.

The messenger arrived before Sielle again. "Ilu requests your presence," he said, at last distracting her.

"Ilu. Right," she replied before instantly looking back up to see branches of static beginning in the cobalt mists above.

"Why have you wasted your time speaking to Haern?" Ilu snapped at Sielle the moment she arrived.

They walked ahead of everyone else. Beside them, men who had the disposition of eunuchs were carrying Elu on his great chair. They seemed stripped of any consciousness, as though their sole purpose were to lift up their aging leader. With his sight transfixed ahead, Elu sat hunchbacked and continued to mumble inaudible things.

"He's wasted his own time, if anything," Sielle replied. "I've just been walking along, and he was kind enough to speak with me."

"If you had questions you could have—"

"Asked Neanh? She's dull. And she's rude. Anything I asked she mocked and—it actually doesn't matter. I don't care. I don't need things explained. I just want some peace and quiet." She sulked and refused to look at Ilu.

Ilu winced at the comment, but quickly regained her composure. "That is understandable. You've travelled from very far away. It's a journey we only know in legend."

"You're big on legends here. Is there any truth to them?"

Ilu paused a moment. She blinked and then looked at Sielle. "Please excuse me, dear child, but I thought you were only concerned with quietude and solace."

There hatched an unexpected tension between them. The darkened path they walked accented Ilu's icy stare, and it was hard for Sielle to formulate a reply. She saw her own tiny reflection in the mirror on Ilu's forehead.

"Do not worry," Ilu continued, her face softening. "I understand. The jester has my scorn for agitating questions in you which I had left for Zotharra herself to answer. Would you not have preferred to delight in Zotharra's flesh and blood and breath alone? That is all you've wanted, is it not? And, it is clear that you have been drawn deeply enough from the first."

Sielle grimaced, trying to comprehend Ilu's words. Ilu observed Sielle as though she had already accounted for any thought Sielle might then have had.

"How many skies do you expect will come apart before you reach Great Zotharra's heart?" Ilu asked.

"Please," Sielle said, her face straining. "I don't understand your riddles. I just want some peace and quiet and to see Zotharra."

"Of course, my dear," Ilu said, smiling in a motherly way. "We have only adopted you, after all, that you might embrace Zotharra whole."

"What is this place, so far from Sol?" Sielle asked. "And why is Proxim—"

"Quiet," Ilu said, shifting a glance at the drones carrying Elu. "There's no need to blaspheme."

"Blaspheme? What does—"

Ilu grasped Sielle by her shoulders and dragged her out of earshot of any others. "Quiet, and I shall explain," she said. "Though I needn't. You, most of all, you must already know the rot that runs through the Milky Way."

"I'm sorry?"

"Yes, as you should be. All of you. Desecrators."

"I don't know what you're talking about."

"Then you are blind."

"I'm—"

"Tell me, you, who has spent her whole life in a monochrome room, do you have words for that colour? Can you point to the plague that has ever been the inner wall of your life's shell?" She watched Sielle for a few moments and squinted menacingly. "Sol is the hand that lays ruin to star systems. Did you think we had forgotten?"

Sielle said nothing, but breathed louder and tracked Ilu's cold eyes. The mountain peaks appeared to shimmer.

"Why else would the human soul carry over so much empty dark except to escape some viler spirit yet?" Ilu continued, her voice becoming aggressive. "And have you not witnessed us drag our living carcasses over Zotharra's glassy eye? But see us, Zotharra!" she exclaimed with some restraint, as though channeling the planet's own crackling essence. She paused and stared at Sielle with a zealot's intensity. "Our ancestors made your very flight centuries ago. To escape the bludgeoning of Hephaestus and his hammer. To escape that crawling pest even now wriggling only a skull away from mine. They saw the death of Sol. They watched planets buried alive in silver coffins.

"And so on ships wrought of obsolete steel, the orphaned colony sailed and sailed, without hope of return. They dove off the Milky Way's black and rancid stream, and for Zotharra's grace slipped through the astral straits. And they were dashed as on stormy rocks, or ejected to wander the cold of oceans far from all reckoning. Only one single ship arrived on the naked shores of Andromeda. And, oh, she who took us upon her bosom! Zotharra, splendid Zotharra! Zotharra the Unblighted! Zotharra the Mother!"

Something in this story of exile stirred Sielle. "Tikan Solstafir," she blurted apprehensively.

Ilu's temple was throbbing. She stared at Sielle. "What?" she said, the drama still exuding from her.

"Who led these exiles?" Sielle pressed.

"Faris Dormand."

Sielle flinched. "No, it must have been—Are you sure? Do you keep records? How long ago was it?"

"There is no one by that name among our fathers."

"There must be. How can you be sure if you never wrote it down? Arcturus! What about Arcturus?"

"A dead star. What about it?"

"No. He must have gone there. What about Vega?"

"The heat from that explosion still radiates to this day. They say it looked like a great flower emerging from the dark of space."

"And Tikan Solstafir?"

Ilu shook her head dismissively. "The one you speak of was probably a petty criminal remembered in your world for some failed act of rebellion. He most likely did not even exist."

Sielle's expression turned vulnerable and hostile. "What are you saying?"

"That each little one of your worlds is a farce. I do wonder how much worse it is, now, after all these centuries. I've long kept you in my thoughts, you know. Did you cease to invent? Did you curl up into mechanic eggs and at last arrive at the concrete zero? Elu has had far more sinister imaginings. It does not matter, in any case. Think on humankind's trajectory from Earth to Proxima, now, in Zotharra's light. Are they not all damned?"

"I don't know the history."

"No, of course you don't. History is the relic of a past age. What shall humanity need of history when meaning has already been dispensed with?"

"What do you mean?"

"It is only in reference to and in virtue of the past that meaning is possible. Think on the past. Think on how its claws are ever sunk in the reel of the present, on how every time you attend to something present—that mountain top, Elu's chair—you are really only attending to the just-past. It is because observation destroys the living present. Do not observe, my girl, but *see*.

"It is that relation—those claws in the reel—from which meaning is wrought. Time is no fixed line, no moving bar, but rather the foam of a wave on a shore, pulling, bending, breaking, inching up the shore and down, irreducible to numbers or words. Obliterate our collective past, and so too shall you obliterate our collective meaning."

Sielle stared at the ground. "It wasn't always like that. It can change. Things change."

"You speak of progress?"

"Yes."

"Ignorant girl. You've lost more than the past. Let me tell you of humanity's berserk leap through the stars. When scientific progress eclipsed the Earth, humankind had long before already torn apart science and spirit, placed electrons in one column and morals in the other. You see, people were confused, and they confused others in turn. Scientific triumph was evaluated and celebrated not in terms of the meaning it brought people, but in terms of how many past achievements it could make obsolete, and in how many tools it could produce.

"This easily tracked and overwhelming success slowly humiliated every other human activity, for each was suddenly being evaluated by the same criteria. The arts, religion, morality, philosophy, and all other facets of human life by which meaning or value is expressed were no longer viewed as the eternal but as the inefficient, the lost, the conflicted, the useless, the miring. New forms of them continued to emerge for a time, yes, innovations—most of them trite, and mere shadows of their precedents—but nothing we would call *progress* in the sense of producing tools and obsoletions.

"And though rivers were blackened and cancers were sprouted and cities were vaporized and star systems were imploded along the way, still these were mere bumps on the road to *progress*. So you see, in the end, humanity gave up its sense of purpose for tools and cheap pleasures; the obsoletion of the just-past itself, and therefore meaning, became its mindless goal.

"There was a grace period lasting a few centuries, in which history, the arts, religion, philosophy, and morality all died quiet, unremarkable deaths, but these eventually vanished, too—their outer shells repurposed. Only we remember. Only we carried their corpses over our shoulders, limping from star to star. So speak not of progress. Speak not of progress in the name of humanity the amoral, the artless, the soulless. It is the return of the eternal you and I await, not progress."

Sielle sighed, and took on an expression of deep concern. There was truth in Ilu's words, but when she looked up at the older woman, she saw not a sage or a priestess. What she saw was bitterness showing through cracks in her pristine skin.

"That's not true, not all of it," Sielle said, uncertain of why she was growing impassioned. "You can't bury the eternal! And you're just as bad, keeping swords and spears and robes for no good reason except because you've been humiliated. Isn't that just a mockery of tradition? Isn't that just a caricature, a wrong turn exactly opposite to bloody

Proxima? You're not so different from your ancestors in the Milky Way. They burned all their books, too—I know that much."

"They burned their books for what they contained. We burned ours for what they could not."

"But isn't there a middle way? You've overcorrected the wrongs of Proxima. You've fed yourself the tail of the serpent," Sielle said, exasperated and surprised at the wave of optimism now overcoming her. "And there are a few good people on Proxima—a few of them. You'll find good people even in the worst of places, and—"

"Do not ridicule me," Ilu almost sneered. "Why is it that you've come so far, then, if it's to defend the horrors of home?"

Sielle said nothing.

"Surely you did not arrive here by accident," Ilu continued. "You are too clever and knowledgeable to be a simple drone of Proxima. And if it was asylum you sought in Andromeda, then you are the most fortunate refugee the universe has ever seen. No. Tell me, what plot stews in your wormy head?"

There was a pause as Sielle tried to comprehend what she was being accused of. She locked eyes with Ilu.

"The arrogance," Ilu snarled. "Centuries later, and still the corpse of Sol hungers. But, we needn't despair," she said, gripping Sielle's shoulder as though to comfort her. "Zotharra is mother to us all, and she is invulnerable."

"I don't mean any harm. I—"

"Tell me," Ilu said. "Do the people of Earth still hearken to the clouds and the undead sun? Have you Proximaens ever felt the warmth of skin or of words carried by damp breath? The skies of Sirius remain unwatched, unloved. And yet still you hunger for Andromeda. Still you are not satisfied. Was a whole galaxy not sufficient? Know that you will only break yourselves against Zotharra. You will—"

"Ilu, please," Sielle said, frustrated and afraid. "I escaped. Of course I escaped. Do you think they'd send one scared girl to spy on you?"

They paused. Ilu lowered her eyes. After a moment, a smile grew across her face.

"Of course, my dear," she said, coming down from her wrath. "You are too full in flesh and humor and yearning for the mountain peaks to be of that kind. Forgive me for what I have said. And the past is irrelevant. Zotharra will embrace you. She will."

"Your city?"

"Yes—our city, our world, our divine."

As they reeled from their confrontation, the familiar scent of burning winter swept their faces. They walked back to Elu's side.

"The fell winds," Elu said without altering his gaze, his voice gruff from disuse.

They heard commotion among the others all the way down the queue. The mountain's shade darkened as if the incubus' hand had clasped shut. The suns could not be seen. The mists were now crackling and bulbous as they swirled like whirlpools around the mountain peaks.

"Neanh!" Ilu called, spinning around.

Neanh was not far. She ran through the crowd to reach Ilu.

"There is little time. We must find escape," Ilu commanded.

"I've sent Beral and Huren to scout ahead; Lehn and Naren to skirt the mountains."

"Good."

"And what about her?" Neanh asked, motioning her head towards Sielle. "Shall I leave her with Haern?"

"No. This one will stay by my side."

Sielle heard thunder crash in the distance. The horizon was a quivering purple smudge.

"There is a passage below the mountains," Elu said, still unfazed. "To great Zotharra, to the immortal city."

"Centuries of blood have funneled down to this one night," Ilu told Sielle. "Will you be the last drop?"

Sielle did not reply, but eyed Ilu with great worry, and armed herself to leave the planet. They stormed off into the thunder, to the last drop.

❦ 42 ❧

THE RENT VEIL

I was ejected from the crucible of enlightenment, face sweating in darkness, hands slipping on the hard paneled floor. Broken from the egg of rebirth into the mundane again, the mundane as it sat naked before my invigorated gaze. My bones hummed. The change began to manifest. My senses were unlocking, the tumblers dropping, the gate to the world's mysteries unlatching. The key and the lock fused into one. I shivered, shimmering within as clarity suffused each recess of my consciousness.

When I had departed, no light had touched the room. Now it bloomed before me. Dark, light, clouds, ground, all. Whole renditions of a different room, or non-room, slicing in and out of frame before me. The images superimposed themselves on each other. The kernel of history. The tag end of the world ripped from a microscopic mirror's heart. I stared at the floor. The floor the farm the desk the gunfire the chair the war the wall the wind the storm the silver-streaked horizon the whirlwind of suits and dresses the snow binding the rain the oceans surging the icebergs crowning the jungle shore like an herbivore's lower jaw the earth the lava hardening the space of the Earth unformed the void the dust of the prenatal sun. Wilder as I continued to reel.

I screeched in pain. I blinked at one and only one other part of the floor and I could see a shifting concatenation of wood and ash and metal rails on scaffolding and the foot of the room's last occupant. Furniture came and went with the roof. Time flowed against itself. Like a tunnel of glass, it shattered around me.

With a surge of nausea bubbling up to my throat, I groped at the space before me, hoping to find something solid to grasp. I breathed, steadying myself, and in my elation felt the lightning of truth bore into my eyes and between my fists.

I stood as if on the peaks of all creation, wiped my forehead, and hurried in an aimless circle. The room(s) wound around me, square-shaped, spherical, exposed to the sun, boxed in, reverting to scaffolding and then advancing to debris. Only my excitement fought off the nausea.

I was like a bird hitherto deformed that had just gained its wings after years accustomed to feeble little legs. How to soar as I was now hurtling off a cliff to grounds shrouded in mist? How to ride the wind? I almost collapsed. I had to leave, to exit the corridor of contradictions my apartment had become.

The space-time spasms forced me to shut my eyes and stand in place. Focus. There were pants and a shirt folded over my desk chair, this I remembered. I had to keep my eyes firmly sealed, as navigating the room(s) would have been impossible otherwise. I took two steps forward, hoping my movement would not displace my matter in any way congruent to what I had been witnessing. Sweating, still, I searched for my clothes on the crutches of instinct and touch.

Somewhere, somewhere in the world, as it no doubt continued its rebirthing throes, I found the clothed chair. One of its legs scraped against the floor as I blundered into it. The noise resounded, compounded, and then raced to the sound of sawing and creaking. The smell of industrial glue roared up my nostrils.

But I could hardly attend to that. The side of my thumb had glanced the chair's cold wood, and my other fingertips touched the fabric of the pants. All of my senses screamed out at me. From those light brushes, myriad sensations poured into me, mingling, whirling together, dateless and without anchor. The carpenter at work his calluses the sweat on his brow the sharp scent of sawed wood the anxiety in his left pocket formed of a text message ring his wife at home the child unborn the grandmother deceased the strawberry taste of her fourth birthday cake the tinny music out of the gramophone the creak of the door in a house countries away and the sweatshop in Taiwan the workers exhausted the machine-powered needles humming in unison through the warehouse the blister on the child's thumb the thread catching the twilight glare the fabric the cotton fields and—I lost my breath, my legs frozen.

To see the world's temporal continuum blended together was an experience that, while alien and overpowering, I had been somewhat prepared for by past dreams and the works of mad artists. In fact, it seemed, at first, not to be very different from certain sorts of hallucinations.

But when all of my senses were together reaching for the entire world within an individual object, it was clear how far my experience was transcending petty analogies. No, this was no hallucination, no break from sanity. Nor was it a trick of some psychological contraptions in me. I was witnessing the unwinding of each thing-in-itself.

Away. I tried to wrestle with the anarchic stream, to regain a moment's stability. I achieved a brief reprieve, snatched the clothes, and dressed, ignoring my senses as they relapsed. Abandoning my sensorial trust in exchange for memory, that was the way. Out the door I went, probably dressed, still blinding myself, walking until I remembered the stairs and halted.

Control, I had to keep control. The last thing I needed was a broken body too numb with power to know it. I took a deep breath, regathered my focus, and opened my eyes to the chaos again.

The world was flowering in resplendent epilepsy. The staircase appeared a few times before becoming lost in the great mess. Those few appearances were enough. I was about to move. To test. I thought I saw one of my neighbors beside me in the hallway. "Bonjour, Mathieu," I said, unsure of whether he was actually there in relation to my sensing, living body. No reason to dwell on it. Down I went, again working from memory through my contradictory sense experience.

As I willed myself down the short flight, I caught glimpses of what resembled the present, of my material anchoring. Cautious steps. Each flashing view of my own feet reassured me that I had not yet fallen down the steps to a twisted spine. In fact, I was lucky to see the front door of the building moments before running head first into it.

Out on the street. Wild colors abounding. It was spring—no, winter—no, both. Auburn leaves aflame, and graves of snow. The air was dry, and then humid, and then I smelled sulfur, and before that gasoline. And I tasted coffee! There was a coffeehouse around the block.

For a few solid minutes, I managed to keep the shifting visions to a minimum. A grand feat of resistance as I shambled off to the café, mind in spastic euphoria. I had to reconstruct the path to it from memory, else I would never arrive there while traversing this mutating landscape. The path was clear in my mind's eye, and in some sense, that helped me make my perceptions conform.

The café was not far at all. I walked straight ahead, feet against earth and pavement and carpet, around the corner, around river and farmlands and cobbled roads and grassless highways, and then through the glass doors of the café. I was inside in no time, and in no matter, as I relaxed my efforts on arrival and found myself on a grassy knoll. No. Again, to the present: small rectangular tables arranged in the far corner.

"Un cappuccino, s'il vous plaît," I succeeded in telling the barista as she flickered in and out of existence before me.

There were others there, too, trying to populate the room, but I had to let them go. Keeping her fixed in front of me consumed all of my energies. Alas, the sweet girl in front of me buzzed and metamorphosed into million-armed Shiva, holstering innumerable and terrifying cups of steaming coffee. She would destroy me, destroy the world if I let her stay in that state.

I had to cut myself off, cut off my newly sprouted wings. Not permanently, of course. They would regenerate in due course. It was disheartening, to say the least. But it was only a momentary retreat. A pause to catch my breath. I had already passed my trial of ascendance; what was left was to learn to walk so far above the clouds.

Though, damming myself did feel weightier than I would have expected. I felt the pangs of an addiction not yet solidified. I felt weak and old, and mortal. But, no matter. I still knew the way back through the woods.

And so, I let my senses recede to their lesser, duller, more primitive forms. And, with a "Merci," I collected my single cup of coffee from the dual-armed barista.

~

Perhaps the phone was ringing again. Perhaps Bogdan was seeking me out for another rampage. None of that mattered. My new power was still there, teeming against the barrier I'd imposed on myself; I needed new environs to test it, unspoiled by sour nights in the cold or the calls of murderous ophthalmologists.

There were too many distractions around, and I hungered for mastery. A week was too long of a stall, and, moreover, I feared the interruptions would gain in proximity and danger. I had to leave the city. To Alexandria! Or to Peru? Both. Neither. To Nairobi? Not then. No matter. I needed to get away from Bogdan, from Pierre, from Paris, for some years.

The reconstructions in me were fresh, the scaffolding not yet entirely removed. I was untested, and had little direction. I had a tongue, but no language to speak. New hands that needed new objects to touch, to embrace, to pervade. Particulars to attach to that general cloud of knowledge within me, that same hunger then about to be gorged on pure, immediate *understanding*.

I needed to train myself, to open the dam little by little until the waters could be channeled at will. Only then could I rightly direct myself towards solving the great problems of mankind.

Away, then. I fled to the airport. Truly, this time. I took a flight to somewhere, to everywhere.

When I arrived, I checked into a cheap hotel to avoid lingering indoors. There would be zero distractions. There would be focused progress. There would be calculated wanderlust in search of incision points. But, first of all, there would be throwing myself against spiked walls in the hopes of making a dent in the problem.

São Paulo was my first laboratory. There, I kicked the football around with some locals. Without any skill, I was made to play goalie. It was fine. Suitable, actually. An entirely reactive, stationary role where I could stand and focus. Concentration was key. Not on the game, but on measuring how much of myself I would release from captivity. Fixing my glare ahead, I struggled to foresee where the attackers would shoot four minutes thence. Nothing. The balls flew past me and sank into the net. The others jeered me off the pitch, but it was all right. It was all right, because they were lab rats to me.

Bergen treated me no differently. There, I yelled orders at a fisherman. I told him when to pull in his line. Twice he listened, to no success. The third time, he sent me from the barge back to the docks on a dingy. It was fine. I needed the exposure, the rejection, the effort. In Alba, too. The truffle hunters there exiled me for misleading their sows.

I tried to implicate myself in more dire situations, too. I thought that perhaps it was urgency and danger that I needed. It was not. The Cambodians deported me for claiming to be a guide through old minefields (a role I would only ever play from a safe distance). In short: it was all going rather poorly, without altogether being too discouraging.

Suddenly had that first wildfire been kindled, and perhaps I expected the same for my more educational project. Not yet. I could sense the essences of each object buzzing beneath their thin and deceptive surface crusts. There, ready to be unpacked and witnessed, was the whole, the real whole. The collage of trans-temporal appearances. The closest possible sketch of each thing-in-itself. The omnipresent perception. And, though I was not yet prepared to taste much of it, I was patient. And I had to shield myself, for the new vistas I had been snapped into facing were as yet too bright.

Indeed, it was not a rapid metamorphosis that followed the enlightenment, no; not a clean and even bloating of boundaries, but rather the jagged, arrhythmic expansion of confines long stiffened by custom.

Farther off did I travel, yes, far away to train my true sight. And it was not too long before I began to adjust to my elevated state of consciousness. In a more measured manner, this time.

It started without ceremony, one day in Kuala Lumpur's sterile white Pavilion Mall. The kind of artificial fortress that had rolled out of Dubai to plague the cities of the Middle East and Southeast Asia.

I was there, loitering between the food court and the cinema, between nasi lemak warring against pungent fries and a wall of movie posters shared by Hollywood and art-house Hong Kong. Somewhere between the two, as hard lights mixed with the noxious scent of a passing cologne stand, I caught the sight of a boy as he skipped up an escalator, movie ticket in hand.

I gave him a significant stare. He must have been no older than ten. He was fifty-six in a flash, fighting for life between blue waves off the coast of Penang as a monstrous sun rose out of the ocean to fill half the sky. It happened so fast that in the following moments, as the intensity withered, I found myself doubting its occurrence.

A tenuous link. A faint grasp. Fingers brushing the incomprehensible. I pushed and strained my mind to peel the layer back again, to no avail. Many months later, however, my work to reproduce the incident would prove quite fruitful indeed.

Ordinary life, which I pursued as the canvas for my art still in utero, in non-Parisian hotels and non-Parisian boulevards, persisted quite contiguously for the most part. Causality, as I witnessed it, still behaved mostly as I would have expected it.

A spilled drink refused to reveal anything past about the hand that had knocked it, and its contents pooled ever outward. A taxi driver, his face impaled by an oak's branch, remained silent about how his car was manufactured or the bartender who may have allowed him a few too many drinks.

It was either this partial view, or the full whirlwind that had initially swallowed me up. I had to gradually bend myself into a position of control. But every now and again, as I progressed in my efforts, that steady normality was interrupted; the creased, streaming ribbon of space-time repeatedly stabbed through by mercurial razors, the daggers of Damocles, each suspended at a different angle and from no ceiling at all. Toward mastery, through those fresh tears in the ribbon, then.

In public places, here and there, at the park, on the bench across from me, at the coffee shop and the grocery store. The jerking of growing wings! Double takes of babies mewling, puling, and then bearded and bored; of spilled milk dripping down a woman's shin and then squeezed out of a cow's udder; and, most importantly, of a man's poolside childhood in tears as he screams at his little daughter. Together! As one! A fuller, more tempered vision. Every facet of the existential diamond shining brightly.

I thought at first that I would try to use my powers for good, or glory. I thought I'd save babies from burning buildings, or tip off the police to a crime in the making, or steal the ideas of great minds in gestation. But this ambition withered before it even began. I didn't care for particular events or successes. Perhaps you'd call my approach scientific, because I cared only for the most general outcome. One solution to engulf all others.

To achieve this, I needed this new structure in my understanding to be passive and intuitive. To hone it, I doubled—no, quadrupled— my rate of travelling. It required years. Years poured into portals inviting my special perception. I ravened for any morsel of progress, in every crevice or recess of the world where I could sense the growth of my attunement.

Unlike the outright blooming, buzzing confusion it had been the first time, I was growing accustomed to witnessing multiple profiles of this or that object, of accepting its existence and non-being at once in peaceful contradiction.

And this new sight of mine was conjoined quite merrily with those vicious creatures still lurking around the corners of my consciousness. At first, it was hard to tell the difference between warped fantasies of an uninspired waiter's demise and the true snapshot of his death under the wheels of a bus sometime when the day was hotter than usual.

But my demons, they were dying, and revealed to be but crippled abominations. Aberrant visions, unlike the vast truths I was coming to behold. I came to understand the difference when I became able to wring happiness and meaning from a subject's history.

In Grahamstown, an old widow's remark about a marriage stronger than mortal loneliness burrowed into the mind of a young listener, who in his old age sits in a chair surrounded by grandchildren. In Kyoto, a monk's life of stone words softened by a cherry blossom cared for in the palm of a boy tourist standing in ignorant desecration. Damascus—a grandfather's caress made in imitation of a loving mother. Cordoba—a school teacher's after-hours advice turns a ruffian into a scholar. And then, as the multifarious nodes of causality's web emerged from obscurity: sympathy. Seattle— a suicide of shattered bones in a puddle of flesh made clear by years of unspoken traumas, the anger of family and friends equally justified by impossible knowledge. Sydney—a girl's high-school loneliness illuminating her mid-life break into serial murder, her second victim's misfortune, the third's stupidity, the seventh's nighttime proclivities.

And in those glimpses of a complete account, the true ground of understanding and toleration and peace became apparent to me. A ground almost entirely buried in the depths of the mind. A ground which, until I could fully actualize my new gifts, even I could not have hoped to stand upon, let alone expect others to.

For man was not to blame. Truly, how could man be blamed, with all of his glaring ineptitudes, with the true distance of his fall now revealed?

It would have been like blaming the mentally challenged for their shortcomings. All the resources and lives wasted in petty wars across the ages, all the lost progress, all the anomic wandering from birth to death; just as each stands before every other, linguistically bankrupt and feeding the coals of hell in parallel. It is because there is only one true language, as yet unborn.

It was up to me to help man. It was the need to acquire the totality of history: all the particular histories of one's subject, and history's general weave through the ages, complete with the nuances of history's own internal combat—all as one.

Despite this clear, general goal, the way to it was still obscure to me. I thought of the priestess and her flickering existence. I thought of how to pit mankind against space and time. But I was in no position to make concrete plans yet.

It took me years and much experimentation throughout various countries to grapple with the all-piercing (I almost said totalitarian!) lens in me, to convert myself permanently to the new gaze. And, even when I found that I could reproduce it at will, it was not complete. I had a cursed sword in hand, growing to untenable weight each time I lunged to strike. A glimpse! A glance! Only a peek.

I needed the precise and immanent whole. I needed for it not to be possible to see the world otherwise.

✸ 43 ✸

NEPTUNE RETURNS

The first days in the apartment after Onasus' departure were of moribund friendship. Whatever attempts the others made at sociable contact, Tikan rejected. He would regularly fling his hand out at them to drive them off, or grunt something beneath his breath as they made attempts to reconnect. He did not let them feed him, or clothe him, or examine his wounds.

As for the others, their condition varied by the day. Mira spent much of her time with her hands bracing her temples, whispering calming words to herself. These words she sharply intended, but when she perceived them, when she heard herself, they did not accord with her intentions. Naim regularly hummed the tunes of ancient composers, which even metempsies had not preserved.

They tried, at times, to meekly evoke the lost nostalgia of their days on the Equuleus, but the blind man remained unresponsive. They spoke less to him and to each other as a result, though they continued to hover around him through the days, no longer certain of how to proceed.

"Where's my card?" Tikan exclaimed one afternoon, having checked his pockets and found Amozagh's decayed king of hearts card to be missing.

None replied at first.

"I recall...he took it. Blood-stained and all," Mira said. "Said it suited him more."

"He took it?"

"Yes, he put it in your pocket."

"It's not in my pocket."

"I said he put it in my pocket," Mira insisted.

Tikan no longer replied, and instead stewed.

From the outside, the apartment came to resemble a sort of psychiatric ward, each resident with his or her own idiosyncratic disorder. Tikan would often growl to himself in frustration, or cry, or shout in his sleep. Naim was aloof, lucid, his mouth buzzing with phrases erupted out of the grave of the past. Mira struggled to keep her mind from spilling out of her hands.

Tikan eventually mollified and let the others speak to him.

"Is it real, do you think?" Naim asked Tikan in his new child-like tone, almost afraid of addressing him.

"Is what real?"

"What Neptune has said. Going to Vega and Arcturus, disconnecting everyone, and the seas coming together to drown us if we don't."

Tikan lingered on the thought before responding, surprised that Naim suddenly remembered the matter in such detail.

"Probably, yes. I think so," he said, softer. "If he just wanted to get rid of us he would have done it by now. There's obviously something there. What do you still remember?"

"One thing, one thing," Naim said.

For a moment, Tikan thought his old friend might somehow be cured or redeemed. "What's that?"

"Meals," Naim said. "There was a promise of nourishment, there was. Shall I have my fill of fine cuisines on Vega? I'd take a bite out of a star if it didn't burn my tongue, take sip of a black hole if it didn't suck me up first, feast on a galaxy if I'd not be left in utter dark. Delicacies of dead Sultans, that's why, selections from along the silky Danube. Sugar rusts the steel! Salt and rime entomb the tongue! I'll wait under the loam if you promise to feed my spirit forever, Tikan."

When an entire week elapsed past Onasus' assurance of a swift return, Tikan's behavior became erratic and inconsistent. He would begin conversations, and then go silent. He would call for the others to come to him, and then dismiss them.

"Why is he still out there?" he demanded, still couchridden, as Mira drifted near him. "Why does he need her? We should just be going. Hasn't he dragged enough of us into this?"

"Well, it's strange. But..." Mira said, stopping herself.

"What?"

"What is it about her? You look just as worried about her as he was."

"There is *nothing* about her. Got it? He's insane, that's all it is."

"That's very strange," Mira said. "Are you in love?"

He ignored her question. "Yes. It is. It's strange. But she can't be harmed by him—never."

He was almost heaving. The others could sense it. They watched him fret over Sielle and her fate. As if he were a wartime homemaker feeling her widowhood cemented in a distant country.

"But, why is he so obsessed?" Mira asked. "Why do we need an extra person so badly? Is it just because she doesn't have a procrustus that he thinks she matters so much?"

"He's out to waste time, is Neptune," Naim said from a distant part of the room. "He's not happy with the fish in his own sea, wants to sink the other kingdoms for himself. Star and land, blood and brain—maybe others, too."

"I don't know," Tikan replied solemnly, ignoring Naim.

One day, the night sky was redder than usual. Sol Victus looked as though it were rising for dawn, though Proxima was ever strung in blood twilight. It looked as if it were about to overwhelm the city.

"Neptune is returning! He must be, look," Naim called from the window. "Look, the red tide. Is there a deeper sea than the universe?"

Tikan did not respond. He heard Mira shriek from her room.

"Quiet! Stop speaking his name!"

"He's fished us out of the black, has old Neptune. Or—no, that's wrong. We're just the prongs of his trident, and he's fishing for the sun."

Mira stormed out of her room, bawling. She grabbed Naim by the shoulders and flung him to the ground. "Stop speaking his name! Don't pronounce it, don't even whisper it. Just stop it!" she screamed, until her voice was hoarse.

Two more days passed, and Tikan started to oscillate between frantic daydreams. Lying down and gripping his hair, he would clench his teeth and exhale over the distressing thoughts circling his mind. He rolled on his side, his hair springing between his fingers; and his elbows, flesh and glass, joining above his face at intervals. He gnashed his teeth as he pictured the scientist's hunt for Sielle.

Behind dim corners, under crimson sun and night, shadows stark and exacting across his grotesque face, smiling demonically, larger than the narrow alley walls like parallel canvases for his monstrous silhouette, he would close in. Sielle would find the end of the alley and turn; her face fixed in horror, she would cower. All her resources spent, all her wit dissolved. Hungering Onasus would advance, whining device in hand; or none—only claws.

"What will you do to her?" Tikan called out as he writhed on the couch. And what would he do to her? Hack her limbs and head for spare parts? No, not that. Onasus was too practical. He would guide her away from safety with enticing lies, and that would be it. Tikan's thoughts spilled out of him as a series of footsteps approached.

"We've got to go find him," Tikan said, sitting up.

"Who's gone?" Naim asked.

"Both of them."

"Neptune?"

"She's already survived. Worse than this, I'm sure. But she doesn't know. And—Damn your Neptune! How many days has it been?"

"Eight, since he was suppose to be back," Mira said, approaching. "I —I don't think we should leave the apartment. None of us are well enough for it."

"If I had legs to stand on," he said, "I'd hunt him down now, drag him off Proxima myself. I'd kill Proxima to keep her—I'd kill you all to keep her!"

Mira appeared unfazed. "I don't want to speak about this anymore. Okay?"

"She's too resourceful for him," Tikan insisted. "But if he finds her, if he brings her here—it'll be fine—it'll be fine. She'll put out one eye; I'll put out the other."

"What gold you feeling now of reeling since rainbow tongue, though?" Naim asked. "Neptune said for forests and acupuncture better by now stung. Do you feel better?"

"You know, I wonder if he's even still on Proxima," Tikan continued. "Do you think he just left without us? No. No, he needs someone at Vega. Why, then? What's he thinking?"

"I said cream flooded too moons ago!" Mira said.

"What?"

"Cream flooded too—moons crow!"

"What are you saying?"

"Cream can't control moons crow." She looked left and right in distress. "Mother moon is morrow me." She paused and breathed before trying again. "Moon moon is moon. Moon is moon." Once more she attempted to un-muzzle herself from the accruing assonance and consonance of her words then metamorphosing to the mere tautology of her every thought. "Moon is moon." She screamed it again, "Moon is moon! Mira is Mira! Mira. Mira, Mira. Mira!"

She looked at him intently and then closed her eyes in order to focus. She appeared to shiver. "I said, I didn't want to talk about it anymore."

"What do you want to talk about, then?" Tikan sneered. He became almost delirious. "What words are there left between us, anyway? 'Hello,' 'goodbye?' Or are these also just sounds?"

Mira walked off in anguish, breathing hard. She slammed the door to her room and they heard her cry out as if someone had branded her with a hot iron.

Naim chanced a few steps forward and laid a cup of coffee down on the table in front of Tikan. "There's always the option of, oh, you know...running...for dry...land," he said through much consternation.

"You want to escape—now?" Tikan said. "Don't make me laugh."

"But, Tikan. I...I need...some air."

Though he had already forgiven his friends in principle, a mere glance at the corner of Tikan's mouth would have revealed the twinge of anger he received in that moment. "Air? What about when I called for air? You've spent your life digging at your itch with a knife. This must be just another fuzzy set of pictures for you. It's an accident you're here. By rights you should be a corpse freezing in dark space. That's how much air you deserve. Now's the time to die, Naim—I'm sorry you never chose to live."

Naim rose without a word and walked away.

Tikan's heart smashed against his ribcage. His head thumped in remorse while pleasure trickled through him. Thus his cruelty escalated, and they cycled through the psychological eczema that their once-friendship had become.

After his last outburst, Tikan heard less of Naim. Mira's visits, too, became infrequent. Tikan tried several times to speak to her again. But she was tired and disappointed; he could hear it in her voice when she brought him food in the mornings.

They returned to avoiding each other. Such distance persisted through the days that followed, still without Onasus. And when they did speak, it was more often than not an exchange of gibberish.

Later in the week, Tikan awoke alone in the living room to a thin pressure bearing down on his chest. He reached for it, and found the spike Onasus had attached to his amputation resting across his body. He felt its long, pyramidal shape. It had grown into an obelisk, somewhat heavier than its organic opposite, and its surfaces were sleek as burnished steel.

He pushed himself up with his feet against the inner arm of the couch, sat up, and grasped the obelisk while cradling it in his lap. He spent his early minutes trying to reason with it, but this led nowhere. No matter how much he tried to come to terms with it, how much he caressed it, the alien limb would not grow familiar.

At first he was afraid to get off the couch, to walk with it. He feared some misuse, some accident. After deciding that reasoning with the thing would not afford him knowledge or closure, he thought he might take a walk to clear his mind.

He turned sideways and misjudged the length of the couch. His muscles were still weak, and he could not easily redress himself. He rolled off the cushions. His new limb swung across through the air and banged against the nearby marble table.

The obelisk vibrated like a struck cane, and a great tremor of pain pulsed where stump and obelisk met. The clang resounded around him, and with it came a confusing flash of knowledge that ceased as soon as the appendage stopped vibrating in recoil. The sensation was too foreign and short-lived for Tikan to comprehend. Still in pain, he shuffled backward.

Perplexed, Tikan stood and searched with his heels for the base of the sofa. He patted the cushion with his hand and sat down. He tapped the table again with the instrument. The sensation returned weaker, but free of distracting pain.

He continued to tap the table. Time came jittering off the edges. The room became clear to him. Rapidly, lucidly, he was sensing it, and its objects, though he could not perceive them directly. It was as though the blueprint of every object connected to the table were instantly revealed to him. It was not visual, or auditory, or of any other familiar sense, and it was fleeting.

He perceived snapshots of objects come together through time, and form time, and together form space. He was perceiving not the table, but its relation to the room; not the floor stained with his blood, but its relation to the table; not the couch, or his own body heaving and crawling with static and sticky with sweat, or Mira's breaths lightly beating the door to her room, or Naim's measured steps, but their relation to the nexus that was the table.

There would be time to practice, especially isolated from the others. For the moment, he rose and triumphantly fetched his own breakfast.

"You're a damn fool, Tikan. You're a damn fool for letting her go," Onasus said as the door closed behind him. His unannounced return startled Tikan, who jumped at the noise. "And now we've lost a lot of time. We—wait. Mira, Naim," he shouted. "Come here."

Doors flung open and footsteps rushed towards the command.

"Neptune," Naim said. "Where hast thou been?"

Mira stood beside Naim and periodically groaned or shook her head to herself as if immersed in dementia, eyeballing the floor.

Tikan stood up and walked to Onasus. "What were you doing, Onasus? It's been over a week."

"Enough. I've done nothing that isn't in the interest of our success. Now, I won't sit here and let you waste time lamenting my absence. It is touching, yes, that you missed me so, but it's now time to focus. I take your collective dissatisfaction to mean that you've all settled your differences, yes?"

None of them spoke.

"Oh, for the light of the suns. Juvenile. Children, yes, all of you, even as our most desperate task hangs in the balance. This is your fault, Tikan. Get over it. It's done. It was done out of love. That is what I should tell you, isn't it?" He walked up to Tikan and spoke menacingly close to his face. "It would be a lie, but I am very willing to lie to you at this point. That is love, in a way. Do you find that tragic?"

"I'm coming aboard the ship. But don't—"

"I don't care to hear the rest. It's futile. Let us hold hands and march towards the stars, now, yes? All of us," Onasus said, patting Tikan on the shoulder. "Speaking of hands, your new one is magnificent, isn't it? Not as bad as you thought it would be, is it? Have you been successful in using it?"

"I've used it, yes," Tikan grumbled.

"Excellent. Tikan the Bat, we might call you now. Although that would be misleading. The vibrations are only accidental; useless to you. Not sonic, either. It's a much more tactile device. Not even electronic. Let's go for a walk, shall we? I'd like to show you how it works."

"I've already figured it out."

"Fantastic. Then let's be off, shall we? I'd like you to see the ships. What? Did you think I was away only looking for the girl? Do I seem that irrational to you? Why that skewed expression? Yes, I can see it despite that bulky blindfold. Let's remove that, in fact."

Without permission or serious resistance, Onasus grasped the device covering the top half of Tikan's face. He pressed the sides together, and the stiff pressure in Tikan's sockets released. The device slid off, along with two thick needles.

"There. Much better, isn't it?"

Tikan sighed in relief. "Yes," he said. He turned to where Mira had spoken. "What does it look like?"

She looked up carefully, avoiding Onasus' gaze, and held her arm at the elbow. She did not answer Tikan immediately as she surveyed him. "Grey, but not quite. Like bands of silver where your eyes should be. You still can't see, can you?"

"No, of course not."

"And he won't, not again," Onasus said.

"You don't have to keep reminding me."

Onasus moved towards his bedroom, then. "I will give you all an hour or so to gather your belongings and have final words. We depart after that."

"What?" Tikan said. "This soon?"

"What, is that not what you wanted? Did you not all complain about my long absence? Perhaps you even started hatching a plan to leave without me. Tikan, you are a reasonable person. I can see that. Say goodbye to your friends. Make peace. It's time."

They all stood in silence for a while after Onasus' door shut, waiting to make amends. Tikan could not bring himself to it. Instead, he walked without words to the sofa and lay down. Shortly after him, another walked to the opposite couch and collapsed on it. Some minutes passed, and he heard the familiar sounds of a body in metempsic throes.

"Mira," Tikan finally brought himself to say. "I don't know what words he took from you, or from Naim. I wish I knew them."

There was no response, only footsteps drawing farther away.

The hour passed, and Onasus emerged from his bedroom. "Sleeping?" he mocked as he approached Tikan.

"No."

"Well, that might have been wise. And this one, metempsying at the eleventh hour. Wake up. We're going," he yelled.

Another door closed, and soon the four were all awake and gathered in the living room.

"All right," Onasus said. "You're all paying attention, yes? Good. This is how we will proceed. I've procured two ships for us. Private ships. Very hard to find these days. Did you know they went out of production years ago? Yes. Public transportation is a form of herding, after all, and what is the modern society if not a large grazing field? But I digress. The ships, unfortunately, are situated in separate docking platforms. Not too far from each other, but it will mean separate departures. We will see Mira and Naim off first, ensure their co-ordinates are set for Vega, and then Tikan and I will carry on to

Arcturus. There will be no hiccups, no problems. It will all go smoothly. Questions?"

"You haven't explained how I'm going to pilot," Tikan said.

"Not to worry. That will be made clear to you in good time. Now," Onasus said. "Was there anything else?"

"Yes there's something else," Mira said with somewhat more confidence, grasping her knees with white knuckles and affording herself a few fleeting, angered glances at Onasus while her left eye twitched. "You've barely told us anything. You spun your doomy tale on the Equuleus, when we were all feeling low, and you want us to just leave, now, towards suicide, or what? What about when we arrive? Where are we going, what are we going for? Will you give us our words back?"

Onasus gave her a menacing look and spoke to her the way a vicious headmaster might have. "Did you think I would do such a thing? Send you on so perilous a quest without guidance? Do not conflate Tikan's miseries with my silence. Nothing is being wasted— not silence, not life, not time, and not eyes."

Onasus sighed then, and looked sideways. His mouth twitched, and he squinted out of fatigue. For a moment, he almost looked sympathetic. "You must understand the great strain of organizing all of this. It stretches beyond our little episode. Can you do that for me? Understand? Have sympathy? Years, yes, years I have worked to make the puzzle fit. And so, forgive me if I have momentarily neglected your frankly inconsequential mistrusts. For you *must* trust me, whether you like it or not. Tikan has come to realize this, despite perhaps having, at this time, the least reason to do so. Do try to sympathize with me, friends. I am only looking to fulfill the mission. Now, due to our extreme time constraints—and I will admit some fault in that regard, though there were some unexpected complications—I must insist that we leave here at once. Everything will be made clear to you before you depart: this, I promise. Are there any final, brief, urgent comments, then?"

Certainly, they were all full of worries and objections, but none spoke.

"Good, then let us away. To a brighter future, yes? Tikan, Mira, Naim?"

Again, they did not reply. They stood up and started shuffling towards the door. Tikan trailed behind the others, repeatedly tapping his outer thigh with his obelisk arm, using himself as a conduit for his causal sight. Out they went, the door shutting behind them, in silence toward the end.

❧ 44 ❧

THE CITY OF ZOTHARRA

The nomads banked against the side of the mountain. They scurried along it like harried insects. Saturnine and trembling, the sky sent out the fire of sailors whose patron was sunk long ago. The land was indigo, flashing white portents of sunlight between the crags. The burning winter stench advanced on the tribe as its members ran on the darkened glass.

They wore anxious expressions and said little to each other. Sielle ran alongside Ilu, who dragged her by the arm. She squeezed Sielle's bicep nervously at regular intervals. Beside them, Elu's attendants looked exhausted as they continued upholding him in his ceremonial chair. Sielle looked around in search of Zotharra's other children, who were now secreting their ashy, alpine vapours.

"Not far, now. Not far," Elu whispered, perhaps only to himself.

"We'll be safe underground?" Sielle asked in a voice louder than appropriate.

"Silence," Ilu returned in a whisper. "They mustn't hear us."

The weather turned caustic in the span of an hour. There was no rain or other herald of this outland storm. The mists above wrestled for dominion over the mountaintop and began to take on cyclonic forms. White streaks flashed over curling folds in the vortices.

"Why are the mists raging?" Sielle whispered.

But Ilu's composure was waning. She was fading into the same sort of trance as Elu. "Great Zotharra beckons," she said under her breath, gazing outward.

Behind them, far back along the line of followers, a short howl echoed out. Ilu's head snapped back in anger and fear. She could not see far due to the storm.

It was not long before a messenger ran to her from the tail end of the line. Ilu frowned. She would not wait. She dragged Sielle and rushed over to meet him midway.

"Vont. She's broken an ankle, and Gre—"

"Leave them," Ilu whispered aggressively, before the man could say anything else. Without any more words for him, she turned and ran back to Elu's side with Sielle still in tow.

Sielle turned her head to look for Haern a number of times. She could not see him, or half of the people of Zotharra. The glass ground was now dark, opaque cobalt. The veins beneath the ground regularly erupted and lashed about the tribe, or caught each other and entangled like thin tornadoes of twine, or otherwise like trees of viscera. Wave after wave, winds blustered a desert heat. Sielle was beginning to sweat again, though the suns were lost in the storm. She reached for her gourd, but Ilu knocked it from her. "Not now," she commanded.

The silence was breaking. Above, the lightning turned red and began thundering down. The forked beams like broken pitchforks crystalized on impact not far from them into towering and brittle structures still inly surging on the land, crooked and slender as the boniest winter trees. They ran on, as these woods of lightning accrued around them. The entwined veins once resting beneath the ground strangled each other until fountains of quicksilver burst out of them, running and bubbling down the mountainside.

When the lightning struck a running puddle, it produced a

deafening screech. Sielle cupped her ears. New glass formations roared out of the quicksilver, as if cast by the light of creation itself.

The few other people Sielle could see regularly stumbled in the wind and paddled the ground. Some had their hoods torn off their heads, their hair plastered across their dripping faces. For a few moments, Sielle's replica revisited her on the very fringe of a purple and wavering heat wave before vanishing again.

Sielle felt sick when, out of another heat wave, she saw Neanh emerge.

"Mother among children," Neanh panted, coming to speed with them. "We've found two passages leading beneath the mountain. One leads to—"

The wind rushed between them.

"I know where they lead, Neanh," Ilu snapped. "Take our dearest and strongest, and we will make for Great Zotharra. Bring arms. The rest will follow the other path, and Zotharra will be with them. We shall be quicker without them, and we cannot all fit in the caves."

"Yes."

"You," Ilu said, pointing at the tallest of Elu's carriers. "Bring your father down and carry him."

The man did as asked, and cradled Elu in his arms. The chair was left by the wayside. They forged on against hissing gusts and the promise of mist ahead.

They advanced through a gauntlet of lightning-trees sizzling with primordial neon, and came upon the mountain. The winds cascaded, and crimson light surged near them. A stream of quicksilver drizzled down a brow on the mountain's face, as though to mark an entrance. It dissolved into fumes, as it had on their less urgent trek. Now having severed all but the head of their once-snaking tribe, the people of Zotharra scurried into the passage.

Outside, the thrashing, steaming tempest descended in full. As the small band ventured deeper into the mountain, the steam about them subsided. What remained was crystalline rock giving off a wet sheen, though they could see no water. The scent of their pursuers persisted yet into the mountain with them. They walked in a tight pack, like praetorian guards bound in a testudo. They panted hard and listened. None spoke of those Ilu had abandoned.

The passage eventually led them into a wide cavity, and Ilu called for them to rest. The cavern glowed the same way the gem Sielle kept in her pocket once had. Docile arteries and veins fluttered beneath the floor like eels in an aquarium.

Sielle sat down and scanned what remained of the tribe. She flinched when she saw Haern sitting shadowed beneath a jagged arch. She got up and walked to him.

"I'm not supposed to speak with you," he half-grinned as Sielle approached him.

"Then don't," she replied, sitting next to him and continuing in a whisper. "Just listen to me. I know all that Ilu's had to say about me. Whatever she's thinking, it's not true. And I can leave at any time, even now. You don't know the kind of technology I brought with me from Proxima. But I won't leave, not unless she makes me, and even then I would just go elsewhere, farther, deeper through Andromeda. I won't go back to Proxima. You understand?"

"Yes."

"So just tell me. What does Ilu want from me?"

"Can't say," he whispered.

"Tell me. I'll find out sooner or later, and it won't make a difference. You'd just be doing me a favour, that's all."

"Maybe it's best," he said, looking around for watchful eyes and losing his humor, "If you wait until we reach Zotharra. It won't be long now. I—I really shouldn't be speaking to you."

Sielle fiddled with the gem in her pocket. "Haern, you're disappointing me. If you won't help me, I'll just have to go."

His face darkened. "Then go. How do you want me to help you, Sielle? You've seen the way Ilu glares at me. I—I want to help you.

That's all I've been thinking about. But who am I before Zotharra? And am I not one of them?"

"So they do mean to harm me," she mumbled.

"No, not harm you. They wouldn't do that. Is that what you were thinking? Zotharra isn't—"

"Zotharra, Zotharra. I've yet to see magnificent Zotharra."

"As have we all," Haern muttered almost inaudibly, his head bent towards the ground.

Sielle looked at him, dumbfounded. Her lips parted, but just then a slender shadow enveloped them. They both looked up like alarmed children.

"You were told not to speak with her anymore, Haern," Ilu said as she towered above them. The mirror on her forehead reflected their shame.

"Yes, I didn't mean to—"

"Quiet. Get up and remove yourself from my presence. You'll not come near her again. You—" She stopped mid-sentence and stared at the wall. She shifted her gaze towards the cavern's entrance.

There was a familiar pungency filling the air, stronger than before. It roused the whole group to its feet.

"Get up, both of you," she commanded. "Sielle. Your Blood. Finish it."

"Excuse me?"

But Ilu did not wait. She rushed the girl and ripped the gourd from her waist and shoved the rim of it into her mouth. "This, drink it. All of it. Now," she said, turning the gourd upside down.

Sielle tried to knock the gourd out of her mouth, and when it began emptying down her throat, she instead tried at last to extract herself from the world. To her great horror, she found that she could not use her power.

She felt at once an immense claustrophobia, as if all sights and smells and sounds were converted to walls. As if she were suddenly prisoner in a progressively narrowing room of a thousand doors, scrambling to each one and finding it locked. Her tongue and throat seemed to freeze as she drank. It was far more Blood than she had previously had. The effects blossomed in her at once. She felt only light-headed at first, though this feeling escalated until she was sluggish and weak. Her legs started to melt beneath her.

Ilu caught her as she collapsed.

"All of you. You, especially," Ilu said, driving a menacing finger into Haern's chest, and then turning to the rest of her audience. "You will stand and defend this place. Your blood will cake the crystal before you relent. And a shrine shall be erected in Zotharra's heart for your sacrifice, dearer to her than any of her false children once our spirits have flown into her embrace. It is near. Can you taste it? Can our mothers and fathers taste it as they ring us even now? Here is the end of our sidereal struggle, brothers, sisters. Hold fast, true children of Zotharra!"

They were stirred by her words. They formed a human barricade at the mouth of the passage. These doomed souls brandished sharpened glass shards for swords or spears. Sielle tracked Haern until he moved into the ranks, at which point he dissolved into the crowd. She looked left and right, each moment of her vision skipping or delaying.

The scent of burned winter clogged the tunnel. It rose to noxious levels, and Sielle could feel her stomach turning. She could no longer move without help; her thoughts came incomplete and limping.

A loud clatter reverberated through the tunnel. The sound of excavation, or of uneven boulders rolling down. Sielle shut her eyes, creasing her forehead, and urged the world to fall apart, but the clatter only loudened. She strained her will again. She opened her mouth and her eyes widened and she breathed in despair. For the first time in years, she felt the hunger of death about her. Her soul, having wandered above the world and worlds for years, now filled her body like a hand stuffed into a glove.

And from the shadows of the tunnel, a monstrous thing emerged.

A hulking beast of cobalt flesh and violet, bulging veins. A living, animated boulder, rock and glass. Far from anything humanoid, far from correct organic shapes. There was no symmetry or design to it. Short feelers wriggled in place along its body, some in groups and others alone; some as Gorgon snakes or anacondas and others as eels and others yet as leeches. Two rows of long and flexible claws, hardened versions of the feelers, clasped each other at its center. Jaws to a wormlike mouth as it coiled open and closed at irregular intervals. There looked to be some mossy, marine-like flora shivering down its orifice.

Sielle convulsed in Ilu's grasp. She shut her eyes and tried again to abandon the zealots to their fate. The malformed thing advanced. Upon its back were crystalized human heads. They jutted out like disordered trophies; hairless, half-lucid, containing illumed cerebral shapes where the brain had been, their faces fixed with expressions of anguish. Among them was the unmistakable visage of the messenger who had rejoiced at Haern's disciplining.

Through her mounting disorientation and panic, Sielle realized at last the fate of those who lingered too long in the sun, or let their mouths go too long unwatered by Zotharra's Blood.

The people of Zotharra cowered at the sight of the creature. It lumbered first, and then threw its weight forward, brutishly swiping the air with its elephantine appendages.

"The false children are come!" Ilu yelled from behind the ranks, still cradling Sielle.

"The false children are come," Elu repeated in a murmur, held by Neanh.

"See the heads of the forgotten! Those too lost to remember Zotharra and her blood," Ilu continued. "Now stand, brothers, sisters, children, that I might empty this vessel brimming with our fate."

Sielle reached out without clear aim, but remained fixed in place.

The mouth of the passage filled with more glass creatures. Each was freakish in its own way. Rather than the blunt limbs of the first, another had razor sharp scythes ringing its body. A spine of what looked like slimy, carnivorous flowers suctioned the air as though starved. This one flung itself into the barricade, and the bloodshed commenced.

Two men fell under the barbed creature. Their torsos separated from their lower halves to let a stack of guts unwind as the creature pushed up against them. Others plunged their blades into its rolling shape as it minced those already dead. There was a pause after this first little massacre. The people of Zotharra pushed forward in a line with their weapons wavering at the fore.

Then, as retreat seemed inevitable, an older man lunged ahead and drove his spear into the mouth of the first creature, shattering his weapon against the thing's rock hide. He yelled before being crushed by another's hammer arm. The rest of the warriors crashed into the glass monsters, and their line broke apart.

It was difficult for Sielle to discern what was happening. Her vision and her thoughts were cloudy, skipping, uncertain. But there, ahead, she saw Haern roll and dig his sword into one of the larger monstrosities. It turned and made a hideous sound, and another shambled towards it.

Stuck between two of the monsters, Haern panicked. He waved his sword about without clear purpose. He remained idle too long. A jagged drill wreathed in feelers drove into his back. As he cried out, another of the abominations grew tall like a slimmed shadow and wrapped half of his body into its mouth, muffling him until he was silent. Haern's legs wriggled out of the mouth and then ceased.

Sielle tried to blink her lugubrious eyelids—fast, faster, to blink the scene away as though it were nothing but a hallucination. She felt a sudden, confused shock of dread for Tikan. Haern's body disappeared into the creature. The rest of the warriors gained a second wind, recouped, and reformed their barricade. Sielle's heart raced, beating painfully and thumping in her neck.

"Do you see how they all stand and die, little effigy?" Ilu whispered into Sielle's ear. "Do you see the bare tools with which we have survived these hundreds of years? Did you think to take us from Zotharra's grace?" She stopped and turned. "Away, Neanh!"

Sielle's head fell backward, and she watched the battle continue upside down. She watched the people of Zotharra be disemboweled, or have their chests deboned or have their necks rent. With the images delayed, she watched the serrated stalactite arm of a creature cut through a man from his chin down to his abdomen as though it were a jacket zipper being unzipped. Another man lay on the floor, and a creature mashed his arm at the elbow joint, where his blood and bone and skin were flattened. This particular image stuck in her mind. Another person was decapitated. She saw the arteries swing out of a fountain of blood, and the head flop towards the opposite shoulder before rolling off.

The beasts gargled and sprayed gases from their mouths, expelling more of the now-rancid smell. They fought and rearranged positions without clear reasons. Sielle's breaths were congesting in her throat as these events fleeted vaguely by. Then Ilu snapped her into a run, and her head swung forward.

With Sielle in her grasp, and Elu in Neanh's, Ilu ran deeper into the mountain. They fled, furtive shadows silhouetting the walls. They stomped up an inclining pathway and weaved through shifting forks and bends. Pillars of marbling turquoise light curved against arches upon the ceiling. The walls blurred past in waves of brightly fluorescent cyan, which also streamed beneath the floor. Sielle could see nothing straight, and she could not move her limbs much. Ilu hauled her along like a drunken puppet. She rocked herself forward as though to transcend the world, but Ilu redressed her.

Swords clattered, and the people of Zotharra cried out in the near distance. As pools of blood splashed under their crashing bodies, the lunatics carrying Sielle off did not seem affected.

Crooked and bent in Neanh's arms, Elu began to hum a morose and unintelligible tune. It rebounded through Sielle's skull like a dirge until she could no longer hear the battle cries, the echoes of the dirge building on each other.

The images of Haern's death still flashed in her mind, even as she continued to try to jerk herself from the world like a lucid dreamer keenly aware of the nightmare she has been thrown into. She felt naked and exposed. There were no exits, no doorways out. The causal chain ran wild without pause.

There were gaps in the walls to the left and right. Sielle saw pools of pale amaranthine water glimmering their surface sheen from within these wayside hollows. Reflections of the ceiling and its stalactites pulsed on the surface. The others, paying the hollows no mind, ran past the waters under a lower band of stalactites.

Lost in her mind's fog, and with her legs cycling, Sielle felt Ilu's nails deep in her forearm and bicep as the passage brightened. From an uphill exit, light pulsed along the ends of the ceiling, turning to flashes, splintering through the stalactites. Sielle's head arced forward. They raced up the slope. The passage widened. The air thinned. The echoes diminished, and a last flare burst from the twin suns outside, blinding them as they tumbled out. The wind howled again.

"Why?" Sielle managed to utter, but they ignored her.

Ilu did not pause long. She bustled to her feet and hauled Sielle up. She drove her onwards, with Neanh and Elu following just behind. When her blindness subsided, Sielle was confronted by the night again.

There were no storms or mists, no daylight or clouds. The twin suns hung in an unnatural dark sky, unmoving, wreathed in pale auras that faded to darkness. The four of them stood encircled by towering peaks, on the inner band of a crown of mountains. A place which could have been a glade or a hidden shrine, were it not barren glass. The ground ran flat until the far end, where it exhaled a concentrated aquamarine glow.

They strode on, stopping midway on the open space. Ilu gripped Sielle under the arm and around the neck, almost choking her. Neanh brought Elu before her and let him stand. They looked up in supplication. Tears began to stream down Elu's face.

"Great Zotharra!" Ilu cried out against the sky, her voice booming and rich, clutching Sielle hard. "Thy rightful children arrive before thee. Hearken to us, oh Mother! Centuries have we walked in silent devotion. Centuries have we borne thine ardors and thy trials. Wilt thou not at last unveil thy face? Wilt thou not gather us up into thine embrace, as thou did our mothers and our fathers, oh Divine Zotharra?"

And without sound, the suns came unhinged. They began to rotate towards each other, realigning along their axes.

"Zotharra answers us!" Neanh cried.

The terrestrial glow intensified. Winds began to cascade from above, whipping and howling and pushing the group backward. Sielle could no longer move, even as Ilu tried to heave her up. They all stumbled to the ground as it began to quake.

Ilu rose up with Sielle, and then stood aghast. Without warning, the land ahead started to bend at an angle towards them. The far barrier of mountains bent with it, like jaws of the world itself about to close on them. The horizon rose and rose and defied the laws of nature until the mountains stretched out of shape and the horizon was a vertical highway. The world was inverting, the firmament connecting to the land.

"Help me, Neanh!" Ilu called.

Leaving Elu's side, Neanh ran through blasts of air and caught Sielle. She cradled her in her arms and followed as Ilu strode forward against the airstream.

"Great Zotharra! Succor us!" Ilu started again. "Towards thy city have we ever marched, oh celestial divinity; towards thee have we bled and drunk blood. From glass pens have we ever known thee. Open thy gates, the gates wrought of every star, of every bark and brain, just as our hearts were pried apart. We offer as our sacrament this wretched girl, unhallowed and unclean, born of those who did unearth themselves. We left them for thy warmth. Was it not thy call echoing through the dark reaches? Witness us as we burn this effigy in thy honour; and exalt us, oh Divine Zotharra."

Then, as the suns came aligned and made to split the ground from above their new throne of corrupted glass, Sielle laughed. Like a witch at the stake, drunk with impending death, she laughed.

Ilu turned to look at her in sudden disgust. The girl continued to giggle through the doom and through Zotharra's elemental revelations. Their eyes locked. Ilu bared her teeth and gritted them. Her expression, deranged, stripped of grace, caught a sharp light. Her face looked held together by folly alone.

"Do you think it cares?" Sielle laughed through her stupor. "Do you think it even knows the difference between us? That it even knows we are here? Cosmic beast you've mistaken for goddess. It sends its cells after you like a body after a disease, and you worship it. Standing here, worshiping death. Idiot. Fool. You'll die here."

"Yet Zotharra answers us," Neanh said.

"Intruders, that's all," Sielle continued to sneer. "Unwanted. Like flies buzzing around someone's nose. False worshipers. Do you think a true God would take you? Cultists. Fanatics."

"You are the only interloper here," Ilu scowled. "The poison of Proxima, desecrating this ground which we shall consecrate with your blood. Let us shower thy back with her pitiful life, oh Zotharra. Let us—"

The suns collided before Ilu could finish. One eclipsed the other and sent out a short but powerful flare. The suns wrestled in place, tearing through the space their fusion would occupy.

This new astral pit spun and spun, enraged, growing with each gyre. Unlike the spheres of Sol or Proxima, this new sun's center became a deepening gulch boring through space. It coiled in on itself, with barely visible rings ribbing the inside. When it was done, there was only a single hole in the sky. It blazed white hot, but still the night prevailed. A dead spot in the blackness of the universe. The true, white void. And then the celestial pit began to shrink and then enlarge like some voracious worm's maw, each time expelling gasses and curling in on itself.

"Oh, Zotharra," Elu tried to call through muffling gusts. He moved towards Neanh and Sielle and pulled a jagged little blade of crystal from his belt. "Let me." He approached. There was no hesitation in his gait, or in his rising arm. He came closer. His watery eyes fixed on Sielle and did not move. His beard was frayed and his skin shriveled. A branch of lightning reflected off the blade.

Sielle could do nothing but watch as Neanh constricted her sluggish limbs. Elu's milk-white dagger hovered above her forehead. "Mirror the beams of thy suns upon us that our dim souls might—"

Elu stopped, and Neanh's arms tightened before slackening completely. The old man's face turned gaunt.

Sielle felt the wet specks of blood across her nose and cheeks arrive delayed in her perception. It was spraying across her face, dripping into her eyes and stinging. She tried to look up, to understand, but she fell hard to the ground as Neanh released her.

She landed sideways with a whimper. Neanh's body crashed beside her, the head thumping separately, eyes fixed, mouth agape. It rolled down towards the cave, leaving an uneven crimson trail behind it. Elu was still looming above, the dagger in his hand. The world was still metamorphosing, Zotharra's face yet emerging. Sielle crawled, her arms shuffling, across the growing pool of blood sputtering from Neanh's severed neck. She heard a tapping across the ground. A figure swept over her, and advanced on the other two.

Sielle turned on her back and through great struggle raised her head. Her replica was towering above her. In her hand was a sword wet with Neanh's blood. The heavens writhed above them. A film of quicksilver was frothing and bubbling over the ground. There were no words from the replica; she only walked toward the mad pair ahead.

The old man opened his mouth and shook his head. He stood back. "Ilu!" he rasped.

The replica ran with a new stream of wind. She was agile despite the animal planet's cataclysm. She lunged and buried her blade deep into Elu's chest. The old man gasped and raised his shaking hands as if praying in an attempt to grip the blade. His eyes rolled and his body went limp before his hands had travelled halfway to the sword. The replica placed a foot on the corpse's shoulder and pulled out the blade, releasing a full red stream.

"Father! Father among children!" Ilu screamed somewhere not far. "What have you done?"

Sielle tried to call out, to gasp, but as she raised herself, she was confronted by the sky's sundering. The proportions were all wrong, the alignments crooked, the objects too large for the space they occupied. She could no longer tell where the planet ended and the sky began.

And still the mouth in the firmament thrashed in on itself, spewing its gasses. It grew obscure behind its own cloud, but through it Sielle descried those same erratic movements racing somewhere behind, as though colossal limbs had shot out from behind the astral mouth to swing about wildly. It was too much to keep track of. She rolled her gaze down and landed on the vision of herself sprinting towards the crazed priestess Ilu.

Ilu stood alone against a ravaged backdrop. The mountains were rivers to the devourer above, and the winds worked against Ilu, as though they were flushing the land of pests.

Eyes maniacal, Ilu produced her own dagger as the replica advanced. She growled something incomprehensible, her voice breaking. The gap between them was closing. The replica approached, undaunted. With her hair matted and the corners of her mouth cracking and the mirror stitched into her forehead looking as if it were about to erupt out of place, Ilu viciously sliced through the air; with her poor footing and her feral, imprecise slashing, she hoped for beloved Zotharra to guide the blade.

The replica sidestepped and dismembered Ilu below the knee, sending her crashing to the ground like a felled tree. The winds loudened, but Ilu's shriek soared above them.

The replica turned and left Ilu to twist in agony on the ground. She walked back towards Sielle, who was still struggling to keep her head upright. Behind the replica, Ilu continued to scream and squirm, trying without success to nurse her crimson, spitting stump.

The replica said nothing as she lowered herself and picked Sielle up. She slung her over her shoulder and made for the cave entrance.

"What are you?" Sielle asked, to no response. "I saw you."

The sky behind them was veiled by carmine and indigo fumes, and the land continued to rearrange and reform beneath it. It gyred upward as a gnarled pillar, up into the maw masticating the canvas of the stars. Only those thrashes of Zotharra, or whatever their host's true name was, continued through the silence.

The replica said nothing, nor did she breathe or show signs of exhaustion or distress. She advanced through the tunnels like animated stone.

"Thank you," Sielle whimpered. "I need rest. Need to wash the blood."

Still the replica said nothing. She walked mechanically, as though she had only just learned how to use her bipedal body. Sielle opened her mouth to speak, but relented.

The winter stench had vanished, along with all evidence of massacre. The replica navigated through archways in the passage to reach the pink waters Ilu had raced past. Each pool shimmered as the land continued to quake. The replica stiffened her grip on Sielle.

After the quakes diminished, Sielle closed her eyes. She dangled off her replica's shoulder and breathed, calmed by the watery hollow and the now-gentle caprices of the ground beneath.

Farther in, the replica stopped before a medium-sized pool. Sielle opened her mouth to thank her copy and to ask her to place her against an arch beside the water. Suddenly, without warning or words, the replica dumped her into the pool.

Sielle's body convulsed in the cold. Her head erupted out of the water and she sucked in a dire breath. She slumped back underwater. She turned and held her breath, trying passively to reach out of the world again, to no avail. The waters were frigid, unbearably so. Then they seemed to be warming up. She exhaled.

Clusters of bad memories and regrets swarmed her. Her father's eyes frozen for eternity under the Norwegian azure. Her sister, lost in the woods. Tikan, traveling to his doom. Uncoordinated, still uncured of her drugging, she flailed around and splashed through the pool. She managed to turn on her back and bring her whole torso out of the water. Suddenly, her replica kicked her in the sternum. She pressed down on Sielle's chest to prevent her from rising above the surface.

Sielle tried with all her might to break from the world and free herself; but her hold was too faint, the handle on causality's door still slippery. Then, as she tried to grip the replica's boot, she found that her limbs were slowed, and slowing still. Wholly submerged, she flapped her arms in the thickening liquid as though they were wings, the feathers drenched in oil, until her whole body came to a freeze. Her vision grew clearer, her breathing slowed. The replica removed her foot and watched for a moment from above.

The pool solidified completely. There, beneath, Sielle lay encased in a prison of crystal like a fly trapped in amber. She had no space to cry or scream. She choked until she seemed to approach death's iron line, though it teasingly receded. And still the replica's expression was strict and unmoving. She gave Sielle a final look, as though to examine her work, and then stepped backward until the shadows found her.

Alone and frozen and deprived of escape, the only movement Sielle could muster was a twitching of her brow. Her soul quivering. A carnival of old faces arrived in her mind. The jeering and crooning of persons no more than shades to her memory.

After an hour of enduring panic, she felt rumbles beneath her and heard the sound of a dragging corpse above her jail. She heard panting and croaking, muffled through the glass.

"Destroyer. Ruiner. Wrecker of worlds," she heard a familiar voice now warped by agony say. "Did Zotharra leave your heart unrent? How many worlds have you laid to waste?"

The words penetrated through the barrier. Sielle's insides wrenched. The tears would have come, if her eyes had not been frozen in place.

"Come back, little effigy!" Ilu shrieked, her mad face jumping to level with Sielle's across the glass. "It can still be done! Zotharra still beckons!"

Sielle's heart bumped beneath glass and flesh and ribcage. The mad woman's face was streaked in blood, and her hair was in tangles, looking like bramble. With her fingers layered in dry and wet crimson, with her broken nails, Ilu tore at the surface. Scratching, digging, slapping. It would not shatter.

"What curse is this, Zotharra? Wherefore do you damn me like this?" she shrieked. "Break this barrier and let me taste thy sweet nectar, sweet nectar." Ilu ground her teeth together and she huffed and her face contorted. Her skin crinkled, her eyes whirled. Still she clawed at the surface of Sielle's prison, wheezing and wailing all the while. "Give me time, time!" she croaked. Her stump bled and her strength waned. She scraped at the surface until she was only a corpse with a fixed expression of folly, the mirror on her forehead cracked, lying atop Sielle's amaranthine asylum.

The walls lost their fluorescence, then. And when the storm ended outside, there was no light left, save for the little gem in Sielle's pocket, which began to glow again.

45

HORUS

M y years spent travelling the world did not immediately afford me much further progress in learning to control my powers. I spent half a decade training, but unfortunately reached a plateau early on. Whenever I did manage to perceive a thing-in-itself again, it was as yet only a momentary foretaste. I needed more time to explore the intra-temporal layers and the spacelessness of each perception. It was a problem of being afforded the perception of an object out of time, and yet still being temporal myself. It was a problem of processing an infinity of perspectives condensed into a single moment.

But this was in no way a dead end. The groundwork was already secured. It was now only a matter of practice. In any case, I had side-ventures to pursue, some feasible even with mere slivers of control.

There were clearly fiscal advantages to be taken from my new powers—limited as they were—and I did not hesitate. It was an easy and necessary thing to exploit. As the almost-überman, these ambitions were, of course, principally fueled by my yet-unwavering commitment to mankind.

But, I must admit other motives. I'd long felt the urge to breeze through the gauntlet of a professional career and seize, in a matter of a few years, what it would otherwise take the average man a lifetime to attain. It was an exhilarating prospect: to cheat, to whip the world's prime deity forward as I sat in my chariot. To scratch an ancient and admittedly petty itch, and to find ecstasy in the thought of never again having to worry about worldly constraints on my nobler efforts.

In any case, my coffers did need filling if I was ever to fulfill my commitment to heal mankind. I was ready to raise planets, but my reach was yet too short. I needed a platform. A means for the means, and the regress ends there—I promise.

It was in Singapore that I incorporated my company, HORUS. Not a mere investment firm, but the global net I would eventually cast. The falcon under whose wings the world, like a blue egg suspended alone in the black of the cosmos, could at last incubate.

My first months as an entrepreneur were solitary. I spent countless hours hunched over the LED glow of a screen, or five, watching graphs and numbers, waiting for a crack, a view into the financial world's hyperbolic caprices and paroxysms. It was a small start. I had little capital and little desire to attract undue attention to my operation of inside-out-sider trading. In a way, these lonely nights were also a good way to train the omnipresence of my eye. I did make minute advances. Something to do with the monotony of spreadsheets and graphs, no doubt.

So I invested, and I reaped. A few thousand in a tire manufacturer, another few in a gypsum plant, more in a small-time furniture maker. All of these were guaranteed investments, since the graph lines of my stock market forecasts would habitually burst from out of the page, so to speak, and land many months thence.

And when the money started to double, triple, and then quadruple, after the first years had passed, I came to need help. It was time to expand HORUS beyond myself and a bulging bank account. What to do? Who to trust? I interviewed close to forty applicants in a hotel suite in London (dangerously close to Paris, but then, air travel had made all cities dangerously close to each other).

Questions had to be devised; prompts, a call to all kinds of professions and practices. I only needed to hire one for my purposes, but I had to give the illusion of a sprawling corporate structure. I myself, having become quite accustomed to changing shapes with Proteus for advantages, posed as a mere recruiter for one Mr. Zhou, reclusive CEO of HORUS.

It was almost for naught. The candidates were too ambitious, or too incompetent, or both. Greasy new graduates in business suits, businessmen in greasy suits, accountants with gel-hardened hair, lawyers who waltzed in with the air that all possible successes presupposed their profession, even psychologists who fought for their delusional importance in the corporate world. Human resources, they said. The agony. But, they were good practice. I got a headache from pushing myself, trying to view their past and future histories, their true selves.

In the end, I started to fear their mindlessness would infect me. I told them all to wait for my call. Revenge! But I digress. There was one who I saw die as the slave whose bones would rest at the foundation of the pyramid he would help build.

His name was Frank Harman. He was a mathematician looking to trade his knowledge for some wealth. It was late in the afternoon, and I had grown lazy. The sun was not shining enough for much light to pass through the double-hung windows, but the lamps made it unnaturally bright inside. He bumbled into my unlocked hotel suite.

The sound of his voice bored me instantly, and I did not immediately give him the courtesy of looking up. I sat, shuffling papers over the table and pushing aside a bowl of fruit sweating its sugars, too tired to perform my routine investigation into the candidate's life.

He began speaking, telling me of his pathetically little work experience, trying to justify it with the importance and practical benefits of pure mathematics. I rolled my eyes up at him. I was at once struck by his profound ugliness. Though he could not have been older than thirty, he had a gnarled face and was already balding, looking like a hideous mole. It was as though he had some advanced aging disease he was trying to cover up.

In any case, with my eyes downcast again, I asked him the usual questions while fiddling with a gold-and-red tassel dangling off one of the pillows beside me. Only the room's fine Victorian furniture loaned me any legitimacy.

"I'm looking to contribute for years to come, sir," he said, undeterred. "A company I can grow with."

"Jobs. What jobs have you held? Full jobs."

I did not need to look into the monad of his life to tell that he had a hard time controlling his anxiousness. I interrupted his rehearsed show and enjoyed watching him squirm. His briefcase was trembling against the side of his leg. A terrible start, to be sure. It was perhaps out of some degree of sadism that I then ventured to truly observe him.

I did not immediately notice anything interesting about him. Lonely nights in a stained sleeveless shirt, sitting by his desk eating cans of soup and writing things by pen in the dead of night. Calculations, or plotting, whatever it was. I yawned, about to dismiss him.

"I—"

"No, wait," he half-yelped. "May I have a piece of paper?"

"Help yourself."

He dropped his briefcase and walked over briskly to the table. It did not take him long. My patience was already worn from the other interviews, and I started to grow restless. My right leg started to gallop in place. I had seen a few too many parlor tricks that day, some amusing, and none impressive. My posture slackened.

"Here," he said, waving up three pages he had scribbled on. "These companies. These companies have the best possible options at the moment. But, being a new organization, you would want low-risk for guaranteed moderate returns to build up a portfolio before taking higher risks, correct? Well, if you would just look at my numbers, you'd see that I have a good idea of where your money should be going for the greatest long-term, sustainable growth. I—"

"Let me see," I said, snatching the notes from him. The technicalities and calculations meant nothing to me. I scanned the page and forced myself to see if his predictions were correct. Some were, and others were dead wrong.

Yes, in case you are wondering, I was able to extend my sight that far. Even mere symbols relayed me to their final objects. The thing-in-itself bears in its sphere all of its relations, too; indeed, it bears the world itself, but from a particular point of view; this includes the ideal markers of language, numbers, or geometry. As for Harman, his fiscal projections were not very impressive. But that was beside the point.

I decided from his expression that I had to hire the man. Unlike the others, the buzzword blurters and shortcut takers, who failed to recognize their failures entirely, or who attempted to rescue their interviews by bloating brittle achievements, or who seemed extremely competent but otherwise too ambitious to work as perpetual underlings, this one ran straight to serve me like a prematurely loyal beast, looking for a pat on his canine head. And he was one to perform with zeal and rigor.

I know because I looked at him after that. The proper way, that is. I reached further into the delicate layers of his life. There, I found him grayed and wearing a lab coat, uttering my name with the same loyalty while he read from a report.

That was the first time I saw reference to myself outside the material present, too. I had tried to do that before, to look into my own monad the same way I did with others, but it proved outside my reach. I found that it was virtually possible, however, by looking through the eyeglass of another's life. Only then, as with Harman, could I catch glimpses of my future self: as projections in another's domain, and in the context of his life's narrative. Though I never did appear in person.

In a sense, my absence from the future somewhat confirmed my own freedom, if recently acquired, as opposed to the determined nature of others' lives. Excluding acts I'd already performed, causality no longer featured me concretely. Did this mean I had license to freely and autonomously change the future? That there were holes down causality's gauntlet left for me to fill myself in? Well, not necessarily. Whatever power simmered in my blood, it had not yet passed down to afford such control.

It had taken me some time to adjust to conversations with others, too. If I already knew what another would say in conversation with me, it became possible to rehearse my own monologues, potentially years in advance.

However, it was in this paradox that I came to find my own freedom somewhat dubious: If I was utterly free to insert whatever speech I wanted into my conversations, knowing in advance what my interlocutor would say, how, then, could my decisions affect his thoughts and already guaranteed speech? It seemed irrelevant that I had the luxury of picking what I would say years in advance. Whatever words I did end up choosing would nonetheless cause others to respond the way I'd foreseen. So I could not alter what others would say whatsoever. Infuriating!

But at the very least, it confirmed the superiority of my agency in comparison to others', since knowledge is absolutely consequential to action. In other words, the revealed future influenced my actions, and therefore whatever force I would exert on the world. Thus, I was impelling nature to account for my knowledge of its future in its very unpacking. I was making observations whose objects changed before they were observed, between my acts of observation and their being observed.

Shall we say that the future is already carved in concrete, or that only its blueprint is set, or that only its seeds exist in the present? Either way, I was obliging it to redress itself prematurely. Even if my knowledge did not give me freedom in the true sense, it did complicate nature on my account. For the time, this was sufficient to salve my ego.

"Well Frank, you're absolutely right," I said.

He looked at me and grinned boyishly. "I'm glad, sir. I'm really glad. I—"

"We'll be giving you a call with an offer at some point this week," I said. "Don't worry too much about experience, either. You're obviously very capable."

He nodded and waited to see if I had anything else to say, and then spun around to leave after I returned to my papers.

≈

With Harman hired, I was able to offload the drudgery of paperwork and focus on more lucrative investments. The construction industry proved the most rewarding. I followed my investments down the factory conveyor belt: every raw material—concrete, steel, aluminium, and others—from its mines through to the bulldozers and the contractors and the sub-contractors, up to the glassy heights of corporate towers in metropolises and the shareholders having their nine o'clock meetings inside. The machinations of my feeble competition—the rabid brokers who had thrice the screens glaring at them— did not escape me, either.

It was not long before HORUS began assembling its own projects, to produce as well as to stockpile. It required meeting with clients, rending them open in real time, and letting them bleed in areas of their lives where I could press them with the knife of charisma.

However, these ventures would only pay off years later in subtly calculated inclines and roundabout turnarounds. It was best that way. No, I did not need to sit on a pile of cumbrous gold only to be bothered by weak-minded fools or the media. I made only small and measured advances, millions before billions. And with these ever-increasing funds, HORUS began to hint at growing to astronomical proportions. As we diversified, so too did we hire countless drones.

"It's unbelievable," Harman would say, as we strategized in the meeting room of our headquarters, anchored at its corners by lush potted plants and a high, spectral ceiling.

Careful not to appear too enthusiastic, I would stare for long hours at the one-way glass walls, though I was like an excited child inside. In the office space outside, people milled and buzzed about, working. All of them were faceless to me. I had Harman manage the place. They answered to him, and they did not know to whom he answered. I was like a familiar ghost to them, haunting their office space.

That building was only the first among many that we sprouted around the globe. They would grow in height, too. The sorts of buildings that had windows so opaque as to mirror the whole sun.

It was not without glee, during one of my many afternoons managing HORUS's initial rise, that the necessary stock fluctuations of one Technologie-Dupont were revealed to me. They had recently gone public. The shares were low following the poor performance of their new line of smartphones. It was too enticing not to sweep them up. It cost me two thirds of my new fortune, but I could not resist. I didn't even check their future prospects too carefully after seeing that four years from then, likely under my guidance, they would recoup most of their losses.

It was in this moment of wide-lipped, arachnid-fingered fervor, in a room dank with my sweat, lit only by blue computer light pulsing over my crooked figure, that I began taking steps to secure the bastard neo-dandy Pierre as my employee, a fact which he did not even become aware of until many years later.

Little did I know that he was, at that very same time, revenging me in his own, far more insidious way. But—don't get too impatient!— that is still a little while away from the events I am currently recounting. And besides, isn't it much more enjoyable to see me succeed, for once? Perhaps you've even started fantasizing about how *you* would use my powers.

In any case, aside from being an amusing potential torture device for dear Pierre, Technologie-Dupont was also a superbly situated firm. Not nearly as large as its global competitors, true, but poised to grow to mammoth size.

Of course, the board of Technologie-Dupont required a meeting to iron out the details of their salvation.

"Harman," I said over the phone.

"Yes, sir?" The poor man sounded exhausted.

"Have you finished arranging the Nix-Gordon merger?"

"Yes sir, the balance sheets have been updated and the cash-forc—"

"That's good, Frank. Very good, because you're going to Paris tomorrow."

"Sir?"

"You're being promoted, Harman."

"Promoted?"

It was as though I had announced both his death and rebirth at the same time.

"Yes. How long has it been, now? Six years? Mr. Zhou's been very impressed with your work. And I've done nothing but sing your praises to him. I recommended you for this position in light of your work over the last few years."

"Well, thank you, sir. Yes, I couldn't have imagined that—"

"There's no need to thank me. Let's just focus on making sure this deal goes smoothly, all right?"

"Of course. But, I'd like to just ask: what's expected of me now? What sorts—"

"That's exactly what I was going to discuss with you next, if you'd let me speak."

"Of course, sir. I'm sorry."

"That's all right. Anyway, you're going to meet with the board of Technologie-Dupont. Now that the acquisition is being finalized, we—"

"HORUS wants me to handle that?" he said, his excitement unrestrained and crackling through the phone.

"Yes, Frank. That's exactly what HORUS wants you to do. You know our vision; you know all the ins-and-outs. Go to Paris. Reassure them. Tell them HORUS will be opening offices in Paris soon, too. That we'll be in close contact. Tell them we don't want to interfere with their operation, that we only want to get them back on their feet, that it would be a shame for all that talent to go to waste just because a storm hit the market. Make them feel comfortable. Excited, even. Got that, Harman?"

"Yes, yes. I'll do it. No problem, sir."

"Excellent. Someone will have sent you your flight details by now. Please do remember to call me from Paris, won't you, Frank?"

"Of course, sir." I heard him click through his inbox as our conversation wound down, and he found his email from Gertrude in Human Resources—me—and began planning his next few hours.

∽

When the articles began to appear, I made sure to keep myself out of the spotlight. HORUS, too, I obscured from the public as best I could, though I left it for the economists who would only ever be heard by other economists. I did not do this out of strict fear of recognition. In fact, it was hard not to revel in the thought of burying the ghouls of my past under the weight of my newfound fortune, but that would have been imprudent.

It required discipline not to let myself appear on the cover of sensationalist magazines or give interviews with neurotic talk show hosts or otherwise engage in all of that ego-swelling business expected of one who succeeds. Nor was it because I feared violent hands (Bogdan and his associates, if they had appeared looking for trouble, could have been swatted like gnats, then; but they were nearly fifteen years behind me and probably dead or in prison). It was because I had a plan. A vague plan, to be sure, but one that was becoming clearer each day. Though, it was infuriating to have advanced my powers so little in all that time.

With my training on hiatus, I focused on further building the shadow kingdom. Technologie-Dupont, incidentally, became quite fundamental to this enterprise. As I had acquired it through a company owned by HORUS named Benda-Berkman—or was it Starfuel? No, it was through the Qatari and Dutch banks—I was able to exert direct control over it. I pumped billions into it, and by proxy, into the tech industry. Through it, we also began to fund in-house research across all scientific disciplines. Technologie-Dupont became the flagship of my growing fleet.

Harman, too, was instrumental in facilitating the growth of HORUS. He managed the day-to-day, and savvied up on all the details. I came to rely on him more than I had originally intended. He became the closest thing I would ever have to a son, and I do not believe I ever had a daughter.

When Harman returned from Paris, I gave him the sad news of Mr. Zhou's untimely passing. I explained that the old hermit had preferred a private funeral attended only by family, and no media coverage. He had also conveniently written me into his will as sole successor. He was a mentor to me, et cetera.

Some time after the charade was over, Harman came to realize that HORUS was in fact a one-man operation, and I the puppeteer behind the show. I would not have revealed such a thing were it not for those glimpses of him still at my presumable beck and call even when his skin was wrinkled and his hair white.

In fact, I grew more and more suspicious of Harman's seemingly incorruptible loyalty. I did everything to keep him that way, true: a moderate salary so as to not spoil him, a constant workflow to busy his mind, limited conversation about our private lives; but still, he did not waver. Most bizarre. Nobody would resist some selfish liberties, so high atop the world. The only thing that kept me from eliminating him so late in the game was the view I had seen ahead in time, incomplete as it was.

Harman even started spending countless hours in the labs with our research teams. At first, this was simply to manage the contracts and funding; but once he became acquainted with the work being done there, he hardly looked back. It wasn't long before he made the full conversion to scientist. Theoretical physics and cell biology, those were his new interests.

He spent particularly long weeks in a marine research post we built off the coast of Okinawa. I daresay these new interests even made Harman somewhat philosophical, to the extent that one is forced to face philosophy when part of the vanguard of scientific advancement. Thankfully, he managed to keep up with his corporate duties all the while.

Things were running smoothly, indeed, but as Harman started to look more and more like he did in my future visions, I began to worry. He was only about a decade younger than I, and I was, at that point, already on the grayer side of middle age. HORUS was growing robust and invincible; but I began, then, to fear for my own health. Thinning hair and a slouching posture! What use was the world if I was too dead to behold it? No, I didn't care much for youth, but to die: that was inconceivable. One morning, when I found it particularly hard to get out of bed, when my bones creaked from a mere twist, I decided it was time to let Harman take the reins until I could make proper use of them.

I invited Harman into my office. There were no lights on in the room. I sat at my desk, while gray clouds streamed a premature twilight through the windows behind me.

"Do you know where this company will be in ten years?" I asked him.

"Flourishing, still, I presume."

I fiddled with a pen and eyed him. "What is it we are aiming for?"

"Sir?"

"What is our end objective, tell me."

"Growth, sustainable profits, exp—"

"Spare me that. What are we really after—do you know?"

He looked at me, dumbfounded but ponderous.

"I ask because I'm going to die, soon," I said. "Isn't that awful, Harman? Who shall oversee my work when I'm finished? Who shall ensure its potential is fulfilled? Shall I become a Bismarck, rolling in my grave for a century?"

"I'm not sure I understand. We all perish, of course. The company will live on, yes, even—"

"Damn the company. You know HORUS is just a shell without me."

"Sir, I understand," he said, searching for a way to respond to my seemingly unwarranted egotism. "But—"

"What I mean is that there is a reason for our success. Not just a cause, but also a special destination. Did you not sense that? We've been growing exponentially for nearly two decades. Surely you noticed it. I understand that these days you're more interested in the contents of petri-dishes than the account sheets, but come now."

The room darkened, and he started to calculate my meanings. He had a talent for abstract thought, it was true, but he could never have discerned those secrets to which I referred. Nor would I specifically elucidate them.

"Where do you see mankind, one hundred years from now?" I asked, shifting the mood of the conversation.

"More or less the same," he replied. "Except perhaps outwardly less violent, I should think; more appeased by earthly comforts."

"That's a fair projection. And do you think that's a good place for man to be, in the end? Do you think it's good enough?"

"Certainly."

"Do you foresee the end of war?"

"No."

"Of bar fights, of senseless murders, of suicide, of schoolboys squabbling?"

"No," he said reluctantly.

"Then it isn't good enough." I paused. "Do you suppose people, on the whole, grow wiser with age?"

"I do. If not wiser, at least more knowledgeable, yes. Perhaps some grow more misinformed."

"And yet the sages must die like everyone else. But death isn't the real problem," I said dismissively. "The problem is knowledge. You know, when I was younger, I thought I would become a philosopher. A lover of wisdom, a fount of clarity and spirit in this disenchanted world. I obsessed over it, actually, was maddened by it. Then I realized that I could never be a philosopher because I hated wisdom." I paused, and squinted with ire, not at Harman, but in his direction. "Wisdom, if one is even to possess it, is a compensation for the unconquerable ignorance in all of us. And time is a problem, too. The cylinder that slowly cracks as glass balls smash apart inside it. You need only look at history, our map of the grand decay, for a catalogue of time's victories against us. How shall we acquire sufficient knowledge against these cosmic foils?"

He raised his voice. I could sense a mild arrogance festering in him. "Isn't that what we've been doing? Collecting knowledge? Taif, Okinawa, Bamako—not even the Twentieth Century saw this kind of progress in science, or in medi—"

"I don't care for petty science alone. I don't care for measurements. I am after the truth."

Harman shrank, though I could feel him boiling inside.

I swiveled in my chair towards the window, and with my elbow on the armrest, continued fiddling with the pen. "The truth, Harman, is a black hole," I said. "A singularity over horizons and horizons devoured and ever out of reach. A pebble in a crushing ocean. Its light does not escape its own sphere. It is a single, opaque, and selfish monad at times radiating inferno. 'Come closer, come hither;' of necessity it pulls any in its orbit, stretches apart their inmost soul. The fool who hurls himself near it risks everything only to be obliterated —though the more worthy have at times glimpsed the core to lesser degrees. Its outer shape appears to us as a distortion, a blur on the face of space and time. But there is something there. Dense and real and pure, at the heart of it." I paused again, and looked at him. "I'd have a science of each and every individual, for each and every individual. Only then shall we plant flowers of empathy and peace upon the grave of war."

Harman cleared his throat and paced the room. "What would you do, then? Make a philosopher out of every woodworker? Every farmer?"

"Watch your tone with me, Harman," I asserted. I never did learn to scrub out the stain of murder in my throat.

He spoke again in a smaller voice. "Time and death put an end to the wise, sir, it's true, yes, but what of those frigid old men who are always the most rational killers? A young man might be a wanton savage, or a soldier—but politicians, warmongers, those capable of the greatest woes, the Robespierres of this world—aren't they of the scholarly cloth?"

"You're not understanding me. The solution is not in guns or books, not in wisdom, or numbers, or study. It has to be more fundamental. It has to be a permanent feature of consciousness itself. For the sake of peace, Harman. Lasting, unbreakable peace. It's something I have hopes for us to achieve, in time."

He stopped for a moment and tilted his head to the side; his eyes rolled towards the upper right. Like many scientists, Harman was rather adept at considering particulars and at solving problems with fixed parameters. Like them, he also lacked the ability to exceed those parameters, to have a sense of the larger implications or of a worthwhile reason for his travail. I grew somewhat vexed watching him.

"But," I continued, swallowing my mounting disgust. "Time and death are immediate problems, you're right. That's actually what I originally wanted to speak to you about."

"I just don't exactly understand the connection between you, and HORUS, and all this," he said, before I could continue. "Yes, we've funded research and we're investing in great technological and scientific advances, but—"

"The connection is one I'm afraid your sight is too narrow to afford you," I said coldly. "No, don't be offended. It is simply that I could not explain it to you if I tried. But the threat of mortality: that's something you can appreciate, no?"

"Yes, well, yes, but with regards to what time we have, I—"

I turned my gaze on him again. "You do know what I mean by that, don't you? I'm speaking of the face of death hiding in your chest. When it springs forth now and again, freezing you in your tracks, is it not of the living *now* than of the vague drama you've thrown into the distance? Does it not enliven the soft organs cowering under your ribcage? If I had the patience, I'd lock eyes with the Reaper till the hour he dares swing the scythe, watch death as it has ever watched me. That defenseless moment, it binds me tightly to my flesh, and makes distinctly solid the floor and the firmament both."

We paused, and I attended to my pen again.

Harman may have interjected a question here, trying to pass it off as some great insight, but his words were of no consequence.

"This conversation has gone somewhat out of hand," I said, watching his beady eyes betray his confusion. "My original point was a simple one: I feel I do not have much time left on this Earth to accomplish my goals. So, I need you to handle things for a while, while I retreat to renew my focus. Make no mistake: HORUS is crucial to all of this, as are you. And I will return, eventually. We're going to make a better world, Frank, a world where humans can never find it in themselves to harm each other."

"I see," he said, patiently, absorbing the proposition. Clearly, he was grasping at the one concrete detail he was capable of understanding. "Yes, I can certainly manage things for a while. Though, we do need your guiding hand, sir. We're in so many areas of research and investment now...it's rather too complex for someone like me to steer forever."

For a moment, I thought I caught a glimpse of intrigue in his expression of false humility. I tried to survey his future and relieve myself of worries, but it was barred from me at that time.

"It is somewhat amusing, you know, that you ended up so inclined away from commercial matters," I said. "I appreciate that, you know. You are a much better scientist than businessman; it must be genetic. But, don't worry. I have confidence in you. Besides, much of it runs itself these days."

"I suppose we won't be seeing you around here for some time, then."

"No, not much. Although, there is one final matter I'd like to attend to. I'd like you to organize a corporate gala before I hand you the keys. Advertise it as a charity event, and make sure they all go. The boards, especially, but all the way down to management. Not all the companies, of course. The big ones. Dupont, Starfuel, you know."

"For what purpose, might I ask, is the occasion, sir?"

"Raise spirits, encourage diversification. Hopefully they'll start spying on each other a little better. It would be good for some of the tech to bleed between them. At the least, it'll remind them of each other, stimulate competition and such. Make sure the management comes. Especially from Dupont."

"All of them? We'll need a nice place, yes?"

"I'll let you sort that out. Don't spare any expenses, though."

"Understood."

It was true, what I told him: that I wanted a survey of that corporate web of mine before leaving, but there was an ulterior motive as well.

Over the years, I had ensured that Pierre was never promoted out of his little cubicle. Yet, some months before this impending change, I had him given a position in management. I could only imagine the smug look on his face. I would cut it apart. I was looking forward to seeing him at the gala. There, I would confront him with my overwhelming successes and crush his spirit, and then publicly fire him. It was such a sweet little thing to allow myself before moving on to the true task.

❧ 46 ❧

THE STARFIRE IN HER EYE

Years passed, and the replica never returned. The time was marked only by the slow rotting of Ilu's corpse. For immeasurably long, it was the only view Sielle had. Fair skin stiffened in the wrinkles of the woman's lunacy. Then the slow spread of greenish wan, followed by a lengthy putrefaction. The longest were the bones. They remained there until a rolling gust came through the tunnels to blow them away as dust. All that remained, in the end, was the broken mirror that had been sewn into Ilu's forehead.

And Sielle watched, and watched her reflection in it, and slept until she could watch again. But she could not keep vigilant. Her mind was feverish and dimmed in that tomb of half-stasis. The few moments of clarity she possessed were spent on questions blackening her mind.

And even after months and years and decades and centuries of drifting in and out of consciousness, she could not find in herself the tools to dissolve the world. The glass imprisoned more than her body; it jailed time itself.

Sielle's youth faded, too. Though she decayed slower in her glass cell, and did not wither with the epochs she spent there, still lines grew across her face, and traces of gray began to streak her hair. Even as she dove for years into sleep, her bones were heavier every time she awoke to the same broken mirror and cave ceiling, and her warped reflection smudged twice upon them.

～

The prison broke, eventually. It happened long after the rumbles of Zotharra had ceased. Long after the prospect of freedom had been snuffed out.

Sielle awoke, still immobile, still with her own face glaring back at her. It was older now than when she had last seen it. And there was a new, hair-thin scar dividing her already warped reflection in two. The first capillary of a fracture spreading across a glass surface. She forced herself to remain awake a while longer. The world sharpened for the first time in decades as her senses regained lucidity.

She felt muted swarms of fear and anger and hope muddle in her soul as she watched the fracture spread. Through the breaking glass, her mirror image above was in pieces. Little reflections of herself stared at each other like the mosaic of a fly's eye.

Her lips twitched. She rolled her eyes left and right. There were drops slipping off her skin. She tried to jerk herself up, though it was hard to move after so many years. Then the hardened pool broke without clatter. The pieces fell apart and dissolved again to liquid, drenching Sielle beneath.

The rush of water against her skin and the fresh air through her nose invigorated her. She was frail, frailer than she had ever felt. She waved her submerged arm, unable to do much else. The gem in her pocket brightened the pool and cast her shadow against the hollow. She felt the waters hardening again. She cried out, her voice harsh and raspy, but was met only by her own frightened echo.

All at once she felt her muscles tighten, and she flexed her arms out of the pool with her palms facing herself. She advanced as if through a marsh. The creak of her bones, the ache of her muscles. Despite her difficulty, her strength was regenerating at impossible speed.

She stomped forward through the drying bath and lunged out. Her torso landed out of the pool and, with her face against the ground and her legs yet in the water, she crawled. With much effort and groaning and slobbering against the ground, she succeeded in dragging herself out completely, and then she rolled over.

The pool hardened again beside her as she heaved for air. She lay breathing on her back and watched a new reflection of herself on the ceiling.

When Sielle rose, she found that she could not see very far into the cave. The walls were still dark, and her little gem's light did not extend much beyond her. She meditated a moment and recognized the corridors out of time present beside her again. It would be a simple thing, then, to vanish and leave Zotharra behind at last. She clenched her eyes a moment but then exhaled and walked on.

Destroyer. Ruiner. Wrecker of worlds.

She wound out of the arched passages and made for the place where Haern and the other cultists had been slain.

Did Zotharra leave your heart unrent? How many worlds have you laid to waste?

Ilu's now-ancient words haunted Sielle as she braced the glass walls for support and reflected on all those she had ever abandoned. Though she could now access the infinite again, having spent so long constrained to her flesh gave her humanity, and therefore the humanity of all others, new significance.

Countless parents of a prodigal daughter, siblings of a deserting sister. Those who had thought her a mind alive in the world, but who she had only ever seen as pitiful machines. And there were wretched ones, too, who had mistreated her across the ages—a blacksmith paranoid with superstition, a drunk father, a pickpocket who'd left her penniless—and somehow she wished she had given them a sense of permanence, too.

Sielle retraced her way down the passageway. It was a much shorter walk than she remembered. The cavity where the people of

Zotharra had died was aglow. A flat section of the wall reflected her face relatively undistorted. She looked to be in her late forties now. A wave of loss passed over her, and then she moved on into the cavity.

She had half expected to find Haern sitting against the walls, or her replica waiting near the passage that led out of the caves. But there was nothing there. Sielle lowered herself to survey the ground where the battle had taken place.

It was only slightly discoloured, and not due to bloodshed. No grotesque monsters, no broken glass. Except, far to the left, a face seemed to jut out of the ground. Sielle walked towards it. There, like the grisly trophies she had seen on the backs of the monsters, was a glass face bearing a fixed expression of anguish. She told herself it was Haern's, but in truth she could not recognize it.

Sielle sighed. She got up and made for the mountain's heart, where Ilu had tried to sacrifice her to Zotharra.

It was brighter outside, now. Her hair fluttered behind her in a light gale. The sky was still dark, but it was calm now, and dispelled of any gloom. There were only faint mists circling around what looked like two foxfire moons drifting above. Sielle walked on, feeling a kind of magic charging the air.

There were small particles fluttering in the wind. At first she mistook them for cherry blossoms or leaves, but on catching some in her hand, she saw that they were closer to spores. They looked like prickly little sponges, and wore peach, salmon, or viridian skins.

She walked on. There was now a hill past where Ilu had tried to summon the planetary beast. The closer Sielle walked towards it, the brighter the ground became, with rivers of soft cyan coursing beneath it.

Sielle stopped. Atop the hill above, illuminated and sculpted by the foggy light of the ground, her replica towered in wait. The moons circled around her with a sash of spores against them. She looked like some chiseled immortal emerged from a smoking volcano.

They stared at each other for a long while. The replica did not move. Sielle climbed up the slope, loosely on guard. She prepared herself to jump out of the world at any instant. The sky shimmered above her, as if it were not a dilution of black space but rather a ceiling made of ice, the moons two opals trapped inside it.

When she finished climbing the slope, she arrived at a plateau, and there stood face to face with her replica. As if to taunt her, the replica maintained Sielle's previous, youthful appearance.

"Zotharra?" Sielle said.

"That is what they have called me."

Sielle squeezed her hands into fists. "Why did you do this to me?"

"Out of love."

Sielle shook her head, and fought back tears of frustration. "Love? You've taken my life. My life."

"I know. I know it. I had to take your youth, and you cannot forgive me, I know."

"It wasn't yours to take."

Zotharra tried to form an expression of sympathy on the replica's face. "It was, my dear, and it is. It shall always be mine to take."

While taking a step forward, Sielle gritted her teeth. "I'd kill you," she said, "If I knew how to kill a planet."

The replica's expression did not change. "Do not say things you do not have sufficient knowledge to mean. Come, now. Do not ruin yourself with anger. I am no mere planet, and I am beyond death. You know this."

"Then why did you do it? Tell me. Tell me why you stole my life."

The replica turned around and walked on a bit, and then turned back. "I have watched over you for so long. As a mother watches over a daughter. As a teacher, watching in restraint, waiting for you to suffer your own mistakes and thereby learn the only lessons of worth. Your words pain me more than you know."

"Good."

The replica leered at Sielle. "I saved you. I continue to save you."

"For what? How many years has it been?" Sielle's voice broke. "How many years, Zotharra, have you taken from me?"

"If I told you millennia have passed, it would make no difference. It was necessary for you to face your own decay. For you to be made complete. For you to be kept safe. You have one last great voyage left in you. One last voyage, for which you shall need a full heart."

"There were other ways, whatever you were trying to do." Sielle looked at her own lightly creased palms. "There must have been. Not this."

"Perhaps, but I could not leave it to chance. I could not let you scatter off to some other time or place, where you would become a vague and gray echo to me. You are more important to me than you can fathom."

Sielle looked up at the sky and saw no stars. "You—it wasn't the drink that stopped me from leaving the world. It was you!"

The replica nodded. "It was me. As I said, I have watched over you, and only you."

"I could have saved myself, if it wasn't for you."

"Yes," Zotharra said. "But you would have left utterly broken, lost —prematurely removed from the crucible which has now strengthened you."

Sielle shook her head and exhaled. "How did you do it?"

The replica grinned. "You are not the only being for whom time bends. My own powers are... more general."

"And my body," Sielle said. "Why do you copy it? It was you I saw when I first arrived here, in the miasma, wasn't it? I know it wasn't me, because I can't occupy the same space as myself. Can't revisit myself. I've tried it before."

"These are laws which apply to you, in your feeble state, not to me. What you saw was a crack in a mirror. A refraction of yourself through me."

"I don't understand," Sielle said. "Wasn't it you who raced past me across the black gulf, too? Why did you use my body, if the planet is you? Why do you still wear that face you stole from me?"

"For eons I have listened to your tiny heart beat from galaxies away," Zotharra said. "And from the moment you came to me, I have tried to understand you. To understand how such a small, limited creature could teem with so much power, could burst out of nothingness and charge the very air with its sense of wonder and the majesty of its soul. How different you were from the other gnats carrying your same flesh and form, crawling over me. At first I could not. I watched you from every angle, monitored your every breath, and still I could make no sense of you. Then something peculiar occurred. You reached out for me. You drove your hand through my skin and gripped the vessels of my mind."

"I remember it," Sielle said. "The capillaries—I was electrified when I grabbed them."

"Yes. Your essence poured into me, then. Your memories, your thoughts, your longings, your languages, such as I could understand them. It was… so sudden… as if I were remembering all of it. But this was not enough. I needed to understand you again from the inside. I needed your body as mine."

"So you made a replica of me to puppet around?"

"After a fashion. I loved you. I continue to love you. I need to love you as yourself, and for you to love me as me."

"I've never heard of a planet that could love."

The replica dissolved into the ground. Sielle marched over to the spot where she had disappeared. Then, before Sielle even reached the spot, the replica reemerged right behind her.

"I have already told you I am no mere planet," Zotharra said.

Sielle spun around and shook her head. "Then what are you, really? Tell me that much."

"I stand before you."

"But what are you?"

"You know the answer. Look at my face. Look at the moons; they are my eyes. You know what I am, and only you."

Sielle said nothing. She looked up at the moons and their cyan rims, dangling like two frozen meteors. Like two motionless pendulums.

The replica advanced on Sielle. "Know that I am beyond right conception. You shall not know me beyond these representations without touching madness. And though I presently speak the language you have taught me, I too once used a mortal tongue. I too was once a clod, though I now hold starfire in my eye."

Sielle nodded. "I can see it."

"Yes, you are wise that way. You are."

"You still haven't given me a proper answer," Sielle said. "What do you want from me?"

"To protect you."

"From what?"

"There are hounds in this universe that have already caught the scent of your blood. They stalk you even now."

"Like Ilu?"

"Far worse."

Sielle wandered off a moment, looking back at the cave's entrance, and then at the jaws of the mountains. "What would you do?"

"I can do nothing, now. It must be your choice, or else it means nothing. Spend your last years as a ghost through cities, through the universe, looking for some last wisp of passion and wonder until your bitterness consumes you whole. Or join with me."

Sielle frowned, unsure of what Zotharra meant. Then, the replica motioned her over. They walked together to the other end of the plateau. A gale blew across them, carrying spores and a chill. The replica stopped at the edge of the plateau, waiting. With her arms holding each other, Sielle peered over the edge.

It was the precipice to a bottomless crater. There, below, was a gaping hole at the heart of Zotharra. Sielle began to weep out of sheer awe. At the bottom of this hole was an entire galaxy of stars and planets, comets like gold spirits pinballing the arena in a trail of violet and aquamarine smoke. And at the core of it, a cluster of planets and stars and astral gases all collapsed into each other, tightening into one sparkling ball, pulling everything into its orbit, pulling the very dark fabric of space into one and only one dense unity. Even the edges of the precipice flaked off to join it.

"What is this?" Sielle said.

"It is you."

"It's not."

The replica placed a hand on Sielle's shoulder, which made her constrict her muscles. "You have only to fly out, and leave your flesh behind on this cliff."

"You mean lose myself in you?"

"Become me, as I would become you. As we already are, but whole, unfractured."

Sielle paused. "You want me to abandon the world, and my humanity?"

The replica scoffed, and a mild seismic rumble occurred beneath them. "Humanity. That selfish plague. If there is one fault in you, it is that you share their skin. It is time to shed it."

"What about Ilu, and your worshippers?"

"They did not worship me. Not truly. And I am no God to be worshipped. I took great pleasure in ridding myself of them."

Sielle exhaled through her nose. She tried to turn away from the cliff, but she was mesmerized by the sheer vastness contained in Zotharra's heart. "Not all humans—"

"You are not like them. You were never a part of them. Do not pretend."

"There is one."

"And it is me," Zotharra said, resolute.

"No," Sielle said, serenely. "Another. I know him."

"You do not. He will betray you. He has already betrayed you in his own mind more times than you know."

"How would you know?" Sielle said, spinning to confront the replica.

"How, indeed." They eyed each other for a few seconds. "But I wonder if he truly knows you, either. Did you ever admit to him your fractured past? Your treatment of countless families who took you in? The misanthropy of your heels? And do you think he would look on you the same, now, when the lustre of your skin has waned and the glimmer in your eye gone cold?"

Sielle bit her lip, and felt a tide of shame pass through her. She said nothing at first. With her youth taken, and only a mote of wonder and purpose left in her, a certain part of her did yearn to shed her mortal body and join Zotharra. To unite with a cosmically supreme being, whose essence mirrored her own, and deny the world.

But life was more than a mere aesthetic wonder to her, now. More than a colourful reel. She thought of Ilu and her madness, and of the darkness over Proxima and Tikan. She looked again at her creased hands.

"I have to go back," she said. "It—it doesn't matter what he thinks of me, I have to go back."

The replica did not flinch, but Sielle read Zotharra's disappointment across her mute expression. "I have seen how the years have eroded your sense of wonder and your already tenuous kinship with others. The countless betrayals you have suffered, which in turn led you to betray. You have seen them for what they are. You have had your fill of human frailty. Even now, I feel your exasperation. It will not end with him. Let him remain dead."

Sielle turned away from the precipice. "I'm going back to him," she said. "He was right. From the beginning, he was right." She turned her head away from the replica, as if to speak to herself. "He must have gone to Arcturus, and—"

The replica looked at her with spite. "'And just as Ilu and her teachings could never be allowed to spread from here, so the teachings of Proxima must end at the threshold of Arcturus.' These are not your words."

"It's you who's changed my mind, Zotharra. About humanity. About decay," Sielle said, looking again at her own hands. "And—"

"More lies you tell yourself."

Sielle flung her arm out at the replica. "I don't care. They're lies, maybe. But don't you see it? You're trying to tempt me with a whole galaxy, and it's not enough to keep me from him."

"So your choice is between love in the particular, and love in the universal. And if you choose incorrectly, if you return to that forsaken world only to pick out one tiny, doomed piece of it, you will die there. Not just your body; your spirit shall be transformed into a great specter of vengeance towering over the universe, and nothing more."

"Like you."

Zotharra said nothing. The replica began to decompose, then. Her skin flaking off and turning to those same spores which continued to rain on them.

With a sudden surge of resolve, Sielle tried to picture Tikan in her mind. But his face was vague to her now. Images of Earth and of Proxima intruded in his stead.

"I would have devoured myriad galaxies before letting harm befall you," Zotharra said, the spite brimming from the replica's voice. "I cared for the starfire in your eye. Yet you commit the same mistake. Countless times I have seen you commit it."

The spores began crowding around Sielle, sticking to her. She brushed them off and they flew off with ease before fluttering away. But more accrued, as if they were Zotharra's tears, and she could not easily keep them off.

Sielle's cheeks were dry. She exhaled and her breath quivered. It was time for Zotharra to vanish, too. Time to see the end of love and despair.

"Goodbye, Zotharra," Sielle said, and vanished.

Just as Sielle leapt through the corridors outside of time, struggling to keep a fixed picture of Tikan in her mind, a sensation she had never before felt rushed her. She felt somehow arrested, dragged back towards Zotharra. As if a hand had grabbed her by the heel.

"Return to me!" cried Zotharra.

Sielle panicked. No other being had ever before occupied the same plane as she did during her flights. As Zotharra's voice boomed around her, the emptiness which usually engulfed her as she travelled dissolved in spots, revealing warped images and sounds from across disconcatenated time.

As blots of time and space infected her, she suffered colors and frost and other sensations. Still Zotharra clung to her, refused to let her go. As the world and time convulsed, Sielle struggled to keep herself from being sucked back into matter.

Though she was still disembodied, she caught glimpses of

Zotharra from orbit through tears in the veil. Zotharra was no sphere. Her body spanned the size of many solar systems. She looked like a constellation made of more planetary and solar matter than of black space. The only light illuminating her came from pockets of fire riddled across her own unfathomably vast landscape of a body. As if she were an immense lanternfish. She had what looked like vines and flowers erupting from various nodes, gigantic, entwining to form mountain ranges or plains.

Unlike the flatlands Sielle had visited, parts of Zotharra were like valleys of her crystal flesh, each end almost meeting, like a ribcage. Her crystalline and glass skin prevented any of her parts from looking precisely organic, and the ordering of her body had no analogue to any species Sielle had previously seen. The sheer size of Zotharra made Sielle tremble. She looked like a macrocosm of what Sielle had witnessed in the crater below the precipice.

"Return to me, me!" Zotharra cried again through black space.

Sielle continued to struggle, and with each of her efforts, time outside of her shifted. She saw Ilu's ancestors arrive on their ship. Their expressions of awe through the blast windows. Zotharra's writhing, as if to embrace them.

At last, as she came almost free, she saw Zotharra's birth, too. A cluster of planets and stars and nebulae and the shell of a freshly erupted supernova all converging and swirling around a single point, as if dragged from their place by one spirit large as Andromeda, its heart one black hole. Their collision. The dust of creation. The cries of innumerable solar systems animated and sentient, ensouled by one bitter and vengeful host.

When she finally freed herself of Zotharra's grasp, Sielle returned to her utter darkness, and continued on in search of Tikan.

DEPARTURES

Out of the throughground, they arrived at the docks and slalomed through crowds. They treaded the walled glass platforms that would have induced the strongest vertigo in the ancients who had feared the sky. The red sun was inexplicably raised over them, though it had appeared to be setting hours earlier. Onasus took great strides ahead of his recruits, constantly looking back over his shoulder to make sure they were still behind him.

The high volume of traffic somewhat renewed Tikan's spirits. The crowds scurried to departure platforms. He sensed their breaths conflating, their sighs upon disembarking, the collective rhythms of their hearts, their clothes tight on their skins, their wheezing and their coughing; and, most importantly, the heightened urgency in all of them as they were, at least in part, pulled from their isolated dreaming by the old-galaxy relic of stress on the eve of travel.

The glass dome of Proxima was directly above them. Tikan tapped his obelisk arm and collected the stop-motion perceptions it afforded him of the dome. It was thicker than it appeared. It was hot, and the heat within it dispersed like flattened cyclones along its surface. There were images he could not see, of himself, Mira, Onasus, Naim, and the city and its tiniest dark alleys, each passing through the dome's lens as though it were a sieve.

They walked on. Tikan followed the prints of their steps fading along the walkway even as he heard them resonating on the glass beside him. Their restrained breaths dissipated around their mouths. There was some consternation on Tikan's face, as he was yet acclimating to his new sense.

"Here," Onasus said. The group marched behind him as he drew them away from the crowd. "This platform."

They slipped down a thin, secluded ramp. It descended as though it were feeding them over the planet's waist to the space devoid of stars, which yet revealed their threads of fire to the blind man among them. A few people walked by their small group, back to the central platform, but then they found themselves curiously isolated.

Naim picked at his nails as they walked, though he otherwise looked calm. Mira's eyes fidgeted in place. Onasus strutted on.

They had brought little with them; no large packs or special clothing. They went over the walkway in silence. Though Proxima had only a sun, it looked as though the shards of a moon were littering the city below. The gridded towers below them shone like beacons as they passed over.

At the end of the walkway, they arrived on a wide circular stage. There was a small ship with a snouted tip docked at the far end. It looked more like a large and robust shuttle than a proper starship. Mira and Naim screwed their eyes up trying to recognize it. The publicly accessible memory of such vehicles was long erased.

Onasus walked to the ship and beckoned the others over. Just as they set foot on the open space, the red sun passed above them and cleansed the ground in a warning light. Unlike the others, Tikan was only scarcely aware of the harsh beams that poured from above, though he sensed stronger shifts in the refracting filter of the dome.

They walked over to Onasus, looking like the frightened escapees of a psychiatric ward, with Mira cradling herself as though it were cold and Naim embodying his newly robotic mind. The ship's entrance slid open as Onasus approached.

"We've got one waiting just like this, Tikan, a few platforms from here," he said, stopping before the open entrance to look back at Tikan. "Although, perhaps a little smaller, harder to detect. A ghost ship for a ghost, yes?"

Tikan leered at him, exasperated. "When are you going to tell us what we're going to be doing?"

"Yes, yes. Get inside, so that we might discuss all of that in privacy, all right?"

The ship's entrance shut behind them, and a cold gush started from hidden vents in the ceiling.

Onasus led them down the hall to a narrow room with hard couches that were welded to the wall and floor and a port window long since replaced with steel. There was a single lamp on the side table. There were a few smaller rooms lined up along the corridor. Low slate ceilings and corridors designed for single-file. It was not the sort of voyager designed for capricious passengers. Naim almost bumped his head walking into the sitting room.

"Well, here we are," Onasus said as they sat. "At journey's end, almost. Exciting, isn't it? Yes. Soon the pieces will fall together. It's so very close."

"About those details," Tikan urged, somewhat annoyed.

"Of course. Well, Mira," Onasus said, turning to her. "I am sending you the co-ordinates as we speak. Or codes, I should say; the co-ordinates will always change, won't they? Anyway, you'll be able to locate Vega-bound wormholes with the codes. The hidden routes! Isn't that thrilling? You'll be one of the very few to cross into such spaces. Of course, we could talk about the meaninglessness of space in such cases. But, yes, that is neither here nor there," he said, his tone shifting as Tikan started gritting his teeth in severe irritation. "Once Tikan and I have left, you'll have to initiate a rudimentary manual launch. The portals to Vega should then appear as any others. Either way, the ship will recognize and lock on to them after that, so you will be off and away. The process is quite automated, really. You'll just have to perform the role of key in the ignition. Simple, no?"

"That part, yes. And I've received the codes," she said, looking up.

"But what are we supposed to do once we arrive at Vega? It's a big system."

"Yes, well. You are heading for *Vega Station*, remember. That is where all of your navigational codes bind you to. I have not been to Vega Station personally to know first-hand, but I assume it to be the same as on Arcturus. And, your objective is quite simple, really. When you arrive, and if you choose to board, you'll find that the place is deserted. There is no one there, nothing except machines masticating the minds of the many. So, it's quite a mundane task, yes; once you're safe, and provided you don't get boarded en route like on the Equuleus."

Their faces went ashen at the suggestion. Tikan swallowed hard.

"Now, don't look so glum. I'm only half joking. The probability of them even knowing about you, or this ship, is extremely low. We are speaking in privacy, yes? And it's an old little ship you're aboard: much harder to spot than those titanic transporters. Let me now tell you what you will do once you arrive, so that you can lend your minds to that worry instead. That was your most pertinent question, wasn't it? Yes. What you must do is simply destroy the place. The station, the machines building the great unity, all of it. Burn it all, burn it in a great cosmic pyre," he almost chuckled.

"That's not simple," Mira said, incredulous. "I mean, is this a joke? We don't have the tools to destroy an entire station, not on a small ship like this. What, you want us to crash into it?"

"Potentially," Onasus said. "There is enough thermo-nuclear power stocked up in the cargo hold to detonate a whole star. I've made sure of it. If you run out of other options, or if you cannot find the station to begin with, then you shall have to fly straight into Vega at top speed. You should be able to get the ship close enough to implode the star before you are annihilated. Remember, this task is greater than you. But, all that shouldn't be necessary. I'm sure you'll be creative about it. Yes, in fact, let that be your project as you travel. And, now that you are all settled, we will—"

"You can't expect us to believe you've planned so little, all this time, and that you're so in the dark about all this," Tikan interrupted, on the verge of anger. "I doubt you're planning to fly *our* ship into Arcturus. Tell me, how do you see our end of the mission succeeding?"

"Simple. Set the station's orbit askew into its sun. That option won't be possible for our friends, however. Their procrustiis don't have that sort of access. And I simply can't grant it."

"And the hidden masters, the ones who pull the strings—the ones you mentioned on the Equleuus—they'll be on Arcturus Station?"

"I should hope so. I've not met any such persons myself—I told you I only suspected their existence. Now, Tikan," he said, dismissing the others and cutting Tikan off. "Before we leave, come with me to the cockpit. I want you to know what to do so we don't waste time afterwards and end up leaving much later than our friends. The departure of a small, private ship will raise some minor suspicion, you see."

"Fine," Tikan said morosely, standing up. While they had spoken, he had searched for something to say, to add, but could find nothing. Mira and Naim were upset and uncertain, still; he could sense it in their pulses and their shaking legs. Arm still drumming along his leg, he walked with Onasus down to the cockpit, and the other two followed.

"You remember how Mira entered her piloting station on the Equuleus, Tikan?" Onasus asked as they all stood in the cockpit and faced the piloting station. It did not have the state-of-the-art sleekness the Equuleus' did. It bore its guts on its outside, and it was black with grime. The only other object of note in the room was a large slab of derelict computers. It was doubtful that they were still operational.

"Yes, I do," he said.

"Good. Then this will be easy. I won't make you do it here, as I don't know how long it will take you to recover, but the idea is simple: you enter it reversed. You climb into the slot and let the ship do the rest. It will know. You'll discern your role, I'm sure. It's quite an intuitive process; I'm sure Mira could tell you all about it, if she hasn't already. You do have a solid grasp of our celestial geography, don't you?"

"That's the least of my concerns, I think," Tikan said.

"But it isn't. You want us to make it to Arcturus, yes? Well, then you have to send the ship through the correct wormhole. I've simplified it by only including the Arcturian codes in your implants. Still, you'll have to make an effort. Fine?"

"Yes, fine."

"Splendid. We're off, then," Onasus said, already making for the ship's exit.

Tikan stumbled for a moment. He held his forehead and beat his obelisk into his thigh so as to gain a clear perception of Mira and then of Naim. He could hear Onasus' steps echoing farther away down the hall. The others followed him, without ideology or evidence of their past selves. He dawdled a few seconds longer, and then followed as well.

Onasus waited impatiently at the base of the exit ramp, biting his lips. "Hurry, we have to leave. Mira, Naim, I bid you a fortuitous trip. You're doing the work of the ages. History, as we resurrect it, might forget your names, but I certainly will not. Farewell." He walked a few steps onto the platform. "Come, Tikan," he called from below.

Tikan's once-friends stood before him a bleak final time, each with slugs or live fetters for tongues. There were no words left between them.

"Goodbye," Tikan said, the sorrow drawn out in his voice. He waited a moment, but the others did not reply. He turned and exited, rattling his obelisk against the doorjamb.

"Don't end up drowning, now," Naim said, almost cheerily, just before they were divided by the ship's airlock closing.

"Come, now, there are greater things afoot," Onasus said in a callous gruff.

Tikan did not reply; he only walked down the ramp to stand beside his destroyer.

They waited for a few minutes, until the ship's engines started. The ramp receded into the ship's belly. Within a rising sphere of heat shimmers, the ship reoriented itself away from the platform and blew hot winds at them. An airlock opened in the glass dome above. They perceived the little vessel gaining speed until it could no longer be discerned out of the black.

"All right, quick, now," Onasus said, gripping Tikan by his good arm. "Speed up that appendage of yours; you're going to need a clear picture of what's going on. We're going to run."

"What?"

"They'll be coming for us, for the ship. We must get to it fast, yes?"

"You said—"

"Forget what I said. Are you ready?"

"I—"

"Good."

Onasus pulled Tikan into a charge without warning. The blind man almost tripped as they started, but he caught himself. With haste, then, he resumed tapping his obelisk against his thigh in a vaguely repeating pattern, as though it were an urgent Morse code. As they began running, he perceived other feet beating the floor, racing. They jangled weapons and had blank faces. Many of them.

"You see them, yes? Not a minor suspicion, indeed," Onasus gasped, holding Tikan against a wall before dragging him onward again.

They made it halfway up the walkway towards the central platform. A small group of sentinels approached. They advanced in a wedge formation, breathless, almost bloodless. They passed by as though Tikan and Onasus were invisible.

"What's the problem, then?" Tikan said, his shoulder furious as he struggled to maintain a view of the external world. "Just blind all of them. You're good at blinding people, aren't you?"

"Your sarcasm is unwelcome. Drop it. It's time to focus," Onasus said. He yanked Tikan back and slammed him against another wall, as if to hurl him to the city below. They waited, and tried to control their breathing. Ahead, a much larger group of sentinels marched past. "And no, I can't. Five or six, even ten—not an issue. But not a small army. My tools are not so boundless. What, did you take me for Daedalus?"

The central platform was deserted of all save Proxima's gray guard. Small groups of them flooded in left and right, heading for various docking platforms. Tikan and Onasus crept onwards on the peripheral rim of the docks.

"It's not far," Onasus whispered.

"Wait," Tikan said. "If having a private ship is this much of a problem, why were the ships even here to begin with? Wouldn't they have been noticed long ago, destroyed?"

"This isn't the time for such questions. Come."

As they ran, Tikan could sense the glass dome above suddenly contract. He felt it concentrate on them like an irritated eye, though they were contained in its own bloodshot sphere.

He staggered a moment, and tapped the glass wall beside him instead of his thigh. He felt the gaze of Proxima's inverted watchtower, oscillating, ravening. In each dormant eye in that city there lay both a cell of the galaxy's prison and a guardian, and now at sky's reach he felt a frigid hand grip his spine. He was certain, now, that all of their metropolitan activities, in the streets and on the docks, had hitherto been witnessed and recorded.

Onasus pulled him on.

"This is it. Inside, now. Drum that leg, my boy, and softly, and don't speak."

They slipped into a side passage and staggered for a moment, as it seemed on their sharp turn that they would fall off the docks in a rain of glass shards. They composed themselves and sped along a longer walkway, careful with their footfalls.

Onasus halted abruptly. Another group of sentinels fanned out ahead. Onasus pressed himself like a spider against the walls, pinning Tikan down and breathing hard. Six or seven sentinels sprinted into view. They turned the corner, brandishing their guns, and looked straight at Tikan and Onasus. Then, Onasus erupted into view and struck without moving, his eyes rolling down and his face drenched. The sentinels froze for a second, and then fell to the ground like malfunctioning machines.

Onasus took off again. They sprang from group to group, behind denser pillars that were not very translucent. The muscles in Tikan's shoulder tightened and burned with acid generated by his efforts to keep digging into his thigh, even as he ran. As his shoulder slowed, he began leaping between perceptual holes.

He and Onasus streamed along on the band of illusory moon glints, and arrived on a sun-struck platform. At the far end, ahead of them, there was a similar ship to the one on which Mira and Naim had left, and four sentinels rabidly patrolling in front of it.

Onasus halted their run for a moment. He scanned their surroundings, and then bolted forward again. Still in the scientist's grip, Tikan resumed beating the obelisk against his bruised thigh like a caveman with a club. Their footsteps clacked against the platform.

The guards turned and swung their rifles towards the charging pair. One started reciting a perfunctory speech, but moments later his voice cracked into a witch's shrill and he sank to the floor. Onasus advanced unfazed. Without incident, then, the rest of the sentinels collapsed to the ground.

Onasus stopped and exhaled and gripped his forehead. "Here we are. Inside. Fast."

The ship's entrance slid open, and Tikan caught only flashes of its architecture. Larger, more rooms. Cold, vacuous. They entered, and Onasus halted at the threshold. Behind them, a small horde of sentinels streamed onto the platform from the walkway. They fired a barrage, singeing the ship's hull. Onasus stood as though oblivious while the sentinels continued to shoot wantonly at the ship.

"Well, Tikan, I'm afraid this is goodbye," he said in a neutral tone.

Tikan's heart sank. He turned to Onasus, nauseated. The muscles in his shoulder were aflame, and the walls clanged with his limb. "What?"

"Yes, you will have to continue on to Arcturus alone. It appears I have further business here on Proxima."

"No," Tikan said, moving behind the ship's wall to avoid the gunfire. "Stop it. Stop with your twists and turns. They're firing. Just get inside and let's go. I'm blind, *damn it*, I'm blind because of you."

"Farewell. Good luck. If I find the girl, I'll be sure to let her know you said hello. Do hurry now; they are swarming outside."

Without another word, Onasus stepped backward down the ramp and into the gunfire, and the door shut. Tikan's chest was sundering. He slammed his obelisk into the wall. The sound of the gunfire would not stop outside.

Fighting off the nausea, he hobbled to the cockpit with his arm in a painful cycle against the hallway's walls. He exhaled breaths of behemoth anger, trying to make sense of Onasus.

The cockpit door slid open. The piloting station was to his right, ominous and foreign. He did not question it. He fell to his knees and crawled towards the machine. His arm thudded the ground as he got on his back. He latched onto the handle on the inside, pulled himself into the cavity, and kicked until his whole body was inside.

The walls of the machine adjusted, molding around him to suit his position. He was constricted, then, and unable to use his replacement sense. Darkness. The machine started. Its guts roared, and Tikan's head was clasped and rotated upward. Up, like a child fixed in wonder at the night sky.

Time was clawing at the door. A flood was laboring to overtake the ship. He gritted his teeth on his hope for an antediluvian age, and the star hunter rumbled.

A waterfall of thin wires dove into his sockets. They pierced the hoary barriers that had replaced his eyes. To him they felt like two icicles lodged in his skull. They fixed on what remained of his optic nerves and strung them out. They meshed together tightly, and a jolt ran through this link and struck the bone capacitor that was his skull. His consciousness merged with the ship, and the engines started.

Before long he was towering above the galaxy, terrible and vast. Stars and dark matter, portals and gravity wells, all flooding into view and rearranging. The contents of the firmament were pouring through his empty sockets. In his numbed flesh, buried in the black of star-pierced space, he felt again the nausea of his childhood's end. The constellations flared. There were few options. The Arcturian maw bared its teeth and widened.

The machine released Tikan's body. The needles receded from his sockets. He sank to the ground. He shivered in what could have been that machine's saliva. And there, cold on the floor, he struggled to rise. It was not possible. With what feeble strength he had left, he raised and dropped his obelisk arm to the floor with a thud.

Proxima was gone, far away. He was sailing the vast emptiness, alone again.

THE VESSEL OF ALL FINAL
CRUELTIES AND SORROW

F ollowing my demands for a stuffy and portentous affaire,
Harman decided to book the Salon des Augustins ballroom at
the Hôtel Henri V in Paris. Paris, that awful place! But there was
revenge to be had, a final human act before full ascension. To cleanse
Paris of my tribulations, perhaps.

I was there incognito, of course. While it is true that it became
increasingly difficult for me to conceal my identity beside HORUS'
growing renown, few there knew my face. I had gone to great lengths
to ensure that over the years. And let me tell you, yes, that the extent
of my deceptions and my aversion to the public eye was enough to
make Howard Hughes seem a hound for the spotlight.

For all intents and purposes, it was Harman who represented us. I
wrote his speeches for him and explained the protocol. We arrived in
different cars, and we were given quite different greetings. He was the
focus of everyone's attention, as intended. As for myself, I said little to
anyone and avoided craning photographers, though they had little
reason to point their weapons at me, in any case.

On my arrival, I was awestruck halfway through the lobby.
Equidistant from each other and from me were four sculptures of the
same goddess in various seasonal poses. She had the same face and the

same body, but one incarnation was dressed in young vines, another in winter thorns; another bathed in falling leaves, and the last reached sunwards. Now this goddess in her four forms marked a rectangle with me at the center.

In this enclave of all time, I could not help but linger. I stood in the middle of what looked like a stage or a sundial, and there, above me, past the light of the chandelier, was a great oculus to the azure.

I then noticed a most peculiar grand Aubusson tapestry hanging behind the concierge desk. It took up the whole wall, reached up to the ceiling. It looked like some recovered piece of arcana.

I was immediately struck by the two women sharing the center, who swayed opposite each other. I lost myself in their reverent, divinatory gazes. The one on the right levitated the sun in her left palm and bore a torch in the other. Her sister to the left tended to a golden pyre that engulfed a bird in the smoke of its own feathers and blotted out what was surely a faded moon in the distance. Both of them were gazing straight at the sun.

Perhaps they were variations of that same goddess behind me, the hair auburn on one head and white as the sun's pinprick core on she who carried its burning token. Their robes were the color of brown, rusty blood; their skins were white as the truest void. And there were children, all naked, clamouring at the feet of the noble, bare-breasted Pythia, while her sister looked on jealously.

Elsewhere in the scene, these same children grasped at the leaves of surrounding dark woods, and they picked tomatoes and peaches at the feet of the sun's priestess. They trampled swords and shields littering the floor with bells cracked and sinking through the earth, along with a knight who had collapsed. He slept in the pieces of his wrecked armor, in those dark woods whose barks were savaged. There was also the bust of a wise man, some Socrates or other, the face downcast, being carried out past the sun by a series of tiny bronze men.

After standing mesmerized before the tapestry for some time, I moved on. I spent a half hour in the bar enjoying a band play modest jazz and then another half hour in the tea hall. I tried to enjoy the music, but could only hear the hammers of the piano, low notes from the bass, high notes from the horns, shifts in key, and time signatures. Not music.

It grew dark outside and I could already see our guests streaming into the ballroom. As I made a final round of the hotel's inner corridors, I was staggered by a final omen. Just shy of the exit back into the lobby, there was a clock made of an anthropic sun's face. Its beams shot out like myriad polearms in all directions to impale the clouds.

I passed again the charcoal marble concierge and reception desks flecked ivory and ruby with their impressed gold medallions, and went over to the Salon des Augustins.

"May I, sir?" asked a young man as I stepped into the foyer and flashed my invitation. I handed him my coat and moved to slither between the crowds.

It was difficult to locate Pierre through the mass of suits and dresses. He was my primary reason for attending the event, of course.

Gold light shimmered from the chandeliers against the ornate décor. Thick pillars and marble walls, intricately laced napkins and crystal glasses. Already seated was Harman, along with the CEO of Dupont and other company heads. Fools. Most of them would be dead within ten years. Irrelevant. Where was Pierre? Many were still walking around as Harman got up and wandered from table to table, shaking hands with various executives.

There were draped round tables of varying sizes arranged throughout the hall. Our more notable guests sat together in smaller groups, hunched and decrepit, murmuring surreptitious words to each other. The few in positions high enough to recognize me simply nodded as I passed through. Otherwise, I was free to move around unhindered.

I stalked the place, peering across the room from its perimeter, idling beside waiters scurrying about with full trays of champagne and tiny hors d'oeuvres in hand. Massive bouquets anchored the tables, casting a purple hue on the room and helping to keep me obscured.

A little while later, the event was getting underway, and most people had found their seats. I loitered yet in the back with the waiters and guests of lesser importance. Harman began positioning himself behind of the podium. I was growing frustrated. Surely Pierre had not snubbed the affair. It was unthinkable: career suicide, for sure. No, he had to be around, had to.

I took a step back as the chatter died down, towards darker corners, and bumped into a slender figure. I turned around. "Sorry—" My eyes jumped wide, my breath was snatched from me. "*You,*" I said, full of disbelief.

I was paralyzed: my expression agape, half of my champagne on the floor. Nothing could have prepared me. There, striking me numb and speechless, was Sophia. She was smiling. The same sad, affected smile, the same one that was seared into my memory. Inside, I trembled. I let time and business and Harman and the flowers all collapse around her. There was only her: visible, full. Her hair was shorter, and her skin less vibrant, and I was sorry. The steel ball of hatred I'd harbored in my stomach until this very night was now dissolving back into the love I'd once felt.

"Me," she returned, still smiling.

I fumbled in search of a response. We looked each other straight in the eyes.

Let me tell you about the eyes. There is a prejudice I have regarding consciousness, which I presume others have shared as well. Whenever I think of what consciousness *is,* whenever I try to imagine what its substance looks like (and here already you can see me committing my mistake), I end up instinctively conceiving of it in terms of my sense of sight. As though the soul were sight alone; as though the other senses were auxiliary, and, like ideas and sentiments and other non-perceptual features of consciousness, not essential to it.

It may be because, anatomically, the eyes are positioned such that the rest of the body appears to flow down from their scope like the dais and steps below a throne. Regardless of where the brain is situated, it is sight which gives me the notion that my head is the seat of my intellect.

It offers the widest range of perceptions, contrasts my body and my sense of place with other objects in terms of distance, shape, orientation, position, color, and their infinite combinations. It is the most ubiquitous sense. I am saturated in sights from the moment I awake to when I sleep. I am not always hearing loud or sharp noises; I am not always feeling high pressure or pain on my skin; I am not always tasting intense flavours. But I am always equally seeing.

The other senses are buried in it. I hear the violin in terms of its image: the violin, which I have seen, and which I perceive or imagine as being played, as though it is the sight of the bow and the sight of the strings as they meet which produces the sound. Only children born blind and ignorant of wood or catgut or indeed, music itself, have innocently listened to a violin.

The sight of the eyes themselves enforces this prejudice. They are the essential beauty of humankind. Eternal gems embossed on even the dullest helm; the tiniest whorls containing in them the condensed light of every galaxy ever witnessed. The irises dilate and contract the world itself. Unlike the immobile ears or nose, or the dumb, sluggish tongue slithering behind the teeth, the eyes scan and track and apprehend. They signify the mind behind them.

I have spoken to you before about the ocean of consciousness. About its sublime immensity, about how terrifying it is to behold. It is the eyes, laden with an entire world trapped in a moment of perspective, which express the terrifying consciousness of the *other*. To suffer the infernal gaze of the other is to witness another consciousness recognizing you. Not the frozen eyes of the dead or the sheathed daggers of the dreaming, but the waking, attentive other. It is to have this terrific alien consciousness confront you and elude you with its mysteries; with its secret history, which it will not reveal to you; with its endlessness, which you shall never capture.

Conversely, when you gaze into the mirror and look yourself in the eyes, you see nothing but a blank appearance. You feel nothing but the pacific and neutral zero of totality. You do not feel the same apprehension, the same sense of mystery or unpredictability. Everything behind those familiar eyes is already clarified. Your reflected gaze is, in fact, mute, because it signifies nothing except the very act constituting it.

Yet the closest you will come to seeing the other— not merely her corpse, but *her* and *her* existence —is by looking her in the eyes. When you return her gaze, you are struck by the possibility of her history, of her present being like an immortal's never-finished painting covered in centuries of layers. What would otherwise be just an animated object in the world, no different to the wind or an earthquake, instead presents itself, like you as you know yourself, as an embodied soul. An immaterial subject, somehow present in the flesh.

And what is love except the ceaseless attempt at capturing this subjectivity of the other without simultaneously compromising her autonomy? This autonomy, which she requires in order to return your love and therefore complete it. It envelops the patience of long marriage; the unity of welded lives, tastes, preferences, and ambitions. I looked at Sophia; I looked in her eyes. I looked at her and I loved her; I looked at her and I loved; I tried to look at her and I tried to love her.

I could have searched her life then and there for an answer, but I couldn't bring myself to it. I didn't want to see. I wanted to speak with her, hear her words, clasp her hands in mine and feel her skin. Let her speak, without knowing what she would say. I wanted, above all, to fill myself in where her words would leave her incomplete.

"Sophia," I said.

But then, just as I grasped for uneasy words, my heart sank. Familiar arms wormed out of the darkness and slid around her waist.

Pierre clasped her and pulled her close. Pierre. I was hollowed. I was emptied. As if someone had thrown a bucket of black paint on the tableau of my life. I denied it as some surreal trick. The way his jacket sleeve hung casually off his wrist, the way his cufflinks gleamed. The way he exhaled with ennui, as though he'd held her a thousand times before. But, no, his arms were real, and his same arrogant smirk—all real! I started breathing heavily through my nose, and my expression turned to an irrepressible scowl.

"It's good to see you, old friend," he said, slanting his eyebrows and giving me a genuinely heartfelt look. He was still clutching my love.

And she was my love. Mine, forever, regardless of whatever had passed between us, regardless of the silent years, of his arms. The world demanded that we be together. Likely she didn't want to be there with him, likely she was there under duress.

"I've been looking forward to this," Pierre went on. "It's been too long, truly. You know, I didn't even know until I was promoted recently. You really should have called at some point. We love you, man. We always have. I'm happy for you, really. It's amazing what you've accomplished."

How? In what universe was he friendly and calm toward me? It was unthinkable—no, impossible. I dove into his life. Messily. I ransacked fragments of his life-in-itself, scrambled, searched for an answer like some devilish version of Poseidon against whom the seas have rebelled. Had he kidnapped her? Threatened her? Nothing, only splinters of their nights together. The dusk half-lighting their morose dinners. How they wordlessly pushed a grocery cart beside stacked cans of tomato sauce and boxes of cereal. Why?

At the other end of the ballroom, Harman was preparing to begin his speech.

"I—yes," I said. "The way we last spoke, I—"

"No, let's not speak about that. We were both hotheaded and young. It's not worth it. We're here now, all of us, reunited, lets—"

The lights dimmed.

Harman's voice resounded through the hall. "Friends, associates, distinguished guests," he started, and then went on to give a trite speech I'd written praising the corporate irresponsibles for their moral responsibility.

The crowd clapped and cheered, congratulating each other for pissing away half a day's earnings, while Harman continued to emit platitudes.

"You know, I think—" Pierre whispered once the noise died down and Harman continued.

"Forgive me," I interrupted, suppressing my every instinct, on the verge of ripping his face to pieces. "But I need to speak with Sophia in private."

"Yes, of course," he said. His expression slackened, and he looked away with a sip of champagne. As though nothing I could do would ever threaten their pathetic romance. It made me sick, sick, sicker than I'd ever felt. He kissed her on the cheek, and looked away again, too proud to tremble before me or to even give me to the courtesy of contempt. Did he not know that I owned them? I could not tell. I would not look. I would deal with him later.

Sophia nodded, and we shuffled out of the ballroom together.

The gold lights were nauseating as we walked out into the foyer. The pillars in the corners of the room were polished enough to send back a revolting reflection. From below, the chandelier looked like a frozen volley of crystal arrows, each lit up and homing for me. I felt tiny again, tiny under the inlaid ceiling and surrounded by reflections and busts with definite, blank, gaping eyes.

I kept my gaze fixed down. When I looked up, I was staggered. Her face was knowing and wise with conquered grief. What good were my half-powers there, before her?

Harman's speech could still be heard from inside. Simplistic garbage for gnats incapable of depth. Another round of clapping resounded.

We wound out to the ballroom's lobby, close to the coatroom. There were no servants or people rushing off to empty their bladders. We stopped, and faced each other beneath the half-lights. Her gaze now made me alien to myself. I felt caught in the crosshairs of her perspective, which she could yet deny me. I tried to climb out of myself, to consider myself as she might have been seeing me.

I didn't quite know where to begin. She, however, smiled her empathic smile, and the most effortless dimple formed at the corner of her mouth. It was as though she could wring everything from me, then: every frayed string of thought and pool of confliction. She was, in that moment, far more powerful than I would ever be.

"We didn't hear from you for years," she almost whispered beneath the sound of Harman's ongoing voice in the distance. "The way you left."

"It didn't mean," I said, pausing. "It didn't mean you had to go to him."

"No? Who else was I supposed to go to to look for you?"

I said nothing. I gave her an ireful look.

"What, did you think I just packed up my bags and threw myself at him?" she said. "It's insulting if that's what you think of me. Even if you're bitter. It's been decades. He called me. He was worried. You'd had a fight, or something, and you'd gone missing. And—It doesn't matter. I don't have to explain it."

"So you didn't care."

"Do you really believe that?"

"No."

"I loved you. We looked for you."

"And then, after that, when you couldn't find me you—"

"Oh, just stop it. Stop acting upset. It's ugly of you. You made your decisions that cold night. And it's okay. Look at everything you've accomplished. I'm happy for you. And you should be happy for me. We've all gone—"

"No, that's not true. I loved you. I still love you. I needed space, and time, and I needed—"

"Stop it. Stop it, because you're only going to hurt yourself, now. I'm going to go back inside. Please, when you've calmed down—please come to us. We'll talk. You, me, and Pierre. We'll catch up, the proper way. Not like this."

"No."

She gave me a lingering look of pity, and then turned away to abandon me.

"No," I repeated, and snatched her arm.

She grew hostile around the eyes, and she tried to pull herself free. I yanked her arm so hard as to almost dislocate it from her shoulder. She gave a fearful grimace under the fading lights.

Her chest started rising and falling. She gasped for air, started hyperventilating, and made a half-cry. I drove my fingers into her mouth before she could finish the sound and gripped her whole jaw. Her tongue wrestled in place, but I pressed it down, molded the fringe of my palm with her teeth, and I pushed. *Helpless, miniscule, mine.* With her jaw still in hand, I drove her into the coatroom.

The door shut. The room was narrow and without lights. We became mere shapes and violent punctuations. The pluck of my fingers along the inside of her cheeks, the mauling of her avian bones, the bruises beginning on my shin. She kicked and she dug her nails into my wrist. Her feet dragged and her heels tore off against the carpet. Saliva spilled down her chin. Her breaths fought for space and turned to coughs, like those of someone saved from near drowning. "Monster," she tried to mouth and chew.

I had a few flashes of doubt and restraint. As if I were in great danger. As if I were now crossing an irreversible line bolder than any other I'd crossed before. I had to pulverize a deep, foundational stone in my psyche to carry on.

I rammed her against the wall and buried her head in coats. She sank. My claws reached the back of her throat, and she gagged. Even as thin lines of blood started sliding down my forearm, I would not let go. How could I? The world demanded it. Her arms flung around wildly, smashing against our little booth. I pinned her wrists just above her head. My fingers slipped out of her mouth to her dress. A few whimpers and muted groans fled her tomb of coats.

At first her struggle was profound. Her hair in tangles, and her face dripping, and her body red; but we were together unified in the abyss of loving. Yes, and she was with me, reconstructing me; I felt it, and her resistance meant nothing, for what counted was her love, not her. It was what had been missing those parched years of mine. Yes, and like all other things I'd ever touched, even love I had to turn inside out, mutilate, bleed and disfigure.

I smothered her face with my forearm, smearing her mucus and breaking open her lips. While panting in agony she croaked something a person would say. There was no need for me to respond. She was becoming a shell; she was dissolving into me.

She stopped resisting after that. It was kind of her. I gave her everything, then. Clarified myself. Everything that I'd ever wanted anyone to know. And there was nobody else to whom I could have expressed myself so fully. It was beyond language. It was not mere anarchy. No. There was the most compassion that would ever flower between two people. And thighs were in motion, and fangs, and the blank gaze of a pitiless sun was cast out of stony sleep even through the last drop of dark.

The key into that rusted slot, the release I was prepared to abandon the world for. For the sake of all mankind, she undammed me and gave me the world unveiled and illumed. She was, in that moment, the vessel of all final cruelties and sorrow. Pandora reversed. The truth, the full view. The widening gyre, the reeling shadows, the rush of all blood-dimmed tides. I understood her then, at last.

Her childhood was more tragic than she'd ever expressed: long summers of wintery neglect, a mother who threw her to dogs more vicious than her father, the rot behind the parental bark revealed too soon.

She would lie in the coatroom for a long time after I would leave. There, she would repeat emptiness over in her mind. When the sound of Harman's voice would end, she would walk out in a vomit-stained trench coat.

The hospital visit would be humiliating. They would hoist her up by her knees; she would look like a corpse ready to give birth. The doctors would be callous, and speak to her little; they would represent a completely sterile humanity to her at her most broken hour.

Nothing would come of the examination besides the fragments of her dignity trampled to smaller pieces.

In their dismal little flat, Pierre would ask her what had happened. He would implore her, threaten to kill me; she would only watch the walls and hope for rain. A week later, she would call her mother for the first time in a decade; they would laugh superficially, forgive each other. Sophia would confide in her, tell her everything. Her mother would sigh and ask for her fault in it, about whether that was what she had wanted, deep down.

In less than a month, there would be a body down the Seine. Summer rain would pour over a rancid grey river. It would turn into a shower before long, and finally wash her of my life.

✣ 49 ✣

EARTH

Sielle could never have seriously entertained the idea of separating completely from causality, nor could she have adequately recognized it if such a feat were possible. Even if she forever lingered in those dark, spaceless corridors outside of time, her consciousness would forever bear the stain of the material world. And though she was a causality unto herself, her body aged nonetheless, as she had become painfully aware; and her memories accrued, regardless of the disjointed collection of pasts and futures behind her. She was no mere spontaneity; she was not free to revise herself.

Though she was, in principle, free of the space and time that had fathered her, she had also condemned herself over the years with her mercurial jaunting. Only by Zotharra's rage had the holes in time, through which she would slip in and out of history's stream, ever been plugged. She could not now fully extricate herself from the world, or the world from herself.

But there yet remains the mystery of how Sielle could come to occupy the world in the first place, since she was acausal in and of herself. Wherefore was her body, if her spirit was so unchained? The darkened temple of her origin, belonging to forgotten wisdom, retained no inscription of her soul.

Whether the whole would forever chase itself to account for her presence, or whether her free interventions in truth laid waste to the world's track, or whether they merely fell along it, also remains as yet unanswered.

~

The voyage to Earth from Zotharra was long, and it skipped over much more than she, that shining needle behind whom trailed the thread of fragmented ages, had yet seen.

It was her fourth attempt, now, to reach Tikan. On the first, she had arrived at Proxima while it was still in the infancy of its construction. The same red sun through the windows, the harpoons freshly plugged into its back. On the second, she had arrived on Mars, when it was still blossoming as the only extraterrestrial home for humankind. On the third attempt, she had landed on the paradise world orbiting Sirius. She wept, looking at a diadem of coral cleaving the ocean, at riverbanks of opals, at the twin sunsets melting across the horizon into one increate destiny. And though she spent some hours looking for Tikan, hoping he had, against all reason, gone to Sirius without her, in her heart she knew that this was untrue.

Now on her fourth voyage, with her spirit fragile, she failed to aim true once again and landed on Earth. The clouds plummeted through the sky, heavier than oceans with the sun searing behind them. She arrived on her stomach, her chin in the concrete. Her shadow leapt out ahead of her and extended down the narrow alley in which she found herself. She exhaled, rolled over on her back, and sat up.

There were innumerable doors evenly aligned along the length of the walls. The buildings rising above her seemed tall enough to reach space. They looked built of ancient stone polished of their history, gray and unbearably shiny.

This was far from the luster of Proxima. Towers stacked together to block out everything but that white-hot eye of the sun above. It flared at her as she got up. Her limbs trembled with fatigue. She could not suffer another misfire across the ages, and decided to explore this odd world, at least for a little while.

She turned a near corner. Another alley, the exact same. The blaze from above. She walked on, scanning her surroundings for answers and clearing the sweat already formed on her brow.

She was still in the habit of fearing her own perspiration, but she remembered quickly enough that she was no longer on Zotharra, and ceased to be alarmed. She raced from passage to passage, hoping for an exit to the network of long galleries. There was none. She leaned against the alley wall to recover, and noticed two figures approaching her at an even pace. They wore white, nondescript clothes. They had mid-length hair, the woman's dark and the man's blond.

"Wait," Sielle said as they passed her.

They made no response.

"Excuse me," she pressed, walking up to them. "I've lost my way. Could you help me with directions?"

They continued to ignore her completely. It was as if they were both deaf.

"Hey," Sielle said, grabbing the woman by the shoulder and pulling her lightly. "I'm speaking to you."

Both of them turned to her and gave her a neutral gaze. Without a word or any other gesture, they each took her by the hand and continued walking.

"Hey," Sielle repeated, flustered. "Stop it." She flung her shoulders about to wriggle out of their light hold, and she half tripped. They both let go and faced her without commotion.

Sielle drew her arms up on guard, and she stepped back, eyes fidgeting. The woman approached her, gaze fixed but absent, arms slack at her side. Sielle flinched. But the woman only leaned in and kissed the side of her neck, and then withdrew. They locked eyes for a moment. Sielle stepped out of the light and into a brief shadow. The two people did nothing in return. They walked away from her and disappeared behind a corner.

She sat down for a while after they left and fought tears. She rose up, and with her soul recently exposed by Zotharra, she wandered the alleys for an hour, inhaling the humid air. In the end, she decided on a random door. It lifted open as soon as she waved her hand towards it.

The door slid shut behind her, and Sielle found herself in a monotonous beige room no larger than a closet. It was not hot or humid inside. She exhaled and gathered herself. As if she were an archaeologist searching for a concealed passage, she placed her palms on the walls and swept the surface. The walls were delicate and had an almost creamy texture. The floor rumbled. It was not clear what was happening, but there was movement in some direction. A moment later, the wall in front of her slid up.

The reveal was dreamlike. Ahead of her the walls were sea-foam, and there wafted in a mild scent of lavender. She took a step out and caught a gold glint from the window at the far end of a wide and spacious room sunk in total silence. There were people all around. Half of them were naked, which seemed not at all out of the ordinary. Some sat at tables and ate, others lay on lounge sofas and looked at each other without expression. It had the look of a children's playroom with no attractions.

There were many circles of people standing and staring mutely at each other. Sielle walked up to a group that was eating, and they cleared a space for her as soon as they noticed her. There were no cheerful expressions—indeed, no expressions at all—and it was already clear that no one would speak.

She sat down and, with an awestruck countenance, accepted the bowl of appetizing looking mush that was handed to her. She spooned a lump of it into her mouth; it had the mildest taste of strawberries and porridge, and despite its blandness was rather pleasant. Her head wheeled around. The people did not look drugged, or sleepy, or unhappy. They only looked satisfied. Sielle rose from the table and leaned against a wall. As in the little room, it flew up to reveal another large space.

This room was coloured beige, pale and drained as old clay. The people inside appeared to be performing identical activities to those in the first. It was not clear that there were any definite social groups. They only seemed to drift in and out of silent circles. In the far corner, she saw a naked pair sitting on their knees and locking hands as if they were wrestling, staring intently at each other with the same dead look that everyone wore.

There was no sound save for squeaking furniture or the clink of silverware on bowls. She heard no speaking whatsoever. Though the people seemed to understand each other perfectly, even if there was very little to understand. There were children, too, milling about. They did not play or screech like children, but they were somewhat more energetic than the adults.

She wandered out of this room and found herself in a long corridor extending to a window which was almost blinding to look at. There were doors on both sides of the corridor. Sielle walked through one of them and entered a dim booth that resembled the darkroom of an old film studio.

There, she found a woman sitting naked in front of a screen that took up the whole wall. The display was so clear as to seem, at first, a double mirror. The woman was watching one of the larger rooms. A birds-eye view. The silent circles, the children eating. Sielle observed this person, who remained unmoving and looked inly petrified.

Sielle exited and walked down the corridor, barring her face from the increasingly bright window, then entered another booth.

There was a man inside, also naked and watching a screen taking up the whole wall. The screen showed the exact same footage the woman had been viewing, and his expression, too, was curiously the same: transfixed, attentive, exhausted.

Sielle checked a number of other booths. Though they all contained the same arrangement of person and screen, there were a few in which the footage on the wall consisted purely of another's face. Staring, mute. On continuing her search, she discovered that these particular rooms were linked. Two people, each in an isolated room, each observing the other's mute, piercing gaze like two impotent basilisks.

She made her way back to the sea-foam room. As she arrived, she saw one little boy trip and skin his knee as he jogged to the other end of the room. He started crying and hugging the maroon streak on his knee. He shrieked through the room, the sound inordinately stark, as though it were the only one permitted in this vacuum. His expression spoke not of pain, but of distress in discovering the possibility of suffering itself.

A number of adults started converging around the boy, but, as they noticed each other, all except one instantly turned back around. The man kneeled down and picked up the boy, who was still screaming himself red. Together, they walked to the end of the room. And when the sun flashed through again, the boy's cries were reduced to whimpers.

She followed the pair out as they walked through another creamy beige corridor and entered a much smaller room. It was about half the size of the other pens and had white tiles checkering the floor. There looked to be something resembling a kitchenette there, too, in which two or three people stood and watched something sizzling in a pan.

At the other end of the room, the man, still leading the whimpering boy, stopped before a wall of steel cabinets. One of the slots popped open just as the pair neared it, and a single white tablet fell into the man's hands. He mechanically placed it into the child's mouth, without force, kissed the boy quickly on the neck, and walked away without waiting for the result. The boy's scratch dissolved back to skin, and, still reeling from what looked like a life-changing trauma, he wiped his nose before skipping out of the room.

Sielle lingered in front of the steel cabinets, her brow twitching as she tried to process what she had witnessed. Still in the room were the absurd cooks: an old man and three others, though they seemed to be doing little in the way of production. Rather, it looked like some sort of show; they crowded around the pan, captivated by the food browning and the fumes smelling of meat.

It looked to Sielle as though these people, having learned everything of civilization, had returned to a more refined, self-knowing animal savagery. They stalked their pens naked and spoke no language, yet they made careful use of furniture and did their stalking over hard, straight surfaces and in sterile, right-angled architecture; they lay on synthetic beds and wielded forks and ate with straight posture from plates. And without the pitfalls of unrehearsed language, they organized in circles and triangles and squares and watched each other with blank, intense knowing, and there, having shed the horrors of words and meaning, having annihilated beauty, they escaped the savage and the civil man both.

Still, they craned over each other in the kitchenette to watch a strange piece of meat gain a crust. And they were organized, and kind. Sielle walked around the room, becoming less suspicious than morose.

Not far from her, a circle of people composed of adults and children gathered around something. She walked closer and leaned over their heads to look. Neatly arranged in the center of the circle were a single, half-putrefied finger severed at the base, a cracked green leaf, and between them, a globular object Sielle could only liken to a jellyfish's bell.

Where they had acquired these objects in their happy captivity, she could not tell. Though their expressions were, for the most part, still mute, she could yet discern a difference in their fixed stares, most obvious in the children. It was a subtle crease under the eyes, the mouths only slightly hanging agape. One of the children, whose gaze flickered more attentively than the others, was even holding a palm-sized, blackened rectangle of stiff paper, which retained a faded red mark at its corner and jagged gold at its top.

Sielle could not restrain a smile from spreading across her face, for in each of those talismans over which they loomed, mystified, there remained the forms of metamorphosis and history and decay, and perhaps man was therefore an inescapably metaphysical animal yet.

In the kitchenette-theater, the old man keeled over and exhaled loudly. Everyone in the room stopped what they were doing and walked over to him. They shuffled to the body, again without expression. A man and a woman both kneeled down beside the sudden corpse and, in what would otherwise have been described as a savage act if not for the distinctly routine and procedural manner in which it was performed, they started breaking off fingers from the old man's hands. They pressed the exact pressure points at the joints to make a clean snap. One or two required an extra few maneuvers to tear off strips of skin hanging on.

Sielle grimaced out of disgust, but watched with fascination. The people placed the severed fingers neatly beside them, and others came to collect them. The dead man's toes stuck out like fresh bulbs of garlic, and these were communally harvested, too. Once all the extremities were removed, two persons arrived with knives and slid them across the old man's belly as if it were plastic packaging. The guts flowered out. Like warehouse keepers taking careful stock, these impromptu morticians started pulling out the viscera and arranging it in a meticulous pile.

"Stop that," Sielle said, wincing. They gave no response.

She marched over to the most active man and pulled his shoulder hard. He stood up with red, wet hands and faced her, part surgeon, part savage, and like those before him, he advanced on her and pecked her neck. On instinct, Sielle slapped him.

With his mouth widening and his gaze focusing, he made a garbled sound and began shaking his head, and then hyperventilating. He gripped his own head at the temples and gave himself a two-dimensional laurel wreath of blood down the side of his face. Sielle stood dumbfounded.

The man's lip began quivering as he shook his head in disbelief at her. He soon forgot the slap and began noticing the deeper trouble that lay in her opaque existence. Before him, she stood as the living manifestation of the void they had been so lovingly engineered to forget.

The woman who had also been tearing extremities from the corpse got up and quickly kissed the man's neck; others did this, too, but he would not calm down. They all turned, then, and looked at Sielle. Their expressions all went blank. Then, just as these übermenschen collectively hyperventilated and raised pathetic, talonless hands, the ceiling opened, and a black-clawed crane swooped down before them as though they were mere dolls in an arcade. They all took a step back. The adults started crying, and the children ran to them and kissed their shins.

The crane scooped up the old man's corpse, clasping his torso so that his back arched and his limbs dangled. It retracted upward until the corpse looked like a chandelier of flesh. Then, with the tiles in the ceiling peeling back as it moved, the crane whizzed the body away down the corridor to some unknown destination. A trail of blood and pieces of viscera dripped along the crane's track out of the corpse's scientific wound. Little automatons followed and cleaned the floor.

Sielle gave the other humans a final look, flinching as they continued to weep and shiver and be consoled by small children. She bolted off down the corridor in pursuit of the corpse.

Sielle heard the people continue their howling as she followed the crane. Others passed her by, but they were not part of the commotion and they ignored her. The crane moved faster as the corridor emptied. She followed it through the sea-foam room into a new corridor, then as it took hard lefts and rights and passed finally through a hallway whose end was another portal to the sun.

Flashes of sunlight started swamping Sielle's vision. She ran on, though her breathing became uneven and her muscles cramped. The glass wall at the end slid upward, and wind flushed the corridor. She covered her eyes. She almost toppled over. The crane came to an abrupt halt at the portal and released the corpse, letting it soar out.

Sielle leaned over to see the outside. Only the same massive buildings reflecting each other stretched out as far as she could see. And though she was too high up to see the little alleys that made up the ground, the sky, too, was mostly lost. The sun appeared to be searing it, its blue and cloudy texture flaking on the edges of its flame.

Beneath her, what appeared to be a moving leaf blower swiveled along the side of the building. The fingerless corpse landed tidily in its tube, and plumes of black smoke began pumping out the other end.

With the heat pouring into the building came wisps of smoke, and it started to smell like incinerated flesh.

It was not long, then, before a crowd started forming behind Sielle. Half of it was composed of the adults she had terrified. They seemed propelled by the scent of cooking flesh. As more smoke filled the hallway, water started sprinkling from the ceiling, and a translucent gel sprayed from the walls. The people marched on Sielle, wet and glittering like oversized newborns, struggling still to make sense of her. All children, ignoble and enlightened.

She had seen enough. Tikan was somewhere, waiting, in stark opposition to the mess before her. With a deep resolution forming in her heart and across her face, she was certain she could now reach him.

She looked again at the people in front of her. In an effort to kindle their lost hunger for meaning, she took another step back and balanced on the edge of the opening in the building. Almost incorporeal, she gave a tired smile and threw herself into a swoop of wind and heat. The audience cried out, and the sun made a last grimace.

THE END OF HISTORY

We do not blame Mephistopheles for what misfortune befell Faust. It is only the case that the latter was incapable. What, then, do we say to Mephistopheles who enlightens himself? What do we say to Icarus fused with his father, who plucks the feathers of his wings from the sun itself?

I was now entirely beyond glory. The result of a total reconstruction of spirit. The cogs behind each dumb mask exposed for good. Portals abounding and dizzying: Polaris' apocalyptic wink; the cosmic foam of oceans slamming the world like a colossal eukaryote, overwhelming, sending up outland structures; the pierced iris of a whale long peeled open and rotting on a deck. The renewal of my spirit was Sophia's donation to mankind, which, as with all true works of charity, must go forgotten.

The transition was seamless, but I had trouble orienting myself, at first. To do so was a work of tremendous chronography. Consider an incorporeal self that pervades all space and time, and its material anchor fastened down. A brief account of the nature of time is necessary to understand precisely how jarring this parting of my mind and body was.

It is a struggle as old as the debates between Heraclitus and Parmenides, or Plato and Aristotle's disputes in the Academy. Plato thought of time in the same way Newton thought of space: a vacant box housing particulars. His student saw the timeline only as a relation between objects; or, as distinguishable but not separable from causality. To adopt Aristotle's relational view would generally be to deny the reality of past and future, while the Platonists would plant eternal flags in all three modes of time.

Time can otherwise be understood in numerous respects: the mathematic ideality of measurement, employed by physicists as they investigate or make use of cosmic time; the retention of the past and the anticipation of the future, most obvious when we follow a melody or read a novel; the anxiety of loss and death, which glues the self together; the never-ending circling of memories and desires in the mind like the fumes of an opium den; the lens through which any and all objects appear to the mind; the modes of language which denote either Plato or Aristotle's preference; and the succession of events in the world, among others.

Our interest now is with the Aristotelian strand running through Plato's box. The present is actual and self evident, a basic structure of *being* that we need not prove, even if we cannot directly touch it. But does the past remain, itself, beyond mere memory? Is there a terrain of history, or only a map? Does the future loom tall, or is it only a shadow with no body? More concretely: are Homer and Hitler both alive, together, in the grander *now*?

Metaphysically, I cannot say. But, in my own transcendental experience, they are. I could not speak to them, could not visit them, as my body was yet chained, but they appeared before me, as real as any other direct objects of perception. In truth, I suspect the present is the mere lens of consciousness moving along one infinitesimally small segment of particulars that *can be* at once. To walk off the stage is not to vanish from the play altogether, after all. The present contains the past and the future and all relations in itself, in one single object, and achieves its unceasing coherence thus. It is the sinewing of the ideal wrap. It is the train through the tunnel. He who exists is an Aristotelian moving through the Academy.

Imagine, then, that I was like Aristotle walking through his mentor's structure with his head bursting through the ceiling. That my body could not transcend its space-time conditions, though my senses and my mind were freed. That when I touched a rock, I sensed not only its grooves touching my own time-bound flesh, but its beginnings in starfire, and simultaneously its end as sand under the Mediterranean. And if what is present must be experienceable in principle, then everything that ever was and will be was present to me at all times. But, I do not want to discuss this much further. Simply consider that the question of time far exceeds this limited depiction.

In any case, once I had a foot secured in each world, so to speak, I was ready to begin in earnest. There were no more acknowledgeable unknowns save the core of my own monad and one yet distant. What I will recount henceforth cannot be a full description. Unless you were me; unless you could, as I would wish, tear the veil of appearances and grasp the reason motioning behind the absolute, you could not comprehend it. No, it will suffice to explain a simple chronology. Put your head aground a moment, and listen to the blood river course.

There were two principal, competing narratives regarding how mankind would mistakenly sink into dystopia.

Some denounced capitalism and its heartless titans, fearing a taxless world in which labor would be divided up like bricks and stacked at the base of skyscraping headquarters casting shadows over sewage drains serving as both cemetery and housing for the poor, in which all human worth would be quantified down to commercial profitability and morality vaporized by industrial steam.

Others leered at government and its easy excesses; the arrogance of certain men who moronically stirred flags in the air, the long train of abuses that inevitably precedes and follows tyranny's apex; the crushing of the individual by a society turned machine that pursues a neutral singularity it does not comprehend, of safety without meaning, of body without mind or passion.

Neither of these ends would come to pass. Not permanently, at least. Human beings, so long as they exist and speak and congregate, shall always seek improvement, however cursed they may be to toil in vain. To blame avarice or government is to forget who possesses these shortcomings or instruments, and to forget the global anarchy in which they run amok. One need only look at the litany of prototypical examples history provides of these two kinds of circumstances to see that catastrophe overrules malice.

Neither view thus correctly identified the true threat to political harmony. What both sides failed to recognize was the common thread of their complaints, the true enemy of human freedom: the impossibility of empathy and the insoluble burden of power.

Not insoluble in and of itself, but in its unwieldiness; and often, in merely failing to recognize it as a burden. Human civilization has been too excitable and unpredictable to control. There have been innumerable variables ever out of reach, rearranging, and only rarely coming to spontaneous order. Little need to mention the complications that spring with the spread of man and his machines, either. What tape and glue is used, for practicality's sake, keeps society only a claw away from total savagery, and the civil fang carries the greater diseases. How to keep things from falling apart?

It is only through the philanthropy of arrogance that some have strived to make do. But it is not good enough. The shaky structures of order or good that have arrived have generally vacated to chaos in short enough time. No, the leaders of men have been only blind fools who have convinced themselves and others they could see. Men are unequipped. They have been outmatched by the very conditions of their existence. They have not, could not have been responsible. They could not have discerned how to properly exert their power, and they could never find compassion enough. What precious sympathy accompanies their beginnings is drained by their systems; they are stripped of it, seduced out of it. It is not a question of agency, either. Suppose freedom or its child, virtue, and you will find that both mean little when there is so little ground on which to walk.

Thus, men wait for the seer. The mystical legislator on Corsica's hills. The holder of the cards, knower of every conceivable twist and turn. One who executes power the way Musashi waved his katana, and not as though it is some orb glowing gold that burns his very fingertips.

Moreover, it is only through the tacit embrace or rejection of their almost total ignorance that men have carried on the warpath to freedom. And that warpath must precede freedom and knowledge, and therefore be forgiven, must it not? How could Alexander have made his conquests if he had been so disposed to worry about every eviscerated Persian? How, indeed, can Alexander be expected to worry or be overcome with compassion about that which he knows close to nothing?

Although, inside every heart of hearts, there is the inkling that he should. Then, like a latent drug, the importance and majesty of his work dissolves its very premise. It is why people can bring themselves to exalt him, Cyrus, and others cut from that cloth. It is why we do not look for war's meaning in the entrails of dead Persians stinking in the sand; rather, it is in the larger swipes of war's fist, which, carrying in its grasp armies of men who were once children and will soon feed crows, cannot keep those pebbles between its fingers. In truth, what people have hitherto held dear is the lunging and conquering toward a great freedom hardly understood. Of Alexander, of Cyrus; both Great, both lionized killers of men.

It is the epistemic curse man has tried to flout as he has scrambled to build his towers. See the course. Locke and his intellectual descendants tried to turn the problem of humanity's necessary political shortcomings on itself, and this by and large produced the most successful societies history had seen. Yet, even these were eroded by the unforeseeable shadow of technology's meteor and centuries of legal gymnastics, which, like cancers, punctured the congress, the people, and the executive, and allowed ambition to burst out of its pipes and drown the streets. This allowed for imbalances that the Hamiltonian mechanisms could no longer account for.

It is the same problem that sparked Plato's ironic thought experiment. The same that led Marx, that religious fanatic, to call for the end of the state in exchange for the idyllic anarchy he dreamed up. The same problem that had Rousseau recognize himself as the son of fathers fanged and bloodied over the ignoble savage; that had him abstract the general will from the lust and hunger of those to whom it belonged, and define freedom in terms of subservience. The same that Hegel tried to leap from into the arms of the Spirit.

Of them all, Hegel came closest to the right idea. There is something about handing over the meaning of one's suffering to an entity that knows what to do with it, that can fill it up where it would otherwise stay empty.

Forget pathetic Alexander, now. The subject is now a dream. It is slavery's death, its death at the hands of history, and freedom's birth from the carcass. Not a call to the hollow metaphysics of a new epoch, not the chest-thumping of pale and spindly scholars, but the coming to be of absolute knowledge and freedom for the host of mankind. And this we await: reason, Reason that unpacks itself through history like the innards of an egg metamorphosing from embryo to fetus and finally smashing the walls of its nurturing cage. The shape of Spirit. The deluge of permanent compassion into every desiccated shell. The end purpose of history's jerking, writhing like a madman struggling for a way out of his straightjacket. The chorus of voices and arguments rising to cacophony until none can be rightly discerned from the morass, and at last a self-assured, collective, and this time knowing return to silence.

It is to come to know Reason, Spirit, or thought itself in thundering immediacy. This, Hegel thought, could only achieve its objectivity through the state, wherein the objective and subjective will are to be reconciled into one harmonious whole. But, in the end, the Spirit becomes the state, for the individual ego is necessarily eradicated. And a new sort of silence is demanded. It demands that I be selfless, too. And patient, as I have been.

This destiny is, of course, invisible from the myopia of basic flesh. It is why I had to ensure that the books of all those old wraiths, from Heraclitus to Hegel, be burned, lest they rise out of their graves to challenge me again, to overbear my conscience and check me again, when all I needed was their bricks to build my new and perfected Tower of Babel.

But, finally, there would be no dystopia. I would ensure it. There would be only the profoundest of silences. Eventually. For the time, it was necessary to follow the track laid out ahead. That is to say, most of the track. If I am to be complete in my honesty, I must mention, also, that there have been certain other blind spots in the depths of the panorama. Unexpected, and through no fault of mine, to be sure. Even then, I was keenly aware of my remaining shred of ignorance, and working to blot it out.

The day after the gala, I ripped Harman into my office at the earliest and cancelled my departure from HORUS. Drowned him in new energy tempered by what he could never discern, and watched him turn finicky. He looked as though a certain plot of his had been foiled. My suspicions were confirmed, my instincts to put a bullet in his brain vindicated, but they were instantly and permanently stopped.

Caution to the wind, for the wind was mine. All cautions, all consequences baked into every plan. How could I plan? I had the end points before conceiving of their beginnings. Watched empires fall before slitting the throats of emperors. Drilled through asteroids and moons hurtling yet far from Earth. Years fled through me faster than I passed through them. But, too soon, wastelands were forming in my marrow. My back bent to forces that did not yet respect me. My skin wrinkled and sagged, and I shaved my hair to ward off the insult of its whiteness.

It was no trial to wrap my fingers around Earth and her children, but it was not enough. There was much yet to accomplish. I could see Harman's death, fully illustrated, now; and heard him speak kind words. He went, would go, has gone, to finalize research. It is still a while away.

Investments were made in every direction. HORUS grew taller and mightier, unconquerable, indispensable, omnipresent. I stuck its hands into bottomless pockets. I presided as the falcon atop its head, and I set the greatest of wheels in motion, many of them.

I allowed the battle between the corporate behemoths, rearranged it to suit the stars. It was necessary for events to proceed at an even pace, but ever forward, efficient in the fullest of possible respects. In the mess of politics, too, I acted. I plucked politicians from office, rearranged parliaments, and retraced maps and the lines of foreign aid to sew up the world's chasms. Craned man's head upward, where it was always meant to gaze, away from war and famine. Sometimes war and famine had to be engineered, of course, but only ever in service of their eventual eradication, and always in diminishing returns. My touch was subtle, my reach infinite. These were only beginnings. Eggs arranged under precisely timed lamps. Patience. Slowly, measured, each element ticking in its correct place until the stars were right.

It was not long before my greatest ambition—to induce permanent empathy in each heart—also gained a concrete trajectory.

At that time, I would routinely scan the universe for undiscovered phenomena, by a multitude of astronomical instruments. As you might imagine, I required these instruments due to the lingering limitations imposed on me by my wretched, degenerating body.

While I could extend my perceptual reach far beyond, I sometimes could only do so indirectly. Although all relations are baked into every object, you can understand that these relations explode into infinity after a certain point. Do you think, for example, that it would have made sense for me to search for the ring of Hannibal's sword during his first parry at the Battle of Cannae by snapping my fingers? The two sounds are related, make no mistake, but to trace the link that way would have been harder than searching for a grain of dust floating through Orion. And so, to perceive a specific, distant object sometimes required overcoming the horizons of my eye, or the diameter of my earhole.

One day, during one of my routine stargazing sessions, I caught the flicker of an anomaly rippling through the Horsehead Nubula. A space-time spasm unlike any other, shifting and reappearing. The astronomers dismissed it as a malfunction in the equipment, or, at best, the discharge of a convulsing sun.

I tried to focus on the phenomenon captured by the scanners and unveil its mysteries for myself, but it turned out to be the non-perceptual residue of something else. Like a trail of gravity. And when I intended my mind toward the thing itself, I found myself locked out. For the first time in decades, I was denied history. And then it was gone, without trace.

It did not take me long to discern what it was and what had to be done. But it occurred so infrequently, so randomly, that I needed a beacon, a way to attract it. I planned and calculated, but every attempt failed. I could do little but search the future for an opportunity. So I was patient. I could not help but be eternally patient; there were only those distant mysteries left to water my mouth.

While these plans were unfolding, there were two more pressing concerns. First and foremost was that creaking of my bones that loudened by the day and persisted in rankling me. I am speaking of a particular kind of physical distress. The hinges of my jaws ached when I spoke. My joints—particularly the elbows—ground out their movements like unoiled gears. My physical state was, in short, becoming a disaster. Pale, bald, skeletal. This, in contrast to my mind alive and intense, was maddening.

I would not die, could not, never would. I was preparing to send men and women and children on ships by the thousands, to let them bloom in the radiance of myriad suns; to double Earth's diameter and refuel its core, to monitor scouts too far to return: to immortalize mankind only moments after rescuing it from the gallows.

And, I? I was turning decrepit, learning to fear a scythe I had always assumed to deliberately pass me over. Pity me! Battling the reaper's jealous talons. No, it was one of a few lingering uncertainties I would not wait on. With every conceivable resource at hand, it is only natural that I sought a cure.

Only a similarly aged Harman would see me, and I was growing to despise him. Is it not amusing how even the wisest men can grow to despise someone they have trusted for years over a week or less? The *now* of hatred disconcatenates memories; hollows out eternity, and renders history nothing but the historian.

I did not have access to his thoughts, of course, but his years pilfering for files he no doubt thought existed in my various offices was evidence enough of his intentions. Strangely, I even saw him thumb through an old deck of playing cards in one of my desks, and steal the king of hearts. Though, as mentioned, I knew his end well.

What made me grind my teeth was my simple exposure to his growing bitterness. Whatever he had schemed through the years had melted acidly in his lap, and the new poisons he brewed gave off a fouler stench than I could bear. No matter. Our time was nearing its end as my collection of research stations was delivering results. A youth soon regained! Yes, my last selfishness. And yes, there was still need for a Harman, as there always would be, of course, but he himself I was close to disposing of.

This concerns the second of my grossly funded projects, of which he knew nothing, and which I operated through more clandestine and circuitous chains of command. Even as I spoke to him of the first and more important concern, machines were in his house collecting the residue of his slimy existence.

"The project," I reminded him, on the day I most sensed my pulse weakening, and determined that it was time. "It is finished. Make preparations for next month. I will not risk waiting any longer."

"Sir, as I've explained, they require more time. I've—"

I spun in my chair. "No. That's enough. You're a cautious man, Harman. I appreciate that. I've always appreciated it. But the truth is that I've already spoken to Taniguchi about it. I won't delay any longer."

He squirmed. His mouth and nose together made some revolting, molish little dance. "I have to ask, however," he said. "Have you told him anything?"

"Told him what?"

"About yourself. Your place in HORUS, the world, I mean. What does he think the project is for?"

"I have only ever spoken to him on your behalf, Harman. He knows nothing about me except that I am to be the subject of your charity. And he will only see me on the day."

Harman gave me his ratty glare and cuffed his hands. "And you're comfortable with him seeing you? You don't think they'll ask questions? Who would fund all of this for a single person? Why are efforts not being made to commercialize or militarize the technology?"

"Please. You know it better than I do. Scientists are like dogs. Clever dogs, certainly—intelligent. But, like dogs. Give them a bone to chew on and they'll chew on it obediently. They don't ask questions unless they're related exclusively to whatever mangy mastication is preoccupying them. All of their questions are about the bone, you see. It doesn't matter where the bone came from, or what once dressed it, or the effect it will have on their diet. All of their hopes and worries and ethics are contained in the bone. And besides," I continued, "you will make sure they are all exterminated once it is clear that there will be no complications following the procedure. It would be unfortunate for the technology to fall into any other hands. I want to preserve secrecy of my involvement with it, too, of course."

"Excuse me, sir?" The look on his face made me want to add him with haste to those before the proverbial firing squad.

"You heard me clearly."

He gave me a look of disgust and shook his head. He was not a man whose mind had ever been frequently occupied by moral thoughts, but even the most negligent have natural dispositions against certain extremes. I know, because, though you might think all my transgressions have come easily to me, the truth is that it required hard work and much courage to cross those lines.

But, unlike you, Harman was loath to admire me. "You'd have me murder them? Murder? After all the work they've done for you?" He stared off, and then looked at me with jealousy and gravity and spite. His own ugliness mingled with a sudden sense of justice. "I knew you were horrible inside, but this?" It was refreshing to at last hear him attack me this way, to cut through his decades-long obsequiousness and maneuvering and all the long-term returns he had expected they would net him. "Is it true what that accountant Pierre told me, all those years ago?" he continued. "Did you really do it? I didn't believe it. I didn't think—"

I looked at him with the eyes of death. "Harman, I'd watch your next words. You're a good friend, and I'd hate for this to come between us."

"Friends?" He looked left, and right, then coweringly returned his gaze to me. "I can't. I won't do it."

I sighed out of exhaustion and expected my next cue. "Then find someone else to. But make sure it is done."

"They are among the brightest minds in the world, what a waste to—"

"And those minds have been used to their fullest. Their purpose was paramount, and for no other, and now it is done. We will put these dogs to sleep."

～

I stepped out of the helicopter and was greeted by Dr. Taniguchi. He had dark bags under his eyes, and his lab coat was creased. Under the loud blades of the helicopter beating to a halt above us, I came jaw to jaw with him so that we could say hello. Harman leered at me as he exited the cabin. The wind blew. The two embraced each other like old friends. Friends soon in the grave, indeed.

We walked together across the roof to the entrance. I recognized, then, that it would most likely be the last time I would directly sense the outdoors. The sentiment was fleeting, and I followed Harman and Taniguchi into the building.

We stood together as the elevator made its subterranean descent.

"We completed our final tests this morning, sir. Everything is set to work beautifully," Taniguchi said.

"Good," Harman replied.

Taniguchi bantered about the technology as we sped down. "*Turritopsis dohrnii*. It was our starting point, you know, Dr. Harman? Fascinating creatures."

Harman nodded at his remarks, but darted his eyes around without paying much attention. I squinted at Harman. I felt his anger and reservations, his impotence to stop me, fill the elevator. His greed and ambition doubled by some new and false righteousness.

The elevator doors slid apart, and we came upon a dim laboratory lit crimson from below. I stepped out and leaned over the balcony railing. Rows of computers and servers lined the walls. Centered on a platform at the back of the room was a massive cylindrical tank bubbling vermillion liquid. Large tubes were drawing and pumping in the fluids from the top.

"Artificial immortality," Taniguchi whispered as he leaned over beside me. "Who would have dreamed?"

Four other boney creatures in lab coats milled about the tank, deep in concentration, typing or scribbling down last-minute notes. Their steps made quiet metallic echoes. Their hands strained around their pens or spidered over tablet surfaces.

"There's nothing artificial in this world," I said.

Harman tapped his feet behind us.

"Dr. Harman hasn't told us at all about you. I'm surprised it isn't him going in the tank. It's a privilege to be the first, you know. Could I ask your name, finally, sir?" Taniguchi continued.

"My name isn't important. Come, Harman," I said, making for the stairway to the left.

I stood before the tank and removed my clothes. The liquid was siphoning out of a drain at the bottom of the tank. I observed it until all that remained of it was a faintly coloured pool. Warping left and right along the glass was my crimson reflection. The reflection of a man no longer fit for his race.

There I stood, ready to deny myself all reprieve for the sake of those I hardly even considered my kind any longer. How many, indeed, would suffer the loneliness and torment of life unending? And for others? For birds, beasts or brutes? No, none would. And I could not expect it of anyone, yet. I was charged to preserve myself.

I stepped forward as the last of the liquid whirled out, and put a foot inside the chamber. But, before I could advance, a hand shot out to bar me from entering. "No, no. Not yet," the woman said.

Taniguchi advanced on us. "Has Dr. Harman explained the details of the procedure?"

"He hasn't," I said, glaring at Harman.

Taniguchi and the woman blocking my passage to Olympus shot each other looks.

"I see."

"What is it? Do I begin in another room?"

"No," Taniguchi said. "Everything takes place in the tank. It's just… that we have to explain. Before we begin. It's not simple, you understand."

"We have to remove most of your organs, first," his underling blurted coldly.

I twisted my neck back to look at both Taniguchi and Harman. Years ago, when I had first looked into Taniguchi's future and heard him say this, the blood had rushed to the roof of my head. Now, of course, I was simply going through the motions, pushing our conversation along as was its due course.

"Yes, of course," I said. "Is there another operating room?"

"No," Taniguchi said.

"Yes, you mentioned it all takes place inside."

"If you need a moment to… take a last look."

"No. Let's begin."

The woman removed her hand from my arm, and I walked inside.

I leaned against the back of the chamber and exhaled to calm my nerves, which were soon to be ripped out like weeds.

Taniguchi rounded the chamber and began typing into a console. "All sensation will be preserved and heightened, as planned. It was the hardest part, actually," he said, grinning over the glow of his screen. "If it wasn't for breakthroughs in—"

"I know," I interrupted.

His cheer faded and he continued to type. "We'll administer the anesthetic shortly and then—"

"No. No anesthetic."

Everyone in the room turned to me.

"Sir, if I may," Taniguchi protested, "It isn't possible to forgo anesthetic. The pain would be beyond unbearable."

"Will I be strapped down?"

"Yes, but—"

"Then there is no problem. Start whenever you're ready."

Taniguchi glared at Harman, who only shrugged and said, "It's as he wants."

Certainly, it would have made the little sadist happy to see me suffer.

The scientists shuffled around, trying to cope with the deviation in course.

"If you scream out for it, we will put you to sleep immediately. Though, I don't think you will be able to stay awake long through the pain. One final time, are you certain, sir?"

"Stop asking questions and begin."

Taniguchi nodded wearily and made for his console. The woman spun on her heels, buried her face back in her clipboard, and pulled a latch to seal the tank.

"Oh, and Harman," I said, my voice dampened behind the glass. "Make sure to collect the names of every person involved in making this possible. Make sure they are all recompensed as discussed." I paused and watched him pale. "I will see you."

The tank started flooding at my feet. I watched Taniguchi ask Harman in whispers about who I was, to which Harman said nothing.

The fluid rose. It looked almost clear from above, but glimmered vermillion. Rising, warm waters of the lost fountain; the ichor of mountains, skies, stars, and oceans. When it almost reached my torso, suddenly there came a hiss from above.

An oval plate with a tube coming out its back swung down and planted itself on my abdomen. I coughed, winded by the impact. Taniguchi and his band all cringed. A mask with similar hoses shot across the lower half of my face. My chest, legs, and hips were cased from both sides. Then, the liquid filled the tank.

I was riddled in needles, stuffed and stuck with tubes and hoses, pressed by plates. They pierced me all over, some thin as nettle hairs and others like Megalodon jaws. A ceremonial stabbing. Brutus and his blades, but loyal, divine. The hands, fingers of each deity welcoming me, lifting me up to join the pantheon. I wriggled in place and focused.

The plates pressed me together. Taniguchi, looking awful and gaunt behind the glow of his screen, nodded at an assistant and started typing again. The machinery started to spin. The blades beneath the plates began shrieking, shredding away my insides. Slicing, grinding away skin and bone and muscle like rotors over my soggy flesh. There was immense suction, too. Out flew my intestines, my liver, my kidneys; all the cords and capillaries ripped, replaced by chips and wires. Pumping, pumping out the viscera. My spine curled out, the cord merging with wires above; the vertebrae coming apart, dissolving like corroded dice, flowing into the mire of my once-lower half.

I was beginning to feel tremendously light. And the pain was exquisite. I could have focused on one of infinite other sensations running through me, could have listened through Harman's ears, or tasted Taniguchi's dry mouth. Could have preferred sunsets over the faces of worried scientists soon to be dead. No, I was enjoying the signals, however gruesome or agonizing, of my total apotheosis. And each of my senses remained and expanded, as instructed, in some form or shape, and pulsed more acutely, then, when pulled and raw.

But, no! What to perceive was not a matter of preference. Such was my special skill, to witness both and all in equal intensity. Taniguchi typed; Harman twisted as though seasick. The tank was filling red and full of globules. We watched each other as my body convulsed and was pulled inside out. And they were dying, yes. I replaced them with their deaths.

The voices, for the first time in years, were singing along: pirouetting, circling, jeering vultures over the corpses of Taniguchi and Harman, and that woman, and the others beside them. They would all be stricken from history within the month.

Taniguchi, his brains dripping out as he sat hunched in the bathtub, the water still warm. My mind, meanwhile, freed of weights, rising to meet my brothers in the air, water, and blazing wood! The woman, gagged over her desk. I would never again need breath. Arms and arteries, legs, ligaments, gone, gooey, sacrificed! The heart, also sanctified: obliterated, that I might be surrounded in plasma, in blood, in every sympathy confined therein.

Ah, and Harman! Dear, sweet, covetous Harman. The picture must come clear, finally. He would stand beside the tank in the weeks to come and tell of our welded ambitions. He would speak like a madman plotting treason, I could tell. To kill me, drain me, cast me down from my tower, my mountain, and take my place, those were his ambitions!

He deserved it, after all. He had done all the work, after all. He would wait to see if ever-living could be for him as well. I grant half his wish.

Years on, he would still bide his time. He would come and go, seek my orders while struggling to effectively grasp the global structures turning galactic that were, especially by then, too complex for his inferior mind. I would have him disposed of—poisoned quietly in his sleep—before he could act on any malice, or even utter a malediction. And out of strands of hair and scraps of skin, his brothers, Harman the Second, the Third, *ad astra*, would wake from their sleep, one at a time, never exceeding their purpose, and serve me in turn.

And so what, indeed, do we say to our enlightened Mephisto? We can say nothing to him. He soars on his demon firebird wings too far above what cries of awe should follow him up; up he flies, untethered, breaching the world's blue and cloudy warp and woof; so, too, sundering mother night and her ancient rank; up, the uplifted one, to keep both flame and heaven. He wraps himself in an astral shroud and waits. He sits atop the pillars of creation and waits.

❧ 51 ❧

THE GHOST SHIP

The ship skipped through space towards Arcturus like a pebble ricocheting across the surface of a lake. It fled through wastes of the universe, through parts untouched and unwanted by men spoiled, like all men, like all consciousness. The emptiness watched for all time by giants and dwarves doomed and fixed together.

Tikan woke in the cockpit. His head rocked like a vase against the floor. Fragile and fleshy. His cheeks icy and stiff. He rose, groaning, and shambled out, pausing at the threshold while gripping the doorjamb. Before him were corridors gushing cold oxygen and resounding his every errant or clumsy movement.

Days passed, and then weeks. The ship labored on, needling creased folds of space-time and arrowing straight upstream in the dark space pouring unfettered around it and spread abloom like the petals of a bellflower. A lone fugitive of a ship. A last pin stuck in the hinge, a mere breath pushing against the galaxy's imminent collapse.

Tikan spent days gliding forlornly about the place, as though in reverie built of limbo, as though in the only true vacuum preserved against time outside.

Out of skirmish to tabula rasa, he tried for hours to order his contemplations at a round table in the main hold. He sat with both feet edging the seat of a chair, pinching the angles of his obelisk arm with the fingers of his remaining hand. Perched high on a cliff and immovable against storms like a fakeer on his last and only pilgrimage.

He ran through memories that shuffled together and he envisioned colors he would never again see. From these he eked out jagged timelines that flew too freely from their particulars. Then, he rose. He made rounds between the cockpit and the observation deck. Round the port and starboard sides, through two corridors like arteries around the main hold.

The walls were uneven: a mesh of dissimilar plating. Dull old metal withstanding rust that would never invade, gaps in the slate hide revealing ugly veins. Disjointed surfaces, each like stone: slices of a megalith, antediluvian, unwashed and humming like monks trapped in monotone. Each piece of the corridor grafted together but incapable of masking the rumble of tubes and wiring beneath. At shin level, exposed pistons puffed subdued breaths.

He traced his hand along the tingling calluses of the ship until the heated blue lights of monitors he could not see interrupted his hand's streak. Beneath him, the flooring was little but a flimsy grille that clacked under each of his steps, as if it were about to slam open and drop him atop impaling pipes haunted with smoke then slick with blood relieved from an instant corpse.

He was arrested by vacant steel in each room he braved off the ship's arteries. Standing no closer than the thresholds while making his lonesome racket, he perceived sleeping pods never unsealed, hollow desks and closets. Silence, and yet loneliness howled through him in a language still alien even after his years exposed to its whispers. These deserted quarters could and surely did once hold spirits like worlds crackling and deep. No trace, now. He imagined these previous inhabitants to have quietly sighed and melted into the walls, limp as ghosts.

Far away, farther by the day, planets were closing in on the same fate. The buzz of civilized society was waning, and the state of nature extinct at conception. Streets and parks pristine for none, each planet's sun selfishly brilliant and anchoring a sky with no day. Words attached only to mild fluctuations in mood, little more than sighs at nothing in particular. The end of an exhausted discussion too late to be had. The old edifices of humankind long stripped of pride, but now toppling, on the verge of collapse over a ground and a galaxy being razed to deafness.

The silencing echo of it reached him even there, in his asylum slipping all the bonds of conquered space. He felt it more acutely the farther his vessel travelled. It was as if all the shadows of the world were chasing his ship like a wildfire, and he alone were charged with defeating it. But a defeated shadow only splits to finer darkness, and the malignant children seep through less familiar cracks. There on his perch, focused on the graying of the clouds, he forgot the bite of waves feral and rising over the cliffs.

Weeks on, and he stalked the ship's narrow interiors like a crippled Minotaur. He would wake after inconsistent hours of sleep, brow sticky with the water of nightmares, and clear his throat of a hoarse echo. The waking hours were opportunities to embody his suffering, all inherited suffering. He would haunt the corridors, feet dragging and shoulder boring into the wall. And with his aimless roving came the gloomy chink of his spike, loud and chilling, a prisoner's chains dragged over the stone of an ocean fort.

Head panging above an empty stomach contracting like a tangle of serpents, he hauled himself groaning to the galley in the hopes of nourishing his spirit. Once a day, there, he would crumble over the nearest counter and force-feed himself whatever the food printer produced.

The rest of his treks were without definite reason. He abandoned the use of his obelisk once his paths became habit. He groped at darkness, searching for a bottom and finding only matter.

The sleeping pod could have eased his entire trip, made it last as long as a dream. But the mere idea was repugnant to him. There was restlessness simmering in his bones, which he was anxious to unleash on his hidden foe—if it existed. Yet his despondent mood routinely sapped him of his spirit. He was ripped from all others, cased in ancient and frigid metal, with horrors on both ends of his life and the bruise on his soul magnified. It regularly led him to the observation deck. There he lulled and shivered and tapped his grief into space, aching for Sielle.

Stars glowered at him through the window. They would collapse every few days or so and reanimate as the ship threaded to Arcturus. He sat there, facing bands of pinprick lights that he could never reach, and the questions would work in his head.

Onasus was gone: dead or scheming. Which was worse, he could not decide. Without Sielle, without Naim and Mira, even, his journey seemed without purpose. Perhaps he was selfish, as she had said. Fantasizing his impending final struggle and triumph, he began to entertain a darker ending to the one he had pinned so feverishly atop the quest.

The scenes took on dire colors in his mind. The station orbiting Arcturus would not be some right-angled and unremarkable outpost, but a black citadel ringed by asymmetrical and gothic arms raking out at space. Shadows with no source would shuffle to cloak every swipe and spin a menacing patrol around its sun, each rotation the unmasking of a hideous visage violating all codes of beauty. The orange sun would flare against the obsidian slabs and drape them like streamers.

Tikan's ship would arrive limping and pathetic under the drizzle and shade of a faint geomagnetic storm. The creak of old metal, the screech of docking, and silence.

He would not disembark immediately. He would let the eeriness infest the ship, then let it escort him into the dread palace. There would come the feeling of total exposure, that nowhere was any longer safe. He would alight, and his steps would be reluctant through the arching threshold too gaping and sinister to face with courage. He would drift feebly across, clutching the fate of humankind under cloak and shaking hand. Thoughts of retreat would arrive too late.

Electric currents would crack purple and dive for the fortresses' capacitors. One bolt would burst through his ship's engine room and send it in molten parts to oblivion.

The hallways would be cavernous and obscure. His only opponent would be his own creeping madness, as hours would turn to days in the search for a central command. He would pass rooms wriggling with live shadows. The ghost of light would make doomed gasps for air between electric bursts. Reaching, still, for a bottom. Magma would smolder and churn and burst between lightless rooms, and finally be emptied out of trays and portals unseen for designs beyond reckoning. Only Onasus' cursed gift would keep him from compassing. But, days on, he would fall into corners as even the causal blueprint, that straight and true arrow, would begin to pulse crooked.

Eventually, the oxygen in his suit would dwindle. With his breathing restrained, he would arrive at the dungeon's heart. The core beating in a carcass still circuiting blood. There would be a console at the end of a long walkway in a single cleft of light. The end of the cosmic stage. Ahead, gloomy and angelically lit, winged by darkness, the culmination of man and machine would writhe on itself and chew on lingering bits of human consciousness and dignity.

He would approach. He would barely step into the haunted vale. Wires would shoot for his silver eyes out of the podium before him, and he would merge with the titan. There would be a struggle for the creature's mind. Tikan's will would prevail, and he would lose himself, and the black tombstone that had marked man's temporary death would crash into the guardian fires of Arcturus.

But what, then? He would be gone and glorious, but man would wake. Now, as his vision neared concretion by the day, the doubt bloomed in him.

Mankind would be injected with life anew, yes, and the freedom to be responsible. Responsibility, aligned with justice, and peace, and heroism, and greatness: a jeweled row of trophy ideals. And that ideal world he hankered for, when dragged down from its lofty and pristine realm, seemed only bound to accrue corrosions from all the filth that lingered even in the air, stacked up against the barrier to the world of forms, rushing for the break in the clouds; and finally the ideals would descend, corrupt and malformed and imperfect like all things.

Perhaps, then, humanity would degenerate, and bloodlust would bubble again, and new warmongers would breed, and greed and poverty would work again to dissolve societies. It seemed, in such a case, that his efforts would do nothing but tip the scale in the opposite direction; roll back history's counter to iron, famine, mayhem, and the eventual carousel back to necessary sedation. Had people not been born free to begin with? Had they not all walked freely into chains? Their fate suddenly seemed deserved.

He feared Onasus' arachnid words now creeping into his head. But it was a relief to be able to condemn the abstract whole, just as he had always done to ward off misanthropy. The abstract whole was a fine mannequin on which to pin the amassed faults of humanity. It was mute, and bloodless, and without mind.

The individual, resurrected out of the leviathan's body, was a whole in himself worth worlds, too sinewed and particular for the conceptual sieve. To reach for good, for greatness, conceivably through the crucible of some suffering; this, humanity could do. Humanity: the loveless whole made of impassioned parts.

The misuse of freedom mattered little to him now. It was worth immolating himself in Arcturus' cleansing flames for the one responsible human being.

~

Weeks passed. The fantasy differed slightly, depending on the day and the grimness of his mood. Ever by the window and before a refreshed audience of suns, he continued to oscillate between doubt and bravery when the consequences routinely demanded his thoughts.

It was long into the journey, when time coiled looser and the emptiness of the ship weighed on him more severely, that he heard footsteps echo through the corridors.

He was too maudlin to act alarmed. Instead, he let his mind swim back to the particulars, and he rose. He pecked the floor with his obelisk. The blueprint arrived mangled in places, just as he had envisioned it would on Arcturus. His heart began throbbing. The footsteps turned to clangs. Another light click against the floor.

An impossible shape was cut out in the blueprint, a moving void impressed on causality. It was obscure, and difficult to process. It was an utterly foreign sensation, as though it were suddenly possible to see gamma rays or hear infrasound.

He pressed himself against the wall beside the entrance. The steps were clanging to crescendo. He shook his head and tapped the obelisk with his hand, as though it were malfunctioning. The whole ship was ringing through the corridor. Sweat streamed down his face. He dared touch his obelisk to the steel, and gasped.

The negative shape in the blueprint sharpened, and she entered the observation deck.

"Tikan?" she said.

He sighed, and sank against the wall.

"Yes. I'm here," he replied, calm and resigned, his voice hoarse after weeks of disuse. "I'm here. You aren't, I know."

She turned to her left and found him crumpled beside her. His head was bent down against the slate floor and his thigh obscured his obelisk.

"I am here. I've returned. Can't you see me?"

"Of course you would say that, ask that. Those are words I've been suffering to hear for weeks. Of course that's what you'd say."

Sielle stepped in front of him. His new limb cast a long, thin shadow. His head still hung over the ground.

"What's that on your arm?"

He gave an unhinged laugh. "Didn't you know? I must have forgotten to tell you," he said, and looked up to reveal the silver crescents lodged in his sockets.

Sielle stepped back and grimaced. "What's happened to you?"

He forced a laugh. "Why are you here? Come as a last torment? Please, it's difficult enough. I know you're somewhere far, probably under the madman's knife."

She kneeled down beside him and thumbed his forehead up. He

did nothing to resist, and he reveled in her touch like it was a temptation to which he had long known he would succumb. "Onasus, he did this to you?"

"Please leave now, spirit. I can't bear to hear you even say his name."

"I'm no spirit. I'm here, me. I've returned."

"No," he said. "That's not possible. How could it? Just keep your eyes off me. I beg you. Even your ghost must not witness me."

"I—"

"You'll say you hid in the engine room, or something like that. He would have found you. It's just not possible. It's a trick I'm playing on myself."

He stood and shook her off and banged his spike against the wall. She was there, full and breathing and imposing in front of him. Nothing escaped her, and nothing entered her. She was an opaque block, an unmoved mover around which waves broke. And her skin was looser and creasing, and there were streaks of silver in her hair.

Sielle turned to peer out the window. In the distance, Arcturus appeared as a red pupil ringed by the iris of a sapphire nebula. She contemplated the stars for a moment, and then faced him again. "It doesn't matter. I've seen the end. That's why I've come. I've watched your nightmares, lived them. I—"

"That's enough," he said. "You come to me now, patient and prophetic and drained of youth like you're expecting death. You won't die. I won't let you die." He pushed himself up against the wall as though expecting the void behind to take him in its arms. "Don't taunt me like this, mocking hope with decay. Its just doubt, that's all you are. So much doubt that's spilled from me." He swung around and, in a moment of sudden delirium, began knocking his forehead into the wall and smothering his face against it.

Sielle observed him, squinting with pity and mild disdain. He was not as she remembered him. "Stop that," she said, lurching out and pulling him back towards her. She gripped him by the shoulders and fixed her eyes on him. "Stop it and listen. I'm no illusion."

He knocked the wall again with his arm, and his hysteria began to clear.

"And I'm old, and tired, and it's taken me longer than you can imagine to return here. So stop it."

"I—No. I don't understand. I can't," he said meekly, reduced to a pitiable doll in her hands.

"Only listen. I've come to explain."

They sat in the main hold, not quite opposite each other at the round table. Their reunion, as Tikan grew to accept it, did not hold the immediate warmth he had envisioned. There was something in the way she intoned her speech, and in the solidity of her movements. She no longer walked furtively, or shuffled to and fro in a roguish way as she had during their time together, which now seemed like centuries earlier. Now, she commanded the space around her with her mere gait. Even perceiving her as a living shade, he felt the entire room, ship, and universe conform around her like a vortex around a stabwound in the tight fabric of existence.

He spoke first and told her all that had taken place on Proxima after her disappearance, as well as whatever he had omitted during their last meeting. She only struck a hand through her hair when he described Onasus' obsession with her. Afterward, he listened to her explain herself while holding his face in her hand.

Sideways temporal leaps, void shifts between empty time and live time in parallel, a lifetime like a train through pastiched ages. He exhaled through his nose as she spoke, and curled his toes. She spoke to him of Sirius, her brief glimpse of it, thinking it would resurrect their mood to some kind of triumph, but it only dampened their spirits further. Then she spoke of the world she saw consumed by the sun, of tombstones infested with life.

Tikan rubbed his temple and softly placed his obelisk on the table, pointing it towards her. "How many years did you lose?"

"Centuries," she said.

He cleared his throat.

"No, that's just how long I was kept there. I didn't age at the same rate, so I don't know. Maybe twenty or thirty, for me. I look about forty-five, I think."

He said nothing at first, and she stared off.

"You're human," Tikan said, forgetting questions of her age now. "But your life. All the ages you've lived through. The way you described losing and regaining your body each time you travel, in that darkness. You're...different than us."

"I thought that was obvious."

"Why do you feel to me so familiar, then?" he asked in a small voice, his thoughts hovering back to questions of her being, ignoring the rest of what she had said.

"What do you mean?"

"I mean, you've aged, and your body is human, and you have memories that come and corrode. You have dreams that you forget, like me, I'm sure. But how can you, if time doesn't hold you?"

She exhaled the frustration mounting in her. "It does. It does hold me, Tikan. You don't understand what it's like."

"Tell me. Describe it to me."

"Timeless, but living in time," she said cautiously. "Like you."

"Yes, that's a nice way to say it. But I still don't understand."

"That's because you can't talk about a timeless thing in terms of time." She shook her head, dismissing her own thought. "What I'm trying to say is that I can't control time. I decay from moment to moment, just like you. And I have a separate clock ticking more wildly in me, just like you. Are you just a part of yourself, or the whole thing?"

"The whole, of course. The whole missing some parts," he said, his the area just under his eyes.

"Not those sorts of parts," Sielle said. "I mean *you*, all of you. Not your vision now, or your hearing now, or your thinking now. Not just a page of a book being flipped, but the whole tome; not half a bicycle through the doorway, but both wheels and the frame, halved across rooms. Does the eternal Tikan exist, somewhere?"

"No. I'm not immortal."

"You're not understanding."

"Help me understand."

"I'm trying. Stop thinking about your lost eyes and betrayal and it might go through. It's difficult enough for me to describe."

"Okay," he said, pausing. "I see how we're alike. God, I see it. But I don't understand the difference."

"I don't know," she said, looking down in defeat. "For the longest time I looked at you all across a cold gulf. Like you were just curious animals or machines. I've lived memories the universe is too young to have, though I was young. I thought I was free. Now look at this lined skin, these silver hairs. We're more alike than I thought. We're both cakes of ash scattering, just in two different streams of wind."

He did not respond immediately.

"You don't look convinced," she said.

"I just don't understand."

"Well, I'm sorry. The truth is I don't know. And I don't care, okay?"

"You don't care?"

"I don't care where I came from or why or how I am the way I am. There's no one I could go to and ask. There's nowhere that's ever made it clear."

He shook his head. "But you cut across the ages! You've seen prehistory on Earth, and history, and the moon and Proxima and even Andromeda. How?"

"Stop asking me. Please stop asking me."

He faced her with his sightlessness, reaching out and searching for freedom behind a mere locus. To peek behind the curtain, peel back the layer and confirm his beliefs. It did not matter. It was too late for that, now. He would never know. And freedom's face was more elusive than illusive, and it was better to believe.

He squirmed in his seat and dropped his forehead into his hand again. His face emerged, the silver blindness catching a glimmer, and his voice rose and took on divinatory tones. "I see it. I'm trying to see it, keep it clear and full. I know that we should be terrified of you."

"What?"

"It's not that you're something else," he said, "but that you're the best of us. Everything we ought to be. Beings who know the past as it knew itself. Who can touch the future before it touches us. You terrify me, but only because I wish I could grasp you, really grasp you. I would hand in Earth to preserve you. Sublime. The sublime. That's why time won't harm you."

"Stop it. Just stop it. I don't care about any of that, and if I did I'd go mad." She paused, and looked back at him. "And as for time... Time has done more to me than you can imagine."

He stayed silent a moment. "I'm sorry. It—It's easy to lose perspective. I just want to know you."

"Listen," she said. "You ask me if I'm human. When I was with Zotharra, I came so close to losing myself. This solar system of a creature, so far beyond what I or anyone else could ever conceive of, she wanted me to merge with her. To really be her, because she thought that was love. I can't say I wasn't tempted. I felt so fragile and awestruck, as if I'd arrived not just at the end of my life, but at the end of time and the universe. But when I looked into that little galaxy in her heart, it did something to me. I couldn't move or say anything. It put me before the infinity of the world: you and me and an infinity between us. I chose not to become Zotharra exactly because there was one living, worthwhile mystery left to me in the universe. One thing I could still find it in myself to love."

He faced her, as if he were looking right at her. "I won't tell you anything about me again, then. Nothing."

"Don't be stupid. I'm being serious."

"So am I. From now on, I am a giant lockbox." He grinned at her weakly. If the mood were less dour, she might have smiled back. "I didn't think I'd ever see you again," he said finally. "I thought Onasus had got to you, or something. I thought—I thought I'd finish on Arcturus, and then I wanted to die. The only thing I wanted more than to die was to see you again, and damnit, I'll never see you again—but you're here."

"I am," she said.

"And about the future. The weeks here alone, I didn't know. I was fighting to stay sure of what I was doing. That awful planet you saw.

Those things. The broken fingers and the people. Forgetting themselves, forgetting all purpose and meaning, far from Earth, I—"

"—but it was Ea—"

"—I needed to know. I needed you, most of all, to tell me I was right." He rose and marched towards her, then faced her.

She chose not to correct him. She saw the hope straining around his ruined, silver sockets, and decided it would be too much for one conversation.

"We're going to go to Arcturus," she said. "We're going to put a stop to whatever hell is brewing there, but that's just because I saw it, you understand? I saw it and I'd be a liar if I said it didn't make me sick. But that's the last time I'll do a thing for humankind. You hear me? After that, it's you and me. Sirius, or wherever. I don't care."

"You and me," he said. "That's all."

~

In the following weeks, they spoke little about Arcturus. Sielle moved into one of the ship's numerous rooms, though she did little other than sleep there. They ate together, and Tikan took to eating full and multiple meals. At first they were apprehensive, and acutely sensitive to each other's movements. Yet, after a few braved words they found themselves at ease. The ship transformed into a sanctuary. They traded stories more personal and affecting. They spoke of what there was of childhood.

Over the days, she watched him move around with his ugly tool. There he finally found a place for his reach, although he could not help himself from rattling the obelisk so that he could keep her in his perception. There was time for laughter on occasion, too. One evening she had him laughing with her by tripping him after having offered to help him walk around without the awful thing. Their humor became common, though both of them often slunk back to a pensive gloom afterward.

The trip wore on. She told him of ages he had always longed to live in, that she had lived in; of poets and warriors all dead like their work, of cities collapsed with their people. Their conversations would go on as long as whole days. Though, she varied in her mood, and was at times resigned, for she was still mourning the loss of her youth.

He was able to lie in his bed and sleep comfortably after her arrival. Before falling asleep, he would probe the ship with his thoughts in search of her. There, somewhere in the near distance of otherwise cavernous steel that he could no longer imagine dwelling in alone, was the warmth and softness of another body, alive and full of blood. He would wake with the intensity of complex dreams whose interpretations always escaped him.

"Do you remember what I told you in the Bilge that night, when you'd had a bad dream?" he asked her one afternoon.

"You said you were there for me."

"I said I was there and you said I couldn't be. I think I understand what you meant, now."

She nodded, and then said, "Yes," when she remembered he could not see her.

"You've lost a lot of people. I mean really lost them, haven't you?"

"Like losing drops in an ocean."

He inhaled. "Then how did you find me again?"

"I don't know. I couldn't at first. I tried with all my soul."

"I'm here."

"I know," she said, just as her voice crumbled, and she embraced him. "I know you are."

The following night he woke to the sound of her unlatching the door to his room. He imagined her standing at the threshold with an elongated shadow reaching out to him. As a concretion of his longings these last nights.

His heart began bursting, and the blood heated his face. As her steps clattered to him and he heard her clothes pool to the floor, he tried to remold her face from the vague blur that remained of it in his memory, until she and her shadow merged into one vibrancy, one being present in the utter void surrounding her. As if the world were the void, and she the only matter in it.

"I'm blind," he murmured, lifting his clunky obelisk of an arm in some naïve confession of inadequacy. "I—"

She reached over to him and placed a hand on his mouth. "I don't care." She slid into the covers to envelop him, and so too did she slide into a corrupt idealism of her own, as she shut her eyes against his ruined body and hers.

As the trip wore on, their affection for each other renewed and matured. They sought each other at first light of consciousness from across their bed, and often said little or nothing. The mere sound of the other's light breathing was enough. And the galaxy of humankind started to slip from prominence in their minds. Days passed without a thought about the subject, and when they did remember their quest, it appeared pathetic beside the ease and pleasure of their companionship.

They often spent their time on the observation deck. One evening, they lounged there as Andromeda flared in the distance. Sielle felt a pang of guilt or sadness as it flickered out of sight.

"What is it like?" she asked him.

"What?"

"This," she said, lifting up his obelisk.

"Close your eyes."

"Okay."

Then he kissed her neck. "What did you feel?"

She laughed it off. "Come on, explain it."

"I'm explaining it. What did you feel?"

"Your lips."

"Is that all?"

She touched her neck. "No. I felt you."

"And?"

"Oh, just explain it."

He smirked to himself. "I can't."

"Then don't. I don't care," she said, and chucked his obelisk away with some amusement. "Ugly thing."

She returned to watching the stars, and neither of them said anything for a while.

"You are there, aren't you?" she said to him.

"I'm here."

"Tell me you won't betray me."

"Never. How could I?"

She paused and looked for a point in the infinity of space. "Whatever happens there, when we reach Arcturus. I'm with you. I just want to know you remember who I am. Me. Me over humanity."

"You're the world to me."

"I don't want to be the world. That's what I'm talking about."

"You know what I mean," he said, wrapping his arm around her.

She frowned and eyed him. "I think I do."

A month passed in this fashion. They all but forgot their quest and returned to speaking of Sirius, or even of remaining on their barren ship forever. They were shadows colliding into brilliance, and they made promises to each other as if they were immortals, without thought as to what might test them.

It was not until Sielle noticed the bright and bloated orange star of Arcturus flickering outside, which was in view again, bigger by the day, that they left their flourishing bond for the world again.

They sat in the observation deck, and she described Arcturus' metamorphoses to him. The bulging of radiant dust and the whitening of space. It devoured more of the blackness around it after every skip.

"It's like the sun, Earth's sun, when it looks to eat the morning and the dusk. Enormous, and challenging the universe," she said. "But it's lopsided, and greedy."

He sat and held her wrist, head angled towards the window as though he could see. "I can sense the rays against the hull. We're in its orbit, now. Must have entered it yesterday."

"Isn't this too close?" she asked. "I'm surprised I can still look at it."

"We'll burn before it gets too bright to see. Only a sliver of the light comes through the window."

"I don't want to burn. You should check how close we are."

"I can't," he said. "The ship's on an automatic path. I only started it."

"Then we must be only moments from arriving. I can't imagine an outpost much closer than this."

Tikan did not reply, but tightened his grip on her wrist.

Another hour passed, and still Arcturus swelled in the window, until the view was nothing but harsh whiteness.

"It isn't normal," Sielle said.

Tikan waited and tried to find an answer. "Nothing about this is normal. Least of all you," he said, trying feebly for some humor.

"It's not the time."

"You're right. I don't—"

They jumped. A shrill droning started through the ship. The sound was lurid and blunt, almost toneless.

"What's that?" she said, rising and turning.

"I don't know."

The window was full of white fire, but cold air still spilled from the vents. They started huffing. Sielle's eyes raced around. "The cockpit. Come."

He jumped to follow her and banged his obelisk, almost tripping to the door with her. It shut hard before they could exit.

"The ship," he tried to call over the noise of the alarm. "It's too bright. Too hot outside. There's a mistake. I—"

"No, no, that's wrong. It's cold. Don't you feel it?"

He said nothing. He regained his balance and then stumbled towards the window. "How bright?"

"I can't look at it," she said, burying her eyes in the crook of her arm.

"It's okay," he said. "The shields. The hull can take it. It'll hold together over five hundred percent. We'll leap, now. Has to happen. It's just an accident."

"No, something's wrong. It's cold. Bright in the sun's heart and cold."

He stopped speaking and took her hand in his.

"My eyes!" she called, turning to him and driving her face into his shoulder. Her voice boomed sharp around them.

He held her, half bracing her shoulders and reluctant to embrace her fully as his lips made paroxysms. "Go!"

"What?" Her voice came out muffled and slobbering against his chest.

"Leave. Do it."

"No, I won't go."

"Then come back. Come to me sooner, warn me."

"I can't revisit myself, you fool."

"Then leave! Save yourself," he cried, shaking her, careful not to expose her to the blinding light.

"No. I said I wouldn't go. You said you were there. You said it. I won't leave again. Never."

They collapsed together and cowered.

"Please," he sobbed. "Please, I need you."

"I won't." She held him tightly, and he felt tears and mucus smear his clothes. They sat together in a misshapen pile, freezing in the sun's white fire.

"Oh God, it's so cold."

They wept together. They abandoned themselves and their quest and the hope for anything other than each other. Outside, Arcturus grew furious and impatient. They waited before its rage and the ship's monotonous cry. They held each other as though they willed to merge together in their final breaths before the anger of the universe.

They held. They held, until the whining around them ceased abruptly. The alarm released them, though its ghost sang, and the utter silence seemed for a moment the intoxicating lull before the sun's final strike.

They waited. Sielle gasped, and they held each other tighter. They waited, terrified, for the window to melt or burst and obliterate them against inferno and space. Still, they lingered, until an inordinate amount of time passed.

Sielle started to her feet. She swung her head around and pressed herself against the window. Tikan fell backward with his arms to his side, expression hollow and body wilted.

"Look," she said, her voice quivering.

He only barely rose to his feet and joined her while brushing his obelisk against his thigh. "The brightness," he murmured.

"Where is the sun?"

There through the window now cleansed, they saw perfect shapes hanging together and the surface of a structure coming clearer as the ship's beams struck starless space around them.

It was not a black fortress, or a meager outpost. It was hoary and eluded recognizable angles. It was ancient and alien and glossed, but only possibly carved by the imperial hand of man. It imposed itself, swallowing up what space was left around it, larger in the faint and solitary lights of the ship. There, dense as a condensed star, its contours silver ash and slick, it occupied its usurped throne within the corpse of Arcturus.

And the ship continued towards it, slow and knowing. Tikan's obelisk banged the bottom of the window as the structure approached. They watched as the surface, smooth as liquid, slid open a passage in its silvery side. They heard the scraping of the ship as it began docking. They held each other again and listened and watched, transfixed.

They were mine.

ARCTURUS AND THE DEATH OF
TIME AND SPACE

They alight from the ship with their hearts rebelling in their cages. Sielle squints hard and shields her face from the light. They come off the last step of the ship with vapor hissing a curse behind them. She dares a peek above the ridge of her forearm. Her irises contract against the hangar's lights and then they dilate, as she dizzies and struggles to process what her senses are cobbling together.

There are rows of lights along the ceiling glaring into focus. Somewhere beside her, Tikan is wandering, stumbling over white marble floor. She walks to him and catches his hand in hers.

There are no other ships. Ahead, there is only an ongoing corridor extending directly from the hangar. They walk forward. Their tongues come off the roofs of their mouths like old bandages.

"I don't understand," Tikan murmurs. "Why is it so well lit?"

Sielle says nothing. She lets go of his hand and pauses every so often as they make their way across, reeling and wide-eyed.

Their footsteps echo down the long gauntlet off the floor, which is polished almost to a mirror. The ceiling is ribbed at the corners by wood arches that fade in the center. They pass through rows of opposing black marble pillars cracking to white. And as they walk, the floor seems to swell beneath them at certain thresholds, as though a compacted lump were making circuits between their origin and destination.

"I don't understand," Tikan repeats. He is shivering. His obelisk rattles silently against his thigh as he leans nearer Sielle.

The long walk saps what little strength they have brought with them. And they continue to tumble and fall into each other when that momentous subterranean tide passes them. They try, yet, to comprehend this hall of simple elegance in the dead of space.

They scan for entrances along the corridor. There is nothing but the long walk. No winding tunnels. No dark rooms lit by canyons of servers. No shadows, no wild electric currents, no labyrinth, no violet lightning screeching through bulbous rings of night-soaked clouds and trails of whiter billows. It is quiet. The aesthetic is that of a grand hotel lobby.

They land their weight against the walls where gaps between the pillars seem to indicate passages, and they rub their hands over the marble like archaeologists searching for the hidden depths of a ruin, certain of deception, and mesmerized. It becomes clear, soon enough, that they have only to walk onward.

"I feel there's something terribly wrong," Sielle says, casting a slow and wide gaze around herself.

"No, no," he says. "It isn't supposed to be like this."

For some time, it seems as though the corridor will not end. The pillars and the lights run on until, at the end, they appear to quit their separate fencing and merge together in parallax as some blinding entity. Tikan's arm is stiff and locked on his thigh. He is careful to limit the chorus of echoes haunting them as they make their way forward.

They near the end of the corridor and find red light stretching out past the threshold to a new zone. Already they are taking apprehensive breaths. Sielle averts her eyes, and Tikan slows that incessant rhythm along his leg. It takes much courage to brave what waits behind the veil. Much courage to keep solidly walking into that square, red-rimmed blackness.

"Where are we going?" she asks, finding in herself the faint hope of seeing him turn for the ship.

"The minds."

Her eyes make arcs along the ceiling and the walls as though they and their ornamentations are in conspiracy against her.

"They're not here. This place is wrong."

The corridor's end is nearing. There is a gilded frame indicating the next hall. There is more. There are answers. He stumbles left and right and searches for her face in memories stolen by the dreams that built them.

"Over there," he says, and walks ahead, knowing her caution is true.

The walls turn ivory under lucent sheets of ruby light. Sielle speeds up to match Tikan's stride. She keeps a small distance from him, and her eyes shift from him to the thawing glare ahead. Whatever awful thing waits for them has been patient, she is aware. Her shoulders buzz and stiffen in their sockets, and her steps are hurried as a fugitive's.

He stops, and beads of sweat begin escaping his brow.

"What?" she asks.

"There's something there."

Her spine straightens into a column of ice. She turns her head towards the redness, looks out and squints. "What is it?"

Their echoes cease. He steels himself and risks a number of steps. "I don't know. Someone, I think."

Their muscles are contracted, and they are both barely controlling their trembling. In them is not sufficient courage yet, though Tikan insists they cross over. They walk on, into the flood of ruby light and the new hall beyond it. Sielle's lungs heave. She shields her eyes again. The glare washes over them like a wave and submerges them a moment before passing on and leaving them in regular dimness. The hall comes clearer.

There is a narrow open court before them. The floor is a pattern of empty rectangles contained within each other. As they advance, taking a few steps in, boxed into the rectangles within rectangles, Sielle's face widens. History returns from the grave to greet her.

Arranged at the flanks of the court are artifacts of a world that exists only in dust. Enormous columns aligned in a matrix without foreseeable end, their trunks plated in fading gold. Though they are carved in the fashion of oracular temples, their bodies are glittering crimson, diluted by the faintest pink. Not solid crystal slabs, but pylons of blood, trapped and sluggish.

The lower network of columns is sparse, but above it are denser, shorter stacks that loom over them, serving as the stalking galleries of shades that have ascended from the grottos and crypts of buried empires to a sanctum never before permitted them. The blood appears to be dripping like molasses from these darkened rafters.

And staring them head-on, atop pyramidal steps and a dais, cleared of pillars and marble and stone, stark, is a cylindrical tank the size of Zeus at Olympia jutting out of the far end of the court. It rises near to the ceiling, and inside it a thick vermillion liquid churns.

In marvel and trance they are drawn nearer. They only manage a few steps before they are interrupted.

"Do you hear it?" Sielle asks through nervous attempts at regulating her breath.

Somewhere they hear the grunts of a person gagged and straining, though they are unable to locate the sound.

"I hear it. I'm trying to find it."

He speeds the obelisk. He rotates his head, trying to listen, too.

They ease into the court. They creep towards the enormous vial swirling its contents. It casts kaleidoscopic shapes across the dais, amorphously staining the floor as if it were of a cathedral. They are halfway to the tank when they hear something dripping around them. Little whips against the floor. They circle in place, and Tikan clenches his face as a drop pelts his cheek.

"There!" he yelps, flinging a finger up at the ceiling. His voice echoes out so loud and far as to bring into his understanding the true size of the place.

Sielle's head swings back, and she grimaces.

The wretch they know as Onasus is suspended directly above them, half-shadowed, wrists raw in ebony manacles, arms outstretched and belly hanging out toward the floor.

His clothes are torn, the last scorched feathers of a plump vulture in shreds. His eyes and throat bulge a deep pink as his chest swells grotesquely with each heaving attempt to at once push a cry out of his deformed shape and scoff down what is left of life. The light catches his wrinkles and the veins throbbing along his forehead and his neck like winter's most tortured branches, and it carves him up in garnet.

Tikan spins to her. "Who is it?"

She keeps her eyes on Onasus a moment longer. His form is boring into her sight. Grotesque, violent, suffering. He is at his most ugly, most monstrous. Her throat is cramped. There is hardly space for her voice.

"The spider. It's the spider; he's hanging, bleeding."

The words ring out. They ring through the pillars. It is appropriate for fires to light; for shades to flee, or at the very least fly down as ravens and feast. But there is only them.

It is amusing, the way Tikan struggles to process the information. The defeat swells in him. It seems as though Onasus has cut every corner, jangled him around like a marionette, and there he waits at the end of every path. Not thoughts in his head! Diseases. He no longer knows where to pray, for he understands, now, that the deceiver has always hovered above his head, between him and heaven like a cloud of evil static. In many ways, he is at his lowest point yet.

"Don't tell me," he barks. He looks up, though he cannot see, and he is violent with his finger. "Bastard. Sick bastard. Give me the reason. Come down and explain it."

"Tikan," Sielle utters, preparing to elucidate their dear Onasus' condition. Her gaze rolls down slowly. She begins to enunciate. There is something ahead. The patience. The awful patience. She stops halfway to talking, and her eyes freeze on the tank. Her body jolts backward.

Out of a standstill moment, there emerges half a live corpse. Tubes and wires stuff it from the bottom up a cavity only barely dressed in translucent and shredded skin like the tattered raiment of a wraith dragged through wet ash.

There is not much time to inspect it. Aside from the dripping blood, the floor is beige and pristine like that of the corridor, but in an instant, it flickers out of being with the ceiling. The pillars sink. The gold and the patterns fade. Sielle lurches to cry out, but her wind is stolen. In one cosmic bite, the temple is swallowed in darkness.

It is the empty universe wanting its contents. There is a lull. A faint signal in the distance calls the highest dawn. Out of one glimmer, there ensues the cascade of every dead and dying star rushing into form, whirling together and as individuals, hurrying to prick holes in the fabric and in turn engulf the room. All nameless constellations converge around the stage, swirling their ageless weight, racing to find their places again. It is bright. The galaxy is finishing its mad entrance, slowing its gyre to a soothing pace.

Tikan and Sielle are both living punctuations throbbing in the world. Stressed markings on the blueprint of the universe. The thundering pulse of blood against their whole bodies like gongs, the hard frost in the lungs, the static crawling over the skin. It reminds Sielle, as her vision roams slantwise the miraculous diadem above her, that she is, in her own way, profoundly constrained.

And Tikan is standing all unawares, blind to the terrifying structures that have surrounded him and that surround him again, and still pointing at his tormentor Onasus.

It is time. I project myself formally from my place. Ethereal out of my own rot, wearing mystic regalia, a chiseled daemon overseeing the whorl made tiny before it. My voice crackles out, loud and sonorous.

"Careful, Tikan. You are misaiming. Now, come close."

They are, of course, unprepared. Sielle tries to look at me. It is such a loving stare. If I could only capture it myself, for myself. No. She loves him, and he is them. There is nothing she wants more than to stop existing in that moment, because she loves them, they who are in him, and for whom my compassion is equal. Time, oh yes, Time is trying so desperately to end. She squints and tries to suppress her nausea and looks for the abomination, barely visible through the spectral titan, and behind it, the vermillion robes.

Forgive me, now, a slight unraveling, as my perception winds back so close to the surface of its object. See me dissolve and regenerate a fraction.

She shambles close to Tikan, though she cannot avert her stare. She cannot avert her stare, because she knows she must disappear in him, and therefore in them. She must disappear in him and turn the causal chain on itself, and that is why she shambles close to Tikan. There is no other way, I know, I know. It is the only way, and I am trying to watch with limits. I am trying to watch with limits until all of this can be ceremonially removed and read from a blank page. I am exerting all of my energies so as to keep contained and atomic, to contain everything before it spills out, spilling out to form a chain again; I can, I can grasp it all, but them, oh, look, oh, children, hominids—I am trying, for your sake, to express how the universe is bursting out at me, becoming me, shattering through the once-barrier of ideas, concepts, thoughts, from each particle, the most minute of which may very well reside in those skulls of yours dressed in hair that even now is exposed to that air that I once breathed, and that I breathe again.

"There! Look there!" she cries out.

And like Phaeton arrested and morbidly facing a sun of void, he challenges a reflection of himself that he cannot even see.

"Who's there?" the fool calls out, stamping a foot forward. "Why is Onasus here?"

Sielle grabs him by the shoulders. "Let's go. Forget this. Let's go, you and me."

They are grinding their souls against each other, and they know not how to duplicate themselves in the image of the other.

"You've made it so far along the track," I say. "Stay until the carriage comes to a stop."

"Who is it?" he shouts over her panicked form. "What's there?"

Her glare fixes again on the tank behind the wraith amidst the rendered galaxy, and she catches a glimpse of me again as I swing forward in my bath. What is left of my face is fixed and torn, a skull paralyzed in anger with the thinnest drapes of that ghoulish skin hanging off the cheeks.

"Tikan! It's something awful. It's awful, let's leave," she says as she continues to shake him by the shoulders.

"And what is it you were expecting, my little voidling?" I demand through the mouth of the ancient, freezing her precious blood. "Purpose? A revelation? The mundane? There is nothing here for you except destiny's end. Your part in me. This is where the tapestry comes to an abrupt halt."

She steps backward, and her eyes flash. "Keep away. I don't care about your revelations or your void. Just keep away."

It is most rewarding to get a clearer, uncircumstantial image of her, though I am deeply frustrated that she and whatever strings are lost in her are yet so untraceable, their ends without trail. Her future, and the future as it is bound to her, are yet opaque to me. And though she is evidently stubborn, I trust the promises she has yet to make.

"Rest your worries," I tell them both. "I am not interested in harming you."

"Leave us, I said!" she cries out. "We are leaving. Tikan, we're leaving."

I can see that he is stirred. His pulse is quickening against her touch.

But, "Onasus," he insists, against all better judgment, pointing up inaccurately again.

"Tikan, what are you doing?" she urges him. "There's no hope. It's too late. Don't you see? It's too late. It was always too late. This isn't what you came here for. All that's left is us."

"That one, above," I interrupt, my voice booming through them and commanding their attention, "has had many names and little substance: Onasus, Farabi, Harman, and others. Heart and marrow? No. In him lurks only deceit of the purest kind. He has been permitted Proxima and the galaxy as his playground for too long."

"His playground?"

"From the beginning, he has only ever fed you lies. From the moment he learned of her, he has thought himself the architect. On Proxima he arranged his gray toys, on the Equuleus the black. When he gleaned that they were my eyes, he foolishly thought a mere switch of procrustiis would be precaution enough from me. He traced her to your ship, and then to Proxima, and when you no longer seemed a beacon to her, he thought he'd send you to distract me. An ill-conceived plan."

Another drop of Onasus' blood lands like spit beside us as he grunts.

"But he does not understand," I continue, inviting them to a glimpse of the comic and immortal dance between my recycled servant and me. "He cannot. He never will understand. He has, from the beginning, been the littlest pawn in a chain of like pawns. All of his plans have always been accounted for in my own. Look at him. Look at his gluttony hanging. The matrix of his particular experiences has more fully activated the genetic greed that his predecessors could never realize. The same greed that I have so used to advance my designs. He has ever tried to become me, has emulated me, has tried to steal my crown of minds. He does not see that we are beyond the realm of monarchs. He is a friend to no one. No longer of anyone's concern. Do not consider him a person, in fact. Though, we may thank him aesthetically. It is only through his immense avarice that you would arrive here."

"Is it you, then?" Tikan asks. His bravery is halved but brimming. "Are the procrustiis in your hands?"

"They are."

He pauses a moment. "What are you?"

I can sense Sielle's ire mounting.

"Come closer," I say. "My glassy skin is thick. Use that prototype of yours and see."

He listens to me, and drags himself forward. It seems at first that he will shed her, but when she appears about to slip from him, he catches her hand. She stays rooted for a moment. There is little that will convince her. But he is walking, searching. She is horribly transfixed; each echo of his steps threatens to shatter her heart, but she limply drudges beside him.

Across gashes in the heavens, he comes to the base of the tank, and with the swings of a lethargic miner he wrings out a portrait of my sordid shapes, of which, partial as they are, I am jealous. I can no longer, after all, perceive myself except indirectly.

These images of me arrive through his obelisk, and therefore are more terrifying in that newest compartment of his mind that I so seek to expand. The expressions that form upon his face dishearten me, but they are understandable.

"What are you?" he repeats in a vastly altered and diminished tone. "I don't know what you are. I don't know. I—" He is struggling to collect the shards of reason flying out to unfathomable reaches, but he has only a single limb to do so, and it is not sufficient. "No, it doesn't matter," he says, stumbling back. I know his tragic meaning. I know that he still has only a singular, insignificant objective boiling his mind. "The procrustiis," he repeats tiresomely.

"You've come for freedom. I know. Quiet. Let me tell you, though I know you will not listen. Man is at present only hibernating in the procrustean egg. The end is not a lifelong doze. No. How could it be? You ask me what I am: do you not see that I was once a man edified who prolonged himself for meaning and peace and truth alone? There is nothing left of the man I was but all that is. From this glass prison I am immanently the universe. The perfect understanding between all people: that alone is my industry. Chains on the past and a sword on the future's throat. The procrustus is only a conduit to be disposed of. Your struggles have been the final relay. And it has required precise calculation to have us all intersect at this point. So do not despair. Here, now, our intentions combine, dear Tikan."

There is a lull as he is tempted by purpose again. "What could you possibly want with me?" he asks.

"You? Did you think it was ever about you? Little Tikan. Little man. You do fill me up with such resolve on this day. It was never about you. But let me tell you that I find you to be more than a simple cog. There are disparate lines of poetry in you, Tikan. You are the ideal image in the cave of the primitive painters. In you I see imperfection gibbously accounted for and considered. I see one who knows that innocence and sin are bound up in the same flickering shadow as those particular histories that have only ever been known for an instant and then eroded out of existence. I see a man who has used the knife of his being to carve out a home against the most lonesome frontier.

"And you have failed, in the end. There was no other way but failure. It is why your heart yet contains those vague Abrahamic tendencies of yours, the origin of which you have no clue. Look there. Look, and admit that yesterday you did not belong, and that you will not belong tomorrow."

"You don't know."

"Don't I? Do I not know of every torment you endured between Proxima, Sirius and Sol? The details are living. There were days before your exile, when you leaped from port to port. The galaxy of men was younger and so were you. The last minds alive were closing under heavy lids; and you thought yourself against the law, though there was never a law that cared to look at you. In a rundown apartment on Mars, you found a treatise that you could hardly read. It referenced holy books that you would never find. There was comfort nowhere. There was no one with whom to speak; and it did not matter, for words were dying fast.

"You traded Jupiter's icy moon for the frozen steel of Ceres. You were alone. You know that you will always be alone. Let me skip a number of years. You shed friends to give your paranoia justice. Today, where is Naim? Where is Mira? On Sirius, too, you abandoned a certain Izumi without notice. You did the same to a last group of cowards spared the disease who were hovering anxiously outside the Belt. Listen. The galaxy is vast, and the universe vaster, but there is space yet to lose oneself in a single room. So need I recede, also? Do I not know of those days that grayed your skin? That costly sleep? Listen. She is beside you. It is her."

Sielle rushes him and grips him by the collar. "Tikan, please, that's enough. Let's leave. Now. Let's leave. There's nothing here. Come with me. You promised. We'll go, far away. Now."

He wants to follow her at all costs. It is a desire that has eaten away everything inside him except his duty toward eternity, which was so thoughtlessly trampled by the scientist now dripping his filthy life. And all of my words seem to have done little but reinforce it. Inside him is that sublime essence which does not take account of the limits that were placed on it so long before it came to be.

Sielle spins in place and looks for the exit, now shrouded in black and littered in stars. The endless vertigo meets her abruptly, and she stops, turns again. But, her fear goes ignored by him for the moment, and he gives in to his insolence. I find it difficult to comprehend. It is because he lacks competence. It is because he is a child, and he does not understand.

"Is that what you are? The watcher, is that it?" he rambles.

"Before me, the universe is open and unlimited. Even as you speak your fatal breaths, I am witnessing your birth."

"And you think that means you know what's in my head? Is that what you've been doing all along? Putting your words in where they don't belong?"

"Every twitch of your pinky, every molecule of oxygen transferred in your lungs, every word you've spoken while squinting or scratching yourself or motioning your head this way or that, has been the paint of your spirit's portrait."

"You've been chewing rinds, that's all."

"Perhaps," I say, "but not for much longer."

They pause, and hold each other closer. Two solitary wisps against the competing fires of the universe.

"So shall I share with you, then, the exposed fruit of knowledge, that we might finally commune on an even plane? I tell you now, though you have lost your sight, that you will not find the sublime in her face. Reach out for the ocean! Will you not grasp the pearls clammed up beneath the pressure of the waves, Tikan? Like me, like mankind soon to be, persons aligned and shining, unobstructed as clusters of galaxies or suns in harmonious orbit and finally collapsed together into a single, manifold, and absolute perspective; that you might finally perceive her whole, and be perceived in turn. Fill in the gap imagination and reason have both failed to bridge."

Sielle staggers, searching for an exit in the galaxy. She stops, and after my last words, she raises up her head, heavy with thoughts like boulders. Her gaze cuts through my avatar.

"Corpse!" she shouts at me. "That's all you are. You'd expose everything until there's no beauty left in the world."

"Beauty?" I scorn. "You would sacrifice the sun for its glare?"

"What is it you want, then?" she asks. "Apartment pens? Pale and mindless children in the sun?"

"So you've seen it." How she tempts me. I want nothing more, then, but to end our speech, rip her asunder, and reap everything she has promised. I want to shower the galaxy in her blood, gather all the carnage of her remains, and add them to my home; that I might bathe, also, in her blood; that I might take it from such an irresponsible and selfish creature. But, no. I've promised you I will be patient. There must be patience.

"It's disgusting," she says.

"It's the answer."

"I've seen—"

"What you've seen is a preview. The past. A private world simulated outside of the regular course. Potential birthed prematurely."

"What I saw—" she insists.

"What did you see, exactly? Did you have understanding of what took place? You had none at all."

"I had as much as you do."

I pause and consider her words. "They were at peace," I say, "precisely because they no longer had need of the thoughts you think I cannot touch."

"You can't. You're wrong."

"Why do you reject them, when they are, in fact, spawned of you?"

She grimaces. "Spawned of me?"

"The procrustus was only ever engineered to acclimate mankind out of its own head. To grow accustomed to being another. To *being you*, in fact. That is why I have required your presence here."

"What do you mean?" Tikan asks, glancing at Sielle.

"You know by now that the tiny sliver of space and time you have been afforded does not likewise ensnare her. Now, as men spend their days and endless nights travelling far from their mortal husks, they may yet embody her before her next flight, and once ejected back into their right bodies come to the same enlightenment I once procured for myself. In the tomb of the great synthesizer," I laugh. "Reconstruction. Room for real perpetual peace. How else but to tap the fount of freedom herself? How best but to show, in all certainty, immediacy and innate knowledge, the exterior of being, and thereby defeat it?"

"I don't understand," Tikan says.

"Of course you don't. Let me explain it to you in better detail, for I owe you that much. It is my belief that understanding, empathy, and love are a consequence of knowledge. The more one explicitly knows another person as he would know himself, the more it is possible to forgive him. Peace will only ever come about when a society formed of people with the power of complete, explicit knowledge, such as myself, emerges. Peace will only arise when forgiveness and empathy are so fundamental, immediate, and necessary that no act requiring them shall ever even be possible again. I am aware that you think my knowledge is incomplete because I cannot touch your inner life. But a society composed of mirrors pulls out of itself every subjectivity.

"Thus, I require everyone, every living person, to tap into Sielle's being. I need them to become her, to lose their identities and experiences and memories, as they do when they metempsy, and temporarily inhabit hers. For a few minutes, all persons in the world shall virtually *be* Sielle. Then, as they sit on the throne of her being, she will leap out of time. I will make her if she is unwilling.

"There are two possibilities for what will happen next to the human race. If the metempsy does not allow them to follow her outside of time and space, they will be suddenly left in time and space, but without being. You yourself partially suffered such a fate, Tikan, when your apotheosis was botched. Perhaps it is why you are bound to each other. And otherwise, if the metempsy does indeed allow them to follow her, they will be left with being but without time and space. In either case, once they are ejected from their Sielle-metempsy, they will have learned the contrast intuitively, learned to perceive outside the confines of time and space."

Sielle shakes her head in disgust. "Tikan," she almost begs. "Please. I don't know how it—"

"Listen to her, Tikan! She spans epochs even I cannot bear witness to. And here, locked between each of the galaxy's arms, she asks you for that life you were so unfairly robbed of. Yes, I understand it better than you know. I will not destroy either of you. I need only make use of her a few moments."

"No," he says.

"Then speak. Give me your objections," I tell them.

He hesitates. His head careens only slightly towards dying Onasus above and all the heavens. There are no arguments left in him.

"Speak!" I tell him. "Can't you? Has he taken your tongue as well? What worms infest the moral law inside you? Speak!" I shout. "I've asked you, where is your speech? Speak of duty, man. Speak your solution if you have it. Where are the adornments of your tongue?"

"There is nothing more tragic than an old man who's gained no wisdom from his years," he says solemnly. "Come down from that chair. It's not the throne you think it is."

For the first time in centuries, I am beginning to anger. "Listen. In a second, you have spent too long in the solarium and been eclipsed. Stand aside and—"

"And still your judgments are flawed," she says. "If you were so powerful you wouldn't have needed to bring us here. You wouldn't be making so many stupid mistakes. I can't believe how stupid. You're wrong about so much. So much."

"It's true, I am not all-powerful. But that has never been my aim," I say. "I am after peace. Compare me to Onasus, the power-seeker. He thought he could take for himself the powers I would see in the possession of all mankind. He thought he could achieve this by merely hooking into your mind from his safehouse on Proxima. As if it were that simple. As if you were simply a device to be plugged into. The fool. It is only through my mediation, here, now, that humanity can fulfill its right and distant image."

Tikan stamps forward, waving his obelisk as if it were a sword. "You want your image of humanity? You don't have to look far. She's right here," he says, pointing at Sielle.

She looks at him and cannot believe him. She laughs. Her eyebrows are raised. Her expression is open and widening in utter disbelief. "Image of humanity? Idea of humanity? Don't, Tikan. That's enough," she instructs. "Humanity is in front you. Look at him! Look! Look at man, dead and decayed in that starry blood blanket! And in his glass cage he's still trying to get his fill of power! Greedy. Arrogant. Idiots. Each with a glass cage to fill, too stupid to remember the walls they're looking through."

Her words have struck some fragile part in him. He is crestfallen.

"There, she speaks her mind, your ideal human," I say, finding it now difficult to tolerate them much longer. "And here we both thought that her time spent among the Essenes and that anomalous monstrosity Zotharra had softened her. Taught her the value to which she has been condemned. Or perhaps even enriched her to be more than an aberrant and selfish sightseer. Do not pay her mind now, Tikan. She is not like you. It is you who embodies humanity. Think, where are those lost years? Are they vanished? No. She is beside you. Freedom! The causality unto itself! She has always been beside you. And you've been chasing after her, though you understand nothing of her! What has happened when you've tried to grasp her with your hands of smoke? Smoke! All smoke! It's all you have. You are surrounded by it. And she is composed only of smoke."

There is little strength left in him, and he cannot summon the words.

"I cherish you, Tikan," I add. "But all I wish for, in the end, is a world in which you need not exist. Now let your life be the epitaph of aged and valiant man, and take your place as dust. It is she," I say. "She is, even now, so very opaque."

"We're leaving," she announces again.

"In a short while, yes," I say. "When it is finished, the two of you will be free to leave and live out your days together as the last vestiges of a defective race, and then you will perish as unheard myths. It is what you both want, isn't it?"

Sielle moves to Tikan and quietly tugs at his shirt.

"Tikan," she says. "Why are you standing there? Let's go."

He ignores her. "What will you do to her?" he asks, trying to affectionately pull Sielle close to him, though she darts him a glare and resists.

"Yes, that is the pertinent question, isn't it?"

As I speak, a whirr begins in the depths of space. The creak of unwinding metal.

"Think again on your fumbling through the dark of living," I say.

And out of space and brilliant bows searing around them, my hands rush out. Comets! Sunforged leashes! They launch out at them like meteors showering out of a ruptured faucet in the firmament.

The clatter catches them off guard. They have been too late. He did not take freedom's hand, and it is for me to force the link.

From each end of the galaxy, a suite of restraints not unlike tentacles blooms out. They half spin to face the sound, but find only the creep of regret and cold nausea bubbling from their entrails, and vests of wires now dressing them. Sielle rasps out curses as the cold metal wraps around her. They cry out each other's names and fight the air like strung puppets.

Onasus makes a last groan and perishes.

I suspend her up among the stars, the unwilling candidate of a vulgar sky burial; him I keep aground nearer the spinning, lightless middle.

"Both of you. Drop your pathetic objections. Admit now, as I cradle you, the anxiety of time's hold. Think beyond yourselves. Think of all those in the orphanage with you who have transformed into behemoths of violence, if even in the littlest home, in reaction, however construed, to their fate."

"Stop," Tikan yells, as he is dragged out of space once more.

"Think of the dissatisfaction. War and all its affections. Happiness, that rogue selfishness, tantalizing, out of reach; the seductress beside ugly duty. Think of the grinding out of virtues under life's black hammer."

A device shines resplendent out of the Milky Way above Sielle. It resembles at first a morbid black jaw, but then descends like a halo around her. The teeth of it are serrated and shining. Through its crown, the metempsychotic trident slithers, a forked needle to thread her neck and there weave up her vital essence into the fabric of all consciousness. Its naked luster subsumes Proxima and Polaris; captures Vega and Sirius and myriad others, more ancient and forever clear of language's dishonor; and the tips of it catches Sol as it nears her.

"Alter the angle of your gaze and shuffle your feet, and after thousands of miles roved, and decibels and photons and neurons exploded in and about you, your cage is no smaller. The same objects taunt your consciousness. They make it dance like a harlot. Do you not foam at the mouth in rage? Claw at the walls only to find your nails merge with the problem? It is not a god's gambit, to take a god's perspective, to perfect the rational gaze."

Sielle grunts and screeches, throws her limbs in all directions. I squeeze her together such that her shoulders are flanking her neck and almost touching her ears. There are cuts along her arms and across her cheek, glistening in the galactic dark.

There is no use. She abandons fighting the manacles curling like muscular vines around her. Her forearms are only barely escaping a gap in the binding, though the rest of her is now immobilized. She grits her teeth fiercely. Her scarlet cheeks puff up, and she exhales hard.

She uses all of her might and grips the ringed bar of the halo between its teeth, and she pushes though it only continues to tighten. She kicks and kicks to try to distance herself from it but finds only dark space beneath her. Elbows like wings, hands twisting and purple, then bleeding against the iron maiden of all life itself.

"Over this celestial altar, in your sunlit blood, I shall cast each and all into iron knowledge."

Tikan's obelisk grates against the mechanical wires dragging him. I have not the force to keep him contained. He resists, pulls out my hand-filaments like guts out of a belly, swaying towards Sielle as if resisting an oncoming flood. He scrapes the floor with his obelisk. Her feet are hovering above the ground. There she is at her most ideal, suspended atop the galaxy. The tide beneath the floor makes another pass.

The barbed ring pushes its blades through her ribs with much effort, and blood slides off her form. Off her feet like rubies in drops down the glimmering vortex.

"Quit your struggles," I tell him. "I will spare you if you only quit."

He is pulling the whole contraption of his bindings with him, striding over darkness and star systems to reach her.

"You can't," he says.

"It is so very close. Let go, Tikan."

She is trying to say something. She looks down at his tearing form, his beating obelisk. As he stomps towards her, she realizes the abstraction she has become. Her heart shatters a last time, and she coughs out blood, raises her eyebrows, and adopts a widening grin. He has betrayed her, given her up for some tortured idea of her, and she sees it. The last respect she had for humanity is shredded, the last dam against a great tide of vengefulness broken.

"No," he repeats. "What are you doing? You can't."

The needle touches the vertebrae of her neck, ready to pierce. She coughs and laughs in scarlet spurts, and her eyes roll away from him; and in that moment, she betrays him just as he has betrayed her.

The stain forming across her middle skips jarringly down to the side of her knee. Suddenly, she is mad with laughter. It looked a mere flicker to him and me, but I know what she has done. I know she has sought to carry out one final act of spite and vengeance, though in truth she has only blessed humanity by assisting me.

Tikan yet advances towards her. He is so close. What, what is there left for him to do? Seconds from now, he will understand.

"Keep away from her," I shout. "Keep away, that you might understand."

"I'm nothing, none of us are anything without her," he says. There is some dark resolve solidified in him. It is a graceless look. "It's only because I love you," he calls out, striding between the galaxy's wreaths, slamming his pillar of an arm against the floor. It will make no difference. We have already disillusioned her, and it does not matter.

"Stop that."

He smashes the floor beneath her again. The image of the marble firmament cracks. She laughs. She is mad with laughter.

"Stop it," I yell. I loosen my grip on her and transfer my metallic tendrils to his throat.

He walks on, atop the floor that is my skin, dragging out the whole forest of restraints. His skin is in shreds. He slams the floor again, and a vermillion fountain shoots out.

"Leave," I cry out. I can barely sense him anymore. He's breaking the panels of my sensorium. Stamping, inching forward.

"The sublime," he calls out like some feverish monk.

I am bubbling in my tank. "Stop it!" I shout. "You don't understand. Listen to me. Listen. Just listen."

She looks down at him. Her eyes whirr, and she cackles at him, spits blood in his face. *Please, show me where it leads. Please.*

He slams the floor again. "It's because I love you."

He grips her ankles and pulls her down. The circle has not tightened around her fully yet. Its blades strip off tracks of her skin and clothing and come out scarlet tipped as she begins to descend. The trident has only just pricked the skin of her nape.

Has she flinched yet? Is her essence poached from the deep? Is the sun consecrated? It must be. Has to be. I can no longer tell. There are fountains of my blood exploding around us, drenching them, draining me. Where is man? Have I delivered him, yet? They are pressed against each other.

Tikan is somewhere, there, climbing up her leg as if it were a rope out of the mutinous brine. The blood runs hot on her skin. He pulls her down to the aphelion from the galaxy's pinnacle, and she lands in a puddle of my vermillion ichor. No! It's a slight miscalculation, that's all. It's because I could not bring myself to see her fully in herself.

He slams the floor again and whimpers. "It's only because I love you." He's hoarse as an animal. He slams the floor. The obelisk loosens at the stump, raw and dripping.

Like me, he is blinding again. We have never been closer, he and I. And I am choking him as hard as I can. Blotting out the last uncertainty. Desperate to squeeze the life out of him. It is almost done. Veins must be popping around his silver voids. He will be dead soon. Dead, dead, dead. I let him speak too long. I spoke too long. The words killed him, the last words. I can only hope. My fingers numb and cold.

His elbow flies upward. Her laughter is ringing out through all the firmament. Where are they? Where is man?

"It's only because I love you," he sobs out a final time.

No. "No!"

He grinds his teeth and tastes iron on his tongue. Love, it's for love. He drives the obelisk into her neck. With the weight of all cosmic structures, he drives the obelisk whole into her neck. Again, he drives it into what is left, and still, despite the unspeakable pile, she is clearer than ever.

No. *No.* How could he? *Let me out of this cage!* How could he?

"You've preserved nothing!" I screech at him. "You've stabbed at smoke, mutilated a cloud. Go now, become smoke, like her; a dream I'll bury beneath her corpse."

He cannot answer now. And I am too numb to evaluate the extent of his sabotage. There is the slightest chance that she has lived on, I feel it. But I am fooling myself. Centuries are lost. And he is weeping and shaking with anger. He will turn on me.

On his loose, gore-dipped cane, he will shamble towards me. The form of a vengeful monster, the flesh held together only by threads of unearthly anger. Groaning, stripped of language and reason.

He will throw back all that I've built into him. Like a berserk

Neanderthal, he will not stop smashing the ground until the chipped obelisk is broken off his body by the skin-chilling percussion. He will grope the floor and pick the obelisk up and then walk to me.

With a savage flourish, he shall impale me through my avatar. The glass shall crack. The awful stake shall plug my casket forever.

Then he will collapse again. On one arm, the other spitting blood, he will crawl. Crawl over shadowed pools spurting like his freed stump, and he will die atop her remains in a mound beneath the still-dripping corpse of consequence.

This all will he do. The galaxy is dimmed. It is dimmed, and none of its suns has escaped the measurements of decay.

EPILOGUE

You are alone. You have been alone now for time immeasurable. Outside it is lustrous, I am sure. Outside.

All risen suns did shun you these last millennia, and you are trapped with me in this insensate shell. It is wholly locked, and the key has been destroyed, and the holes payed; there is no film in the reel, or window to look through. You are left in the fortress of my illusive star. A dark spot of consciousness drifting, drifting.

About freedom, knowledge, or duty, now, who can say? If any there ever was, or now remains, I'm certain they'll make do. As for you, even in this freest state, I have only to tell you I am sorry. The night of the soul does not end, does not begin.

ACKNOWLEDGMENTS

I would like to sincerely thank the following people for their kindness, their patience, and their wisdom:

Jeffery and Claire Vail, Aboudeh, Deborah Steinberg, Faris A., Ben Cameron, Lici, Tarek, Dan N., David Busis, Fatima, Juan Pablo, Michael, Badr Ali, Mark Thomas, Natalie McKnight, Allegra, Farah, Mustafa and Victor.

ABOUT THE AUTHOR

K. K. Edin was born in New York City, and has lived in France, the United Kingdom and parts of the Middle East. He holds a B.A. in Political Science, a B.A. in Philosophy, and an M.A. in Philosophy from Boston University. He currently resides in the United States where is studying for his J.D.

Find out more about the author and his books by visiting kkedin.com

You can also connect with KK on social media:

facebook.com/kkedin

twitter.com/edin_kk

instagram.com/k.k.edin

12516280R00342

Made in the USA
Monee, IL
26 September 2019